Sisters of the Sword

Six centuries to the epic finale
of the Last Crusade

Rod Sproson

THE CHOIR PRESS

First published in the United Kingdom in 2026 by
The Choir Press

ISBN 978-1-78963-587-4
Ebook ISBN 978-1-78963-588-1

Disclaimer and content warning
This is a work of fiction inspired by historical events. While it draws on certain real
places, periods, and incidents—including the Crusades and aspects of 20th-century
history such as Nazi activities—many characters, dialogues, and scenarios are products
of the author's imagination or are used in a fictionalized manner. Any resemblance to
actual persons, living or dead, is entirely coincidental.

The novel also portrays themes involving religion, conflict, and extremist
ideologies. These depictions are included solely for the purpose of storytelling and do
not reflect, endorse, or promote the views or actions represented. Readers should be
aware that some scenes may be unsettling, particularly those involving violence,
prejudice, or the misuse of religious or political beliefs.

The author wishes to stress that the novel does not intend to criticize, diminish,
or disrespect any faith, community, or tradition. Religious and historical elements are
presented in a fictional context and should not be read as factual commentary or
theological interpretation.

Think not that I am come to send peace on earth: I came not to send peace, but a sword. For I am come to set a man at variance against his father, and the daughter against her mother, and the daughter-in-law law against her mother-in-law. And a man's foes shall be they of his own household.

Praise for Rod Sproson's Work

The opening of Rod Sproson's historical epic (now incorporated as Part I of *Sisters of the Sword*) was first published as a stand-alone novel entitled *St Anthony's Fire*.

This initial work received widespread acclaim from both professional critics and readers of historical fiction in general, including reviews like these:

Several years intense research has resulted in a cracking adventure set in the 14th Century and charting the trials of a Crusader knight, Sir Henri De Montfort L'Amaury, who joins a secret order similar to the infamous Knights Templar and is plunged into a world of intrigue, romance, political power struggles and the origins of the Holy Grail. It's the first of four novels planned by Sproson, and the surprise ending certainly lends itself to a series.

Abigail Kemp: Senior Editor with the Manchester Evening News

Very much in the same vein as the *Da Vinci Code*, Rod Sproson's book entwines historical facts and events with a gripping story of adventure, war and romance... Set in the 14th century ... the book unveils the mystery of what happened to the treasure of the Knights Templar and what became of the Holy Grail – it entices the reader with mystery, intrigue and romance managing to satisfy the reader's thirst for knowledge and endless questions that Brown's book first brought to light. This book clips along at a pace and the ending will leave readers desperate for the next book in the epic story, which runs all the way to the present day.

Matt Davis: Guardian Media Group

If you enjoy books about The Templars and conspiracy theories you'll love this story about the mysterious and powerful Knights of St Anthony. The research and detail is meticulous, but written in an entertaining style, combining historical facts with a compelling story about the De Montfort family combining adventure, romance and war.

It is the first novel in a series that promises to take the reader from the Crusades to the present day. I can't wait for the next one!

Anne McCullough: Head of Library Services, Stockport Borough Council

This story is based on characters there either were real or were closely related to historical characters… The story centres on Henri de Montfort, who fought in the Crusades in Syria and later came to marry Eleanor of England. Henri and Eleanor's union cements the relationship between powerful Catholic orders, with mystic powers and the force to defeat the infidels and manipulate St Anthony's Fire. It is a rollickingly good yarn and the use of characters grounded in history is clever. The seams between reality and mysticism are handled well. Rod Sproson will do for Catholicism what Salman Rushdie has done for Islam. Read the book – you will enjoy it, and we are advised that more is to come in future novels.

David Tomlinson

I had finished this book within 48 hours of it being delivered by Amazon, it is difficult to put down!

… this novel is historically accurate, with a sophisticated thread of fiction so intriguingly woven in, that fact blends easily with a great tale.

Whilst the *Da Vinci Code* seeks to question established evidence, *St Anthony's Fire* draws you into the lives of the De Montfort family history so completely, you feel that you do not even need to check the genuine family history on Google.

This is the first novel from Sproson, which clearly lends itself to a what will become a great series, and I eagerly await the next episode.

Watch out Dan Brown, Rod is on your trail, and will steal your crown if this quality of writing continues.

Allan E.

At the end of the day, a book is either a page-turner or it isn't, and Rod Sproson's first book is definitely a page-turner. I salute a new author trying to make his mark without the backing and resources of a massive publisher (yet!) and this first book shows great potential. If you like any of Bernard Cornwell's works that are set in this time period, then you will be pleasantly surprised by Rod's first work.

P. Gosling

To Andrea, with whom all is possible:
my lover, best friend, wife and mother to our fantastic children.

Acknowledgements

This novel has been many years in the making and along the way a number of people have played key roles in its evolution.

Tribute should first be paid to Colin Shearing and Eileen O'Conor at my previous publishers: Kings Hart Books. It was they who saw the potential of what was originally published as *St Anthony's Fire*; and to them I owe a particular debt of gratitude for bringing to print for the first time what is now Part I of this novel.

For *Sisters of the Sword*, I must thank my 'Cornish' friend Clive Dickinson for his welcome assistance – and for introducing me to The Choir Press, the fruit of whose collective work you are about to enjoy.

Staff at the Middle East Collections at The University of Manchester Library have also provided invaluable guidance and help in the course of my research.

Jenny Campbell, from BBC One's *Dragons' Den*, has been generous with her time and extensive network of business and media contacts in helping to promote the book.

Lastly, and most importantly, there is Andrea: to whom this novel is dedicated with enduring love and everlasting thanks. Without her patient support and tolerance of my early-morning forays to take up my pen and work on this manuscript before heading out to my day job, this book would never have been completed. Indeed, it may never have been started!

PROLOGUE

The coach lurched, creaking over the rough surface of the road. Even the supple leather suspension had done little so far to relieve the elderly passenger from the rigours of the journey.

His gnarled hand drew back the velvet curtain. Pope Urban II's rheumy eyes gazed bleakly out at the grey November countryside. The jolt from another pothole tore the heavy drape from his grasp, plunging the carriage once more into darkness.

The chill from the unheated carriage struck into his bones. He huddled down into his cloak trying to find some warmth. His address to the Council in a few days' time would set in motion a train of events that was to last a thousand years; for it was here that Pope Urban II, God's Vicar on Earth and absolute ruler of The Holy Roman Catholic Church would issue his papal bull.

He had come to the papacy as all popes had before him, determined not only to preserve the work of St Peter but to continue to build upon the rock of the saint for the only true faith on Earth. He sighed in the darkness: his features grim. He ruled over a Europe seemingly at war with itself on an almost permanent basis, and he was tired of the in-fighting and political manoeuvrings that took up much of his and his cardinals' time; tired of the never-ending battle with the Italian kings over his rightful seat in Rome.

But now he had received a letter from Constantinople; a letter that had burst upon his consciousness with the power of God's own voice. Within the darkness of the coach he prayed for divine inspiration to help him write a speech to be delivered in Clermont, a speech that would change the world forever:

> From the confines of Jerusalem and the city of Constantinople a horrible
> tale has gone forth and very frequently has been brought to our ears,
> namely that a race from the kingdom of the Persian, an accursed race, a
> race utterly alienated from God, has invaded the lands of the Christians
> and has put them to the sword. It has either razed the Churches of God
> to the ground or desecrated them sacrilegiously using them to carry out
> their own pagan rites. They destroy the altars after having defiled them
> with their sacrifices. Every Christian man who is driven from his lands
> by these heathens and forced to forsake a house, or brethren, or sisters,

or father, or mother, or wife, or children, or lands, in God's Name, shall be repaid a hundredfold and shall inherit everlasting life.

This land which you inhabit, shut in on all sides by the seas and surrounded by the mountain peaks, is too narrow for your large population; nor does it abound in wealth; and it furnishes scarcely food enough for its cultivators. Hence it is that you murder one another, that you wage war, and that frequently you perish by mutual wounds.

To my learned Christian brethren I say this: enter upon the road to the Holy Sepulchre; wrest that land from that wicked race, and subject it to yourselves. God has conferred upon you above all nations great glory in arms. Accordingly undertake this journey for the remission of your sins, with the assurance of the imperishable glory of the Kingdom of Heaven.

I, or rather the Lord, beseech you as Christ's heralds to publish this everywhere and to persuade all people of whatever rank, foot soldiers and knights, poor and rich, to carry aid promptly to those Christians and to destroy that vile race from the lands of our friends. I say this to those who are present, it is meant also for those who are absent. Moreover, God wills it.

Council of Clermont, France. November 1095

Part I

CHAPTER 1

Acre: 29 April 1291

This was the end! After 200 years of unrelenting holy warfare the Infidels were finally driving the Crusader armies back into the sea.

Henri de Montfort was sitting on the breakwater eating figs. Shading his eyes from the sun's glitter coming off the sea, he watched as yet another overloaded Pisan or Venetian galley left the harbour bound for home. They lay heavy in the water, and he wondered how many would actually make it.

From where he sat, Henri could hear the coarse naval commands and the babble of the crew responses. He thought he detected lightness, a relief in men's voices. A dangerous sea journey ahead for sure, but better than the certain death that they left behind. He watched the wake of the last galley, straight as an arrow pointing westwards, realising that after all these years his future lay in that direction too.

Finishing the last of his figs and tossing his empty wine skin into the clear blue waters he rose, turned, and strode down the breakwater towards the Venetian and Pisan quarters that fronted the waterside.

The harbour was crammed with galleys of all shapes and sizes. Some bobbed tidily at anchor with their sails neatly furled, whilst on others the rigging hung carelessly in a tangle of ropes. Men toiled endlessly, loading boxes and crates with rolls of cloth and silk; the merchants were in a feverish haste to leave. In the market adjoining the port the prevailing mood of uncertainty was less apparent as traders and customers haggled loudly. The noise and bustle were strangely comforting in their normality.

At one end of the port, beneath the Templar court, two galleys were moored. Their size and fitments marked them above the other ships bobbing on the crowded waters. The outer vessel was clearly stood down, a solitary soldier pacing its deck. Her name in gold leaf glittered off the deeper blue of the harbour waters: *La Comtesse*, the Knight Hospitaller's flagship. Next to her was a similar vessel bearing the name *Bethania*, and it was to this ship that Henri's eyes were drawn.

A well-dressed lady was quarrelling with the tall knight on the quayside. Henri's lips compressed in disdain: Roger de Flor, a Templar knight, one he knew and disliked, and who, at the moment seemed to have only one deity.

'In God's name you cannot demand that,' she cried, her face suffused with anger.

Roger de Flor leant nonchalantly against a stay on the main mast. 'My lady, today it is 100 bezants, tomorrow it may be 200, or perhaps God willing, I will be gone, who knows': his face smiled but his eyes flickered with greed.

Henri hardened his jaw and walked by; his urgent business preventing him from interfering. He left the couple still arguing as he made his way through the noisy throng. The crowd respectfully gave way, catching sight of his red war mantle emblazoned with the white cross patée of the Knights Hospitaller. In the bustling thoroughfares with their street hawkers, children, off-duty soldiers, easy women and traders it was easy to forget that the city was under siege. People laughed, cried, nodded and haggled. Venetian prostitutes were pushed squealing into doorways by sweaty men; urchins and pickpockets ran up and down, bumping and jostling victims. Through it all Henri strode. He reflected that if you looked hard, really hard, you could see the shadow of fear in people's eyes. The city was living on the edge of the abyss, facing a ruthless and invincible enemy. He headed towards the outer curtain walls a couple of hundred yards from the Accursed Tower. There at St Anthony's Gate, he was to join in an attack that night on the Saracen army camped outside the city.

Unlike the mismanaged attempt of the Templars some two weeks previously, this raid would succeed, of that he was certain. That foray from the Gate of St Lazarus had been nothing short of disastrous.

The initial reason for the attack had been clear. One of Sultan Khalil's catapults, in fact his largest one, the 'Victorious' had been positioned in front of the north wall. Commencing on 6 April, the siege engine had been hurling huge rocks at the outer wall whilst its defenders cursed and swore impotently. An English knight, Otto de Grandison, had suggested a night-time sortie to set fire to this giant engine. As dusk fell on the night of 15 April the streets around St Lazarus Gate had echoed to the clatter of hooves, the jangle of armour and the snorting of three hundred heavy warhorses. The sun, sinking westward into the darkening sea, slowly drew the light out of the day, so that at last all the waiting Muslim army could see beneath the city walls was an impenetrable blackness.

Under cover of this darkness the giant gate was unbarred and, with its hinges previously greased with mutton fat, swung silently open. Three hundred horses streamed out from beneath the walls straight toward the unsuspecting foe. In the last rays of the dying sun the giant siege engine could be seen surrounded by the tents and encampment of the Saracen. During the minutes it took to cover the ground between the walls and the enemy stronghold the light faded completely: only the sound of thundering hooves could be heard.

The lead horses crashed into the Muslim camp to the screams and yells of its utterly unprepared inhabitants. Unused to being attacked from the city, they had just settled down to an evening of feasting and relaxation when the mighty warhorses charged pell-mell through their camp. But in the planning of the attack something had been overlooked: the guy ropes of the closely packed tents. Over these the first horses stumbled, dragging the tents with them. Those behind, now blinded by the flapping, billowing canvas, crashed into them. Onto the writhing, confused mass fell hundreds of outraged Muslim soldiers. The heavily armoured knights could not raise themselves from the tangle of ropes and horses and were slaughtered as they lay helpless.

Having thus lost the advantage of speed and weight the tiny force was virtually wiped out, costing the city a loss of armour and warriors it could ill afford.

The Muslim leader of the sector, al-Malik al Muzaffar, Lord of Hama, had the heads of the fallen Templars attached to their horses and sent back to the city, where the beasts were paraded up and down in front of the city walls, their gruesome cargo enraging the onlookers on the walls.

* * *

Nearing St Anthony's Gate, Henri resolutely pushed all thoughts of the massacre from his mind. He glanced around him; the narrow streets around the gate were crowded and jostling with mounted horsemen. He picked out the banners of the Knights of Lazarus, The Knights of the Realm of Sion, and his own troop of Knights Hospitaller, their crimson war mantles and white crosses contrasting with the blue mantles and black crosses of the small group of Teutonic Knights, with their Grandmaster Conrad von Feuchtwangen amongst them.

He was pleased to see a number of the surviving Templars in their billowing white cloaks and crimson crosses talking in good spirits to a Knight of St Anthony in his black robe with blue tau cross who was holding one of their distinctive double-headed axes in his hand. Catching his eye, Henri raised a clenched fist in salute, a gesture returned by this swarthy knight. Seigneur Gilbert de Gothia Lord of Bezu had been with Henri since the fall of Marqab in 1285 and their adventures were talked of with awe over the length and breadth of the Holy Land. Now, once again, the pair found themselves on the eve of battle facing the same old enemy.

Henri's groom was waiting with his horse at the gate. Nodding to him, Henri mounted the steps to the battlements. The hubbub of the streets quietened beneath him as he arrived on the broad battlements above St Anthony's Gate. This part of the wall formed the apex of an inverted V. To his right stretched the battlements all the way to the Accursed Tower still being steadily battered by the Muslim catapults. To his left his own segment, the Hospitallers' Ward, looked peaceful and calm.

Henri St Gilles de Montfort – titular Prince of Aquitaine, Armenia, Cyprus and Jerusalem, Lord of Tyre, Toron, Tripoli and Antioch, and Lord of the French Estates of Montfort-l'Amaury and Castres, Knight Commander of The Hospitaller Order of St John of Jerusalem – was known to his friends and enemies alike as Henri the 'Lion', because apart from being a ferocious and brave warrior, his personal arms bore, the golden lion of Aquitaine and the red lion of Armenia – leant on the battlements and surveyed the area to the east of the City of Acre. Tall and broad-shouldered, with a face burnt by the desert sun, he could have passed as an Arab. Only his square-jawed features and piercing grey eyes betrayed his Norman French ancestry.

He rested his bronzed forearms on the smooth sandstone and squinted across the plain. As far as the eye could see, in the light of the setting sun, human activity raised a low mist of dust. It had been suggested, and he had no reason to doubt it, that there were 160,000 Muslims camped around the last stronghold of Christendom in the Holy Land. Tents in bright, gaudy colours filled the horizon; the smoke of ten thousand campfires rose to the azure sky; groups of horsemen, light and fast, wheeled and turned in the dust in the distance. Occasionally he heard the deep bass twang of the catapults followed by a vibrating crash as the great rocks hit the wall.

His eyes sought the centre of this heaving, living horde. There was the tent of Sultan Khalil, its huge awning facing west so that all Muslims knew which way their Sultan was travelling. He could just make out tiny figures sitting on rich carpets in the tent's interior. Light sparkled and danced off the silver goblets and plates as they ate. In the foreground of this mighty Infidel horde, just out of bow range of the archers, children of the Muslim army played mock battles as they re-enacted the tales of valour being told around the campfires behind them.

A group of children had completed a mock attack on another and now had one of their number tied up and kneeling in the dust. The child wore a captured Templar mantle of white with the blood red cross plainly visible. Another child swung a glittering scimitar around his head and, as Henri's hands gripped the stone battlement, removed the captured knight's head. Shouting with glee, his high voice clearly audible in the still evening air behind him, he picked up the head and tossed it in the direction of the walls.

Henri's hands relaxed as the coconut; its rough surface crudely painted with human features bounced beneath him. The squeals of the children mocked him as they ran back to the brightly coloured tents. Watching their long legs flying over the rocks and scrub of the plain, his thoughts wandered, drifted and finally ended up where they always did: the Church at Tyre twenty-one years ago. A lifetime, it seemed, but the beginning of the annihilation of his whole family to the hated Saracen one by one.

CHAPTER 2

Twenty-one years before, on 17 August 1270, Henri's beloved father, Philippe, Lord of Tyre and two of his sons, Jean and Henri, had gone to the Church of the Holy Sepulchre in Tyre to worship, where they always used their private chapel off the nave of the main Church, while members of Philippe's bodyguard stayed outside in the early morning sun playing quoits in the dusty square.

The three of them had entered the cool darkness of the church and knelt in silent prayer. Henri, at twelve years of age, knew his father's capacity for prayer and the likely loss of feeling to his own knees. Not for Philippe the effete modern custom of kneeling on padded cushions in front of the altar: for him it was the unforgiving stone floor for up to an hour.

Once Henri was sure his father's eyes were closed in supplication, he slowly rose from his knees and moved behind one of the large stone pillars supporting the timber roof. He still prayed, but from a more comfortable position – he was sure the Lord would understand. He closed his eyes and clasped his hands together. The silence of the church grew as the minutes passed.

Suddenly a door creaked. The rasp of metal cut through Henri's quiet contemplation. Reflecting that he could still pray with one eye closed, he opened the other. Sunlight slanted into the church through the now open door. Soft, swift footsteps approached. Who was risking his father's wrath by disturbing his prayers? Leaning forward to peer round the pillar he saw the tall form of Batu Al-Khalid, a Muslim who had converted to Christianity under the tutelage of his father's priest.

Batu had arrived in Tyre some four weeks previously from the mountains, professing a desire to be converted. He had been accepted readily into the community of Tyre as an example of Christianity's triumph over Islam. Now, Henri thought, he had obviously come to worship with his father. As Henri watched, Batu slowly and silently approached Philippe and Jean at the altar.

Nearing the kneeling figures, Batu's right hand disappeared into his robe. Steel flashed in the sunlight. Henri watched, transfixed, as the blade descended. His father rose, half turned, clutching at his throat. A glistening redness spread through his fingers. Batu struck again, the blade entering Philippe's chest. He fell heavily, his blood already spreading across the stone floor.

Jean, eyes wide in terror, screamed shrilly. At his cry the church door was flung wider and Philippe's bodyguard rushed in. They found their master choking and gasping in a pool of blood. The assassin whirled to face the guards. Jean wavered uncertainly in between the dripping blade and the fast-approaching guard. Batu lunged at him, but the boy was too quick and he hurled himself away from the flashing blade. Its tip caught his shoulder and a fine spray of bright red blood glittered for a moment.

Two of the guards had pinned the struggling assassin to the floor and another knelt over Philippe. His father's motionless body and the expression on the guards' faces told Henri everything. He had risen and backed away from the dreadful scene.

One of the guard's rose from his knees and thrust his sword into the still wildly struggling assassin, who jerked spasmodically and lay still.

Suddenly a powerful arm had encircled Henri's body. A sweaty hand silenced his scream of terror. He choked on a smell of spices and herbs as he was dragged, kicking frantically, to the rear of the church. Then his head exploded in a burst of stars and bright lights and he sank into darkness.

* * *

The harsh jolting of the crude wooden cart brought him slowly back to consciousness. He was lying face down in a foul-smelling mixture of straw and animal excrement. He tried to struggle up but found that he was bound hand and foot. However, by the position of the setting sun he knew he was moving north.

The voices of his captors came to him over the rumbling of the wooden cart. They were the voices of men who had tasted success and who looked forward to returning home.

'Better to sell him in Sidon,' said one. 'A few bezants now would be better than waiting until Damascus.'

'No, Yousef, trust me. The boy will make a fine Mamaluke at Emir Baibars' camp, and the emir will reward us, mark my words.'

Henri lay petrified. Mothers accompanying the Crusaders, in order to terrify infants into good behaviour had used the threat of 'Baibars'. Everyone knew the ferocious reputation of the former slave. Henri felt an overpowering sense of loneliness and grief steal over him. He began to weep uncontrollably.

His father, grandfather Guy, and his great uncle the infamous Simon de Montfort, had all felt the kiss of Saracen steel. When Henri was seven years of age, Baibars had personally executed 200 Templar Knights in front of the walls of Castel Safed and followed that up two years later by the execution of over 1,000 soldiers outside Acre.

Henri panicked briefly in his stinking, swaying prison, but suddenly he seemed to see the stern face of his father, and in spite of his despair he took deep calming breaths. Baibars would not be interested personally in the fate of a captured child, and of the two options the chance to be trained as a soldier, albeit for the Infidel, gave him the best hope of survival. It was a tradition of the Egyptians adopted after they realised that the Turkish bowmen and horsemen, whilst brilliant in the field, gathered their possessions and went home when the money or fight ran out. The meagre subsistence of the nomadic tribes was often strained by the birth of too many children, so that the young males between ten and twelve years were sometimes bought by the army to be trained in the use of the sword, horse, bow and battleaxe. Often little persuasion was needed, as the choice to be trained in one of the finest armies in the East was one which most young boys, given the alternative of herding goats for a lifetime, leapt at.

Young Henri, in his terror and anguish, instinctively knew that to survive he would have to appear as extremely promising fighting material from the moment his bonds were released.

The cart entered a body of water and was immediately flooded. For a moment Henri panicked. Then recovering his wits, he gulped gratefully at the cool, fresh liquid, which, at the same time, was thankfully sluicing away most of the foul-smelling detritus he was lying on. Refreshed, and now with the knowledge that they had crossed the River Litani to the north of Tyre, he relaxed, falling into a sleep of pure exhaustion.

* * *

Henri was released from his bonds as soon as the group reached the mountains above Damascus. He was then tied to the saddle of one of the Hashashin horses, for it was they who had kidnapped him after the bloody murder of his father: they had had no way of knowing that the small boy cowering behind the pillar was Philippe of Tyre's son. In their euphoria at the successful assassination of one of Christendom's most feared and ruthless Crusaders, they had grabbed the solitary child with nothing more in mind than selling him later to the highest bidder as a slave. Henri, remembering his thoughts on the subject, had fought savagely with his captors once his bonds were removed. He was restrained none too gently amidst much laughter and ribald comment, and by the time the group arrived at their mountain hideout all talk of selling him in the slave market had come to an end.

His neck halter remained, and he was issued with a flowing white djellaba like any young Arab boy. The group relaxed, comfortable in their mountain lair, and Henri was left to himself. He wandered aimlessly around the clusters of huddled fighters as they talked and indulged in boisterous horseplay. They ignored him utterly. When they cooked, someone would throw him scraps as they would to a dog. He felt utterly alone and dejected.

After three days, he was huddled in his cloak as near to the fire as he could get when Yousef al Malik approached and sat beside him in silence, during which Yousef observed his young charge, before he nodded slowly and spoke. 'Tomorrow we start. Tomorrow we begin to make you a warrior.' Then he nodded briskly and went striding away.

The next morning the group began to school Henri in the art of battle.

Already an experienced and gifted horseman, he took to the small light Arab horses as if he had been riding them all his life. Yousef-al-Malik, the leader of the small band who had urged caution about Henri's disposal on the first day of his capture, was especially keen to watch his young charge.

One day Henri's halter was removed and he was given a small battleaxe mounted on flexible bamboo, which the Hashashin had adapted from those used by the Mongol army. Galloping down a small ravine at full speed, Henri had to remove a melon from the top of a pole stuck in the earth. At his first attempt he cleanly cut the melon in half. The watching band of Hashashin erupted into spontaneous applause. Henri made a mock bow to Yousef, but his half-closed eyes glittered with hatred. One day, he thought, the melon will be your head, Yousef al Malik.

As a sect of the Shiites, the Hashashin had achieved an importance far above their actual military capability. Known as 'seveners' in Islam, they believed that the missing seventh Imam, Ismail, would return as the 'Mahdi' or chosen one, being a blood descendant of the Prophet. Their sect had already slaughtered the fourth Imam, Uthman, hundreds of years earlier, thus creating the Shiite movement, arguing that only descendants of the Prophet – and not 'companions – should lead Islam. They claimed the right to slaughter anybody who stood in the way of their search for the Mahdi.

Having been seamlessly absorbed into this little mountain group led by the bearded Yousef al-Malik, Henri gradually realised that his birth in Tyre and life amongst the Arabs of the Christian court had played a large part in saving his life. Dirty and evil-smelling as he was, there was little to distinguish him from a native-born Arab. He was, like most foreign aristocrats in the Holy Land, a fluent Arabic speaker, and understood fully the daily demands of the Muslim faith. Taking care to seek the east in order to pray five times a day, and eating only with his right hand, he was quickly absorbed into the band. When it was discovered that he could shoot an arrow with considerable accuracy, so much that he could bring down a wild goat at over two hundred paces, he began to earn the grudging respect of the band of Hashishin.

CHAPTER 3

The year passed quickly, and Yousef al Malik watched his charge mature into a tall, strapping young man. One morning, in late spring, the group rose from their beds in the honeycomb of caves above the tumbling stream, and rather than the usual communal breakfast around the re-kindled campfire, packed hard wheat cakes, figs and dates into their saddle rolls. In the distance, appearing like a rolling bank of winter fog, a dust cloud approached.

Normally for the group this would have signalled an instant dispersal: not so today. The cloud metamorphosed into thousands upon thousands of men; walking, riding, carrying weapons and hauling huge siege engines. At this vast column's head, a group of a dozen horsemen, mounted on beautiful Arab stallions, rode up to greet Al-Malik. Whooping and yelling 'Allu, Allah al Akbar' ['God is Great'] they dismounted and embraced like long lost friends.

Yousef sought out the tallest and most brilliantly robed horseman, and after a few moments of boisterous laughter he turned to Henri and beckoned him. Henri stood patiently at Yousef's side, looking expectantly at the tall, arrogant leader before him. Piercing blue eyes, unusual in an Arab, regarded him from beneath black dense eyebrows. Henri felt a shiver run through him in spite of the morning sun.

'We acquired this little Mamaluke during our mission in Tyre', Yousef said, 'I know of no finer bowman and horseman in my entire troop. When he has sampled the delights of the seventy-two houris in heaven he will be a fearless soldier for Allah.'

The tall emir nodded, grunting. He extended his hand to Henri. 'May I present Al-adin your eminence,' continued Yousef, using the name of the legendary Saladin's brother, which he had bestowed on Henri as a special honour. 'Al-adin, this is Sultan Rukn al-Din Baibars'.

Henri's hand had already been firmly grasped by Baibars. But at the sound of his name he recoiled. As he bowed his head his eyes flashed hatred. Here was the very devil incarnate whose deeds had terrified Henri during his childhood; the man who had sent his assassins to murder Henri's father; the sole cause of the loss of his family's lands and their flight to the borders of the Mediterranean at Tyre.

He raised his eyes. They were without expression. He studied the man's face: he would remember it. In the confusion and general euphoria no one noticed him trembling as he fought to control his rage.

Henri's group joined the mighty caravan as it continued its journey north. The huge siege catapults of Baibars' army had been broken down into their separate parts, and it took over a thousand men to transport them: progress was a painful five miles a day.

The caravan's destination was the fabled Knights Hospitaller fortress of Krak de Chevaliers, a bastion enshrined in Muslim lore as the one that even the mighty Saladin had failed to conquer. But when, after several weeks, the huge cliff-top edifice came into view the caravan merely wound its way along the valley floor. From the beleaguered but still defiant garrison came the loud, derisory blast of trumpets and clashing of cymbals, followed by raucous laughter and catcalls as sewage and other waste was hurled down the cliffs at them. Later, huddled round the campfire, Henri questioned Yousef as to the reason for passing it by. Yousef smiled and nodded, pleased that his young charge had questioned the tactics.

'First Safita, then we come back for the Krak de Chevaliers. Sultan Baibars does not want to fight with another garrison at his back.'

In the late summer of 1271, Baibars' arrival at the smaller, light-coloured stone castle at Safita, sometimes known as Castel Blanc, had caught the defenders unaware. The garrison, under Templar Grand Master Thomas Bérard, was seriously undermanned. In spite of its eleven-foot-thick outer walls, the position was hopeless, given the overwhelming forces surrounding it.

Essentially, Baibars required that the Fortress of Safita be neutralised so that he could concentrate on Krak de Chevaliers. He had opened negotiations with Thomas Bérard and agreed that he and his Templars could leave, making their way back to Tortosa on foot. He surmised that news of his clemency would do him no harm in future negotiations. With Safita neatly out of the way, the column had returned to the business at Krak de Chevaliers.

Henri darted around the engineers as they erected the giant catapults and watched as they hewed large pieces of rock with which to batter the walls.

Brought up in fortresses and fortifications, he had a low opinion of the catapults in their ability to destroy walls many feet thick. These catapults were fashioned from timbers over a man's forearm thick. They took nearly a thousand men to transport them, and it took a week to erect them: three days merely to fill the trebuchet's large counterweight that gave the engine its power. Using a windlass manned by thirty brawny Egyptians, the giant arm was winched down and a large boulder of easily two men's weight placed in the basket. At a signal the windlass was released, and the counterweight plummeted to earth. The catapult's main shaft thicker than a man's torso could be seen to bend as the power of the counterweight was transferred to the end of the bucket. It seemed as little an effort as the flicking of a marble to make the huge boulder fly skywards before it crashed into the gatehouse of the mighty fortress, so hard Henri felt it through his feet. Great lumps of shattered masonry began falling from the crenelations above the gate.

After a day of incessant pounding the towers above the gatehouse were reduced to rubble.

As the defenders retreated to avoid the falling masonry, the more agile of the Muslim archers climbed the walls either side of the huge gate. Fighting off frantic attempts to repel them, they managed to open the gate, and the leading groups of Muslim soldiers poured into the castle. Those who had not sought the sanctuary of the inner keep were doomed. Servants and native-born soldiers were shackled and later sold into slavery. However, a group of thirty or so Hospitallers, some wounded, were taken prisoner. Henri stayed close to Yousef as he watched the group of proud knights being stripped naked and forced to kneel in the baking sun.

Baibars had selected a patch of ground within the inner walls, but in full view of the remainder of the garrison clustered on the walls of the inner keep above him. The sultan had his men erect his travelling tent, a gaudily striped affair, so that its opening faced the inner keep of the watching Hospitallers. Parading up and down in front of the naked kneeling knights he offered them their lives if they renounced God in favour of the One True Prophet by the time he had finished his afternoon refreshment.

As he sat on his Persian carpet in the shade of his tent, he slowly sipped a goblet of effervescent sherbet. Draining the glass, he rose and took up a small knife and a pair of tongs used to place lumps of charcoal in the night braziers. Two huge gleaming Nubians dragged the first knight in front of the tent and forced him to kneel holding his arms outstretched. Baibars approached the man and swiftly ran the knife down from his shoulders to his navel in two parallel strokes. The man screamed as blood spurted. Making a further sideways slashing movement Baibars now had a thin strip of skin from the victim's chest to his navel. Without pause he took the tongs and gripping the top of the flap of flesh he pulled the entire strip from the man. Without heeding the victim's screams, he again slashed with the knife. The man was being skinned alive as the two impassive Nubians held him. Pausing when he had a pile of skin at the victim's knees, Baibars cut off a piece and forced it into the screaming knight's mouth. The horrific sounds died away slowly, and the Nubians released their charge: twitching and moaning the knight bled and choked to death. Every other Hospitaller was then beheaded in full view of the garrison.

For ten days they camped inside the inner walls. Then Baibars agreed that the garrison could leave without weapons or food and return to Tripoli on foot – an act that formed part of the legend of Baibars: sometimes ferocious cruelty, other times he displayed something almost bordering on compassion. However, the message was clear to the inhabitants of the next city on Baibars' route.

There was good reason for Baibars' apparent softening of heart in not massacring the rest of the garrison, though. A new Crusade led by the youthful but brilliant tactician, Prince Edward Plantagenet, accompanied by a certain Teobaldo Visconti, had arrived in the Holy Land: in years to come these men would become Edward I of England and Pope Gregory X. Baibars had naturally little to fear from another few thousand Crusaders, but the Mongols in the east under their supreme leader Kublai Khan were stirring again. Baibars had already received threatening communication from Kublai's son, the Ilkhan Abaga, demanding that the Egyptians bow to the Mongol Khan. At the same time, Thomas Bérard, the Templar Grand Master and recipient of Baibars 'mercy' at Safita, had good reason to believe a treaty with Baibars was possible. All this intelligence came to Henri via his fireside lessons from his mentor.

One night Yousef had joined Henri at the dying embers of the campfire. The group had eaten well, and drunk large quantities of kumis, so that the fire was surrounded by sleeping men. The two were now on their own. Yousef leant towards Henri conspiratorially: since Henri's acceptance by the group he was treated almost as an equal. 'Very soon I shall have my seventy-two virgins in heaven my friend.'

Yousef's expression was unreadable and Henri looked at him questioningly.

'I have been given an assignment by Baibars himself,' he went on. 'I am to go to the court of Prince Edward of England and ingratiate myself into his company, then ...'

Yousef paused and glanced quickly over his shoulder before removing a small bundle from his cloak. It contained a wickedly curved dagger. He wrapped it up quickly and returned it to the folds of his garment. 'And you are to accompany me! Though you need not sample the virgins just yet,' he added wryly.

He was to take his young Mamaluke as witness, and as part of his rite of initiation. Yousef's eyes gleamed in the darkness as the promise of eternity with seventy-two virgins beckoned. The boys and young men of the camp had, of course, discussed these matters loudly and at length with the young Henri.

At certain times the normal routines of the group were suspended. They sat around all day smoking hashish or eating it when it had been baked into sweet cakes. One or two of the group, usually the boys aged eighteen or nineteen, and sprouting wispy hairs of manhood, were fed more than the rest. When virtually unconscious they were taken further up the valley to a small walled area around a splashing mountain stream. In their advanced hallucinatory state, they found themselves alone and naked in a lush walled garden, with six or more beautiful young, sexually accomplished, women called houris. All day these women would tend to their every whim and need, including some they had never heard of before. By the time the effect of the hashish eventually wore off the girls would have disappeared, and the young men's incredulous tales to their compatriots would be gravely interpreted as a vision of heaven, available to all young Muslims for all eternity if they sacrificed themselves in the name of the Prophet. Yousef had now been given his own personal jihad by Sultan Baibars himself and was ready to die.

* * *

The peace treaty with Prince Edward was not thirty days old when the pair were sent to his court at Tortosa. As an emissary from the Sultan Baibars, Yousef was received warmly into the English court, accompanied by Henri in the guise of his page. Yousef professed to be negotiating the finer details of the ten-year treaty with Baibars. At the same time he was ingratiating himself he was also alluding to being a secret admirer of the Christian faith. After a few weeks, Yousef and Henri's attendance at the daily Mass attracted scant attention, and Edward spent many hours with Yousef discussing the finer points of Christianity versus Islam. Eventually he dropped his guard sufficiently to allow himself to be in Yousef's company outside his quarters, with only the minimum number of bodyguards.

One morning Henri awoke to find Yousef on his prayer mat, facing east and holding the long thin dagger, the blade of which he could now see was discoloured: he knew it was poisoned. Henri watched in fascination as Yousef prepared himself for the journey into the afterlife that the assassination of Prince Edward would bring for him.

For several days Yousef had gone alone to the royal quarters in order to distance himself from Henri. The plan was for Henri to witness the murder of Edward, then slip away and report back to Baibars. Accordingly, on the day in question he dressed himself in a scruffy djellaba so that he was indistinguishable from any other young man around the castle. He positioned himself at the far end of the courtyard and busied himself around the water trough. Watching the horses drink, he also watched as Yousef swiftly entered the royal apartments.

A scream of pain and a bellow of anger brought the guards pounding across the courtyard. Henri went racing towards the royal quarters followed by the prince's young wife. A small but growing group of courtiers, bodyguards and personal retainers had begun to gather around an inert form on the marble floor. Edward was laying there his robes ripped from him.

The princess pushed her way through the crowd and knelt at her husband's side, ordering everybody away as she did so. 'Water! Quickly!' she cried. Then she held up the knife, the one Henri had seen earlier in Yousef's hand. Only the tip was stained with blood, showing that the penetration into Edward's body had been minimal. To Henri's astonishment she bent her head and covered the bloody gash beneath Edward's ribs with her lips. Her body heaved, and she spat a stream of blood and spittle onto the pale marble floor.

The crowd had parted in obedience to the princess's command, and Edward twisted his head to look at the soldiers holding Yousef, whose face had taken on a dreamlike calmness. He raised his arm and pointed. 'Guilty!' he managed to croak, 'Execute the heathen bastard now!' Then he slumped backwards, unconscious.

Yousef was dragged roughly into the courtyard. His eyes caught Henri's and he smiled in complete happiness. He was still smiling as he was forced to his knees; smiling still as the swift sword removed his head and sent it rolling in the dust.

Henri shrank into the gathering crowd and headed towards the castle gates. He walked in the heat without feeling, his mind numb. It was only after several miles that his thoughts calmed. Even though Yousef and his group had kidnapped him during the most appalling event in his life, whether Henri wanted to admit it or not, Yousef had been kind to him and kept him safe. And he had taught him skills that would prove invaluable. Yet the shock of the brutal removal of Yousef's head faded somewhat as he remembered his own father's death. With renewed strength he took the road to the mountains again.

Some days later Henri stood shaking in front of the tall figure of Sultan Baibars. Baibars's emirs regarded with some amusement the ragged dirty sixteen-year-old, dusty from the long road from Tortosa. 'Sit, sit my child,' Baibars said slowly, his eyes glittering. 'Did you see the prince breathe his last?'

'No, no,' Henri, whispered. 'I did not, Lord, but I saw how his lady held up the bloodstained dagger in her hand.'

'But Yousef is in paradise?'

'Yes, Lord, executed on Prince Edward's orders.'

Baibars turned briefly to a hawkish looking emir next to him. 'Go! Confirm Edward's death. An assassin should leave no room for doubt.'

Turning again to Henri, he smiled benignly. 'Go now with our thanks. Rest and refresh yourself. You have done well.' Relieved, Henri stumbled from the tent.

If there was doubt in Sultan Baibars' mind about the outcome of the assassination, there was none in the camp of the Hashashin. They danced and whirled the night away to the relentless thump of the kettledrums as the campfire burned brightly, hurling effervescent sparks towards the inky heavens now alight with a thousand stars. Henri sat on the edge of the group, neither with them nor apart from them. He had survived the last few years, and he was grateful to the Hashashin for that. This had been better than a life sold into slavery.

However, his thoughts had increasingly of late turned to the moment of his capture, and to memories of his father: never a warm figure, but a tower of stability and strength, who had run his fiefdom in Tyre with a firm but fair hand, and who had been slain at a moment of prayer by a murderous Infidel. And in an echo of that evil event, Prince Edward of England, stabbed by a man in his confidence for whom, just for a moment, he had let his guard down.

Henri spat in the dust and clenched his fists. His toes were gritty with sand and his lice-infested djellaba itched unbearably. He suddenly had a vision of his quarters in the keep at Tyre: fresh water from the well, meals on tables in front of roaring fires, and the basic simplicity of his privileged life. He lowered his head and his eyes glittered in the darkness. He clenched and unclenched his fists. Suddenly the tears came.

In the morning he joined his group as they prepared to return to their mountain lair. Henri set off with them, galloping together towards the distant purple mountains. He knew now what he had to do. One slip and he was dead, but if it took a lifetime, he had to return to his family and take his rightful place. Only from there could he be certain of avenging his father's death. He whooped and cried with his fellow Hashashin as the dust rose around their horses' flying hooves, but his heart beat steadily and coolly as they thundered into the band's mountain lair.

According to custom, the responsibility of the training and equipping of Henri passed to Yousef's brother: Ayub al Malik. Whilst an accomplished soldier, Ayub was not as communicative as his late brother so that once each day's training and skirmishing had come to an end, Henri found himself at a loose end around the camp.

Whilst the group of fifty or sixty Hashashin formed an independent unit, they kept themselves abreast of the latest intelligence via a network of spies, not only in Baibars' camp, but in the Christian strongholds and the Mongol army, ever-present and threatening to the east.

In the summer or early autumn of 1276, Sultan Baibars sent word to the group, that they were to move on to the Cypriot land of Anatolia to the north. The recent death of the Seljuk leader had left a four-year old on the Sultan's throne, controlled by a greedy emir named Suleiman. Whilst he paid tribute to the Mongol Ilkhan Abaga, who prudently kept a garrison of horsemen in his country, he helped himself to the country's riches and ignored the plight of the people. Sultan Baibars had perceived this opportunity and promptly invaded. Whilst the Hashashins were not part of the invasion, their particular skills could be called upon.

Baibars moved on Anatolia, seeing little threat from the small Mongol garrison. However, news of his success reached the ears of the Ilkhan Abaga, and in fury he mobilised the entire Mongol army. Sultan Baibars was a brilliant tactician, and a courageous leader, but even he feared the gathering Mongol hordes. Quickly, he retired into Syria.

In 1277, secure in the heart of Damascus, Baibars burned with rage. Not only had he had to give way to the Mongol army, but also a young Syrian prince, al-Qahir, was receiving more than his fair share of praise for the recent military actions. Baibars was acutely aware that the prince was a descendent of the legendary Saladin, and finally he could contain his anger no longer. The young al-Qahir, now invested as the Prince of Kerak, was invited to a grand banquet. Henri's Hashishin were also invited.

Over five hundred people sat down under the stars to feast and consume vast quantities of kumis, that was so highly regarded by the Mongols.

As the evening wore on, Sultan Baibars and the young prince staggered about among the royal entourage in a display of affection and respect. Henri had a large leather gourd and was replenishing drinks as fast as he could when he approached Sultan Baibars, whose guards were familiar with his presence.

Baibars had collapsed onto a large silk cushion, and the young prince had done the same. Both men's eyes were struggling to stay open. As Henri bent with the gourd, Baibars fumbled under his cloak. He held in his unsteady hand a small phial containing a milky liquid. Henri watched, mesmerised, as

Baibars' fingers crushed the top of the phial. With his left hand pointing unsteadily, he drew the prince's attention to a group of beautiful young houris dancing nearby. With the other hand Baibars quickly tipped the contents of the phial into al-Qahir's goblet.

Reacting almost without thinking, Henri smoothly removed the goblet from the prince's hand: the young man, his eyes still fixed on the houris, could see nothing else.

Henri now took the drunken Baibar's and the prince's goblets and, with his back half-turned, made as if he was refilling them before respectfully offering the goblets to Baibars and the young prince. Waiting until the drunken pair had toasted each other and swallowed deep drafts from their poisoned goblets, Henri moved on past the recumbent emirs and the snoring soldiers to the campfire, where he settled down to sit in the glow of the fire behind a group of sleeping men. Around him the camp quietened down for the night, the odd snoring or guttural retching of someone being the only sounds in the inky blackness. He dozed fitfully, his mind alive.

The first screams of terror and anguish woke everybody in the camp. In the ensuing confusion it was not immediately clear that they came, not from one throat, but from two. As the soldiers, still dazed with drink, milled about in anxious disorder, first the sultan, and then the young prince, al-Qahir, emerged, staggering and stumbling, from their tents, hands tearing at their bodies in fearful agony.

Their skins glistened with sweat and their eyes were swollen to twice their normal size. Against their pallor the whites of their eyes stood out as they howled and writhed in torment. Clutching at their stomachs they collapsed at last and lay still in the grit of the desert.

Henri watched with a strange feeling of detachment as Baibars' emirs tried, with one potion after another, to revive the all-but-lifeless forms. As dawn streaked the sky, first the young prince, and then Sultan Baibars, howled and breathed their last. Henri, clenching his fists, watched in triumph knowing that Christendom's most ruthless enemy was now dead.

That was how Henri had slipped away into the darkness to make his way back to his own people, taking with him the skills that he would now use against his mortal enemies.

Had it really all happened so long ago?

CHAPTER 4

Fourteen years had passed, during which time the sacred realm should have been won back from the Infidel. Henri ground his teeth, hands clenching on the stone battlements. His eyes took in the Muslim hordes led by Khalil camped just three hundred yards from the walls of Acre. It would take no less than a miracle for them to fail to push the Christians into the sea at Acre. This was the last bastion of Christianity, now just a breath away from extinction.

Henri's thoughts grew darker as the sun sank towards the sea. For years, under the continual onslaught of the Infidel, the Holy Land had fragmented; each part ruled separately by the various chivalric orders, all in direct competition with each other. They stupidly preferred to war between themselves rather than concentrate on keeping the heathens from the gate. How had Pope Urban II's rallying call from Clermont proved so fruitless?

Henri took a deep breath, straightening his shoulders. He looked forward to the coming combat. He had spent most of his life in one battle or another since he had escaped from the Hashashin after assassinating Sultan Baibar all those years ago. But tonight, although he was confident in his planning of the skirmish, he felt a certain pessimism, doubting that the raid would really affect the result of the coming battle for Acre. He watched the Saracens around their campfire as they squatted on the ground beating their large copper kettledrums. The rhythm began to increase as their excitement and euphoria grew. Their eyes would be glittering with hatred, and their teeth would be bared. Jubilant, they knew that only a few stones stood between them and the last Christians in the lands that were now all but theirs. The end was not in doubt. It was merely a matter of time.

Henri's thoughts drifted back to when his mother, Princess Maria of Armenia, after her initial joy at her reunion with her youngest son, seemingly back from the dead, had encouraged Henri to join the Knights Hospitaller under Jean de Villiers. She had inherited her late husband's conviction that the Templars, with their posturing and quarrelling, had cost Christendom the Holy Land. In her own capacity as Princess of Antioch, she had met a previous Hospitaller Grand Master, the thoughtful and subtle Hugues de Revel, before his death in 1277. As a direct result of that meeting, Henri had found himself fighting at the side of a certain Gilbert de Gothia at the siege of Marqab in 1285. It was not only to be the start of a lifelong friendship, but it would also change Henri's life forever. Henri's mind drifted further as he remembered the occasion that had forged their friendship.

Sultan Khala'un's catapults had been battering the gatehouse at Marqab, whilst his archers had kept up a deadly hail of arrows. Simultaneously, his miners were excavating the rock beneath the castle's foundations. The truth was that whilst the catapults had proved a small success, the height of the fortress of Marqab, mounted as it was on a rocky promontory, meant that they expended most of their force throwing the rocks skywards. With this in mind, Khala'un had ordered the use of thousands of miners, who had been cutting away at the cliff beneath the walls. When they had enlarged a sufficient area, they propped up the roof under the castle foundations with pitch- and naptha-soaked timbers. Eventually the creaks and groans told them that the weight of the foundations was now supported solely by these wooden props, which they then set on fire. Far above the miners, the garrison could smell the vapours of the naptha as it was being poured on the tunnel's props and feel the vibrations of the miners beneath their feet.

To reconnoitre, Henri had braved the showers of arrows and had just reached the battlements when a particularly large boulder crashed into the wall in front of him.

As Henri leapt forward over the falling masonry, a rumbling came from under his feet. Incredibly, an enemy foot soldier appeared suddenly before him. Henri, slowed by his bulky armour, was a fraction later than the other man in recovering the initiative. As the swarthy warrior's scimitar swept murderously upwards, somewhere from Henri's right came a bellow of warning, and the blade was deflected by a blow from a double-headed battleaxe. The same weapon, continuing its deadly arc, disappeared into the face of Henri's assailant. Henri was pulled backwards over the fallen stones. Recovering swiftly and fighting to raise his sword arm against this unknown force, his struggles were cut short by a tremendous roar.

The timely action of Gilbert de Gothia had saved Henri from disappearing into the enormous hole where the gatehouse and ramp to the castle once stood. This same hole had prevented any further incursions into the castle, and as a result both sides retired to plan the next move. After three days, Sultan Khala'un called a truce and, to the knights' astonishment, gave terms that each knight could leave with his horse, armour and personal weapons, whilst the foot soldiers were to leave with nothing.

Henri had, of course, witnessed this kind of diplomacy under Baibars, and appreciated the sultan's game. When the hungry knights and soldiers found their way back to Tripoli, Sultan Khala'un would not be seen in too unfavourable a light, and this would make the defence of a large city difficult if there was seemingly little to fear from the Saracen hordes. As the disconsolate knights and foot soldiers streamed slowly out of Marqab, Khala'un's masons had begun dismantling the mighty fortress stone by stone. Henri, Gilbert de Gothia, and what was left of the garrison wound their way down the mountain track. The stones that the masons hurled down the cliffs bounced and reverberated along the valley. The pair rode side by side without speaking until the noise of the destruction faded in the distance.

'The road to Tripoli is long, Henri,' muttered Gilbert.

'And there is only the sea beyond that,' rejoined Henri.

The pair lapsed again into an uneasy silence. Henri felt waves of alternate rage and despair wash over him. He sat slumped in his saddle, caring little if a loose Saracen arrow should find its mark. He was twenty-nine years old. He bore his father's title of Lord of Tyre. He had inherited his mother's estates in Armenia, Antioch, and Tripoli and his elder brother Philippe's estates in France, of Montfort L'Amaury, Ferte-Alais and Castres, following his recent death in Tunisia. He was, in theory at least, a wealthy and highly placed young man. Again, and again the Templars had retreated, conceded or been beaten back towards the sea. Those taken prisoner had either been killed on the spot or sold later as slaves. To be sure, Henri had tasted his share of victories, but they had been battles won in a losing war. His mother had barely been restored to him when she was murdered in a Muslim raid. Before she died, she had been raped by a succession of drunken Cypriot bowmen.

Three years later his elder brother, Jean of Toron, had died in a fight with Muslim traders in the Port of Tripoli, and finally, so had Humphrey, his closest brother, the year before the fall of Marqab. His only remaining family lived far away in France and England.

The memory of Humphrey's death was still painful and fresh to Henri, and now he was the last of the de Montfort family left in this godforsaken land. But he had inherited one thing from his noble line: a steely determination to overcome his enemy. The one thread that had run through his life so far had been the violent contact with the followers of the Prophet Mohammed. His father, his mother, his three brothers, gone now, murdered by the Infidel, and aided not a little in his eyes, by the incompetence, greed and internecine rivalry of the Knights Templar.

And then the blackness in his heart had been suddenly replaced by a burning passion; a heat so fierce it made him grip his sword, force himself upright in his saddle and swear silently that he would not rest until the forces of Mohammad were defeated and pushed back to the burning barren sands of Arabia, as Pope Urban had decreed.

He had glanced across at Gilbert. They had only met in the last weeks of the siege at Marqab, but already each man felt a deep sense of brotherhood towards the other. There had been times in battle when death threatened, and each had found the other at his side. Gilbert had caught Henri's glance; he had seen that fury in his friend's eyes. Then Henri's anger faded as he threw off his black mood and the pair smiled briefly at each other, tight lipped.

'The last to Tripoli buys dinner,' shouted Henri, digging his spurs to his charger's flank. Gilbert did likewise and the two galloped past the despondent column, heading towards the glittering sea in the far distance. Roaring and whooping, the two exorcised their gloomy thoughts and exchanged them for the promise of the food and carousing awaiting them.

* * *

Henri pushed these thoughts and memories to the back of his mind and turned to make his way back along the battlements. That was when he saw a figure approaching, and paused, recognising the familiar gait. 'Gilbert, dearest friend how are you tonight?' he called.

Gilbert bowed mockingly, 'Ready to blunt my sword on the Saracen's head, my Prince.'

The two men embraced warmly. Gilbert, a Knight Commander of the Order of St Anthony, had parried and teased Henri's probing questions about his order, giving little away. On the occasions that the two were parted, Henri had from time to time found his friend wandering around the oldest churches of Acre, and the chapel at the Gate of St Anthony where they now stood. As the pair relaxed after various forays, especially in the last twelve months, Gilbert's journeys to the other churches in Acre had become more frequent. Henri had questioned his friend but to little avail, save that Gilbert's apparent quest appeared to have begun from the moment a messenger from his home in Villandraut, in France, had delivered a letter to him. All that Henri had discovered was that Gilbert had lost his father in a jousting tournament when he was four years old and had been adopted by his uncle Bishop Bertrand de Gothia who lived at Château Villandraut; and that he had a sister, Eleanor, whom he loved deeply, who was versed in the healing arts, and was newly arrived in Acre.

Gilbert leant on the battlements, blocking Henri's path and nodded in the direction of Khalil's tent, 'Observe the chest with the carrying poles next to Khalil?'

It was a statement as much as a question. Henri stared at the Infidel encampment and grunted in acknowledgement, his brow puckering. 'That would be a greater prize than setting fire to a catapult,' he said. Gilbert spat in derision. 'That chest carries the world's first written Koran by Uthman, who was murdered whilst reading it in 656.'

Henri's frown deepened. Until now he had assumed that Gilbert's off-duty knowledge was restricted to eating and wenching.

Gilbert continued, his voice deepening, 'You may think, my Prince, that a unified army of Islam opposes us. Nothing could be further from the truth. The Koran in that tent, not more than a thousand yards away, was written by the third Caliph after Ali, called Uthman. As he sat writing in the book he was murdered by the followers of Ali, who claimed that the word of God should pass down the bloodline of Mohamed the Prophet and not his companions: the murderers were from a sect known as Shia, whilst Uthman was from the Sunni sect. That Holy Koran is still stained with Uthman's blood. After his murder it was rumoured that the Koran was taken to Ethiopia, the original homeland of the Knights of St Anthony. Subsequently the Islamic empire expanded and within seventy years of Uthman's death in Mecca, the Infidel had conquered northern Africa and Spain, and had begun to move into Aquitaine and Gaul.'

'Fortunately for our holdings in France,' Gilbert continued wryly, 'our ancestors under Charles Martel defeated Al Ghafiqi at the Battle of Poitiers in 732. That Koran was at the battle and narrowly avoided capture at the hands of Martel's troops. Some of the group of Muslims carrying the Koran whilst fleeing back to Andalusia disappeared in the Languedoc and it was rumoured that part of their Holy Koran went missing during a skirmish in that area too.'

'Go on,' Henri said glancing curiously at his friend.

Gilbert continued, 'So, as you can see, there are two forces opposing us, my Lord: the followers of Ali who was a direct descendent of the Prophet –I believe they call themselves the Shi'at Ali or Ahl al Boyt; and the followers of Uthman who call themselves Sunni.'

Then Gilbert fell silent and Henri was surprised to see by his friend's expression that there was a struggle going on within him.

When Gilbert began again, he spoke in a lower voice, 'There are some who say the contents of Uthman's Koran, if it is complete, could divide the Infidel in a manner that would make our battle for the Holy Land seem a child's game. I don't know if this is true. However, one thing is certain. Seize that holy Koran and you will split the heathen forever.'

If Henri wondered where his friend had obtained this knowledge he did not ask, but he thought if the foray tonight got anywhere near the Sultan Khalil, it would be worth a fight to win their sacred book.

The pair continued to chat companionably on the walls as the blood-red sun sank into the darkness of the sea. Then gathering themselves, they made their way down the narrow unguarded steps into the throng of men and horses waiting behind the Gate of St Anthony. Gilbert preceded Henri, his black cloak and blue tau cross merging so that he cut a dark and menacing figure. The throng of tense armed soldiers parted as the two made their way through the crowd; Henri and Gilbert had a reputation for enjoying a hard fight. Men respected them.

Henri sometimes felt Gilbert held back from describing the Antonines, although nominally under Hospitaller command he suspected that they also had some kind of papal favour. He felt glad that Gilbert was fighting by his side. However, thinking of the imminent raid, he suddenly felt an inexplicable sense of unease.

As usual he and Gilbert were in the vanguard of the knights, and he watched the gleaming, sweating torsos of the gatekeepers as they pulled back the oiled timbers holding the doors closed. The great barriers swung inwards silently, and a cool breeze fanned the waiting horsemen. Just beyond an arrow's flight away, the fires from the enemy camp glimmered in the darkness.

Bearing in mind how the previous raiding party of Templar knights had been upended by the guy ropes of the Infidel tents as they crashed into them with predictably fatal results, Henri had given this problem great thought. After much experimentation, he had lashed a small flexible bamboo-handled battleaxe – spoils of war from a Mongol soldier – to a section of broken lance. He discovered he could ride at a tent and, whirling the now extended axe round his shoulders, effectively cut any guy ropes before his horse tripped on them. The further honing of this technique had led Gilbert and Henri to create an arrow formation of horsemen, with the outer edge comprising more agile local horsemen wielding these axes, while in the centre of the group rode the armoured knights.

Obeying muted commands, the battle group formed up in the deep shadow of the walls. Eschewing the usual bellowed battle cries they moved off on a steady canter, building to a full gallop as the last rays of the dying sun faded into an indigo sky. Henri crouched on his black stallion, the warm evening air streaming through the slit in his visor. This was his world, and he revelled in it.

With the creak and jangle of the galloping armoured knights loud in his ears, he focussed on the darkened encampment ahead. Through his wind-seared eyes, he saw the angular shapes of the Muslim army's tents come into view. He urged his mount onwards, and the bunched arrow formation loosened a little. Now his blood was up and he hefted his sword, anticipating the bloody havoc he would wreak with it. The tents were now only seventy yards away. He could make out the individual campfires, and soldiers passing to and fro before them. Suddenly his straining eyes detected something else. Small pinpricks of light were moving rapidly and erratically along the line of tents. With some difficulty he made out shadowy forms holding flaming torches.

The Infidel army had perfected the art of using naphtha oil obtained from underground deposits in Persia. They had often used it to great effect to fire the timbers supporting Crusader castle walls that they had mined. Henri, finally grasping the enemy's intention, was a fraction too late to shout of the danger. As the soldiers touched their flaming torches to the ground, lines of bluish flames leapt towards the galloping horses. The flattened area before the enemy camp was lit up, showing criss-cross channels filled with the flaming substance. Where the lines intersected, small piles of brushwood burst into flames in front of the galloping formation.

Henri tried to rein his mount in, but it was far too late. The horses on the edge of the formation turned in panic at the approaching conflagration. Screaming with terror, the lighter mounts collided with the heavier destriers of the knights at the centre. Speed, weight and momentum ensured that the smaller horses were rammed and trampled by the armoured chargers. Henri tried vainly to hold back his horse as it collided violently with another. The impact splintered the other rider's leg. He screamed in agony, and was thrown to the ground, to be crushed to a bloody pulp by his own falling horse. In the confusion Henri now heard an altogether more sinister noise: the whirr and hiss of hundreds of arrows as the Cypriot bowmen stepped out from behind their tents.

He knew in an instant what he must do. His armour and horse were only of any use on the move, and at speed. Slowed to a halt, surrounded by fallen, struggling, men there could be only one outcome. He wheeled to his left as Gilbert did likewise, the pair acting uncannily as one in the heat of battle. Henri had completed his left wheel and was searching for a gap in the chaos towards which he and Gilbert could head. The dying sun had illuminated the skyline of Acre, and Henri flattened himself along his charger's back and dug his spurs in. As he did so, a metallic twang reverberated around his head, and an arrow bounced off his steel helm. He grinned grimly in the darkness as his horse turned and raced back to the safety of Acre.

The second arrow made no noise when Henri felt a searing, red-hot agony low down on his right side. The pain took his breath away. His fingers loosened on the reins. He felt himself falling. Strangely, as he hit the ground the pain disappeared, and for a moment he felt that he was floating on his back as he looked up at the star-filled sky. His breath came back suddenly in great shuddering gasps. Dimly he heard horses being drawn to a halt and the rattle of armour as dark figures surrounded him. He felt hands lift him and he shouted in agony as the blackness descended.

* * *

Henri did not know how long he had been unconscious. He felt his brow being wiped gently with a cool cloth. He heard Gilbert say, 'The arrow must have broken when we put him on the horse, sister.'

'We must remove the arrow before putrefaction sets in,' a female voice said firmly. It continued conversationally; 'Did you capture the Koran of Uthman?' Henri at this point opened his eyes and saw Gilbert shake his head at someone he could not see.

Then a female figure came into view as she leaned over him. She rolled him onto his side and a blinding, searing pain shot through him. This woke him fully. The woman continued, 'See, the arrow has only penetrated his flesh, the barbs are just below the skin. We must cut around the head of the arrow using the Egyptian spoons and draw the whole shaft through his skin.' Henri's pain came again, stronger this time, and he felt himself floating away.

Gilbert looked at the fresh-faced nun and a smile lifted the corners of his lips. His younger sister had arrived by boat in the besieged city the week before. Ostensibly she had arrived at the beleaguered port of Acre to care for the wounded knights. Gilbert, however, knew that the news of his discovery of the ancient manuscripts and bound volumes of the treasury of St Anthony would have caused his uncle Bertrand de Gothia to send his sister to take them all back to France.

Her eyes, a deep intense blue, shone and sparkled at her sunburnt, swarthy brother, tall and lean from years of fighting in the Outremer sun. 'If you want your friend to live, my brother, we need to cut him now and remove the arrow.' She looked hard at Gilbert.

'You have our book now, haven't you?'

He nodded mutely.

'We will need some of its knowledge, if we are to stop this wound putrefying.'

Eleanor moved to the curtain over the doorway of the small chamber where they had laid Henri. Sweeping it to one side, she motioned in one of Henri's troop and bade him stand at the foot of the wooden table upon which Henri lay. Stooping, she picked up a small leather bag and took out a long apron, which she tied around herself. Rolling Henri onto one side, she motioned Gilbert to hold his arms, whilst the soldier was pressed into holding his legs. 'Firmly, man, firmly!' she snapped, 'This knight looks very strong.'

Then she bent over Henri, and with a sharp knife cut his woollen vest to the armpit, exposing his finely muscled torso. The arrow had entered Henri's body below his breastplate, but above the rear pommel of his large saddle, nicking his side as he twisted away from the flaming naphtha. A bloody haft of splintered wood protruded from his back. The line of the shaft could plainly be seen beneath his taut flesh. The larger protuberance of the arrowhead was visible below his ribcage in a small roll of body fat. Eleanor's fingers traced the arrow, feeling the beginnings of the heat of putrefaction. She pulled a small blade and a pair of long narrow bronze spoons from her bag.

The ancient Egyptians had pioneered the use of these spoons, primarily to extract the contents of the skull prior to mummification, and that was fully explained in the manuscripts and volumes that Eleanor's brother had found. These were, amongst other things, a treasury of healing knowledge that had been gradually added to since the time of the patron of their order: St Anthony.

Currently under the control of Bertrand de Gothia, their uncle and its Grand Prior, the order had in fact, been founded in Ethiopia in 370AD by the king, Prester John, for the defence of Christianity. It was the oldest order of chivalry in Christendom, and as Ethiopia had been under enormous influence from the ancient Egyptians, the use of these bronze spoons in surgery was well developed from the time of the pharaohs.

In addition, the order's volumes recorded the early beginnings of Islam, and the turmoil created in Mecca and Medina following the murder of the Caliph Uthman in 656, when elements of the Infidel fled to Ethiopia with the first written Koran. As brother and sister knew full well, it was Uthman's writings that were of great interest to their order.

For the moment, though, their focus was the wounded knight before them, lying prostrate and in dire need of the order's medical expertise. Moving gently, Eleanor's fingers sought beneath the skin for the sharp tip of the arrow. Finding it, she made a small cut across the skin, digging deeply until she felt the blade strike something hard. Henri convulsed on the table.

'Hold him!' she snapped, as she worked the twin spoons deep into his flesh guiding their shapes around the barbed arrowhead. With one hand she held the two spoons as they cocooned their deadly cargo, and with the other she enlarged the slit her knife had made. Henri writhed and moaned.

'Hold him down!' she shouted, and pulled strongly upwards with the spoons. Henri's body twisted, and he bellowed in pain, but Eleanor triumphantly held aloft the bloody remains of the arrow shaft.

Dropping the spoons into a small dish, she took a pitcher of clear water and poured it into the cut. It flowed from both wounds bloody and streaked with clots of dark venous blood. She continued to pour until the water ran clear. Taking a handful of Hypericum leaves mixed with potassium crystals, she packed them in the wound and wrapped a long bandage around Henri's torso, stretching round his girth as she fed the bandage under him, her cheeks pressed to the damp curls on his slowly breathing chest. When the bandage was in place and secure, she rose and looked at Gilbert, 'Rest for ten days – he mustn't leave his bed.'

Then, without waiting for a reply, she swept out of the room. Gilbert watched her depart before turning back to the sweat-drenched form of his friend.

Eleanor came back each day to change Henri's dressing. She was alarmed to see after the second day a trickle of weak pus seeping from his wound. She administered more of the purple potassium crystals, and for good measure, smeared his wound with wild honey and garlic, following the edicts laid down in the documents her brother had discovered – and all to timely effect, for within ten days Henri's wound had dried, and a firm crusty covering had appeared.

If Henri wondered why Eleanor had come to Acre at such a dangerous time, he refrained from enquiring. The news reaching his hospital bed was disastrous, and he fretted and became impatient with his immobility. Eleanor would not countenance his rising from his bed, however, and he found this female authority over him frustrating. Outside the walls a seething mass of Infidel soldiers were encamped. The thud of the miners as they drove tunnels under the foundations could be felt in his bed in the quiet of the night. Khalil had gathered all his great war drums outside the walls near the Accursed Tower. Their incessant beat warned the inhabitants of what to expect when the walls finally fell.

Gilbert entered Henri's chamber during the first week of May with the welcome news that King Hugh of Cyprus had arrived by sea with 2,000 men, and whilst the numbers could not hope to influence the final battle, he did bring some authority to the various factions. He had attempted to arrange an armistice with the Sultan, and had sent his envoy, the Knight Templar Guillaume de Conran to convey his request. In a farcical example of the behaviour of the wilder elements of the various orders, a missile from the city had landed amongst the little party as they spoke with the sultan. Narrowly avoiding instant execution in front of the furious sultan, the knight was sent hurrying back to the garrison with unconditional terms of surrender.

Henri grunted as he listened. 'Grand Master de Beaujeu needs to keep his Templars more in line. Does he not recognise their responsibility in arriving at this perilous stage?' he asked contemptuously, remembering his father's oft-repeated axiom that there were elements among the Templars that would rather die fighting than win any kind of lasting peace.

Gilbert nodded in agreement. Within two weeks of the attempt at diplomacy the walls around the Accursed Tower and the St Anthony's Gate were showing distinct signs of instability. Cracks had appeared, and parts of the extensive machicolations had tumbled into the streets below, as terrified citizens shrank back into their doorways.

Henri had become increasingly impatient and frustrated. The neat scab over his wound had healed, but its incessant itching was driving him mad. On the tenth day Eleanor had allowed (allowed!) him to sit a little in the sunshine in the alleyway outside his quarters. She appeared regularly after sunrise to change his dressing and smear more honey over the area. He had once protested that he saw little need in changing the dressing now that it had healed, and she had paused for a moment in her ministrations, looking at him with icy blue eyes, to explain, 'If you would like to see your estates at Castres and elsewhere, my Lord, we will do it my way.'

Reflecting on this afterwards, he could not fathom why on earth he had not exploded in rage at this impertinence.

A few days after he had begun to sit in the alley, he was taking his first unaided steps. It was not as if he had broken any bones, but the violence of the surgery had made him stiffen and walk as a man twice his age. However, a few circuits of the port area on the arm of Gilbert soon started to ease his stiffness.

The next day as Henri, Gilbert and Eleanor started their walk down to the harbour they passed the Templar Grand Master de Beaujeu. He was sitting astride his horse, urging his men on in their efforts to repair the walls with the fallen masonry. Out of a shower of arrows the Infidel had fired over the walls, a single shaft found the gap in his armour under his armpit. The three friends, watched, aghast, as the grand master's sword fell from his hand. His charger lurched to one side as it clattered onto the cobbles, and the Grand Master fell heavily to the ground. He made as if to rise then slumped back again. The soldiers, seeing their commander fall, let out a great cry of rage and dismay.

Henri and Gilbert hurriedly ran over to the fallen knight. His white cloak was now stained with his own slowly spreading blood. He looked up at the two Hospitallers. 'Gentlemen, I can do no more, look at my wound, I am dead.'

His head slumped as the two dragged him to the shelter of the stone arch. Eleanor bent over him. After a moment she glanced up at the two knights, shaking her own head.

Later, as darkness fell, and in sombre mood, Henri and Gilbert climbed the narrow steps outside the makeshift hospital ward to the flat roof of the tiny stone building. As they stood, they were slightly below the level of the battlements across the narrow street, but they could see in the distance the seething mass of Khalil's army, and its gaily coloured tents. The last rays of the dying sun caught the conical tops of the tents and illuminated them like miniature volcanoes.

Beneath the walls in front of them, and out of their sight, they could hear the raucous exchanges of the Infidel troops and the thud of the miners as they burrowed beneath the mighty walls. To their right stood the Accursed Tower, its upper battlements still bathed in light. As they watched, the tops of a pair of scaling ladders appeared, and three or four turbaned figures leapt over the walls. Others followed, their features dark and swarthy.

Henri and Gilbert instinctively grasped their sword hilts, but the gap between the flat roof and the battlements was too wide. In unison they shouted to the watch on the tower, who thus far had remained ignorant of the threat beneath them in the darkness. Quickly the battlements were filled with running soldiers and the ring of clashing steel, and desperate shouts echoed across the rooftops. The garrison soon overwhelmed the little group, and the scaling ladders were pushed back to the screams of the unfortunate Infidel still scaling them.

Henri and Gilbert relaxed, and then the menacing throb of the kettledrums began again. 'They grow in confidence,' Henri said. 'Tomorrow or the next night the wall will fall ...'

'We have the sea at our backs Gilbert. We should make our peace with God before we die fighting with steel in our hands.'

Gilbert nodded slowly. 'We fight for the one true God indeed, Henri, but our orders come from Pope Nicholas IV here on earth.'

Henri looked at his friend in the same manner he had during their discourse on the battlements before the abortive sortie.

Gilbert continued, 'God's fight will be won, of that there is no doubt, and we shall bring the light of His Word to the Heathen. But to that end Henri, we will need an army to defeat them.'

'Indeed, my friend, but we have taken an oath, a sacred oath, to defend to the death that which we hold dear.'

'And what did we do at Marqab and others?' Gilbert demanded.

Henri nodded but did not reply. The pair stared out over the walls at the darkening tips of the enemy tents. Over the muted noise of the drums came a more sinister sound.

'Shields!' snapped Henri. They squatted down on the flat roof, holding their battle shields above them. Not a moment too soon. Dozens of arrows clattered onto the roof around them. Somewhere in the alley beneath them a man screamed. Henri cautiously peered round his shield and grimaced as he saw the shaft of an arrow embedded in it. Angrily he snatched it out of the leather surface, making as if to hurl it away, his eye was drawn to the discoloured tip. 'Hashashin, Gilbert. See the poison?' He pointed to the sticky residue on the arrow's tip.

The pair, holding their shields above them, made their way down the stone steps as further arrows clattered harmlessly behind. Henri was in no doubt as to his fate should his previous captors get hold of him. He shivered involuntarily.

Once in the quiet of his chamber he turned to his friend. 'So, who remains with the authority to order the Grand Masters to leave?'

Gilbert smiled, tight lipped.

'The orders are here already Henri, it's just that you haven't seen them.'

Henri shook his head annoyed, irritated. 'Orders? Orders! Gilbert, by God's word I know not of any order other than your dearest sister's orders. She treats me as a child! In God's name I swear that I am struck dumb at her words.'

Gilbert did not reply but turned and picked up a worn leather bag from behind a curtain. Henri glimpsed manuscripts and rolls of parchment before Gilbert tied it shut. A slight noise at the door drew Henri's eyes. Eleanor stood looking at the two knights. She had changed from her light clothes and wore a dark cloak. She carried a small bag.

'We should go,' Gilbert said quietly.

CHAPTER 5

As the three made their way to the harbour, the streets were seething with panic-stricken inhabitants, and as they neared the port the more congested the streets became. It was late summer, and although the air was warm from the last of the sun's rays, people huddled nervously around braziers on every street corner. From the doors of taverns came the bawdy songs of Venetian and Pisan traders and sailors.

A swarthy drunken sailor, reeling from a tavern, stumbled against Eleanor. Grinning tipsily, his arm went around her. Gilbert's arm shot out of his dark cloak and with his large hand he grabbed the sailor's throat, slamming him against the wall. Terrified the sailor gasped out a choked apology. Gilbert released the man who, coughing and spluttering, collapsed in the gutter.

They continued down the narrow street, the smell of the sea becoming stronger. Henri heard the running of bare feet behind them and turned his hand on his sword. Gilbert was faster. The rasp of steel and the flash of his blade in the moonlight came as one, and the dark, rushing shape was run through. The man screamed horribly, his knife falling from his lifeless fingers as he died. Other shadowy shapes that had appeared behind him turned and fled back into the darkness.

Stooping, Gilbert wiped his blade on the man's clothing, then sheathing the sword, turned and caught up with Henri and Eleanor. Not a word was spoken. Minutes later the three reached the quayside, leaving behind them the dark confines of the narrow streets.

The port was bathed in moonlight. All the colours were grey and silver, the noise and bustle of the town faded behind them. Already the harbour had almost emptied and Henri watched grimly as a galley put to sea; ships normally never sailed at night. Behind the Pisan quarter he could see the walled fortress of the Templars from which the final battle would be fought.

Eleanor moved ahead, walking briskly around the port to the outer breakwater. Here were moored *La Comtesse*, and the Templar galleys *Bethania* and *Bethel*. Lines of soldiers carried crates and bundles from the lowered drawbridge of the Templar fortress to the ships. Henri noticed the distinctive bald tonsure of the Templar treasurer, Thibaud Gaudin. He was bowed over a makeshift lectern in the stern of *Bethania*, making entries in a large ledger by the light of a guttering lamp. Already the vessel had settled substantially in the water, and it bustled with activity as the banks of oars were being removed from their swivels to be greased ensuring a swifter progress. Jean de Villiers, the Hospitaller Grand Master, wounded the day before, and Conrad von Feuchtwangen the Teutonic Knights Grandmaster had just been taken on board *La Comtesse*, and that galley was almost ready to leave the chaos behind. The *Bethel* was also heavily laden, but only Roger de Flor stood at the gangplank, whilst his crew laboured, stowing away the cargo.

The three friends passed the bustling *La Comtesse* and *Bethania*, and Eleanor spoke as she bade Henri and Gilbert wait in the shadows of some large crates. 'When I signal, join me, but do not draw your arms.'

Henri's mouth opened but no sound came. He shook his head resignedly. 'By God, Gilbert, I would rather fight the Infidel than your sister, I swear.'

Eleanor stepped confidently across the quay to the leering Roger de Flor. Reaching him, she made a small curtsey, her voice carrying clearly over the bustle of the harbour. 'Good evening Knight de Flor. I believe you have a passage to Cyprus for sale?'

'Full, my Lady. Full to the gunwales, I'm afraid,' he sneered. He glanced over his shoulder to where his sailors were manoeuvring heavy crates and bundles on deck.

'I come with good authority, my Lord,' Eleanor said softly and deliberately, offering her hand to him.

De Flor bent in the moonlight and straightened quickly. 'Authority without question, sister,' he frowned. 'But without gold bezants, even that is worthless.'

Henri, watching from the shadows, whispered to Gilbert. 'What has she in her hand, my friend?'

'The seal of Pope Nicholas IV, Henri,' Gilbert said, without emotion.

Henri's mind reeled. This woman, sister of Gilbert, nurse to him, carrying the papal seal!

Eleanor continued, 'I have more bezants than you can carry, but I want exclusive passage for me and my escorts.' She motioned to Henri and Gilbert, who went quickly towards her across the quay. They stood impassively either side of her diminutive figure, staring at the Templar knight.

Roger de Flor spoke contemptuously. 'A Knight of the Temple takes instruction or threat from no-one, madam. As I stated, my berths are full, and we sail tomorrow. My passengers have delivered to me their valuables.' He paused, motioning towards the galley. 'We shall sail at first light, unless of course those Infidel dogs get here before that.' He cocked his head at the low, incessant murmur of the drums.

Eleanor's tone hardened. 'You do recognise the seal, sir ? Refusal can be construed as treason ... even heresy. We are on papal business under direct orders of Pope Nicholas IV. We carry documents that must not fall into Sultan Khalil's hands –'

'I care not for your seal, Lady: I have a full complement of generous, fare-paying passengers,' De Flor interrupted. 'Now if you will excuse me ...'

Gilbert and Henri exchanged a glance above Eleanor's head. Swift as the gesture was, it was enough to cause de Flor's hand to fly to his sword hilt. Before the two Knights could act, though, Eleanor's own hand had appeared from under her cloak, going swiftly for the knight's throat. His eyes bulged. Then a thin trickle of dark scarlet ran down Eleanor's pale, slim hand. De Flor slid to the ground without a sound.

Eleanor stood, the moonlight gleaming red on the long slim blade in her hand. De Flor's eyes rolled up and he fell backwards. There was a barely discernible splash in the waters between the boat and the quay where the weight of his armour carried him swiftly beneath the dark surface. Eleanor, breathing hard, turned to her brother, her eyes glittering, 'Take over command Gilbert. Double the crew's rates. We sail for Narbonne at dawn.' So saying, she took Henri's arm and led him unresistingly along the quay to the Temple Gate.

The speed at which Eleanor had dispatched de Flor would have impressed even the trained killers of the Hashashin, Henri mused. He also realised that his reluctantly growing admiration for Eleanor de Gothia was tempered by the possibility that one wrong move on his part could well prove fatal.

Eleanor continued conversationally, as if the incident had not occurred, 'You lost your father to the Infidel, I believe?'

She paused, and Henri spoke forcefully, his feelings high, 'And my brothers and my mother.' He stopped suddenly. 'And you wish me to flee now?' he asked her.

'Not flee my lord, no, not flee. Rather to lead the fight for the one True God from elsewhere'. She held out the Great Seal of the Pope: the bronze key of St Peter embossed with Nicholas's IV insignia. 'Our presence here is no accident'. She gestured back to the boat where Gilbert was watching. 'Neither is yours'. She looked directly at him with cool blue eyes. 'Our late friend de Flor has accumulated a king's ransom, but Gilbert has a document that dwarfs even that.'

She smiled, thin lipped and pale, at Henri. 'The Templar ship, *Bethel*, looks as heavily laden as the *Bethania*,' she continued, 'This new grand master, the one who'll be sworn in following William de Beaujeu's death – what is his name?'

'Thibaud Gaudin, their treasurer,' offered Henri.

'That's his standard flying on the *Bethania*,' she rejoined. 'He's ready to leave with the Templar coffers. It's only good fortune that Khalil's Egyptian friends have not sailed into Acre. If they do ...'

Henri saw at once the opportunity to acquire another vessel laden with treasure.

'If I can persuade Thibaud to sail early, we would have two valuable vessels on the high seas.' He paused uncertainly.

Eleanor spoke softly, 'Vessels that contain the remnants of the Christian wealth which we can use to continue the fight.' Henri noticed her use of the plural and increased his pace as they entered the Temple courtyard.

'I believe Thibaud Gaudin knew my mother ...' he murmured.

Eleanor watched him approach a portly tonsured figure holding court amongst a group of knights.

Previously the treasurer of the Knights Templar, now its newly elected grand master, if anybody knew what treasures to load aboard their vessels, Thibaud Gaudin did. Watching, she saw him bow his head as Henri spoke softly into his ear.

Dawn streaked the pale blue sky, and the tempo and volume of the rumbling kettledrums increased. The loading of the vessels had continued throughout the night, and they lay with sails loosely furled, ready to leave at a moment's notice.

Henri and Gilbert had returned in the small hours to St Anthony's Gate. Though Henri accepted the authority of the 'Great Seal', he was still reluctant to be leaving. He wrestled with his conscience, memories of his father, mother and brothers drifting through his mind. Were they calling him to fight and remain in the Holy Land, or was a higher authority urging him on? He shook his head as if to clear it.

Standing with Gilbert on the battlements looking along their length Henri could see jagged gaps in the wall even in what remained of the darkness. Watching from above, the ground outside the city seemed to ferment and seethe, as the approaching dawn signalled hundreds of Infidel soldiers beginning to pace menacingly towards the walls.

The drumbeats increased their rhythm – and then Khalil's war trumpets added their strident tones.

Henri glanced quickly at Gilbert. Grim faced, the other man nodded. Down in the harbour the early rays of sunshine had yet to reach the calm waters, yet they could see the two vessels being pulled along the breakwater. The lead vessel, the *Bethania*, carrying the Templar grand master unfurled its snowy white sail, the blood red Templar cross billowing bravely as it caught an offshore breeze. Slowly the first vessel cleared the breakwater. As one, the pair turned and ran down the narrow steps from the battlements. Hastening down the still darkened streets, their mantles flowed behind them and their boots rang on the cobbles. As they entered the harbour, they saw the *Bethel* was nearing the end of the breakwater.

'Quickly!' Henri shouted as they hurtled along the quayside. Breathing hard, they leapt the widening gulf between the ship and the quay as she followed *Bethania* out of the harbour.

Eleanor flashed them a furious look for their tardiness. The *Bethel*, heavily laden as she was, had, of course, sailed without her compliment of paying passengers. Nevertheless, a dozen of Gilbert's knights lay gratefully on the bulging cargo more than a little relieved to have survived thus far.

'I thought it best to bring an exchange crew, Henri, should we have to run more than one galley,' Gilbert said.

'I wasn't aware you spoke for your sister,' Henri replied teasing his friend, watching Eleanor give directions to the coxswain to follow the wake of the *Bethania*.

Eleanor finished issuing her orders and joined the two men on the forepeak.

'King Hugh de Lusignan of Cyprus is with de Villiers on *La Comtesse*,' she said. 'That means Cyprus is our first port of call. We should await developments there, I think.'

'I have cousins in Cyprus who will be pleased to see me and perhaps help us,' Henri replied. 'So Cyprus is a very good place to begin a new life.'

The three vessels made steady progress away from the rising sun. Shading their eyes against its dazzling rays, only the outline of Acre could be seen, but already several plumes of smoke were climbing into the blue morning sky. Henri stood with Gilbert and Eleanor on the gently heaving deck. For a long time they watched in silence, until at last Henri spoke, 'Let us not in this hour of defeat harbour a single thought that this is the end. Rather say that this is the beginning of the end for the Infidel across the world. Urban II's call will be honoured, if it takes until the end of time.'

Somewhere amongst the gaily coloured tents, under the crumbling walls of Acre, an obscure Arab historian was penning his memoirs:

With these conquests, all the lands of the coast were fully returned to the children of Allah. Thus were the Franks expelled from all the lands of Syria. May the Prophet grant that they never set foot here again.

CHAPTER 6

The three vessels cleared the coast and turned towards Tyre and Sidon, the next two strongholds rumoured still to be in Christian hands. Little was said as the galleys slipped northwards in the calm waters. On the shore a cloud of dust from a group of galloping horsemen kept pace with them.

The captain of *La Comtesse*, unwilling to contemplate that the entire coast was now hostile, made to turn into the Port of Tyre – surely a safe haven, held, as it was by Almaric, King Hugh of Cyprus's brother. As they approached the harbour a small vessel was leaving, flying the Red Lion: the Cypriot flag.

Henri and Eleanor, from the deck of the *Bethel*, further offshore, could not hear the shouted warnings between the crews of the two vessels, but as the Cypriot vessel continued to sea, *La Comtesse* performed a graceful arc in the mouth of the River Litani and continued north in the wake of the *Bethania*. As the vessels regained their close formation, it became clear just how near they had come to sailing their treasures into the hands of the Infidel: Tyre had been surrendered without a fight to Khalil's emir, Shujai.

The little flotilla continued north, still accompanied by the dust cloud from galloping horsemen. As darkness fell the three vessels moored at the last outpost of the coast, the Castle of the Sea at Sidon. Aptly named, this stood on a small rocky island just offshore that protected it from the pursuing horsemen.

The ships' companies disembarked and ate frugally at the castle, grateful to be on terra firma after the unfamiliar motion of the galleys.

It was a sombre affair: now Grand Master of not very much, Thibaud was painfully aware he was fleeing the Holy Land. He sought out Henri, who listened politely, offering little comment. It was decided the castle be abandoned before Shujai's engineers completed the causeway they were constructing from the beach. Putting on a confident air, Thibaud declared the fight for the Holy Land would continue from Cyprus under the protection of King Hugh. There at last the Templars could regroup, lick their wounds, and beg further funds from the Pope for a new and greater Crusade.

At dawn the following day, as the three vessels set sail for Cyprus the two knights stood close together, watching the land they had fought for so desperately slip away from them. Each felt an almost unbearable sense of loss; of something integral having gone from their lives, and which perhaps would never return.

For Henri, a pall seemed to settle over the ship as the day passed and the true nature of their situation became clear, bound for Europe, a place of which he knew little, not only with Gilbert, but also with Eleanor, who was beginning to fill more and more of his thoughts. It was his growing uncertainty about what lay ahead that finally drove him to question Gilbert directly about his mysterious order: the Antonines.

Henri already knew a little of their history from the discussions back in Acre. Strange though it seemed, although they came under the jurisdiction of the Hospitallers, each order maintained a large degree of secrecy from the others, in the same way that the Order of Notre Dame de Sion did under the Templars. Henri, inheriting his late father's contempt of the posturing Templars, had, of course, under his mother's insistence joined the Hospitallers.

Originally a monastic nursing order, founded by the Blessed Gerard, and confirmed by a papal bull of Pope Paschal II in 1113, their origins stretched back to 600AD, when Abbot Probus had been commissioned by Pope Gregory the Great to build a hostel in Jerusalem to treat and care for Christian pilgrims to the Holy Land. That was subsequently destroyed by Caliph el Hakim, and then rebuilt in 1023 by merchants from Amalfi and Salerno, by permission of Caliph Haroun el Rashid of Egypt. From their origins of caring for the sick pilgrims, the Hospitallers soon expanded into providing armed escorts, due to the rapidly growing tensions between Islam and the Christian world. By Henri's time, most of the actual nursing had been delegated to the Benedictine monks, as the Hospitallers developed into a smaller, more compact version of their brothers, the Knights Templar.

Now that he was seeking a greater understanding, Gilbert and Eleanor looked at each other with a strange half smile. 'Our line stretches back nearly one thousand years,' began Gilbert. 'St Anthony was the first monk to attempt to codify our existence in pursuit of the Kingdom of God. He was a hermit who lived by the Red Sea, and he died on 17 January 356.'

Gilbert paused, glancing at Eleanor. She continued, her eyes shining, 'The Knights of St Anthony is the oldest chivalric order in the world and was officially formed as part of the defence of the Christian King Prester John in Ethiopia. However, our own legend has it that the original knights came from a troop of nine of the Roman Emperor Constantine's 'Golden Knights' who were sent to Egypt to bring St Anthony to Rome to meet Constantine in 322. But that when Anthony the Hermit refused to go to Rome they stayed and were taught by him, and that at his death they went to Ethiopia to aid Prester John, calling themselves Knights of The Order of St Anthony the Hermit.

'There were also nine Knights of St Anthony at the Battle of Poitiers in 732, with Charles Martell. In 1095 they formed close links with the Pope and founded the Hospitaller Order of St Anthony.'

'Wasn't that the date of the Council of Clermont, in which Urban II started the Crusades?' interjected Henri, not wishing to be left behind in this sudden erudite discussion.

Eleanor nodded, smiling slightly. The wind had risen, and the rhythmic slap of the waves had taken a deeper resonance.

'The founder of our Hospitaller order, Gaston de Dauphine, who was an Antonine, had a son who fell ill in 1095, and he was praying before the relics of St Anthony in the Church of St Didier la Mothe, near Vienne, when he had a vision of how to cure his son's illness.

'Several weeks previously a number of his villagers had fallen to the same disease afflicting his son. First of all, they scratched themselves so hard their fingernails drew blood. Then they went berserk and ran screaming around the village, yelling and shouting that they felt as if they were on fire. All the while their eyes rolled until just the whites were visible and they frothed at the mouth. Within a day, their hands and feet began to turn grey, then black, as the flesh rotted. Infection set in and raced to the centre of the body. Even so, death took many days. The poor wretches kept up their screaming and writhing until the last'.

Eleanor fell silent. All were aware of the dreaded disease that afflicted young and old alike. Sometimes, and no one knew why, limbs merely withered away, and the victim became a leper, outcast from society, condemned to a living death.

It was Gilbert who then continued, 'Gaston saw in a dream a concoction he needed to defeat the disease, which later became known as St Anthony's Fire. When this succeeded in curing his son, he went to Clermont to offer his life to God and the Crusades. He met Clement V, who persuaded him to write his remedies down and continue his work in France. During his work, Gaston also discovered what caused the disease as well as how to cure it.'

Gilbert paused and glanced at Henri, who was watching his friend with a newfound respect: he had not realised that his comrade in arms of the last six years was so erudite.

Eleanor continued smoothly, 'We, that is, the Antonines, then had the power of both creating and curing the disease, which gave us the freedom to roam Europe, curing doomed people. Gaston's book of remedies was then brought to the Holy Land, where it was used by our order in their hospitals.'

She paused, glancing towards Gilbert. 'You mean that was what Gilbert was looking for?' asked Henri.

Eleanor nodded, 'The book was lost to the order during the earlier Crusades, and it is only through Gilbert's diligence that its whereabouts was discovered. Now our order's knights and Hospitallers have preceptories throughout France, and other lands. We are heading back to one of our nine preceptories at Rennes-Le-Château which is not far from your estate at Castres.

'I should also tell you that our order differs from other orders in that our members do not take vows of poverty or chastity, but only holy obedience to our Grand Nautonier. Actually, we encourage marriage between members of our order and our children inherit their parent's obligations.

'Within the order there exists a small band of extremely capable men and women called upon to undertake the most dangerous tasks: they are the Sons of Sion. Our own family and the families of our commanders trace an unbroken line from the original nine Golden Knights of Constantine.'

The conversation lapsed as one of Gilbert's men brought around coarse bread, olives and a small flagon of wine each. The waves had eased a little and the sun glittered off a brilliant blue sea. Henri got to his feet and paced about:

they were completely out of sight of land. Uneasy, he sank down again on the deck. Eleanor watched him as he ate. From time to time, she licked a crumb from her lips, took a sip of wine. After a while both she and Gilbert, having finished their evening meal, rose, and smiling at Henri, left him to his thoughts.

It was as the sun was setting that Henri sought them out, wrapping his cloak about him against the chill. 'We sail from the land of our God after being soundly defeated by the Infidel hordes. All our lives we have fought and plotted and planned for the return of Jerusalem to the one true faith, and for nought. As if our God has forsaken us, we are cast out upon the ocean, whilst hordes of filthy unbelievers run rampage over our sacred land.' He spoke in bitterness and in deep anger.

'And yet, and yet,' he continued softly, 'we flee in ships containing fabulous wealth. And we have, if you are to be believed,' looking hard at Eleanor, 'a book giving us power to create and cure disease: the power of life and death.'

He paused. Gilbert and Eleanor gazed at him. They did not speak, but Eleanor's eyes shone in the approaching dusk.

Henri continued softly, 'We would not be the first in history to be fleeing our Holy Land, nor the first to be carrying great wealth and knowledge. I only can hope and pray that somehow this . . . in which we find ourselves will enable us to acquit ourselves with honour.'

As the three huddled on the open forepeak of the *Bethel*, the only one of the three ships not to have an enclosed cabin, and in spite of his solemn vows, Henri could not but be aware of the small heat Eleanor's body generated. Eventually, after much deliberation, he rested his arm around her shoulder, and she snuggled back into his arms as they slept.

* * *

On the fifth day the low mountainous bulk of Cyprus came into view, and on the evening of that day the two vessels, *Bethania* and *Bethel*, slipped into Larnaca Bay to dock at Skala, where *La Comtesse* was already moored. The Templars had an interest in the island of Cyprus, on which, although they had sold the bulk of it to King Hugh, they still maintained a healthy presence.

Within the sheltering arms of the bay, against the backdrop of the dun-coloured mountains, the waters were as smooth as glass. For the first time in many days the motion of the boat stabilised somewhat. The *Bethania* and *Bethel* headed for the harbour behind the long stone breakwater. Gilbert's troops became boisterous and loud in anticipation of being on dry land: these were not seasoned sailors, and the constant motion at sea had caused much sickness.

The vessels dropped their sails, whilst the crew manoeuvred the boats alongside the quay using the oars. Henri was first off and he leapt the narrowing gap with ease. He was a little unsteady as he stood on the stone quay, swaying, with his arms outstretched as he attempted to regain his balance after days of pitching and rolling at sea.

Gilbert likewise landed on the dock and weaved unsteadily towards the large stone bollards by which the ships were moored. To much muttered protest, Henry and Gilbert gave orders that the ships be turned around with their bows pointing towards the harbour entrance. Only when the sails had been furled correctly and the little ships made ready for sea again did Henri pay off the crew, warning them to stay close to the harbour.

When they were satisfied that the vessels were secure, Henri, Gilbert and Eleanor made their way to the cluster of taverns and stores lining the rear of the harbour. From one of the narrow streets shouts and laughter could be heard, accompanied by feminine screams. The sun shone and the air was warm and still. Henri, walking on the edge of the quay, could see into the clear blue waters where fish of many brilliant hues swirled and darted amongst the little fishing boats. He felt an immense sensation of relief and wellbeing flow through his body. His eyes took in the pretty, peaceful harbour; he savoured the smells of cooking, the relaxed air of the port. For the first time in his life the Infidel were just distant memories. He welcomed this feeling – it was one of hope and of a growing confidence in the future.

He glanced behind to where Eleanor was strolling arm-in-arm with Gilbert. She was conversing earnestly with him, but she smiled at Henri, her eyes sparkling. Henri filled his lungs with the sweet salty air and strode ahead to the tavern.

* * *

It was not long after their arrival that Thibaud Gaudin hastened to consult with Jean de Villiers, Grand Master of the Hospitallers, who had arrived on board the Hospitaller's flagship *La Comtesse* and was Henri's direct superior. The two grand masters accompanied by Henri and Gilbert talked long into the night. It was evident that the sensitive political situation of the island kingdom precluded a long stay there. Jean decided at last that the best course for the Hospitallers was to attempt to secure the Island of Rhodes upon which a long-lasting and secure base could be built, leaving Cyprus for the Templars and King Hugh to squabble over.

Gilbert and Henri spent the next few days on horseback exploring the lush island and visiting with Henri's cousins. However, unbeknown to Henri, every evening Gilbert and Eleanor would spend hours alone poring over the book that they had brought with them from the Holy Land. After several days Gilbert disappeared into the cellar of their quarters and returned with shallow trays covered in damp cloths. These were filled with mouldering rye seeds, which Gilbert turned over gently with a small wooden paddle, before returning them to the cellar. Later, he dried them, and then ground the mouldy seeds into flour, before preparing a number of small, unleavened cakes.

Eleanor took a batch of these to Thibaud Gaudin's court during her ministrations to a sick soldier. Thibaud had been in a black depression since arriving in Cyprus. The loss of the Holy Land had weighed heavily on him. In spite of his vow to return to Sidon with a Templar army, he had been unable to do so.

Within several days of Eleanor's visit, rumours swept the island of Thibaud's strange behaviour. First, he had spent some days furiously scratching himself. After that he had complained that his skin felt as if it was burning, and in obvious distress, he had taken to dousing himself continuously with cold water. King Hugh, fearfully hearing of the presence of the dreaded St Anthony's Fire on his island, confined himself to the mountain-top fortress, leaving the *Bethania* in the harbour under the guard of a dozen men.

Gilbert took himself to the quayside and gathered his men around him on the *Bethel*. Ribald shouts and laughter drifted across from the *Bethania* as the crew, taking full advantage of their lack of leadership, cavorted drunkenly with the harlots of the port. Gilbert left shortly afterwards, and whilst some of his men quietly continued with preparing the *Bethel*, others collected fist-sized pebbles from the seabed.

Later in the day, nobody took any notice of the cloaked and hooded woman as she walked the quay with a basket of freshly baked loaves. A sergeant-of-arms, lolling against the hawsers of the *Bethania*, hailed her, looking hungrily at her and her basket of bread. Eleanor's tones, rebuking the leering drunken sergeant as he purchased the entire basket for his men, could be heard across the harbour.

* * *

Jean de Villiers, an old friend of Henri's as well as his master, looked down at the kneeling figure before him. Sir Henri de Montfort would indeed be a great loss to the Hospitallers, as well as to any future Crusade.

De Villiers attempted to remonstrate with him. 'Your family, Henri,' he said. 'You have lost much, but to leave the order now would surely be a grave mistake for you and a great loss to us.'

Henri nodded, 'I cannot serve both you and my heart, Master, and I will not break my vows. I beg you release me from them so I may at last try to follow my true feelings for the Lady Eleanor de Gothia.'

There was no doubt that the union of the de Montfort and de Gothia families would be a mighty force working for the One Tue God, of that much he was sure. Jean hoped that Henri's strong resolve and clarity of purpose, joined to Eleanor's wealth would lead on to greater triumphs for the Holy Church.

With a heavy heart, Jean formally agreed to Henri's request that he be released from his vows of chastity as a Knight Hospitaller. Inclining his head, he reluctantly gave his blessing.

* * *

The entire troop guarding the *Bethania* had succumbed to the same illness as Thibaud Gaudin. They lay on rough palliasses around the harbour, thrashing and moaning, whilst pouring seawater over themselves. The salt water on the fresh scratches made them howl even more. The more fortunate inhabitants of the harbour buildings had fled up to the hills in an attempt to avoid the fate of the soldiers.

Gilbert went down to the *Bethel* in the harbour. He took one of the bamboo axes from its housing on the gunwales and gave it to one of his troop. Rapidly he passed round another half a dozen of the wicked-looking spikes, bidding his men follow him along the quay. Jumping down into one of King Hugh's galleys, he placed the tip of the spike on the bottom of the hull. After striking the top of it sharply with the fist-sized stone he wrenched it out of the wood to be rewarded by the gurgle of water. He returned to the quay. The whole process had taken less than a minute. He motioned his men to do likewise to the other vessels.

The next day Jean de Villiers stood gazing out at a harbour bereft of vessels. Empty, that is, of floating ships, for under the gently swelling surface the outline of the galleys could be seen, their masts and rigging giving the harbour the somewhat surreal look of an exotic reed bed, only his own ship *La Comtesse* remained intact. Of the two vessels, *Bethania* and *Bethel* there was no sign.

It was a little while before King Hugh ventured from his eyrie to view his sunken fleet. The monarch ranted furiously from his mountain fortress, for the *Bethania* contained a goodly portion of the Cypriot king's wealth. He also vented considerable anger on the two possible successors to the late Thibaud Gaudin: one Hugues de Pairaud, the Templar Treasurer and Jacques de Molay, who would eventually become the next Grand Master of The Temple.

Whilst the two protagonists argued and debated the rift between the Templars and the Hospitallers, a discussion that was going to take the best part of a year, the two galleys, the *Bethel* and the *Bethania* slipped silently westwards, followed the next day by *La Comtesse* with Grand Master Jean de Villiers on board on his way to Rhodes.

CHAPTER 7

A voyage of almost two thousand miles lay ahead of them and Henri was now under no illusion as to the ruthlessness of his companions or the hazards and dangers facing them. Whilst their vessels were arguably the finest in the Templar fleet, they were also heavily laden and severely under-crewed. Henri had no experience of maritime warfare, but during his time on Cyprus he had heard enough about the Sicilian pirates to know that the narrowing of the ocean in between Sicily and the North African coast could be very dangerous.

However, with the promise of a little gold now and a lot more on their safe arrival at Narbonne, the services of a dozen Cypriot bowmen had been acquired before they had embarked. Their short stubby bows would be issued in time of need, and a prodigious supply of arrows was held on each boat. Remembering the actions of Khala'un's miners, several earthenware urns containing flammable naphtha from Asia had also been procured.

As the two ships headed ever westward towards Narbonne, Henri found himself gazing more and more often at Eleanor. When on occasion she happened to notice this, she returned his interest with complete equanimity, her cool blue eyes giving little away.

Once a long, long time ago, he had hunted in the mountains of Armenia on his mother's family estates, and after a particularly long and arduous climb at the end of which he found himself quite alone, he had rounded a rocky outcrop to find himself face to face with a mountain leopard, so close he could smell the rank animal odour. Henri had frozen to the spot as, tail lashing ominously, the cat's great yellow eyes blazed into his. Then with an explosive grunt the animal had leapt from the path in front of him and away down the cliff. Henri had no doubt at all that the cat's decision not to kill him was hers and hers alone.

Disturbingly he brought the little scene from his past to the fore whenever Eleanor regarded him. He was also reminded of the ease with which Roger de

Flor had been dispatched back in Acre. He could not quite bring himself to admit it, but he did harbour the suspicion that in some strange way his destiny was pre-ordained.

Henri did not rebut this, but he became puzzled and not a little envious when some of the looks she shot him were preceded or followed by a long discussion with Gilbert. Try as he might, he could not persuade his friends to share the contents of their discussions: he felt isolated and frustrated.

From Cyprus their natural route would have led them to the island of Rhodes but given the appropriation of the Templar treasure they decided to head for Crete. Here they berthed at the end of the breakwater in the Byzantine port of Chania on the north-west coast of the island, as far away from the centre of the harbour as possible, to ensure a rapid and unimpeded departure. Gilbert, having divided the crews up more evenly, had moved to the *Bethel*, leaving Henri the sole use of the luxurious aft cabin of the *Bethania*.

Without allowing the crews to rest, orders were given to revictual and replenish the water supplies aboard the vessels. Only after this was accomplished to Gilbert's satisfaction did he allow the crews to head towards the taverns of the harbour: they would need all their strength and resolve for the passage ahead.

* * *

Henri had never learnt to swim. All his life had been spent in dry, gritty lands, where the provision of water in any quantity was deemed a privilege of the rich. During the years of his captivity by the Hashashin his one recurring dream had been of the servants fetching warmed water from the kitchen fire to fill his bath at his father's castle. It was therefore with some fascination that he watched Eleanor, after Gilbert had released the crew onshore, remove her outer garments and wearing a simple cotton shift, dive gleefully from the deck into the warm blue sea. He was even more amazed to watch her swim and splash confidently around the schools of cavorting dolphins that accompanied them from time to time and were gathered around the harbour entrance.

One day she had cajoled him to join her in the water, where her floating cotton shift held a fascination he could not quite erase from his mind. The diaphanous display of long legs beneath the flimsy material became too much for him. With an oath he stripped his soiled, sweat-soaked garments from his body and vaulted onto the wide rail around the stern of the vessel. Eleanor squealed and covered her eyes as her laughter rang out. Henri paused, balanced precariously on the rail, his muscular figure showing not an ounce of spare flesh. He glanced around. It was midday, and the port slumbered under the hot sun: the harbour was deserted.

It did occur to Henri as he stepped into thin air that perhaps he should have taken some lessons in the art of swimming, but it was too late. He landed with an almighty splash next to a shrieking Eleanor. He had barely taken in her wet laughing face when the green waters closed above him. He had no difficulty in opening his eyes in the clean, warm aquamarine sea as his jump carried him deep beneath her. Glancing upwards towards the light he saw instantly her slim star shaped figure silhouetted against the sunlit waves. For a moment he was spellbound, then the pressure on his lungs became too great and with rising panic he lashed out at his watery prison. As he watched the silvery surface draw nearer, his lungs felt as if they would explode, and he burst from the water gulping great quantities of clean fresh air. Eleanor's peals of laughter rang around him, and he had barely chance to catch his breath, before he felt long smooth legs grip him in a scissor movement. Even in his perilous state his mind registered the thick curly bush of hair in the fork of her legs as she momentarily held his torso in her grip. Then he was under again, and she was gone. This time when he surfaced, mucus and water streaming from his mouth, he weakly paddled to the sides of the *Bethania*.

Later, as the sun touched the blackening sea, he sat in his aft cabin. The door opened confidently, and Eleanor entered. She had dried and brushed her lustrous wavy tresses, and the shift she was wearing floated around her body. The last rays of sunlight danced in her hair briefly as she closed the door. Henri stood, uncertain for a moment. She drew close to him. Her warm, feminine odour assailed him, and the drawstring around her shoulders holding up her white cotton shift held a fascination all of its own. He made to speak, but with a small shake of her head she picked up his hand, brushed it across her lips and put it on the drawstring.

* * *

Dawn several days later found them between the coast of Tunisia and the distant mountains of Sicily. For the first time in weeks the wind deserted them, and they made slow heading with the oars in the still, oily sea. Just before the sun reached its zenith Henri, hearing Gilbert's warning shout, looked up quickly: two vessels were approaching with a considerable degree of speed.

Gilbert shouted to Henri to hoist, 'Le Drapeau Jolie Rouge.' This little red flag emblazoned with a white scull and crossed leg bones was the feared battle flag of the Templar fleet, and Gilbert hoped that the sight of it might deter the approaching corsair raiders.

Putting every available man on the oars, the two knights began issuing bows to the bowmen. A pot of naphtha was given to each man and, after much coaxing from the supply of tinder, a small guttering candle. The corsair vessels had an edge on speed with to their double-banked oars, but Henri and Gilbert turned and aimed their vessels straight at the oncoming ships. The corsairs' tactics were to ram a vessel broadside on and, using the weight of their fast-moving vessel, push the victim's ship under the surface. Henri's plan demanded that they aim straight for the pirates head-on, and at the last possible moment before a collision, pass closely down one side of the oncoming vessels.

Closer, closer the pirate ships drew. Henri could not tear his eyes away, but he knew Gilbert watched closely on his port side. 'Hard to port!' he bellowed, fearing he had left it too late. The bow of the *Bethania* veered slowly to the left, and the pirate vessel appeared on the starboard bow not ten yards away.

'Starboard oars in!' he shouted. His oarsmen instantly pulled their dripping blades into the vessel. The prow of the *Bethania* ploughed into the double-bank of the pirates' oars, snapping them off like dry twigs or forcing the long wooden shafts into the oarsmen's bodies, to screams of agony. Simultaneously the Cypriot bowmen stood up and rapidly poured arrow after arrow tipped with flaming naphtha into the corsair ships.

In minutes it was all over. The two ships' combined closing speeds caused them to pass each other rapidly, quickly redeploying their own oars the two vessels continued their westward journey. Behind them the corsairs had slewed around and lay dead in the water, whilst their devastated crews were torn between attempting to redistribute their remaining oars or put out the rapidly escalating fires beneath the decks. As the screams of agony and outrage drifted steadily astern, the flames took hold, and presently all that remained behind were two fiercely burning hulks.

CHAPTER 8

From the moment the two vessels had left the sweltering coast of Outremer, it was as if a shutter had descended on that part of Henri's life. He had of course been with Gilbert de Gothia since Marqab in 1285, and the two had become as close as brothers. Then Eleanor had come along fitting so neatly, dovetailing into his life and thoughts.

They had landed at Narbonne in the late summer. The two Templar galleys now flying the blue tau cross flag of the Order of St Anthony, had attracted some local interest, but the sudden appearance of a group of particularly burly monks had fended off the townsfolk's attention. Smitten with Eleanor, Henri had paid scant attention to the rapid unloading of the vessel's cargo onto a convoy of some thirteen ox carts that mysteriously appeared on the quayside.

Henri had spoken volubly regarding his estates at Castres and l'Amaury near Paris, as if he were somehow seeking to impress the companionable beauty at his side. Suddenly and without warning he understood the attraction of spending his life with Eleanor, and to enjoy with her both his estates, neither of which he had ever seen.

Located about three days' ride from Narbonne along the River Agout, the old fortified town of Castres clustered around the ancient Abbey of St Benoit, in which he now stood.

His titles of Lord of Castres and of l'Amaury had not, in truth, meant a lot to him during his life in the Holy Land, but since his arrival in the Languedoc his memories of his father's journeys through his estates in Tyre came flooding back. As a small boy he had derived childlike pleasure watching the local population treat his father with deference and respect. Now as he rode through his ancestral lands, he sat a little higher in the saddle and looked forward in anticipation of showing his estates to Eleanor. However, he had given little thought to the location of the actual estate and so was forced to ask for directions.

Hailing a small group of shabbily dressed men on the side of the track, he called, 'Good day, I am Henri de Montfort, Lord of Castres. Have the goodness to direct me to my estate.'

Used as he was to a certain level of servility, the dark looks and mutterings of the first group took him a little by surprise. A negative answer of sorts forced him to ask a second group further down the track, and a third. After each enquiry the result was the same, and he found to his chagrin a rising sense of fury and bitterness at this unexpected atmosphere of surly truculence. Two or three scowling individuals had even hawked and spat in the mud beneath his horse's hooves, scuttling away into the dense woods as he uttered an oath and made to draw his sword.

Their disturbance of the undergrowth had startled a small flock of birds, which in turn made Henri's horse prance and circle in the middle of the track. Exploding with rage Henri drew his sword with a shout and gathering his horse's reins made to dash into the forest in pursuit of the insolent group. Before he could do so he felt a firm grip on his arm. Eleanor was regarding him with cool blue eyes. She said nothing but raised her hand placatingly. Henri returned her gaze, unsure as to why she had halted his headlong rush into the undergrowth. After a moment Eleanor dismounted and approached a group of women who had been observing the little scene. She soon discovered the reason behind the resentment of the populace.

The town remembered with anguish the Albigensian Crusades against the Cathars some ninety years previously, in which Catholic was set against Catholic on the direct orders of Pope Innocent III. The papal legate charged with destroying the heretics was Arnaud Amalric; and in turn, one of his more enthusiastic generals, and proponent of the Pope's wishes, was Simon de Montfort: Henri's great uncle.

Encouraged by the papal promise of land, which included Castres, in return for crushing the Cathar population, and accompanied by his Dominican inquisitors, he had watched as the heretics were burnt at the stake, proclaiming arrogantly in the nearby town of Béziers, as over one thousand Catholics were herded together in the church of St Nazaire, 'Kill them all. God will know His own,' as he set fire to the building. Understandably, then, the de Montfort name was still accursed in this part of France.

Eleanor thanked the group of women politely and remounted her horse. She took the lead and cantered off down the track, followed by Henri. After several turns and a steep climb, the two of them emerged from the forest and found a large, fortified house built on the edge of a precipice. Surrounding the house was a substantial stone wall with a huge wooden gate. The gate leant drunkenly against the pillar, and through it Henri and Eleanor could see an overgrown track leading to the house.

Henri reined in his horse, 'My grandfather Guy de Montfort left this place fifty years ago,' he said, before dismounting and bidding Eleanor to do likewise. The two picked their way past the remains of the gate and struggled through the waist high weeds to the front of the house. The huge wooden door, battered and scarred, resisted all attempts to force an entrance. Henri circled the great house, to no avail. All the entrances were boarded up and had obviously not been disturbed for many years. He sat down on a fallen tree trunk as Eleanor joined him.

He had given little thought as to what this moment would bring, but now, faced with the cold reality of his homecoming, he was momentarily overcome by despair.

In the distance the sight of the snow-covered Pyrenees under a leaden sky sent a shiver down his back. He got up after a while and, followed by Eleanor, walked slowly to where his horse was tethered. Henri had looked forward so much to showing Eleanor the house of which she would soon become its mistress. The pair headed back to the town and the comfortable quarters of the abbey.

CHAPTER 9

The cold winter sun streaming through the windows of the Benedictine Abbey of St Benoit's in Castres lifted Henri's heart. Waiting now at the altar of the abbey, where Elanor was to become his bride, he resolved firmly to overcome his sense of betrayal and disillusion. They were young. The future, with all its promise, lay ahead of them. He turned at the peal of trumpets to see his bride approaching slowly. Briefly the sun illuminated her face as it shone between the mighty pillars of the church. She smiled radiantly back at him. On her right, linking her arm walked a burly figure. His usual tonsure was covered by his bishop's mitre, and the cross on his staff glinted in the sunlight as the couple made their way towards Henri. The Bishop of Bordeaux, Bertrand de Gothia, regarded Henri impassively, acknowledging by the merest inclination of his head the man who was to become the husband of his niece Eleanor de Gothia.

Henri had met Bertrand a week or so after their arrival at Castres, when he and Eleanor had visited him at the Gothia family estate at Villandraut. Putting aside his bitter anger at the condition of his own estates, Henri had rapidly realised that if, as he had long suspected, Gilbert and Eleanor were driven by some strange, secret purpose, then its catalyst was Bertrand de Gothia. Theoretically Bishop of Bordeaux, which at this time was an English dominion, his influence extended to the papal court and the group of cardinals who, due to the Pope's declining health, were now jostling for position. Henri had no knowledge of the machinations of the papal court, but once when he entered a room Bertrand, Eleanor and Gilbert had been in deep discussion, as often as not with of a couple of the Antonine monks wearing their Tau crosses.

He had questioned both Eleanor and Gilbert independently as to the whereabouts of the *Bethania*'s and *Bethel*'s cargoes but had received little response. He was no fool and resolved to put the question off until after the wedding on the 17 January. The date itself meant little to him, chosen as it was by Eleanor, until he realised that it was the feast of St Anthony, and that the abbey's entire complement of Antonine monks would be present for the ceremony. Again, he did not object or question this but felt drawn by currents stronger than his own will.

Having been bitterly disappointed by the condition of his estates in Castres, he had taken the step of sending a party of monks, chosen by Gilbert, to his holdings at l'Amaury on the outskirts of Paris. If he were to make a home in that cold, damp land he would need to know what sort of welcome awaited him before he undertook the long journey north.

To his delight, he had received a report back that confirmed his estate at l'Amaury was in robust health, and contained large parts of the Forest of Rambouillet, being well run and in substantial surplus by the current tenants. He resolved to reward them generously upon his reclaiming of the estates and mentioned to Eleanor that he would be settling there after a short stay in Castres. She had merely nodded and said that before they travelled north she really would like to visit the Monastery of St Anthony at La Val Dieu, a few days' ride away. Then she had that look in her eye and Henri had pushed the obvious question to the back of his mind.

* * *

Eleanor, on Bertrand's arm, had reached him, and now stood by his side. Henri looked at her, beautiful and radiant. Managing a small blush, she gazed back at him. Her sparkling eyes met his, and his heart leapt. Henri turned as he heard the priest approaching along the chancel to begin the solemn ceremony. Through the rood screen the eyes of the priest regarded Henri for a moment before the doors of the rood swung open.

The priest asked, 'Who giveth this woman?'

Bertrand stepped forward and offered him Eleanor's slim hand. As he did so, Bertrand's and Henri's eyes met. In that moment Henri felt as if the depths of his soul were torn open to this man. He felt – no, he knew, with utter certainty – that only death would part him from Eleanor.

Bertrand offered the signet ring to Eleanor on a small velvet cushion. Its golden buttery finish contrasting with the engraved double-headed eagle on a black shield with an engraved gold band. She placed it on his hand and looked deep into his eyes. Henri felt as one. He was complete.

* * *

As Henri left the abbey with Eleanor, he saw that low grey clouds had replaced the wintry sun, and the first flakes of snow were beginning to fall. Fully expecting to be housed on his own estate, Henri had been unable to obtain quarters for himself and his new bride, and it was with grateful thanks that they had accepted the offer of the abbot's rooms for a week.

Bertrand had taken over an inn in the village, across the raging River Agout. One evening, soon after their wedding, the radiant couple accepted the bishop's invitation to dine in his quarters above the inn.

When they entered, Bertrand had already taken the large throne-like chair at the head of the table. Henri noticed that surprisingly the man who was, in effect, his father-in-law was wearing the black habit embroidered with the blue tau crosses of an Antonine monk. A gold chain of office proclaimed him Grand Prior of the Order.

Bertrand motioned them to be seated but said little as the food and wine were being served. When the door closed behind the serving women, he rose and drew the heavy curtain over it. Returning to the table, he seated himself again, lowering his voice to a murmur so that Henri and Eleanor had to lean across the table to catch his words. Their three heads close together in the guttering yellow candlelight, Bertrand began to speak. 'I want to talk to you of the responsibilities that your marriage to Eleanor brings. The de Gothia Family is as ancient and distinguished as your own Henri. We have both fought the Infidel side by side on the same battlefield many times before. Although your family has its origins amongst the Norsemen and ours stems from Visigoth nobility, we have common ancestors from the royal houses of both Aquitaine and Aragon. In fact, our coat of arms is the same as the Aragon's.

'Lady Eleanor holds the de jure title of Marquise of Gothia, because Gilbert is the progeny of my brother Wilfred's morganatic marriage, and therefore unable to inherit his father's title. Now, through this marriage, this title passes to you. At your wedding ceremony you also became a knight of St Anthony. Both these titles bind you to King James of Aragon's fight against the Infidel in Spain, so your holy war is by no means over. I am confident that you will undertake your responsibilities very seriously.

'As regards the Templars, they have a new grand master, a Jacques de Molay, who is plotting and planning the return of the Crusaders to the Holy Land, but there is little enthusiasm for such a venture in France.'

Henri himself was no admirer of the Templars; he blamed them personally for the loss of the Holy Land, and as Bertrand continued he began to understand the strong undercurrents of resentment against the Templars in France: the envious and debt-ridden French king, Philippe le Bel, and the overt posturing of the Templars, flaunting their wealth and their secret banking system, made it worse. Even so, the rest of Bertrand's whispers around the table that wintry night in Castres left Henri's amazed at the implications of his marriage to Eleanor.

The next morning a chill wind sprang up, turning the snow to a crisp crust. As Bertrand had arranged, two beautiful fresh horses had appeared at the inn. Eleanor, already dressed in furs for the journey ahead, was the first to vault into the saddle. With a laugh and a shout of, 'Come on, my darling Lord, race me,' she galloped off up the muddy track. With a resigned oath Henri followed, glancing back as his mount cleared the outskirts of the village. In spite of the southerly location of Castres the sky was leaden, and snow-filled flurries of wind gusted around the heavily wrapped riders. Henri had pushed Bertrand's conversation regarding his obligations to the back of his mind as he galloped off in pursuit of Eleanor.

However, Bertrand de Gothia, Bishop of Bordeaux, and secretly much, much more, stood in the centre of the road, solemnly making the *signum crucis* after the departing couple.

* * *

After two days of alternate furious, breathless galloping and long sensual evenings spent in small taverns, Henri was surprised to come upon a mule train laden, as he recognized to his amazement from the day they arrived in Narbonne, with the cargoes of the *Bethania* and *Bethel*. The train was winding its steady way along tree lined tracks. He and Gilbert, who was leading the train, exchanged shouts of greeting and although Henri found it a remarkable coincidence that they were together again, he said little.

Aeons ago at the end of the last ice age, the mountains of the Alps and Pyrenees had discharged their swollen melt water into the basin of southern Gaul and Aragon. Drained by the rivers Madeleine, Aude, Sals and Rialsesse, the former seabed of the inland tropical sea had risen inexorably with the lessening of the weight of the ice, and the outpourings of glacial melt water had exploited the natural characteristics of the limestone beds to provide deep valleys and swift rushing rivers. Occasionally the rivers would run fast and furiously down a valley only to disappear down a sinkhole, leaving the downstream section of the valley mysteriously dry. Sometimes the river would surface further down the same valley, whisps of steam rising from small gushing tributaries.

Wonderingly Henri dipped his hand into the water of one of these to discover that it was at blood temperature.

'These hot springs feed my bath,' Eleanor said, as she watched his face. Her use of the word conjured up such a long-lost memory of childhood domesticity that he shook his head sadly and then, remembering the night before's lovemaking, smiled at his lovely bride.

'Ice falling from the sky,' he mused, indicating the dying flurries of snow. 'Bath water that comes from the ground. What other magic awaits us?'

Eleanor smiled at him before turning and galloping off with a peal of laughter, calling back to him, 'Me, me!'

The little convoy wound its way through this mysterious region of the Massif du Canigou. At every turn, monstrous cliffs and hanging valleys revealed themselves. The wooden wheels and muted conversations did little to disturb the cry of buzzards and kites as they circled overhead in the azure-blue sky.

Presently Eleanor called a halt and to Henri's puzzlement supervised the ripping of many hessian sacks into long lengths, which she had the carters wrap around the wheels of the wagons. Smaller pieces were tied to the hooves of the horses and the feet of the carters. Soon after starting off again, they came to a deep, fast flowing river more than fifty yards across, its currents and eddies apparent on the surface as it flowed swiftly on.

Henri rose slightly in his stirrups, casting curious glances up and down the river. The trail had led them directly to the riverbank. To his left and right the river ran fast and deep in between walls of polished limestone. Only the track they had been travelling on penetrated the steep walls. An occasional creeper dangling in the current gave an indication of the speed of this obstacle and he half-turned in the saddle, ready to halt the convoy.

'Keep onwards, Henri,' came Gilbert's urgent shout. Henri looked at him a moment longer, then urged his mount forward.

The lead wagon was about to enter the water following two of the escorting monks. The horses had shied at first, when the thick sacking had been tied round their hooves. They looked comical, almost as if wearing slippers, but once they entered the water and it rose above their fetlocks they forged onwards against the pull of the current. Below the translucent surface Henri could see the outline of huge paving blocks; the continuation of the track under water, upon which the hessian wrapped wagon wheels travelled. The blocks had been carefully fitted together, and at their edges Henri could see into the green translucent depths of the river.

By now the two lead horses, obviously accustomed to the crossing, had neared the halfway mark. The reason for the wrapping of the hooves and wheels became clear; the slippery strands of waving algae on the smooth paving blocks would have afforded little grip in the strong current. Without this clever addition, the horses and carts would have been swept away downstream to the roaring plume of spray just visible as the river rounded a bend.

Henri's horse clambered up the gently sloping bank, and he turned to watch as the laden wagons crossed the river. He mused that if this marked the outer defence of their destination, then it had been incredibly well engineered, with more than a hint of a military mind, some considerable time ago, which did seem curious considering that he had been told that their destination was a monastery not a fortress.

Gilbert halted the convoy as the last wagons cleared the river, water cascading from them, so that the hessian wrappings could be removed.

That night the convoy dined on the plump rabbits abounding in the lush valleys. Knowing no fear of man, it was a simple matter to approach one from behind and dispatch it with a single blow. It was as though the river crossing had led them to a secret kingdom within a kingdom, and having crossed the river, Henri swore he felt the mood of the convoy lighten.

Gilbert and Eleanor, wise in the ways of this hidden world, ensured that all the bark was removed from the wood that had been gathered for the fire in order to create clear burning, almost smokeless embers on which to roast the small carcasses. All seemed at peace – except that Henri could have sworn that he had observed dark-robed figures on the rocky ramparts above the track watching them; although when he shielded his eyes against the bright sun, they had gone. Travel weariness, must have been making his eyes play tricks on him, he thought, and yet ...

Eleanor woke him at dawn with a light ethereal kiss on his eyelids. Instantly he wrapped his arms around her. Alert in a second and rolling nimbly away, she grinned and rolled her eyes at the sleeping forms around them. 'Not now, my stallion!' she chuckled. 'By tonight we will have completed our journey.' She paused. 'Home.'

'Home?' Henri gave a wry smile. It was a word that had been absent from his life for many years, and certainly nothing to do with either his long-neglected mouldering estate in Castres, or his ultimate destination of l'Amaury.

'How could a monastery be home?' he wondered. Yet again he felt himself being pulled in a direction of which he knew nothing.

The mood in the camp was light-hearted that morning. For the first time many of the monks that had accompanied Gilbert with the convoy threw back their dark cowls and revelled in the bright early sun. Used as he was to dealing with fighting men under his command, Henri recognised that these Antonines also bore the same military stamp. Hard, tough-looking men, bronzed by suns far fiercer than those of southern Europe, they were clearly anticipating with relish the moment they arrived back at their headquarters.

Henri caught their mood as he rode at the head of the wagons with Gilbert. Again, he glimpsed shadowy figures on the surrounding hills, and this time there was no mistake. However, Gilbert either didn't notice or abstained from commenting: chatting easily the two men – the questioner and the questioned – rode onwards.

Gilbert gave little away to Henri's insistent probing but did admit that the place –he spoke of it as the sanctuary – for which they were heading had been in existence for over 500 years. Construction had been started shortly after the

Battle of Poitiers in 732 and continued during the reign of Charlemagne. He did not elaborate further.

A shout from ahead alerted Henri. One of the soldiers who had accompanied them from Acre was wheeling his horse around, muttering and cursing. Henri could see a cluster of derelict buildings and hovels and, amongst them, movement. He spurred his mount forward, and two men rose from where they had been squatting. Dressed in rags and with their heads wound about with crudely wrapped bandages, they shuffled towards him. He stared, transfixed. In places the bandages had slipped to reveal horribly disfigured faces covered with open running sores.

He recoiled, but Eleanor's calm voice cut through to him. 'Lepers, Henri, lepers. Only the ignorant think their ailment is transmitted by touch. These men can do you no harm.'

Her cool-voiced authority calmed him, and the soldier and the little convoy trotted past the colony of bedraggled wretches.

Gilbert turned and glanced at him. 'These are just some of the guardians of the Valley of God and the Monastery of St Anthony.' Hearing this, Henri's heart raced: at last, an answer, a reason.

Ahead, the trail curved slightly to the right, joining the bed of a small stream, no more than a bullock's cart wide, before disappearing between two towering limestone buttresses. At the top of the buttresses, sentinel-like, stood two dark-robed figures, each armed only with a staff. They remained there as the convoy splashed up the narrow stream bed, its clear, warm waters barely covering the horses' hooves. Mist filled the narrow defile. For almost 500 yards the convoy continued in silence, the blue sky glimpsed through the ethereal vapours, framed by the top of the polished limestone walls either side. Occasionally the shell of some long dead sea creature showed embedded in the rock. Henri turned briefly in his saddle and saw that the entire convoy was now close bunched inside the towering walls. He frowned: a perfect ambush, he thought.

The shallow waters of the steam gradually petered out, and now the horses were walking through the fine limestone dust of the dry stream bed. Ahead the narrow band of blue sky began to widen. Henry felt excitement rise in him. With an exultant cry he suddenly urged his horse forward and came thundering out of the narrow defile into open country only to stop just as suddenly, causing Gilbert to utter a colourful oath as he almost collided with him. The two riders paused: an incredible vista had opened in front of them.

Ahead lay an enormous valley, what would have been perhaps a sinkhole or lake: a relic of the end of the last ice age. As the water receded it had left a deep depression some half a mile in diameter, ringed by vertical limestone cliffs. The valley was completely enclosed save for the narrow entrance to the defile from which they had just emerged. The ancient alluvial lakebed was obviously highly fertile, and stooped figures could be seen in the neat, ordered fields, which were bounded by low stone walls. Carts piled high with crops made their way across them. Figures, dwarfed by the distance, slowly followed bullock-drawn ploughs. Below the rim of the bowl, under dangling creepers, natural caves gaped, set in the limestone cliffs. Gradually, on closer inspection, these seemed to take on a more ordered look. Crudely carved steps could be seen running up the cliffs and disappearing into the entrances many feet above the floor of the valley. Henri was able to make out lines of regular mortar joints, and the outline of windows in the walls, behind which he could see movement. The sound of distant voices floated down. The inhabitants of this extraordinary basin lived in the rock face itself!

As he watched, entranced, he saw children playing on the steps and balconies, women leaning out of windows yelling and scolding. His horse whinnied and stirred impatiently. Still Henri stared. For it was not the ordered fields, or the dwellings of the troglodytes, or the teeming abundant life he saw that transfixed him. In the centre of this secret sanctuary, dominating everything, was an incredible vision – a castle. It was a magical sight. Massive walls of mellow, dressed limestone soared to crenelated buttresses. Beyond them, reflecting the light, the conical tile rooves of the inner keep gleamed. From the four corners, pennants of the Order of St Anthony flew bravely in the light breeze. The whole scene glittered and shone like a jewel in the pale sunlight. A broad road, beginning at the entrance to the defile from which the rest of the convoy was still emerging, ran straight to the foot of the mighty walls, ending at a portcullis. Even as Henri watched, this, began to move slowly upwards. Now with Eleanor and Gilbert at his side he urged his mount forward down the long road that led to the bewitching castle, beaming with almost childlike glee.

On either side of the road stretched fields, interspersed with orchards, their trees in neat orderly rows. Well-kept beehives nestled beneath them. Even though it was winter, the sky was a clear blue and all around there was a feeling of rich husbandry and contentment. As the friends drew near Henri saw, with astonishment, that the castle had been modelled on the great castle at Jerusalem, where Henri had never set foot, but whose recapture was not only his own reason for existence, but that of all Christendom.

However, this castle did not have the hordes of colourful, teeming noisy humanity, nor the low, crowded dwellings that Jerusalem had lapping at its walls. As the party drew nearer, Henri made out tiny figures patrolling the battlements: figures in glinting armour, figures with the flapping black surcoats and the emblazoned blue tau cross of the knights of the Order of St Anthony.

He turned in bewilderment to Gilbert, and then to Eleanor. The pair were watching him intensely, their expressions giving nothing away. Gilbert spoke at last, as if to break the spell,

'Welcome to La Val Dieu, Henri.' His voice was impassive.

'And to our future,' added Eleanor.

Her eyes seemed to sparkle suddenly, and an odd little smile played briefly about her lips. For a brief moment Henri experienced a feeling made up in equal parts of anticipation and apprehension.

Entering the courtyard, after an exultant gallop along the roadway, the friends stopped in the centre of the wondrous castle. The dozen or so wagons from Narbonne followed them and then veered slowly to the left, where they disappeared down some kind of curved roadway. Watching them, Henri's eyes narrowed, 'Four missing, Gilbert?'

'Not missing Henri, we sent the last four northwest to La Rochelle.'

Gilbert paused, and Henri spoke impatiently. 'Go on man, why? Why have four wagons gone to La Rochelle?' He saw that Gilbert did not quite meet his eyes.

'I've sent Claude, my best sergeant, and a dozen men to escort them. They're to seek a ship at La Rochelle belonging to Prince St Clair, bound for his castle at Roslin, in Scotland: for he is our grand prior in that land,' Gilbert replied.

Henri, realising that his question had not so much been answered as deflected, decided not to press the matter.

Chapter 10

Eleanor remained closeted for many hours during the day with Gilbert in the large, panelled library of the inner keep, while Henri explored the estate alone. On one occasion he had knocked on the doors and without waiting for an answer had entered the room. The two were seated with an elderly brother of the order at the huge circular table. The monk quickly pulled his habit across his chest, but not before Henri had glimpsed the crimson breast and gold chain of office of a cardinal.

The three had been poring over a large, somehow familiar ledger bound in leather. A worn dusty satchel, last seen by Henri being carried by Gilbert from the Gate of St Anthony in Acre, lay discarded on the floor. Gilbert had risen, smiling easily, indicating that he and Eleanor were busy with affairs of their estate. Still smiling, he had led Henri gently but firmly back through the library doors.

Barely able to conceal his chagrin, Henri had left the inner keep and found his mount tethered in the stables. Riding furiously along the causeway he had galloped through the narrow defile until he brought up at the fast-flowing river. He jumped from his horse and angrily kicked at a stone, sending it hurtling into the water.

'In God's name!' he muttered to himself. 'Thrown out of the Holy Land with a king's ransom in treasure; married before I can shake a stick; and now shut out of affairs and plots of which I know nothing, as if I were a child. And what of the obligations that Bernard had discussed?'

Across the years the memory of his austere father flowed back towards him. At once his burst of temper evaporated, to be replaced by cold, angry logic. He stared at the figures high above the valley, their cowls up, their dark robes flapping in the wind that blew across the Forest of Rialsesse. Setting his jaw, he jumped on his mount and galloped furiously back through the defile.

This time, finding Eleanor alone in the library, he entered, slamming the door behind him. She turned, startled, from the blazing fire. A half-smile froze on her lips as she saw the look upon his face. 'The roof turret, now!' he snapped.

The circular turret room at the top of the keep had a steep, conical roof. The chimneys from the great hall and the kitchens below meant that the stone inner walls seeped warmth into the narrow room. It was a place of utter privacy as the couple had discovered before. It was also soundproof, high above the bustle of the castle. Henri and Eleanor were both breathing heavily as the door closed behind them and he turned to her, his eyes cold.

'Ever since our departure from Acre,' he began, 'I have allowed myself to be guided along this gilded path by yourself and Gilbert, not questioning, but believing that in some way a future awaited me ... And now I find myself, whilst not a prisoner, a hostage in this great castle, itself unknown and hidden from the world. I have been forced from the land where my father was so brutally murdered, with no chance now of ever avenging that deed, save to languish on my estates. I have no role to play here, Eleanor, except that of your husband, and it is plain that the order to which you both belong is averse to involve me in any way.'

His outburst had the effect of calming him somewhat and he was puzzled by Eleanor's silence. She merely leant against the door and observed him quizzically. His jaw clenched and he continued. 'Before sunset tomorrow I will travel to my estate at Montfort l'Amaury in the north.'

Eleanor looked at her husband, her face uncharacteristically betraying a fleeting series of emotions. She shook her head suddenly, as if making up her mind, and looked directly at him, reminding Henri – and not for the first time – of the mountain leopard of his youth.

'We did not meet by chance Henri. Your great uncle Simon was utterly ruthless in the destruction of the Cathars, previously loyal to our cause, but on the verge of revealing La Val Dieu to the world. History will remember Simon de Montfort for the massacres at Béziers. But before him, your ancestors defeated the Infidel at Poitiers, a battle that my ancestors also fought at, repelling the attempted invasion by the Infidels in 732. It was during the pursuit of the defeated followers of Mohammed, that they discovered La Val Dieu. So, you see, Henri, our journey has been long.'

She paused a moment, looking at him with those penetrating blue eyes. Not for the first time did Henri feel he could have no secrets under her gaze.

'We still have a long, long way to go,' she concluded.

Henri's mood had become calmer. He leant against the parapet watching Eleanor without speaking, letting the warm breeze caress his face. She returned his gaze with equanimity. The silence hung between them. At last Eleanor stirred, 'Wait here.'

Then she turned and was gone before Henri could protest. He stared out of the roof turret. The scene around him was one of utter contentment, which he felt beginning to permeate his soul. Somehow, he knew that in spite of his ultimatum to Eleanor he would be part of this place for a very long time.

He heard the door open behind him and suddenly Eleanor was by his side again. Her face was flushed, and she looked at him with shining eyes. She began softly but with calm authority, 'Our battle for the Holy Land is temporarily lost, but our war with the Infidel continues for us and our future generations. Let there be no doubt, here at La Val Dieu we have the means of our victory, God willing.'

Letting these words sink in, she paused before holding out her hand to Henri, 'There is something you must see. The time has come.'

Leading him back to the library. Carefully closing and bolting the doors behind her, she walked to the table. A lamp stood there. In its pool of amber light lay a vellum map, weighed down at its four corners by heavy golden coins. Taking up one of the coins, Eleanor began. 'The centre of the map is the castle you now stand in, and represents us, our world, our kingdom, our home. All around us lie the valleys and foothills of the Massif du Canigou, the Razès and the forest of Railsesse all of which form our veil from prying eyes and the attentions of the world.'

'At seven or eight open points in the valleys we came through earlier are our first lines of defence. As you already know, l'Ermitage and others are our own leper colonies. Our other centres contain sufferers of St Anthony's Fire.' She seemed not to notice Henri's sudden look of horror. 'As I said earlier, leprosy is not contagious, and we have the knowledge to control St Anthony's Fire.'

She paused, glancing at him. Henri nodded, remembering Cyprus. 'The only villages in the vicinity are the two Rennes: Rennes-les-Bains and Rennes-le-Château. These are now mere fractions of their ancient size, as much of the original Visigoth settlements were demolished to provide the means to build La Val Dieu. In both those villages we have our own eyes and ears.'

Henri waited for her to elaborate on this. Instead, she went on, 'Inwards from the colonies, we patrol the heights of the valleys ourselves, and as you've seen, the final approach is well concealed. We have been here for over 500 years and no one knows about us who should not.'

The 'we' seemed to hang in the air between them. There had been a sense of implacability – a kind of baleful malignity in her words that had sent a chill through Henri. For a moment the expression of agonized shock on the face of Rodger de Flor as Eleanor's steel entered his brain flashed before him.

In what seemed an oddly conciliatory gesture, Eleanor took his hand and kissed him lightly. 'Please, my Lord, keep your questions until later. Now, we go to the vaults.'

Leaving the inner keep, they entered the main courtyard inside the massive portcullis through which they galloped on that first day. To the left of this a road curved into what Henri saw was the entrance to a passageway, after which it descended steeply. Pausing only to provide themselves with flaming torches, the pair began the journey that would lead them deep into the bowels of the castle.

The surface of rough-hewn cobbles had been worn in two parallel grooves by the passage of countless wheels over the centuries. Overhead the walls curved into a smooth arch, and Henri marvelled at the skill of the ancient stonemasons: not a feather's thickness could penetrate the joints of the stone blocks. Down, down they went bearing constantly to the right. It seemed to Henri that they had turned back on themselves three times, and still the flickering light revealed the passageway stretching downwards. A fresh, gentle breeze coming from somewhere moved gently around them, making the light from the torches dance and sway. Still they descended until, at last, they arrived at two immense iron-studded wooden doors.

Eleanor gave Henri a reassuring glance and then knocked seven times. A small section of one of the doors slid open, and a single eye regarded them. The sound of heavy bolts being drawn back echoed along the passage. Before the door was fully open, Eleanor slipped through, drawing Henri with her. Taking both torches, she extinguished them in a vat of water standing by.

Henri froze. They had stepped into dazzling sunshine. The light poured down past hanging creepers and lianas. They were in a huge roofless chamber, at whose furthest extremity Henri could barely discern a number of robed figures moving, apparently engaged in some kind of labour. To one side a long column of untended carts such as he had escorted to this place stretched away from him. At the head of the column, where the carts were being unloaded, furnaces glowed. Clouds of smoke and steam coiled skywards, dissipating slowly.

Henri gazed in wonder at this mighty roofless cathedral; its natural rock walls sloping inwards to the patch of iridescent blue hundreds of feet above his head. The vertical rock walls would have ended in a jagged gash framing the sky but for the softening effect of the flora hanging into this secret world.

Letting go of Eleanor's hand, Henri walked slowly down the line of waiting carts, his fingers lightly brushing their coarse bodywork. Different styles of construction, some ornate and carved, some plain workaday farm carts, spoke of their origins from different countries, different regions. The carts he had seen being loaded at Narbonne with the cargoes of the *Bethel* and the *Bethania* had now been joined by many others, all crowding into this enormous cavern. The single factor linking all the wagons – he calculated that there must be about eighty of them – was that, judging by their sagging bodywork, they each carried a very heavy load.

He turned as Eleanor's light footsteps sounded behind him. Wordlessly she took his hand and led him further along the chamber to the roaring furnaces. There were three of them, standing against the sloping rock wall. Henri watched as one by one the wagons, having been emptied of their precious cargo, were broken up and pushed into the furnace to feed the hungry flames. The heat was intense. Moving aside a little to try and escape it, Henri glimpsed what, to his overwrought imagination, seemed to be a vision of Hell.

To each furnace was attached a large bellows made of wood and covered with animal hide. These were connected by a crude, yet complicated arrangement of rods and wheels. The whole system was kept in motion by the pumping feet of three small dark creatures wearing heavy iron collars around their necks, which were attached to the wall behind them. Moving between the three bellows, carrying an ox hide whip, strode a huge Nubian: a slave-master.

In the flickering light his black skin shone with sweat. His rippling muscles bulged as with liberal use of the whip he urged the three slaves to greater efforts on their tread mills.

A pair of sweating, leather clad foundry men was ladling molten metal in a golden stream into moulds of sand. The fiery liquid hissed and spluttered, sending showers of sparks into the air.

Eleanor touched Henri's arm. 'Come,' she mouthed and he followed her to a stone wall, twice the height of a man. A door had been let into it, which opened at Eleanor's touch and Henri followed her through it. At once the noise and heat were silenced as she closed the door behind them.

They now found themselves in a place of pure magic. To the faint sound of rushing, tumbling water the walls danced and spun with a myriad of shifting light patterns. All was brightness, radiance and dazzling luminosity.

At a table sat four men wearing the dark habit and blue tau cross of the Antonines. Henri saw that they were engaged in carefully dismantling a great mound of gold and silver relics, chalices, swords, chains of office: all richly encrusted with jewels. It was these that were giving off the brilliant dancing colours that raced across the grey stone walls.

Henri was accustomed to a fairly ostentatious show of wealth. But here, jumbled and piled like so much flotsam and jetsam, lay much, much more than even a king's ransom – the spoils of war from two centuries of crusading against the Infidel.

Behind each of the brothers there stood a large reed basket. As the treasure was dismantled, using crude picks, hammers and chisels, the golden metal mounts were put into the basket. Once these were filled, they were moved by other robed figures to the arched door leading to the furnace room. The precious stones, extracted by the delicate picks, were placed in a leather container. Henri saw that it was three quarters full of gemstones, from small pea-sized pearls to rubies, emeralds, sapphires, and diamonds, many as large as a bird's egg.

'There's more,' Eleanor whispered in his ear, disturbing his reverie.

He glanced at her, and then about him and saw that there were passages leading off the main chamber like the spokes of a wheel. Colossal wooden racks could be seen at the entrances to these passages, each rack was made up of four shelves on which were stacked row on row of yellow-gold ingots. The racks, burdened with their gleaming bars, stretched into the passageways until they were lost in darkness.

Henri turned to look at Eleanor. Standing quietly there, she seemed both fragile and indomitable, a paradox set against a backdrop of incredible industry. Smiling, her face pale in the glancing light, she took his hand again,

64

leading him this time towards the sound of running water, to where, in the farthest reaches of the chamber, a broad, fast-flowing river ran. Here there was little light. The river, black and swift and somehow ominous, both appeared and disappeared into the rock itself. A small rope bridge precariously spanned the rushing, swirling torrent. Eleanor confidently placed her foot on the bridge, beckoning him to follow. In a moment, though it seemed longer to Henri, they found themselves on a wide rock shelf, with only the rushing depths separating them from the rest of the cavern.

Yet another door was set into the rock. This opened onto a narrow stone staircase. A thick rope was attached to the walls with rusty iron stanchions. There were no torches here to light the way. Leaving the sound of the rushing waters behind them they began to climb into darkness using the rope as a guide.

The stairs seemed to go on forever., and after a while Henri's calf muscles began to ache, his heart to pound. About to protest, he heard Eleanor ahead of him fumble with something that sounded metallic, and immediately the narrow staircase was flooded with radiance. They stepped into a room of light; a circular room panelled on the floor and walls in the palest of oak. The source of the amazing brilliance came from the many wide windows let into the walls of the room; windows that had nothing in common with the more usual arrow-slits.

Wonderingly Henri walked across this silent glowing room and touched the translucent material. Slight imperfections in the surface made the reflection of the countryside beyond shimmer and dance. Outside the banners streaming from the turrets snapped and cracked in the stiff breeze, yet the room was a haven of light, air and tranquillity.

Since he was little more than a child Henri had heard talk of this wonderful new material called 'glass', brought back from the wars by Flemish soldiers. It was so expensive, it was said, that only the very rich, the nobles, the merchants grown fat on prosperity, could afford it. His fingers stroked it gently. He turned to see that Eleanor was standing at the opposite side of the room. While he had been musing she had slipped off her voluminous cloak. What he saw behind her made him gasp.

Upon the altar standing over six feet high stood a huge golden, seven-branched menorah.

'As you know Henri, my ancestors were Visigoth nobility, and when they sacked Rome in 410 they captured this sacred menorah, which the Romans had looted from the Temple of Solomon in Jerusalem, and brought it here to Rhedae their capital. In 700 it was returned to the Jews in Narbonne, where their royal family resided. Just before Narbonne fell to the Infidel in 720 this menorah and other of their holy treasures were taken by them and hidden at the monastery of Saint-Guilhem-le-Désert, and when our sanctuary was ready in 895 it was brought here. From that point on this place has been the treasure house of our order's wealth that we guard on behalf of our Holy Church and use on its behalf to fight its Holy War.'

She stood there in a simple white satin sheath, which fell sheer to her ankles. Her slim waist was circled by a broad leather belt, from which hung a sword, a thing of ancient, jewelled beauty that glittered, throwing back the light. Her hand rested lightly on the hilt. 'This is Joyeuse, the sword of Charlemagne and this ...' In her right hand she held a golden chalice, tall and thin stemmed; it flared almost sensuously into a bowl flanked by two graceful handles.

Without asking – hardly daring to breath – Henri knew what that it was.

One of the reasons for the bloody crusading quests into the Holy Land, started by Urban II in 1095, and urged onwards with fanatical zeal by subsequent popes, was the race to find the most sacred vessel of Christendom: the Chalice of the Eucharist, the cup from which Jesus had drunk at the Last Supper, and which was said to hold a drop of his holy blood. It was thought that possession of this sacred cup not only gave the alluring promise of eternal life, but also of temporal power greater than anyone had ever known.

When Joseph of Aramathia was cast into prison following the death of Jesus, Christ himself had miraculously appeared to him and had given him this vessel. By it he was sustained in his solitary confinement, which lasted for two years until he was freed by the Emperor Vespasian. According to legend, Joseph, or his colleague, Lissan, had taken the Grail to Glastonbury in England. Following Joseph's death, the Grail had mysteriously disappeared, to the anguish of the Christian world.

All this passed through Henri's mind as, unable to speak, unable to move, he watched Eleanor pour the flagon's contents into the gleaming bowl.

She offered it to him. Trance like, he took a deep draught of the aromatic ruby wine, then watched as she did the same. She then unbuckled the Sword and handed it to him. 'This now belongs to you my prince, and in turn it shall belong to our descendants'

Then she turned and walked towards the huge bed that stood under one of the windows. Sunlight streamed through her fine satin garment, which she now let slip from her onto the flag-stoned floor. Holding his gaze, she stretched out on the bed, cat like, languid, smiling. He moved towards her, towards the promise in her smile, knowing that somehow a point of no return had been passed: he had finally and irrevocably been accepted not only by his beloved, but also by the power she represented. She was preparing to lead him, with her secret, mystic force, into something shadowy-deep and profoundly mysterious; something as yet unnamed, but that would shape his life and the fate of his family forevermore. There were sudden tears in his eyes, but his heart soared as he walked towards her.

Chapter 11

The sun casting its fiery rays through the windows woke them. They dressed without speaking, but sending each other faint, smiling glances. Something had changed between them – now there was no looking back.

Finally able to take in the details of the room, Henri saw that there was another door opposite the one they had entered – how long ago that seemed now! A spirit of joyous, almost childlike mischief made him turn the handle and peer round the edge. The door opened onto a balcony running round the walls of a great hall. He frowned, not recognising this part of the castle.

From behind him Eleanor said softly, 'We are not inside the castle now, my lover. We are in the Observatoire La Pique.' Smiling at him in her enigmatic way, she led Henri along the balcony. In the hall below them, two mighty chandeliers hung over a table spread magnificently for four people. Used as he was to displays of wealth, Henri marvelled at the richness and opulence of the surroundings, at last realising that all this wealth was theirs to dispose of as they wished. His own small estates now seemed irrelevant: he was now part of something much larger than being yet another feudal baron.

Eleanor opened a small door that led onto the roof of what Henri now realised was the monastery. The stiff breeze had freshened, become almost fierce, causing the streaming banners to flap noisily. At one end of the roof stood the figure of a man in a billowing robe, his back to them. He turned as they approached. His eyes were cold and grey, his face set. He extended a large hand. 'Henri, it's good to see you again.' His expression gave nothing away. Henri wordlessly returned the handshake.

Eleanor said, 'Hello, Uncle Bertrand,' and embraced him affectionately.

'But of course,' Henri thought, 'of course.'

Now he knew his place. Now he knew that because of these two people he had become a part of something extraordinary. But a part of . . . what?

Bertrand put his arm around Henri's shoulders, and with Eleanor on his other arm began slowly to pace with them the length of the roof. 'You must know,' he said, his head turning slightly in Henri's direction so that there was no doubt about to whom he was speaking, 'You must know that following the recent death of His Holiness, Pope Nicholas IV, the Council of Cardinals ...', his voice taking on a faint edge, '... have done again that which they do best, they have elected a frail elderly hermit, Pope Celestine V, because they could not agree on anybody else. Since he is approaching eighty years of age it gives us a little time to prepare the ground for our next candidate.'

Henri glanced quickly at Eleanor. For a bishop to be discussing the College of Cardinals' choice of the next Vicar of Christ betrayed an extraordinary level of confidence, he thought.

'We shall choose a pope who will stand up to the intrigues and plotting of Philippe le Bel,' Bertrand said. 'The King of France makes new demands daily, taxing the Church in order to fatten his own purse, and to fund his war with England. I tell you, Henri, that the King of France is heavily in debt to the Knights Templar, and is even now looking for ways to abrogate that debt.'

Henri frowned. 'And this election of a weak, eighty-year-old pope will achieve what exactly?'

Bertrand acknowledged this question but did not reply directly. Instead, he led them from the roof down a narrow staircase to the peace and warm tranquillity of the great hall.

The figure now seated at the magnificently set table rose as they approached. Bertrand made the introductions. 'May I present my niece, the Lady Eleanor, and her husband, Lord Henri de Montfort l'Amaury. Eleanor, Henri this is Cardinal Gaetani.'

The introductions completed, he seated himself, motioning the others to do the same, and clapped his hands sharply. Soft-footed brothers of the order appeared carrying steaming dishes.

The meal that followed was superb and during it nothing of importance was discussed. When the last dishes were cleared away, the dying fire was replenished with logs and the serving brothers retired, closing the door with respectful bows. For a while there was silence. Then Cardinal Gaetani rose and stood before the fire nursing a large goblet. 'The war in the East is over, as you know, Henri,' he said. 'We cannot fight a thousand miles from home from a fractured Europe with indifferent support. The Saracens are united in purpose and fear no man: indeed their death in battle is taught as an immediate entry to paradise itself.' His eyes sought and held Henri's.

This man knows of my Hashashin past Henri mused as he listened.

Gaetani continued, 'You have seen today our preparations for the continuance of that war, which our learned Urban II began 200 years ago in Clermont. Nations divested themselves of knights and warriors to head eastwards. However, on our very own borders in Al-Andalus, the Infidel has been in occupation since 711 and has changed the beliefs and social structures in that country so to be unrecognisable to Christian men. Whilst the Holy See watches and wrings its hands at failure in the Holy Land, the Knights of St Anthony, shielded from the world by their brothers in the Order of St Anthony, have been fighting the Infidel from here for over 500 years.' Henri's thoughts went swiftly to Gilbert's comments as they were approaching the castle for the first time.

'Groups of Knights,' continued Gaetani, 'brought by Guillaume de Gellone Comte de Razès, from their home in Ethiopia, assisted Charlemagne in 778 as he entered Iberia with the Neustrian Army to receive the homage of Solomon ibn-al-Arabi at Zaragoza; and it was their skill that prevented the massacre at Roncevaux Pass turning into a rout. I believe you and Gilbert attempted to capture the Uthman Koran at Acre, an attempt also made when the Caliph of Baghdad, Harun-al-Rashid was lured into contact with a unit of knights in 801. That particular manuscript contains a message that we have fought to obtain for over five centuries. So, you see, Henri, our fight is long, and may grow longer, but God is on our side.'

His voice cracking with passion and fanatical conviction, he paused to take a long draught from his goblet.

'We use our resources to help the kings of and Navarre in their battles against the Caliph of Iberia. The Islamic hordes do not rule easily, and now they have declared war on the Jews and the Visigoths, we must press this advantage'

He suddenly threw up his hands. 'However, I have not come here merely to ask the help of a courageous knight for an adventure in foreign lands.' He smiled. 'We will win in Al-Andalus not only because it is our home, but the basis of this,' he indicated the large, silent hall, 'the home of the Antonine order, and its battle for the Holy Land. A battle which may take us into unknown waters, for I fear in future we may not rely merely on brave men in armour, but on our cunning and our great wealth, to cause our return to Jerusalem, and in time, God willing, to bring the light of Christianity to those afflicted by the laws and customs of Islam.'

Henri waited deferentially for the cardinal to finish before he spoke. 'Sire, with respect, how can you base your future on those assumptions if the Holy Father decides to pursue a different policy, and not our order? You plan for hundreds of years in the future, yet all is at the mercy of the decision of the incumbent pope.'

Cardinal Gaetani regarded Henri with cold eyes. 'Then we shall be requiring a new, strong-minded Pope, Henri.'

The fire had not burned down all that much, but Henri felt a shiver run through him, and he realised that with its great wealth and power the Order of St Anthony was in control of the Vatican itself. This was its – and now his – great secret.

CHAPTER 12

Henri's forays on behalf of the King of Aragon eventually grew less as the Moors were pushed further and further south in Iberia, and it came as something of a surprise when one day he idly calculated that he had not left the castle for over a year.

While he had occasionally fretted about the lack of action, his life had become filled with the day-to-day concerns generated by maintaining the large estates, supervising the work being undertaken in the secret cavern, and his growing delight at fatherhood, now that his son, whom he named Raymond after his beloved grandfather, had been born.

If he felt that he had been somehow been excluded from Eleanor's plans so far, it was as nothing to the exclusion he had experienced at his son's birth. Eleanor's body had swollen enormously, and at times Henri harboured the thought that their child would cause her to burst like a ripe plum. Two older women from the estates attended Eleanor as the first pains arrived. Gently, but firmly, they shooed Henri from the apartments: his leaving and his acceptance of their authority as much a surprise to him as to the two women.

He paced the battlements watching, but unseeing, for half a day until Eleanor's screams drove him to their bedroom door. As he reached for the door handle, a lusty cry of a newborn baby slowed his panic-stricken rush, and he entered the room in time to see an exhausted but triumphant Eleanor cradling in her arms a small, wrapped bundle, while the women made their excuses and left.

As the door closed behind the two midwives, Eleanor slumped back in the bed, her face weary, and her eyes watchful. Henri carefully took the tiny bundle in his arms. His eyes met Eleanor's, and she nodded. 'A boy Henri. It's a boy, the beginning of a dynasty that will sweep the Infidel from the face of the earth.'

Henri nodded, understanding.

When he suggested to Eleanor that they call the boy Raymond, she had laughed in delight and said, 'Truly, Henri, you prophecy well, with all the wealth that he will have at his disposal he and his descendants surely could become Les Rois de Monde, Kings of the World'

* * *

Bertrand, who had significantly enhanced his status as Archbishop of Bordeaux, had arrived one morning to announce this to his family and to discuss the latest political machinations; and Henri listened with interest to his accounts of the public rows between a rapacious King Philippe of France, and Pope Boniface VIII. The king's refusal to return the wealth of the Holy Mother Church to Rome that he had misappropriated, was becoming ever more strident.

Boniface VIII had used the approaching turn of the century to call all pilgrims to Rome with their offerings. As the last years of the old century drew to a close, almost two million pilgrims filled the ancient city. Two priests reportedly stood all day and night behind the beautiful altar of St Paul using rakes and shovels to drag away the steady stream of gold and silver offered by the faithful in exchange for remission of their sins. Bertrand wryly remarked on one visit that Boniface had interpreted rather too literally the words from his papal investiture, 'Take the tiara, and know that thou art the father of princes and kings, the ruler of the world, the Vicar on Earth of our Saviour, Jesus Christ.'

Emboldened by his newfound wealth, Boniface had determined to bring to a head the problem of Philippe IV of France, who by now had resorted to confiscating Church lands and property in lieu of unpaid taxes. To make matters worse, Boniface's sworn enemies at the papal palace, members of the Colonna family who had railed against his investiture, had been given sanctuary by Philippe IV. In fury, Boniface summoned the Council of Cardinals in Rome, but Philippe's strength lay in his total control of the French clergy, and by way of their weekly sermons he rallied the French people around him against what he believed was a vicious and greedy pope.

Philippe forbade any French prelate to attend the council, called, he said, to denigrate the throne of France. Disobedience would be repaid by the total confiscation of the entire papal French property.

A further expedition into Castile on behalf of the King of Aragon provided Henri with much needed intelligence as he travelled, as a monk of the order, over the Pyrenees. The content of many of the sermons he heard preached by local priests provided him with irrefutable evidence of Philippe's meddling in the Church's affairs. He felt at times that the whole country was seething with indignation at the politicised antics of the Holy Father.

Henri had fought with many men, had killed many more, and had spent the majority of his life at war for his One True God. If he was anything at all he was an utterly loyal servant of God's representative on earth, but there were occasions when it took all his self-discipline not to reach for his sword.

One day, on returning to the castle after such a foray, he was pleased to see the personal guards of Bertrand de Gothia practising the new two-handed axe-play in the courtyard. Eagerly he sought out Bertrand, whom he had come to regard as a father-in-law. He found him in the library in deep and quiet discussion with Eleanor. They were sat by the fire with their heads almost touching, the murmur of their conversation lost against the crackle of the logs.

The two drew apart at Henri's entrance. Not for the first time did he feel himself in the role of a junior partner. Throwing off his frustration, he made to speak to Bertrand. Bertrand shook his head, and rose, pointing to his mouth and ears, indicating they should go onto the roof, the place of all their confidential discussions. Once there, he paced between Henri and Eleanor, saying little whilst Henri told him what was troubling him.

'Philippe le Bel is bound to grant me an audience if only from curiosity,' Henri had concluded.

'Provided you keep your name from Guillaume de Nogaret,' cautioned Eleanor.

'He remembers that his family were burned as Cathars by Simon de Montfort and he still hates the de Montfort name: he has the king's trust and is a dangerous man.'

'The question,' interrupted Bertrand, 'is this. Will Philippe's desire to abrogate his debts to the Templars cause him to be less cunning when dealing with Abbot Henri of the Order of St Anthony, supposing that he is under the impression that the abbot can assist him in his desire?'

Henri glanced quickly at Bertrand. An archbishop, maybe, he thought, but a clever, scheming one.

Eleanor added, 'Perhaps Henri could intimate to Philippe that only through the offices of Bertrand de Gothia, Archbishop of Bordeaux and the Order of St Anthony, may it prove possible to achieve the downfall of the Templars, and the abrogation of his debts.'

Henri frowned at her. She was regarding him with a strange intense look, as if trying to compel him to follow Bertrand's lead.

Bertrand spoke softly. 'Just supposing the Pope was to assist Philippe – in secret, of course – to acquire the holdings of the Knights Templar ...'

Henri's face was furious, his fists clenched. 'The Knights are pledged to the Pope, My Lord! They have fought and died for him and his office. That would be treachery of the basest kind indeed.'

Bertrand raised his hand and his cold eyes bored into Henri's. 'What if the holdings were empty? The treasure gone? What if the majority of the knights simply disappeared? A pyrrhic victory, perhaps?'

Leaving Henri staring after him, he turned and walked with Eleanor to the far corner of the roof. Henri stood for a long time at the battlements staring over the green and pleasant fields surrounding him. His mind raced and seethed with bewilderment and indignation. He stared balefully at the couple at the end of the roof. Their heads came together briefly. Then Bertrand turned and descended the steps to the library. Eleanor regarded Henri coolly as he approached, his face flushed with anger.

'In God's name Eleanor, you seem to have woven a spell far too strong! At every step, events that I have marvelled at turn out to be the result of long-laid plans and plots conceived even before I was born. I am defeated in the Holy Land, only to be brought here, to this secret place of fantastic wealth and then to find that I am a pawn in a game of which I know little. Now, unless I am very much mistaken, I am being asked to commit treachery against the Most Holy Order of the Temple.'

Henri paused, calming himself a little as he took Eleanor in his arms. 'Knights, I admit I have no love for, but who, nevertheless, have given their lives in the cause of God's Vicar on Earth. Eleanor, this man, your uncle, archbishop, whoever, is asking me to betray men whom I have fought alongside all of my life!'

He pulled angrily away from Eleanor and went stamping down the stairs to the library. Bursting in, he found Bertrand by the fire regarding him with equanimity. The door closed behind Henri as Eleanor joined them.

'Boniface would never even speak to Philippe IV, let alone negotiate secretly,' began Henri forcefully, thinking as he said it that it was stating the obvious.

'I concur, but perhaps Philippe may be unaware he is not negotiating with the Pope,' Bertrand shot back.

Henri acknowledged the reply with a furious shake of his head. 'You still haven't answered my point,' he said vehemently.

Bertrand regarded Henri for a moment, his eyes flicking between him and Eleanor. 'An Archbishop of Bordeaux, may I remind you; and under English fealty what is more, would not offend Philippe so deeply.' Bertrand said softly, his eyes dark and direct.

Henri laughed sarcastically. 'You have my utmost respect, sir, but the King of France is not likely to confuse a chaplain to Boniface VIII with the papal office itself.'

Bertrand replied coldly, 'So long as I remain merely the chaplain, I agree.'

A long silence followed this, each alone with his thoughts, until Eleanor interjected quietly, 'The English connection is a good point indeed. Philippe's war with the aggressive Edward of England is a huge drain on his resources. I am told that even now he seeks an alliance to marry his sister to Edward and his daughter to Edward's son. That union may well prove not to be as fruitful as Philippe hopes. My sources tell me the Prince of Wales prefers the flesh of men.' She smiled wryly.

'But with England placated,' mused Henri, 'Philippe could turn his attention elsewhere.'

CHAPTER 13

Henri knelt before the Vicar of Christ on Earth at the high altar of St Peter's. It had been a considerable undertaking to gather the band of the brothers of St Anthony and journey to Rome. Surreptitious visits days in advance of the tiny band of monks had ensured that a selected village had an outbreak of St Anthony's Fire just as, God be praised, the brothers appeared. Usually, one or two of the poor afflicted wretches would have died in agony, their limbs blackening as their terror-stricken eyes watched their own bodies putrefy. It had never occurred to the suffering villagers to connect the catastrophe that had devastated their population with the visits a day or two earlier of two merchants selling rye grain and flour.

* * *

The Monks had come to Rome to have the Order of St Anthony ordained under the rule of St Austin by Boniface VIII; a method, as Bertrand explained, of distancing themselves from the Hospitaller and especially the Templar orders. Accordingly, in the late summer of 1297, members of the order were finally ordained as canons regular, giving them the established monastic way of living that would protect their dark secrets even more.

Henri, now officially the abbot of the order, along with his wife, Eleanor, had knelt before Pope Boniface VIII to receive his papal blessing. Raising his eyes to the cross in the small private chapel of St Peter, he caught sight of Archbishop Bertrand de Gothia, as chaplain, standing to the left of the Pope. Flicking his eyes back to Boniface he felt immediately that the power of the most Holy Office on Earth had already shifted. Importantly, he was utterly at one with his new feeling, an innate sense of inescapable destiny. He knelt in silence and remembered the peaceful quietness of the church at Tyre moments before his father's brutal assassination, sensing as though his father had laid his hand gently upon him.

After the simple ceremony the chapel had emptied of the Curia and scribes, and Boniface once more placed his hand on Henri's bare head, looking down at the couple in front of him.

'May the blessing of God the Father be upon you, Abbot Henri and to you, Abbess Eleanor.'

He raised his eyes and his voice thundered suddenly 'Be it God's Holy will that the forces of evil that live within the Infidel unbelievers are finally banished from this earth.'

* * *

Boniface had continued his public war with Philippe IV, and had raised the stakes considerably by his bull *Unam Sanctam*, the strongest claim of papal supremacy ever issued.

'It is a condition of salvation,' he had thundered at the King of France, 'that all human beings should be subject to the Pontiff of Rome.'

In return, Philippe's loyal servant and lawyer, Guillaume de Nogaret, had prepared a legal assault on the Pope, affirming that the Church had been, in God's eyes, married to Celestine V, and that therefore Boniface, while Celestine still lived, had committed the sin of adultery by stealing away the bride of God.

De Nogaret then produced a list of twenty-nine charges against the Pope, including stealing Church property, heresy and the murder of Celestine V. Henri knew that the people of France, through Philippe's control of the priesthood, believed these charges. It came as a shock, however, that the French Templars under Hugues de Pairaud sided with the French king against their spiritual leader. Bertrand had confided in Henri that Hugues de Pairaud, against all Templar law, had become the godfather to King Philippe IV's son, in addition to lending considerable amounts of money to the French king from the order's coffers.

Bertrand had walked with Henri from St Peter's, after the ordination, through the crowded streets of Rome, the noise and bustle providing the perfect cover for their conversation. As always, he came straight to the point. 'You should go back to Paris, Henri. Now would be an opportune moment to talk to the French King Philippe. Your wife's perception of the situation is correct. De Nogaret may indeed pose a threat, but my spies tell me he has left the French court, bound for Anagni.

'Anagni?'

'He seeks an audience with Boniface following the announcement that the entire French kingdom was to be excommunicated.' Bertrand paused as Henri raised his eyebrows. 'I have a suspicion the audience may not be entirely peaceful, as fifteen hundred of King Philippe's soldiers are accompanying him.'

'Are you not normally at his side?' asked Henri.

'I am chaplain only to the Office of The Holy Father, my dear son,' Bertrand smoothly replied.

* * *

Henri and the members of the order had not dallied long in Paris and were soon returned to their mountain sanctuary. Henri, leapt from his horse, weary after two weeks of travelling, but invigorated by the prospect of being with Eleanor again. He found her in the large airy room beneath the turret roof of the castle. The bed had been removed, and the room had become a repository of the order's records.

Every golden plate, every bezant and precious stone, had been painstakingly recorded in these red leather-bound volumes. The Order of St Anthony was now the wealthiest institution in the world. The light, streaming through the Flemish glass, bleached the corners and edges of these rows of volumes, but every time one was removed from its shelf Henri saw in his mind's eye Gilbert descending the stone steps of the Gate of St Anthony all those years ago in Acre. Henri's strong arms encircled his wife and her swollen stomach, and he nuzzled her affectionately. 'A girl this time, I know it for sure,' he murmured.

Eleanor regarded him, eyes shining. 'Of course it is, my dear, of course,' she smiled and rested her head against his shoulder.

A clatter of hooves came from the courtyard below. Eleanor peered down through the distortions of the glass. 'Uncle!' she said, her smile widening. 'Uncle Bertrand, at last, I haven't seen him for over two years!'

Eleanor had begun to be somewhat concerned when Bertrand's visits dropped off dramatically, but he had sent word that he had been at the Court of Philippe IV for a considerable time. Henri had nodded silently when he heard this.

His own sojourn there had not been in vain. Indeed, Eleanor had greeted his return with considerable relief, elated to find that Henri had used the ratification of the order to conduct negotiations with Philippe IV as Abbot Henri of the Monastery La Val Dieu.

Later that day a messenger arrived shaky and nervous. He eventually summoned the courage to speak. 'In the name of the Father, Son and Holy

Ghost it is my sad duty to inform you, the people of this holy place, that I bring news of a dark and tragic nature.' He paused, looking around as if seeking the courage to continue. His pale face bore a sheen of perspiration. He stood for several moments, his mouth opening, but with no sound issuing. Presently he took a deep breath and continued, 'Our Most Holy Father, Pope Boniface VIII, has died following an assault on the papal palace at Anagni.'

Henri leant to Eleanor and whispered, 'Anagni, that's where Philippe sent de Nogaret. Somehow he is involved in this.'

'Further, there has come a proclamation declaring Niccolo Bocassini as the next Holy Father. He has taken the name Benedict XI.'

Bertrand nodded gravely, remaining silent.

CHAPTER 14

Five months after the inauguration of Benedict XI, Bertrand, who had spent several months at the castle, only occasionally disappearing for a few days, bade Henri saddle up. The pair had ridden out of the castle, and in silence traversed the causeway between a sea of early spring crops. Pausing at the narrow entrance to the defile they turned and looked back at the castle's walls: to Henri, they had taken on an almost ethereal quality.

This unaccompanied ride was a sufficiently rare event to have put Henri on his guard. Ruefully he remarked to Bertrand, 'Is it always the case that you need to tell me your darkest plots surrounded by nature?'

Bertrand roared with laughter as he regarded Henri's expression. The horses fidgeted anticipating a good morning's exercise ahead. The movement snapped Bertrand into action and wheeling, he urged his mount down the narrow passage. The defile became wet as the path returned to the riverbed, and Bertrand's horse threw up a swirling mist of water droplets into which Henri followed.

Bertrand was a fast and confident rider, and as the trail widened into one of the valleys of the Razès, he abruptly turned onto a path heading diagonally up the side of the valley. Cresting the top of the ridge, horses and men breathless with effort, they paused to look back. As far as the distant Pyrenees, their snow-clad peaks evident even at this distance, the rolling, undulating hills and the tree-clad slopes of the forest of Railesse stretched. All around them was a huge spreading canopy of green. Of their secret kingdom there was no sign.

'When man achieves the abilities of the birds,' Bertrand said, eyeing the circling buzzards above, 'then we shall have to think again. Until that day I should say our secret is safe.' He smiled at Henri, but his eyes were cool and watchful. 'You are a soldier, Henri. Tell me, what is the quality you would look for most in selecting men for your troop?'

Henri paused a moment before replying carefully, 'Courage, fitness, a strong sense of purpose, and above all, loyalty.'

Bertrand nodded, his eyes on the distant horizon. 'You are well settled here Henri you have two fine children, Raymond, and, I believe, the latest addition, Maria.'

'In honour of my mother who was killed by the Infidel.'

Bertrand nodded briefly. 'You are building our sanctuary well.'

Henri noted his own inclusion into the partnership.

Bertrand continued, 'So that we may continue the fight against the Islamic hordes.'

'A new Crusade?' Henri interjected, his pulse quickening.

Bertrand glanced at quickly at him. 'A Crusade. Yes, my dear son, but not in the way you think. We have spoken before of the need to change the fight. We must no longer think in purely military terms, or indeed even winning the battle within our own short lives. Like the Infidel, we may have to sacrifice ourselves but, in our case, it will be to cause that which God wishes us to do. Could you do that, Henri?'

Henri nodded without hesitation.

'We may,' Bertrand said softly, 'have to betray others. Some strangers to us, yes – but also those close to us.'

Again, Henri nodded. He had reflected earlier on his time with the Hashishin, the fanatical band of Islamic fighters that Bertrand kept alluding to in his conversations with Henri. He felt now, more than anything, that a task was soon to be set for him that would change his life forever.

Nothing more was said as the pair rode through the valleys, enjoying the late summer sun. Later in the day, as the sun lengthened the shadows, they re-entered the narrow defile, and paused again at its opening into the fertile bowl of the sanctuary.

'I need you to go to Perugia, Henri,' said Bertrand suddenly. 'It is the home of Benedict XI. He gripped Henri's arm. 'I need you to practise what you learnt in the mountains above Damascus near Baalbek. See to it, Henri.'

He pulled on the reins, whirling his horse about, and galloped furiously down the straight road to the castle.

That evening Henri saddled up and clattered back out of the castle gates, with Bertrand's word's ringing in his ears, 'Do not fail me, Henri. I shall be in Paris with Gilbert.'

CHAPTER 15

Henri was accepted quickly into the court of Benedict XI, and the Order of St Anthony had sufficient importance in the life of Boniface, his predecessor, to gain him a personal papal audience. Benedict and his court of Curia, selected now from both the Orsini and Colonna families of Italy, showed polite if scant interest in one Abbot Henri as he discussed the monastic rule of the his order in the context of the new papal reign.

The court at Perugia was not the largest or the most opulent of papal residences, but Henri's sparsely furnished cell below the Pope's apartments became his home for a few months. As an Abbot of the Order of St Anthony he attracted little attention compared to the arrogant scarlet-clad cardinals that swept in and out of Benedict's court. The Pope's great age and the identity of his likely successor formed a major part of the conversations in and around the papal palace. Henri was not altogether surprised to discover that Archbishop Bertrand de Gothia had been retained as private chaplain to the Pope following the previous incumbent's unfortunate demise.

Henri had brought with him copies of pages from the red leather volumes in the castle, and since the reputation of the Order of St Anthony had gone before him, it was no surprise when his cell began to take on the appearance of a miniature apothecary's shop. Neither did his excursions into the surrounding countryside attract any attention as he returned carrying small samples of plants and roots. Indeed, it was only a matter of time before members of the Curia began calling at his little cell with their own particular aches and pains, to which Henri benignly prescribed some of the specimens.

He busied himself with his work, content just to watch and listen.

One evening, when the bustling court quietened, Henri's thoughts turned to his Hashishin mentor, Yousef-al-Malik. He remembered how he had prepared himself for his task and subsequent death with calmness and an utter faith in his personal destiny. He remembered, too, how Yousef would justify the murder he was about to commit in the name of Islam, and the arguments he would put forth as to the requirement for Islam to triumph over the world. Henri remembered all this with a certain amount of irony as he set about his task.

Methodically, and with great care according to the instructions he had brought with him, Henri prepared the paste of ground hemlock roots using a small pestle and mortar. He mixed the paste with a fiery spirit he had brought from the Cognac region to the north of their sanctuary. Next, he collected plums from the fruit trees lining the avenue approaching the papal palace, and for several days let these dry on wooden trays outside his cell window in the fierce Umbrian sun. When they had shrunk to a fraction of their previous size, he took half a dozen and with a sharp knife slit them open and removed the stones. These he carefully replaced with some of the stiff paste he had prepared earlier. He carefully re-formed the dried plums and concealed the cut with a miniscule drip of wax. Then he hid them carefully under his bunk. The rest of the plums he soaked in the cognac spirit, placing the bowl near to his cell door, and waited.

It was not many days before the aroma of fermenting fruit and the fumes of the cognac began to attract people as they passed by. The contents of the first bowl disappeared rapidly. Within days Henri was required to produce another batch. And it was not long before the effects of these succulent fruits began to have a dramatic result on the Curia's bowel habits. Presently the entire palace was alive with rumours of the wonderful laxative effects of Brother Henri's stewed plums. His skills as an apothecary were applauded. It was not many days before he received a request to attend His Holiness in the papal apartments above him.

Pope Benedict XI was standing at the open window as a member of his Curia bade Henri enter the room. The elderly pope sat on a couch and indicated to Henry to do likewise.

'My courtiers tell me you prepare some wonderful fruits with some interesting properties!'

Henri smiled and offered a small plate with a dozen or so plums in the rich juice. Benedict took one and chewed on it, letting a little of the juice run down his chin. He was an old man even by papal standards, and Henri marvelled at his thin stick-like hands as they picked among the plate of fruit.

'I believe you know my personal chaplain, de Gothia?' Benedict said conversationally, his mouth continuing to chew.

'Indeed my lord, I fought with his nephew in the Holy Land.'

Benedict raised his eyes from the plate. 'A soldier?'

Henri smiled 'A knight, Your Holiness.'

Benedict nodded slowly. His eyes darted around the room whilst he continued to chew. The contents of his mouth were obviously causing some discomfort. Suddenly he held his hand to his mouth and spat out the handful of stones.

Pope Benedict XI apologised to Henri whilst wiping his mouth. 'Pity these fruits do not come without the stones!' He opened his mouth to Henri to reveal a perfect set of pink, shining gums. The two laughed together.

It was not long before the palace was rocking with laughter at the effect the fruit had had on the elderly Pope. Blessings and services were disrupted, as the Vicar of Christ needed quick access to his portable commode. Henri's fruits grew ever more popular. The sedentary life of many of the Curia led to a permanent battle with their digestive systems when allied to the rich diet of the papal palace.

One day Henri noticed an increase in the tempo of palace life. Members of the Curia and palace staff were rushing hither and thither, and preparations were being made for a grand banquet. An ambassador from King Philippe of France had been summoned in an attempt to heal the rift between king and pope, caused both by the refusal of the king to allow revenues to leave his domain, and the widespread opinion that the death of the previous incumbent of the Holy See had been murdered on the direct orders of the King of France. Abbot Henri was not involved in the visit, but he did receive a request from the Curia for some of his fruit for the Pope personally.

He knelt long, as his father had done, on the cold stone floor of the cell: the moment Bertrand had spoken of was at hand. He retrieved the fruit, from which he had carefully removed the stones, and put six of them on a plate. Climbing the stairs he headed for the papal apartments, but his way was blocked by the pope's personal guard. No amount of persuasion would gain Henri access to the Pope, so he had to be content in handing the plate to a courtier, giving strict instructions that the fruit was for the personal consumption of the Pope.

Having taken the precaution of providing a second plate of whole fruit for Benedict's personal staff, to prevent their surreptitiously dipping into their master's, Henri retired to his cell, having watched the arrival of the French ambassador.

Later, he was awakened by the sounds of running feet outside his door. Donning his robe, he joined a group of worried-looking Curia at the foot of the stairs to the papal apartments. Benedict's screams could clearly be heard as various physicians and Orsini and Colonna cardinals came and went, wearing ever more dismal expressions.

For Henri, the terrible sounds forced him to relive those moments in Baibars' encampment all those years ago. As he knelt on the stone floor of the cell, sounds of the old Pope's agony echoed throughout the castle. Various cardinals swept in and out of the papal apartments all night, or gathered in small groups along the corridor; bitter rivals at court, but united in the belief that, yet again, this was somehow the work of Philippe IV and his ambassador.

CHAPTER 16

Some nine months after the death of Benedict XI, poisoned, it was widely believed, on the orders of King Philippe of France, the College of Cardinals was still struggling to elect a successor. Although the smaller French faction that had flourished under Boniface held the balance of power between the warring Orsini and Collonna clans, under no circumstances would the people of Rome accept a French pope.

Towards the end of September 1305 a small group of horsemen appeared at the entrance to the defile. They were not expected, and Henri had the drawbridge raised as a precaution. He watched from the battlements as the new arrivals, no more than five, cantered leisurely down the causeway. Even at a distance he could see they wore rough travelling clothes, and that their horses bore the foam and fleck of a hard ride. The riders' appearance was unkempt. Worried that they had found this place, Henri descended to the gatehouse and watched them through the iron grill of the mighty portcullis as they dismounted and approached, gripping his sword as the tall leader swept back his coarse hood with a sudden gesture. A dishevelled but unmistakable Bertrand de Gothia was revealed.

'Fine way to greet your father-in-law!' he called.

Eleanor shouted in pleasure. Henri cast his eyes over the archbishop's retinue as the portcullis ground slowly upwards. 'Gilbert, what of Gilbert, Bertrand?' he cried.

'We'll talk about him later, but you need not concern yourself – he is at the court of Philippe IV as we speak,' replied Bertrand. Henri frowned but held his tongue.

Later, the three of them had retired to the library and Bertrand was poring over the red leather volumes, painstakingly completed by Eleanor, recording the progress of the work in the cavern. Eventually he laid his small eyeglasses down on the table and sat back. 'This will be my last visit for some considerable time,' he began. 'It will not be sufficient in future merely to travel incognito. The French court has spies everywhere, and it will be necessary to remain in France after next month.'

Henri glanced at Eleanor, who was regarding Bertrand with rapt attention. When Bertrand did not continue, Henri prompted. 'Next month?'

'Next month a new pope will be elected by the College of Cardinals.'

Henri looked up sharply. How could he know this in advance?

Bertrand continued, 'The new pope will be French, and thus unacceptable to the people of Rome. Not only that, but his life would be at risk if he ever returned to Rome, so the papal residency would have to be in France under the jurisdiction and protection of Philippe IV.'

'Protection, Bertrand?' Henri said. 'Philippe was virtually at war with Boniface, and people have come to their own conclusion about the death of Benedict.'

A wry smile spread of Bertrand's face. 'Protection does not necessarily mean co-operation Henri. Gilbert, my own nephew, has had to remain at the court of Philippe as personal surety to certain negotiations that I have been conducting of late.'

He rose and paced the room, his shadow dancing round the richly panelled walls in the light of the guttering candles, his face bowed and in darkness. 'Gilbert may be away a year or more until our plans can be executed. When the time is right, Henri, I will send for you and you will return to our sanctuary with Gilbert, for that you have my word. Until then we must keep our association and your family title a deadly secret, especially from the ears of Guillaume de Nogaret. He will, above all, have cause to suspect you of treason. History will judge me in a treacherous light my friend, of that I am certain, but if you take to your heart our recent conversations, and recall your time in Damascus, then you will have the strength and courage to understand the task you have before you, both of you.'

Henri nodded slowly. Yet another ambiguous message, full of portent, he sensed, not only for himself. 'You still haven't said what's happening to you next month,' he pressed.

'Now that Philippe has his hostage, my nephew, Gilbert de Gothia, he will deliver his promise. As I am Archbishop of Bordeaux, and therefore under English fealty, the Italian Cardinals will have no difficulty in agreeing.'

'Agreeing to what?,' said Henri, exasperated.

'Having me elected as the next pope, taking the name of Clement V.'

An awed silence filled the room until Eleanor's firm voice announced, 'We should kneel to thank God for His blessing.'

Bertrand nodded gravely as the three figures knelt together in the softly glowing room. He raised his hand. 'In nomine Patri…'

In fulfilment with Bertrand's prophesy, it was to be almost two years before Henri and he met again. Not that the inhabitants of the castle were short of news of him, for Eleanor had a constant flow of reports from the outside world brought by visiting monks of their order.

Having been ratified under the late Boniface VII, Anthonites enjoyed the support of the clergy in France, which in turn was well politicised by Philippe IV. The parish priest's weekly homilies, whilst addressing the spiritual need of his flock, contained in no small measure their sovereign's insidious propaganda against the Church, and, increasingly, against the alleged excesses of the Templar Order.

Some ten months after Bertrand had left the castle, and nine months into his papacy, in July 1306 it was announced that Philippe had ordered the seizing of all Jews and their possessions within his kingdom. Overnight, every Jewish home and business was raided by his soldiers. Henri knew that after the Knights Templar and the Catholic Church, the Jews had been a substantial lender to the French Crown. It came as no surprise to find that all documents recording debts to the king were destroyed, whilst monies owing to the Jews were directed to the royal coffers. Eleanor's opinion was that it was 'A rehearsal, Henri, just a rehearsal'.

'De Nogaret's hand is in this. By one event co-ordinated all over France in one night, Philippe has cancelled a third of his debts,' she said softly, linking his arm as they strolled in the heat of the day.

Then she released her arm and turned to face him. 'Uncle Bertand has sent a message for you Henri. You must go to the prison at Toulouse. There is a man whom you may have met before as the prior of the Templar preceptory of Montfaucon, near Périgueux, called Esquieu de Floyran.

Henri nodded vaguely.

She continued, 'He was removed from office following various irregularities, but his bitterness and fury grew daily until it consumed him and he murdered his superior in an ambush one night after a failed attempt to regain his position. A character I think, not unlike Roger de Flor in Acre.'

She paused, and Henri watched her face. He seemed to see the narrow knife in her hand, and the final look of astonishment on Knight de Flors' face as his life ebbed away.

She continued, her eyes cold as the leopard's. 'Esquieu de Floyran is in prison in Toulouse, with an Italian informer called Arnolfo Deghi.'

She held up her hand as Henri sought to interrupt. 'De Floyran is attempting to obtain money and a pardon from the King of France in exchange for betraying the Rule of the Knights Templar. This bears all the hallmark of

De Nogaret. Do not forget he originates from Toulouse and attended the university there after the death of his parents. The man they have placed in the cell with him, Deghi, is de Nogaret's puppet and they are attempting to use Floyran's evidence through his confession as to the heresy and witchcraft practised by the Templars.'

'And what have I to do in Toulouse?' Henri asked.

'Escort de Floyran and Deghi to Philippe IV's Court of Inquisition to be put on trial for their lives.'

CHAPTER 17

The narrow streets of Paris around the Temple preceptory echoed to the clatter of horses' hooves. It seemed half of Paris had turned out to witness the arrival of Grand Master Jacques de Molay of the Order of the Poor Fellow-Soldiers of Christ and of the Temple of Solomon: the official title of the Knights Templar. Accompanying him was a personal escort of sixty armoured knights, their helms and weapons burnished with a mixture of birdlime and sand until they shone like silver. Their snowy white surcoats, emblazoned with the crimson cross, made for a stirring sight that Parisian morning.

Not content with his sixty knights, de Molay was also attended by his personal retinue of black-robed squires and sergeants, who guarded a pack train of twelve horses carrying 15,000 gold florins: there was nothing 'poor' about this order. The entire procession wound its way through the narrow streets in an impressive display of invincible power and wealth.

De Molay had languished in Cyprus for ten years or more, beseeching each successive pope to authorise and declare a fresh Crusade to recover the Holy Land. Until the investiture of Clement V, of whose previous machinations he knew nothing, all his plans and pleading letters had been to no avail. Now he had received the papal command to attend an audience with Clement at the court at Poitiers.

Jacques de Molay knew that his time, and more importantly, the time of the Knights Templar, had returned. He had absolutely no intention of attending a provincial court; he was marching to Paris to stake his claim, before no less a personage than the King of France himself. Ultimately, Jacques de Molay saw himself as the leader of the next Crusade.

He would have arrived a little less ostentatiously had he known that Philippe's lawyer, Guillaume de Nogaret, had been behind Clement's summons of the grand master. De Molay was more concerned that a movement begun by another priest and lawyer, Pierre Dubois, had given birth to an idea that could herald the end of his beloved Templars. Dubois' document *De Recuperatione Terrae Sanctae* cited the advantages of uniting the Hospitallers and the Templars in order to recover the Holy Land. Another Dominican priest, Ramon Llull, had, with no sense of irony, suggested the head of this new military order, was to be called Rex Bellator, or 'War King,' and should be King Philippe Le Bel of France. Furthermore, Philippe should have control over the joint organisation's considerable assets.

* * *

The monastery and church of St-Germain-des-Prés had stood on the same site since the sixth century. Reputedly built by King Childebert I of the Franks, the church was constructed to house a relic of the True Cross brought from Spain in 542. It had been destroyed by the Norman invaders some 200 years previously, but its new incarnation soared above the surrounding neighbourhood, rebuilt with the patronage of the current King of France.

De Nogaret deemed that his examinations of Esquieu de Floyran would be better served if he involved the religious authorities from the start. Accordingly, he had arranged for the inquisition to be held in the great hall of the Abbey of St-Germain-des-Prés.

He had laboured behind the scenes to persuade the Palace of Justice that the trial of a man accused of murder should be held some distance from the scene of the crime, and before the Grand Inquisition. The Lord Chief Justice of Paris had questioned the setting of the trial with King Philippe, and to his surprise and embarrassment had been overruled. Now de Nogaret surveyed the magnificent court as he rose. Above the suspended candelabras the ornate wooden ceiling soared away into the darkness. Across the courtroom floor and opposite the judicial bench rose the tiered seats of the public gallery. Today they were full of the good burghers of Paris, here to see a man on trial for his life. De Nogaret knew that as the trial progressed and the likelihood of the prisoner being sent to the scaffold increased so would the public's scramble for a place in the court.

Seated on de Nogaret's right was Guillaume Imbert, the Grand Inquisitor of France, appointed by the Pope, and personal friend of Philippe IV. On his left was Pierre Dubois, author of the document proposing the union of the Templars and Hospitallers. He nodded to the jailer at the rear of the court, and a bowed, shackled figure was led to the dock.

'It is the duty of this court,' de Nogaret began, 'not only to try you for the murder of your superior from the preceptory at Toulouse, but also to ascertain the nature of your allegations, the rumours of which have reached us from the jail at Toulouse.'

De Nogaret knew that in order to move against the Templars it would not be sufficient to prove that one or two errant knights had transgressed, no matter what the crime. Individuals could be rooted out and punished. For de Nogaret's plan to succeed, he had to prove that the very Rule of the Templar Knights encouraged heresy.

Rule was of course not in written form: most Templars were illiterate, including their Grand Master Jacques de Molay. So, The Rule was communicated to each knight orally at his initiation; perhaps there were no more than a dozen leading knights who knew the entire Rule. Each knight was forbidden to discuss it with anybody else. The secrecy of this situation made it ripe for rumours and hearsay. It was against this background that the Court sat in rapt attention at de Floyran's evidence.

On trial for his life, Esqieu de Floyran's first charge was that of murder for which, if he was found guilty, his noble status would bring him the merciful attention of the headsman's axe. On the second charge of heresy (hence his appearance at the Court Of Inquisition) he could expect nothing less than the excruciating flames of the stake.

Earlier, in the jail at Toulouse, de Floyran's erstwhile cellmate, Deghi, had listened in fascination to his lurid account of his time at the Toulouse preceptory. Deghi, a habitual thief, could reasonably expect to be flogged before being forced to join the king's army, with an altogether uncertain lifespan. He was a larger-than-life character, with whom de Floyran would not normally have found himself in conversation. One day during their sojourn in the prison at Toulouse, Deghi was hauled from the cell by two jailers. It was couple of days before the door clanged open again, and a bruised and beaten Deghi was thrown back into the cell.

De Floyran knelt to attend to his companion but was stopped in his ministrations by the silent appearance of a man of diminutive stature dressed entirely in black.

De Nogaret had not introduced himself but spoke in a soft voice that caused a shiver to run through the knight's body. 'You are from the Templar preceptory, I believe?'

De Floyran had merely nodded.

De Nogaret continued, 'There are certain actions within the Rule of the Templars that would be of great interest to my principal'. He had shrugged. 'But here you are on trial for your life, so that even if we were to reward you for your information, you could not spend it from the gallows.'

De Floyran had risen to his feet, towering above the sinister little man, wishing fervently for a moment that he still had his sword. 'Then there is little point in my imparting my full knowledge of the Rule, if, as you say, only my executioners would benefit. However, I doubt you have come all this way in your expensive attire merely to tell me that!'

De Nogaret feigned a sigh of resignation and raised his hands expressively. 'A bargain then, a bargain, it always comes down to that in the end.' He gestured for de Floyran to sit, and with the battered Deghi still semi-conscious on the floor, he began to speak.

* * *

After the second day of the trial Guillaume de Nogaret left the Abbey of St-Germain-des-Prés wearing a satisfied expression. He had spoken little, preferring to let the Grand Inquisitor perform his role before the court. He had waited whilst de Floyran had unburdened himself at length, and listened whilst the lawyer Dubois had conducted a detailed examination of the denials.

De Nogaret had cleared his throat and spoken quietly, 'You will be aware, Knight de Floyran, that if a Catholic has no access to his priest he may, in those circumstances, confess his sins to another. The confession is witnessed by God and can only contain the truth.'

When he had received an affirmative nod from de Floyran, de Nogaret's eyes had gone to the rear of the court and he called 'Summon the witness!'

Arnolfo Deghi was led in to the court wearing new clothes, and with his hair carefully attended to. Flicking a guarded look at de Nogaret, he took his oath in front of Inquisitor Imbert.

De Floyran had risen to his feet to the consternation of his two jailers, his face dark and furious. He recognised his cellmate from Toulouse and exclaimed, 'sir, I must protest! Surely the court would be beneath contempt if it were to take the word of a common criminal!'

Before he could continue, one of the jailers clamped his hand over his mouth and forcibly wrestled him to the ground. For a moment de Floyran fought, and the onlookers rose in confusion as the men spilled kicking and punching onto the court floor. Grand Inquisitor Imbert shouted, his face furious, 'Remove the prisoner from my court! Take him to the cells and teach him how to behave!' A vicious punch to his groin left him doubled up in agony as he was dragged away.

De Nogaret had sat silent and unmoved during the disturbance. For a moment he thought de Floyran had over-played his hand. However, as he watched the faces of the crowd in the public gallery after Deghi had taken his oath in front of the Grand Inquisitor, he nodded to himself satisfied. They were listening in rapt attention to Deghi's testimony.

Pierre Dubois had paced the courtroom floor, choosing his words carefully as he addressed Deghi, 'The oath you have sworn before this court carries the penalty of death for perjury. You are fully aware of this fact, are you not?' Deghi nodded emphatically.

Dubois paused for several long moments as the silence of the courtroom deepened. It was as if the breaths of the assembled crowd were being collectively held. Then he continued,

'In summary then, you are prepared to swear before this court that during the confession of the accused, Knight de Floyran, held in the cell at Toulouse, and witnessed by God Himself, certain practices now disclosed to the court took place in the Templar preceptory, attended to and witnessed by Knight de Floyran.

'All that I have spoken is true, sir,' affirmed Deghi.

A sigh went round the court with the realisation that a crucial part of the trial had been reached. Surely now the burghers of Paris would be entertained by the flames of the stake.

Dubois raised his hand and the court was silent.

'Bring back the prisoner!'

De Floyran was dragged across the courtroom floor. His jailers supported him on either arm, his head hung low. He was barely able to stand unaided and was propped up in front of the judicial bench.

Dubois returned to his seat, cleared his throat and continued, 'Knight de Floyran of the Templar preceptory at Toulouse, we have heard in this court today, by virtue of your own confession to God, that in your time at the preceptory, and with full knowledge and indeed participation of your superiors, certain ceremonies were undertaken as part of the initiation to the order: namely that you and members of your order did spit upon the Cross of Jesus, and that you did indulge in lewd and immoral acts upon the altar of God Himself, by kissing the base of the spine in between the buttocks of a naked man whilst he was prostrate over the altar.

'Further, as if these sacrileges were not enough, the severed head of a goat was worshipped, using the salutation of Bahomet. At this point perhaps I should inform the court that learned opinion has it that this title of Bahomet is a corruption of the word Mahomet: the Prophet of the Infidels. We have documentary evidence linking the word with a Templar prayer used in the Holy Land. I shall read these words to the Court taken from a Templar prayer: "And daily they impose new defeats on us: for God, who used to watch on our behalf, is now asleep, and Bahomet puts forth his power to support the Sultan."'

De Floyran raised his weary head, 'My Lord, anybody with an ounce of intelligence would know that the Infidel do not worship idols of any kind – ' But any further words were cut off by a blow from his jailer.

Dubois continued silkily, 'But this is your confession to God, taken by the court's good servant Deghi. Retraction of holy confession is heresy.'

De Floyran slumped, held only by his jailers. Dubois nodded to the dark-robed scribe in the rear of the court, who hurried forward with the transcript of de Floyran's confession. With a shaking hand de Floyran scratched his mark on the vellum.

Collectively, the courtroom sighed. This was the moment that they had been eagerly anticipating – all the evidence, denials and accusations at last summed up in that one word: 'heresy'.

De Floyran's head fell forward in defeat but not before he had looked towards de Nogaret, who gazed back coolly.

Grand Inquisitor Imbert rose and the court fell silent.'On the charges of heresy brought before this court, Knight de Floyran, we find you guilty and sentence you to death at the stake. Further, as the sentence is to be carried out in the morning, I propose not to waste any more of the court's time on the charge of murder, as its outcome would be pointless.' He then dismissed the court.

In minutes the room had emptied. Only de Nogaret sat for long moments, his face a mask. Presently he rose and, holding a silk kerchief to his nose, descended to the cells below the courthouse where his ominous authority sent the guard scuttling away as he entered de Floyran's cell.

'Thank God you've come,' spluttered de Floyran. 'I am but hours away from the stake'

De Nogaret motioned him to be seated. 'It is necessary for the machinery of state to proceed in the correct and legal manner, my friend. Tomorrow you will be taken to the Ile aux Juifs, the place of execution. You will be bound to the stake and faggots piled around you. But you need not worry. Only Grand Inquisitor Imbert can light the fire. He and I are to dine at the palace with King Philippe, and when you next see the Grand Inquisitor, I shall be accompanying him bearing the royal pardon ... with of course, the payment we discussed in gold.'

De Floyran leant back against the hard cold walls in relief.

'Until tomorrow then.'

* * *

At dawn de Floyran was taken to the gloomy, mist-shrouded island in the centre of the Seine and bound to an iron post upon a raised stone dais. He protested little as the bundles of faggots were placed around him. The little courtyard fell silent as the crowds awaited the arrival of Grand Inquisitor Imbert. Moments passed and the crowd grew restless. De Floyran's eyes switched to the door in the corner of the courtyard. It opened and Grand Master Imbert strode across the yard. Alone.

CHAPTER 18

De Nogaret hurried through the late afternoon's warmth, heading for the royal palace at Fontainebleau. His familiar diminutive form gained him rapid access to Philippe IV, and he found the king deep in conversation with his chancellor, the Bishop of Narbonne, Bernard Saisset.

The bishop glanced up at de Nogaret's approach, a fleeting look of frustration crossing his face. Philippe's upstart lawyer seemed to have a call on the King of France far above his station, the bishop reflected. But Philippe nodded and beckoned de Nogaret closer.

'I bring news from England, sire!' The lawyer began. 'Edward is dead, his son has succeeded as Edward II.'

Philippe raised his hands in triumph, a smile creasing his face. 'Praise God, at last, relief from the rapacious English!' He clasped his hands and knelt briefly in prayer.

For a moment, their differences forgotten, three Frenchmen were united by the death of an English king who had for so long fought and harried their country. When he rose de Nogaret spoke for them all, 'Now, my Liege, the threat from England, a heinous and heavy drain on our country, is lifted. Edward's son, although now King of England, is no match for real men.'

The news had transformed the king. He strode vigorously round the room, and his voice boomed with confidence. Dismissing the bishop, he turned to face de Nogaret.

'Tell me of de Floyran,' he began.

The bishop moved away, but he had heard enough. That night a figure slipped from the bishop's palace and headed for the papal court at Poitiers.

∗ ∗ ∗

Some weeks later, in August 1307, that same court, rang to the harsh thrilling fanfare of the elite royal trumpeters. On his papal throne, Clement V sat waiting to receive His Majesty, King Philippe of France. Known widely as Philippe the Fair, this was a reflection on his good looks rather than on any tendency to equanimity in his dealings with others, as Clement wryly reminded himself.

While he waited in the draughty, vaulted great hall of his palace, he surveyed its pitted walls, its uneven floor and its shabby furnishings with disgust. He thought of how he, himself, would oversee the building of the new palace at Avignon. That would indeed be a fitting repository for part of his wealth, as, God willing, his plans over the coming years unfolded.

Then, at the appointed time, Pope Clement nodded graciously at the approaching figure of the king and extended his hand bearing the papal ring to be kissed.

Later, in the privacy of the court gardens, and with the sound of the river muffling their conversation, Philippe began, 'A knight has come to the Court of Inquisition held by Brother Guillaume Imbert.'

Clement noted wryly the King's use of the Dominican title: not 'Grand Master Inquisitor Imbert.'

'He brings shameful evidence of the activities of the Knights Templar,' the king continued. 'The Templars have put their order before the interests of Holy Mother Church. I doubt there are many who are not in debt to them,' he added sardonically.

'In addition, they have taken a secret oath to defend and enrich their order by any means. They have communicated secretly with the Infidel and indeed use a term in praise of Mahomet. Whilst their secret initiation rites require novices to spit on the cross, and to deny Jesus. The Templars omit the words of consecration in the Mass, and it is through the treachery of the Templars that the Holy Land is lost. Further, the use of satanic idols in their castles and preceptories, in the shape of a bearded goat's head, and a cat, is widespread.'

Hearing this, Clement's face had become rigid, his eyes hard. 'Philippe, my son, do you give credence to any of this? Surely these are the rantings of the enemies of this most holy order?'

'I would not, Your Holiness, have travelled here in person to discuss mere rumours,' was Philippe's reply. 'There is a witness to the events I have described. He has been thoroughly cross-examined by Pierre Dubois, and also by my lawyer, de Nogaret.'

'Ah, of course,' murmured Clement. 'De Nogaret.' His eyes were lowered in apparent distress as he murmured that he would, of course, call a papal enquiry in the remote chance that further evidence would be forthcoming.

Then, he thanked Philippe for being a true son of the Church, and watched as the king and his entourage galloped away.

Later, as he sat thinking, a knock on his door woke him from his reverie and, seeing who was entering, he rose to greet his old friend. 'Bernard Saisset! Welcome to Poitiers.'

Saisset took the proffered seat and began to confide, 'De Nogaret is almost ready, sir. He has for some months been stockpiling chains and manacles, and daily a stream of spies report to him the levels of manning and readiness of the preceptories. I cannot yet be sure of a date for his plans, but I think we can count on early October.'

Clement regarded Saisset with affection. 'God knows, Bernard, you have served the Papacy well. Yet again you have put your life at risk for the one true Church.'

Bernard Saisset bowed his head in gratitude.

'I have one last request,' Clement continued. 'Go to Paris and seek out Brother Henri de Montfort, and my nephew, Gilbert de Gothia. Gilbert has been a "houseguest" of Philippe these two years, but he is free to leave now.' He did not elaborate on this.

'Seek them and these other six knights,' and he handed Bernard a rolled parchment bearing the papal seal. 'Seek them urgently. Tell them I require them in Poitiers within the week.'

CHAPTER 19

Henri, had slipped away from the court at St-Germain-des-Prés. Until now he had retained his guise of Abbot Henri, merely escorting the two knights from prison at Toulouse. Upon his being presented, de Nogaret had glanced briefly at him without a flicker of recognition. It was a different story some days later when he had sought an audience with Philippe IV. Giving his full titles of Lord Henri de Montfort l'Amaury Prince of Armenia, Marquis de Gothia, to the courtier at the entrance to the royal apartments, he had not long to wait.

Rapid footsteps approached before the huge, gilded doors were flung open. An astonished courtier could only look on in amazement as Philippe boisterously greeted Henri as a long-lost friend. As the king engaged in a most unroyal-like bear hug, Henri reflected that it was indeed fortuitous that his own grandfather, Guy de Montfort, had been so pivotal in the life of Philippe IV's grandfather following the end of the Albigensian Crusades.

Philippe IV burst out laughing, a deep rich laugh, and his eyes twinkled. 'Not as an Abbot tonight, my dear de Montfort,' he gently chided.

Henri smiled back. 'I have taken orders in truth, sire. I am an Abbot of the Order of St Anthony. However, as Your Majesty will undoubtedly appreciate, fine houses of God cannot run on prayer alone. I am here to collect my tithes from my estate at Montfort l'Amaury.'

'Of course, of course, murmured Philippe.

'Tithes which I need to rebuild Castres following the local population's desecration of it due to my uncles' part in the Albigensian Crusades,' Henri continued.

'People's memories are long indeed, de Montfort.'

'My father had a low opinion of the Templars, sire. In fact he blamed them for the loss of the Holy Land itself.'

Philippe glanced at him, unsure. 'You never took the cross?'

'I did indeed, sire,' Henri protested. 'As a Knight Hospitaller, I was pushed out of Acre by Khalil himself.' He allowed a trace of bitterness to enter his voice. 'The Templars did not save us then.'

Philippe watched him in silence for a long moment. 'There are many who share your thoughts, Henri. At this very moment I am instigating an enquiry on behalf of our Holy Father, Clement V, to ascertain the truth of the confessions of a Templar knight with regard to the Templar Rule.'

He hesitated, biting his lip, as if for a moment thinking perhaps that he had said too much. Then he placed his arm round Henri's shoulders and walked with him down the darkened corridor of the royal chateau at Fontainebleau.

The king was murmuring into Henri's ear as they entered the Chapel of Louis VII that had been personally consecrated by the English cardinal, Thomas à Becket. For many minutes the two men stood talking in muted tones. At one point, Henri pulled violently away and his voice rose in protest. Then he became quiet, listening as the king whispered on in the shadowed silence of the chapel.

* * *

It was late when an outwardly calm Henri retired to bed. In a sense much of what Philippe IV had disclosed in the sanctity of the chapel had been expected, but as he tossed and turned in his apartments overlooking the royal hunting forest he felt again the mysterious powerful force that had seemed to guide so much of his life: a force that seemed to have been with him since the dark days of Acre.

He drifted off to sleep and Eleanor came to him, a vision of beauty, calling him in whispers and behind her stood Clement, impassive, eyes boring into him. He sat up suddenly in the darkness and knew with absolute clarity what he had to do.

He had of course previously observed Gilbert in one of the many courtyards; whilst from last night's conversation he knew that Gilbert had taken up the duties of hunt master to Philippe IV during his enforced stay. Henri had struggled to retain his composure as Philippe disclosed that His Holiness had sent him a witness of good faith, Gilbert de Gothia, a member of his own family, to undertake the inquisition on behalf of Clement.

As dawn broke Henri made his way to the great stables of the chateau. Hunting in the forests around the palace was a daily occurrence, and Henri soon found Gilbert bellowing at a pair of hapless grooms. He had been careful to avoid a public greeting before, but now in the bustle of the yard, with noisy steaming horses milling around waiting for their morning exercise, he grasped Gilbert in delight and relief. Gilbert grinned openly at him, and then with a surreptitious glance to his left indicated caution. Two figures sat immobile in the bustle of activity next to a stable door. They regarded Gilbert coolly. Henri drifted away feigning interest in his horse.

* * *

De Nogaret was not in the best of moods. He had been roused from his bed by a furious knocking on his door. Answering, he found a trembling figure. His anger had abated somewhat as he listened to his informant, and now he stood wrapped against the early autumn morning chill in a garret overlooking the assembled hunt. His eyes narrowed as they found Gilbert de Gothia's figure near the impatient horses. The abbot, Henri, who had accompanied Deghi and de Floyran from Toulouse, was in close conversation with Gilbert.

De Nogaret knew of Gilbert's purpose here, indeed it was his own observation to Philippe IV that the wily Clement V would need some leverage to fulfil his promises that had led to Gilbert's enforced sojourn in Philippe's court. He watched as Abbot Henri wheeled and manoeuvred his horse, his face flushed with excitement as he conversed animatedly with Gilbert. He coolly formed the opinion that firstly Henri was a master horseman and secondly that his friendship with Gilbert de Gothia was a good deal deeper than this casual encounter would suggest.

CHAPTER 20

Candles cast a flickering light over the room, whilst a log fire's dying embers shed a ruddy glow onto the faces of the room's occupants. King Philippe sat relaxed by the fire regarding the diminutive black-clad figure before him. He waited as de Nogaret framed his statement – always the lawyer, always cautious. Some four years previously, in February 1303, this had been the man who had bought charges against Boniface VIII: the man who had had the skill and cunning to take on the power and the might of the Holy Roman Church. So now the king waited.

'We have sufficient witnesses and evidence to proceed, sire,' said de Nogaret simply. 'My plans are complete, my jailers await and the seneschals have been warned to expect orders on Friday 13 October.'

Philippe nodded. He had expected nothing less. The fire burned lower and the room remained silent. He had waited for a long time for this moment, and he derived no small measure of satisfaction from it as he reviewed his options.

Clement V was on French soil, and under Philippe's protection. Grand Master de Molay was even now planning his next Crusade, but crucially resident in France. And here was de Nogaret, Keeper of the Royal Seal and author of the grand plan about to unfold.

Philippe could almost see the Templar treasure pouring into his coffers. For a moment his mind allowed itself the luxury of imagining the treasures of the various Templar preceptories now to be his in no less than a week.

He turned to de Nogaret. The dour lawyer continued. 'All in one day, sire, all on the 13 October. The inquisitors are waiting for their orders. We will have our confessions before Clement goes to bed that night.'

Philippe exhaled. The confessions – part of the Court of Inquisition's role was to extract confessions about the heretical acts undertaken, under torture if necessary. Confessions under duress were widely held to be the absolute truth, as God would allow true believers to speak only the truth. Naturally any knight that then retracted his confession became a relapsed heretic whose automatic fate was to be handed over to the secular authorities, to be burnt at the stake.

'Do it swiftly. Make not any mistake, and do it for the King of France and the Holy Roman Church,' Philippe said simply.

De Nogaret's face bore a flush of pleasure as he rose to his feet. 'I shall see to it immediately, your Majesty.' He bowed stiffly and walked calmly to the door. His hand on the ornate door handle he turned. 'Sire, there is one small thing. The nephew of Clement, he who has been our houseguest for two years; I saw him with the hunt this morning. He seemed very familiar with a Brother Henri, the abbot who accompanied De Floyran and Deghi from Toulouse ... ' Then, he paused, inviting comment.

'Abbot Henri,' the king looked puzzled. 'Oh yes, de Nogaret. That would be Lord Henri de Montfort l'Amaury. He was here only today. His grandfather and mine campaigned together long ago, he is a good and loyal servant.'

De Nogaret nodded and made his exit. As he gently closed the doors behind him his eyes glittered, and his lips compressed. A name that had stalked his childhood, that of the man that had burnt his parents alive amongst hundreds of others in Béziers. Simon de Montfort, the most vicious evil commander of the Albigensian Crusades in southern France and Aragon. A man who had carried on his personal vendetta in the region long after a truce had been called. And now another scion of that accursed family was here, his trail only hours old. Abbot Henri, indeed, De Nogaret's legal mind turned the facts over. The de Montforts were strong allies of the papacy; and he had heard stories of their bravery in the Holy Land. His mind stalled. There was more, he knew. More – but what was it? A fact – something vital he was sure – was eluding him.

He walked slowly down the corridor, his eyes unseeing. He ran over de Montfort's name again and again in his mind. Something of huge significance was teetering on the edge of his memory. He stood at the head of the beautiful staircase looking over the marble tiled floor.

A woman! That was it! Henri de Montfort had married, that he knew. He almost fell down the stairs in his excitement. Of course! He had married one Eleanor de Gothia, niece and goddaughter of Bertrand de Gothia, now His Holiness Clement V. Gilbert de Gothia, her brother, had been a hostage of Philippe these two years to ensure that the secret negotiations of Philippe IV and Clement V bore fruit. That was it, indeed! Eleanor had sent her husband to rescue her brother on the eve of de Nogaret's move against the Templars!

He went hurrying from the Porte Dore to the palace stables. It had been early morning when he had seen the pair, which meant that they had almost a day's start. There was no time to lose.

* * *

'Today,' Henri had whispered in Gilbert's ear, his voice almost lost in the stamping of the horses, steaming in the early morning chill. 'Today, Gilbert, you go home. Watch for my signal.'

He had wheeled away in an instant, excitement coursing through his body.

For much of the morning the hunt streamed in pack formation through the thinly wooded areas around Fontainebleau and Rambouillet. As each boar or deer was brought down, either by arrow or hunting dogs, a small party of the hunt retinue would detach itself and set off back to the chateau.

Henri sought Gilbert as the autumn sun reached its zenith. They slowed their horses down to a walk, ostensibly bored with the hunt and deep in conversation. Presently they lost the pack and were following a faint track through a glade. The two sour retainers who had accompanied Gilbert these last two months looked questioningly at Henri as he dismounted.

Eyeing Gilbert, he took from his saddlebag a bulging skin of wine and two goblets. Gilbert, taking his signal, dismounted, and the two took seemingly long draughts from the goblets. They were large pewter goblets and, when being drained, quite covered a man's face. Making a show Henri wiped his lips with the back of his hand and made to offer Gilbert a further draught from the skin.

'We should share our wine, Brother Henri,' rebuked Gilbert. 'These men have become separated from the party and have brought no refreshments.'

Feigning a show of embarrassment, Henri half-filled the two goblets. With perfect split-second choreography he and Gilbert offered them to the two retainers, who took them with surly thanks raising them to their lips.

They had had no refreshment since early dawn. Greedily they drank, heads thrown back, the poison acting instantly as they slumped heavily to the ground.

Wasting no time Henri and Gilbert leapt onto their horses. 'Paris, quickly, one last call at the preceptory then we ride for home,' Henri shouted, spurring his horse down the glade.

* * *

Two days later, the two horses were walking sedately down a Paris street towards the Templar preceptory. Grand Master de Molay was in residence and had only just returned from a royal funeral. He had been acting as pallbearer for the body of Princess Catherine, the dead wife of Philippe IV's brother Charles of Valois. He had been all day in the company of kings, dukes and archbishops, and was tired, so it was with some reluctance he agreed to meet Henri.

'Grand Master, we must speak alone,' said Henri, indicating the ranks of courtiers and sergeants, waiting until a weary de Molay had motioned them away. Henri fumbled under his garment and produced a small seal, which he presented to the grand master. 'Know this; I am on Clement's business, sir. Ask me not how I know, but your train has arrived with 150,000 gold florins from Cyprus.'

De Molay's eyes narrowed, but he remained silent. Henri continued speaking softly as horses and men milled around them out of earshot.

* * *

Sometime afterwards, two riders left the preceptory gates. They sat astride their two horses, looking casually up and down the almost empty street. A clattering of hooves at one end made both riders look in that direction. Guillaume de Nogaret, mud-splashed and filthy from his ride from Fontainebleau, raised his voice, a deep powerful voice that carried the length of the street. 'Arrest them! Arrest them in the name of the Inquisition, a gold florin for the man who brings them down!'

The group of riders escorting de Nogaret spurred their horses down the street. Promptly, the two riders in front of the Templar preceptory dug in their heels and fled in the opposite direction. De Nogaret's deep voice could be plainly heard urging on his guards to even greater efforts as they pursued the two horsemen.

Peace returned once more as the street settled back into its quiet afternoon. A little while later, the huge double doors of the preceptory opened again, and a creaking cart piled high with the stable's waste of straw and stinking manure turned into the street. Henri rode alongside the groaning cart. Considering it seemingly carried just straw and manure it was protesting loudly from every creaking joint. Gilbert glanced at him, his eyes twinkling behind the mask of flour and grains that covered his face. His left hand holding the reins was blackened, and in his other hand he carried a small bell. He grinned painfully as his mask cracked.

Henri shook his head in amusement at Gilbert's predicament. 'You should be safe getting out of Paris, my friend. In a day or so I'll send some brothers to escort you, the journey will be long, but you must get to La Val Dieu. I will ride for Château Bezu tonight to warn them. God speed, Gilbert, Eleanor awaits both of us.'

Without further ceremony he galloped off, his horse's hooves echoing on the cobbles.

CHAPTER 21

Henri drove his mount hard that night, his mind was as alive and active as its flying hooves. He thought of Gilbert plodding slowly southwards, his face smeared with a pox-like paste, and he smiled in the darkness. He thought too of his other six knights carrying Bertrand's letters to various preceptories. Templar preceptories that by now should have begun to move their treasures to the Monastery of La Val Dieu. He laughed out loud in the rushing cool night air as he imagined de Nogaret's face after the raids. With the majority of the French army tied up guarding prisoners and empty Templar fortresses, the roads of France and Aragon should be safe for a few weeks to come.

* * *

Friday the 13 October 1307 dawned clear and bright. De Nogaret had personally taken charge of the assault on the Paris preceptory. It had all been so ridiculously easy. Bearing the king's letters and seals, and invoking the name of God and the Holy Roman Church, they had demanded the doors be opened to a small group of court officials. The moment the huge doors had swung open, de Nogaret's heavily armed group of men had ridden straight into the preceptory courtyard.

Now, after several hours, the sixty knights and attendant squires and sergeants stood chained against the walls. The air rang with shouts of protested innocence, of lives devoted to God in the pursuit of the Infidel. De Molay alone stood silent and glowering, his fall the more astonishing. Only the day before a pallbearer for the body of the wife of King Philippe IV's brother and now shackled as a common criminal whilst this weasel-faced lawyer supervised the erection of various instruments in the courtyard.

De Nogaret had the huge gates barred to the seething mob, greedy for sensation in the street outside. In no particular order a tall knight was brought from the walls, escorted by two black-clad members of Imbert's inquisition. Roughly and without ceremony they flung him down on an iron bedstead arrangement shackling his feet, arms and torso: bizarrely his feet overhung the short bed. Guillaume Imbert motioned with his hand, and a small writing desk was brought to the side of the terrified man. Smoke briefly hid the little scene as silence descended on the courtyard, and a charcoal brazier was lit. Kneeling at the bedstead, one of Imbert's assistants delicately anointed the knight's feet with oil.

Imbert began. 'Have you ever denied Christ as part of the initiation ceremony of the Knights of Jerusalem?'

The shackled figure shouted his denial.

'Have you ever been ordered to spit on the crucifix or worship an idol of a bearded head and a cat?'

Again, the protestation of innocence.

'We have heard that during the secret Templar ceremonies, held after dark, new members of the order indulge in the osculum infame, or kiss of shame, in which you kiss the prior on his mouth, or his navel, or below his spine. Would you agree?'

Again, the hoarse, 'No!'

Imbert laid his quill down with a resigned look. 'God will protect the innocent from the pain,' he remarked and nodded to the two figures at the foot of the bed. The coals in the little brazier were now glowing and virtually smokeless. It was pushed under the knight's feet. His screams echoed around the courtyard as the oil thinned and dripped. Presently it began to heat and give off wisps of smoke. From his writhing heels blackness and blistering began to spread up the pale skin of his feet.

The knight's screams were indescribable. Several prisoners retched against their chains. Only when his skin was completely blackened was the brazier pulled away: it did not stop the screaming, however, as the hot oil continued to cook the wretched man's feet. Imbert resumed the questioning.

Allowing himself a thin smile of satisfaction de Nogaret turned and went into the preceptory. All around him, oblivious to the sounds from the courtyard, soldiers were carrying all manner of hangings, precious objects and items of furniture. He grasped a burly sergeant and questioned him.

'What of the gold? And the jewels we know are here? All I observe your men carrying are the trinkets of a great house.'

The sergeant shook his head and indicated his men were now searching the furthest outbuildings of the preceptory. Frowning, de Nogaret continued his own meticulous examination of the buildings. For such a wealthy order he had expected more gold and silver. Much more. King Philippe had remarked several times that when he had to borrow from the Templars they had been able to supply the money extremely quickly. Still, it was early days yet, he mused and dismissed the nagging worry from his mind.

It was sometime later that the truth began to dawn on de Nogaret, as he inventoried the contents of the preceptory. It was as he remembered the futile chase of the two knights from the gate of the preceptory the day before the raid that everything began to make sense. His band of soldiers had eventually overtaken the fleeing knights and forced them to halt. In an act of fury and frustration at discovering two sergeants who claimed to be merely exercising their mounts, Guillaume had them thrown into the inquisition dungeon.

He went quickly to the stable, which, as with everything in the preceptory were orderly, and beautifully kept. All the horses' tack, gleaming and polished, was suspended from the walls, and a selection of working carts were reversed in ordered rows against a wall. One, though was missing. Guillaume de Nogaret stood in its empty berth and nodded slowly.

Miles away by now, the missing cart creaked alarmingly as it laboured under its heavy load. Five other brothers of the Order of St Anthony, who now accompanied the protesting cart, had joined Gilbert. Bales of cloth and barrels of ale had replaced the straw, but it still sagged and swayed at the limits of its capacity. Gilbert and two others sported the flour pox mix, as they called it, whilst the remainder of the black-robed monks tolled small hand bells. The little group was left quite alone as it journeyed south.

*　*　*

Guillaume stood for a long time in the empty stable. His anger had abated somewhat and now his cool legal brain was analysing his problem. Not for nothing had the Templars been called the bankers of Europe. They had invented a system of debits and credits that did away with the need to transport gold the length and breadth of the continent. Merely depositing a sum with one Templar preceptory meant that, with suitable documentation, an equivalent sum could be withdrawn at another in a different town, or, for that matter, country. Musing quietly to himself he made his way to de Molay's quarters.

The large, well-lit room was quiet, and many of the more portable valuables had been removed. In a corner, its surface splashed with light from the leaded French-glass windows, stood a lectern. Guillaume fingered its sloping surface thoughtfully. Turning, he observed a double row of oak shelves, quite empty, above it. He minutely examined their surface. There in the faint dust he could see the outlines of many books or ledgers.

That was it! He had it now. He had been using his time as if he were a frantic hound, trying to locate hidden vaults and rooms. The key would be in the missing volumes. And he hurried from the room to draft another question to be put to the screaming knights in the courtyard below.

*　*　*

By the end of the first week, Grand Inquisitor Guillaume Imbert stood before Philippe IV, clutching in his hand a sheaf of manuscripts. 'Fifty-two signed confessions, Your Majesty.' He bowed slightly.

'Sixty knights were held, were they not?' questioned Philippe.

The man before him nodded and smiled dryly. 'One died under questioning, whilst seven recanted their confessions, claiming they had only confessed to prevent further agony. They were burnt at the stake immediately. As relapsed heretics the law demands this,' he added simply.

Philippe nodded. This was welcome news indeed. The papal court at Poitiers had erupted in fury at the arrest of the order, reporting direct to the Pope. Philippe had cunningly recalled his conversation with Clement only a month before, when he presented the rumours of the heretical Order of Templars. Clement had said, 'My son, you must look into their deeds with diligent care, and report to me what you make of them.'

The fury of Clement, in public at least, had led to the suspension of his Grand Inquisitor Imbert. Now, clutching his evidence, Philippe had, with a great show of piety, taken the confessions to the papal court. By 22 November, just over a month since the arrests, Clement V issued a bull *Pastorallis preeminentae*, praising the actions of Philippe IV, and recognising him as a True Son of the Church, and loyal Defender of the Faith.

Clement's bull formally recognised the truth of the charges against the Templar Order and commanded all Christian kings to move against the order in their own kingdoms.

* * *

Eleanor's finger traced gently the entries in the ledger before her. It was, in appearance similar to the one her brother had rescued from Acre. However, instead of wisdom and the knowledge of herbs, these additions to the library at La Val Dieu contained the inventory of two centuries of financial investment and acquisition. Apart from housing the well-organised accounts of the assets continually arriving deep within the cavern, this well-lit turret room was her operations centre, it housed her records of the Knights of St Anthony's mighty financial empire: a storehouse of treasure the like of which the world had never seen before. An empire that only a handful of people would ever have the knowledge of. An empire that would finance and guide the future of the most powerful Church on earth.

CHAPTER 22

Henri turned from his reverie. He had been mesmerised by the currents, flows and eddies around the stone pillars of the Pont St Bénézet at Avignon: secretly summoned from La Val Dieu by Clement V, he had waited patiently.

The bridge was indeed a miraculous structure, and he had surveyed its twenty-two arches from the bank leading to the fortress of Phillipe le Bel. That such a narrow bridge could remain upright against the powerful flow of the river was astonishing. As he watched, a sodden tree trunk, a victim of a storm further up the river, maybe as far as Lyons, struck the pillar on which he stood. He felt the vibration as the current built up behind the log. Then with a rasp and a shake it was driven down one side of the pillar and released to continue its journey to the Mediterranean.

As he turned away, a monk approached, head bowed. Henri, in recognition, made as if to kneel.

'No, Henri, we are being watched, my friend,' Clement said.

The two men leant casually on the stone parapet, the ripple of the current muffling any conversation. Henri gave Clement V a brief summary of all that had been achieved in the last six years. Even so, the cavern was still full of unloaded carts of Templar treasure. Eleanor had had to take on additional bookkeepers, and the metallurgists had resorted to smelting much of the precious metal at night as a permanent haze of smoke was beginning to hang over the forest. Henri described the amounts of oak needed for racking in the long corridors underground, and the problems of disposing of the ash from the furnaces after each smelting. He attempted briefly to describe the amounts of gold and jewel encrusted artefacts he now held but found it difficult to convey the idea of the vastness of the accumulated treasure.

'At the rate of progress, sire, it will be another two years before we see the end.'

Clement nodded with deep satisfaction. 'Your task is indeed an onerous one, Henri. Even as you struggle to record our fortune, de Nogaret is reaching a frenzy of activity. He has had the King appoint Philippe de Marigny as the Archbishop of Sens against my personal wishes, and as a result fifty-four knights have been burnt at the stake in Paris over the last two years. Thank God, as the flames burnt and blistered their skin, not one thought to save his life and reveal the whereabouts of the records of the treasures of the Knights Templar. Not one, Henri!'

Clement watched Henri's eyes grow sad at the fate of these brave knights. Then Henri crossed himself, his eyes hardening. Clement continued, 'That fifty-four men should choose to die in that manner without a thought of saving themselves, does it not leave you with a sense of our destiny, Henri?' He dabbed a silk kerchief at his eyes. 'It is indeed God's will, nothing less. King Philippe is sated at present. He has sold off numerous holdings and lands. Of everyone involved I think only de Nogaret has an inkling of the true extent of our subterfuge, and of how much we have prevented falling into their hands.'

Henri absorbed his words. He met infrequently with Clement, and then it was always done clandestinely. Eleanor had told him that Clement had moved to the Dominican priory of Avignon. He waited for confirmation of her words.

'We will build a new papal palace here to rival anything we had in Rome and it will be built under the protection of King Philippe himself,' Clement grimaced wryly. 'Here at the centre of Europe, at the first bridge of the mighty River Rhone, we will build in veneration of God, and with the Order of St Anthony not too far away, it will be the basis of that which I discussed with you some years ago.'

Clement paused as he watched the swirling eddies of the river below. His face betrayed his inner struggle as he spoke lower, and in a resigned tone.

'History will judge me harshly, Henri, as I have intimated. Our journey transcends generations to come and the destruction of the Infidel is undoubtedly a task too much for one man's lifetime. I believe, I hope, my actions will one day be regarded as the cornerstone of our achievement, but I fear I will be called to judgement for those actions. On the other hand, Henri, no such fate awaits you or your descendants, for you are invisible, an unknown force without which we could not contemplate the fight to come. Guard the secret well, Henri.

Guard it with your life.'

Henri nodded silently. It was his way. The Pope's desires and wishes were transmitted orally only. He clasped Clement's hand and turned to go.

'One last thing, my Henri.'

Henri turned to look into Clement's implacable eyes.

'It is almost over now,' the other man continued, 'De Molay and de Charnay are to be publicly paraded in front of Notre Dame. King Philippe and Guillaume Imbert want their confessions to be made in public. You must go, but do not let anybody recognise you.'

Clement bent to Henri's ear, his words lost in the river breeze. At one point Henri recoiled, but Clement gripped his arm fiercely. 'In this you must not fail; listen to de Molay.'

In an instant he whirled and was gone. His robed figure joined other several dark-clad brothers at the end of the bridge. He did not turn round.

CHAPTER 23

Henri had, with hundreds of tense and expectant Parisians, waited patiently since dawn on that chilly grey March morning. The air in the square hung heavy with the scent of cut pine and rang to the sound of hammers and saws. Since first light carpenters had been toiling to complete a huge platform in front of Notre Dame. Here the four remaining knights of the Temple of Jerusalem were publicly to confess their crimes, and the profanities regularly performed by their order.

Over the last few years public suspicion had been growing that the brutal suppression of the order had more to do with Philippe Le Bel's greed for their riches, than anything else. De Nogaret had arranged the public confession to quell the increasing hostility to the persecutions. De Molay, now approaching seventy, had confessed all that had been put to him. This was partly from his terror at the thought of more of the horrendous torture planned for him if he did not comply, but at the back of his mind was the thought that if he could somehow put his case directly to Pope Clement rather than to Philippe IV and de Nogaret's prosecutors, then the whole misunderstanding could be cleared up. Clement, of course, had no intention of meeting the Grand Master face to face. Henri already knew that through a process of bargaining, the four knights had agreed to accept a lifetime's imprisonment in return for their lives.

Henri pondered Clement's last words as he slowly inched his way to the front of the crowd. Usually, his monk's habit and his greying stubble was enough to persuade the surliest of Parisian to make way, although he occasionally heard a muttered curse as to the arrogance of the man of God. Presently he stood at the foot of the wooden staircase leading to the platform. A disturbance at the back of the restless crowd drew his attention, and shortly the four knights, resplendent in fresh snowy white robes with their famous crimson cross patée, escorted by grim-faced members of King Philippe's personal guard, arrived at the foot of the platform.

Their humiliation was there for all to see as, weighed down with chains and manacles, the frail elderly men gasped their way up the wooden steps to the platform. Presently they stood shoulder to shoulder gazing out over the crowd. Not one of them bowed his head. Grand Inquisitor Imbert stepped to the edge of the balcony above and raised his arms. The crowd fell silent, men lifted their faces to the platform, women stilled impatient children.

'Burgers of Paris, you are gathered, under the auspices and guidance of King Philippe IV, finally to lay to rest the rumours and half-truths surrounding the fall from grace of the once mighty Knights Templar. You will hear the confessions of heresy and immoral practices that have alone caused their downfall. Not through the greed of our mighty king, but through their own monstrous deeds. Listen carefully, my friends, for you shall not hear their voices again. They will leave this place for a lifetime of imprisonment in atonement for their sins.'

He stepped back and motioned a guard toward de Molay. A rough shove sent the silver-haired grand master to the edge of the platform. For a moment he said nothing as his rheumy eyes surveyed the crowd. He gripped the rail in front of him and began, his voice frail but gaining in strength. 'I think it is only right at so solemn a moment, when my life has so little time to run, that I should reveal the deception which has been practised on you all, and speak up for the truth.'

An expectant tremor ran through the crowd. Henri watched as Imbert's face paled at de Molay's words. The Inquisitor made a sudden movement, but he was powerless. De Molay continued, 'Before heaven and earth and with all of you here as my witnesses, I admit that I am guilty of the grossest iniquity. However, you should know that the iniquity is that I have lied in admitting to the atrocious charges levelled against this Holy Order. I declare, as I stand before you, that the order is innocent of all mortal sin. There has been no heresy. The purity and saintliness of the order is beyond question.'

A low murmur ran through the crowd. This was not what they had been told to expect. In defying the Grand Inquisitor these must surely be the words of a condemned man. Surely a man on the point of death would not lie. Silence fell again in the vast square, broken only by the quickly stifled cry of a child. De Molay's thin voice, gaining strength, continued. 'I have indeed confessed that the order is guilty, but I have done so only to save myself from the most horrific tortures. Others of my dear brother knights who have retracted their confessions have been led to the stake, yet the thought of dying is not so awful that I shall confess foul crimes which have never been committed. Life is offered to me, but at the price of infamy. At such a price, life is not worth having. I do not grieve that I must die, if life can be bought only by endangering my immortal soul.'

Inspired by de Molay's words, Geoffrey de Charnay stepped forward, loudly proclaiming the innocence of the order. An angry crowd, believing the words of a condemned man, and having had their long-held suspicions of the complicity of the French king, confirmed, drowned his words.

Furiously the guards and officers of the inquisition bundled the four knights down the steps. Henri caught a glimpse of Imbert's face suffused in dark anger. At the foot of the stairs, de Molay and de Charnay were roughly stripped of their Templar robes before being bundled into a crude tumbrel. A crowd followed as best it could down the narrow Paris streets to the river. There the two men were thrown roughly into the bottom of a riverboat, which cast off and headed downstream. The crowd milled uncertainly, but several jumped into other craft and followed. Henri did likewise, caught up in the macabre pursuit of the two condemned men.

A little island in the centre of the river, Ile aux Juifs was their destination. Without further ceremony the two men were chained to two posts, and their executioners set about stacking bundles of wood around them. Henri splashed ashore with about thirty Parisians who had come to witness the spectacle. He saw with a sense of creeping horror that the bundles of faggots and twigs were a mix of cured and green wood, specially chosen to produce a slow-burning fire of intense heat that would slowly roast the men from the ground up, in order to prolong their lives and agony for as long as possible.

Without any further delay, flaming brands were thrust into the piled wood. The flames took a hold of the dried bundles, causing the green twigs to splutter and begin to smoulder. The two men were enveloped by swirling white smoke. They began to cough; great, harsh racking coughs as they fought desperately for air. The heat intensified as the flames licked upwards towards them. Their desperate, gasping coughs were replaced by their screams of agony as the first flames began to lick at their feet. Their agonised features swirled and swam in the heat, and they strained at the chains holding them. The dancing flames took hold of the cotton shifts they had been wearing after their armour had been removed, and their screams became one. Then de Charnay's head fell forward and he was silenced. As the flames caught at his silver hair, de Molay cried out, his face twisted into a rictus of suffering, as he yelled in torment, 'Within a year I call unto King Philippe to meet me in heaven to answer these charges. I call upon Pope Clement V to meet me there also.'

The small crowd grew silent as the flames engulfed the two men. Several of the crowd sank to their knees in prayer. Here had died most horribly two innocent victims, that was certain. Later, as the flames flickered lower, individuals darted forward and picked still smouldering bones from the ashes. They wrapped them in anything they could find and scurried away.

Henri lingered long after the last of the crowd had gone, unable to tear himself away from the burnt and twisted remains of the brave knights. His mind drifted to another place and time; a time when he had fought alongside men like these against a common foe. Men he had depended upon, and on whom he could trust with his life. Granted authority from the highest source in the world for his current undertakings, he could only wonder as he turned sadly away.

Henri now had two final tasks entrusted to him by his father-in-law, friend and Holy Father to the Roman Catholic Church, Clement V: two tasks he would relish.

CHAPTER 24

De Nogaret bent once more to the open volume before him. It was late, and the light was fading as fast as his frustrations were increasing. For six months following the execution of de Molay and Charnay he had scoured the length and breadth of France, searching ransacked preceptories and castles. Granted, King Philippe was highly pleased with the sale of lands and valuables that the dissolution of the Templars had brought to his coffers, and for the moment he was sated.

But de Nogaret was reluctantly beginning to realise that something was wrong, very wrong. He scratched his ribs, not for the first time that day. In fact, his entire body was beginning to itch like the Devil. He stood up, his concentration ruined and cast off his tunic. He saw the angry red weals stretching across his body and bellowed angrily for his bath to be filled. Later, in the darkness of his apartment, he tossed and turned, scratching frantically. He was bathed in sweat, and he had a raging thirst.

Over the next few days, he found he could not bear the feeling of clothes on his body and ran around naked as if possessed. His servants cowered in fear at his rage.

By the fourth day his fingertips had begun to blacken and rot, but he continued to scratch frantically with the putrefying stumps. He was unable to close his staring eyes, and his bloated tongue hung grotesquely from his mouth. His servants belatedly recognised the onset of St Anthony's Fire and sought out one of the monks of the order.

Abbot Henri's timely arrival was seized upon with considerable relief. He went to de Nogaret's room and, having drawn the heavy curtains, seated himself in the gloom next to the victim's sweating, writhing form. Insisting on the servants leaving the room, Henri knelt and prayed for the soul of Guilaume de Nogaret.

De Nogaret could not drink, for his tongue was horribly swollen and beginning to blacken, but Henri administered a goblet of liquid to his patient's grateful thanks. The diluted saliva from a rabid dog which was contained in it gave de Nogaret an ever more raging thirst, which he could not assuage without Henri's help.

For two days Henri sat quietly as his patient tossed and turned, moaning incoherently. Then he rose and drew the curtains, flooding the apartment with light and provoking a scream of pain from de Nogaret. He crossed to the bed and holding de Nogaret's head, gently, offered a small goblet to his lips. A little of the liquid dribbled past de Nogaret's swollen tongue. Henri stood up and swept his hood back.

Against the light of the windows de Nogaret could see only a dark silhouette, but the words he heard were all to easy to comprehend, 'Extract of Belladonna, my friend. Shortly you will be unable to move a single muscle of your body. You will remain in agony from now until your last breath.'

His assassin turned abruptly and left the room, leaving de Nogaret lying still, his eyes staring blankly, his tongue thrust out the length of a man's forefinger.

CHAPTER 25

Pont-Sainte-Maxence: 29 November 1314

Now there remained Henri de Montfort 'The Lion's' final task, entrusted to him by the late Pope Clement V: Clement himself having died, a month after de Molay's execution, almost certainly poisoned by de Nogaret.

Henri's hand strayed to the tiny sheath in his rich leather boot, as, just before dawn, he headed for the royal estate at Fontainebleau.

His title of Lord Henri, Grand Prior of The Order of St Anthony, meant he had little difficulty in persuading the stable hands he was a guest of honour for that morning's hunt. He waited patiently. Presently the cobbled yard rang to the clatter of many hooves as the royal entourage assembled. Philippe stood in his stirrups, his face flushed and arrogant as he surveyed the assembled knights. His eyes fell on Henri and he nodded in recognition, a smile touching his lips.

'You are most welcome to grace us with your presence, de Montfort, I was not aware you were at l'Amaury this time of year.' His horse fidgeted, and he whirled away before Henri could reply.

The hunt streamed from the chateau walls, huge thundering chargers, their breath like clouds on the cold air, the jingle of chain mail mixing with the calls of the horns.

The quarry was elusive that morning, and before long, King Philippe, always in the lead, was accompanied by just two knights, one of whom was Henri. Entering a heath of low scrub and stunted trees, Henri bent forward in the saddle. In his right hand he held the bolo of knotted rope and heavy weighted stones. Keeping it shielded from the king's view he whirled it briefly, then, with a fluid movement, flicked the spinning rope under his horse's neck, towards the royal mount.

The whirling rope and weights wrapped themselves around the forelegs of the king's horse, and in an instant horse and rider crashed to the ground. Henri was at the fallen king's side at once. He glanced up. The second knight had turned and was galloping back. Shouts behind him warned of the rest of the hunt's approach.

Reaching down, Henri extracted the slim blade from his boot. Cradling the king's dazed head in his arms, he placed the point of the blade in his ear.

His smile held Philippe's eyes for a second, and then he rammed the blade home. The King's eyes widened fractionally. Then he grew limp.

Henri withdrew the narrow blade and re-sheathed it. Scooping up a handful of earth, he pushed some of it into the King's ear to stop the flow of blood. Quickly he smeared the rest of it over the King's face. He pushed the bolo out of sight as the other rider galloped up.

'The King is badly hurt,' he shouted. 'We must get him back to the chateau.'

The other huntsmen arrived in a flurry of concern and chaotic anxiety. Nervous, frightened figures dashed about aimlessly, calling for help and getting in each other's way around the king's lifeless form; while startled horses whinnied at the unaccustomed commotion.

It was all too easy for Henri, the assassin, to melt away silently and unnoticed into the forest.

Dieu le veut

Part II

Part II

CHAPTER 26

Zatow, Poland: 1942

Easing his right foot off the accelerator the sound of the 7273cc Skoda 8 eight-cylinder diesel died away quickly, as simultaneously his left leg depressed the heavy clutch pedal. Jan Wojack deftly brought the huge brass-topped lever back towards himself with an oily click. His faultless double-gear change was a source of deep pride, but his expression never faltered. Leaning forward to save the jarring ride rubbing his spine raw he scanned the road through the grimy screen. He had the three minuscule wipers at full speed, but his best visibility was through the open split windscreen, giving a pillar-box view of the road some twenty yards ahead.

Jan had left the warmth of his bed and the soft curves of his wife, Helena, as dawn stole over the eastern sky. To the loud squawk of the chickens, he had coaxed the ten-year-old Skoda 506 lorry from its shelter in the barn. He was lucky to have such a vehicle, he knew. But its acquisition had surely been divine intervention.

It was 3 September, during the outbreak of the war back in 1939, he had been guiding the cumbersome plough behind his four heavy horses. A loud thump and tearing sound accompanying the screech of tyres from the nearby road into Krakow signalled one thing. The huge pantechnicon from Katowice had failed to negotiate a notorious bend. Miraculously, the driver, a man from Piotrkrow to the north, was climbing stiffly out of the passenger door when Jan arrived.

The bend had claimed many victims before, but on a clear dry day, the reason for the forty-foot vehicle's argument with the old oak tree was difficult to discern. Not for long. The driver, recovering quickly, shielded his eyes to the north. Specks in the sky filled the horizon. Jan, breathing hard from his run across the heavy ploughed field screwed his eyes against the glare of the late-summer sun flashing off the tumbling aircraft. Watching for several minutes, Jan's breathing quickly regulated, and a pattern emerged. The planes were circling like vultures. From one corner of the circling, droning mass, individual aircraft would tumble out of the sky, accompanied by a wailing shriek. This was the 'blitzkrieg' that the village gossip was alive with: Hitler's new method of lightning war. Columns of smoke rose skywards from the skyline as the two men turned to each other.

In the chaos of the early days of war Petre had been trying to return to his depot with a consignment of new duck feather mattresses for the Warsaw hotels. Now, as the two men surveyed the dormant vehicle, it was immediately apparent that it would not be seeing Warsaw again. Shouts from across the fields brought the two men out of their reverie as men arrived to pull and tear at the wreck. Shortly the quiet road was alive to the sound of horse-drawn carts, sledgehammers and saws as the aluminium bodywork, in useful flat sheets, was cannibalised and the prized mattresses went to replace worn out ones in many a local farm.

In no time at all the hapless driver was given a lift back to Katowice, there to join his reserve unit of cavalry against the German Panzers and Jan was left by the side of the road surveying the beautifully bent chassis and untouched cab of the once pristine Skoda lorry. Glancing northwards at the plummeting black specks his jaws hardened, and he whirled and ran back over the disturbed earth of his recently ploughed furrows. His four massive shire horses stood mournfully observing his clumsy approach, their liquid brown eyes regarding his haste with disdain. The heavy plough took only a moment to disconnect, leaving its curved plates firmly embedded in the heavy earth of southwest Silesia.

Turning the team, he set off across his neatly ploughed furrows, before shackling the them to the rear cross-member of the stricken vehicle and pulling it gently out of the slight ditch and away from the tree which showed singularly little damage. Unhitching the unwieldy team after a stint of manoeuvring saw them hitched again to the front of the vehicle. Jan found that by turning the steering wheel in opposite lock to the bent chassis the whole could be made to crab sideways down the still, deserted road.

Helena Wojack stood in the farm doorway, her hands dusty with flour, as she surveyed the strange contraption being towed across the farmyard. Jan reluctantly made eye contact with his wife. 'Jan Wojack, what on earth are you doing?' she yelled, her hands now resting on her hips and her ample bosom straining at her blouse, her face suffused in red as her anger grew. Four mouths to feed, the crops not yet in the ground and the ploughing two weeks behind after the recent wet spell and her husband had turned up with yet another of his 'projects'. She followed the vehicle and horses purposefully into the huge double barn.

'Well?' she demanded, 'What now Jan Wojack?'

Jan loved Helena deeply, but he loved her especially when she was angry. Letting her see his amusement would only arouse her more; so for the moment he cast his eyes down.

'God has truly answered our prayers today, Helena,' he began. Helena relaxed slightly and eyed Jan carefully. 'With help and a good blacksmith, we'll have this on the road in no time. With this beauty we can take our pigs and potatoes to a bigger market where the prices are higher. Not only ours but every farm around would pay to use this.'

The words 'God' and 'pay' were usually enough to mollify Helena: this time was no exception. Slowly she walked round the twisted vehicle, casting quizzical looks at her husband. She loved him dearly but, as with all men, he needed a firm hand to keep him on the straight and narrow.

'This will repair?' she said, pointing to the bent chassis.

'Yes, yes my love,' said Jan bounding round the side of the vehicle. 'Father will help,' he explained at length and Helena began to see the possibilities.

'Three days, Jan Wojack; then we need the ploughing finished. Three days to repair it, otherwise Mikel at the scrapyard is coming.'

Keeping her face stern, she swept out of the barn. Jan watched her backside under the old skirt sway through the door, and a grin crossed his face. Shortly a bowl of thick pork and potato soup and two large brown bread cobs arrived in the barn to be put down next to a growing pile of components as the lorry's chassis was stripped back to nothing.

Jan's father, whiskered Andrzej Wojack, was summoned on the second day, arriving in the yard with his horse-drawn trailer piled high with his long-retired forge. The outfit disappeared into the barn.

That night the blackness of the farmyard was replaced by an amber glow emanating from the chinks in the woodwork of the old barn. For a second night Helena tossed and turned in a cold bed to the sound of hammers and the wheeze of the bellows in the barn.

Late on the third day Helena kept coming to the door looking expectantly towards the barn. As the sun started to dip her face grew determined. Enough of this playing, the farm had to be run by someone. As she prepared to call time on the activities in the barn the huge door opened and, with a cough of the diesel engine, the Skoda re-emerged from the barn.

Jan's eyes, red rimmed in his blackened face, beamed at Helena as her face softened at the sight of the amazing contraption. Somewhat shorter than when it had left the factory, the vehicle now sported a simple body that would hold many tons of produce: its gleaming deep blue finish on the cab incongruous in the farmyard surroundings.

Father, son and wife surveyed their acquisition over three cups of dark, strong coffee. Old Andrzej's eyes watched the black specks overhead. Looking back at the gleaming vehicle he scratched his head.

When the coffee was finished the Skoda was reversed once more into the barn. Much to Helena's annoyance and frustration, for a third night she went to a cold bed. Only as dawn was breaking did Jan creep exhausted into her arms. Curious, she later visited the silent barn. As the huge door swung open her jaw dropped, the gleaming vehicle that stood proudly in the yard only yesterday had gone. In its place stood a dirty, dented specimen that looked like it had been painted with the contents of the cow byre. Mouth agape she walked around the vehicle.

* * *

In Jan's village of Zatow the vehicle had proved a huge success. Within months Jan had loads of fresh vegetables going into war-torn Warsaw and then just when he thought it could not get better found a contract to run coal back to the village and outlying areas direct from the mines of Katowice. Soon he had a small mountain of brown coal behind his barn, which he sold at a tidy profit to his neighbours.

Life was good to Jan Wojack, even after the Nazi grip on Poland tightened. Too good. One evening the family was sitting down to evening meal. Beaming he watched Helena ladle out the thick soup into the well-filled bowls which reposed on a long gleaming oak table. Crystal glasses winked and shone at him in the soft light of the gas mantles. Life was good, very good.

The knock at the door caused everyone to start. Visitors after dark were uncommon. The curfew and the preponderance of German patrols on the highway ensured the farm remained locked and in darkness until dawn. Helena glanced at her husband: Jan shook his head and continued to spoon the steaming soup into his mouth. The knock came again, more insistent this time.

Taking a slow breath, Jan put his spoon down on the plate, its chink unnaturally loud. Rising, he reached for his shotgun above the fireplace. Standing behind the barred oak door he called out; 'Ja, who is that?'

Helena watched her husband's shoulders stiffen as he caught the reply and quickly drew the bolts. A slight figure in a black cloak slipped into the warmth as Jan stepped outside to check if anyone had seen the visitor enter. Bolting the door again he turned to him. The figure had swept his head back to reveal his frosted hair and pink features from the cold outside.

'Father Krzysiak!' Jan exclaimed, shaking his hand, 'What in God's name are you doing here?'

Helena interrupted smoothly, 'I think what my husband meant, Father, was that it is not a usual time to visit, but will you sup with us? Come, give me your cloak.'

Father Krzysiak gratefully handed it to her, still holding onto a small holdall, which, from his white knuckles, was evidently heavy. Sliding the holdall under a spare chair, he sat down, blessed the meal and tucked into a bowl of soup much larger than Helena had given to Jan.

Presently he spoke. 'These are treacherous times, Jan and Helena. What I am about to say may put your own lives in danger: yours and that of your family.' He indicated the heads of the children who were ignoring him while chasing a bread roll under the table with their feet. Taking the cue, Helena firmly told the children to go to bed, and after a little protest they duly scampered upstairs.

Silence returned. 'So, Father, tell us what brings you here now that couldn't wait until Sunday?' Jan said leaning back in his chair.

'We are fortunate in Poland, Jan – some more than others,' the priest began, casting a look around the richly furnished room.

'I work hard, Father, for family and church...' Jan said, his neck suffused a shade of red.

Father Krzysiak, held up a placating hand, 'I do not mean to doubt your faith or your character, but certain groups of our community are disappearing, and we have a duty to our fellow men.'

Jan knew he referred to Polish Jews, of whom he had several friends. Ever since the invasion, the Germans had singled out any 'Juden', forcing them to wear the yellow Star of David. He had seen lines of them, each with assorted possessions, at the goods yard in Warsaw where they were being pushed into cattle wagons. Once he had seen an officer beating a man on the ground as he passed. Inexplicably, and to his shame, he had ignored it and carried on.

The priest went on, 'The rumours of the death camps are more than just rumours, Jan. We may not like what is happening, but it is truly taking place, and we have a duty to help: a duty to God and to ourselves.'

Jan stared at him, the warm euphoria seeping away now under the stare of the priest's eyes. He knew. He knew alright. His change of fortune had blinded him to the rumours. He had pursued self-interest above all else: ever since that lorry had arrived in his farmyard he had but one goal, to raise himself and his family out of the aching poverty and backbreaking drudgery of life as a Polish farmer. As if the scales lifted from his eyes he looked at Helena who had remained silent so far. She watched him proudly and, reading his mind, nodded imperceptibly.

'Go on Father,' he said, slowly leaning forward and resting his large open hands on the well-scrubbed wood. In answer Father pushed back his chair and hefting the small holdall let it thump on the table. Unclipping the broad leather clasp, he delved deep into the bag and brought out a small parcel wrapped in brown paper and bound with string.

Repeating the manoeuvre, he soon had six small parcels on the table. He selected one, carefully undid the string and wrapping before tipping its contents onto the table. The darkened room danced with light as a thousand refractions of the glowing oil lamp leapt around the walls. The contents of the little parcel glowed and winked as Jan's jaw dropped at the sight of a collection of diamonds, rubies and precious stones, interspersed with various items of gold jewellery.

Father's fingers dipped into the glowing pile and selecting one item he held it aloft in one hand, while repeating the action with his other. Holding the two items between his index fingers and thumbs he turned to Helena. 'Jacob Drozd's wedding ring and his wife's,' he paused, 'they were put on the train last Tuesday.'

Jan swallowed, fingering his own ring, 'You mean...?'

The priest shrugged and returned the rings to the parcel, which he neatly retied. Helena poked at the other parcels. All bore the name of friends and neighbours. 'The Cieslas!' she said, her hand flying to her mouth and her eyes filling. 'Oh, dear God. They've only just been married – why Leila is expecting their first child. Surely, she hasn't been put on the train?'

Father did not reply, clamping his lips together in silent affirmation. He re-packed the holdall. His gaze, previously so directly into Jan's eyes, slid away. 'For safekeeping ... and the greater good', he explained

CHAPTER 27

Jan strained to peer through the windscreen, and he barely saw the checkpoint in time out of the gloom of the winter's afternoon, his meagre headlamps scarcely picking out the red-and-white-striped pole of the roadblock. Swallowing quickly, he slid open the window, greeting the coal scuttle-helmeted figure who stared sullenly at him. Glancing in his mirrors he saw three or four soldiers begin to poke and prod in the load of loose brown coal in the rear of his lorry.

'Hurry up my friend, we don't want the monks getting wet coal do we?' he grinned at the bespectacled officer who had stepped out of the guardhouse.

'Where are you bound?' the officer's quiet voice somehow instilling more fear than the solders' brusque efforts.

'Jasna Gora, sir, at Czestochowa.'

The officer paused a moment and swiftly crossing himself he raised his voice at his troop. 'Leave it men, let it go.'

As the barrier raised Jan pulled smoothly away with a nod of thanks. Father Krzysiak had been right, Pope Pius' secret accord with Hitler in 1933 confirming the inviolability of the Vatican State had permeated through most if not all, of the German war machine: although they could not be certain, it was a powerful talisman that enabled the activities of the Church to continue virtually unhindered.

* * *

That night, all those months ago, back at the farmhouse Jan's life had changed. Contact had been made with the Archbishop of Krakow who in turn had sent an emissary, one Karol Wojtyla, north to the monastery at Jasna Gora. Now Jan was on his ninth – or was it his tenth run – to the fourteenth-century fortress high above the town of Czestochowa.

His arrivals had settled into a routine; reversing his vehicle carefully through the medieval portcullis he would stop next to a barrel window that once would have been a cell. Undoing the slatted sides of the truck, he would shovel the contents of brown Silesian coal down a stone chute into the bowels of the monastery. As he stood in the rear of his vehicle, pausing on the long-handled shovel whilst the brown coal dust settled and swirled round his feet, he surveyed his surroundings. The monastery at Jasna Gora was home of the fabled Black Madonna and, as such, its place in the centre of Polish Catholicism was assured.

The icon had originated in the Ukraine but was brought to Czestochowa by the Pauline monks led by one Prince Wladyslaw of Opole in 1382. Believed to be a copy of a painting by St Luke, it was made on a piece of wood, said to come from the table on which the Last Supper was held. The icon was held in a church above the town and the same prince ordered a fortress to be built around it, resulting in a heavily-armoured medieval monastic complex, subsequently extended during the seventeenth and eighteenth centuries. In the dark days of the German invasion the monastery's history held particular appeal for Poles of all denominations.

During the seventeenth century the all-conquering Swedes had invaded Silesia and occupied the monastery. Victorious and invincible in their eyrie above the town, they had inexplicably retreated from the castle and were subsequently driven from the country.

What had happened to one past invader, was not lost on the occupying Germans. As the icon was uncovered every day before Mass, hanging above a beautiful ebony and silver altar, so the queue of the faithful remained, snaking out of the monastery and into the town. The Germans tried everything to dissuade the faithful from displaying their loyalty to the icon and what it represented. They imposed snap body searches, tried forced registrations and even drove convoys of heavily laden vehicles past the queue in an endless circle around the town. But they would not lift a finger to touch the two orders that inhabited the monastery: descendants of the original Pauline monks and a small band of the Sons of Sion, of whom Jan knew little.

It was always members of the latter that would slip up to his truck in the dark as he unloaded. Usually, a pair of them would materialise, their hooded cowls keeping their features pools of black. As Jan shovelled the loose coal down the chute into the cellars, so the brothers would go silently to work on the nearside of the lorry.

When the Skoda had left the works near Prague it had a long body, much longer than it carried now, with two huge fuel tanks slung either side of the chassis. As a result of the altercation with the oak tree near Jan's farm, Jan and his father had removed one of the large tanks. However, subsequent discussions with Father Krzysiak had seen the tank reinstated with slight modifications.

Jan paused again on the shovel, his exertions sending clouds of his breath rising around him. Dimly he could see the two cowled figures working at the side of his vehicle, a small kerosene lamp set in the cobbles their only light. Behind them, on a small-wheeled dolly of indeterminate age, sat an identical fuel tank. Presently, to the screech of a bolt being pulled through a hole, the two figures sat down heavily on the cobbles accompanied by most un-brother-like oaths. Pausing only to gather their robes around them and readjust their hemp belts, the two manoeuvred the second tank on the dolly under the vehicle. Quickly it was offered up and secured. The original tank, to some considerable effort, was lifted onto the dolly. Then and only then, did the two straighten up and push the cowls back from their faces. Breathing in the cool night air they glanced at Jan.

'Heavy work eh?' said Jan conspiratorially.

'Dieu le veut, my friend. Dieu le veut,' replied the smaller of the two.

Bending without further word, the pair balanced the long tank on the dolly and set off across the uneven courtyard.

Jan looked thoughtfully after them. Bemused, he wondered how the production of six small parcels of personal possessions on his farmhouse table one dark night had come to this.

Unquestioningly he and Andrzejw had cut open his spare fuel tank on the barn floor. Following intricate instructions and drawings supplied by Father

Krzysiak, they had fabricated at one end of the open tank a fuel section, so a suspicious removal of the filler cap – or worse a dipping of the tank for black market fuel – by German troops revealed just that: fuel. The remaining two-thirds, however, became a secret compartment accessible only by removing the entire tank from its place nestling against the chassis members.

Startling him from his reverie, the shout came a second time. The two brothers had crossed the courtyard and now stood in a half-open door facing him and beckoning him to them. He put the shovel in its bracket behind the cab and walked across the cobbles. It was his tenth visit that year, but he had never been offered so much as a bowl of stew: merely delivering the coal, exchanging a few curt words with the brothers and out again back to Zatow.

Now the two brothers looked at Jan as he approached. 'Come, my friend,' called the taller of the two, indicating the tank at his feet, 'you'll have to sup with us tonight, the Germans have brought forward the curfew, you won't have time to return.'

Jan put his back into lifting the tank over the low stone lintel. It took the three of them, grunting and puffing, to manoeuvre it through the door. At the final push Jan felt them leaning against him, fleetingly he felt hard angular shapes under their robes and a muted clatter as one of them pushed past the door frame. They were armed.

Accompanied by the rumble of the steel shod wheels on the ancient stone floor, the trio set off down the long corridor. It stretched into the distance, only broken by several right turns. Jan surmised they had circled the courtyard and now were in the oldest part of the monastery perched on a rock promontory overlooking the town: the original fourteenth-century fortress. One final turn led them to a dead end revealing a stone wall from floor to ceiling. The dolly came to a halt and the trio straightened. Without hesitation the shorter brother went forward and reaching up touched a block of stone high above his tonsured head. Stepping back smartly he was accompanied by a grating and rumbling sound as the bottom section of the wall swung outwards.

The first thing Jan noticed or felt was a blast of hot air that came at him. It carried a faint burning aroma, but the warmth was welcome in the cool passageway. Moving the dolly forward, the huge stone section swung back again with a muted thump. Casting his eyes over his shoulders, Jan saw the reason for the smooth operation of the door. The wall was mounted on a massive oak frame of ancient vintage, out of which protruded two extremely large cantilevers supporting huge cast iron weights: the door would pivot at the touch of man's hand.

Moving forward they approached another cowled figure seated at an oak lectern. Silently gesturing he pointed at the contraption in front of him. A balance scale hung from a chain: the tank was hung on it by the three men, while the dolly was wheeled to one side. A silent brother behind the lectern made a note in a large damask, leather-bound ledger of indeterminate age.

To silent gestures from the two brothers, more cowled figures approached. With effort the tank was freed from the scale and placed on a section of oak bench. Swiftly the locking mechanism was released and the contents spilled across its surface. Jan saw that the pile in front of him contained similar parcels to those revealed by Father Krzysiak in his kitchen. In addition to the parcels wrapped with diligent care and bearing handwritten labels, there were steel strongboxes of all shapes and sizes carrying tags with the name and address of the owner. Moving forward Jan fingered one such tag: Hans and Juna Gospedare from Oswiecim. Oswiecim! The location of those rumoured death camps of Auschwitz and Birkenau! Jan kept his counsel and passed along the table.

* * *

Members of the cowled brotherhood sat on various benches in silence, they were hacking and twisting and prodding industriously at the mound of parcels and boxes. Gradually Jan could see a pattern emerging. Parcels were opened immediately, and the golden contents moved to one side. The strongboxes took a little longer, but at benches equipped with vices, hydraulic clamps and hissing blow torches they were discarded: smoking twisted carcasses in a large pile behind the sweating brothers. There was little evidence of a calm, contemplative order here, he mused silently.

A soft rumbling raised Jan's eyes to the end of the room. Pushing a small-wheeled trolley, yet another burly monk – what on earth did they feed them on? – passed down the front of the table. With a practised sweep of his arm the golden pile fell into his cart and without pause he turned and walked back from he came.

Without bidding Jan followed in his footsteps. As he reached a doorway, the source of the heat became apparent. Flinging up his hand as the hot air seared his forehead, he squinted into the fiery glow that greeted him. A brawny, leather-clad figure, gleaming with sweat that made the hairs on his body glow like a shiny black pelt, stood in front of an open furnace. Using a small pair of tongs, he was gently placing various items of glistening metal in a crucible that itself glowed with ruddy heat. Jan watched fascinated as each item briefly discoloured the crimson surface while it cooled, then succumbed in an instant to the searing temperature, sinking gracefully beneath the surface. Periodically the sweating figure would take a flat ladle and skim off the crust of impurities that rose to the surface.

As Jan turned to leave the stifling room, the sweating foundry brother poured the glowing molten contents into several moulds and placed the whole onto a small, inclined conveyor belt that disappeared through the walls of the monastery. Jan ducked through a low doorway and followed in the direction that had been gestured to him.

By comparison the next vaulted room was an oasis of peace and calm as the still hot bars exiting from their conveyor belt through the wall entered its vast space. Cooling quickly, they were stacked on a large metal-faced bench awaiting the rhythmic attentions of a final brother. He pushed each ingot under the jaws of a huge press and pulled the lever down. Then the ingot was ejected to be added to a growing pile on the floor.

Not for the first time that night, Jan's eyes caught something that caused his heart to lurch. Slowly he walked over the uneven stone floor to stare down at the pile of ingots reposing in wooden ammunition boxes. Neatly stamped in the golden surfaces, the crooked symbol of oppression of an occupied continent stared back at him.

CHAPTER 28

The big, open car hurtled down the dusty roads of Gory Swietokrzyskie on the eastern flanks of the Polish Jura and to the north of the meandering Vistula. It was July and the countryside hummed with life: the sky of an iridescent blue shone on the occupants of Horch three-litre, eight-cylinder, staff car bearing the swastika pennant on the nearside wing, with the oak leaves of a full field marshall on the offside wing, flanked to the rear by two heavily armed motorcycle and sidecar units. The upholstery in rich dark leather insulated its passengers from the thrumming of the wheels.

The young staff sergeant driving was grateful at having to concentrate on keeping the big Horch out of potholes, for the atmosphere in the car was decidedly icy. To the left of the driver sat Lieutenant Orzo Zeitler, political officer of the Waffen SS, dressed in black from head to toe, only the silver jagged SS on his collar flashing in the sun. Tight-lipped and staring straight ahead over the sun dappled bonnet, he waited with interest to see how the two senior commanders behind him would execute Hitler's directive that Lublin would, not should, be held as a fortified area by the German 3rd Panzers as part of the Army Group Centre under commander Field Marshall Busch.

The fact that thirty-seven divisions of Germans, supported by some 400 tanks, were all that stood before General Rokossovsky's 1st Belorussian army who fielded some 166 divisions each of 10,000 men supported by 4,500 tanks was of little interest to him. The Horch began to climb gently towards the east in the direction of Kielce. There the two generals hoped for an overview of the invasion of Belorussia and Eastern Poland by the Soviets.

Field Marshall Georg Kuchler and Colonel General Lindeman sat comfortably in the rear of the speeding staff car. With its hood stowed, and motoring in clement weather, it was an extremely agreeable mode of transport. Stretching their immaculately booted legs out as far as possible they did not even reach the rear of the two front seats. With the road and wind noise it was possible to confer in low tones without being overheard by Zeitler. Of course, he knew they were talking, the discolouration of his neck betrayed his anger.

Kuchler glanced skyward at the twisting vapour trails, Lindeman too glanced upwards. Both remembered not four years previous when they, Adolf, Goering and others, had stood behind the Atlantic wall staring at white cliffs not twenty miles distant across the English Channel. Then the RAF had seemed finished, its remaining minnows darting in and out of the massed German squadrons. Defeat had seemed ludicrous then, but now in July 1944 the minnows in the sky above were the tattered remnants of the Luftwaffe, once the world's mightiest air force. Relentlessly the Russian Yak fighters pushed onwards, seemingly oblivious to the losses.

Glancing at each other Kuchler raised his hand in caution, indicating the front passenger. On the outskirts of Kielce they slowed briefly at Third Army Group checkpoints. Alert sentries spotting the two pennants approaching, raised the pole and snapped the Nazi salute at the passing car. None of the occupants returned the stare but all three snapped the salute. Kuchler, out of the corner of his eye, caught the hull down silhouette of the Panzers either side of the roadblock. No use, he thought: Tiger Mk IV only – the German's faced the much heavier SU152 and ML20s of the Russian army. They needed the Mark VI, now but he knew it was already too late.

Latest intelligence put Rokossovsky and his divisions at the outskirts of Lublin some forty miles away. Was the man inhuman? Lublin already. Why, he only took Grodro three days previously: that was over 120 miles in three days with full infantry and ten divisions in this zone alone. Privately, Kuchler despaired.

Driving through the as yet untouched town the two generals nodded and returned regular army salutes to groups of soldiers wearily digging in and sandbagging their positions. On the outskirts, overlooking the Vistula river, there was a small park some two hundred feet above the river plain. In bygone times the benches here would have attracted lovers of the eastern sun: children would have played in between the trees and old men would have negotiated a game of chess in the leafy shade. Now it was deserted, the once luxuriant trees cut down and discarded, victims to the fields of fire demanded by the embedded Tigers behind them.

The car drove through the remains of the park gates and stopped at the low wall, its radiator facing east. Lindeman rested his hand on the driver's shoulder, 'Wait here,' he said. Then he stepped out of the vehicle following Kuchler and Zeitler. All three stood at the low wall and took out their field glasses. Silently they traversed the horizon. A light wind came from the west, behind them, pressing their leather coats to the backs of their legs. As one they stared at one section of the horizon and swept slowly to the right. Moments passed as the operation was repeated. Kuchler sighed deeply and lowered the glasses.

CHAPTER 29

The day before, Colonel Van de Goltz had leant wearily against the turret hatch ring of his Tiger IV. A sideways movement of his hand, saw the rumbling diesel engine quit. The silence assaulted his senses. Battered by the clanking tracks, turret mechanism and the occasional deafening detonation of the 88mm gun, Van de Goltz's ears rang with the silence. Drawing on the cigarette in its elegant silver holder, he waited for his hearing to return.

As he surveyed the plain in front he could see the town of Lublin to his left and behind the escarpment climbing to Kielce. Lublin was lost he knew, his forty-four remaining Panzers out of an original 320, were battered and mauled. Every day they lost more to breakdowns than to the feared T34s of the Russians.

The rear hatch clanged open and Van de Goltz's crew tumbled out into the sweet-smelling sunshine. Exhausted, they fell into the long grass around the tank. Birdsong returned to his ears as he made a full 360-degree search. Then he lowered the field glasses with a sigh: God he was tired. For three years he had ridden his Panzers across these vast steppes, for two they had chased the Russians to Stalingrad, and then ... He wiped his hand across his forehead, pushing up his battered cap. Then hell itself had descended upon them. He thought they could defeat the Russians; he thought they could handle the weather, but not both. Dear God, not both.

* * *

In October 1942, all German forces were ordered to prepare for winter defence, to dig in and wait for spring: the Führer having confidently claimed that the Russian army would be destroyed in 1943. In fact, Stalin and Zhukov had spent most of September and October preparing for a major winter offensive. As the German Panzers dug in and attempted to catch up with their maintenance schedules, on 19 November 1942 one million men, 13,500 field guns, 894 tanks and 1,115 aircraft had attacked the German 6th Army at Stalingrad. Some fifteen months later Van de Goltz's Panzers were still running across the Russian steppes. Now they were being pulled back into Poland. Wearily he loosened his top button.

A crackle of static interrupted his thoughts. Wilhelm, half-asleep at his feet passed the cumbersome microphone and headset up to the turret. Adjusting the earpiece over his cap, he snapped, 'Colonel Von de Goltz'.

Listening intently, a frown crossed his forehead. Raising his wrist he studied the large dial, 'Not before dark, sir. Yes, yes, ten o'clock tomorrow at the square in Kielce.'

Then he thumbed the off button, 'Dig in boys, I've been summoned to a field conference at Kielce tomorrow morning. No doubt to hear how we can roll this lot,' jerking his thumb over his shoulder, 'back to Moscow.'

A series of sarcastic muffled replies came from his exhausted crew. Manfred, the driver, crawled out of the underside hatch onto the grass and growled 'You'd better bring fuel back with you. This heap won't make it to Kielce on orders alone.' Van de Goltz chewed his lip. He didn't say he might not be back.

* * *

The tiny küblewagen with its air-cooled engine covered the dusty road to Kielce quickly and without incident. Even the Russian air force must have been asleep that glorious morning. Leaving it at the gates to the old park, Van de Goltz marched swiftly towards the three leather-clad figures surveying the plain. His boots in the gravel announced his arrival and as they turned he snapped the Nazi salute. It was returned by the black clad SS officer, but the two older generals in crumpled field grey merely acknowledged his salute with a curt nod of the neck. Van de Goltz relaxed and started to grin at Kuchler: the two were old friends and held each other in high regard.

Kuchler's pale blue eyes flared in warning. 'Colonel! Your plans to defend Lublin?'

Van de Goltz stiffened, catching his friend's warning. 'Sir, we're well dug in, but low on ammunition and fuel, perhaps supplies will arrive soon?'

Kuchler's jaw grimaced, not a chance he thought.

'But you will hold out, Colonel?' The silky tones of Zeitler smoothly interrupting.

Kuchler took an unobtrusive step forward, looking directly at Van de Goltz he raised his binoculars with a startled gasp to study something past Van de Goltz's shoulder. His elbows at ninety degrees to his body he gasped again, seemingly staring at something facing him from the other side of the park.

Zeitler took a step forward, 'What is it Field Marshall? What do you see?'

Kuchler swung to the left then, without pause, brought his elbow back, smashing into Zeitler's nose below the bridge and flinging him backwards with an explosive curse. The low parapet wall overlooking the plain had been built with ornate iron scrollwork along its length. Since it was missing, Zeitler's legs caught the stone just below his knee and with a cry he tumbled backwards over the precipice. The three men stared at each other, Van de Goltz uncertain, but then Kuchler opened his arms, binoculars falling to his chest. 'Now for the truth,' and without a backward glance the three left the park.

Kuchler's driver had the big Horch running and turned around. If he noticed Zeitler's substitution he didn't say: he just sat lower in the big seat. The three climbed in, Kuchler and Lindeman looked to the east one last time. The breeze had eased and now smudges of oily smoke dotted the horizon; evidence of the carnage on the ground. Distantly the crump of antitank weapons could be heard, followed by the answering bark of the advancing T34s.

Kuchler tapped the driver, 'Go, my friend, go like the wind, Jasna Gora monastery at Czestochowa before nightfall.' The driver raised his eyebrows at the destination but stamped on the accelerator and slewed the big car out of the park.

* * *

Van de Goltz gambled correctly that the roadblocks would take little notice of a staff car bearing these pennants but just in case slumped low in the seat with the peak of his cap pulled down. He had trained under Kuchler when the Panzer divisions were first formed back in the thirties and the two had maintained steady contact. Kuchler had first broached the subject of 'what if?' some four years previously, but then victories in North Africa and with the communists fleeing eastwards Van de Goltz had merely kept his counsel out of respect for his friend. Back in July 1942 Kuchler had again tackled him, but then on the outskirts of Stalingrad frankly he had been a little short, and

Kuchler had spent a couple of nights worrying whether his then young captain would betray him.

During the fifth week of the Russian onslaught the two had shared a dugout in a ruined cellar on the outskirts of Stalingrad when, temporarily, one day they had been cut off and had watched mesmerised from under the fallen beams as column after column of fresh troops marched past, followed by at least a hundred brand new T34s: so new, their exhausts were burning off the paint as they ground down the road. The two men had looked at each other, knowing what it meant to have provoked the Russian bear, and from then onwards it was not 'what if', but 'when'. He knew little of Lindeman, but Van de Goltz was not fool enough to think Kuchler was the only field marshal to be laying plans for after the war.

* * *

A little after Koniecpol, as they approached the Jura Krakowska mountains, the previously iridescent blue sky swiftly turned grey, then black. Soon the storm burst and large drops of rain as big as marbles hit the car. Swiftly the driver, slowed the vehicle and opportunistically drove under a large ivy-clad limestone overhang as he fiddled with the hood fittings. While he folded the hood over and fitted the perspex side screens, Kuchler, Lindeman and Van de Goltz stood with their backs to the cliff sharing a cigarette.

With a muted roar, a half-track, lights blazing carelessly in the dark downpour, hurtled towards them. In the rear they could see armed soldiers, seated facing inwards. The three cursed, surely no one had missed Zeitler yet? To a man the three of them dropped their hands to the Luger in each belt, then the speeding half-track was past in a cloud of spray and half executed salutes. Watching it flee down the road, Van de Goltz wondered idly how many more would follow it in the headlong rush to evade the triumphant Russians.

As it sped past and cleared the overhang under which they had taken shelter, another deeper roar could be heard. The three men had started to duck and cover their heads as a Yak 3, dull red stars on its underbelly, flew down the road, it twinkled and spat four lines of tracer down the road. Fascinated, the sheltering men watched the four neat lines of bursts on the road surface intersect at the rear of the speeding half-track. It was over in seconds, the crump of exploding fuel and the blast of hot air reaching them as the vehicle slewed violently off the road and flipped upside down in the undergrowth.

The sound of the fighter's engine died as swiftly as it had arrived, and except for the crackle of flames from small fires in the brushwood up the road, silence returned. The driver stoically completed fitting the hood as the three looked at each other.

The journey continued to Czestochowa, slower and with great circumspection, Kuchler and Lindeman taking turns to sit in the small rear-facing seats and scan the following sky for danger. The rain continued unabated. Sodden soldiers manning checkpoints waved them through and it was this more than anything that saw their safe arrival at the towering bulk of Jasna Gora in the late evening.

The car pulled up outside the sturdy oak doors of the darkened monastery. The curfew and blackout was being rigidly adhered to and it was some moments before Kuchler found the bell chain in the stonework to the side of the doorway.

Pulling it firmly he waited. Patiently he stood as the rain, lighter now, dripped off his cap. The darkness was near absolute, only the jagged crenelations of the monastery against the dark sky giving him a sense of perspective. He was about to pull the chain a second time when a small panel slid open with a rasp and a pale face appeared at the rusty mesh.

If Brother Gregor was surprised at who was standing outside the monastery gates at this hour, he gave no hint as he observed the uniform and clean-cut features of Field Marshall Georg Kuchler.

Kuchler's eyes grew frosty under his dripping cap. Not now, he reminded himself, not now. Taking a deep breath, he began politely, 'Good evening, brother: Abbot Papee, please.'

The soft enquiring tones of this senior Nazi figure outside the door was too much for Brother Gregor. Stifling a gasp he slammed the little panel shut and Kuchler heard his footsteps shuffle away.

As the damp penetrated his neck he opted to sit in the vehicle and await the brother's pleasure. Now – not so much two senior officers, a driver and a colonel of the Wehrmacht – as four uncertain, nervous men, for the first time in four years they waited for an audience with someone whom they had never met, but one who, at his discretion, held their fate in his hands.

CHAPTER 30

Jan Wojack sat at a long, rough-hewn table in the abbot's refectory. Deep within the monastery, light blazed, and the roaring fire was not the only thing keeping him warm. In front of him sat a huge pot of Bigos, or hunter stew.

Living on the farm Jan had not had a difficult war but even so the largesse of the catering of the brotherhood surprised him. Comprising chopped white cabbage, sauerkraut, and dried mushrooms, with pork, bacon and Polish sausage, the dish was well beyond most of the population's ration books: coupled with his fourth glass of the fiery Wyborowa vodka, Jan was beginning to perspire freely.

He glanced up as Brother Gregor silently entered the room and whispered in the abbot's ear. Abbot Papee, who had yet to even acknowledge Jan's presence, put down his knife and fork. Slowly the colour drained from his face as his eyes took on a distant rheumy look. His hand involuntarily strayed to the signet ring on his finger. After a long moment he whispered back to Gregor, who promptly disappeared.

Four brothers on the right of the abbot rose, cleared their plates and set four more places. These were piled high and four glasses duly charged as the four grey clad figures entered the room. Jan was chewing a particularly succulent piece of bacon as he looked up, but it immediately turned to the consistency of chalk in his mouth: in the silence of the room his knife clattered to the stone floor.

The abbot rose as the four slid along the worn benches and sat down. Blessing the food with the sign of the cross he added, 'We welcome our fellow men, running from persecution.' A large brother opposite Jan growled and made to rise. The abbot's eyes, implacable, bored into him and he gestured with his hand. Uncertain, the burly brother half rose from his seat then slumped back. Chewing viciously and glancing up the table, Jan noticed the knuckles on the hand holding his knife were white with anger.

Later, still none the wiser, Jan was shown to his cell. He would have to wait for 'association' after dawn Mass to speak to the brotherhood. A fitful night passed and just as first light was breaking Jan found himself in the dark courtyard. Near the gate, under a solitary lamp, stood his truck. At least it looked like his, but something was different. Not once in the four years of contraband running had anyone so much as checked the vehicle's registration or papers. Now, however, it stood in the half-light, a uniform dull grey, the still soft paint the hue of the large German staff car parked in front. Whilst the lorry carried no livery, the car sported the swastika pennant and oak leaves, presumably belonging to last night's surprise guests.

Walking slowly around his vehicle, as was his wont, checking the tyres and oils, Jan noticed how much lower the tailboard was. Flicking his eyes to the large leaf springs under the rear chassis, he saw at once that instead of their graceful elliptical shape they were completely horizontal and in fact several of the thick leaves had parted, almost buckling under their load. With an oath

Jan flicked the canvas back, peered into the gloom and gasped. The lorry, his lorry, Jan Wojack's own lorry, was full to the brim with wooden ammunition boxes, that he had witnessed being filled in the cellar the night before.

Suddenly lights around the courtyard came flickering on and a party of six or seven men came towards him. Abbot Papee came directly to Jan as the four rested, bathed and fed officers climbed into the car, confiding, 'Father Krzysiak has spoken great things of you, Jan Wojack.' Jan bowed his head in embarrassment. 'These are dark and dangerous days, and the coming years may be worse.' And, as if to drive home his point, a rumble of artillery fire boomed in from the east.

Abbot Papee laid his hand on Jan's shoulder. 'Let these...' he paused. 'Let these gentlemen escort you to Krakow: you'll be quite safe. Go to the Bishop Hudal at the Wawel Palace. You will wish to see your family, so I've had Father Krzysiak take them there. The area around Zatow and Osweicim has become too dangerous. At Wawel you must make up your own mind, Jan Wojack, how much further you can help your Mother Church.'

Jan frowned, bewildered and uncomprehending. But further discussion was arrested by the large car starting up and heading for the gates.

Jan clambered into the cab and in a moment rolled out of the yard following the Horch. Glancing backwards he saw Abbot Papee and Brother Gregor both blessing the departing vehicles, but it was the look on their faces that disturbed him most.

CHAPTER 31

The little convoy followed what is known as the Trail of the Eagles' Nests along the border between Upper Silesia and Malopolska. The area is characterised by caves, wild gorges, gentle valleys and variegated woodland.

At midday they stopped at the highest point, Podzamcze Ogrodzienieckie, a 500-metre escarpment overlooking the river plain of the Vistula. It was a glorious day again and, as Jan remained in the lorry, the three occupants of the car alighted and took out their field glasses. The entire horizon to the east was obliterated by columns of smoke and flame. In spite of the distance sporadic gunfire could be heard and overhead tumbled and wheeled the opposing air forces.

Their route had been well chosen: only an aeroplane flying directly over the road would have a chance of spotting them. It ran in a seemingly endless succession of gorges, followed by overhanging trees, followed by deep ravines.

Twisting his neck upwards, Jan caught sight of medieval castles, their ruins stark against the vapour-trailed, crisscrossed sky. Rounding a particular hairpin bend, Jan cursed as he stood on the massive brake pedal bringing the laden lorry to a shuddering halt. The big Horch had stopped in the centre of the road and Colonel Van de Goltz had started to climb out of the front of the vehicle. Beyond the stationary Horch the reason for the sudden halt became clear. Resting half on the road and half in a shallow ditch a Tiger MKIV lay stationary, its long barrel pointing seemingly at Jan Wojack's heart. The rear engine covers had been folded back like some giant butterfly and the long oil-stained legs of two of the crew could be seen. The turret hatch was open, its machine gun pointing aimlessly to the sky, whilst its captain sat on the front armour observing the two vehicles in front of him.

Van de Goltz straightened himself and sauntered across. Saluting firmly, they introduced each other in a low monotone before moving to the rear of the tank in comradely discussion. It was then that Field Marshall Kuchler alighted, the slamming of the car door unnaturally loud in the silent gorge. The tank captain turned, Van de Goltz continuing to talk to the crew invisible in the engine bay save for their protruding legs.

The Tiger captain stiffened when he saw Kuchler's red stripes. With a sneer he walked towards the car, 'Well, well, what have we here?' he leered. His manner caused Jan to study him closer. The captain staggered a little and his top tunic button was undone, his cheeks were an unnatural cherry red, and his eyes appeared glazed. His words slurred as he said, 'Going the wrong way to the front aren't we, sir?'

Kuchler's voice cut like ice, 'Captain, you will address me correctly!

'Do you require assistance?'

'Oh yes, oh yes, we require assistance all right, just some fuel, ammunition, food, drink and some Polish whores would do,' he laughed and staggered. 'I think I've found some deserters lads.'

At the last phrase his voice rose and he fumbled at his holster. Kuchler saw the move and attempted the same, but his greatcoat hampered him and in a trice the captain's Luger was an inch from his chest.

'I don't think so, sir,' he sneered, 'now let's see what's in the truck.'

Van de Goltz moved silently away from the tank, the two crew unaware of the scene unfolding on the road.

The Tiger captain spun Kuchler and rammed the Luger under his chin from behind. 'The gun Colonel, slowly.' Van de Goltz stood frozen.

'Now,' hissed the captain, forcing Kuchler's head backwards.

* * *

Reluctantly, Van de Goltz dropped the pistol and kicked it away. Smiling the captain turned and, waving his pistol towards the lorry, bowed mockingly, 'Shall we?'

As he straightened, a muffled report came from inside the Horch. The bullet took the captain under his chin in exactly the same place as he had pressed his weapon into Kuchler's moments before. At such a range it exited the top of his skull in a fine spray, sending his cap and earphones spinning away. His last conscious action was to tighten his finger on the Luger and send a round ricocheting down the gorge.

The two gunshots caused the pairs of legs under the rear of the Tiger to wave frantically as their owners sought to extricate themselves from the engine bay. Lindeman stepped elegantly from the rear of the Horch, then paused to finger the single hole in the thin perspex and caught Kuchler's eye.

Taking in the scene immediately, he strode over to the rear of the Tiger, lithely mounted the front-sloping and lightly ran up over the hull.

Jan froze at the wheel.

Crouching at the rear of the angular turret, Lindeman paused, gun in hand.

Gradually the tank crew had pushed themselves backwards from the depths of the oily engine bay. Startled by the shots, they knew nothing of the drama that just taken place. The pair rolled on the aft ventilation louvres and blinked in the bright light. Lindeman rose swiftly and stepped lightly behind them.

Later Jan swore there had been only one shot, but the two crew rolled limp back into the engine bay as Lindeman jumped lithely back to the road. Reloading his Luger as he walked, he nodded curtly to Van de Goltz and Kuchler, and within seconds the Horch had squeezed past the Tiger followed by the Skoda.

No sooner had the hull passed into Jan's rear mirror than they stopped again. Tense, Jan squeezed the steering wheel as Kuchler and Lindeman strode back towards him, only to pass down both sides of the truck and meet at the silent tank. Fascinated, Jan watched as the two officers dragged the late tank captain to the rear of the tank. Kuchler scrambled up and bent briefly under the rear engine deck. As Jan watched, a growing pool of liquid spread from under the tank, diverted briefly by the tank captain's body. Then the two men walked backwards, away.

Lindeman spoke to Kuchler and harsh laughter rang out. Pausing, Kuchler took a smooth object from Lindeman and lobbed it in a graceful arc towards the tank. It flew flawlessly down the open hatch and without waiting the two ran past the lorry, slapping the doors and shouting, 'Go, go.'

Jan needed no bidding. He accelerated as the two officers fell aboard the stationery Horch and it too raced away from under Jan's bumper. The two speeding vehicles were round the next bend when a double crump and pillar of smoke in Jan's rear mirror told of Kuchler's actions.

CHAPTER 32

As night fell the two vehicles made it to Krakow. Behind them, even over the roar of the engines, the rumble and flash of the approaching battle could be heard. The road was filled with ox carts, bicycles and laden cattle carrying men, women, children and their worldly possessions as they sought sanctuary in the countryside. Only the speeding Horch sporting its pennants and swastikas – and with liberal use of the horn – had kept up any progress at all. The populace had obviously taken the fate of Warsaw to heart and were not in the mood for staying under the curfew.

At Brama Florianska a coal scuttle-helmeted trooper walked slowly round the Horch, fingering his Schmeiser. Van de Goltz barked at him, but he only took a step back and began to unsling the weapon. Jan tensed, but Lindeman alighted elegantly from the rear and straightened himself in front of the trooper. Rank won out as the trooper took in the double flashes on Lindeman's tunic collar and with a shout the barrier was raised. Snapping a perfect salute Lindeman returned to the car.

Except for the headlights of their vehicles, Grodzka Street was in darkness and not a chink of light showed as they exited the long street into Rynek Glowny Square. One of the largest medieval squares in Europe, excepting St Mark's in Venice, it was utterly deserted. Jan had been here only once when it had teemed with life and laughter on market day. Now, however, the rows of baroque buildings frowned down on the moonlit square, with only the swivelling multiple barrels of an anti-aircraft unit in the corner providing any movement. Without pause the vehicles accelerated across the huge, cobbled space and came at last to Wawel Castle.

Although Jan had never visited its cathedral, both Father Krzysiak and Helena had spoken glowingly of this place. Now as the two vehicles coasted to a halt outside the Kaplica Zygmuntowska, Jan shivered. Not a light shone until, just as the darkness seemed it could go no blacker, the moon burst from the clouds. Above them shone the Sigismund dome in ornate gold leaf, and beyond the fabled three towers of the cathedral itself.

In front of him the officers slowly got out of their car and took in their surroundings. Built as a royal palace between 1038 and 1596, the complex of buildings rising high above the Vistula comprised defensive walls, towers, the royal castle itself, cathedral, treasury and armoury. Each architectural genre, from Romanesque and Gothic to Renaissance and Baroque was represented. The castle's three-storied, arcaded courtyard into which they had driven was one of northern Europe's finest examples of Renaissance architecture.

* * *

Jan watched the three officers in the moonlight. They were totally relaxed, as plumes of cigarette smoke issued skywards to sounds of low laughter. Kuchler tapped his belt and to Jan's astonishment the three removed their uniform belts and pistols. Leaving them in the car the three mounted the steps of the chapel and pulled the bell.

Almost immediately, as if they were expected, the door to the chapel opened. A dark habit-clad friar of advancing years stood on the step, his simple garb belied slightly by the ornate gold cross around his neck. For several moments he surveyed the three officers, capless on the steps below, then with a strange smile he gestured to the vehicles and disappeared into the darkness of the chapel.

Van de Goltz walked briskly to the car and then to Jan's window, 'Come, my friend, tonight we are all on one side.'

Inside the chapel a table had been laid for supper. The elderly friar now took his place at the head of the table, whilst the five men and two other monks duly sat along the refectory table. Inclining his tonsured head he intoned grace.

* * *

Bishop Hudal had known this moment would arrive, as if the last five years of occupation had been a rehearsal. Some two dozen of these arrogant grey-clad men had passed through the monastery with their booty in the last few weeks. And, as instructed, he had sent them onwards to France and a place he had never visited: La Val Dieu.

However, Allied advances from the west and from the east had brought about a change in those orders and a new destination for the accumulating wealth. He was sending them on a far more dangerous route. But he was not taking the risk, was he?

Bishop Hudal watched as the three officers – the sergeant driver and the civilian driver – sat awkwardly in the surroundings. Smiling benignly, he nodded to the young novice sat at the end of the table. Hudal counted his blessings that he had had the opportunity of meeting and teaching such a young man. Back in 1942, as the persecutions of intelligentsia had reached epidemic proportions, the Dean of the Jagiellonian University had visited him. He had suggested, no he had begged, the bishop to take in four of his brightest students and hide them in the palace. Somewhat reluctantly, treading the fine line between his independence and protecting the Catholic community, he had agreed. One of the young men from Wodowice had lost his father, a retired Polish army lieutenant, only months before and it was a delicate matter to embed them in the seminary.

* * *

Taking his cue from the bishop's benign smile, Karol Wojtyla rose and began to ladle out the thick potato soup to the small group. As he moved silently down the table not one of the officers looked up to thank the novice, nor even acknowledge him. The bishop's brow furrowed as his eyes cast over the scar on Wojtyla's head. Six months previous whilst on a clandestine mission from the palace, Karol had been knocked down and left in the gutter by a speeding German truck. There his life would have ended but for another passing German vehicle which took the unconscious novice to hospital. He spent thirteen days recuperating from serious head wounds before being released, with mercifully few questions, into the abbot's care. Again, not three weeks ago, as squads of SS had ruthlessly searched the city, Karol had chanced upon a cellar in which he had managed to hide despite it being searched by the soldiers.

The bishop breathed deeply, Karol was his favourite student and he was convinced he was destined for high office: something in his manner gave him a calm maturity beyond his years. Even after tonight he doubted Poland had heard the last of Karol Wojtyla.

Lindeman cleared his throat as the plates were tided away. Putting his finely manicured hands on the table he looked the bishop in the eye. Jan watched, uncertain. Feeling his gaze, Bishop Hudal, clasped his hands and waited: he was not the one in a rush.

Lindeman spoke softly. 'We have some valuable merchandise outside Father which would help a great cause.' He paused, waiting for a reaction from Bishop Hudal. There was none, save for his sipping his wine reflectively. Lindeman raised his hands, palm upwards, slightly off the table. 'Father, the war is over for us, we have no wish to fall into Russian hands, nor,' he said meaningfully, 'to remain here in your sanctuary.'

The bishop merely raised his eyebrows. Marshal Rydz-Smigly commander of the vanquished Polish forces had stated years before, 'With the Nazis we lose our freedom but with the Russians we lose our soul.'

Five years of occupation had taught him many bitter lessons. Russians at the gates or not, he was not about to put a noose around his neck himself. Leaning forward, his fingertips together, he looked down the table. God knows he had had some sinners in his flock before, but now, as his eyes moved from the promising young novices on one side to the burly farmer who had driven the truck, so highly spoken of by Father Krzysiak, and then to the very devil incarnate in the shape of the three grey-clad, cold-eyed monsters, he reflected on the need for forgiveness. Pope Pius may have been right, his secret accord with the Nazis in 1933 had meant they had survived, had not they? However, the approaching rumble of gunfire troubled him deeply. At least under the Nazis most churches had remained open, and a reasonable dialogue had been possible. But under Stalin? Who knew?

He shrugged his shoulders impassively. 'Kapitan,' he said deliberately lowering Lindeman's rank 'how do you expect a poor abbot, a man of God, to help?'

For a moment Jan thought Lindeman would lose control. His lips hardened and he expelled the air in his lungs through his nose in a frustrated hiss. Giving Jan momentary concern as his hand strayed to his belt, Lindeman tugged out of his tunic a smooth bulky object and flung it with disdain on the table with a thump. The novices leant forward in astonishment, neither speaking. The bishop leant forward likewise, scarcely glancing at the golden ingot and raised his eyebrows in question.

'Good God, man,' Lindeman exclaimed, 'We carry your gold, four tons of it, in the truck outside.' A drop of spittle escaped his lips and he wiped it with the back of his hand. Sweat beaded on his temple.

'The stamp, Kapitan. The stamp on the gold. Forgive me. I can't quite see from here. What does it mean?' Bishop Hudal squinted, as if short-sighted, down the table.

Lindeman turned the ingot: the outspread wings and the eagle clutching the swastika winked upwards. He understood and slumped backwards. Three German officers running west with four tons of Reichsbank gold. 'But we collected this from Jasna Gora...' he protested.

'Of course you did, dear Lindeman, of course,' and Bishop Hudal smiled benignly.

Now it was Kuchler's turn smoothly to intervene, placing his hand on Lindeman's arm. 'What we are trying to obtain, is some small assistance, in return for escorting this to its destination. Perhaps Amadeus would help?'

At Kuchler's utterance, Hudal grunted. Of course. These were not the first and they would not be the last. If short-term help, even to the devil's disciple, was necessary to fight the devil himself then so be it.

'You have a plan?' he asked. But as he listened to Kuchler's reply his eyes rose to the wall above Kuchler's head from where Van Eyck's scarlet robed Urban II seemed to stare at him from across the centuries. Hudal compressed his lips and subconsciously nodded to the scarlet figure.

'Yes, yes, Father,' Kuchler stuttered. 'Zagreb first, the Ustashas, you understand, then perhaps on from there.'

Hudal nodded, 'Go and see Father Krunoslar Dragonovic in Zagreb, if you get that far,' he indicated the table. 'But you must get to Rome, then onto Genoa for a passage to Argentina.'

Father Papee leant forward, 'The password is "Amadeus", go to the Basilica di Santa Maria Maggiore, seek Father Golik of the Sons of Sion, he will arranged Red Cross passports and onward transport to Buenos Aires ... with a quarter of our cargo.'

Lindeman rose, his face flushed. 'A quarter! Why you robbing...'

But Kuchler restrained him with an effort, 'Franz my friend, is it a quarter chance at life after this?' he said, rolling his eyes, 'Or death?'

The colour drained from Lindeman's face. Then after standing in silence for a moment, he saluted and clicking his heels he bowed firmly. 'To Rome and one quarter then.'

* * *

Helena Wojack shielded her eyes from the late sun, her features impassive, devoid of emotion. It had been so since her beloved Jan had driven from the farmyard a cheery wave and a promise to be back by tomorrow. Many tomorrows had come and gone but no Jan. To the children, scampering around the dusty farmyard she kept a cheerful countenance, fending off questions about their father with an unconcerned laugh. At night her tears soaked the pillows in the large empty bed.

That was until the afternoon when a solitary horse and rider had appeared at the end of the farm track as it joined the road. Helena, born and bred on the plains of Silesia, recognised the steady gait of a working cob as it approached. She stepped back over the threshold and glanced upwards to where Jan's shotgun was hung.

Uncertainty flooded her as she realised her loneliness. The cob was at last responding to the urging of its rider and had broken into an ungainly trot. Then its rider's cries reached Helena and she stepped forward, a strange mixture of anger, fear and overwhelming love coursing her veins.

Later, when they came downstairs and while the children played and scampered in the warm kitchen came the questions. Jan's journey had not been without risk, they knew, but neither had they wanted to confront their fear. Helena, glowing and contented paid only scant attention to her husband's story, content with him merely being back home. Only when she raised the issue of the missing lorry did he focus on her. In answer, he rose and went outside to the darkened yard. Presently he returned carrying the horse's heavy saddlebags over his shoulder. In front of Helena's slowly widening eyes he laid the six heavy bars of buttery yellow on the well-scrubbed table. 'The price of silence, my love,' he said looking her straight in the eyes.

That night the chinks in the barn door glowed red again as the imprinted crooked symbol of Europe's oppression disappeared into a fiery crucible.

Part III

Part III

CHAPTER 33

Chiroya, Guatemala: 1998

The two pickups bounced and jarred as they flew down the track, the heavily armed thickset men in the rear cursing as they hung on with one hand and held their AK-47s in the other. Behind the two Toyotas came a Bedford 4x4 open tilt, also carrying a group of heavily armed men. Within yards of the rear of the speeding Bedford followed a black Range Rover Mk II, its interior an impenetrable mystery behind tinted windows. Bringing up the rear followed another Toyota pickup.

The small convoy had left the regional capital of Coban in Guatemala in the early morning and, having run out of metaled roads, was making its way along the dusty and potholed highway 89 towards Chiroya in the northern highlands. With the exception of a pause in Chisec, in which the occupant of the Range Rover had briefly disappeared into the Church of St Mary Magdalene whilst the armed entourage had stood uncertainly round the vehicles, the convoy had kept up a blistering pace. Periodically the last Toyota would drop back and park unobtrusively at the side of the road, usually behind a stand of vegetation or building to make certain they were not followed.

No vehicle passed them. The convoy was secure.

* * *

The Rotax 912 four-cylinder engine was using all of its eighty horsepower and emitting a shrill high-pitch buzzing which in turn propelled twenty-seven feet of RQI Predator unmanned aerial surveillance aircraft (UAV) through the bright clear skies of Guatemala. At an altitude of 23,000 feet and moving at just ninety miles per hour, it was completely invisible to the speeding convoy far below. On board the unmanned aircraft three electronic systems tracking the target were being operated by the same number of personnel from the 11th Reconnaissance Squadron United States Air Force, usually based in Indian Springs, Nevada but currently sitting in an extremely hot and sticky RAF C130 parked at the end of runway 3 at the British military base of Belize some 450 miles away.

As the convoy sped along the infra red camera tracked its progress, even through the overhanging jungle canopy. In addition, the ground-facing radar followed the vehicles effortlessly.

The systems in the C130 had logged their earlier pause at fourteen minutes thirty seconds, whilst the satellite navigation system identified the nearest building as a church, and the data stream from the Predator was transmitted in real time via the military Comsat system to CIA headquarters in Langley, Virginia. Not that they were the only recipient of the data stream.

One hundred and fifty miles away in the Maya Mountains, Sergeant Mike Walters, late of the Royal Green Jackets but now serving under the winged dagger of the Special Air Service, hunched over the video link to the UAV. Following the convoy, he had calculated they were no more than three miles from the ranch complex they had had under surveillance for the last three months.

Clicking his throat mike once, he asked 'Are you receiving? Over.'

'Affirmative,' came back immediately.

'Target three miles and closing. Begin your entry. Out.'

Two clicks were the only response. Mike glanced through the camouflage netting of the Land Rover to see and hear the Islander twin-engine begin its run. Almost immediately it left the ground from the short runway and banked away to the west: its short stubby wings carrying the bright orange logo of the Guatemalan Earthquake and Seismology Department. The fact that it took off with no more than fifteen minutes of daylight left aroused no suspicion at all.

* * *

Approaching his ranch, Ortiz Scalabrini stretched contentedly on the soft Oxford leather of his Range Rover. He would soon be surrounded by friends who were gathering for the party planned for later tonight and Ortiz was particularly anticipating the girls his brother Martinez had brought in specially. He had not a care in the world. At his feet, in his briefcase, lay half a million US dollars and nowhere on his vehicle or the escorts was there anything to connect him with the drugs that fuelled his empire. He had many visits from his friends the Policia Nacional Civil, sometimes accompanied by the serious Americans from the Alcohol, Tobacco and Firearms department. Each time they had raided his warehouses they had found nothing. Nor would they, he thought wryly, fingering the small crucifix round his neck.

* * *

In the rear of the Islander, also approaching the ranch but at a height of some 9,000 feet, sat four men, silent with their thoughts as they prepared to jump.

Led by Ben, Pete, Phil and Chas, all four late of Hereford, England and serving members of Her Majesty's armed forces, looked anything but that. Dressed in jeans and logging boots, the unshaven group were wearing heavy quilted jackets to guard against the chill during the descent.

They checked their weapons: an AK-47 and a Ka-Bar commando knife strapped to each leg. Chas also carried the standard SAS sniping rifle by Accuracy International, its long barrel and scope broken down and strapped to his pack.

Ben pushed the earpiece of his comms unit to his ear to override the droning of the aircraft's engines. He heard two clicks: 'Two minutes to drop boys.' He stood up swiftly and slid the large door open. Leaning out he grasped the handle on the wing stay supporting the high mounted wings. A further click in his ear sent him diving into the deepening gloom followed by the other three. The Islander was just still in sunshine, but the ground below had swiftly descended into tropical night.

Jack-knifing to a cruising position, Ben streamlined his arms to his sides and twisting himself, aimed his body towards the silver oxbow of the river almost two miles below. He sensed the change in temperature as he fell and with an effort he checked his altimeter on his left wrist. At 300m he reached across and bracing himself pulled the aluminium D-ring. With a crack above him and a jerk that he felt through every bone in his body he was drifting gently down, suddenly surrounded by night sounds of the approaching jungle canopy and smelling its warm rich odour.

As the copse of thinning trees rushed towards him in the gloom, he bent his his legs and landed lightly, rolling immediately forward and to one side, bringing his AK-47 to bear in one movement. Silence. Three successive thuds to his left and right confirmed the troop had landed as planned not a hundred yards from the promontory overlooking the river, on the other side of which lay Scalabrini's ranch.

Gathering the four chutes, Pete swiftly dug a small hole and buried them with a quantity of pepper to prevent discovery by tracker dogs.

Ben called them together by clicking his tin snipper. 'Right,' he whispered. 'Chas, OK?' He raised his eyebrows. He need not have done: Chas flashed his grin, the rifle already assembled and a round clicking into place.

'Wait for my signal and then we'll go in when you shoot after first light'.

Chas nodded and melted away to the top of the small cliff that formed the opposite bank to the ranch. Pausing only to attach vegetation to the long barrel of the gun and around the Schmidt and Bender 6x42 telescopic sight, he warily approached the skyline. Taking several minutes to feed the gun in front of him, he cautiously parted a small bush and with his Gerber multi-tool snipped and cut an aperture just big enough for himself in the centre of the bush. Then he lined the interior of the bush with his camo net and dug a small pit for his elbows and pelvis to make it bearable for the next few hours. Finally, he set the weapon up on a small bipod and peered through the sight. It took a moment or two for the pale walls of the ranch to come into focus, but when it did his position was perfect, overlooking Ortiz's patio and barbecue area.

A large tree with overhanging boughs was growing to the right of the barbecue area and in due course Chas spotted the small flash of light he had been looking for: Ben was in position. Similar flashes came from the rear of the villa near the south road.

Not long after the last flash, the sound of the approaching convoy could be heard. Shortly the two lead pickups, Bedford, Range Rover and final pickup entered the compound. Chas watched the guards being deployed and the ranch spring to life. Soon the compound was illuminated as bright as day, and Chas watched as the open pool in the courtyard became the centre of a drunken orgy. A dozen or more scantily clad girls, probably no more than seventeen or eighteen years old, were busily entertaining the various guards from the convoy, uninhibitedly frolicking in the water.

Loud rock music blared out. In the crowd, Chas could see Ortiz surrounded by three or four older girls. Amid the noise and lights of the central courtyard he was pointing to one of his guards. The man turned and ambled slowly across the yard and into the far wing of the ranch. Presently he returned with a tall figure in a long dark robe.

Chas watched: the robed figure had the open sandals and garments of a religious order, a monk no less. Walking towards his host, he was smiling and laughing and holding out his arms. Ortiz embraced him and placed a glass full of amber liquid in his hands. As the two toasted together Ortiz said something to the girl on his left. Moving seductively, she took the glass from the monk's hand and led him out of the courtyard into the main building. They reappeared on the large patio overlooking the river but now in complete privacy. The girl pushed the monk against the low table and with a swift movement undid the cord holding the robe together. Chas grinned as he watched her kneel swiftly in front of the monk.

* * *

The party died down after several hours and eventually the girls were put in the back of one of the pickups which drove away to the accompaniment of high-pitched screams and laughter. The ranch quietened for the night, and Chas watched the guards desultorily patrolling the building. The night was interminably long and dark, the jungle deafening with its cacophony of night-time sounds. With every nerve stretched to breaking point, Chas waited for the dawn.

When it came, he flexed each muscle cautiously before focussing the cross hairs on the patio doors overlooking the river almost opposite him, below and 200 metres away. He had been recruited when he was at Bisley, hitting targets no more than an inch across from 600 metres and he did not anticipate a problem here.

When the doors were flung open Ortiz Scalabrini, wearing a white silk gown walked slowly onto his patio. Chas eased the bolt forward to the breech and the 7.62mm x 51mm round slid home. Taking the first pressure, he exhaled slowly. The big man stood still, a large cigar clamped in his mouth, his gown open to the front. The phrase 'hung like a donkey' came briefly to mind as Chas briefly considered changing the primary target. At 841 metres per second the round left the one-metre barrel. Designed to penetrate body armour, at 600 metres it entered Scalabrini's head just above the bridge of his nose. Exiting the rear of his skull in a fine red mist, it buried itself in the flower bed to the right of the patio doors. So swift was the bullet's entry and exit it left him dead on his feet for a second or two, the look of total surprise on his face remaining as he slumped to the floor in a growing pool of darkness. Behind him, framed for a second in the doorway, stood a tall slim girl with long straight hair. She was wearing a blue baby doll nightie that concealed little. Unsure of what she had seen her hand flew to her mouth as she stood in indecision. Running forward, she knelt at the fallen figure then threw her head back and screamed. The second bullet entered that screaming void and did not exit.

Now firing erupted from all sides, the guards running into the centre of the courtyard found themselves dropped one by one by short taps on the AK-47s of Ben, Pete and Phil. Within minutes it was over, and Chas could see Ben and Pete as they methodically checked every room, occasionally a single shot breaking the returning silence. Shouldering his weapon, Chas slithered down the slope and with the gun at high port waded across the languid river to walk still dripping into the central courtyard.

'Sixteen males, two females, all accounted for', Pete coldly tallied up.

Fetching his haversack, Ben fished out handfuls of spent Chinese 7.62mm cartridges and scattered them around. 'Just another drugs' fight,' he shrugged.

* * *

Later in the commandeered Toyota, Chas said, 'Who shot the monk then?'

'What monk?' Ben said derisively.

Chas explained the night's events. Silence.

Then, Pete exploded in laughter, 'Piss off, Chas. You've been chewing coca leaves again'.

Ben looked across warily.

'I know, I know', Chas said, 'but seriously guys, I saw him with my own eyes'.

By now the Toyota was rocking with mirth as the pent-up stress of the firefight gave vent to hysterical laughter.

'Seriously Ben, I know you've got religion and all that', Chas said in between gasps, 'I'm serious!'

But, back at base in the debriefing session, nothing was mentioned about Chas's strange observation. Much later after the debrief Ben was sitting in the late afternoon sun when Sergeant Walters found him and passed him an official looking envelope.

'Thanks Mike', said Ben, looking at the letter. 'Thank you'.

Rising, he walked to the base perimeter near to the now silent C130. He leant against one of the huge wheels under the wing and stared at the envelope. He loved the army, he relished every waking moment, but he knew, deep down when he stopped, his yearning had not gone. He remembered the day, the hour, the minute, six years ago, turning to wave farewell as Father Ryan stood in the door of the Magdalene Theological College. He knew then he would be back –and he knew the time was now.

CHAPTER 34

The Mountfords had lived at Mountford Hall overlooking the River Wye in Herefordshire for over 600 years. The crest of the double-headed eagle on a black shield and engraved gold bard having been awarded for the original de Montfort family who had served in the Crusades, then helped considerably in restoring King Charles II to his throne.

Throughout the ensuing ages the family had been hugely successful in various business ventures particularly from the booming port of Bristol as the New World and East India routes had opened up. This, coupled with the fact that they had managed to conceal their Catholicism, had meant they also benefitted under Henry VIII as he redistributed the more overt Catholic holdings. Their interests in shipping, agriculture from the large fertile holdings in the West Country, and shrewd investments in the tin and China clay industries meant the family had ridden well the economic storms of the last six centuries.

One little known fact, however, drove the family. The male line, almost without exception, either went to fight for the monarch or served the Catholic Church. In the latter case, in earlier times, it simply meant that one or more sons simply 'disappeared' until either they died, or they came out of the priesthood to reclaim their family title. This was how Benedict Cadogan Mountford became destined to fight for country or Rome.

Ben had an elder brother James who was his antithesis. Quiet, studious and a deep thinker, it was apparent his path lay solely with the church. Ben, however, was different. Even before his birth at ten pounds two ounces, according to his mother Elizabeth Mountford, he had kicked and fought the previous three months. So, it was with considerable relief that she brought him into the world, only to find her problems just beginning.

From the first day, his head, a mass of unruly dark curls, would rear above the maternity ward cot and it was only a matter of days before his dark eyes, ready smile and dark good looks began to captivate everyone who visited the Mountford family. It was a pattern that was to repeat itself throughout Ben's life. He discovered that his impish smile and handsome features could and did get him out of any number of scrapes. His exploits became legendary: once he had found out he could beat his elder brother at sports or usually fighting, he moved on. Whether it was kicking his football through the glasshouses of neighbouring fruit farms or catapulting ball bearings at passing cars, his mother and father, Sir Roderick Mountford, always knew just which son to address when the authorities came calling.

One characteristic, which above all gave his parents hope, was that whatever he had been doing to get into trouble, and whatever the adrenalin rush he had experienced, seemed to be followed by long periods of studious melancholy. Elizabeth saw this as an inward penance; perhaps Ben's way of revealing his repentance and learning from whatever experience he had just been punished for. Sir Roderick, on the other hand, thought he was calculating how much better he could have carried out his latest escapade. Only Ben knew.

When he was fifteen and broadening out and upwards physically, Ben was unfortunate to receive at St Ambrose Catholic High School in Hereford a new French teacher for his final year before his O-levels. Sitting at the rear of the class, as was his wont with Harry Crawford, they waited for the first French lesson of the term to begin.

Footsteps approached along the wooden corridor and the door opened swiftly. 'Bonjour, mes élèves, je m'appelles Miss O'Connor and I am your new French teacher'.

The silence of the classroom was broken only by Ben's pen falling to the floor: he had never seen such a beautiful woman in his life. He felt his chest squeezed tight. His throat grew dry, and he stammered his full name to his immediate embarrassment as Miss O'Connor read the register.

As she stood at the lectern in front of the sloping classroom and its tiers of oak desks, she became uncomfortably aware of Ben's open stare. Subconsciously feeling her top button she turned to the board.

By home time Ben had his wager with Harry. 'Bet I can put my hand up her skirt while you watch'.

'Twenty pounds says you can't', scoffed Harry, almost banking the wager straight away.

Until now Ben had achieved high marks in his French and over the next week Claire O'Connor was perturbed by the rapid fall of the marks in his written work, to the point when she told him to stay behind one afternoon after the lesson had finished.

As the class dispersed, Ben winked at Harry who, making sure he was last out, shut the door loudly, while keeping the catch turned to open it immediately afterwards to peer through a small crack.

Ben had seated himself at one of the front desks so that Miss O'Connor had to stand over him in full view of the door. Claire leant forward, her thick hair brushing Ben's shoulder. Behind her Harry could see Ben's hand hovering at the back of her shapely calves.

Claire sensed a slip of control as she bent to his work, conscious of a presence she had not experienced before. Again, she started to blush and her nipples acquired a tightness that was not altogether unpleasant.

'See this is how…' But her voice deserted her and her mouth was dry as her eyes became trapped in his. Unconsciously, she licked her lips with a small pink tongue and Ben broke his gaze to stare at her beautiful slightly pursed lips. Sensing the right time, his hand disappeared slowly up Claire's mid-length skirt.

For an eternity it seemed, Harry stood open mouthed, watching the motionless couple. Then Miss O'Connor suddenly straightened and delivered a swinging right-hander to Ben's left ear, sending him sprawling. At this Harry bolted down the corridor, but not before Claire's subconscious had registered the click of the door behind her.

Rapidly she hissed, 'Get out', and, as Ben's previous confidence deserted him, he fled the room. A short while later she left the classroom, closing the door firmly behind her, the muted click reminding her of the noise she heard as she had cuffed Ben's ear.

She set off determinedly, her heels clicking on the wooden parquet flooring. As she neared the headmaster's study, she rehearsed her words of indignation and demands for summary justice. She had knocked on the large, panelled door, and her hand was on the brass handle as the gruff 'Enter' came from within. That was when she suddenly saw all too clearly Ben's dimpled smile, unruly hair and twinkling eyes. Simultaneously a warm feeling spread across her lower stomach. Committed though, she pushed the door open, popped her head round and said, 'Goodnight headmaster'.

'Goodnight, Miss O'Connor,' was the bemused reply.

* * *

The next day Harry Crawford became twenty pounds the poorer, but for the rest of that week Ben was at a loss at how to pursue Miss O'Connor further. He had to dodge a few questions about his cauliflower ear, but by and large he had escaped any undue consequences. He was, however, intrigued by Miss O'Connor's blushing when she caught his eye. It stirred his passion mightily, although he was at a loss what to do. Then, as the class filed out, at the end of another afternoon lesson, Miss O'Connor asked casually, 'Mountford, would you help me carry these books to my car?'

With alacrity Ben picked up the class's twenty exercise books and followed Miss O'Connor's swinging skirt to the staff car park. As he placed the volumes on the floor of the Mini he felt a small hand enter his pocket. Squeezing his erection so hard he gasped, she breathed, 'So you want a real French lesson?' It had taken considerable amounts of her courage, but she had been unable to sleep for days, so aroused had she been by this angelic devil in her class.

Later that evening there was a knock at the door of her flat and when she opened it she was met with the sight of Ben Mountford: no school uniform now, just an open shirt, jeans and trainers, and a curious, amused nervous grin that had Claire's legs to jelly in seconds. They never made it to the bedroom, finding the tiny hall sufficient for that first time. Ben left in the early hours with knowledge that would never be taken from him, a self-satisfied smile and severely aching loins.

His parents were initially impressed at his sudden desire to spend his own time studying French. Harry Crawford was beside himself with curiosity and soon the whole school knew. Not long after came the day when Ben saw Miss O'Connor walking swiftly to her car, her head down and then driving rapidly out of the gates. While Ben was still staring at the gates, he was startled to see his father's maroon Bentley coming through them and parking briskly. Later, leaving the headmaster's study at St Ambrose for the last time, Ben was accompanied by a very embarrassed Sir Roderick Mountford. The drive home was silent, which was more than can be said of Sir Roderick's study when Ben met his father's belt not for the first time, but certainly for the most painful.

The Roman Catholic schools around Hereford had all heard of young Mountford's expulsion. As one, they declined to take Ben for his final year. Eschewing the alternative of state schools, a series of tutors was engaged and a room was set aside in the Hall in which his 'home schooling' could take place. The newfound college-like freedom had suited Ben and he was pleased with his subsequent results. Especially surprising was his 'A-star' in French.

CHAPTER 35

Although the Mountfords had always given a freedom of choice to their sons, when it came to it the family's two career choices there always seemed just the two: the army or the Church. Ben hankered for the military option, but his expulsion meant he had no references with which to apply to the Royal Green Jackets, the regiment of choice and the recipient of previous Mountfords. With his hopes dashed of following the family down the path of a military career, he sought sanctuary with the local priest, with whom he had always had a steady relationship. Father Murphy regarded the tall strapping lad in front of him with resigned amusement. Whilst he was grateful for vocations within the church, he doubted the church would cure Ben's restless temperament; although, if it did, he thought it would gain a mighty ambassador.

Mindful of the frosty reception the request for a referee would receive from St Ambrose, Father Murphy called a friend in the Magdalene Theological College in Birkenhead. An introduction from Father Murphy proved to be sufficient and a short time later Ben found himself on a damp gloomy Wirral afternoon in October knocking at the large doors of an ex-Victorian workhouse in Birkenhead.

Ben's spirits had plummeted rapidly. The journey through the North-West's grim industrial heartland had been bad enough, so he was surprised and gratified to find the large door flung open and a beaming rotund figure in a long brown cassock welcome him with open arms.

'Benedict. Good to meet you. Come in. Come in. Father Ryan. Pleased to have you,' he said, introducing himself.

He fussed around Ben, taking his large suitcase and seeming not to be bothered at all by the weight, he set off along the hall. Ben trailed in his considerable wake as he burst through a door on the left, just before a large staircase disappeared up into the gloom.

'Elizabeth,' the priest called. 'Meet Ben, our latest victim ... sorry, applicant,' he burst out laughing, his round chubby face twinkling with merriment. 'Ben, this is Elizabeth, our registrar, who knows everything, and I mean everything,' another burst of laughter, 'about you'.

Ben's spirits had soared with his greeting and Father Ryan's ebullient introductions, but they were damped as Elizabeth stood and proffered a small hand in greeting. She was about five feet three or so, but her broad shoulders continued at that width seemingly to the floor, a grey cardigan of indeterminate age buttoned at the centre struggled to contain that within. A pair of stout legs protruded from her warm tweed skirt ending in flat black brogues. Her grey-blonde hair was scraped back in a severe bun and her half-moon glasses rested on a nose that was quite the broadest nose Ben had seen on a woman. It appeared her mascara was doing double-duty as thermal insulation. But her eyes were the palest, iciest blue and they regarded Ben coolly before she cast her gaze down and with a small old-fashioned curtsy welcomed him.

A few formalities later and Father Michael pressed a small bell on the desk and the door opened to reveal Ian the elderly porter of the college. 'Would you be so kind as to show Ben to his room?' Father Ryan beamed. Ian picked up Ben's cases and with a nod to father and Elizabeth guided Ben out into the hall and up the stairs.

Glancing at his watch Father Ryan nodded to Elizabeth who was already bowed over her elderly typewriter, 'Must dash, or I'll be late for Mass. Would you leave Benedict's file in my office so I can become acquainted with him later?'

As she murmured her acquiescence, Father Ryan left the office, closing the door behind him. As soon as he was out of the door, Elizabeth pushed back her chair and crossed the office swiftly, opened the door a crack and watched him disappearing into the gloom towards the chapel. Closing the door softly, she picked up the large folder marked 'New Appellants' and took out Benedict's records. His family, background and educational results were all there, along with a reference from Father Murphy detailing the family's past prowess and Catholic history. Her long slim manicured fingers rifled quickly through the next pages. When she was sure she had it all, she crossed to the photocopier and within minutes a neat copy lay ready and waiting.

At five o'clock precisely, Elizabeth left the office for the day and made her way through the dark, wet streets to Wavertree Library. There she found the fax machine supplied by the council, dialled a number she had written on a scrap of paper in her purse and began feeding the papers into the machine when her call was answered at the other end. As the sheets disappeared through the machine she collected them and, paying a further small charge, fed them through the shredder. When the slip confirming the fax had been sent emerged, Elizabeth shredded that also – it bore the international code of 0039: Italy.

* * *

Two nights later she was at home in her small, terraced house just outside Toxteth when she heard her letterbox open. When she went to look, she found a small jiffy bag on the doormat. Inside was a mobile phone. The screen displayed a long number. Elizabeth pressed 'call' and she listened until several clicks later she was connected. The voice she heard spoke for one minute, after which Elizabeth simply said 'Understood' and pressed the 'end' button. The chances of the conversation being overheard were remote; and in any case few people these days understood Latin. Even so, on her way to work the following morning, Elizabeth dropped the phone's main body into one waste bin, the battery into a another and the sim card into a third: the Nokia had served its purpose.

* * *

Ben settled surprisingly well into college life. After his enforced break and various tutors back home, he found the strict regime behind the dark brick walls almost comforting. The college was housed in the same building as the monastery of the Sons of Sion, a collective of monks dating back to the Middle Ages. Ben rarely saw any of the dark figures, but on occasion one would come in to the lecture and either sit silently at the back of the room or sometimes himself lecture on the early teachings of the church.

Once in a while, it was possible to provoke these monks with the lively debate that formed his training. Whilst the class of twelve young Catholics had all felt a calling to the Church, the fact remained that for all their seriousness they were still young men questioning and debating as they sought to move the Church to a more modern stance. This debate was neither new nor exclusive to the Catholic faith: all religions had their younger members thrusting for change against the establishment of the elders.

During one debate on the ethics of the modern church and the leadership of the Holy See, Louis, a close confidant of Ben's, sought to enlarge the discussion into the area of papal infallibility. The class was being led by Father Gregory of the order of Sion. A large well-built man with a full beard and piercing eyes, he could be intimidating at the best of times. Although he was usually fully robed as he discharged his duties around the college, today he was wearing olive green fatigues, almost military in look.

Louis had been cornered into agreeing with the concept of papal infallibility. As Father Gregory sensed victory, citing the Holy See's direct connection to God and the fact that his pronunciations were in fact God's Holy Word on Earth, Louis interrupted him by raising the topic of the Inquisition. 'How could the Church accede to and partake in torture and murder? Did this not prove the Pope was human and now some 500 years later should apologise?'

Father Gregory paused, turning to Louis. 'If it were the case that it was God's will to cut out the canker of the time, would you follow your calling?' He spoke gently, but a silence descended on the class. 'What if the forces opposing you, the Devil and all his works, were too great, would you defend your Church?'

Louis paused, the argument turned on its head. 'How could I kill having taken my vows?' he replied. 'If you did not, your vows would be worthless if the Infidel defeated us'.

Ben stuck his hand in the air. 'I would fight for the Holy Roman Church as it is the only true church, Father.'

'I believe you would', Father Gregory replied. 'I believe you would, but some of your compatriots may not'.

Ben pondered this and later asked Father Ryan what he thought. To his surprise, Ryan was dismissive of Father Gregory's arguments, citing the divisions in the Church as being between the orthodox and progressive ideas. 'When you take your vows, Ben, you will go far in this church. You may even make Rome, and there you will witness the rise of the Opus Dei amongst others, and the internal struggle that has carried on for a thousand years or more'.

* * *

It was Father Ryan's custom, once a month or so, to encourage his appellants to go out 'on the town' and circulate within the wider Liverpool society. One of the greatest difficulties his young priests had was the vow of celibacy. Struggling against a lack of vocation and the requirement of celibacy as well, he was fortunate if twenty-five percent of his appellants made it through to the priesthood. So he cleverly wove into the syllabus the doctrine of temptation and then encouraged his flock to go out into Liverpool, usually the night after those very sins of temptation had been discussed. Strangely, although sins of the flesh were discussed painfully and at length, at no stage was it deemed a sin to go out and get completely roaring drunk: a habit that seemed to be peculiar to the Roman Catholic Church. Accordingly, Ben, Louis and one or two others had formed the habit of visiting the Star and Garter public house on the corner of Henrietta Street, a stone's throw from the college.

At nine-thirty on a Friday evening the atmosphere in the pub was warming rapidly, when Ben pushed open the door and made for the bar. Over the pulsating music and through the haze of cigarette smoke Ben's tall figure led the way: that evening he was out with Louis, Pete and Jordan after a particularly difficult week. The first year's exams were under their belts the foursome were looking forward to a good night out.

Father Michael had benignly bade them well as they had left, telling them to be wary and to be careful on the streets. Elizabeth had slipped out too and had walked a hundred yards or so with the young men. Unusually for her, she had engaged the four men in lively conversation and out of politeness they had invited her along. Muttering something about her housework she had scurried off down a side street, somewhat to their relief.

The 'Star' was a well-known watering hole for the clergy of the college and, as is the way, the young girls of the neighbourhood, as with homosexuals, found the attraction of something they could not have irresistible. In fact, O'Leary's Tote on the corner ran a book on the percentage failures in the college down to sins of the flesh. Confirmation of the figures came from a secret source high in the abbey, which cost the landlord of the 'Star' and O'Leary's a case of malt every year: well worth it when the amount of young, unattached females in the 'Star' caused the establishment to be the most popular for miles around.

As Ben, Louis Pete and Jordan settled into the corner by the open fire the talk was of the Derby the following day: Liverpool versus Manchester United at home. The arguments were loud and vociferous. A couple of local lads were trying their best to wind up the students, knowing that unusually for Liverpool they would not retaliate,

'Same again, boys?' Ben asked. Not waiting for the answer, he elbowed his way to the bar. 'Four again, George', he told the barman.

At the sound of his voice the slim blonde girl with shoulder-length hair turned to face him at the bar. 'Excuse me,' she said icily, 'I was first'.

'I ...' stuttered Ben, 'I'm terribly sorry, can I buy you a drink?'

'Hang on a minute, you're the one pushing in! That's a new line of chat if ever I heard one!'

Her eyes were bright and pale blue, but twinkling, or steely? Ben felt himself blushing.

'OK, OK', she said graciously, 'I'll have scotch ... Large', raising her eyebrows fractionally.

As the drinks came Ben invited her to join them near the fire. 'I'd better not', she said, inclining her head to the door where a large lad in a coarse donkey jacket stood scanning the crowd.

'You …!' said Ben.

'Thanks for the drink', she said smiling and then slipping the coaster from her drink onto Ben's tray. It had a phone number on it and a name: Maria Yates. Shaking his head amusedly, Ben slipped the mat into his pocket and went back to the others.

* * *

Several days later he was at his desk in the shared bedroom completing his essay on the doctrine of celibacy. His mind knew the arguments: his mind knew what he should write; but his hand would not. From Claire O'Connor's face taunting and teasing him, he saw the long blonde hair turn repeatedly to him at the bar: the eyes, he decided it was the eyes. Finally exasperated, he pushed the paper away and fetched the dog-eared coaster from the top pocket of his Marco Polo shirt. The number seemed to stare at him, challenge him, dare him. The physical stirrings in his pants were interspersed with the vision of the Devil on his shoulder as he watched himself struggle with his essay.

Maria's number had a local code, and she answered immediately. 'Hi, it's Ben', he simply said. She sounded pleased and, never very good on the phone, Ben swiftly secured a date for the next Friday.

'I can't break a vow if I haven't taken it', he thought to himself as he put down the phone. Maria smiled as she replaced her receiver; the job was not so bad after all, she thought as she ironed her medium-length tweed skirt ready for work on Monday morning.

The following Friday Ben strolled into the 'Star' eagerly, looking forward to his evening with this alluring girl. She was against the bar, laughing with Jim the barman, throwing back her head so that her long throat caught Ben's eyes. Jim acknowledged Ben with a nod sending her blue eyes flashing towards him.

She turned slowly, the smallest roll of hip stilled as she welcomed Ben. It was early and the pair had the snug to themselves for over an hour, which went too fast anyway. Ben found her open and amusing, delighting in her company. He noted with not a little pride the envious looks of the regulars later on, as they saw the willowy blonde giving her full attention to him.

So he felt as if the wind had been knocked out him when Maria suddenly caught her watch with a gasp. 'I must go, I've a train to catch to Derby tonight. It's my sister', she explained.

Crestfallen Ben offered to escort her to the train station but at that moment, as if by magic, a dripping wet taxi driver yelled into the pub, 'Taxi for Maria'. She had jumped up before Ben could say a word, planted a light, ethereal kiss on his cheek and was struggling with her coat through the door.

Ben finished his drink, bemused and went back to the college intending to finish his essay.

How did she get a taxi that quick in such a foul storm? He couldn't wait for the weekend to pass. On Monday he rang expectantly – and got no reply. Tuesday. Wednesday. Thursday: he was going mad. Then, on Friday she said 'Hi'.

'Where've you been?' he gasped explosively.

'At my sister's,' she replied. 'Didn't I say it was for the week?'

'Oh, oh, no you didn't' said Ben, feeling foolish.

'Sorry', said Maria, a smile playing her lips, having watched his number come up on caller ID all week.

* * *

El Casa, the local Spanish restaurant around the side of the precinct, was packed, but Ben and Maria did not notice. Sitting in the farthest booth from the door, they were oblivious to all. The sautéed scallops with lentil sauce had gone down extremely well, followed by a bottle of Señor Felipe's excellent Muscadet.

Sliding closer to Maria, Ben put his arm round her and kissed her gently. 'Thanks', he said, 'I've really enjoyed tonight,'

Amusedly she looked into his green eyes as a lock of his dark curly hair fell over one. 'What's the point?' she said abruptly, sounding harsh but not meaning it.

Hurt, he drew back. 'What?' he said.

'What's the point?' she repeated. 'We can only ever be friends.' Angry now, she slid out of the booth and beckoned Felipe to bring her coat.

'Maria', said Ben, 'Maria, don't go please', the last word softly pleading.

The other diners looked on, the striking blonde with her trench coat half-on, half-off and the tall young student.

'Hmph', she snorted and tugging free, strode from the room. She paused at the door, fished for her compact and watched Ben paying the bill in its tiny mirror.

He strode out, following her as she flagged down a taxi. But, as the dark, low shape pulled up at the kerb, he caught her arm. 'Let me take you home'.

She turned, almost ready to pull away, but tears blurred her vision and she crumbled into Ben's arms. The cabby remonstrated impatiently as the two leant against the open door of the car.

'Falkner Street, please', she said through her tears.

The cab pulled away, its driver surreptitiously adjusting the rear-view mirror and smiling sardonically at the huddled couple in the rear.

Ben would remember the number for many years to come: 218 Falkner Street, a smart dark green door with the numbers in polished brass at eye level. Maria ….' he began. But that was the last word he spoke all evening.

Slim arms curved around his neck as her wide full mouth came down on his, her eyes the brightest strongest sparkling blue he had ever seen. Somehow the door opened and they were in.

His initial memories were of a plainly decorated minimalistic look with polished wood-effect floors and soft lighting: very single and very feminine.

First it was the hallway wall. Next, onto the large settee in the front room. Before progressing with slowly declining levels of energy to the main bedroom upstairs: the small unobtrusive fish eye lenses in every room caught it all. Channelled down micro coaxial audio and video cable, the pictures fed four flickering black and white monitors in the upstairs room next door. In turn these downloaded the writhing images and close-up shots to a video recorder While the monitor's flickering images were reflected in the large mirror above the professional-looking dressing table where a single line of naked bulbs surrounded three sides of the glass, below which lay neat tubes of camouflage make-up, Derma wax, eyebrow plastic and an orderly pile of various latex sponges in different shapes. On an old-fashioned tailor's dummy in the corner of the room hung a grey, well-worn cardigan buttoned at the front. A tweed skirt completed the dummy's ensemble, along with small pair of half-moon spectacles lying in front of the mirror.

CHAPTER 36

Father Ryan had risen before dawn to prepare for the Lenten address. Hearing a creak on the landing he pushed his door silently open to see Ben's tall figure, shoes in hand, tiptoeing down the landing: dawn was still one hour away. Compressing his lips and shaking his head wryly, he returned to his writing.

Later that morning, showered, fresh and on top of the world, Ben bounded downstairs with a sheaf of papers to copy. After a perfunctory knock, he entered the registrar's office and asked, 'Elizabeth, can I photocopy these…?'

His words cut off as Elizabeth, with the phone to her ear, held her finger to her lips and pointed to the large photocopier on the far wall of the cluttered office.

Ben mouthed 'Sorry' and tiptoed across the floor.

'Yes, my name's Elizabeth Fitzpatrick of 216 Falkner Street. You tried to deliver my fridge last night and I told you I wouldn't be in. Can you do the same tonight?'

Ben stopped feeding his research into the maw of the machine. 216? 216? It could not be. He felt an unexplained heat rising up his neck.

'Yes, that's right', Elizabeth was saying, 'tonight please at six pm.'

'Really, you can't depend on anybody,' she told Ben with a tut and rolled eyes. 'Now, what did you want?'

'Nothing. Nothing, it's fine. I can work the machine', Ben said.

He hid his smile. The vision of Elizabeth, combed, lank hair in a bun and broad of beam interspersed with his night's activities in turn. 218? 216? 'Well, well', he thought.

'Sorry, I couldn't help overhearing, Elizabeth', he said seriously, 'I have a friend at 218 Falkner Street. I was there only last night. What a small world'. He shook his head, worldly wise.

'I think you'll find you're wrong, Ben', Elizabeth said smoothly, 'It's been empty for two months. Old Mrs Jones' family have been trying to let it after her death'.

'No', said Ben, 'I'm sure that was the number, 218'.

'Yes', said Elizabeth, firmly. 'That's next door, but it's decidedly empty. I was in this morning, collecting the mail to forward on'. Understanding the confusion, she said 'Why don't you come round to give me a hand with the fridge and you'll see that you've probably got the wrong street'. Her eyes gazed frankly at him: serious eyes, overlooking her half-moon glasses. Blue eyes. Ben left the room, confused.

During lunch break he phoned Maria. 'The number you have dialled has not been recognised', came the monotone electronic voice.

'Sorry, we have no Maria Yates listed at that address', the directory enquiry lady replied to his question.

The day wore interminably on. After his last lecture, he hurried to the registrar's office. 'Elizabeth, I'll help you if you want', he volunteered.

'Thanks', she said, 'Come round at six. Hopefully the fridge should arrive on time'. She smiled: a small dry smile of thanks.

* * *

Ben rounded the street corner off the Dock Road just as last night, with the corner newsagent's window blazing brightly out into the drizzle. Above the

162

window he remembered the street name Falkner Street: above the large *Liverpool Echo* sign, proprietor E & L Daly. Thirty yards down the street a large Currys van was parked and two burly figures had just deposited a polythene wrapped box on the pavement; the figure of Elizabeth could be seen signing a chit on the box top.

As Ben approached, the older of the two deliverymen looked up and seeing the glance between Elizabeth and Ben flicked up the tail lift and said cheerily, 'As you've got help, we'll be off then', and a moment later the van was pulling down the street leaving Ben and Elizabeth looking at each other.

With a shrug Ben walked the big box into the house, down the neat floral-patterned hall and into the tiny kitchen where a space had been left by the old one. Elizabeth fussed around him ensuring its corners did not touch her pristine paintwork.

As she busied about Ben could smell a faint rubbery smell, not burnt, but rubbery or plastic. He could not place it and said nothing. Although Elizabeth offered him a cup of tea in thanks, she was hopping uneasily from foot to foot: plainly unaccustomed to strangers, she kept glancing to the crucifix on the wall and her watch.

'I'll be off. Thanks for the tea,' Ben said. 'By the way, could you show me next door; it's been killing me all day'.

'Yes, yes', and she fished the key out of her small brown purse.

'218. Yes, this is it.' His heart was pounding. The smart green door and the brass letters: Ben knew he was right.

Elizabeth put the key in and swung the door open, snapping on the light. A single naked bulb hung from the ceiling illuminating the dingy walls with their faded wallpaper and an ancient dado rail marching into the gloom at the end of the hall. The floor was covered with a hideously patterned carpet of indeterminate age, and the smell of mothballs hung in the air.

Elizabeth looked on with steely eyes as Ben stooped and peeled back the carpet. Yellowing copies of the *Liverpool Echo* covered the dirty floorboards. No wood effect here.

Before Elizabeth could stop him, he darted down the passage. Surely in the front room was a large settee in beige, with an ornamental Chinese rug in front of the gas fire where Maria and he had ... But the room yawned emptily, the old brown stained cupboards either side of the empty fireplace revealed shelves lined with newspaper; the single bulb hung shadeless from the centre of the room.

Elizabeth watched from the door as he swung his head round the room. 'I'd have sworn ...' he said.

'Perhaps it was Falkner Square?' 'Perhaps ...?' She left the question hanging.

'No!' Ben exclaimed. 'The corner shop, the painted door ...' His eyes rose to the ceiling. 'So sorry Elizabeth. I didn't mean to explode, but I am, was, so certain. May I just go upstairs?'

'She was a good friend then?' the question soft, her eyes cool. 'Yes, I ...' But Ben was reluctant to go on. He brushed past Elizabeth and taking the stairs two at a time up the central runner of brown carpet, paused on the tiny top landing. The bed was huge and brass and had a plain white duvet. The lights that had been so bright it was as day. He opened the door and saw nothing. Nothing. Had he dreamt everything, he wondered?

He made his farewells to Elizabeth, who watched him until he turned the street corner, and made his way back to the college. Feeling foolish, he sat at his desk, where the coaster from the 'Star' mocked him with Maria's name and her number. He threw it across the room.

* * *

Days later he had found himself in the Royal Albert Dock, Liverpool dutifully filing past models of the Navy's finest that had been berthed here during the war years as well as merchant ships that had plied the Atlantic in peacetime. He came to the section marked 'Emigration'. Without realising it, he stood in front of the large grainy black and white photograph in which hundreds of grim-faced men, women and children were queueing to board the *Gloucester Castle* bound for New York. 1921: the caption, 'A fresh start, a new challenge' seared his soul.

Sometime later, he could not remember how, he had entered the mobile recruiting office of the British Army on the dockside, where the slogan on the front of the Challenger MkII tank in front of the office read: 'Be the Best'.

The recruiting sergeant had been shuffling his papers preparing to finish the day and realising he had a convert on his hands he raced through the paperwork. 'Which college?' he said.

'Magdalene Theological,' Ben replied.

The sergeant's pen paused briefly, then continued. The name Benjamin Cadogan Mountford once entered in the British Army records ensured things progressed smoothly, and with his indiscretions at school concealed by his approach from the college his ten-week training course at the Pre-Royal Military Academy Sandhurst was confirmed.

* * *

While waiting, he had found himself twice in Falkner Street. On one mid-evening visit, he had thought Elizabeth's curtains had twitched, and he had walked swiftly on. Ben felt that somehow a fragment of his life had been stolen from him: but by whom?

Father Ryan observed his young charge carefully. Having heard from Elizabeth, he assumed Ben's fall off in effort was in some way connected to his 'friend's' mysterious disappearance; and there were occasions when he caught Ben gazing wistfully out of the windows in a semi-trance.

'You know, a calling is a difficult vocation,' Father Ryan told him gently, when he had drawn Ben aside for a quiet chat. 'It is not always one straight road. Sometimes Ben you have to fight your own battles before you can fight the Lord's'.

Ben looked at the pink-faced, earnest priest. 'Father, I feel lost. Perhaps this calling is the wrong one for me.'

'Ben, your family has a long and illustrious history of fighting for right and justice. If you need me, my door is always open'. Patting Ben benignly, he walked away along the corridor.

Ben stared silently after him. The letter in his jacket pocket seemed to radiate heat and he pulled it out. The buff-coloured envelope, addressed to him using his full name, had been handed to him by Elizabeth that morning. He had ignored her quizzical looks and had hastily stuffed it in his jacket. The postmark read Sandhurst and the rear of the envelope bore the motto 'Serve to Lead'.

Back in his room and breathing heavily, Ben tore it open.. 'On behalf of Her Majesty's Government ...' the letter began. A flash of clarity coursed through him: all doubts dispelled in an instant. Within minutes he was packing and not long after he was carrying his holdall down the stairs to knock on Father Ryan's half-open door.

The cleric did not attempt to talk Ben out of going, but made sure Ben knew there was a always place for him when he chose.

Father did ask one thing, 'Could I photocopy your placement to Sandhurst, just for the records?'

'Of course,' Ben said handing the letter to Elizabeth who had silently appeared. As the copy slipped out of the machine in the next room, the blue eyes over the half-moon glasses read the lines. 'Damn, damn, damn', she dug her nails into her palm.

She placed an extra copy under her blotter before taking the original and Father Ryan's copy into his study and the two bade Ben farewell, Father accompanying Ben to the doors.

'Pity about Ben,' said Father, as he and Elizabeth locked up for the night. 'But do you know, I have the oddest feeling we haven't seen the last of him'.

She murmured something polite and slipped away. The library was nearly closing but the single sheet went smoothly through the fax bearing the same 0039 prefix. That, and the confirmation slip, were neatly shredded just as before.

CHAPTER 37

Leaning against the large wheel and enjoying the sun's warmth still radiating from it Ben stared at the envelope Sergeant Walters had given him. That corner of the base was quiet; he was alone, surrounded by the noise of the Belize jungle, smelling the deep rich aromas of life, death, decay. The envelope contained the closing of a chapter of his life. He had signed up for the shortest time, somehow sensing in his rush from Magdalene College that even this was not his ultimate goal.

Ben had just a couple of weeks left in the sortie and week's leave due. Back in the offices he had dialled the UK code, Liverpool area, and instantly the familiar voice of Father Ryan had picked up the phone. 'Good to hear from you Ben,' he had chuckled.

Ten minutes later Ben was streaming down the coast road on an Armstrong courier bike borrowed from the pool. He planned to travel to Guatemala City then leave the bike to be collected before flying out back to the UK.

Sunday evening, 26 April 1998 to be precise, Ben had sought out Sergeant Miguel Faberlé for a last meal in South America before his flight in the morning. Miguel and Helena, his beautiful dark-haired wife, were both serving members of the new Policia Nacional Civil (PNC). Helena had been liaison officer with the tracking team in Belize in an effort to coordinate the two countries' anti-drug operations. Although they had never met, all three were familiar enough to enjoy a superb evening out at a Mayan restaurant in the new Zona Viva area of the city. Mindful of his long flight Ben had bade them farewell outside the restaurant, declining the offer of a taxi to savour the warm night air.

'Don't worry, Helena, Ben can look after himself'. Miguel had looked at Ben. 'Mejor amigo, God be with you'.

Embracing Helena, Ben had turned and walked away, doors closing in his mind behind him. It was late evening and the illuminated façade of the San Sebastián Church seemed to be beckoning him as Ben walked towards it. To the right the large notice board proclaimed the Mass times followed by the preacher for the day.

Bishop Juan Gerardi Conedera had been speaking today. Conedera? That was the name of the author of the human rights report published days before critically naming the army and the paramilitary patrols, or PAC, as being responsible for the worst of the civil rights abuses. Helena and Miguel had discussed it over dinner; Helena nervously agreeing with the report, whilst glancing at her fellow diners. Miguel's approach had been more sang-froid in attempting to understand the military needs to control insurgents. The storm the report had unleashed had left them both voicing concerns for its author.

Seemingly untouchable, and with the full backing of the Catholic Church worldwide, Bishop Conedera had continued to preach openly against the government and its agents, accusing them of corruption and aiding and abetting the international drug trade. In particular he had singled out an army death squad called the Jaguars, whose existence the government vehemently denied.

Heading towards the church, Ben would not have noticed the two young men dressed fashionably in pale, loose tops, dark, baggy trousers and trainers, except for their haste. As he passed the pair, he noted that they were breathing hard and their eyes were flicking nervous glances. Uneasy, he continued and approached the door.

The sharp sweet smell of incense emanated from the open door, bringing back as it always did a host of childhood memories. About to enter, his progress was halted by a scream from the parish house next door. The scream came again, this time an anguished wail. He turned swiftly to the house and noticed the small garage door was open and through it stumbled the figure of a nun; she held her hand out as if it were not hers. It gleamed with a shocking redness. Her eyes locked onto Ben's. In the microsecond it took for her to scream again, Ben's eyes took in the motionless figure at her feet, its deep cream silk robes stained and dark. Her screams echoed through the night as Ben entered the garage. A glance was enough. The skull had been fractured by a single blow that had left the soft contents oozing over the concrete floor.

* * *

The Honda Motorcycle Co of Japan had made so many of the Cub 50cc motorcycles it had recently confessed to not knowing the production figures. Renowned throughout the world for their cheapness and reliability, it was the cough of the foot-operated starter that startled Ben out of the reverie surrounding the tragedy on the floor the garage. The sound of the motor bursting into life carried over the continuing screams of the nun.

Ben whirled and ran through the ranks of anxious church staff approaching the scene. As he pushed past them, the two figures he had seen earlier were mounted on a Honda Cub. The pillion passenger glanced back and his eyes met Ben's just as the heavily laden motorcycle swung round and headed off to the right of the church.

Ben shouted and started to run. He saw that he was gaining on the overladen Cub until, fortunately for them the ground began to slope downwards from the side of the church and the little motorcycle shot out of Ben's reach and continued to pull away.

The crowds were thickening and the motorcyclist was having to weave in and out of angry pedestrians. Keeping them in sight Ben pounded along maintaining a steady rhythm; but it was no use, the two figures on the machine were pulling away, the pillion passenger flashing a grin of defiance.

He was about to give up, when he spotted them swiftly bank to the left. The disappearance of his quarry lent fresh wings to his feet, and he swiftly came on the street where they turned, the sign above, unmistakable in any language, indicated: 'Dead End'.

With his heart and lungs pounding Ben made his way down the centre of the street where walls, high and uninviting, stretched on both sides. The street bent left again, and Ben saw two huge doors in an arch at the end of the road. Outside sat two monks in long brown habits having a smoke under a lantern which illuminated a sign, 'Sons of Sion, Blessed are the Poor'. A monastery! But of the bike, there was no sign.

Ben walked the last twenty yards towards the monks. Taller and of far heavier build than the two on the bike, they looked curiously at Ben, obviously mildly embarrassed at the cigarettes in their hands.

His enquiry, 'Est donde motorcycle señor?' met with a shrug and a blank look. He must have mistaken. The pair would be miles away by now. But walking back to the church amid a rising cacophony of sirens and hooters he suddenly stopped. That was the strangest cigarette smoke he had ever smelt, in fact . . . it was. Yes, it was! Engine exhaust fumes! He was right! The motorcycle had gone down that street.

All his instincts told him, pulled at him, to go back. Then it dawned on him: he had less than six hours left in this country; his flight journey to another life beckoned. So, putting his suspicions behind him, he strode purposefully on back towards the church.

∗ ∗ ∗

Back in his hotel the receptionist had handed him a note to ring Miguel at the PNC. Miguel's direct line rang once before his sultry tones came down the wire, 'Si?'

'Hi', said Ben. 'You rang?' No names, even then conscious of eavesdroppers.
'Have you heard?'... began Miguel.
'I was there', replied Ben. 'I ... There's something I need to tell you'.
'Go on', Miguel', said slowly.
'There were two...' But, was the line sounding hollow? Almost like listening at a seashell. 'Miguel, I'll ring you from the UK', he said firmly.
'OK, Ben, have a good journey'. The line clicked, twice.
Downstairs Magda, the long limbed, dusky receptionist fingered the small cross round her neck. She pushed the phone buttons rapidly, looking furtively round the lobby.
'Sons of Sion, good evening,' came the reply at the other end of the line.

* * *

The next morning Ben caught a cab to the airport, grabbing a paper as he boarded South American Airways flight 405 to Boston, USA. He caught the headlines 'Father Mario Orantes arrested following bishop's murder!' Shaking his head slowly he pushed the newspaper into his baggage and left South America.

After the chaos of the southern continent, Boston's O'Hare's spick and span, gleaming concourse and efficient transit felt like a cold shower. Catching BA 902 to Heathrow Ben could not help being glad to be going home. With Guatemala now behind him, he looked forward to his last night at Hereford's Stirling Lines with the regiment.

* * *

Lieutenant Colonel Parker, CO of B Squadron, turned from the window overlooking the base and motioned to Ben to sit down. 'The regiment will miss you and I suspect the compliment will be returned. Your fight against the dark side is not over but is merely changing; store what you have learnt and use it well'.

Opening a drawer behind his desk, the colonel slid across a small plain business card. On it, engraved in copper plate, was the legend 'George Parker, antique books bought and sold' and a Hereford telephone number. 'If you need me or', his hands spread round the office, 'call anytime'.

Keeping his teeth clamped together, Ben saluted smartly for the last time, strode down the polished corridor and into the sunshine. Fifteen minutes later, in jeans and his Berghaus jacket, he was collected by taxi and driven from the headquarters of 22 SAS for the last time.

CHAPTER 38

'Magdalene College, you say? Yep, I know. Down by the docks. OK, gov'. The cheerful cabby pulled away in a sharp U-turn outside Liverpool station in the wet, gathering gloom of a winter's afternoon.

Eight years, it was not really that long ago, Ben mused, gazing from the steamed-up taxi windows. The grey streets slid by.

'Falkner Street', he said impulsively. 'Falkner Street, do you know that?'

'Mm . . .' came the driver's reply between puffs of a cigarette dangling from the corner of his mouth. 'There's a Falkner Court there now, been up five years I dare say, any good?'

'No' said Ben, but worth a try, he thought, his mind briefly back to Maria. Many times that strange encounter had flashed through his mind and each time he was no wiser.

* * *

The large doors in the old Victorian workhouse were as he had left them, if anything they were even more bereft of paint. Only the sign to the right of the door 'Magdalene College of Theology' was still polished and burnished, inexplicably bringing to mind the swinging sign of the Sons of Sion in Guatemala City.

Father Ryan had lost none of his beaming benevolence. His bald head shone a little more through his tonsure, but his out-flung arms betrayed his genuine delight to see Ben again. 'Older and wiser, eh? Well, I'm sure you have lots to tell us about your adventures. I always said we need more mature entrants: men who have lived, and I mean lived!' he chuckled.

Guiding Ben down the hall, he started to climb the stairs into the gloom. 'Don't I get to meet Elizabeth again, Father?'

'No, no, we have had to let her go,' said Father Ryan seriously. 'The diocese decided we could do our own administration with the help of a small computer. I believe she works for a closed order in Northern Ireland now. Progress I believe it's called,' he said, rolling his eyes and clicking his tongue.

* * *

Ben felt as if he had never been away as he rapidly settled back to college life. A few of the fresh entrants, clones of himself eight years ago, gave him sidelong glares but his easy manner and his confident contributions to the lectures made him a firm favourite. The Star and Garter was still in business, although it had now become the focal point for a brand-new housing estate. Its change to a fake historical interior and memories of Maria meant that Ben avoided group outings there preferring to concentrate on his studies. After the first few weeks, when he had found it difficult to concentrate on the written and classroom work after so long Ben found himself relishing his change of direction. Although he had not realised it at the time, he had studied hard when he had first graced the college and Father Ryan decided he would need little more than a refresher course of eight or nine months before he could pass out as a novice and be seconded to a parish.

The diocese was clearly happy with this arrangement, as vocational calling from UK nationals was running at an all-time low. Ben was made to feel very welcome and special, and he repaid the faith shown in him by attaining top marks month after month.

One afternoon, sitting with Father Ryan in the sparse study, the topic drifted from theological attitudes to various factions within the church. Ben had noticed a lesser degree of contact with the monastery next door and a reluctance on Father Ryan's part to enthuse about it as he used to.

Oddly, when Ben raised the issue, Father Ryan frowned, rose up and crossing the room closed his study door gently. 'Use your skills well and carefully, Ben. Parts of our wonderful Church have no intention of moving into the twenty-first century and would willingly take us back 700 years.' Ben saw an immense sadness cloud his eyes.

Strangely, furtively he glanced at the door. Ben frowned at him. He realised with a start that Father Ryan was petrified.

Pausing for a long moment his mentor took a deep breath. 'Next month, Ben, Bishop Gordon permitting, and of course subject to your final results, the diocese is sending you to your first parish.

'No, no!' he laughed. 'Not the Vatican! Although I doubt it'll be long before they spot you. You'll see!' But nothing Ben could do would persuade him to reveal where he his destination might be. He did, however, tell Ben that his mentor would be one Father Raffique Alambra. Ben's spirits soared: Raffique Alambra, it must be an exotic location!

* * *

The next month simply flew by and, as expected, Ben left Magdalene College with straight 'A's. The investiture ceremony for that year's seminarians in the cathedral at Shrewsbury was full of anxious, proud parents as the assembled hierarchy of the diocese processed glittering and serious down Pugin's nave.

Glancing around as Bishop Gordon blessed the new incumbents, Ben caught a glimpse of his mother and father, and his brother James. His father looked strangely content, whilst his mother dabbed a tear away. James looked proudly at his sibling, no doubt reflecting on their childhood and, up to now, very different paths: the Mountford Way.

CHAPTER 39

Father Raffique Alambra! The name had sent him into paroxysms of fantasies about the whereabouts of his new parish: there wasn't an exotic corner of the world he had not thought about as his possible posting.

A characterisation of Ben's favourite form of transport was that it did not let the occupant have any illusion about the outside weather. Ben's fifteen-year-old ex-RAF air-portable Land Rover rattled and banged over the appalling road, its pathetic wipers seemingly fighting for independence, wholly losing the battle to control the water sluicing down the split-front windscreen. Likewise, inside, the hugely noisy fan completely failed to clear the condensation forming on the interior of the glass. Wedged in his warm flying jacket and his windproof trousers, his ears assaulted, his arms challenged and his backside pummelled, Ben roared with laughter as he made his way across a rain-lashed Donegal to the Parish of St Mary and The Apostles of Burtonport, headed by Father Raffique Alambra – Raffy to his friends – a convert from Islam and a refugee from Iraq.

* * *

The same rain, driving westward off the Atlantic, ran down the large presbytery windows. The view across a grey Gweebarra Bay distorted by streams of water transforming the dark, sullen swells and clouds into a mirage of shapes and movements. Turning from the windows, Father Alambra placed the cup of neat tea back on the saucer and smiled broadly: he had learnt a lot in three years but still could not take tea the Irish way with milk and sugar. No, it would have to be neat tea with a slice of lemon, just a small reminder of home, in a cup and saucer of course.

Home. The smile faded, the eyes grew moist and distant. God helped him, guided him, but no matter. He had welcomed him with opened arms, but even

He could not empty Raffy's memory. On the outside Father Raffique Alambra bore the cosy confidence of the parish priest. At first cautiously, suspiciously, welcomed by the conservative population of fifteen hundred souls in this staunch centre of Christianity he had worked hard for their trust. As a convert he could look back with pride at his achievements. And yet in the quiet times he was there again; back where it everything had changed for him. Back where all this began.

* * *

From his vantage point 115 feet up in the minaret of his local mosque in Halabja, the orange disc of dawn was one finger's width above the dry arid landscape. Raffique had listened to the sounds of dawn: chickens scratching in little pens at the rear of the flat-roofed houses; washing flapping in the slow-moving breeze; the kick of a starter of a moped and the subsequent whine as it passed down the main street out of sight but not out of earshot.

Hakim stood next to him. Tall in his white robes, he threw his head back and in the manner of muezzins the world over called the faithful to prayer, the first of five such calls that day.

As Hakim paused and drew breath after the first verse, Raffique's ears detected another tone, a distant rumbling and squeaking, almost a chorus of dawn sparrows but without their sweet clarity. Losing the sound again as Hakim's chords echoed forth, it was there again as he paused: louder this time. Raffique turned into the early sun feeling the warm breeze on his face. As he shielded his eyes, he saw the waving antennae and long barrels of the Soviet T72 tanks. Following these, just breaking the skyline, he could see numerous towed and self-propelled artillery pieces. His eyes, now sharply focused, in the clear morning light made out the pennants of the elite Republican Guard: Haras al-Iraq al-Jamhuriy.

For some considerable time there had been rumours of Saddam Hussein's murderous pogrom against the Kurds. Raffy saw half a dozen of the self-propelled units come to the forefront of the formation. As if in a trance he saw the flashes from their menacing barrels. Long before the rumbling crack of the salvo reached his ears, in the near distance fountains of dust and debris shot skywards. Instantly the sun and the skyline disappeared in a brown swirling fog. The crack of the salvo caused nearby chickens to erupt in a cacophony of noise, and muffled shouts of alarm could be heard from within sleeping households. All this happened in seconds, and Hakim had started down the flight of over one hundred steps.

For a reason he could not fathom, nor could afterwards, Raffique remained at the balcony of the minaret. The surrounding area was waking rapidly now, and the narrow streets were full of men, women and children heading for the central square; half, no doubt in panic at the gunfire, and half obeying Hakim's summons to prayer. The cloud of dust that had arisen after the explosions now drifted slowly towards Raffique. As he watched, its topmost swirls and clouds were rapidly falling to earth and he realised that he was already above the cloud as it drifted into the neighbourhood.

Raffique had once watched an American baseball game in which the crowd had demonstrated the 'Mexican wave' – a ripple of human movement swirling round the stadium like the current flowing down a stream. Now, the villagers furthest from the mosque and nearer the brown cloud started their own 'Mexican wave'. In a macabre dance, their hands flew to their throats: turning round and sagging to their knees they slowly toppled silently into the dust.

None moved. The effect spread across the square. The quicker-witted ones saw the approaching wave of collapsing villagers and ran away as fast as they could. Presently the square turned into a mass of humanity trying to flee down the narrow lanes either side of the mosque. But the brown fog, by now no more than two or three metres high, rolled on relentlessly, silently enfolding them. Before the fog there had been the sounds of rising human panic: after the fog there was silence. Complete silence.

Horror-struck, Raffique had stepped back into the shadows of the top of the minaret. There he remained, rooted to the spot. Eventually, harsh guttural military commands broke the silence. As he peered through the balustrades, he could see soldiers advancing with full face masks and respiratory systems. After they had kicked and rolled over a few bodies they started removing these now that the brown cloud had dissipated and began methodically looting the bodies and buildings of the square. Below, Raffique could hear boots being kicked off and the thud of knees on the mosque carpet as the killers came to morning prayer. Guiltily he too fell to his knees.

As a student under his mullahs at the University of Baghdad, Raffique had been intrigued by the Westernisation, or Christianisation, of God's word. Stunned and in state of profound shock following the events he had just witnessed devastating his home and everyone he knew in it, he prayed now to Allah using the words of one of his prophets: Jesus, son of Mary, 'Allah forgive them for they know not what they do'. Sensing safety in the minaret, Raffy had stayed there all day as various army units came and went, and lorries laden with loot from the ransacked shops and houses pulled away, grinding heavily up the slope out of the square.

Now in the safety of his study in Ireland, as the Atlantic threw its worst at the windows of the presbytery, he decided that it was the moment he saw one of the mullahs from his university days surveying the carnage with the local commander of the Republican Guard that he had to go – and not simply leave Halabja and his homeland, but abandon the faith in which he had been raised: Islam.

That single defining moment transcended the following weeks of evasion and risk as he travelled overland to Turkey and then to Italy, and the Vatican to seek succour and help from the most powerful church in the world.

Raffy was surprised at the ready acceptance that greeted him as he was absorbed into the workings of the Vatican. Initially, he pursued his goal of obtaining assistance for his fellow countrymen in exile. However, not many months had gone by before he found himself becoming absorbed by the history and teachings of the Catholic Church. Inclined to be studious, he was to be found in his flowing Arab thawb at all hours in the Vatican archives. Bemused priests would exchange glances and mutter comments seeing the robed figure hunched over library desks.

Eight months after arriving in Rome, Raffique travelled to the outskirts of the city. Taking off his flowing thawb he put it on the ground poured lighter fluid over it and lit it. That same day Monsignor Albertoli, Raffique's mentor, was pleased to accept his request to join the holy Roman Church as a convert and priest. Three years later, Raffy was in this north-west corner of Ireland leading a small, thriving parish, with only his olive complexion and dark eyes betraying any hint of his past life.

CHAPTER 40

Father Raffique Alambra proved an easy taskmaster for Ben. Brought up under the rule of the Koran, in one of the three Abrahamic faiths in which Judaism and Christianity were of considerably lower importance, Raffy struggled deeply with the largely Christian notion of democracy. Indeed, up to the late 1890s there was no Arabic term for it. In Islam, power belongs only to God. The man who exercises that power on earth is the Caliph. The Koran is the divine word of God thus immutable and protected from distortion and corruption for ever. In his previous life the mullah's word literally carried the power of life or death. Sometimes, Raffy yearned for the certainty of Islam when faced with the more benign democracy of parish affairs, but he was content to let his young charge take over some of his more mundane duties. Ben effectively became his manager when it came to running the running the parish, as Raffy slipped into the more scholarly aspects of a priest's life. But, when Ben's workload increased sharply, it caused him an occasional flicker of frustration to find Raffy in the study surrounded by history and catechisms of the Catholic faith.

* * *

It had become a habit of Ben's to slip down to Maggie's Bar on the sea front on a Sunday night. Since this was an accepted habit of the Irish priesthood, no eyebrows were raised when the priest was to be found supping Guinness and enjoying a game of darts. One particular Sunday night in April, Ben had stayed beyond midnight at Maggie's being regaled by Pat O'Connor, the local Garda officer, about the antics of the IRA in these parts. Ben listened politely, hinting only at a minor military background before joining the priesthood, and others joined their conversation.

'Anyways Pat, it shouldna be the Republicans you're after', remonstrated Seamus, 'What about that bunch in the monastery at Dungloe?'

'If you ask me,' he said – no one did, but he continued anyway – 'It's a weird set up, mark my words.'

'Now, Seamus, don't you go worrying our new priest, with your scaremongering. You're just jealous you get no work on the building out of them,' retorted Pat.

'I've told you; it's not just me,' Seamus replied, part of the head of an indeterminate number of pints of Guinness forming a comical cream moustache above his upper lip. 'You talk to Dr Daly. He's never been there. O'Malleys, the funeral parlour: they've never been called. Only the postman goes regular, and he never gets past the gate. I tell you, it's not right'.

Later Ben weaved gently up the hill to the presbytery. The spring air was soft and cool off the ocean and against the few lights of the village the stars shone brightly. He was utterly content and at peace. Seeing the study light on when he got back, he popped his head round the door.

His entry was silent and he obviously disturbed Raffy, who started nervously. 'It's only me', laughed Ben. What are you reading?'

'Oh nothing really,' Raffy said, moving another book over the open volume.

The movement was not lost on Ben, who sauntered across the room chatting easily. 'What's the problem with the monastery in Dungloe? Seamus hasn't a good word for them.'

Raffy's eyes flickered towards his research volumes on his desk. 'Oh. You know, these villagers, someone will have upset them in the past and they never forget'. Then, smiling openly at Ben, he suggested, 'A nightcap, perhaps?'

'That would be nice,' but while Raffy poured generous measures into two tumblers, Ben quickly looked at what he had been reading and his eyes took in the words 'Prieuré de Sion and the Pope ... '.

The two priests clinked glasses and sipped their contents. 'Sometimes you know Ben,' Raffy said, 'we have to rise above our flock's day to day concerns'.

'I know, I know'.

'I shouldn't worry about the monastery, Ben. These Sons of Sion are a closed order and many people don't comprehend that'.

'Mm, yes. I suppose you're right. Anyway, cheers'. The two men chattered amiably until Ben said 'Good night' and left. As he went out of the door Raffy once again was seated at the desk hunched over his volumes. Thoughtfully Ben climbed the stairs.

* * *

Several days later, Ben's day off was being taken up by settling the presbytery's domestic bills in the shops of Burtonport. Lost in his thoughts, he stood behind a small, well-built lady with scraped back hair. As the queue shuffled slowly forward Ben idly watched her. She finished her banter with the assistant in O'Malley's and turned to leave the warm, steamy bakery As she did so her eyes met Ben's and locked onto them momentarily before she dropped her gaze and scuttled rapidly out of the door, leaving him with the image of half-moon spectacles and blue eyes of an intensity Ben hadn't seen for many years – hadn't seen, in fact, since before he had joined the army.

The last piece of logic clicked into place like the mechanism of a giant clock.

'Keep it,' Ben told the astonished assistant as he dropped an over-generous note on the glass counter as he set off after the woman.

The blonde scraped back hair was seventy-five yards up the street and moving rapidly. Ben crossed the road and followed on the opposite pavement. Periodically the woman turned her head but did not see Ben on the other side. From her gait and manner, she seemed to be talking animatedly; possibly into the new kind of portable telephone that was fast becoming all the rage.

When the woman ended the conversation, she looked around one more time and then did a curious thing. Twisting what Ben now saw was indeed a mobile phone, she removed the battery and dropped this discreetly in a convenient waste bin. She did the same with the body of the phone a further twenty yards on and then stood waiting at the nearby the bus stop.

Ben ducked into an estate agent's window and was browsing the properties from behind the window when the bus to Dungloe pulled up. When it drew away, the woman was gone.

Crossing the road swiftly and feeling slightly foolish, Ben went to the first waste bin and retrieved the battery case: the second receptacle revealed the phone. He jammed them both into his pocket and headed back the presbytery.

That night at Maggie's Bar the conversation was interrupted by the bleep of someone's mobile phone, to loud choruses of dismay the unfortunate owner embarrassedly answered it.

'Do many of those get pinched around here?' Ben asked Pat O'Connor in what he hoped was a nonchalant tone.

'Now that's a funny thing, you're asking. There didn't used to be: the coverage isn't so clever around here. But I've four phones at the station been handed in by various folk and the last number dialled always begins the same'.

'Go on', said Ben.

'Well, the code is 0039', said Pat triumphantly.

'And?' Ben said.

'That's Italy! So, our thief must be Italian,' concluded Pat with devastating logic.

* * *

The next day Ben was sitting in the presbytery study reading the front page of the *Catholic Voice*. The headline ran 'John Paul II to receive Alvaro Arzu, president of Guatemala' and the date was 22 April, 1999.

Ben's thoughts cast back twelve months to that fateful night. He had heard some details from his friend Miguel in the PNC. The crime apparently remained unsolved, but a priest had been taken into custody. Casting his eyes down the typewritten columns he noted that Arzu was to visit Cardinal Angelo Godano. As he reached that sentence the door behind him opened softly and Raffy walked in. Glancing at the headlines Ben was reading, he muttered something under his breath before standing with his back to the fire, slowly shaking his head.

Ben took the cue, and asked, 'Raffy, what's the matter?'...

He had barely finished when Raffy answered furiously, 'Ben your – I mean our – church is not ...

'What I mean is, if you ever go to Rome just be very careful', he finished lamely.

'Raffy, what on earth are you talking about?' Ben asked, bemused by the passion in Raffy's voice.

'Ben, when I was in Rome I was approached by all sides at the court of John Paul II and believe me there are some people you don't wish to meet. Godano is one.'

'Don't be daft, Raffy. There are always different opinions . . .' but he didn't finish.

'Opinions, yes! But this is a war!'

'Bit strong, that, Raffy, isn't it?' said Ben.

Raffy didn't answer but instead reached for an elderly volume on his desk. As the large pages fell open under Raffy's careful fingering, Ben, who was peering over his shoulder, became aware of the book's musty odour, and the wafer-thin sheets of fine tissue protected its colour plates of Renaissance paintings.

Raffy turned the pages carefully and then stopped as he gently removed the aged tissue paper to reveal the picture beneath in its full glory. On the right-hand side, in twelfth-century robes the figure of Urban II was seated on mighty oak throne with the twin towers of the cathedral at Clermont behind him. Brilliant light streamed from the heavens around the pope. In his right hand he held his mitre using it to point to the lower left side of the canvas. In front of Urban was amassed a fantastic array of horsemen and soldiers, each faithfully wearing the cotton singlet and cross patée of the first Crusades. In the foreground were pictured the mayhem, riotous colours and ethnic backgrounds of the armies of Saladin. The painting, noted Ben, was widely attributed to Van Eyck: the court artist to Philip the Good of Burgundy, who had also completed the well-known Ghent altarpieces at the cathedral of the same name. Ben instantly understood the thrust of the painting: there was the Pope directing his forces to crush the Islamic infidel led by a fearful Saladin.

The two men studied the painting in silence, but when Ben was about to speak, Raffy put his forefinger to his lips and crossed to the windows, peering into the blackness. Then he swiftly drew together the heavy drapes. With the windows now blanked out, he closed and locked the door.

Ben looked quizzical and Raffy walked back to the open volume on the desktop, where he covered the left half of the painting with a sheet of paper, leaving the image of Urban II on his throne pointing at the room with his mitre.

'That picture, or a copy, hangs in the Magdalene College,' he exclaimed.

'And the original is in the Vatican', continued Raffy. 'When I was in Rome undergoing conversion, many people sought my counsel. One day I was introduced to a group calling itself the Priory of Sion. At the time I was still of the Islamic faith, you understand.

'I was taken, blindfolded, to which part of the city I know not. Once in their chambers, the painting you see half-covered was at one end of the corridor. The story goes that when the two original halves of this painting are reunited, so Islam will fall and Urban will have his final victory'.

Ben's eyes met Raffy's. Long moments passed, each alone in his thoughts and respective backgrounds.

Now it was Ben's turn with the paper, which he pulled away and tilted the small desk light full onto the book. Its message leapt down the centuries. Urban's eyes seemed to blaze, and the shaft of light, depicted in silver and gold, illuminated his crown and robes. His Crusaders' task was to crush the Infidel and they did it with his blessing. Ben remembered from his studies that a plenary indulgence was granted to all who undertook the journey 'pro sola devotione' ('For devotion alone'); and the 'Truce of God' was extended to those who wore the cross patée.

Ben stooped and in the stillness of that Irish presbytery read the caption on the painting: 'Let them turn their weapons dripping with the blood of their brothers against the enemy of the Christian Faith. Let them – oppressors of orphans and widows, murderers and violators of churches, robbers of the property of others, vultures drawn by the scent of battle, let them hasten, if they love their souls, under their captain Christ, to the rescue of Sion'.

'There was a Monastery of Sion in Guatemala,' he told Raffy without elaborating.

'Yes, and here too', Raffy said.

The silence that followed was interrupted by the soft rattle of the letterbox in the outer hall.

'Ah, well', said Ben. 'Back to reality. That'll be someone dropping in the rota for church cleaning!'

Behind the heavy front door lay a small buff envelope inside which a single sheet of paper read: 'Dear father Raffique and Father Benjamin, Would you do me the honour of the reading and gospel at our Mass on Sunday next?' The address at the top read 'Priory of the Sons of Sion, Dungloe.'

Ben passed it to Raffy, with the comment, 'Well, we'll get some answers now!'

'Hm', Raffy replied and returned to his desk indicating that the conversation was over.

One thought did occur to Ben, though: why both of them? Militarily that was wrong.

'Don't be silly Ben, we're talking about the priests going to a monastery,' he told himself.

CHAPTER 41

The breeze from the south-east that had favoured Talib from sunset faded as silently as it had began. In the lee of the island of Bubiyan situated in the northern Persian Gulf, the only warning was the receding slap of the bow waves. For a moment the motionless figure at the helm did nothing, before shaking himself from the reverie of the star-filled sky above and moving forward swiftly to the halyards supporting the big triangular lateen sail. Its dirty folds landed on the deck with a soft rumble to be wrapped up with a length of hemp. With several grunts, Talib kicked aside the mounds of silver fish he had kept on the deck and, fumbling in the slippery warm blackness, he slid back the heavy cover revealing a dark hole into the bowels of the dhow, from which arose a faint mechanical, oily smell mingled with that of rancid fish. He felt around under the coaming and the small hold was suddenly illuminated by the soft light from small fluorescent tubes beneath his feet, so arranged that it was only visible from directly overhead.

Shutting one eye to preserve some of his night vision, Talib nimbly slithered down into the small hot space. His sandalled feet landed in five inches of dark, fetid bilge water, and he leant forward to the large tarpaulin-covered lump in the centre of the boat. With its cover off this was not just an engine. Oh no, this was 'One of the finest most reliable engines ever made', as Michael would have said. Not that a casual glance would reveal that; for it was red with rust and streaked with black rivulets where its very blood had leaked out, or so it seemed. The myriad of pipes and cables and pulleys attached to it were festooned with old rags, wrapped round many times, held in place by crude lengths of wire twisted into knots.

Talib surveyed it for a moment then leant forward to an ancient control panel on the bulkhead in front of the engine. His finger stabbed at the large button that was once green but now hid behind layers of fish scale and grease. The large starter motor whirred for a second. The engine caught and steadied into a deep purr. Watching the rev counter hover steadily Talib turned and lithely leapt back on deck, switching off the light and pulling the hatch cover in place in one practised movement.

The beat of the engine could barely be heard. He nodded to himself, and his mouth pressed into a self-satisfied grimace. Resuming his place at the stern he pushed the small hand throttle forward a notch heading the boat once again towards the flat open lands to the east of Bubiyan. The next two weeks would see success or failure. Navigating the Shatt al-Arab waterway at dead of night was not for the faint-hearted. If he could avoid the countless wrecks sunk in the Iraq–Iran war and avoid the two countries' patrol boats equipped with radar, heavy machine guns and the penchant to use them, then all he had to do was sail into Bandar Abbas Iranian naval base to sell his contraband. Simple, really. He leaned against the teak gaff rail and softly hummed a tune feeling the faint vibration beneath his feet as the chords of the 'The Rose of Tralee' coursed softly in his throat.

CHAPTER 42

He had been one of ten born to Betty and Louis in the small town of Burtonport, in north-west Ireland thirty-five years ago. By the time he had come along his arrival was acknowledged by the need for Louis to repair more televisions and radios, in order to support yet another hungry mouth and pay the bar bill at Caseys on the harbour front. At sixteen, tiring of kicking footballs through the church windows in an effort to emulate Best and Keegan, he had run away. Not intentionally, you understand, but he had somehow forgotten to get off the bus as it drove through the town after visiting his favourite uncle at the mysterious Sons of Sion monastery. In the way of families, he had perhaps a closer bond to his uncle than his father. The beat of the engine in the old AEC Routmaster had somehow willed him to stay aboard, so three hours later when it pulled in the depot behind the Shankill Road the bus driver was bemused to find a tired, hungry Thomas O'Neil in a world he found unfamiliar and new.

Saun Daly had felt sorry for the lad and taken him to his two-up-two-down in Rafferty Street, where his girlfriend, Mary, who had never had children, had immediately taken a shine to Thomas. In a trice he was in a hot bath downstairs, while his only clothes spun and clanked in the electric dolly tub in the scullery. After that he had been clad in one of Saun's heavy woollen shirts that all but drowned him and as presented with a large plate of steaming liver and onions that he wolfed down. After two days of unlimited hospitality Saun introduced his new-found-son to Michael at the Belfast and Western Ireland Bus Company.

Michael (Thomas never did find out his surname) was in charge of maintenance for the seventy-four buses and coaches parked in the depot. When they were not being used as barricades or burnt for entertainment, they provided a much-needed service for both communities. Most of the depot's workforce were of the Catholic faith and, from time to time, furtive men in jeans and parkas would board the bus glancing suspiciously round as each and every passenger quickly covered their face.

As he had with Saun, Thomas quickly found an easy rapport with Michael who seemed to spend his entire life in oily overalls, wiping his hands on an equally oily rag and tutting over the engines in his charge. Thomas suspected that the hearts of the seventy-four buses and coaches were a surrogate family for Michael, and he quickly learned to distinguish the two engines in the depot: the deeper, throatier Gardner 680, and the purr of the AEC Routemaster.

'Clean air, clean fuel, and clean oil: last for ever,' Michael used to mutter when, yet another smoking bus pulled into the depot, its terrified driver casting glances around for Michael's presence. Michael would wait for the hapless driver to descend before marching him to his office. Doors slammed, voices were raised, and the driver never saw the cab of a bus in Belfast again. Michael would then stay after work, locked in the large echoing hangar with Thomas until the huge diesel was once more running sweet and true. Then and only then would he drop Thomas off at Saun's house with a muttered, 'Don't be late in the morning' as dawn streaked the sky.

Occasionally, Thomas noted, a bus would pull in the depot and drive through to the yard at the back where the scrap buses and spare mechanical parts were stored: that was particularly the case with runs from Newry and Armagh. These were also the only times the buses were locked out of the depot.

One evening Michael was frustrated at an AEC 7.7 and curtly told Thomas, 'Bugger off, lad, and make a brew'. While the kettle boiled Thomas had wandered in the silence towards the doors leading the yard. For no good reason he had put his eye to a chink in the small access door. The yard outside was bathed in the full silvery glow of moonlight; only the dark shadows between the long dead buses remained impenetrable.

Suddenly he tensed and pressed his forehead harder to the chipped woodwork. Three figures appeared ethereally on the top of the high brick wall and jumped down onto an oil storage tank. Silently and confidently, they made their way to the rear of the 595 to Newry, its destination board visible in the moonlight. Swiftly kneeling at one of the side access panels, the leader of the group took out a small silver key. Thomas knew the purpose of this key: on certain vehicles, he had to ask Michael for the access key for the small panel.

But every time, Michael had put down the item he was working on to explain, 'These keys are tricky', before brushing off Thomas' request.

Now the leader had the panel open and was reaching in quickly. The next thing Thomas saw was him handing the other two four parcels about fifteen inches long and wrapped in what looked like heavy greased paper. Then, as silently as they arrived, the trio melted into the shadows over the oil tank and were gone.

The rising crescendo of the kettle's steam whistle drew him back inside only to run smack into the firm figure of Michael who gripped his collar and lifted him effortlessly up the door. For what felt like minutes, Michael held him fully twelve inches off the floor. Thomas' vision began to cloud, and he beat his hands against the panelling until the mist began to clear from Michael's eyes and he slowly let the lad slide down the door. But from that moment it was as if Thomas had stepped through a portal to a secret world.

Slowly he began to notice the sub-culture of the depot; how certain mechanics only appeared on Friday afternoons, their clothes conspicuous by the absence of oil stains, to collect their wages from Pat in the small glass-fronted office. One afternoon the three-fifteen to Antrim was about to pull out when Michael frantically flagged it down and indicated to the driver that he should wait, totally ignoring the driver impatiently tapping his wristwatch. Five minutes passed when into the depot ran a lithe figure clutching his bloodstained left arm. At Michael's bidding he rolled swiftly into the large access panel at the rear of the bus and the vehicle duly rolled out of the garage. Minutes later two British Army armoured Land Rovers squealed to a halt in front of the doors and disgorged grim-faced soldiers. The ensuing search revealed nothing: the icy stare of the young officer returned with equanimity by the silent staff.

Gradually, then, Thomas was sucked into the everyday activities of the 'RAH' as the IRA was known. Thomas was a quick learner, and he had a natural affinity with engines of the stolen getaway cars, coaxing them to life often with no more than his penknife and a length of wire. What the vehicles were used for he had scant idea. He rarely read newspapers or listened to the media. His life comprised work at the bus depot, running nefarious errands for the RAH and his social life. Of his parents and siblings in Burtonport there was scant contact or thought.

One Friday, after an unexpected early finish, he was in O'Tooleys Bar on Derry Street with two or three of the drivers. The evening was warm and light, and the craic was flowing. It was Thomas' weekend off and he was looking forward to going fishing with Saun in the morning. Kieran stood up and announced he was having an early night, and his daughter had come to collect him. Making her way towards them across the crowded bar was one of the most beautiful girls Thomas had ever seen. Seizing the moment, he sprang up and awkwardly offered her a drink. Her cool grey eyes appraised him for a second, her lips compressed in a faint smile. Then, equally coolly she declined his offer, and linking her father's arm in her own she left the bar.

With dogged determination, Thomas found out that they worshipped at St Theresa's off the Shankill Road. To the amusement of Saun and Mary, who had tried unsuccessfully to encourage him to go to Mass, Sunday mornings now found Thomas scrubbed and suited and sitting dutifully in the back row of St Theresa's. On the second Sunday, she noticed him and by the eighth Sunday he had a date.

Kieran, her father, was a widower having lost his wife to a premature detonation of an RAH bomb some six years before. He was fiercely protective of Clodagh and if it had not been for Thomas working at the bus depot, he doubted he would have been allowed to see her. As it was, Kieran accepted Thomas but remained defensive and faintly aggressive towards him. For her part, Clodagh was a vivacious companion and as long as their social life was conducted within the confines of St Theresa's social club and O'Tooles, everybody was happy.

After a while Thomas worked out that every Sunday afternoon Kieran left the house for the bowling green at two o'clock, he seldom returned before seven. With an eye on Kieran's door from the corner of the social club, Clodagh and Thomas would watch as the clock chimed two, whereupon Kieran would exit the little terraced house holding his brown, polished leather bowls bag to set off down the street. Minutes later the couple were in the house and upstairs.

Thomas was a comparative novice but Clodagh, a year or two older, was no beginner. As the 'Sunday sermons'– as the pair laughingly described them – progressed, it became a game to invent new parts of the house that they would make love in, or on. From the kitchen to the scullery, to the hall floor. One room at the rear of the house remained closed, however. Thomas raised the question as he bent Clodagh over the banisters for the third time.

Immediately her body tensed and she expelled him. Then, she quickly scooped and collected her clothes before running, goddess-like, downstairs. 'That was me ma's room before the bastards in the RAH blew her up. Dad keeps all her things in there.' The tears coursed down her cheeks while Thomas held her.

Presently she paused stock still as if making her mind up. Looking at him in the crook of his arm, she asked, 'Would you help me nail those bastards, Thomas?'

'I don't know how I could,' he replied, surprised.

'Come on, that depot's up to its eyes in it,' she said directly. 'My dad's always been for them up to six years ago, now . . .' and she let the sentence hang.

Then followed an amazing transformation, as she mounted Thomas on the floor and, climaxing again, she bent to his ear and whispered, 'I'll pay'.

All that week he could think of nothing else. Initially he was strong and resolved to tell Michael. Several times he walked purposefully across the garage to unburden his secret and each time as he opened his mouth he failed. Later in the week as Sunday approached, a different pressure came to bear from his trousers. By the following Sunday he had given in.

Her organisational skills surprised him, among them arranging for a savings account to be opened in his name on the Isle of Man. Curiously, all the documents and forms relating to that came via her: not one item arrived in the post at his home with Saun and Mary.

Two Sunday's later Clodagh gave him a folded piece of paper. It was a bank statement bearing his name at the top; but his heart nearly missed a beat when he looked at the balance and saw there was £1,000 in it – twice his monthly wage. His lips went dry as he looked at Clodagh.

'Tell me what goes on at the depot and it's that per week.' She smiled, but her eyes remained cool and watchful.

Thomas licked his lips and swallowed. She made up his mind for him when she loosened her top button.

At first he was terrified, but gradually as each week passed, he realised all he had to do was to tell Clodagh a potted version of the preceding week's events before they could tumble upstairs to bed. And so it continued, for three long years.

After twelve months, unbelievably, Clodagh asked Kieran if Thomas could move in, and to their amazement he agreed. The arrangement caused a few raised eyebrows at St Theresa's and much ribald comment at the garage, but Thomas was such a valuable worker, and under Michael's wing, that nobody dared question his domestic arrangements.

Over this period, Thomas became increasingly involved in the smuggling of cigarettes and alcohol from the south of the border. He was fortunate in that one weekend on a trip to Newry with Michael, he had collected a crate of ex-Nato 5.56 x 4.5mm ammunition and two stolen Heckler & Koch SA80s. On the way back, they had stopped so that Michael could take Thomas to a small wood to demonstrate one of the weapons. Thomas' attempt at handling and firing the gun nearly killed both of them and thereafter Michael would gently steer requests from the 'active' members of the brigade away from getting Thomas involved. 'No, no, you don't understand,' he would chuckle. 'Leave him to his engines'.

CHAPTER 43

Judging from Michael's demeanour at the garage, the struggle had been going badly lately. One month he had lost five buses to hijacking by the UDA. It was becoming well known that the green and yellow buses represented a major IRA lifeline and it was merely a matter of time before the security forces became involved. Strangely, the buses the UDA seemed to hijack were all carrying valuable contraband of one form or another. And then it was only a matter of time before Thomas's world changed for ever.

He was humming 'The Rose of Tralee' as he walked across the darkened depot towards Michael's office one evening: a beacon of light against the dark green and yellow shapes. Without pausing he swung the door open to find Michael at the filing cabinet with his back to him. 'I'm off home Mike,' he said easily, 'Fancy one in O'Tooles?'

'Nah, you get off,' said Michael without turning round. 'Oh, Thomas, pass me that piece of paper on the desk, would you?'

Thomas stepped forward in the light and collected the A4 sheet in his thumb and oily forefinger. Then he stopped. In fact, his life stopped at that moment. He saw he was holding a copy of the bank statement Clodagh had been in the habit of giving him. Only this was a full list of all the credits going to the account in his name at the Isle of Man Bank, in Douglas. At the bottom a neat total revealed £152,000 in credit.

That was when Michael turned, the Beretta 9mm dwarfed in his hand.

Thomas stepped back involuntarily only to gasp as a hard steel barrel rammed into his skull, behind his left ear. 'Saving to get married, me boy?' said Michael, his eyebrows raised but his eyes, once genial, were black and cold.

Behind him Thomas could hear footsteps and a dragging, shuffling noise. Two of the many roof arc lights came on with the customary crackle and hum. The gun barrel in his left ear became a kick in the shins, as hard hands spun him and escorted him from the office.

In the centre of the dark depot twin pools of light illuminated a four-wheel dolly trailer, its bed of rough timber scarred with years of work. It sat on two sturdy axles that had solid rubber wheels of at least a foot in diameter. On the small trailer two hooded figures stood, one a female from her torn stockings and only shoe, the other, from his uniform trousers an employee of the bus depot. From their necks, looped in bright silver against the blackness ran nooses of the fine steel cable that was used to repair the large handbrakes of the older buses. Behind them in the soft shadows stood six masked figures.

Michael pushed past Thomas, his hard shoulder betraying his contempt. Striding purposefully to the two figures he stepped up onto the dolly causing it to sway and making the two figures gasp. With a swift brutal movement, the hoods were ripped away, making Thomas sag against his captor, fighting for air and retching violently.

Keiran stood stoically and only identified by his tousled grey hair that betrayed the dull yellow of a habitual smoker: his brutally beaten face was unrecognisable. Clodagh's on the other hand had been left unmarked, which made her pale desperate features seeking Thomas all the more unbearable. Her blouse had been torn off leaving one proud breast jutting forward. Her stockings had been left in tatters. While the fresh cigarette burns on her chest glistened with the tears that coursed down her face to drip from her nose and chin.

Both of their arms had been tied around their upper body at the elbows leaving their wrists flat against their thighs. Silently from behind the captives, a hooded figure stepped forward. Moving swiftly behind Keiran with his right hand, he produced a thick iron bar, and with a short vicious stroke smashed it sideways into each of Kieran's wrists. The crack of the bones could be heard across the depot. His screams masked the same treatment dealt to Clodagh.

The same masked man then sliced the bindings of the two figures, so they cradled their smashed wrists in front of them. Kieran sagged to the dolly floor only to be brought up sharply by the silver noose. Wildly he struggled on his two feet, the agony of his flapping wrists contorting his face. Clodagh stepped to one side and using her thigh steadied her father.

Meanwhile, Michael had turned to face Thomas. 'What intrigued us was that he never went to the grave, Thomas. You know the story: a loyal soldier's wife blown up in a terrible accident. But we never found a grave, and we never found where he came from. It seems that our friend Kieran and sweet little Clodagh go back no further than seven years. But to be fair, Thomas, it wasn't us that found them. Never let your old landlady wash your clothes if you leave valuables in them,' and he let the statement from the bank flutter to the floor.

'You're lucky, Thomas. You're just a grass. We shoot grasses, simple really. But officers of the British Army. Well ...'

He left that sentence unfinished. From his waistband he took a Browning army-issue revolver and sauntering up to the pair on the dolly, he paused in front of Kieran. With the muzzle pressed to his right kneecap, the shot and Kieran's scream came as one. Without pause he moved to Kieran's left kneecap and pulled the trigger again.

The effect was immediate: Kieran's heavy body sagged on his shattered joints. The noose became a rigid silver line, perpendicular from the darkness above as he danced and jigged his life away. It took several minutes. Clodagh stood, her shoulders shaking, head slumped in defeat.

Silence returned. Michael turned, gun in hand and came to Thomas. Standing in front of him he snapped the chamber left and ejected two cases. Their innocuous polished brass reflecting in his coarse hands. Clicking the chamber shut he reversed the weapon and pushed it to Thomas' chest, telling him, 'Do it and you live'.

Thomas' chest contracted. A band of steel crushed his breath. Past Michael's cold eyes he could see the dangling figure next to Clodagh. She stood proud now staring at him, her face expressionless. With the heavy Browning dangling at his side, Thomas walked towards the pool of light. His eyes never left hers, as the gun became heavier with each step.

He reached the dolly. Her knees, so fresh and pink, shone from the tattered dullness of her stockings. Behind, Thomas could see seven pairs of jean- and overall-clad legs, a gun or two in relaxed hands and half their upper bodies.

Michael spoke slowly from the blackness, 'Either her or her and you. You choose.'

Seconds dragged out. Each sound of the depot was magnified in Thomas' mind: the loose roof board in the light breeze and the gentle hiss of the compressor. He started to turn to Clodagh, his grip becoming firmer as he lifted the weapon.

When he was a child at school, his old form mistress at St Levine in Burtonport used to delight in lining through his work with red biro: 'Can do better' she would scrawl. Now red lines appeared in the dark connecting each member of Michael's brigade to different locations high up and around the garage. Each line ended in a red dot on each man's head.

Michael sauntered forward unaware of the dancing addition to his forehead: the dot moved with him. Standing full in the light and drawing on his habitual cigarette, from which the smoke momentarily highlighted the red beam, his right hand moved towards the Beretta tucked in his waistband. Without warning the small red dot on his forehead disappeared instantaneously, to be replaced by another that seemed to grow and leak red. Stone dead, Michael began to crumple.

'British Army. Lay down your weapons,' rang out a metallic megaphone order.

One figure at the end of the line of hooded men started to kneel and put his weapon down. Not so the others and the crash of gunfire that followed was deafening. Bullets ricocheted and whined, and the men's moans and screams filled the blackness. It was an unequal battle.

'Hold your fire,' bellowed a young, commanding voice.

But a new and terrifying noise was now replacing the deadly staccato of the automatic weapons. Ricocheting bullets had found the paint store next to Michael's office and the building was filling with black, acrid smoke. Rolling behind the dolly in the confusion, Thomas made his way quickly under the large workbenches lining the rear wall. It was completely black, but he knew of a space in front of the wall in which he could scurry the length of the depot behind various spare engines. The roar of flames was becoming louder as he found his way to the door into the waiting room. It was the only room with an unbarred window and without hesitation, holding the heavy weapon in front as a ram, he hurled himself through the window.

Thomas landed lightly and, trying to ignore the pain in his glass-slashed shoulders, he was back at Clodagh's house in moments. He had to gamble that the events at the garage had taken care of Michael's cronies and inside four minutes he had thrown his clothes into a rucksack, collected his bank statements from under the floorboards near his bed, and was out of the front door, ahead of the first armoured Land Rover seventy-five yards away, when it came careering round the bend.

The first ferry the next morning carried a single figure spending his journey at the rails watching Ireland slip below the horizon. After calling at Douglas on the Isle of Man, the ship reached Liverpool one passenger short.

CHAPTER 44

Lieutenant Al Zubair swung lightly up the steel stairwell to the open bridge. Nodding curtly to the figure at the wheel, he began his watch. It was only after Mansur, the helmsman, had clattered down the bridge ladder that he exhaled slowly. The night was black with a rich velvety intenseness. Slowly, he let the breeze from the way of the ship steady his senses. Glancing round, he took out his silver cigarette case and extracted a half-smoked cigarette, which he lit and placed gently next to a protruding bolt, where its smoke wafted freely. Then, after a second check that he was alone, he furtively opened the rear of his cigarette case and took out a far more compact, perfectly shaped Marlboro, which he ran under his nose, almost as if savouring a fine cheese. 'At last, a decent smoke,' he thought.

Lieutenant Al Zubair was a rising star in the Iranian navy at Abadan. Although he would indignantly deny it, the lower decks knew it was because his uncle, General Saeed Izadi, was a Commander of the Quds Force in the Islamic Revolutionary Guards Corps or IRGC. Here on the bridge in the middle watch, Al Zubair could wallow in his most private thoughts. He dared not speak it, but he knew that the stories from his uncle and from the Iranian state radio, Seda o Sima, did not tell him all.

It had started with the cigarettes. For months the authorities had tried to obliterate the steady stream of alcohol and cigarettes being smuggled into Iran. For months he had watched, satisfied, as the cartons of expensive cigarettes had bubbled quietly under the waters of the Shatt al-Arab waterway. The pungent odours of the whisky and tobacco had perfumed the night air as their cases were riddled with machinegun fire. One night, as he personally executed a captured smuggler, the man had exhaled directly into Zubair's face as he died and before his body hit the river, Zubair knew he had to try one.

But these western cigarettes had none of the pungent odour that characterised local brands and he had to think up ways of masking the smoke: hence his first cigarette. That had found the chink in his armour.

The second major blow to his contempt of America, the great Satan, was when he found out his beloved *Khasmin* craft in the Islamic Republic of Iran Navy, was in fact American. The Kennedy Class Type 52 corvette was a revelation in 1964 as it had a complete fibreglass hull and body. At the time this gave it a fantastic advantage against the magnetic mines favoured by the Russian navy, in addition to its lightness and speed. Pensioned off in the mid-seventies, she became the *Coquimbo* of the Chilean navy. Later in a deal for oil for the cash-strapped junta, she sailed west to join the Iranian navy. And from the moment of his appointment Zubair had loved this boat. Its smooth underwater profile and powerful twin Caterpillar diesels outshone anything his comrades commanded. Usually on exercise in the Northern Gulf, it was the *Khasmin* that outperformed and never broke down. Zubair had lost count of the number of times he had been called to recover the other vessels in the anti-smuggling patrol, especially the fast OSA Class boats from the USSR. Chatting with dockyard managers one day, as yet another OSA boat was dragged smoking into the dry dock, Zubair heard one of the workers comments 'Good job we don't have more of the *Khasmin*: we'd be out of a job! The Americans do know how to build a boat.'

The manager had exploded and threatened to report the man for blasphemy, but as he walked back to her Zubair looked afresh at his boat. It was the start of a love affair. From then on, he drove his crew mercilessly. Twenty years of neglect and abuse were polished, painted and cleaned away.

With no money for spares, he scoured the waterway for parts, cannibalising the hundreds of half-sunken vessels for everything from winches and stays, to bridge screens and lifeboats. Within four months the *Khasmin* was the talk of the base. His greatest triumph was the engine room. Reading somewhere that Caterpillar engines were always yellow, he had managed to find a stock of paint just in the right shade. It took a month alone, but a surgeon would have been proud of the engine room of the *Khasmin*. His watch always featured a trip to the hot, noisy bowels of the ship. There he would stand nodding and scowling at his crew. Standing on the gleaming mesh walkways he would move his ear defenders slightly to hear the song of the twin turbocharged caterpillar engines. Satisfied, he would nod and walk away. He never discussed that the gleaming immaculate *Khasmin*, jewel of the Iranian navy was a living testament to the engineering and naval skills of the Great American Satan.

* * *

Since the end of the Iraq-Iran war both sides warily patrolled their respective banks of the Shatt al-Arab waterway. The dredged channel in the centre had been cleared following the war and traffic of sorts had begun to navigate the waterway. Whilst money had been found to clear the deep centre sections where two ocean-going ships could pass carefully, the shallow edges were still littered with wrecks. In was in this steel graveyard to the west bank of the waterway that Talib now guided his gently throbbing vessel. Steering to port of a large sunken vessel, he caught the muted murmuring of the approaching twin diesels. Guessing it was a river patrol, he eased back the throttle and glided silently down the towering hull. Masked by the vessel the only sound was the slap of the water in between the two hulls. The dhow silently and swiftly lost way pushing Talib slightly forward on the balls of his feet. He had grounded on a mud bank.

Instinctively, he opened the throttle a touch to maintain his momentum. Instantly the mud gave up its suction and the boat surged forward. Talib quickly pulled the throttle back, but it was too late, the dhow exited the lee of the sunken vessel fractionally too quickly showing a tumbling phosphorescence at its bow. It was this flash of bow wave that caught Zubair's attention.

It was not much of a chase: Talib's boat was outpowered and outgunned and a burst of machinegun fire convinced him to throttle back the surging dhow. He was not too concerned; his cargo of Marlboros and Johnny Walker was destined for the base commander anyway. If he reached there alive, he should be OK and in preparation, as the gun-wielding sailors powered up to his wallowing dhow, he dragged a few cases up from the hold on deck.

Lieutenant Zubair leant against the dhow's mast with hand-rolled cigarette gripped between forefinger and thumb, gently inhaling the foul smoke before rapidly expelling it. He studied the small figure in the filthy white dish dash in front of him and screwed up his nose at the smell around him. There was a pile rapidly decaying of river perch, that he would not have fed his dog; and the small vessel had not seen a coat of paint in years.

His men were waiting for his order to throw the cargo overboard. But there was something that made him pause and his four crew members stared blankly waiting for his command.

The burly Damiri grinned under his moustache, 'Come on Zubair, sir, now is not the time to be dreaming of Sukaynah'.

Zubair grinned back. 'Does not the Koran forbid jealous thoughts,' he teased, knowing the awe in which his crew held his beautiful girlfriend. Still, he paused. Something was missing. The deck vibrated gently under his feet as the exhaust burbled away. He had stood on the deck of many smugglers' dhows, and this one smelled no better than any other, but the smooth purr under his feet caught his attention.

He ordered the contraband be thrown on the *Khasmin*'s deck and the hapless Talibto handcuffed on to the stern rail: that was where they executed smugglers. From his belt he took a large Maglite which may have been heavily wrapped in old tape but was still another piece of superb engineering from the Great Satan. With the light from the torch showing the way, Zubair opened the small engine hatch and jumped down into the stinking hot space.

The was something definitely amiss. On the face of it, the engine was a mechanical nightmare but to his trained ear that gentle purr was emanating from something in far better condition. Zubair grabbed one rag-clad pipe which came away with a large section of the rough cladding to reveal gleaming brass work winking at him in the torch's beam. Rapidly he tore at the remaining pipes with his hands and small clasp knife, and in a matter of minutes the engine's camouflage lay in the swilling bilge and instead he found himself admiring an immaculate, glossy green, six-cylinder diesel. On the large rocker cover lay an unfamiliar badge with the letters AEC in a blue triangle with a red dot in its centre. To the left and right of the inverted triangle silver wings extended. Now he knew why he had hesitated on deck. This dhow was not powered by the usual Russian tank or truck engine with its attendant knocking and thumping. The engine in this dhow was professionally maintained, and it most certainly was not what one found plying the clandestine waters of the Gulf.

The dhow was taken in tow; the *Khasmin* performed a graceful arc in the waterway and headed back up the river.

Zubair made his way to the fantail at the stern of the vessel, where Talib stood stoically by the ensign staff to which he had been manacled. Zubair sat on a capstan, and looked his prisoner up and down trying to get the measure of the man before asking, 'So, my friend, where did you learn your diesel craft then?'

Talib raised his manacled hands, 'Bey, I beg of you I am a poor smuggler, it is not my boat. I have a wife and family with sick children to provide for.' As if to reinforce the point, he dropped to his knees and would have prostrated on the deck himself if his bound wrists had permitted.

Damiri stepped forward and viciously kicked Talib on his side. As he rolled sideways, his filthy dish dash rose above his knee to reveal a flash of thin white flesh.

'White? Strip him,' commanded Zubair curtly. At which Damiri took out his knife and swiftly cut the filthy robes off Talib. 'In the name of Allah,' chuckled Damiri, surveying the curious figure he had revealed.

Talib's arms and legs and head were of the darkest walnut and his skin wizened and creased. But from his knees and elbows inwards his body gleamed a pale waxy white: the kind of pale whiteness only seen on westerners. He was, in fact, a very definite European colour.

'Mmmm. Well, well, Damiri. Cover him up,' Zubair said silkily.

Back on the bridge he reached for the thick rubber-covered radio, and ordered, 'Get me my uncle, General Saeed Izadi, at Khatam Al Anbiya Headquarters at once'

CHAPTER 45

Dr Schlatter glanced at his watch. Seven o'clock. Damn. He felt the beads of sweat on his forehead. Why could not he remember to finish on time?

His eyes glanced over the huge bank of dials and controls on the curved panel in front of him. With main power output reading at 28GV, the room hummed with energy. But he needed to concentrate and put aside his own thoughts while his hand hovered above the large accelerator control.

The particle stream round the large Electron Position Collider was focused down to the thickness of a human hair in the collider in front of him. Invisible to the naked eye, protons and electrons were being forced round the twenty-seven-kilometre underground tunnel at 10,000 times a second. The head-on collision of these particles and the energy produced was Dr Schlatter's raison d'être – and his passion, to find the solution to the unlimited power these particles promised.

Since he was a gawky schoolboy at the high school in Lucerne, he had followed this same path. He had never forgotten reading about Oak Ridge in Tennessee, USA and the experiments of Ernest Lawrence. How they had created a whole new science and industrial base from scratch in the eastern mountains of America. How they had built machines of such fantastic complexity with unlimited funds from America's Manhattan project, using over $300,000,000 of silver borrowed from the treasury for the electromagnets to separate the U235 isotope, so that in 1945 the Second World War could be ended in a flash of light and a release of energy not seen since the dawn of time.

Even at 10,000 laps per second the particles only had a one in 40,000 chance of colliding. As his hand hovered, his mind raced, calculating the effects of increasing the energy load and focussing further the stream of opposing particles.

The room hummed with energy. More sweat formed on his forehead. His hand pushed up the thick spectacles which were beginning to slide down his aquiline nose. The movement broke his concentration enough for the purr of the telephone to get through to him.

'Dr Schlatter ...' the soft female voice stopped. All the secretaries knew to pause while Dr S's mind 'came back', as they put it. 'Dr Schlatter, your wife's been on. You should have been home an hour ago....'

'I ....' mumbled Dr Schlatter.

'It's OK,' the soft voice returned, 'Judi's on her way with a change of clothes for you. When she arrives, I'll show her to the hospitality suite so you can meet her there.'

'OK. OK. Thank you,' Dr Schlatter answered, before replacing the handset in its cradle. Mild panic set in as he blinked owlishly behind his thick pebble lenses. She would be angry again. It would cost yet more of his salary to buy her a new bauble. Then his haunted expression turned into a grin. It was only money, after all. And he, Dr Pier Schlatter had the most gorgeous wife in all Geneva: who cared about irritating letters from the bank?

As he left the LEP laboratory at the European Centre for Nuclear Research (CERN) Geneva and headed for the surface some ninety metres above him, Piert Schlatter reflected with some satisfaction on the surprising change in his domestic fortune.

By the time Judi had reached fifteen she had come to understand that her affluent Italian upbringing in a classical villa nestling in the foothills of Mount Lesima, just north of Genoa, was no accident: nor was it the product of an industrious family business. When she questioned her mother, Chiara, about her working arrangements, Judi fared little better than she did with her father.

She loved her father dearly and counted herself lucky he was always around to drop her at school and collect her at the end of the day in one of his stable of exotic cars. She saw less of her mother whose hours appeared to coincide with her sleep patterns. The reason for this became all too evident after Judi had rashly accepted a lift into Genoa on the back of the Vespa belonging to one of the village boys. That was when she had spotted her mother alighting from the Mercedes limousine and being welcomed into a stucco palace of fairytale proportions. Judi watched agog from the back of the Vespa, with her slim brown arms encircling the boy, and scarcely heard him when he laughed and said, 'Your mother works at a bordello da notte!' Flushing with shame, she had slipped off the scooter and caught the bus back home.

However, she had not gone unnoticed. Chiara had stepped elegantly from the rear of the Mercedes 500 SEL and seen the Vespa with her crestfallen daughter astride it. Well, it had to happen someday, she supposed. Her beloved daughter Jolanda – how she hated the Americanised 'Judi' of her peers – would someday discover the truth. Chiara saw it as a rite of passage. It would mark the end of her childhood and her entry into the world Chiara had tried so hard to protect her from.

It was at times like these that she envied her eastern clients and their arranged marriages. Not for them the gnawing worry of launching children into adulthood, with barely a single chance at putting wise heads on young shoulders to secure a 'good marriage'.

Still, her profession did have its compensations, she thought, as she stepped through the ornate cut-glass doors of her 'hotel', felt her feet sank into the rich carpet and inhaled heady aroma of expensive clothes and perfume that greeted her.

Chiara switched on her famous dazzling smile as she surveyed the room. A dozen beautiful women adorned an equal number of tanned, fit men; always the same when he was in town she mused: the entire delegation straight from Geneva for the whole weekend. She knew little of the purposes of the IAEC or International Atomic Energy Commission, suffice it that when the Iranian delegation took time off from their work in Geneva to fly to Genoa, she had to lay on extra girls for frustrated Muslims freed for a moment from the oppression of their faith.

She smiled even more radiantly as a tall, well-built, olive complexioned man disengaged himself from a willowy, scantily clad blonde. Without a backward glance, he strode towards Chiara, made a formal half bow and his lips brushed the flawless diamond on her fingers when she extended her hand to him. 'Such impeccable manners', she sighed to herself.

'Hussy', she began, Hussein Famel's eyes screwed in pleasure when she called him that, 'Hussy, my oldest and dearest friend. When you have finished with Roxanne, I would be very grateful for your advice'.

Hussein Famel's eyebrows raised fractionally, 'But of course my dear Chiara, of course'.

The delights Roxanne bestowed kept him well occupied, so it was sometime later that the elegant couple strolled along the harbour front arm in arm.

'It's Jolanda,' Chiara began. 'It's time she was away from this'. She swept her arm around the darkening waterfront. In the shadows of the Aquaria de Geneva on the Ponte Spinola, leggy street girls could be seen weaving in and out of the thinning crowds. This was where her own early days had started, she remembered. Then a flush of achievement overcame her and she continued. 'My mother introduced me to the "trade" and in truth it has not been a bad life. But you understand, Hussy, don't you? My Jolanda deserves better.'

Hussy nodded reflectively. 'She is a beautiful young girl, Chiara.' But when her face began to cloud with anger, he added quickly, 'No. No. Your girls in the hotel: that's pleasure. But your daughter: that's business, Chiara.'

If she wondered on his choice of words, she let it pass. 'You have connections in Geneva, Hussy?' A statement, not a question.

He nodded, thinking hard. Sometimes a wine was too young to be drunk now, he reflected. 'If I can help, Chiara, darling, I will. But first she must attend a finishing school in Switzerland. I have an establishment in mind. From there we can place her in the correct circles.'

Chiara smiled and kissed him lingeringly. 'I will be very grateful,' she murmured.

* * *

Gradually it all began to make sense to Judi: the house parties with endless parades of gorgeous Italian girls, and the drive crammed with every exotic vehicle from every European manufacturer. And the men, all sunburned, good looking and dressed expensively. It was not long before Rimoldo, the scooter owner, came calling for her. It was not much longer when she took him to her bed.

The pair had frolicked by the pool completely naked for most of the early evening, secure in the knowledge that they were alone as Genoa was hosting a welcoming party for the latest British aircraft carrier. By now Judi was growing tired of the quick frantic thrusting's of her peers and she had taken home an older boy by four years. Not a boy she told herself. A man. And Jose had been stunning so far, gently leading her down the paths of pleasure until she could take no more, then equally gently easing back just when she wanted him most. Eventually she tired of this and resolved to have him at last. But as he rolled across her parted thighs, to her horror the poolside lights came on and the small gate next to her father's garage burst open.

In a blink of an eye Jose was held by her father at the poolside, his arms pinioned behind him as the rustle of her mother's skirts swept through the bushes.

'Well, well,' Chiara said, smiling. 'While the cat's away ...' Then the smile disappeared.

Judi had rarely seen her mother so furious. Jose was clearly terrified, shaking like a leaf the confident, smooth bearing of his nineteen years as limp and wilted as was his magnificent member.

That was when Chiara did something that Judi was never to forget. Approaching the shivering Jose, she lifted the small Malacca cane tipped with silver that she was in the habit of carrying as 'the Madam of Genoa'. Thrusting it under Jose's scrotum she lifted his genitals forward. Simultaneously she took from her thigh a small, silver-plated Derringer 9mm and put the muzzle to Jose's head. 'These,' she said, lifting fractionally Jose's genitalia, 'are absolutely no use whatsoever without these.'

When she pulled the trigger Jose's brains emptied across the marble patio as blackness descended on Judi.

* * *

Four years later, having been forced through a finishing school at Thonon, Judi had presented herself at the administration offices of CERN just outside Geneva. Settling in behind the reception desk, she watched patiently for the first six months as the academic cream of the world's universities came and went in the search for knowledge of nuclear fusion with which to enrich their governments.

Dr Schlatter was invariably the last to leave of an evening, much to the unspoken displeasure of the resigned looking security guard who summarily switched off the lights around him, leaving the good doctor to smile myopically at the two duty girls on reception before he entangled himself in the swing doors as he tried to make his exit into the cool Geneva air leaving barely stifled giggles in his wake.

'He's the cleverest man in CERN: that's who he is,' Judi's companion confided. 'Don't even think of talking to him unless you've a battery of PhDs.'

That was the just the cue that Judi needed, and it wasn't many afternoons later that she excused herself, grabbed a clipboard and made for the lifts. With no security pass or swipe card for the deepest level, she waited patiently until one of the scientists punched in level G8 and accompanied him down. He was flattered by the attention of the head-turning girl at reception and completely failed to spot that she had no security clearance to be there. Judi, though, knew that all she needed was a cup of Dr Schlatter's favourite ground Brazilian coffee and the radiance of her renowned smile to get where she wanted in Laboratory G8.

Later that evening she had grabbed her coat as Dr Schlatter arrived in reception. Winking broadly to an astonished Anna, she proprietarily linked her arm with his and whirled them both through the glass doors.

On their third date, Judy gently kissed Dr Schlatter (as she still insisted on calling him, coyly) at the door to her apartment, said 'Goodnight' and firmly shut the door – but not before she waited to see him feel wonderingly at his lips as he gently turned a deep shade of crimson.

Their wooing was unlike any she had known before. She sat patiently while he droned on about neutrons and positrons, dipole magnets, up quarks and down quarks. After a while, she would look at him with large, doe-like eyes and slightly parted lips, and confess she still did not have a clue.

Pier Schlatter's heart melted. He swallowed hard and began again gently, as his arm slowly crept around Judi's shoulder. She let him talk about his work for only so long, then sweetly asked if they could talk about something else at which he became effusive with embarrassment, and when his jealous colleagues suggested, frequently from barely disguised envy, that she was a gold digger he knew differently.

Dr Schlatter had never had a girlfriend, but steadily an astonishing change came over him. Gone were the woollen jumpers and misshapen corduroys. In their place came smart jackets, designer suits and fitted Italian trousers. His shoes went from scruffy brogues to the finest from John Lobb in London. He became a familiar, bespectacled figure in the swankiest restaurants of Geneva and always with the gorgeous Judi on his arm.

All this of course took a great deal of his money. Slowly, her appetite for his salary was becoming as large as her appetite in bed, but no matter. Who cared? For the first time in his life Dr Schlatter was having a ball.

CHAPTER 46

So it was that some months later a deeply contented Dr Schlatter had entered his apartment building. The time showing on his watch provoked a frown. Late again. Still, when Judi heard about the latest project on the SPS and his probable role he was sure she would forgive him.

Five minutes later, with a ringing in his head and a feeling of utter bewilderment, he had been pushed back into the corridor to loud screams of feminine rage.

She had never, ever, hit him before. For once she had actually said she did not care about his dammed neutrons. In fact, it had been a great deal more heated, as the heavy glass tumbler hitting the door behind him had confirmed.

Puzzled and bemused, he had sought solace in the flat of a colleague on the second floor. Half a bottle of scotch later, his hosts prepared for bed after settling their guest on the settee.

'Sounds like a visit to Adlers,' Hank confided.

'Really?' said Pier. 'You think so?'

Hank had gazed frankly at him. 'Trust me. One little bauble from Adlers and you'll be back in her bed in no time.' Then he had turned off the light with a wink and softly closed the door, leaving Pier reassured and resolved to be at the famous Geneva jewellers as the doors opened the next day.

And so it proved. In exchange for a goodly part of his monthly salary, a small burgundy velvet box sat on the glass table in his apartment later that day. Further advice from amused colleagues had encouraged him to light several aromatic candles surrounding bouquets of the finest flowers in Geneva; and he had ordered in outside catering from the Geneva Grand Hotel.

Pier had stationed himself in the large white leather sofa from where he would see the apartment's door across the room. He heard Judi's key scrape in the lock and watched her step firmly into the room. She held her head high and her shoulders back as her fine stilettos click across the wooden flooring.

Judi got four paces into the apartment before she absorbed the softly guttering candles, the flowers, and the exquisite meal laid for two. She approached the table silently, holding Piers' eyes in her own steady gaze. Softening perceptibly, she allowed the corners of her eyes to smile at him as she slipped off her full-length fur. She sat down without comment only to freeze at the sight of the small box on the table in front of her. Opening it with a dull snap she gasped. The stone had been cut in brilliant form and the candlelight shone and reflected a thousand colours from its flawless heart. The meal so carefully prepared in Geneva's finest kitchen was not designed to be eaten cold; but it was the only food in the apartment for the next two days.

When Dr Schlatter eventually returned to work it was obvious that Hank's discretion could not be assured. Knowing female glances followed him everywhere. The immaculate and bespectacled professor of nuclear physics and his glamorous wife were the talk of the town.

The only cloud on Dr Schlatter's horizon blew in once every month when a discreet buff envelope would be among his morning mail. No names or insignia adorned the envelope, but he came to dread the letter from Credit Suisse. In the envelope would be his neatly typewritten statements, now many more pages than before. Pre-Judi, he called it. Accompanying the statement would be an extremely polite letter informing Dr Schlatter that once again his overdraft limit had been raised to 'take into account his spending patterns'. While the bank in no way appeared concerned, the monthly raising of his indebtedness caused extra lines to appear on Dr Schlatter's forehead.

Gentle requests to watch the money were met by pouted lips and flashing eyes and invariably another visit to Adlers, at whose establishment he had a further small but growing line of credit.

One summer evening as they strolled back to their apartment block, an elderly Mercedes drew up next to them. With a flash of white teeth, the driver hailed Mrs Schlatter, 'Hey Judi! How are you?'

Puzzled, she shielded her eyes against and squinted towards the car. 'Oh! Hi, Zak, I didn't recognise you.' Walking in front of Pier, she stood at the car chatting idly to the two male occupants.

Pier wandered on, casting looks behind. When she caught up, she gave a small card to him with a phone number and an e-mail address. 'Zak wants you to ring him.'

'What for?'

'He says he might be able to help with the second of the month.'

As today's date was the third, Pier's thoughts leapt to his financial situation straight away. 'Who is he anyway?'

'Just one of the couriers who comes into reception.'

The explanation seemed logical, and Dr Schlatter brushed it way.

One month later and a day after yet another letter from the bank, Judi mentioned again ringing this 'Zak'. The bank's tone had been a little more formal, this time suggesting a meeting with one of their 'financial planning officers'. Still feeling uncertain, Pier had put Zak's crumpled card back into his pocket. As Professor of Nuclear Physics, he was now heavily involved in CERN's latest accelerator. The so-called Super Proton Synchrotron was set up to study the quark gluon plasma which followed on after the 'big bang'. He had tried to explain that one to Judi, but she had stopped him by nibbling his anatomy in his favourite place. Zak's card had remained hidden for a further month.

The following month's buff envelope sent him reeling. Dr Schlatter had never received such a formal letter in his life. The bank's icy tone suggested his overdraft was 'repayable on demand' and dictated an appointment for Dr Schlatter at three o'clock the following day. Attendance was not an option.

The thought of interrupting his work to discuss his finances with a complete stranger sent him into a blind panic and he blundered into the local park with Judi reluctantly on his arm. She was in no mood to compromise having had her credit card declined as she had filled the Mercedes SLK. Embarrassingly, she had had to leave the vehicle and walk the few blocks to the office.

'Maybe you should phone Zak. He seems friendly enough. Maybe he wants to offer you work'.

'Work! He's a driver Judi!'

'Yes. But he seems nice.

'Very well,' one phone call. Then I'll have to go to the director and get help'.

To Pier's surprise the address Zak had given him turned out to be an extremely expensive small private hotel in the financial heart of the city.

He was further surprised to find Zak in an expensive suit talking animatedly to another moustached and tanned gentleman. Zak ordered coffee and invited Dr Schlatter (as he insisted on calling 'this eminent scientist' to sit with him in a discreet corner. Apart from the barman desultorily polishing the display of fine crystal wine glasses, they were alone.

In the true eastern style, the conversation ebbed and flowed around every subject under the sun. It was obvious that Zak's companion was either in no rush at all or the whole exercise was a waste of time. On their third cup of the bitter dark coffee, Zak smoothly interrupted, 'I'm so sorry, Dr Schlatter I assumed you'd met.

'Dr Schlatter, Dr Ali Akbar Saleh.' The two rose and shook hands. 'Head of the Iranian Nuclear Facility at Nantaz,' continued Zak.

Dr Schlatter leapt back as if stung, but Dr Saleh held his hand in an iron grip. His eyes bored into Dr Schlatter as he watched the colour drain from his face.

Back in their seats, the conversation descended into swift rapier-like questions, but with questions to which they always knew the answers. 'Life must be difficult if you earn \$11,000 a month but you spend \$13,000!' observed Zak.

'So much easier if you tripled your salary.'

Dr Schlatter's chair hit the floor with a mild thump as he quickly got to his feet and fled the darkened lobby.

When he told Judi that evening, holding her hands on his knees and rocking back and forth, all she could repeat was, 'Three times your salary?'

'You don't understand, Judi. You know what they'll want me to do.'

'Well, you work for one government now. So, what's the problem working for another government? Lots of my friends get job offers'. Behind the large doe eyes, she was swiftly calculating what effect three times more money meant. To Pier, the most endearing part of Judi was how she was utterly removed from his work and life: she was his breath of fresh air and nothing in him wanted that to change.

He slept fitfully all night. Rising early, he left Judi and was sitting in his office next to G8 by six o'clock. He did not find it difficult to concentrate: all his life he had focussed on this one problem. Now the Giant LEP machine, twenty-seven kilometres of curricular accelerator under the Swiss Alps would give him the answers. They would soon begin accelerating the positrons and neutrons in opposing directions at over 15,000 laps per second. Pier was convinced that it would not be long before the secret of fusion from the beginning of time would soon yield its secrets.

The shrill of the telephone eventually broke his thoughts, but when he picked up the receiver he heard nothing. Frowning he went to replace it, only to realise the shrill tones were still ringing out. He looked across and saw the single line flashing on the control console: the one that was only used by accelerator technicians in the tunnels. No one was at work yet, but still the telephone rang. This was not what he needed and, grunting in exasperation, he propelled his chair across the console and picked the instrument up.

The silky voice cut to his inner self. 'Your overdraft can be cancelled to day Dr Schlatter. Just do as we ask and funds will be credited in a matter of hours.' Then the line went dead.

Frantically Pier scanned the banks of monitors that kept watch along the miles of tunnels: nothing. He dialled the front desk and demanded to know who had been put through to him.

'No one, Dr Schlatter. We didn't even know you were in so early.'

The chill that ran through him brought an awful clarity: he knew now what he must do. Picking up the internal phone, he left a message on the Director of Finance's voicemail requesting a meeting at nine o'clock the following morning, confident that his value to the institute would count for a lot more than a mere overdraft. Before settling back to work, though, he made sure to set his desk alarm, so he would not be late for the bank.

* * *

The stiff frock coated officials were extremely polite, over tea and biscuits they illustrated gently the spiralling curve of Dr Schlatter's overdraft. With his analytical mind he could see the dip in the figures from credit to debit starting four months after he had married Judi. He was further shocked to find that they managed to allude to the account at Adlers. Pier was slightly mollified by their deference, but by the end of the formal meeting the demands that the overdraft be repaid in full by the end of the year were in place. Astonishingly he also agreed to agree by the formal repayment schedule by signing his salary over to the bank. It was only when the gentle but firm request for his credit cards came that the enormity of his situation sank in.

It was late when he returned home after making an uncharacteristic stop at a small bar where he downed several large drinks. When the effect of those began to dull his senses, he had locked up the car and completed his journey home on foot.

The moment he opened the door, he knew what had happened. One of Judi's elegant gold-strap shoes was in small hall and the Chinese rug had been pushed to one side. The main room was a shambles. The whole apartment had been ransacked: exquisite porcelain lay smashed on the oak floor; his precious bookshelves and CD collection had been flung around the room.

Relief was beginning to seep in as his mind adjusted to the thought of a clumsy burglary. But this slight relief was short-lived. Judi was no longer there but the keys to her beloved Mercedes were lying on the marble mantlepiece.

Pier was processing the implications of what he was looking at when the phone rang. Panic set in as he could not find it. The ringing stopped while he was flinging around cushions and shifting furniture. He found it, just as the ringing started again.

'Got a pen?' asked the caller.

Dr Schlatter's panic stricken attempts at questions were cut short abruptly by a feminine scream down the handset. Not just any female scream: Judi's scream.

His shaking hand had written the instructions on the back of a hastily found theatre programme. Then the phone went dead.

A website? He had been given the address of a website. The bar on his laptop screen marched from side to side, searching, searching. Momentarily an image flashed up with what he thought was Arabic script, then pixel by pixel a picture appeared. A pale cross took shape in squares on the dark background. The download bar at the foot of the screen kept reading and receiving: 45% GiF; 56% GiF; 75% GiF.

The pale star appeared to be rotating, but as it came round again, Dr

204

Schlatter could see it was a human form, manacled to a bar at the top and with its feet likewise spread to the ends of a similar bar below. The pixels were becoming clearer now as they continue their teasing parade. His legs buckled and he sagged to the floor. The picture was complete now and he looked at Judi's stricken face as she swung slowly round, suspended like an exotic starfish. The webcam picture depicted her beautiful naked form; swinging round again, her puffy swollen features caused him to gag.

His breath came in short gasps as the webcam pulled back and a smiling Dr Saleh came into the picture. He was carrying a silver-topped cane with which he gently stroked Judi's body provoking a violent reaction as she arched her head back and swung her spread-eagled legs around her. To little avail, the effort simply displayed her perfect figure to the even greater delight of the perverted eyes looking on unseen but menacing.

The picture remained some forty-five seconds then faded: 'Connection lost' the screen stated. Pier's fingers skimmed the keys frantically. 'The server does not recognise the following website'. In despair Dr Schlatter sank to the floor.

The doorbell caused him to start, and he staggered to his feet to open it. Outside stood dark figure with a raised arm. Dr Schlatter's last memory was of a slim needle entering his arm.

After that: blackness.

CHAPTER 47

The low moan of the air raid siren penetrated his fitful dream. He was fifteen-years old and in an old film, Lancaster bombers were sweeping in. The siren sounded again, this time accompanied by the whoosh and crump of missiles. Startled he sat up. Flashes through the curtains the width of the room gave him his bearings as he fumbled on the small cabinet for his glasses. When he could not find them, he swung his legs from the bed and encountered cool tiles. Tiles? His bedroom had oriental rugs; it was one of his secret pleasures feeling his toes in their warm richness.

He made his way uncertainly towards the windows and the flashes of light beyond the curtains. Once he had succeeded in battling through these, he gazed myopically at the indigo sky, criss-crossed by vapour trails below which lay the silhouette of a city he had never seen before. Bright green streams of tracers arced skywards accompanying the wail of sirens and the explosive flashes on the horizon.

The curtains clinging to his back began to slide sidewards accompanied by a low hum. Free at last of the enveloping fabric, Dr Schlatter felt a firm hand take his and his glasses were put in his palm and quickly transferred to his head.

In front of him stood an immaculately uniformed bellboy. His rich maroon tunic, trimmed with gold, bore the name Espinas Palace on his breast pocket. He moved away and busied himself at a low table with various ornate silver teapots. From under a domed cover he revealed two plates of steaming eggs, tomatoes and large mushrooms. Bowing formally to the immobile Dr Schlatter, he switched on the large flat screen TV, turned and exited the room. The door closed with a curious double click. The screen showed a pile of smoking rubble and a group of Arab-looking women on their knees beating their heads in grief.

But it was another moan that next grabbed Pier's attention. This came from beneath the duvet on the large double-bed; and when he pulled back the soft white cover onto the mattress weeping: Judi lay foetal-like on the edge of the bed. Clad in dark silk pyjamas she stirred, slowly groping for him. Her wrists and ankles were bound with neat surgical dressings and her still sleepy face bore the swellings and puffiness of her ordeal. They embraced instinctively and tears of joy ran down their faces as they held each other tightly.

It was only when they were tucking into the very welcome breakfast that Pier spotted the clock and date on the wall near the small desk showing 17 July. His meeting with the bank had been the scheduled for 15 July. What had happened? He remembered the fading webcam picture and the silky tones on his mobile but then nothing.

The wailing of the call to prayer brought his senses into top gear. Where the hell was he?

* * *

They lived in the suite for four days without once leaving it. Wardrobes revealed sets of clothes for them both, all fitting them perfectly. Food was served promptly three times a day, but the same bellboy would only shake his head when questioned. The room door remained locked, and the glass windows led only to a balcony some twenty floors up. It did not take a genius to work out where they were; all they could hope was that their elegant comfortable prison remained safe until they knew of their fate.

Every night they watched the attacks on the city and Tehran's missile defences. By the fourth day Judi's face had regained its elegant self and she had removed her bandages. Perking up no end at the wardrobe of designer clothes, jewellery and shoes, she appeared unperturbed at her predicament.

* * *

On the morning of their fifth day breakfast the silent-ever Mahmood was accompanied by a smaller suited gentleman, who told Pier, 'Please be ready in one hour Dr Schlatter'.

He then took the small remote control and switched on the TV tuning it to the BBC's international news channel and then left the apartment as enigmatically as he had entered it.

'And now in a late item,' began the news anchor, 'it has been reported from Geneva that the respected nuclear physicist Dr Pier Schlatter and his wife Judi have perished in a tragic road accident. Their car was apparently hit by a petrol tanker on the main motorway out of the city. The accident happened yesterday, but identification was impossible until dental records could be accessed. The couple had only recently married, and Dr Schlatter and his wife will be sorely missed by his colleagues at CERN: the European nuclear research facility near Geneva.' The TV picture showed the emergency services hosing down the remains of a large tanker and small sports car tangled together. Pier sank onto the sofa.

One hour later to the second, there was a soft knock on the door and Dr Saleh and another gentleman in an olive-green uniform entered the apartment. 'Good morning, Dr and Mrs Schlatter,' Saleh said smoothly. 'I hope everything is to your taste? May I introduce Major General Mohammad Bagheri of the Iranian Armed Forces? He will be escorting us on our visit today.'

Dr Schlatter glanced at the TV.

'Ah, yes,' Saleh continued. 'We welcome you to our country Dr Schlatter, but in view of the annoying habit Mossad has of assassinating our scientists, we thought it best if your visit remained secret'.

He did not wait for a reply, simply bowing slightly to indicate that Dr Schlatter should leave the apartment. Judi made to follow, but an upraised hand stopped her. 'So sorry Mrs Schlatter: your husband has to work'.

The lift took them directly to the hotel basement where four blacked-out Mercedes saloons bearing the pennant of the the Islamic Revolutionary Guard Corps, were parked waiting for them. As cars sped from the underground car park and split up to take their individual routes, Pier wondered whether he would ever see Judi again.

Their journey took them southwards, judging from the position of the sun. Weaving and sounding the horn continuously, the car and escort carved through the Tehran morning traffic.

Once they reached the main highway south, the vehicle picked up speed leaving the escort behind: its occupants seemed to relax, and Pier nodded off to the hum of the tyres on the smooth tarmac.

Rough hands shook him awake and pulled him from the car, stiff and blinking into the bright daylight, 'Please put on these Dr Schlatter,' he was asked as a pair of pale grey overalls were thrust into his hands. These were several sizes too big and the large gumboots that came with them hampered movement as he shuffled to join a group of men clustered round Dr Saleh and the general, who were receiving the damage report of the past few nights' raids. Dr Saleh closed this with an air of resignation and waved to the group to board a line of small golf trolleys in which they were driven into the complex facing them.

Low buildings appeared scattered across the dusty landscape. Behind each one soared earth berms some hundred feet in height. From their smooth contours it was apparent they would contain any blast and limit the damage to the nearest structures. As they cruised down the smooth highway, Dr Schlatter observed the enormous electrical cables of a thickness familiar to his work at CERN: 'At least 100 megawatts supply,' he surmised.

The journey continued past huge industrial warehouses. Some were completely intact, but others – even those in their protected berms – were completely destroyed, their smoking steel skeletons now open to the sky.

At one point Dr Saleh ordered the little convoy to halt so that he could lead a panting Dr Schlatter to the top of one of the berms. Up here, a gentle breeze blew fine desert dust in the air. The sun created eddies of heat swirling the images around into shimmering shapes. Gradually though, as his heavy breathing subsided, a pattern emerged, and chessboard of gigantic proportions unfolded before them. Each square was tens of acres in size and further was bordered by vast earthwork berms. Millions and millions of tons of desert soil and rocks had been shaped into the thirty-degree slopes enclosing most of the buildings.

Dr Saleh handed Dr Schlatter a small pair of binoculars and told him to take a close look at the unit immediately below, which had been ripped apart by a huge explosion. The roof had disappeared completely, and scanning the interior Dr Schlatter could see neat rows of huge machines some of which merged with each other in the hazy distance. Even so, he counted thirty-six machines, or their remains.

As a schoolboy, his first experience of the world of isotopes and fission had been the gift of a book called the *Manhattan Project*. In it a young brilliant scientist Ernest Orlando Lawrence had, at university in California, deduced that introducing matter between the poles of very large electromagnets would eventually lead to the separation of the isotope's uranium 235 and 238 so unleashing enormous power. The first crude machines built at Berkley before the Second World War comprised ion sources, collectors and very high, regulated voltage. So high was the amperage required by Lawrence and his team, that they had been required eventually to inform the power generating companies what was causing the 'brown out' in the fashionable areas surrounding their laboratory.

Whilst Lawrence had succeeded for the first time in history in separating his isotopes, the amounts involved had been so infinitesimal that they were scarcely worth the effort it had taken. Eventually they realised that they would have to link the machines in what was called 'racetracks.' And, at Oak Ridge in Tennessee, as the weight of the American nuclear bomb programme under the auspice of General Groves swung behind them, the beta calutrons were positioned in two rectangular tracks, each containing thirty-six calutrons in two parallel arrays and joined at their ends by iron yokes in order to make a closed magnetic circuit.

That was an image engrained in Dr Schlatter's memory; and when he handed the binoculars back to Dr Saleh, he told him, 'That's Oak Ridge, Tennessee. You've rebuilt the Manhattan Project. It is true, then. You're creating fissile material.'

'We were,' Saleh replied. 'That's why you're here. But that technology was finished in the fifties: it's so inefficient. What worked for Groves at Hiroshima would again.'

'You're mad – insane,' stuttered Dr Schlatter.

'Perhaps so, but you're alive,' replied Saleh silkily.

Something bothered Dr Schlatter, however. Something was missing. In spite of the destruction, something was not quite right. Turning again he examined the building. Huge power convectors sat undamaged in the lee of a berm. The thick cable suspended in mid-air leading to the building. Power. Oak Ridge needed fifty megawatts. The power services Dr Schlatter had witnessed clearly exceeded that. The twisted skeleton shimmered in the heat.

That was it! Cooling. How did they cool all that energy? Oak Ridge had its own dams and cooling towers and produced enough hot water for a town of 10,000.

'You're not showing me . . .' he began, but Dr Saleh had started down the berm to the waiting cart.

As Director of Research of CERN, Dr Schlatter had been privy to many of the UNSCOM inspections in an attempt to negotiate away the Iranian nuclear enrichment programme. In particular, he had ensured that its inspectors had the necessary knowledge to recognise nuclear technology when they found it. Iran's presence on the board of the International Atomic Energy Commission and its signing of the Non-Proliferation Treaty in the late sixties had, at least in diplomatic circles, ensured it was innocent of clandestinely developing nuclear weapons. Until the overthrow of the Shah, Iran was a favoured nation with the West in its bloody war against the growing threat of Islamist extremists. Using its immense cash reserves and unlimited manpower, Iran had in fact built up a large nuclear research industry, routinely asking for and obtaining clearance to import power generating equipment, gas centrifuges and large amounts of uranium oxide. The fact that a country with the second largest oil reserves in the world needed nuclear power to generate electricity never seemed to concern anyone.

Over the next five days, Dr Schlatter and Dr Saleh, accompanied now by Iran's leading nuclear physicist, toured the Esfahan technology centre, the Bandar Abbas production plant and finally the secret Fordo plant under the mountains near Qom.

CHAPTER 48

The elderly man leant on his son, walking stiffly to the marble bench by the side of the tranquil lagoon. His right hand was stiff and immobile since the assassination attempt in 1981 and he needed his son's care to guide him onto seat with a murmured, 'Praise be with you my son, Mojtaba.'

The pair waited in the ornate gardens of the Ferdowsi Mausoleum, Mashhad, the old man's home town. As a lifelong student and lover of Farsi literature, it was one of many locations he came to visit in his search for security from the forces of Zionism: particularly the Israeli secret service, Mossad.

Today, the grounds had been emptied of visitors and members of the elite Quds force were stationed out of earshot around the walls. Footsteps announced the arrival of the three visitors, all summoned in secret using couriers and code words since not even mobile phones could be now trusted.

After bowing to the Supreme Leader they sat around the marble bench, where General Bagheri began, summarising the damage the Zionists had wreaked on the nation's missile sites and nuclear facilities.

It was a lengthy statement and the Supreme Leader's head was bowed while he listened to the catalogue of destruction. When the general had finished and he had digested fully what he had had been told, he looked at them all and said angrily, 'God will bring down the fires of hell on the Zionists and its American puppets. They shall feel the wrath of the Iranian people as never before!

'What progress at Fordo, Mohammad Abbasi?' he asked, addressing a suited man next to the general.

Fereydoon Abbasi swallowed. 'We have succeeded in convincing the International Atomic Energy Agency that we have only managed to achieve sixty percent purity. This will do little to cool Zionist ardour; but in reality, with the facility at Fordo and our new Swiss recruit we have successfully been running at over ninety percent. In fact, I can announce today that we have sufficient material for ten devices. Should Your Excellency decide of course', he hastily added.

The third man, silent until now spoke strongly, 'Then Tehran can open the Gates of Hell upon our enemies!'

The Supreme Leader struggled to his feet and they stood to attention. After fixing each man with his piercing stare he made his way towards the entrance. When he was out of sight, the three sat down, visibly relaxing, listening in silence to the gentle burble of the fountains.

It was General Bagheri who made the first move, slowly raising his hand to remove his epaulettes from his shoulders; Hossein Salami and Saeed Izadi took their lead and did the same with theirs.

Next, Salami picked up three strands of grass and offered them to the others to pull straws. Salami took the shortest. It was a ritual the three friends had observed since they all were recruited into the military and studied at Tehran University. They trusted each other. It was not a common commodity in Iran.

'We may wish to use our weapon,' Salami began. 'We may want to use our weapon. We may,' casting his eyes towards the departing Supreme Leader, 'believe we can. But the reality is we have no delivery system. We simply cannot risk our small stock on our inaccurate Shahab 5 missiles. We struggle to hit an entire block in Tel Aviv, whilst our enemies enter through windows and doors. The American president sends B2 bombers that can hit a refrigerator door from 50,000 feet.

'None of us want to admit that our missile systems are not as good as they should be for the money invested. But the truth is, we are schoolchildren throwing paper darts at an enemy armed with rifles.

'We send hundreds of missiles and drones into Israel – and we may claim success, but the reality is different. The Shaheed drones behave just as badly for Putin. The Russians are lucky to even hit a city.' He sighed and there was a long uncomfortable pause.

General Bagheri nodded slowly. 'What, then, is the solution, Hossein?'

'What we lack in strength, we must make up in cunning. The precision attacks on us, whether personal or military, all have one thing in common: intelligence. Irrefutable knowledge. Eavesdropping. It is that which is missing.

'We can by-pass sanctions all day long and have procured astonishing machinery in the face of denials; but the knowledge our enemies have, evades us.'

Now that he had the group's attention, he let what he had said sink in before continuing, 'We need to blind them like Samson. We need to take out their eyes and ears. By the grace of God, we have in Bandar Abbas a smuggler of extraordinary talent and background.'

'Meaning?' snapped Saeed.

'Meaning, my esteemed colleague, that if he could smuggle in, could he smuggle out?' When he recalled that moment afterwards, General Bagheri would swear that the ensuing silence had lasted minutes. Hyperbole aside, there could be no denying the profound impact of what Salami had started coursing through their minds.

'I believe he is currently under sentence of death,' General Bagheri said at last. 'You had better hurry then' he told Izadi.'

'I hear your man in Bandar Abbas is Irish, Saeed?'

'It is so my General, and if my hunch is right a fugitive from the IRA.'

Bagheri frowned, trying to remember. 'A long time ago we sent a consignment of weapons and explosives to the IRA by way of our colonel in Libya. It was the fourth such shipment with the aid of Libya, but the vessel, I believe the *Eksund* was arrested by French customs on an unrelated matter. There was a fixer in Ireland by the name of Maher at the time. An extremely capable man, he took a device to Manchester.'

* * *

Thomas sat in the back of the open Mercedes wagon that had taken that month's prisoners to the sharia court. The harsh ride and biding manacles meant nothing now. His identity as the smuggler Talib had been stripped away long ago and he had been charged with smuggling alcohol and tobacco; and running the black-market in Bandar Abbas. The base commander had done his best to plead Thomas's case with the mullahs, but they had remained unmoved. The sharia court's decision was final: death by hanging in the square following Friday prayers.

The decision to execute a foreign national had to be referred to Tehran, of course; but that would only be a matter of a few weeks. Thomas knew that his pending fate had not been helped by the discovery that his Irish nationality had been checked out and found to be that of an ex-IRA terrorist who, according to British records, was dead anyway.

Commander Raffique al Qasim was a gentle man and he shared some burden of guilt for Thomas' predicament. Not that he knew of his Irish origins, but he had turned a blind eye when fine American cigarettes and malt whisky kept up the morale at the naval base. In the brief conversation he had managed after the verdict had been handed down, Thomas had asked a strange question. He said that would like to speak to a brother from the Sons of Sion, based within the Order of St Anthony in Turkey. Thomas had muttered something about a relation in the order back in Ireland. The sharia court's verdict was inevitable and final. So, with a resigned shrug, Raffique placed a small note in the hand of a trusted messenger and using his friends in the Revolutionary Guard, secured his route across Iran's northern border into neighbouring Turkey.

* * *

It only took the staff at the Espinas Palace one look at the convoy that had arrived at dawn that morning for them to apply themselves industriously to their duties and to avoid making eye contact with any of the new arrivals.

Everyone recognised General Bagheri and the feared IRGC commander Hossein Salami. The small contingent of Basij, the fanatical volunteer wing of the Iran Popular Mobilisation force with them did nothing to settle the anxious members of staff, who watched as Dr Schlatter was escorted to the Mercedes limousine awaiting at the kerb.

With a pair of heavily armed jeeps following, the convoy left Tehran and sped through interminably drab scenery, whilst the inside the car an icy silence gripped its occupants. In due course the mountains of Elburz came hazily into view and after while the car cruised to a halt.

Dr Schlatter looked around. There was nothing to be seen for miles and silence still reigned in the car. He swallowed.

After consulting his expensive watch, General Bagheri announced, 'Nine minutes to the next spy satellite. We wait'.

Minutes passed slowly. The soldiers in the jeeps were sweating. Eventually, after another look at his watch, the general nodded and the car leapt forward, heading directly for a craggy cliff face in the distance. As it approached, a ravine opened up and immediately Dr Schlatter should see the beginnings of a tunnel, with large, dilapidated doors.

The doors swung open automatically and the car entered the darkness: fluorescent lights flickered into life, shining off stainless steel. A lurching sensation told Dr Schlatter they were in some kind of lift. A large lift. Large enough for several commercial vehicles. The lift descended. His memories of the lifts at CERN enabled him to calculate that the depth, of whatever facility this was, was at least a hundred metres.

Back in the 1930s the Anglo-Iranian Oil Company had test drilled in the area and discovered huge reserves of natural gas. Some forty years of extraction had led to the collapse of the porous shale leaving a vast underground chamber.

The lift sighed to a halt and doors opened to reveal a sight that left Dr Schlatter awe-struck. Used as he was to the state-of-the-art facilities at CERN, he had sarcastically dismissed (at least to himself) the status of the Iranian nuclear programme. However, stretched in front of him, housed in the largest cavern he had ever seen lay a full-scale modern industrial complex.

Forklift trucks glided around. Huge centrifuges bearing the name Urenco stretched into the distance. Urenco! The European enrichment consortium led by the German engineering firm MAN. Why, this was technology that CERN had only just developed. Next, Dr Schlatter recognised the familiar machines and control systems manufactured by H&H Metelfarm GmbH, and Schonblin SA of Switzerland. There were the GI form of the centrifuge he had recently visited at Almelo in the Netherlands.

Saying nothing, Famel, Judi's mother's old flame from Genoa, led the dumbstruck Dr Schlatter further into the huge cavern. Again the huge power cables that had been so in evidence at Tunwaitta and other sites filled the floor space: and then the penny dropped.

'That was what was missing! You've no method of cooling at all the sites you've shown me. One hundred megawatts needs vast amounts of free flowing water and cooling towers. Those facilities could not possible work!'

Famel smiled and nodded, 'But they look as if they might.'

He walked on, leaving Dr Schlatter to catch up. 'So how do you cool it here?'

'If you follow the scientific reports, for years international geologists have commented on the falling levels of water in the Qom River. They've accused us of draining the water tables and causing huge environmental damage. But do you know what? No one has ever asked where the water goes.'

To make his point, he indicated upwards where Dr Schlatter could see huge two-metre pipes exiting the ceiling before being split into coils around the huge centrifuges. 'Yes. But where does the hot water go?' he asked, still puzzled.

'Simple. We pump it south into our oldest oilfield to keep the pressure up and the oil flowing. Oil floats on water does it not?'

'Clever, very clever,' muttered Dr Schlatter. 'No heat signature for the satellites either!' 'Correct, Doctor,' said a beaming Saleh. 'Correct'

* * *

Dr Schlatter's days merged as the project gathered pace in a complete industrial complex deep, and undetectable beneath the arid Dasht-e Kavir desert where, he estimated one hundred to 150 people worked in various locations. These facilities were all of impeccable quality, rivalling anything he had had at CERN and, for the first time for many weeks, he immersed himself enthusiastically in his task never concerning himself with the end result: his sole focus was the research – the pure research and the prospect of what it promised to achieve that filled his thoughts.

After a week in the luxurious surroundings of his underground prison he was overjoyed when Judi was brought to him. She questioned little but revelled in her new life of carefree opulence.

Although the Iranians had spent the money well, the project had been failing because of the inferior quality and limited knowledge of the engineers deep in the bowels of the earth. As Dr Schlatter gradually synchronised the operation of the giant machines, production started to increase.

Most of the nuclear enrichment had been attained at Natanz, but it took the special equipment under the mountains of Fordo to take it to over ninety percent fissile material. Dr Schlatter was under no illusion as to its purpose, but he was mollified by the presence of Judi and the considerable rewards his efforts were delivering.

Furthermore, he enjoyed the quiet satisfaction that without him, the project had little chance of success. Here, at the frontiers of this rarified science, he was much an artist as a technician, a fact that others slowly began to appreciate as they watched him slowly tune the huge machines, playing with the control panels as he smoothed the current that sent the fragile centrifuges spinning at phenomenal speeds to separate the isotopes. Only a small interruption of the power could cause them to spin out of control, wrecking the entire plant. And yet, after a mere four weeks he had single-handedly enriched most of the stock of Uranium 235 that the Iranians held.

The four men who had attended the mausoleum at Ferdowsi had now come to the plant and were sitting, waiting in the luxurious boardroom, into which a nervous Dr Schlatter was shown and invited to sit at one end.

There were no formalities, and they got straight down to business. 'You have enough material for how many devices, doctor?' was General Bhageri's flat enquiry.

'Five hundred kilos, enough for ten, General,' Dr Schlatter replied beaming with pride.

The four sat back in their chairs. Hussein Salami picked up an old-fashioned telephone and dialled. At an unknown location, Mojtaba answered and then whispered in his father's ear. The Supreme Leaders rheumy eyes looked into the far distance. Then he nodded, and a moment later the phone was put down.

Azadi spoke, to tell the meeting, 'Inform the Supreme Leader's office we have 450 kilos, enough for nine,' there was a silence but the look of the others' faces expressed their surprise. 'Remember,' Azadi reminded them, 'Mossad has ears closer than our own The Great Satan will know soon enough.'

* * *

Israeli attacks on missile sites on the northern border had delayed Commander Raffique's messenger to the monastery in Turkey. It was only now, two weeks, before the smuggler's execution that Father Sebastian heard the cell door slam behind him as he embraced a pale Thomas.

The coarse dark material of the uncommonly brawny monk's habit, bound by the familiar braided belt, brought memories tumbling back for Thomas. His Uncle in Burtonport had been a member of the Sons of Sion: a secretive order not known for its hospitality.

This unlikely pair sat and talked long into the night. Although it was Thomas who did most of that talking, rambling on about his life while Father Sebastian listened benignly.

It was Thomas' smuggling activities that seemed to interest him the most, to the point when, at one stage, feigning discomfort in the heat of the cell, the monk loosened his habit enough to reveal to Thomas the olive-green fatigues he was wearing underneath it.

Thomas' birthplace too evoked much enquiry, although Father Sebastian did emphasise that he had never been to Ireland himself.

* * *

Two weeks later, the mullah had preached his last and the crowd had dispersed into the square for the afternoon's entertainment. Three prisoners were due to have their hands removed for stealing, and two were to be executed.

The amputations proceeded quickly. Each man had his crimes read aloud to the crowd before the curved silver scimitar came flashing down, with cheers and applause greeting each sickening thud.

Hanging was not a formal affair in Iran: two small hire cranes were parked in the corner of the yard. The first prisoner, a terrified forty-five year old, had raped the daughter of the local baker. Feelings had run high since his capture two weeks before and the guards had some difficulty in beating back the crowd as he was brought forward. The father of the raped girl had demanded, as was his right under sharia law, that no blindfold or hood be given to the prisoner so he could watch and see him die. Neither were his limbs to be bound.

The hook from one of the cranes hovered above the man's head as a noose was placed around his neck. With two guards holding his struggling arms, the mullah nodded to the crane driver and, with a cough of black diesel smoke, the hook rose skyward with its grotesque, kicking, scratching cargo provoking cheers from the crowd.

Thomas swallowed hard. In the cell, Father Sebastian was waiting to take his body out of Iran and was twisting his fingers around his small signet ring which bore the engraving of the double-headed eagle on a black shield with a gold band.

A stifling hood was forced over Thomas' head as he was pushed forward. His knees gave way when the noose slipped round his head. With the coarse cloth now blinding him and muffling his hearing, he was unaware of the three black Mercedes saloons that had swept into the rear of the small square. All twelve doors had burst open and uniformed figures had run to the back of the crowd. Thomas heard shots over the revving of the crane engine ... and then it was all over.

CHAPTER 49

The strains of the elderly organ died away as the congregation gathered their hymnbooks and orders of service. Father Ben surveyed the small gathering, but his thoughts were elsewhere. A shuffling noise from the aisle indicated that Brandon, the elderly churchwarden, was snuffing out the votive candles and was preparing to lock up for the night.

Ben had taken Mass that evening although he was rostered to be off duty. For three days since that envelope inviting them to the monastery in Dungloe had dropped through the letterbox, Raffy had retreated into himself. Ben had come and gone in the study to be met with only grunts of recognition as volumes of open books had surrounded his colleague. But tonight, as the church door slammed behind him in the porch and Brandon made his farewells and shambled off down the path in the direction of Burtonport, the little town's twinkling lights made up Ben's mind for him.

When he had left Hereford, he had jettisoned most of his previous life. The day he walked back into the seminary in Liverpool had wiped his conscience clean and for months now his life in the army had been a memory he rarely visited. However, Ben had kept some items from his past and it was to his battered kit bag he now went, with sense of purpose and resolve he had not felt for a very long time.

* * *

With a stream of faintly blue smoke trailing his old Land Rover, Ben had accelerated hard out of the presbytery's drive and turned north. The few minutes he had taken to remove the canvas hood, door taps and windscreen now gave his evening drive an air of exhilaration. The Land Rover's eager coarseness and whining transmission somehow dispelled the cloud that had dogged him for the last three days, and he bucketed down the road with the damp early evening air streaming at him he suddenly feeling invincible.

The narrow road to Dungloe was deserted and once away from Burtonport's lights its limestone-chipping surface reflected a pale eerie glow in the moonlight. Ben leaned forward and twisted the large rotary switch on the small aluminium dashboard to turn off the headlights. Tearing along the road without forward illumination further heightened his sense of anticipation. He had not brought a map, preferring to commit any details of the terrain to memory, and when the pale silver road swept gently to the right, he could see the old Dungloe Head lighthouse and the regular pulse of its light flashing through the night. The monastery lay over the next rise and Ben slowed as he sought the small lane he knew was there.

By folding down his windscreen, he had to make do without his rear-view mirror. As such he had had just a flash of an approaching headlamp in his tiny wing mirror before the big bike was on him. One of the attributes of BMW's boxer engine is its relative silence and, with Ben's thoughts elsewhere, the silver BMW K100 swept past him before he knew it was there. Startled, he had barely time to notice that it did not have a rear number plate, before the powerful machine was swallowed up in the darkness.

Not the best start, he acknowledged. He must have lost his edge. And with this sense of annoyance gnawing at him at being taken unawares, he continued towards the top of the hill in the distance. When he came to a small lane to his left, heading towards the sea, he turned down it to leave the Land Rover out of sight behind a stone wall. Just to be sure, Ben pulled out the camouflage net and draped it over its angular shape.

Ben followed the patchwork of fields, keeping in the shadow of the uneven stone walls, only crossing them swiftly when he needed to. At the crest of the hill, inching forward on his belly in the lee of the wall, he caught a glimpse of the monastery. It lay in a natural bowl some half-a-mile away where the land sloped gently downwards and then rose sharply, giving the monastery a good defensive position he noted.

It was a large building with ornate gothic turrets. Built by a cotton baron in the last century it mimicked a German schloss with its curving walls and soaring turrets. Surrounding this incongruous edifice the reason for much of the monastery's self-sufficiency could be seen neatly laid out in a neat patchwork of turned earth and crops. But these well-tended fields were silent now: just an occasional light lit up the austere facade and the tolling of a sole bell carried to him across the valley.

Ben lay there listening to the bell for several minutes. Its sound lulled him but despite a gathering chill from the earth he stayed motionless, remembering similar situations from times past. What would the old troop make of it, he wondered, if they knew he had staked out a monastery? That led him to recall the drive away from that ranch in Guatemala. Chas in the rear of the Land Rover explaining about the monk he swore he had seen in the compound and the rest of the lads exploding with mirth. Yes, that was a blast – and he exhaled deeply at the memory.

Then the memory vanished and he froze. Some forty centimetres above him a bright red beam revealed itself through the ethereal swirling of his breath. Instantly alert now, Ben gently breathed out again and watched fascinated as the invisible infra-red beam sliced through the pale cloud.

Not too low to be triggered by small nocturnal animals, but not high enough to duck underneath with any speed, the beam maintained its vigil while Ben lay beneath for long moments breathing into it as if to blow it away.

Once he had its coordinates clear in his mind, Ben he slithered on his back using his elbows and knees to edge along the lee of the low wall, where the beam was being emitted directly from a small hole right in the centre of a stone. Cupping his hands around his miniature Maglite, and using his breath to reveal the beams presence, he carefully examined the large stone. It took a while, but then he found the power source at the base of the wall buried under undergrowth, where the conduit and armour-plated cable disappeared into the base of the wall.

This was no temporary infra-red security device; it was competently installed, and a permanent early warning system. Experience had taught him what would happen if the beam were broken and he gently passed his hand through the thin red line of light. He was instantly rewarded by a low click to his right, which drew him to a small lens, again set in a stone to the right of the beam. A night vision device, he was sure. But why?

Retracing his approach to the monastery in his mind, he was sure he had found the outer perimeter warning system, as the other fields he had crossed all had large livestock, whereas none of the fields around the monastery showed signs of cattle. No, this beam was the first point at which anything larger than a cow or sheep could be detected. Time to leave.

Back in the dry ditch at the side of the road all was quiet until he picked up the faint, almost indiscernible beat of an engine steadily approaching. He sank down, remembering his instructor at Hereford, 'Understand the earth, sink into it, be part of it'. The approaching motorbike engine became louder, and without raising his head he knew what was coming: the cylinder head of the horizontally opposed BMW engine swept past no more than one metre away. Moving at fifteen to twenty miles an hour, the unlit bike continued down the road without a pause. Raising his head through the vegetation Ben watched it depart with the two figures astride it peering carefully from side to side. For the second time that night, its two helmeted figures rotating their heads side to side as they patrolled the road.

Two? On a motorbike! his mind flicked again to Guatemala. A warm final evening, the shocking discovery in the church and the cough of the motorcycle engine outside.

* * *

Ben had driven back to the presbytery and had not seen the motorbike again. He had parked quickly in the open garage, shut the doors and, using the back staircase, had appeared in the study nonchalantly sporting slacks and T-shirt and yawning elaborately.

Raffy turned from his books. 'Hi Ben. Nice drive?'

'Mm, yes thanks, just needed to clear my head.'

'Don't we all,' Raffy observed wryly, before turning again to his books. Ben watched him, bowed in study. He wondered about his outburst the other evening and his curious reaction to the mentioning of the monastery. One thing Ben was certain of: there had been pure fear in Raffy's eyes as he had closed the curtains and locked the door.

'Raffy ...' he began, 'the monastery ...'

'Oh sorry, I forgot. They rang half-an-hour before you returned to ask if we were able to attend Mass and do the homily. I've said yes for both of us but explained you were out. Is that alright?'

Ben nodded.

CHAPTER 50

Whenever Ben had come back from 'ops' in his previous life, release from the tension and constant adrenaline surges had been of an alcoholic nature. Wild nights out, mixed with intense training in the day, led to a camaraderie and team spirit investing the troop with an air of invincibility. Now he was on his own, lying in the darkness of the silent presbytery, unable to sleep.

Out of the blue, following a whim, something had changed. Everything screamed at him to probe further and yet, something he could not explain was preventing him.

Raffy made a superb priest. His depth of knowledge and spiritual understanding of the faith was no doubt helped by his experience 'on the other side' – an experience few 'cradle Catholics' ever had.

Was Ben overreacting, he wondered? Was the use of security devices belonging to the twenty-first century any different to a fence or wall keeping out unwanted visitors hundreds of years ago?

The motorbike, he decided, was the difference. Not only that motorbike, but the snarl of the tiny Honda back in his past filled his mind as he drifted off to sleep.

* * *

By midweek Ben's curiosity had the better of him. Yet again, as he popped his head round the study door, Raffy had muttered 'goodnight' and returned to whatever volume he was poring over that evening. It was time for Maggie's Bar; early he knew, the sun had barely dipped to the horizon, but Ben was looking for someone.

He found him, off the small hall in what would have been the front room. Sitting in the corner with his feet carelessly resting on a cane chair, Burtonport's sole police officer was deep into the *Donegal News*.

'Same again Pat?' Ben asked.

'It'd be rude not to, if you're buying,' came the hearty response. Only when the two glasses of smooth dark Guinness had been ceremoniously and laboriously poured and set down did Pat O'Connor put aside the paper with a resigned look. Ben would be tolerated but his arrival had interrupted the study of form for the next race meeting where Pat fancied his chances.

'Shouldn't drink on duty,' he confided, eyeing the cream-topped glass thoughtfully. 'Still, my shift finishes in twenty minutes. Cheers Father!' at which a third of the contents smoothly disappeared before the glass was set carefully down and Pat slowly exhaled.

'Hard day?'

Pat grunted in reply.

'Not often we get to chat properly. This place is always full,' Ben gestured to the silent chairs.

Pat's eyes grew wary. 'Father I'll take your drink, but this ain't no confessional'.

'No Pat, it isn't. And I've not got my collar on.'

The two men lapsed into easy conversation. It turned out they shared a military background. Pat had joined the Irish army in 1973; first as a driver, then progressing to their equivalent of the engineering and heavy logistics division. The two ex-soldiers chatted easily, a bond established, no longer priest and parishioner, just two men having a quiet pint with a common background.

Eventually, as soldiers do, after the second glass of Guinness was nearing the end Ben said casually, 'Ever wondered why you joined Pat?'

Pat stiffened and stillness settled over the corner of the darkening room. 'It was after the bombing of Claudy in '72', he finally said. 'You see I was there. I was nineteen when that car destroyed the village. A wee girl, no more than nine or ten had been cleaning her parents shop front; the car had been parked right next to her.'

Pausing he took a reflective sip at his pint. 'The blast pushed her through the walls, but she was alive when I reached her. She had the most amazing eyes: they were the only thing left intact and she died in my arms.'

The narrative was delivered in calm, soldierly fashion, but Ben knew he had touched a nerve. 'Couldn't see what uniting the country would have done for that little girl; before,' pause 'before that,' Pat said, gathering himself.

'I was a firebrand I suppose. Looking back, I probably would have ended up in the IRA, but that wee girl's eyes changed everything for good. After that, each time Sinn Fein spoke on TV or visited the village, I'd see her and I wondered why. I used to be angry and carried that day with me for years, but all they'd say was it was a war.'

'So, you joined the army,' Ben's cautious statement carrying neither praise nor rancour.

'Hah! I cocked up my basic training and convinced the doc my eyesight was no good for combat. But I made damned sure I excelled at driving and mechanics.'

'And now, Pat? What do you think?'

'That day in 1972 never left me, you know. I came here twenty years ago during the Troubles. I'd been all round the world with the army and I land a dream beat for the Garda, and do you know what?'

Ben remained silent.

'My first day on the beat, shiny new patrol car and all, I see him standing at the bus stop.'

'Who?' said Ben.

'Him, Father Chesney from Claudy.'

Ben's face remained curious, So?'

Pat sniffed, 'Jim Chesney was for the 'RAH' alright. A true Republican. He used the Claudy pulpit like his soapbox: we were all only eighteen or nineteen, but the presbytery was full of them. Men with Ford Cortinas and Granadas, big men, silent men, men with darkness in their hearts. The Brits knew them for what they were, of course. Helicopters were all over the place, and up above Claudy they'd built one of those eagle nest observation posts.'

Ben nodded.

'After the bombing, of course, came Bloody Sunday and it got wiped off the front pages. But we knew, and what's more the Bishop of Derry knew.'

Ben summoned Maggie with a nod, indicating the empty glasses. 'Knew? The bishop knew of Father Chesney's activities? I'd doubt that.'

'You would, Father Ben, but you're not of here, see? Bishop Daly knew fine, but he couldn't prove a thing. So after a while they moved him. I think he went to Head in Derry, but he was definitely here and on more than one occasion. I saw him after in the town and at the bus stop.'

'Bus stop Pat? You mean on the Dungloe Road?'

'Aye, the one past the monastery.'

There it was again: the monastery. But, either from the Guinness or the need to reflect, the conversation lapsed. Pat idly checked the miscellaneous sales column. Ben examined minutely the dregs in his empty glass until Maggie's bustling entrance broke the ice and Ben continued, 'So you never followed it up?'

'Nah, he was never charged or even under suspicion; it was just gossip.'

'Nothing to do with the monastery then?' finished Ben idly.

'Oh you've been listening to Seamus again. If you ever let another joiner work on the church apart from him, he'd have all the west coast thinking you and Raffy were Druids, I'd bet!' he chuckled to himself. 'They just keep themselves to themselves that's all,' he finished lamely.

And there the conversation should have ended.

Both men sat savouring what was, by silent understanding, their last point as the front door opened and footfalls announced the arrival of the rest of the evening's hardcore drinkers. 'Mind you Father, there is one thing ...'

'Go on,' said Ben softly.

'Years back, they sent me on a course. You know, completely irrelevant to my day-to-day work, but so someone in Dublin could tick the box marked "international co-operation".'

Ben nodded, sagely.

'Anyway, I ended up in Manchester, studying inner-city methods. Fat use here, but still. I was partnered with a chap called Kieran O'Leary, an ex-marine and now in their Tactical Aid Group for Longsight and Mosside. They're the big immigrant inner-city areas, Father, used to be called the curry mile,' explained Pat.

Ben nodded, but his attention was frankly drifting. He had never been to Manchester, but the dreary surroundings of the seminary in Liverpool some forty miles away had made visiting another northern city a low priority.

'Well, we'd been to a party one night – Kieran had some new post to go to, something with the new police helicopter what with him a marine and all that – and we were all sat in one of the curry houses in Longsight. Anyway, as the waiters came and went the evening got more and more raucous and the banter between the groups, police, Indians and Pakistanis grew we were all having a ball.

'I'd said something about the Indians and Pakistanis being great folk, something obviously I don't see here. The Manchester force was then undergoing the early stages of political correctness, and a lot of old attitudes were being stamped on. But then Kieran leant across and whispered, 'Watch them Pat. Watch them real careful. Four years here,' rolling his eyes at his surroundings, 'and not a sudden death in a community of 10–15,000 people.'

'So, what's the point?' Ben said sliding lower in his chair.

'Well, in any community, anywhere in the world someone will die sudden. Really old? Not always. Sometimes an accident. But anyways, the first to be involved are the police'. Ben nodded understanding. 'What Kieran was saying was that no one in that community died suddenly; naturally, yes, with doctors around, but no accidents.

'That was in order to keep the social paying for benefits – and that scam went on for years, probably still does.'

Ben's face began to frown in puzzlement, 'But you don't have immigrants here in this part of Ireland.'

'No father, we don't. But in twenty years, not one elderly novice from the monastery of Sion has ever died suddenly. I've often wondered. That's all.'

Ben glanced at his watch, 'Mm, must be off. Diocese meeting tomorrow.'

Pat gathered his paper, 'I'll come too, both of you having a chat with me makes me nervous.'

'Both?' Ben queried, as they left the narrow front door and stood on the darkened street.

'Father Raffique was quizzing me about the monastery two weeks ago,' Pat said over his shoulder as he strode away into the gathering gloom.

Ben watched him go. Policeman didn't wonder about things; they were by nature suspicious or not.

CHAPTER 51

The elderly Renault's tyres swished along the road, wet with last night's downpour but sparkling in the early sun. Ben decided it was impossible to be suspicious on such a glorious God-given day. The sky shone a pale luminous blue; fields reflected a deep richness of varying greens and hues, and over the tyre noise and rattling engine birds sang in the hedgerows.

Relishing the peace in the surroundings, Father Raffique smiled at Ben, taking his eyes off the road for a moment. 'I have a good feeling Ben, today. Maybe today God will wash away my doubt.'

Ben nodded, smiling back. It troubled him greatly, his mind was reacting as it would twelve months ago, but he had wanted to leave his former life and follow his chosen path. He almost regretted his nighttime foray to the monastery, pushing it to the back of his mind. He was on his way to serve Mass for the Order of Sion.

* * *

The little car crested the rise where only a short while before Ben had hidden his Land Rover. In the sparkling early sun, the peace of the woodlands and fields seemed to be mocking him.

To Ben and Raffy's surprise they joined a queue of various vehicles turning into the large abbey gates. At the stone archway the two novices were welcoming every vehicle's occupants. As their Renault approached, one of them came to the window. He was large man, aged around thirty-five, Ben guessed, and his fresh features displayed an openness that made Ben's heart sing.

'Good morning, Fathers,' he said in a rich melodious voice. 'Ignore the car park and sweep left around the walls. You'll see the vestry door on the right.'

'Thank you, thank you,' beamed Raffy as the vehicle left the stream of cars and came to a halt next to a small, studded door, where they stood awkwardly until the appearance of another large rotund figure who emerged from the doorway, as if squeezed out from the massive walls. With a swift movement of his left hand, he swept the dark hood from his head as his right hand extended in welcome. 'Father Padraic, pleased to see you. You must be Father Benjamin and Father Raffique?'

Ben and Raffy followed him through the doorway, where he held a finger to his lips a finger to his lips, gesturing that theirs was a silent order. Through the door, and with it carefully bolted, Ben and Raffy followed Father Padraic's billowing figure along the smooth stone passage silent except for the slap of his sandals on the smooth stone slabs.

It was a large passage, some two yards wide and stretching to the front of the monastery, where, Ben sensed, they would be approaching the chapel. Along its length he counted fifteen oak doors: all identical and firmly shut.

Silence pervaded the whole building. Only the rustle of their garments, the odd squeak from their suitcases and Father Padraic's sandaled feet betrayed their progress. At the final door Father Padraic double knocked twice and paused. There followed a scuffle from behind the door and then it was opened by a beaming figure in half-moon glasses, who bowed and indicated with a sweep of his arm that they should enter.

As the trio entered the vestry an overwhelming odour of male sweat assailed Ben's nostrils: a strange smell for a vestry, he thought, more akin to a gymnasium than a place of worship. The room was richly furnished in a dark oak. Individual wooden wardrobes lined the walls and in front of each cupboard, in various stages of undress, stood a line of novices. Nodding politely and following Father Padraic's lead in clasping the flat of his hands together in front, in supplication, Ben acknowledged the nodded greetings in a similar fashion.

As it was nearly time for Mass to start, most of them had donned long brown habits and robes and were busy tying the heavy silk plaited cord around themselves. A couple, who were obviously late were still struggling into their attire. Ben was struck by the clothes they wore underneath. The two brothers had on a one-piece overall in a dull olive-green. In fact, Ben thought, their get-up was more reminiscent of army workshop gear than novices in the service of God. Nor did their Vibram-soled commando boots go unnoticed.

A double clap summoned his attention to Father Padraic and the fully dressed column of novices positioned itself facing the door into the chapel, each figure cowled with head bowed and hands concealed in voluminous sleeves. Without further ceremony the column proceeded into the nave of the church to the faint accompaniment of 'Handel's Vespers' high above.

Uncowled and head high, Ben observed the congregation. In common with all Catholic churches, it was full to capacity with the faithful, row upon row of men and women gazing upwards in expectation.

Without exception, the men of the congregation wore dark suits of various vintages. White shirts with stiff starched collars and dark ties supported pink, scrubbed and shaved faces. Faces worn by the ceaseless winds of the Atlantic. Faces used to work on the land. Traditional faces thought Ben. It had been a long time since he had seen all the women wearing the mantilla of the high Catholic Church; but here, every woman did. Another striking detail was that there was not a person in the church under the age of thirty.

The faint strains of the opening vespers still carried around the church as the brothers entered the doors of the rood screen. Originally designed in the early centuries of the Church, its purpose was to keep the uneducated faithful away from the highly educated and learned priests. Ben had not seen a rood screen in operation since his childhood, and the magnificent examples that survived were now permanently open, the mystery of what had lain beyond lost and forgotten.

Father Padraic turned as the processions entered the portals of the rood, indicating with a gesture and bowed head the two small lecterns to the left and right of the doors. Without waiting for an answer, he resumed his journey through the rood. As Ben and Raffy hesitated and glanced at each other, the doors of the screen shut firmly.

Confused, the two priests turned and took up their places at their lecterns. Opening the parish Mass book at the ninth Sunday, both men paused and waited. The silence was long and drawn and broken only by the occasional cough or sniff.

Ben glanced sideways at Raffy, eyebrows raised before they were drawn upwards to admire the magnificent screen stretched from one wall to another, fully twenty feet in height. Above the ornate doors soared a golden cross: the only symbol the congregation could see. The screen itself was an intricate lace work of dark, carved wood, displaying panels of mathematically precise patterns and symmetry next to beautiful figures from biblical history: the beheading of John the Baptist being directly behind Ben.

Twisting further and for a moment forgetting the congregation, Ben stared at the carving. He had never seen such beauty in wood: the limbs, the expressions, the faces of the executioner all captured as if on film, with not the smallest detail omitted.

Lost in thought and still ignoring the congregation, Ben turned the opposite way and, from down the centuries, Van Eyck's painting leapt at him, except this was a faithful replica in wood. There was Urban on his throne outside the Cathedral of Clermont, in front the massed armies of Christendom looked reverently up at him, weapons raised. Ben looked at the fiery horseman in the forefront of the armed throng. His eyes fell upon the double-headed eagle on the black background emblazoned on a young man's breastplate and he felt a shiver run down his spine.

But his mind was drawn back to the morning's proceedings by the deep, melodious baritone voice that began soaring upwards from behind the rood screen. 'Gloria Patri, et filio, et Spiritui Sancto' sang the deep lonely voice. 'Sicut erat in principio, et nunc, et semper, et in saecula saeculorum. Amen' came the response.

The plainsong of the early church had been with Ben since childhood and in his eventful journey to the present there were times when he had thought the music more important than God. Much to the mirth of his old SAS troop, his tapes of vespers and psalms cluttered whatever vehicle he was using at the time: the soaring chords and deep baritones of the early church chants lifting him as never before. A strange combination to take him into battle, but in a way his battles had always been God's battles in Ben's eyes. His last seven years merely an extension of his deep faith. But once again his mind was dragged back when the melody stopped, and silence ensued.

Father Padraic began the *confiteor*, or priest's confession. The doors behind Raffy remaining firmly closed. Ben looked at the rows of faithful in front of them and he was suddenly reminded of an old black and white film he had seen, he could not remember when, but a long time ago: there was a missionary preaching to the local population somewhere. Somewhere poor and backward, where the priest represented authority, bureaucracy, justice and God. He did not feel part of the Mass; he did not think the congregation did either, but there they stood, row upon row of placid, peaceful faces.

Something was missing, Ben realised, as he watched the congregation mouth 'Christ have mercy', to the faint chants of Kyrie Eleison from the other side of the screen. He racked his brain: everything seemed so normal and yet … He glanced at Raffy who was mouthing the Antiphon to the Priests' chant behind him: eyes closed, hands clasped, his olive features calm in prayer.

Ben felt suddenly guilty. Moving his hands, palm together he stretched his neck backwards and closed his eyes, raising his face upwards.

At the rear of the church, above the entrance stood the organ loft, its silver pipes stretching in neat order across the rear wall. The church's only lighting came from four large, nondescript candelabra fittings hung some fifteen feet above the bowed heads of the congregation. Their effect was, from the floor at least, that the ceiling was shrouded in darkness by the brightness of the lamps shining downwards. Thus, Ben's upturned face could see nothing beyond the lights when he opened his eyes.

From above the organ loft, however, it was different – and there Maria stared down into the church from her tiny balcony; her hands clasping and unclasping on the wooden rail in front. It seemed light years ago and equally just a matter of minutes. But here he was, now! And her stomach fluttered at the memory. Her firm figure leant forward, prompting the dark, cowled figure next to her to ask, 'Well is it him?'

'Oh, yes,' she breathed heavily, 'It's him, alright'. Her chest rose and fell. 'My only failure, and now he's back'.

'Sure, we still want him after these years?'.

'He would have been perfect at the time,' hissed Maria, 'if he hadn't upped and joined the army. By now he would have been in place.'

'We had everything ready: a soft appointment with an elderly sleeper, his exam results, and that tape'. She smiled softly to herself at the last observation.

'And what has he been up to in the British army then?' came the deep, measured question.

'Regular appointment in the Royal Green Jackets. Two tours overseas. No combat experience. No mention in dispatches. His family always served, but to no great distinction'.

'Maria, are we sure?' Without waiting for a reply the tall figure went on, 'What we are pretty sure about is that he was up on the outer fence the other night. He was definitely out of the presbytery, and Liam saw him on the Dungloe Road'.

Maria pressed her lips together. 'Mm, well, let's run a check again in London. Maybe we should try a different approach. Perhaps from a friendly embassy?' At the last words she looked directly at the figure behind her. Nodding briefly, he moved off down the dimly lit corridor, with Maria following in his wake.

Through the door at the end, the couple entered a richly decorated room, some forty feet in length. Dark oak panels covered the walls in between bookshelves stacked with old leather-bound volumes. At three intervals along one wall, large French windows opened out onto an ornamental balcony at the top of the monastery The room's deep rich green carpet complimented the softly gleaming woodwork, but in spite of the richness of the decor, it was not for that, that the room demanded attention. Behind the carved oak chair at the head of the long, polished table, stood a motionless figure. Gleaming and polished as if his suit had left the forge that morning, a tall, armoured figure in full face helm stood motionless. But it was not the burnished armour of the thousand-year-old suit that drew attention. The white linen surcoat, now stitched to a nylon mesh to support its rotting fabric, had softened over the centuries but still the blood red cross patée dominated the room.

'I'd better go and find Elizabeth,' she said with a smile to the tall figure.

'Don't rush. Make it perfect,' he replied.

He had taken off his long brown robe revealing an olive-green one-piece suit such as Ben had witnessed earlier. As he hung his discarded robe in the wardrobe next to the armoured figure, a flash of a Cardinal's scarlet caught Maria's eye. Nodding she left the room closing the door softly.

The tall lithe figure moved swiftly down the room to press the spine of one of the richly bound books, at which a panel swung forward revealing a bank of eight small screens, which sprang to flickering life at the touch of buttons on an adjacent panel. The lower two screens showed the service in progress in the church beneath his feet.

The finger stabbed again. This time a greenish tinge lit the top screens as the video ran. Slowly the camera focused on a shapeless mass in the gloom, who raised a hand and passed within inches of the lens, and then it was gone. The tall figure's mouth compressed, as he switched off the flickering evidence.

Behind Ben a shuffling of feet and a click indicated the rood doors opening. They revealed Father Padraic, cowl swept back, beaming openness directed at the congregation as he welcomed their two 'guests'. Beyond him Ben caught sight of the row of cowled figures all with their backs to him.

With a nod from Father, Raffy got to his feet and the rest of the congregation sat down and made themselves comfortable as they listened to the Homily. Raffy had chosen well in preaching the need for greater evangelism, not only between local churches, but also in the wider world beyond Donegal. He thanked his host for the invitation to address the congregation that morning, observing softly he had been parish priest of Burtonport for four years and yet the appointment of a young priest, indicating Ben, had produced an invitation to visit within weeks.

Ben watched Father Padraic as Raffy's soft chiding reached his ears. His eyes flickered and stared upwards to the ceiling. Ben followed his gaze but could see nothing through the light of the candelabras.

As Raffy concluded, Father Padraic nodded to the rear of the church and three catechumens came forward with the Mass offerings. As the three members of the congregation approached he turned and led them through the rood screen. The trio, with Father at their head, moved up the nave to the ornate alter as the ranks of novices began the offertory psalm.

'Suscipe, Sancte Pater ....' Ben and Raffy let the rest of the congregation mutely shuffle forward in an orderly line to the altar rail to receive the body and blood of Christ. As the last member entered the rood doors, Ben and Raffy turned and walked up the mosaic tiles.

They knelt at the altar. To their left the last of the congregation had received the bread and wine and had begun to rise. The first novice approached with the nearly empty silver plate in his hand. Placing the thin wafer on Raffy's proffered tongue he uttered, 'The body of Christ' and moved to Ben repeating the words. Some distance behind him came the second novice bearing an ornate silver chalice. For no reason Ben's eyes watched as he offered the cup to Raffy. But, with the cup barely a fraction of an inch of Raffy's expectant lips, and his hands raised to tilt its base to sip the wine, the chalice was firmly taken away and was offered to Ben, who took a deep draught to the blessing of 'The blood of Christ' from the cowled novice.

Glancing upwards as the rich fluid passed his lips Ben could see two dark eyes from the depths of the novice's cowl. He could almost feel Raffy's surprise when the two rose from the altar rail and walked slowly down the nave and exited through the rood screen doors, which shut firmly behind them.

Ben and Raffy stood next to Father Padraic at the porch as the largely silent congregation shuffled out. Ben was struck by the lack of warmth in the congregation but put it down to the monks belonging to a silent order, and when the last had gone on their way they followed Father Padraic back to the vestry to de-robe and collect their bags.

'Father Ben,' said Father Padraic. 'The most Reverend Colm Hegarty, Chevalier of our order here in Ireland would very much like to meet you. Could you spare half an hour?' The tone indicated it was not a request, but as Ben turned to Raffy and opened his mouth to discuss it, Father Padraic smoothly continued, 'I'm sorry, only Father Ben has an invitation, Father Raffique'.

Raffy's face darkened as he nodded to Ben, 'Sure, Ben, I'll wait outside, the Chevalier must be very busy'. But as he picked his case up and went out of the vestry door he looked back at Ben, to say, 'See you in half an hour', his eyes dark and direct – overtones which Father Padraic either missed, or ignored missed as he held open the door.

'I believe you've met Elizabeth,' said Father Padraic, gesturing to the rising figure behind the desk. 'Good heavens Benjamin, is it you?' Elizabeth smiled gently as she came round to greet him. The same scraped back hair; the thick mascara; the same below-the-knee tweed skirt. Ben's mind reeled. So, it was her he had seen in the village weeks before. Those eyes, he knew then but could not place her. He was suddenly back in the seminary in Liverpool: a raw eighteen-year-old, his life in front of him. Was it really eight years ago?

Elizabeth had rounded the desk and grabbed his hand. 'So glad you came back, Ben, I knew you would'.

Ben was touched by her expression of faith, but before he could continue the conversation, Father Padraic had ushered him through the office and past yet another open door. It led to the room so recently vacated by Elizabeth, and at its table head sat the figure Ben had come to meet.

'Excuse me, Chevalier Hegarty. I've brought Father Ben for you'.

Ben couldn't help noticing the transition from bustling priest to efficient servant, as the tall figure rose, putting his pen down firmly. Ben strode up the room and to shake hands. Six foot two, or three, this man had a rangy soldierly look about him, his face creased and weathered, and bright blue eyes twinkling beneath greying eyebrows. His attire was similar to the novices Ben had noticed in the vestry: olive green fatigues and soft boots.

'Tea and sandwiches, Padraic,' he snapped. 'And send Elizabeth in, won't you?' And that was not a question either. 'We're part of an order, not members of a democracy', he told Ben curtly.

* * *

Ben gazed round the room, taking in his surroundings. He was familiar with Van Eyck's work and that seemed to be in some way to be connected to the order. His gaze fell on the armoured figure behind Colm, which the other man noted.

'We are the oldest order of Christ's soldiers in the world, Ben. We don't run parishes. We don't participate in the diocese. We are a contemplative silent order dedicated to overthrowing the enemies of Christ'.

Ben glanced again at the armoured figure and lightly countered, 'And here's me thinking the Crusades finished with De Molay's death'.

Colm's reaction surprised him. The man threw back his head and guffawed: a deep amused laugh. 'A lost battle in the eternal war!'

He was still smiling to himself when their sandwiches arrived and Elizabeth poured tea for the three of them.

'How's Father Raffique, Ben?' Colm enquired.

'Well, you could ask him yourself', chided Ben.

Colm stopped chewing, and answered reproachfully, 'We pride ourselves here on fighting for Christ. Not one man would surrender his principles for the other side'.

232

This comment pulled Ben up short. 'Hardly ecumenical that.' Angry now, he stood his ground as the atmosphere grew tense.

'How many sides has your family fought for in the past 500 years?'

The question floored Ben. 'Well, I ...'

'Precisely,' sneered Colm.

'Now, now boys,' interrupted Elizabeth, 'You've only just met.' She looked at Ben critically and glared harder at Colm. That did the trick.

'Sorry Ben. Apologies. Anyway, how's parish life?'

And that was the start of a conversation that ebbed and flowed as Ben felt increasingly sure that he was being carefully probed by the two of them. In spite of that, he had spent way beyond the half-hour Raffy was expecting when he checked his watch and realised he had to go.

The Renault remained silent as drove out of the gates and the familiar cowled figure closed them behind. The silence continued as the car swished along the still wet roads with both men deep in their private thoughts.

It was Ben who spoke first. 'Did you see Van Eyck's image in the rood screen?'

Raffy nodded.

'And it was there again in the Chevalier's office'. Raffy looked at Ben, momentarily taking his eyes from the road, but still he said nothing.

Back in the presbytery, Eileen, the elderly housekeeper, had lit a fire and the rain began to beat against the windows. Without a conscious decision Ben poured two small measures and the clink of glasses broke their silence.

Neither mentioned their unsettling visit to the monastery, but their attempt at small talk was ended when Raffy asked, 'Ben, have you moved any of my books?'

'Raffy, I've my own desk. Why would I do anything like that'.

'Well. Someone's moved things here, and it's not Eileen. She knows it's the only place in the house she doesn't touch'.

He decided to check his computer. 'Ben, someone's messed with this too.'

'Raffy, don't be daft'.

'No Ben. I'm serious. 'Someone's accessed this since we left this morning'.

* * *

Twenty-four hours later the shrill tone of a telephone rang along darkened corridors, four floors beneath Pall Mall in London. It rang a dozen times or more and was eventually answered by a smartly dressed WAAF: 'Records Office. Staff Sergeant Campbell speaking', frowning slightly she listened intently to the smooth well-educated tones in her ear.

'Do you wish to hold on, or shall I ring you back, sir?' her back stiffening as she listened to the voice.

'Yes, sir, one moment', at which, she placed the receiver down on the desktop and disappeared down a long dimly lit aisle of files. Dragging a small-wheeled stair trolley behind her she began searching, 'M, Mount, Mountford. Got it,' she muttered, 'Benjamin Mountford'. She took the buff manila file back to the the little office, picked up the receiver and said, 'Here we are, sir, I have the file. Not much in it, I'm afraid. Officer entry from Sandhurst. A letter from his father detailing past family history. Royal Green Jackets. Two overseas tours. No mention in dispatches'. The conversation paused.

'Very well, sir. Thank You'.

Staff Sergeant Campbell replaced the receiver. It had been one hell of a party the night before and her head hurt a lot. Still, something worried her. Not in five years had she taken an enquiry from an overseas embassy. Requests usually came through the normal channels upstairs. When did the first secretary of a British embassy ever make a call like that?

Thumbing the buff folder reflectively, she set off down the aisle to replace it. But the nagging doubt persuaded her to take a seat at a small desk and look through it again: more carefully this time. But the sparse contents, yielded no further secrets: nothing of any interest at all. She was about to close the file when she spotted something at last: the record of access stamped on the inside cover. Another enquiry not ten days before, and what's more Mountford's discharge reference.

This comprised his military number, date of birth and payroll reference, which were followed by the triple three code she recognised. Mountford had been involved in covert operations and his superiors needed to know if someone was digging into his past. According to the record, the previous enquiry had not been logged upstairs. Feeling vindicated, Sergeant Campbell headed to the lift.

CHAPTER 52

Twenty-four hours later a telephone rang again. This time it was followed by the scraping of a chair as Father Raffique put the receiver down in the study and called upstairs for Ben, 'It's Father Ryan from Liverpool.'

'Father Ryan, good to hear from you! Still growing seedlings for us?' Ben chuckled with genuine pleasure at hearing his old friend's voice once more.

'Ben, how are you?' and the conversation rambled on about nothing in particular for a minute or two, until Ryan explained, 'Someone called George Parker rang for you, Ben. Something about some antiques belonging to your family? Anyway, I wouldn't tell him where you were, but I promised to pass on the message.'

'Thanks Father,' said Ben, jotting down the phone number Ryan gave him on a small part of Raffy's note pad and stuffing the fragment in his pocket.

This was a call that Ben could not make on the presbytery phone. The phone booth on the main street in Burtonport would suffice, although the ill-lit, deserted and the single bulb illuminating the kiosk seemed to mock Ben's approach.

Not so the person he was telephoning. His call was answered immediately with a single word, 'Parker'.

'Mountford, sir,' countered Ben.

'Secure line?'

'Public booth sir.'

'OK Ben. One minute only. Someone's been accessing your official records.' Ben gripped the receiver, the kiosk feeling fragile suddenly.

'Two approaches. One, I'm afraid to say, taken by a temp in the MOD and not properly logged. The other from our embassy in Rome. Any reasons why? Are you OK?'

Ben fell silent a moment, fingering the small silver crucifix under his jacket. 'Rome!' Suddenly Elizabeth's face swam into view, coming round the desk. 'You've met before . . .' from a beaming Father Padraic.

'Ben! Ben! Are you there?'

'Yes, sorry sir. Of course. Let me know if access is tried again? Thanks.'

* * *

As he let the heavy door of the booth slam shut, the green and cream single decker bus passed down the street, on the way out of town. Behind the driver, unmistakeable with her hair swept back, sat Elizabeth. Her head bowed, she was talking animatedly into a small handset.

Later that evening in Maggie's, at further cost to the parish funds, Ben extracted a promise to Pat O'Connor to let him have the parts of the mobile phones that Pat had collected in the course of duty around the town.

Pat eyed him warily. 'I have a friend in England who sends old phones and the like to the Third World. You know, our castaways are their necessities. Mm . . . Yes. I don't see why not. They're not part of a criminal investigation as such.'

Nodding his thanks, Ben arranged for Pat to drop them at the presbytery in the morning.

He was awake in the darkness before dawn. It was these moments Ben savoured: warm, snug and secure, yet with the open presbytery windows facing the soft onshore breeze. The silence of the dawn not yet broken by birdsong, was still enough to hear the crashing breakers nearly a quarter of a mile away.

Something else had woken him, though: a sound, or the cessation of a sound. Dimly his memory dredged backwards through the curtain of sleep. An engine switching off. Wide awake now, he rolled sideways, keeping on his knees as he peered around the open window.

Out on the road, making no attempt to conceal themselves, stood a dozen motionless, dark clad figures. Behind the large minibus that had brought this mysterious group, a dark car pulled up. A door opened and the interior light revealed a peak capped gentleman of ruddy complexion. What on earth was going on?

Four hammered brisk knocks hammered on the presbytery door. Down the cool tiled hall, the shadow of the tall inspector's cap spread towards him. Ben flung open the door to the ruddy faced inspector.

'Good morning, sir. Sorry to trouble you. Father Raffique Alhambra?'

'No, Father Benjamin Mountford actually. What on earth is going on?'

'I have a warrant to search these premises and interview Father Alhambra.' Then he moved to step forward, but Ben stood his ground bringing the ruddy complexion to within inches of his own.

'And your warrant?'

Snapping his fingers at a bemused constable, Inspector O'Neill, said, 'The warrant man. Now!'

Eventually, the folded piece of paper was produced and proffered to Ben.

'Thank you, Inspector. Now if you'll wait just there, I'll go into the study and read this'.

He entered the room to find Raffy already standing at his desk, visibly trembling.

'Ben. Ben, what on earths happening?'

'Don't panic Raffy; they'll have the wrong address or something,' he said lightly as he skimmed the terms of the warrant.

'You don't understand, my friend,' Raffy said. 'Where I come from, a visit from the police at this hour means only one thing'.

Ben laughed quietly, 'Raffy this is Ireland, not Iraq!' The details on the warrant seemed frighteningly accurate, however. Ben frowned.

'Something's not right, Ben?' Raffy asked nervously.

'They want to take away our PC for "forensic analysis," whatever that means.'

'Pah. I knew it. I told you. Someone has messed with it'.

Ben looked across at his friend. 'Raffy this is a legal document. We have no choice but to comply'. This was not what Raffy needed to hear, and Ben shook his head hoping to reassure his friend.

'Raffy, look. Let them search. Let them examine our PC. I'm sure that the Women's Guild cleaning rota and next week's sermon will make riveting reading! They'll be back all sheepish before the day is out'.

But Raffy was anything but reassured. He grabbed Ben's arm and told him anxiously, 'If I'm taken ... What I mean is if they get me; clean the tabernacle for me, won't you?' Then he went into the hall and announced, 'Is it I you seek, Inspector?'

* * *

Soon it was over. The presbytery creaked and thudded to the steps of twelve large policemen as they methodically searched room by room. A thin faced man, who did not introduce himself seemed to concentrate around Raffy's desk. After boxes of his historical volumes had been loaded into the waiting van, the small computer hummed as the nameless man switched it on. Thin pale fingers skimmed the keys, while the screen changed so fast Ben could hardly keep up. Rolling columns of phone numbers from the internet access history flashed up, and a moment later Ben caught the look between the seated expert and Inspector O'Neil.

Dawn had broken, by the time they had finished and driven off. They had not handcuffed him but, in all but name, Raffy had been arrested and put in the back of the unmarked car. As he had left the presbytery, Raffy had turned to Ben and shaking his hand firmly before had executing that small formal bow that he used at Mass to pass the host to Ben. That troubled Ben more than the astonishing events of the morning.

He needed coffee – several cups of coffee, as he tried to gather his thoughts. A list would be a good start and he jotted down everything that came to mind. At the top was contacting the diocese office as soon as it opened, to inform Bishop Casey. But just as he was about to pick the receiver to speak to the bishop's secretary, the phone rang.

Startled, he picked it up. 'Father Ben Mountford speaking, Saint Mary and the Apostles'.

'Good morning, Father,' replied the soft southern Irish accent. 'Greenhalgh, Lindsell Phelan and Co, Limerick. We're Raphoe Diocesan solicitors. I understand you have a small problem?'

Stunned at the immediacy of the call, Ben could only agree, and within two minutes David Greenhalgh, holding the entire conversation, had informed Ben he was on his way and would be with him shortly after lunch the day after.

The next day fortunately, was not a holy day and his parish duties were light. Following a home visit to sick Mrs Malley, Ben was cycling down the main street. From his chat with Pat O'Connor, he had realised the constable was on nights and would be leaving his station about ten o'clock. Sure enough, on the dot, the burly figure of Burtonport's finest, strolled out of the tiny constabulary office. Dismounting, Ben caught up with him.

'Ah, Morning Father Ben, thought you'd be around. I've got those phones, me boy,' he said flicking his eyes over his shoulder to a battered knapsack.

'Never mind the phones,' snapped Ben, a trifle uncharitably. 'Sorry, I didn't mean that. But how's Raffy?'

'They're interviewing him now, Ben. I'm out of it as I'm local,'

'What do you mean?' Ben glared at him.

'Well, this lot turned up last night from right out of the blue, from C3'. Ben looked questioningly at Pat. 'Sorry: jargon. Special Branch Department, C3: anti-terrorist unit'.

'What?'

'Whoever called this up pulled some very high strings indeed, Ben'.

'What's the charge? Do we know yet?'

Pat sighed and looked awkward.

'Come on Pat!'

'Ben, they suspect him of indecent acts and the use of the internet for pornographical reasons.' Pat wasn't smiling. 'But I have it good authority that was just to remove him from the presbytery,' he said tapping his nose.

Ben's lips compressed. This was almost funny … almost.

'That's the most ridiculous thing I ever heard, Pat.'

'I know, I know. But part of me is also a police officer too. And I've seen many strange things in my time'.

Putting the small knapsack on the pannier of Ben's bike, Pat indicated the topic closed and with a nod, headed off towards home.

Ben stood uncertainly in the middle of the street. He could not get Raffy's face out of his mind. Shrugging, he glared at the tiny knapsack and went to the post office: puzzled and angry at the morning's events.

After buying a large, padded envelope and many more stamps than were needed, to avoid having to have the parcel weighed, he wrote an address, slipped the contents of the knapsack into the thick envelope and pushed it through the slit of the post box, hoping that entrusted to the Irish postal service, they were in safe hands.

With that task completed he sought solace in the church: a place of sanctity and solitude while he wrestled with the conundrum facing him. He knelt at the oak altar and set his gaze on the curtained tabernacle in front of him.

'Clean the tabernacle,' Raffy had said. 'Clean it!'

What did he mean?

The small shelf holding the tabernacle had a semi-circular porch affair sporting the tiny curtains. When these were parted, the immaculately polished tabernacle gleamed at him.

'Clean it?' Ben fumbled under his cassock, selected the smallest key on his keyring, and opened the carved doors. Inside everything looked in order: the chalice and paten freshly polished and gleaming. It was as he was closing the doors that Ben saw that part of the internal mahogany panel was standing proud of the brass frame. Without thought, he pressed his thumb to the wood. It sunk back into its rebate with a discernible click. But as Ben released his thumb to close the door, irritatingly the panel sprung back out again. He pushed it back once more and a second time, it sprung back.

A closer look revealed feint scratches indicating that the panel may have been eased out in the past. Carefully using his Swiss army penknife, he gently prised the quarter inch thick panel away from its rebate, and as he did so out fell a thick manila envelope. 'What in the world?' he thought as he pressed the panel back into the door and locked the tabernacle. On the front of the package, written in Raffy's neat handwriting, was the solitary word: 'Benjamin'. Inside, it was the opening sentence on the loose sheet of A4 paper that caused a shudder to run through him, 'When you read this, I am probably beyond help,' it read.

* * *

Even at ten paces from the front door Ben could hear the shrill of the parish telephone in the tiled hall. 'Raffy?' he wondered, as he fumbled with the door lock and hurried to catch the call. 'Saint Mary's Presbyter . . .'

'Is dat the church?'

'Yes, it is,' Ben replied, a trifle impatiently.

'Mike O'Leary: *Donegal Gazette*. Can I speak with Father Raffique?'

The use of Raffy's first name rang alarm bells in Ben's mind. He pictured the caller now: O'Leary, the stout, loud-check jacket wearing ferret of local news, his residency in Maggie's bar a local legend.

Ben cursed for answering the phone. How many times did he tell Raffy to let the answer-phone screen calls? 'He's not in Mike' he answered, with a forced conviviality. 'Can I help at all?'

'No, no, it was Father Raffique I wanted'. A pause followed, 'Is it true, Father?' his soft brogue slipping under Ben's guard.

'Mike ...' said Ben sighing. 'Mike, can you find it in your heart to keep a lid on this?'.

Mike O'Leary laughed at the end of the line. 'In a town like this? If I printed it today the *Gazette* would be the last to know, it's all over the town. Ben, I just want the facts. Just the facts Ben, then we're fair'.

Ben knew there was little point in obfuscating with the man. He began with the morning's knock on the door, impatiently knocking the envelope against his calf, willing the call to end so that he could read its contents. When it did, it was in a way Ben could never have imagined.

He was outlining what happened and how Raffy had been taken into custody when he spotted a darkened figure outside the front door. His conversation faltered then stopped, leaving O'Leary's metallic voice, sounding in the silent hall, 'Hello! Hello! Father, are you there?' But Ben placed the receiver it in its cradle and cut him off.

CHAPTER 53

She came forward through the open door, carelessly left ajar by Ben moments before, the single bulb of the hallway lighting her soft blonde hair. The smile playing ever so slightly on her lips was the same, and those icy blue eyes sparkling just as he remembered them. Ben found his head nodding, his mouth dry; the eight years had not changed her. Ben's mind searched for words; his mouth opened, but none came.

'Ben,' she said at last. 'Or should I say Father Ben? It's been a while!'

'Maria?' and he held his arms to her where she joined his embrace, kissing him fully. The blonde at the bar in the 'Star' in Liverpool. Their final meal and the journey back to her house, 218 Falkener Street. There had not been a time in the last eight years when he had not thought of it. Elizabeth, yes again: Elizabeth. Opening the door to the yawningly empty terrace house. The house, only shortly before, the scene of one of the most sensual and fulfilling episodes of his youth. Gone, empty, as if it never happened.

Maria's arms had encircled him, and her body was pressed against him, leaving him in no doubt. He felt his resolve slipping. Swiftly it seemed, her slim cool fingers slid inside the buttoned back of his cassock. Feeling flesh, she instantly raked the small of his back with her nails. He arched, control abandoned. His arms came round her. He clasped her small firm buttock in one hand while the other still held the envelope. Somehow in the rising tide of passion, he realised that there was more, but he was drowning, losing control. Her fingers raked his back again, lower. Ben's last rational act was to slide the envelope under the blotter next to the telephone. With an animal grunt he pushed her against the low table. Feeling his arousal, she rolled her hips beneath him, leant backwards and brought him over her arched body. Slowly and confidently as she put her arms around his neck, pulling him to her parted lips, she softly undid the white collar of his office. As Ben bent her backwards over the table edge, her arm flung something away and the collar rolled across the tiled floor. Just as before, the hall was merely a prelude to what was to follow.

* * *

Later, Ben came down to the darkened hallway, intending to take up a bottle of his and Raffy's wine. As he came down the stairs and turned to the kitchen at the rear of the building, the half-opened door of the study made him pause. Raffy's desk gaped emptily in the moonlight, the gap from the missing PC triggering his thoughts and he crossed to the table, still slightly askew from its normal position and extracted the small envelope from its hiding place. The envelope had come from Raffy's desk and inside the top drawer, Ben found a matching one. He quickly copied Raffy's writing onto the envelope, found several sheets of loosely typed sentences, folded them, and slipped them inside the second envelope. As he passed the hall table with the fresh bottle of wine, he slid the envelope back under the blotter. His bare feet lightly kicked something across the floor. Barely visible in the gloom, the shape of his discarded dog collar mocked him. But the enticingly lit bedroom doorway beckoned him and mounted the stairs lightly.

She lay flat in the single bed, the ends of her blonde hair plastered damply across her forehead, eyes closed. Her arms gracefully flung upwards, tautening her breasts. Ben ran his finger down the sweat-smoothed cleavage as he watched her. Instantly her nipples hardened and her eyes blinked open. Silence.

'So, what happened, Maria?' Ben said softly. Her eyebrows lifted fractionally. 'Falkener Street, eight years ago!'

She closed her eyes again and the corners of her mouth lifted. 'All in good time Ben, all in good time'.

Ben slumped back against the wall, his hand continuing its downward journey. Playfully, his finger circled her navel. She grabbed his hand and cat-like, rolled away. She grinned at him, leaving the bed and stooping to recover clothing from the floor. The sound of the shower galvanised him too and he dressed rapidly and went downstairs.

Over sandwiches at the large kitchen table, they chatted. For Ben, it was as if the last eight years had never happened. To gentle probing, he told her of his various duties in the army, sticking to the official version.

'So, you never travelled the world then?' she said playfully.

'No, no, nothing exotic,' he replied.

She smiled with her lips, but her eyes gazed frankly at him. His stomach churned. She knew. She knew he was lying, but the moment passed.

He pressed her gently, but could get no further, other than she was in human resources: for whom, she didn't say.

But Ben didn't pursue the matter. Maria's time in the shower had given him the chance to assimilate his thoughts. He would watch, wait and let the game come to him.

When the time came for her to go, dressed as elegantly as her initial entrance, almost as if she had been paying a visit for afternoon tea, she parted from Ben's farewell embrace and made to leave the prestbytery. Approaching the front door, her eyes fell on the silver framed photograph showing a dusky Father Raffique Alhambra smiling broadly on the steps of St Peter's Basilica in Rome on the day of his investiture. Unnoticed by Ben, the alluring Maria momentarily transformed into the real Elizabeth and for an instant the sight of that man in the photograph transported back into that awful backyard in Hackney all those years ago.

CHAPTER 54

Ishmal was as British as she was. His parents had fled the persecutions after the fall of the Shah in Iran. With a little money and marginally more industriousness they had sent their only son to the London School of Economics. Elizabeth would never have met him but for a school trip in her last year from the convent attached to the Abbey in Ealing.

From their cloistered environment they had toured the LSE's impressive facilities. After inauspicious beginnings their romance had blossomed in spite of her background and, as she later discovered, his family's disapproval.

With Elizabeth's results in with a trio of 'A' grades, there was no doubt in her mind that it was the London School of Economics for her. Life had stretched so invitingly ahead, the prospect of a university place, a dashing, exotic, westernised boyfriend and an intoxicating fusion of cultures. Even Ishmal's parents grudgingly accepted the vivacious blonde into their closeted world. It was a different situation, however, when Ishmal's uncle came visiting. He was a mullah at the local mosque, whose sinister, disfigured looks caused made Elizabeth's deeply uneasy. He never spoke to her, preferring instead to stare right through his nephew's vivacious girlfriend as if she did not exist. Ishmal's demeanour changed as well to one of patronising sarcasm, much to Elizabeth's considerable chagrin.

That was how it started. Its ending began with Ishmal's frantic phone call, 'Izzy, Izzy! Don't come. Don't come at all! Not, ever again!'

'Ishmal!' she never abbreviated his name, preferring its exotic connotations. 'What on earth's the matter?'

She calmed his gasping voice slowly, but he continued sorrowfully, 'Izzy, it's over. You don't understand. It can never be: for it is written, I should be killed for cavorting with infidel women'.

The uncle! 'Stay there,' she snapped. 'I'm coming over right now,'. Without pausing for an answer, she slammed the receiver down. It was a simple matter to tiptoe out into the cool evening and presently she was standing outside Ishmal's parents' home in Hackney. The little terraced house opened directly onto the street, and she was somewhat surprised to find the front door ajar. With rising indignation and determination, she had not felt before, she pushed the door open and went inside. There was no light on, but Ishmal stood framed against the light from the kitchen with a strange expression on his face.

Elizabeth took a step into the darkened room. The door slammed violently behind her, and she felt her arms pinioned to her sides. She tried to scream, but a foul sweaty palm clamped over her mouth and nose. Then she was being frogmarched across to Ishmal. Only now in her own panic-stricken struggle could she see the fear in his eyes. He too had his arms pinioned to his sides by a darkened figure behind him. He was dragged backwards as she approached, through the tiny kitchen and into the high-walled rear yard.

Elizabeth felt herself starting to suffocate and she bit the soft sweaty flesh covering her mouth and nose. With a curse, the hand was whipped away as, with some satisfaction, she tasted her assailant's blood. But a sharp blow to the side of her head caused blackness to descend.

When she came round, she found herself bound to a small chair; a gag of indescribably foul taste filled her mouth and was knotted painfully behind her head. Her eyes flared as she recognised Ishmal in front of her, but it was not her Ishmal that stared lifelessly back. His head had been shaven to reveal a glistening polished skull. He was now dressed the simple dish dash of an Arabian peasant, and he was kneeling on the hard flagstones with his hands bound behind him. He looked at Elizabeth through dark, defeated eyes, his features betraying the beating he had received. Through the gap in his grubby garment, Elizabeth could see angry weals and smaller blisters on his chest. Her eyes swivelled sideways to a small glowing brazier in the corner of the yard, at the same time a faintly cloying, sickly smell assailed her nostrils; with shocking clarity she realised he had been tortured: burnt, by his inquisitors.

Before she could react, a droning monotone began, chanted by four sinister hooded figures behind Ishmal.

When this stopped, there was silence: a deep, menacing silence that chilled her to the core. It was broken by a slow, grating sound above. The group of figures behind Ishmal looked up. Elizabeth twisted and did likewise. The upstairs sash windows had been opened and against the soft glow of the night sky Ishmal's uncle was framed from where he spat out an unintelligible stream of rhetoric to the group below. When he finished, the window slammed shut behind him.

Watching in disbelief, as if what she was seeing was a horror film or the ghastly terror of a nightmare, Elizabeth saw three of the hooded figures withdraw long, curved knives from the folds of their shamas. Almost in slow motion to the now resumed chant of their colleague, they fell upon Ishmal and the blades flashed down on his exposed neck. It was over in seconds: dark glistening blood spreading across the worn flagstones between the severed head and twitching body.

She was incapable of sound or movement, but with quick strokes, her bonds were cut and she was pushed back into the kitchen. Terror flooded her veins and adrenaline leant her strength she staggered and turned into the front room. The darkness made her stumble and bump into unfamiliar furniture. Then hands caught and tore at her, four men, semi-naked in the cloying shades threw her over the sofa and fell on her. She was remote from the writhing, thrusting mêlée, as if the violent attacks to her physical body allowed her mind to float free and detached. She was silent until the first of many pains tore her from within. She saw the knives they had used before. Before? The base instincts if survival flooded through her, and she meekly submitted. For how many hours she knew not, but dawn was breaking as she was thrown from the back of a filthy car many miles away. One of them had stopped another when he held a knife to her throat. 'Leave the harlot, her punishment is for all time knowing our brother Ishmal has his virgins in heaven'.

For six dark months following her ordeal, Elizabeth had scarcely left her home. The usual fleeting police investigation led to a sorrowful look in the inspector's eyes as he called yet again. Ishmal's parents had, through the official interpreter, insisted that he had left for a pilgrimage to Mecca some days before 'alleged incident' and they did not know when he would return. Not a scrap of forensic evidence had been found in the yard of their house, and the cleric, whose name caused the inspector's face momentarily to flush in anger, had a perfect alibi from fellow members at the mosque where he had been leading a study session from the Koran at the time.

* * *

During Elizabeth's recovery, Father Gregorus had come, spasmodically at first. He was part of the abbey community, although she was unsure of his precise role. Presently his visits settled down to a twice-weekly chat. He rarely discussed his background, referring only to the 'Church'. Elizabeth had heard of Opus Dei, of course: who had not. But during their chats, it was never actually mentioned by name.

This time was intended to be Elizabeth's gap year, and it gave them a chance to go over what she was planning to study once her course began. This interest in her strengthened their relationship and Elizabeth started to see him more often, as he gently tutored her in the early Church's history which had taken on a growing fascination in her mind.

Neither he nor Elizabeth ever referred to her assailants directly, but she gradually allied her mind with the scholarly father's abhorrence at the spread of Islam, fuelled by her own deep feelings of anger and revenge. As the months passed under his careful tutelage, she found herself drifting further from the mainstream of conventional abbey life to become an ambassador for 'their' church.

The Neocatechumenals taught an early orthodox version of Catholicism that sometimes pre-dated even the extremes of Opus Dei. She observed how its very name caused concern to mainstream priests and laity, but increasingly she saw them to be at fault, not her 'Church'. Indeed, she sensed there was more as Father Gregorus led her on deep behind the façade of Opus and the Neocatechumenals and she saw the deep medieval power of the secretive Sons of Sion within the Order of St Anthony. Direct descendants from the last Crusades, and with a simple deadly agenda Elizabeth had surged onwards within their secretive world.

* * *

At the presbytery door, she pecked Ben's cheek and walked quickly down the drive. Even before she got to the gate, Ben had lifted the corner of the blotter

– the envelope had gone. Watching her from the door, she turned to wave and Ben raised his hand thoughtfully.

A small man in a long trench coat had come in the gate, just before Maria reached it. He stopped, and with a curious half-bow, lifted the dark homburg from his head. Ben could not hear what was said, but the two exchanged words, and Maria curiously touched his arm before leaving.

The little man raised his hat again when he greeted Ben at the front door, 'David Greenhalgh: Lindsell Plelan and Co. Father Benjamin?'

'Yes, yes. Come in' said Ben, 'I thought you were coming tomorrow?'

'Yes, indeed,' David replied, struggling off his trench coat, 'but Bishop Casey wanted this sorting out urgently'.

'You've done well to travel from Limerick this morning,' Ben observed.

'Yes,' a brief pause followed. 'Yes, I suppose I have.'

'Is this the study?' he asked, changing the subject, and walking into the room leaving Ben gazing thoughtfully behind him; Raffy's handwritten note seemed to be burning in his pocket.

CHAPTER 55

The buff envelope, warmed from its proximity to her skin, skidded down the long table. Colm Heggarty reached for it and wafted it under his nose. The movement was not wasted on Maria. 'Too close, Colm, too close'.

'Don't worry, Elizabeth,' the smooth tones replied. 'Father Raffique's in custody and he'll be out of harm's way soon.'

'It should never get this far,' she hissed. 'You know the rules.'

'We can't change history, you know.' The look she shot back made it very clear that was a truism which had cut painfully home.

'When do you receive Father Raffique?'

'Just as soon as David bails him, in the morning'.

'Too late!' she flared. 'All night in the cells with those chatty Irish coppers. I'm warning you, Colm …' but there was need to finish the sentence. Colm Hegarty understood well enough – she was sure of that.

He picked up the envelope and ran his finger under the seal. The folded sheets crackled softly in his hands and then he glared down the room at Elizabeth.

Her eyes blazed. 'What now?' she snapped.

'I fear your stud may have as much between his ears as between his legs,' he finished dryly, letting the sheets of paper fall to the table where Saint Mary's and the Apostles' cleaning rota and the minutes to Burtonport's Women's Institute mocked the silence of the room.

* * *

David Greenhalgh sat at the desk in the study, Ben at the furthest point on the small leather sofa. Ben watched as the dapper man, thinning on top, wrote down Ben's witness statement in his careful longhand. Anywhere in the world, and you would know he was a lawyer.

The pages filled and the questions continued. But Ben said nothing about Raffy's suspicions of the Order of Sion, nor the monastery; but did comment that Raffy had been convinced that someone had interfered with the computer.

David looked up and, removing his glasses, smiled. 'That really won't do, Father Ben. You see, in every case like this the standard defence is that someone or somebody had placed items on the hard drive or buried them somewhere in the computer's memory. He simply wouldn't be believed. Or worse, you'd be implicated'.

'Why aren't I?' said Ben softly.

David smiled, replying 'I just operate on instructions from the diocese Ben. At the moment, Father Raffy is under arrest, not you'.

'Who brought the charges David: do we know?'

David went to his file. 'I can't say I'm afraid. The client relationship, the client relationship ...' he tailed off, spreading his hands and looking at Ben. 'You understand.'

They were interrupted by phone ringing. Ben was up and across the room before the second ring died away. 'Saint Mary's Prest ...'

But a deep, educated voice cut in without preamble, 'David Greenhalgh of Linsell Phelan please.'

Ben gazed at the receiver in irritation and then popped his head round the door.

David was already halfway across the room. 'It's for you.'

David went into the hall, his neat steel capped shoes clicking loudly. 'Hello? Yes sir, I'm doing it now'. Ben didn't hear the rest because David reached across and pulled the door to. Moments later, he re-entered the study. 'Sorry Ben, got to dash. Can we finish this tomorrow?' and, without waiting for an answer, he began to gather his papers.

'Are you coming back?' Ben ventured.

'No, no, I've rooms in the town, thank you'. Odd really, thought Ben, he hadn't asked if he was staying the night.

Still, Father Benjamin Mountford had a more pressing matter to attend to and, in the darkened comfort of the church, he knelt at the altar rail, holding the previous evening's discarded dog collar, clasped his hands and bent his head. 'Father, forgive me, for I have grievously sinned,' he began.

He did unburden himself he was sure of that – and trusted that the Lord would hear His penitent servant and show His mercy and forgiveness. But Ben also found himself deliberating the events of the last few weeks with the Almighty. Explaining that he felt as if he had been swept along by a series of seemingly unrelated events. His night of passion with Maria had been the motive for his confession, of course, but as he knelt he was not so sure it was the only reason.

His intertwined fingers unravelled as his eyes rose to the figure on the altar before him. He twisted the ancient signet ring around his finger. Smooth and buttery, its great age almost concealed the engraving of the double-headed eagle on a black shield with engraved gold bard. His mind drifted as his fingers worked around its smooth familiarity.

The church had been part of his life since childhood: always there, unchanging, a bulwark seeming at odds with fast-changing society. His younger days in the seminary had, he supposed, been full of youthful impetuous demands for change. He, along with countless others, had railed at Rome's stance on women priests, contraception, and homosexuals. He could go on and on, but the time in the SAS had opened his mind to the real threat to society: indifference to the rise of extreme enemies of Christendom; and the watering down of long-held beliefs so as to offend no-one.

In a way, though, his unit had been fighting enemies of society in just the way he attempted to from the pulpit. This thought brought Colm Hegarty clearly to mind, and his odd words at their last meeting, 'We are members of an order, not a democracy'. Then there had been David Greenhalgh's almost military answer on the phone, 'Yes sir'. what lawyer ever said that? And to whom?

Ben turned and twisted his dog collar as he prayed. His gaze fell upon the tabernacle. He remembered the envelope. Slowly, determinedly he refitted the collar, genuflected and left the dark church. In the study he remembered Raffy that night and, feeling vaguely foolish, drew the curtains and locked the front door.

* * *

Elizabeth had composed herself. The contents of the envelope so carefully lifted from Ben's hallway carried a message. How much did he know? She pressed her fingertips together pursing her lips. Colm watched her carefully, the length of the polished table no defence against her tongue.

'We could get the boys to bomb the Garda station,' he suggested.

Her gaze held him in contempt for a brief moment. 'What have I said about using the RAH direct, Colm?'

'But under the circumstances ...' his voice trailed.

'And what of the contents of the envelope?' Maria asked. 'And how much attention do you want?'

'I was only trying to help,' he raised his hands expansively.

'Leave your bandits out of this. Let David do his work. Get him here and finish it.'

They were silent for a moment, each working through how events might unfold.

'The local brigade commander, who is he?' Elizabeth asked.

'Maher.'

'Can we speak?'

'Well, as a matter of fact he's in the gallery downstairs, trying some new sniper scope. Shall I get him now?'

'Yes.' Then Elizabeth's voice took a softer tone, 'No. On second thoughts, give me half an hour: he only knows me as Elizabeth.' Then she rose and left the room.

CHAPTER 56

When Maher had answered the telephone in the nondescript, pebble-dashed house in Portadown, General Bagheri did not introduce himself but used a codeword that Maher had not heard for twenty years – so long ago that it took a moment for him to acknowledge it.

Later that day the letter box had rattled, and a buff envelope had landed on the doormat. Inside was a mobile phone which rang soon afterwards, displaying an international code. When the call had finished, Maher did as he been instructed and left the house to walk through the village, disposing of its various components, unseen, in different bins.

Maher had morphed from his Republican days and his success with Manchester. Much of his work now was with the Dublin gangs who had a substantial appetite for assassinating each other and even more substantial budget. Often his contracts came from a Dubai number and that was the same code as his conversation. This time, however, there was no need to negotiate the fee: it was so large and the risk so small. He would retire, perhaps to a small golf course in southern Ireland.

Delivery only: that was all that was involved. And to a small provincial town in southern England. He had only heard of it because of the horse racing and the Gold Cup. It would be detonated from thousands of miles away.

And now he lay at the furthest end of the long, vaulted gallery. Buried deep below the monastery, where the cellar of rough-hewn stone ran the length of the building. The Order had given substantial support to him over the years with the tacit backing of the Catholic Church during the 'Troubles': he was comfortable here and felt secure.

Maher really needed a half mile or more to test the new scope, but the advantage of not being heard outside the thick walls outweighed any disadvantage. To simulate a longer distance, he had found a postcard-sized picture of a bear-skinned guardsman outside Buckingham Palace. At over 125 yards, the picture was barely bigger than a postage stamp. The weapon kicked slightly. Maher inhaled gratefully, scrambled to his feet, and flicking a switch to his right, walked softly down the sandy floor towards the target. He heard the iron door open as he was halfway down the range, he ignored it and walked on to retrieve the postcard. Where the soldier's face had been, a neat hole had been punched clean through.

'Heggarty wants you', said the cowled figure who had entered. It was not a question, and Maher followed the rustling robes and climbed out of the range.

Colm Heggarty watched him sit down, midway down the long table. Maher nodded briefly at him, ignoring the stocky Elizabeth seated at the opposite end.

'How's the scope, Maher?' Colm asked.

'Just practising,' remarked Maher flatly. Colm expected little more out of him: no emotion, he was just a killing machine with dark brooding eyes, which had been the last ones to watch as a dozen or more Brits in Belfast over the years had succumbed to his marksmanship with the Barrett M82 rifle the Libyan had supplied.

He liked his killing, did Maher: not for him the easy option of skulking behind the lines.

'Your package is on the way,' Elizabeth told him, using the same codeword he had received.

Maher swivelled, confused. The mousy haired secretary stared at him over her small glasses.

'Get your team together, Mr Maher. Bring them here via the usual route.

CHAPTER 57

The handwritten note had arrived two months before: Saint-Bénézet bridge, and a date. Heggarty had ignited the note and watched its ashes fall into the grate. Only once before had this occurred.

The Eurostar carried him smoothly to the south of France and on to Avignon. There, he had made his way with the tourist throngs to the famous bridge. The mistral was blowing and people spent only moments at the end of the structure before scurrying back to the myriad bars and restaurants. But Heggarty waited patiently.

An elderly lady, hooded against the wind, joined him above its swirling eddies. Moments passed and then she placed her sun-blotched hand on the worn stone balustrade. The golden ring with the double-headed eagle gleamed. Heggarty looked into the most icy-blue eyes, in a face that was once beautiful and still framed with luxuriant titian hair. Without preamble she began. 'By the grace of God we have been sent a gift that will fulfil Clement's prophecy. You will receive it soon.' Then she bent closer and gripped Heggarty's arm fiercely, 'Remember Urban's words.'

* * *

'If you'll just sign here and here, sir,' the burly desk sergeant indicated with a stubby finger, as David Greenhalgh's pen hovered. 'And if you, Father Raffique, can sign here. We can complete the bail paperwork'.

Father Raffique watched the small dapper man, who had sat with him the previous evening during his 'interview'. From experiences in Iraq, this was a very soft brush with the law indeed. All the same, he swallowed uneasily as the pair left the rear of the tiny police station, and sped northwards in David's hire car.

'How's Father Ben after all this?' Raffy asked, breaking the silence.

'Fine, fine', rejoined David, offering little more.

'Good', enthused Raffy, 'I'm looking forward to seeing him'.

'You're on bail. We're going to a safe house until the investigation is complete.'

Raffy exhaled, 'Can I see the Bishop then?'

'Oh yes, you'll manage that alright.' said David.

'Good. But where are we going?' Raffy asked as they cleared the outskirts of Burtonport and turned right up to the bulk of the Glendown Mountains.

As they climbed the narrow twisting road, Raffy glanced out of the window. There across the fields, maybe a couple of miles away, the soaring turrets of the monastery were revealed. A short while later, as the road steepened into the mountains proper, David took a left turn down a shaded, unmade track which was running parallel with the main coast road.

After about a quarter of a mile, the car's headlights illuminated a green mailbox, leaning at a somewhat drunken angle at the end of a small drive. Beyond this stood a small bungalow: the attempt at a garden and the wheelbarrow abandoned under one of the windows drew the conclusion from Raffy that this was probably one of Belfast's holiday homes. But as the car approached the garage door, it began to open smoothly and swing upwards. Raffy looked at David in surprise but he was answered by a stabbing pain in his thigh. Glancing down he saw the small silver object in David's hand disappearing as if by magic. 'What!' he exclaimed.

David had removed his spectacles and now, moving the car forward, inched onto the blackness of the garage. Raffy went to move his hand to rub his thigh but found he could not. What he did sense was a warmth, a numbness, spreading up his body. He looked at his hand, willing it to move. But it lay there motionless, along the seat edge while the numbness spread up his chest.

* * *

Lights flickered on to either side of him. He could not move, but his eyes were open and his chest rose and fell. He heard David wind the window down and something clicked. The walls of the garage in front of him, hung with rakes and miscellaneous garden equipment, slid upwards. A sinking feeling in Raffy's stomach told of their descent. He found he could see to the extent of swivelling his eyeballs and hear the low moan of the lift machinery. However, to move even a facial muscle or a limb was impossible; it was as though every part of him was covered in heavy lead.

The lift stopped softly in front of a stone arch, through which David Greenhalgh gingerly piloted the vehicle. Astonishingly, a large well-lit garage revealed itself, lined with various motor vehicles and large silver motorcycle took up space by one wall.

David nosed the car into a space next to a large black limousine bearing Dublin registration plates. Raffy had seen the car before but could not think where it had been. His door opened and olive-green clad arms reached in for him. He let his mouth fall open, but his tongue refused to work; a faint grunt was all he could utter. He was placed on some kind of upright chair, almost a litter of sorts. In front of him, two of the olive clad men who had unloaded his inert form from the car, took up positions at the two poles supporting his chair. Raffy felt a pressure on his wrists and legs, and at the lower limit of his eyes, yet another pair of hands was fastening rough bindings around the frame of the chair. He was immobile.

The litter was lifted from the floor, and to a gentle swaying movement, he was carried down the vast underground garage. To a chorus of grunts and gently muttered curses, Raffy was carried up several flights of stone stairs, to exit eventually into the cool night air. He was in some kind of courtyard. Vertiginous black walls surrounded the large, cobbled area, only slightly distinguished from the cloudless dark blue of the evening. Around the walls guttered dozens of torches, their uneven flare and curls of black smoke lending the courtyard a medieval tone.

The oak chair on which Raffy was bound and immobile was marched across the courtyard and deposited on some kind of raised dais. The poles supporting the chair were withdrawn and footsteps receded.

In front of Raffy, under one of the guttering torches, a large door was flung open with a crash. The interior light shining from it was bright and it completely backlit the large figure as he entered the courtyard. Behind him, Raffy watched as dozens of cowled figures entered the same and lined the walls. Raffy attempted to squint to see the figure, but the light from behind was too bright. Their outline was odd, strange even.

As the figure advanced to him, Raffy felt a shiver of fear when the shape of the medieval helmet came into focus. The door had closed now, but around the walls, soft lights came on, enhancing the guttering torches and bathing the courtyard in a soft ethereal glow. Ranks of dark cowled monks, their faces an impenetrable black, faced him. The large single figure moved decisively into his line of sight. Raffy's pupils widened in terror. In front of him, in full armour, helm and hauberk, stood a medieval knight Crusader. His white surcoat emblazoned with a fresh crimson cross patée. A mailed hand rose and tilted his visor upwards. The piercing eyes of the most Reverend Chevalier Colm Heggarty gazed at the olive-skinned, inert form in front of him. With his other thickly mailed hand, he held up a small silver syringe. The same as Raffy had last seen in David Greenhalgh's hand just after the short stabbing pain in his leg. The voice from the helm was slightly muffled when he held the silver vial near to Raffy's eyes, 'Eighteenth of March in the year of our Lord 1314 was the last time this was used by the inquisition Mohammed'.

Heggarty's use of Raffy's Islamic title caused his eyes to swivel around wildly. 'Then, of course,' the muffled voice continued: 'Mandragora was merely added to wine to dull senses of the condemned'. Raffy's eyes widened further, but he was immobile. 'With a little help from the twentieth century we use it today. But now, distilled and refined, we can completely immobilise a heretic, while keeping the nerve endings live.'

Then the hand disappeared from Raffy's sight; the figure turned and with surcoat billowing, took up position next to a small table clad in white altar vestments. Hooded figures appeared silently, to place the chalice softly on the white surface, only to withdraw as silently as they arrived. Raffy became aware of a regular tap-tap on the cobbles. Several of the hooded figures in front of him turned towards a small door at the extreme left of Raffy's vision. Stooping slightly, the ornate mitre only just clearing the arched stone doorway, another figure clad this time in flowing liturgical purple chasuble and alb, entered the courtyard. Rows of darkened hoods bowed their heads as the figure made his way, tapping his staff on the cobbles.

When Raffy had first sought sanctuary in Rome and then immersed himself in its teachings, he had absorbed far more details of the vestments and traditions of the Church than perhaps a normal priest would have.

Around the figure's purple clad shoulders, lay a circle of fine white wool. Wool supplied in Rome by two lambs presented annually as a tax by the Lateran Cannons to the chapter of Saint John on the feast of Saint Agness, usually solemnly blessed on the high altar after the pontifical Mass. Where the circle of fine wool touched the shoulders, breast and back, were small black crosses held by an ornate pin from which a precious stone dangled. The pallium symbolised the *plenitudo pontificallis offici*, or participation of the supreme power of the Holy See.

The figure busied himself at the small altar, holding the chalice aloft for the assembled novices. A strange rustling noise around the back of Raffy only increased his sense of panic. Then, in the periphery of his vision, figures came round both sides of his chair on the raised stone dais. Raffy's heart began to race when he saw that they carried neat bungles of twigs, freshly cut wands of holly and willow bound in bark. These they placed in an upright position around his chair.

In no time at all, he was sitting up to his waist in a circle of bound twigs. His breathing laboured as his heart accelerated wildly. The figure at the altar raised the chalice skyward and began to celebrate the Mass. 'In nomine Patri, et filli ...'

Raffy heard no more for, from behind the altar two figures emerged, hooded and carrying a guttering torch, that so recently had been lighting up the courtyard. Without preamble, the pair thrust the flaming torches into the faggots either side of Raffy's chair. Raffy's eyes wildly sought the bishop's through the first wisps of smoke. But the bishop simply raised his right hand, palm slightly crooked, and the flapping sleeve of his alb obscured his face.

Through the smoke Raffy caught a glimpse of the man's face. In a split second the face was staring at Raffy from the rear of the vehicle he had seen in the underground garage, only last time it was leaving the Dublin grounds of the Episcopal Palace of the Primate of all Ireland after the synod of bishops and clergy, not three months before.

His voice, as deeply melodious and resonant as it was when he had chaired that distant meeting, rang out over the crackles of the flames. 'Know this, Mohammed. Even as you pry and enquire under the cover of adopting the one true Church, our mission has been 700 years in the making and is not to be deflected now.' His voice rose to the darkened assembled of brothers, and he continued, 'My brethren, I give you the first infidel of the final Crusade! Dieu le veut! Dieu le veut!'

Male voices, hesitant at first, joined his rich baritone, and through the first wisps of smoke he made the sign of the cross. As the heat reached Raffy's legs, his mouth opened, and he heaved against his bonds. The fire roared softly, and the flames were clear and hot.

* * *

When the presbytery telephone rang, a crisp female voice told him without preamble, 'Father Benjamin? I have Bishop Casey for you, hold the line please'. The line clicked and hissed as Ben marshalled his thoughts.

'Benjamin, how are you?' boomed the fruity tones of the bishop. Ben frowned. Up to now they had not exchanged a dozen words. Without waiting for a reply, though, the bishop went on, 'Difficult time this. Father Raffique is bailed at present, but under the circumstances we … Sorry, I want you out of there'.

'But Bishop.'

'But nothing Benjamin', the tone hardening. 'I heard great things from Liverpool about you, and with considerable help, I've secured a year's placement in the Vatican for you. But you must leave tonight. It's a great opportunity, Ben. I only wish I was younger'.

Ben pressed his jaw closed. Through the open study door he saw the envelope, its contents spilling out under the soft glow of the desk lamp.

Ben protested mildly, deliberately trying to provoke a strong, forceful reaction. He succeeded when the bishop left him in no doubt that he would be leaving that night.

On one point Ben was adamant, however. He would have to drive the Land Rover back to his parents then catch the flight from Heathrow.

To this the Bishop had grudgingly agreed.

Ben smiled. Between Burtonport and Heathrow lay Hereford.

* * *

The pale blue eyes observed Bishop Casey down the long, polished table, 'Well done. Well done,' he was told.

She rose and opened the French windows to the night air, which was cool but with the lingering heat from the fire in the courtyard that reached her nostrils. She wrinkled her nose and withdrew into the room. 'Any news from Father Sebastian?' she asked Colm Heggarty.

CHAPTER 58

The red hat lay on the desk's rich tooled leather surface: its silk brocade catching the late evening sun as it slanted through the cardinal's windows domain. Albioni studied it intensely and then clasped his hands together and shut his eyes. 'Dear Lord and Father hear me …'

The rumours were malicious, of course. Albioni did not pretend to be interested in the politics of the Council, but even so at times like these a man could dream could he not? He would be only sixty-six years of age, a ridiculous age to attain high office for sure. Why most of the conclave were a good twenty years older! But still his diligent *assessore*, Pedro, had been diligent in collating numbers and gathering opinion and it was possible – just possible.

Damn these thoughts. Albioni shook his head in frustration, again clasping his hands together, 'Dear Lord …', but he got no further. This time there was a soft knock and Pedro stood on the threshold, 'So sorry, Your Eminence, but I thought you wouldn't mind,' he stammered.

Albioni sighed and pushed the red cap of his office away. 'No Pedro, it's fine. What is the matter?'

'Your brother, Eduardo, sir: from Agardo.'

'Yes, yes,' said Albioni a trifle irritated.

'He wants you to come now. There's been a terrible accident down the mine, and he needs you quickly.'

Albioni rose, blanching. 'Eduardo – He's OK?'

'Yes, Father. I should have said, it's not him but your old pupil at the Technical Institute: Ricardo da Silva. He wants you to take his confession. Only you Father.'

Albioni stiffened: a personal request for a last confession could never be refused, nor would it, he sighed. 'Alright, Pedro, alright, organise the car.' Pedro nodded and disappeared.

'Organise the car,' he could not help but smile. The office of cardinal, his since 1963, had given him the trappings that many chairmen of huge corporations would covet, but he, Albioni Luciani, genuinely cared little. True his apartment was warm in the icy Rome winds sweeping down from the Apennines, but the associated finery he could do without. Even after Vatican II had stripped the Church of much of its public pomp and posturing, behind the scenes little had changed: but no matter. He really loved the car. The long black Mercedes Benz would pull up to his door in minutes and he could have it whisk him anywhere.

Frowning at his covetous daydreaming, a habit that seemed to be growing as fast as the rumours of Paul VI's illness, he shrugged on his black cloak. Outside, in the evening sunshine of August 1978, Pedro awaited by the open door of the Mercedes. 'I've packed your garments for a few days, Father, just in case. Don't worry about here.' Then he inclined his head and confided, 'I'll let you know if they're about to call a conclave.'

Albioni smiled and his eyes twinkled. 'If I didn't know you better, Pedro, I'd say you're enjoying this.'

* * *

During the drive he tried to push these thoughts from his head as he looked forward to meeting Eduardo again, maybe away from the pressure of Rome they could walk in the hills and enjoy a glass of Frascati in the sun. But what did Ricardo da Silva want, he mused? What was so important that it could not be entrusted to the current chaplain of the Institute for Miners in Agardo? Agardo: the place of his birth. His mind wandered as the passing scenery speeded up.

Canale d'Agardo, the mining town in the north nestling in the lower foothills of the Appenines, with its tiny chapel, so often the final resting place of burly men crushed to pulp by another fall in the *miniera di stagno*, the tin mine that kept the village's 8,000 souls in food and drink, but provided a miserable back-breaking life for men called to be *minatori*.

Oh sure, when fresh from school the back-breaking work developed those young bodies to near-Herculean proportions, and their appearance from the pithead at four o'clock every afternoon would always be accompanied by a gaggle of leggy, pubescent girls, ogling the muscle-bound, sweat-oiled bodies. Worked hard, played hard: those were the *minatori* from Agardo.

The mountains were unforgiving in their labyrinth of passages and chambers developed over years of burrowing and tunnelling by generations before. Predictably, every so often workings collapsed into old unmapped tunnels, or the honeycombed mountain simply slipped into itself, pinning men like insects under thousands of tons of rubble. Then, of course, the tiny chapel held the raw deal boxes bedecked with flowers, containing nothing more than rocks.

Albioni's eyes grew misty as he remembered how they knew, the whole town knew. It was the wheels of the pithead; spinning with timeless elegance in the morning at eight o'clock and again at the end of the day when the endless ropes whisked steel cages of men the hundreds of metres down to the workings. Somehow their turnings attracted the eye, no matter where in the town you were: if those wheels began to turn at any other time of day – you knew.

* * *

It had been just after the war, in the winter of 1946: a particularly hard winter when the snow lay on the ground for weeks. It was no later than ten o'clock in the morning, in fact he had just finished weekly Mass for all the wives left at home. He had been standing on the steps of the Miners Institute bidding farewell to the shuffling mantilla-clad housewives as they gossiped animatedly heading to the market for the day's provisions when the wheels had started turning. Conversation died away to be replaced by sharp intakes of breath and quick signs of the cross as the older women understood quickly what they were looking at.

Albioni had stood at the door of the Institute and saw the grey despair on the faces of the women. At once his nervous fingers let slip his rosary as he gathered up his long vestments and with the women flew down the street towards the spinning pit head.

A gaggle of white-shirted management had gathered at the exit from the pithead. The cables vibrated harshly against the steelwork as the cage rose to the surface. To accompanying wails, the cage hove into view. The backs of burly miners could be seen, streaked and lined with sweat, but also the crimson of the disaster below. Wails turned to shrieks as the double mesh doors slid open with a hiss and half the cage emptied to leave on the floor a residue of broken, twisted bodies. The women pressed forward keening in their grief to gape into the battered cage where four men lay: three of whom would not see another sunrise.

The fourth, a giant of a man, looked at Albioni with bright eyes, 'Father! Father! Thank, God!' His words belying his dreadful wounds. Big as he was, but from his waist down his body looked as if it had been crushed by a giant fist. He lay on the rudimentary stretcher, flattened and limp, with the rising and falling of his mighty chest indicating his struggle for life within.

Father Albioni sensed a tugging as his robes where a waif of a boy, no more than six or seven, had wormed his way between the voluminous skirts of the wailing women. Father Albioni never, ever, forgot the moment that small, grubby hand found his and with a light squeeze and a look from welling brown eyes the child begged him to save his father. 'It's OK, *papà*, Father's here. He'll help. You'll be OK now.' If only that could have been true.

* * *

The funerals of the four men killed that day had been Albioni's last at Canale d'Agardo. The four had left six children between them and four widows. Young Ricardo was taken in by his aunt, but he had always smiled at Albioni: that same smile as that awful day at the mine. And so it was that as Albioni had progressed up the hierarchy of the Roman Catholic Church, leading to his elevation as Bishop of Vittorio Veneto in 1958. Ricardo, by then a strapping young man, had called on him to say Mass at his wedding, still in the chapel at Agardo and again, when he was Patriarch of Venice in the late-sixties, he received the call from Agardo: this time for a baptism. He could never refuse, nor did he wish to. It was as if each time a significant event happened in his own career, the call from Ricardo would come too. No matter how efficient his personal assistants became over the years, the one call that always got through to him would be the one from Ricardo.

CHAPTER 59

Albioni's call to the Vatican Council, and his red cap came in 1973, and just a month after that he listened to Ricardo's broken voice on the line, 'Father,' for he never recognised any further rank, 'Father, its Amelia, can you come?'

Of course he could, and he did, only this time the trip to Agardo revealed the wasted body of the tall attractive girl he had married to Ricardo fifteen years before. Amelia tossed and turned in her delirium. Ricardo and Cardinal Albioni took it in turns to wipe her brow and force water between her cracked lips. It took three days for the leukaemia to finally claim her and yet again the tiny chapel held a flower-decked coffin.

After the service Albioni and Ricardo had walked down the street: two men with a common start in life. 'Not got out yet?' Albioni nodded his head towards the stationary minewheel.

'Well, yes, Father. That's the tragedy. Some outfit in Rome wanted tunnelling specialists and I'd got the job and was ready to move then – Amelia.'

'What'll you do?'

'I've signed the contract, Father, and given my notice in at the mine. The money's nearly treble and they're laying off down there now: so, I've no choice. Amelia's mum will look after the boys, and I'll have to find lodgings.'

* * *

That had been nearly five years ago, reflected Albioni as the Mercedes glided up the winding road to Agardo. What was it this time? Eduardo had phoned, not Ricardo, why?

As he had done on every visit to his home town, he first stopped at the Institute of Mines and visited the tiny chapel where his service to God had started so many years before. Kneeling in front of the simple altar, his eyes caught the marble tablets on the walls with names of the village dead. Some from both world wars, yes; but on a separate tablet, the victims of the town's mine. Some of the early names leapt out at him as he clasped his hands together.

* * *

As he had been requested, he did not go to Ricardo's simple house near the pithead, but to his brother, Eduardo's. The younger brother had never married and a simple two-room apartment on the outskirts of town was Albioni's destination. Telling his driver to wait in the car park, he made his way to the eighth-floor apartment.

Eduardo answered the door and the two had embraced. But before they could talk, a hoarse whisper had reached Albioni's ears, 'Father, Father, in here!' Through the door into the tiny lounge, with its views over the town, Albioni stopped short. A man sat in the armchair by the large picture windows, but it was with difficulty he recognised the gaunt form. Ricardo smiled at him as he had so many years ago, even his emaciated face and frame unsuccessful in dampening that brilliant, confident smile.

'Ah, you're here now, please sit down.' A bony hand directed his visitor to the chair next to the frail figure. Eduardo brought in a small tray with two glasses of white wine. Ricardo's sunken eyes regarded Eduardo as he raised his glass with Father Albioni. 'I know, I know, I'll leave you two now,' he grumbled.

Nothing further was said until the door banged shut, followed by the whirring of the lift in the corridor. Ricardo struggled upwards and slid open the bedroom doors, leaning on the rail, he watched Eduardo walk across the car park into town.

'I'm dying, Father,' he said simply, 'dying because of a job I took just after you buried Amelia for me.'

Albioni nodded, recalling their conversation. Ricardo fumbled under his clothing and squeezed a small inhaler into his mouth.

'I've watched you, Father, all my life. What I'm going to tell you will make your future difficult, if not impossible. It may even kill you. If you get the vote from the conclave, then God knows what you'll do.'

Cardinal Albioni raised his hands in mock protest, at the same time marvelling that a simple miner was echoing the political machinations going on back in the hotbed of the Curia in Rome.

'It is not my desire to accede, Ricardo, believe me.'

Ricardo accepted his protestations with a wry smile. 'When I had laid Amelia to rest, I went to Rome a few days later to meet the consortium that was handling the tunnelling contract. The job was to the south-west of the Stazione Termini, directly underneath the Basilica di Santa Maria Maggiore'

Albioni nodded. The area around the railway terminal was a rundown district of olive warehouses and cheap hotels, three or four storeys high and of little interest to the city.

'When I arrived, I'd already signed the contract, but they made me sign again with very strict rules on confidentiality. They said it was a new commercial development, and it was important that as much of the work was completed before their rivals knew what was happening. In fact, Father, the clauses of confidentiality and the way they were put to us, well it made one or two of us stand up and nearly walk out.'

'But you didn't,' interrupted Albioni.

'No, you don't when your family and your life is threatened.'

'Physical threats against you for a tunnelling contract?' interrupted Albioni.

Ricardo looked uncomfortable and then continued. The company that had the contract was Argentinian, which was odd: Europe is full of very capable engineering contractors. They were good, very professional, but the strange thing was the hold the brothers had over them. They were from some order or other, I can't remember but the company was called Amadeus.'

'Go on' said Albioni watching Ricardo struggle with himself.

'Well we told ourselves if it wasn't for the money . . . but it was nearly treble the going rate, so we got stuck in.'

Ricardo's tale rambled on; several times Albioni rose and refilled his empty glass, saying little, just letting the story unfold. The time passed in a blur and he was getting confused.

'Can I write this down?' he pleaded.

'No, not ever!' came the explosive answer. For the first time Albioni saw fear in those sunken eyes.

Eventually it was finished and Ricardo sat slumped back in his chair studying the bottom of yet another empty glass. Albioni eyed his own reflectively. 'Ricardo, your confession is confidential you know that, but I am bound to act somehow. Can I ask, is there any proof of all this?'

Ricardo sighed heavily and struggled to his feet. Shuffling across the room his progress was interrupted by the shrill of the telephone. Lifting the receiver he said 'Si?' simply and to an obvious question he replied that Eduardo was not here and replaced the instrument. Reaching under the small table he took out a small parcel with which he returned to the chair by the window. Placing the parcel on the table between the two of them, he spoke slowly. 'Open it on your way back to Rome, Father, not before.' He paused for a moment, the tortured heaving of his chest as it fought for oxygen the only sound.

Then he continued doggedly, 'The dust from the vaults we carved out of the volcanic pumice, and the sawdust from the shelves of oak as thick as a man's leg we built to carry the weight of this,' he gestured weakly to the table in between them. 'It's done for me, Father. You will not speak to me again.'

Albioni eyed him quizzically for a moment before blessing him and collecting the small parcel. It was surprisingly heavy. Leaving the frail figure in the chair, he let himself out and took the lift down. His driver pulled up outside, right on cue, and Albioni sank gratefully into the soft leather seats with the small parcel next to him. Moments later he was startled from his reverie by the abrupt application of the Mercedes' brakes. A stifled curse from his normally placid driver sent him scanning the front of the vehicle. The dark robed figure of a monk, his face hidden in the shadows of his cowl, passed down the right wing of the car.

Normally the smooth journey down the autostrada would have sent Albioni to sleep against the soft nappa leather, but now his thoughts were racing. His eyes flickered across the carriageway and into the passing villages, seeing nothing: his mind in turmoil. By the time the car pulled up outside his door he had clarified everything. Ricardo was undoubtedly a sick man, a dying man definitely. The dust from his mining days was slowly clogging the alveoli of his lungs day by day. Albioni would have to have words with the correct apostolic authorities, but he felt he had the problem in perspective. As he ducked out of the car, the driver called after him, 'Your Eminence, you left this,' handing him the small heavy package he had put on the rear seat.

After gratefully accepting the glass of brandy left for him by the ever-attendant Pedro, Albioni sat at his desk and used his small ivory-handled letter opener to tear at the parcel's wrapping until the contents lay naked on the desk, solid and gleaming with the dull glow of pure gold. Albioni looked at it wonderingly, but his thoughts were wrenched away by the telephone call that came next.

'Your Eminence,' said the melancholy voice of Pedro. 'We've just heard from Castel Gandolfo. His Holiness Paul VI has passed away following his heart attack.'

'May his soul rest in peace,' the two men muttered down the line.

'The conclave will soon be meeting,' Pedro added. 'My prayers are with you.'

Albioni Luciani replaced the receiver, a great sadness stealing across his face. The ingot on his desk glared up at him, the stamped insignia with the outspread wings and swastika searing his soul. It was not, however, for the ingot's past that Luciani was concerned, it was its latent threat to the future that desperately worried him. He was still pondering it half an hour later as the telephone rang again and he heard with surprise his brother blurt out, 'Albi, is that you?'

'Eduardo, what is it? What's the matter at this hour?'

'Albi, it's Ricardo. He's dead!'

'So soon?'

'No, you don't follow. They found him in the carpark. He fell from his flat not half an hour after you left.'

'How do you know, Eduardo?'

'Cousin Luigi. The police in his unit knew you were there, and that you left at about four-thirty, but the strange thing is they seem to think a monk visited Ricardo also; but no trace of him and we don't have any monasteries up here.'

Albioni murmured his condolences and asked to be kept informed about the funeral. Replacing the receiver, his mind filled with the dark cowled figure that had caused the driver to stop so suddenly.

CHAPTER 60

Silvio Barzini sat back in the swaying coach surveying the rest of the carriage's occupants minutely. He remained satisfied no one was paying him any attention and instead stared out at the darkening countryside. Mentally he saw the balance in his account at the Banco Ambrosiano increase comfortably. Mind, he did not think this one would have gone so smoothly. He had been on the verge of crossing the nondescript car park when the large black Mercedes had swept up to the block of flats. His garb did not encourage him to meet with the scarlet-capped figure who alighted and entered the flats, so he had tucked into a nearby churchyard from where he saw someone emerge from the flats and cast frequent glances up at the block. Following his gaze, Barzini saw a gaunt figure at the balcony rail and even at that distance he had recognised the face from the picture he had been given.

All afternoon he had hung around the little church, on two occasions praying with the elderly couples as they came to lay flowers at the graves of their loved ones. Eventually, to his relief, he had heard the engine of the Mercedes start discreetly and had seen the same scarlet capped gentleman leaving the car park. In his haste, though he had only narrowly avoided being mowed down by the speeding limousine. He made a mental note to seek the driver out: Barzini did not allow loose ends.

When his press on the entrance buzzer was answered, he had mumbled into his fist, ending with the word 'plumber', which was enough to let him through the door. Taking the lift, he rose to the eighth floor and stepped out. Luck was with him, the flat number he needed was directly opposite the lift and the door had been propped open with a scuffed shoe. He could see the pyjama-clad figure of a man against the balcony railing looking down. Grabbing a cushion and a convenient towel he placed the cushion at the top of the man's spine and pushed hard as the figure let out an explosive gasp of surprise. He wrapped the towel around the man's ankles and, in one smooth movement, he lifted him over the rail.

The cushion was back on the settee and the towel over the back of the chair as Ricardo's body hit the concrete eight floors below. Before he exited the flat, fumbling under his habit he extracted a coarse canvas bag. Then he stuffed his monk's habit in the workman's holdall, took the stairs, left by the back entrance and was walking to the railway station whistling in his stained overalls and scuffed boots as a small crowd gathered at the base of the flats.

A second-class ticket conveyed him to Milan, and once at Milan's busy concourse he exited the station and re-entered using a different way in, all the while surreptitiously checking he was not being followed. After that, one further train journey carried him to Rome, where it rumbled into the darkened Statzione Termini. Down the side of the station and away from the bright lights of the centre, Barzini threaded his way through the maze of streets reeking of genteel decay. Hotel after hotel offered vacancy signs with garish prices in flickering neon. There was not a hundred lira difference between one side of the street and the other. The only decision that needed to be made whilst selecting a bed for the night was the differences in the peeling facades or the brightness of the naked bulbs inside.

To his left, behind the basilica, a small cul-de-sac opened and Barzini took it at a steady pace. In the corner the neon-lit sign of the Hotel Ambrose beckoned. The receptionist glanced upwards, momentarily irritated at leaving the nails to which she was applying a deep scarlet polish. At the sight of Barzini, she nodded curtly and lowered her head. The hallway carried a faint, pungent odour of long-used bleach and cigarette smoke. Behind the receptionist's blonde head rows of hooks with numbers reached either side. One key remained on the top row and Barzini retrieved it with a grunt.

'Better ring upstairs and tell them Silvio's back,' he muttered to the blonde head. Without acknowledging him, she reached out with her scarlet-tipped fingers and delicately picked up the receiver so as not to spoil her nail varnish. She was speaking rapidly as Barzini entered the lift. Mirrored on three sides by chipped and flyblown glass, the lift smelt worse than the lobby. His stubby finger jabbed at the number four, it being the highest digit on offer. As the digits climbed, he took the small key and inserted it just below the control panel. His stomach felt the lift slow as the number four glowed. Turning the key, the lift speeded up again momentarily, before coming to a halt. The doors slid open, and he stepped into another world.

Barzini's feet sank into a deep pile carpet, while around him glowed oak panelled walls, interspersed with softly illuminated lights from expensive fittings. Scarcely glancing at his surrounding, he opened a door immediately in front of him and went in.

Throwing his bag in the corner, he leant in the stainless steel and glass cubicle and turned on the gushing spray of hot water. Fifteen minutes later his soft Rockports sank into the carpet as he strode towards the double doors at the end of the small corridor. Dressed from head to toe in black he grasped the two golden handles and pushed them decisively inwards. Four dark habit-clad figures turned to him as he entered the room. The doors clicked shut behind him and he took the proffered fifth chair. The meeting had been in progress some time, a decanter of amber liquid that was presently residing next to the burly figure opposite Barzini was half empty and the room had an ethereal layer of cigar smoke. To Barzini's left, the eldest man spoke first in clipped American tones. 'Good Trip.' It was not a question.

Barzini began to nod and the burly figure opposite expelled a stream of pent-up smoke in relief. A smile cracked his features and his hand drifted to the decanter. Ortolani's black eyes watched him and narrowed, 'There is a but isn't there?'

Barzini continued nodding as the mood sharpened around the small table. 'Albioni spent three hours with him in his flat before.'

* * *

Archbishop Casimir Marcinkus' hand, which seconds before had halted its progress to the decanter, continued its journey and poured a slug into his empty glass before he passed the decanter to Carone, chewing his cigar all the while.

As one, the five figures slumped backwards, absorbing the news. Barzini had failed spectacularly to prevent the knowledge reaching Albioni. Cardinal Albioni Luciani who would soon be ensconced with 115 cardinals in the Sistine Chapel while a conclave convened to choose the next pope and, if rumour were to be believed, may himself even have a chance of being elected.

Vincent Carone leant forward, recovering first. The professional New York policeman and senior member of the Grand Order of Sovereign Knights of Malta spoke in soft tones. 'Whoa, whoa! Out of one hundred and fifteen how many can we count on? Marcinkus, how many with you?'

A pause, 'Twenty-one, maybe twenty-three,' he muttered from behind the dampening cigar.

'Calvi, how many with the IOR?'

'Perhaps thirty,' said the moustached man to Barzini's right, who had so far remained silent.

'Ortolani, the southern cardinals and Sicily, how many?'

Expressionless, his dark eyes unfathomable, Ortalani replied, 'Sixteen,' in a precise, clipped tone.

'OK. OK. Sixty-seven. That should do it.'

Ortolani leant forward, almost snakelike in his menace, 'Gentlemen, gentlemen, is Albioni more dangerous as a cardinal or as Pontiff? That is the question. If he's elected, then we have a delicate problem with the head of the Catholic Church, if not,' he paused and raised his palms, 'well, then we have just another ageing cardinal.'

Marcinkus grunted and leant forward, his thick forearms appearing from his habit. Not for nothing was he called the 'gorilla': the tough, streetwise archbishop from Cicero, Illinois and bodyguard to the previous pontiff. 'Are you crazy? We'd never get away with that; not even here.'

Calvi interrupted smoothly, 'It might, of course, be a decision that could cost the results of seven hundred years of struggle.' The table fell silent. Calvi paused, well used to presenting difficult arguments to powerful committees, and he watched each man around the table. 'Our plan requires the Pole, Wojtyla. Only he can bring down the communists, that is a greater goal than this little matter,' he continued. 'This has been all our lives, and others before in the making. Not only the resources but the intelligence we have garnered. Gentlemen, we stand ready, as the end of the twentieth century approaches, to complete what Urban II started. That is our goal, and we must not be deflected.'

'Casimir!' Calvi gestured through the gently swirling smoke, 'was it not you who once said we can't run on Hail Marys alone? Well, you weren't just talking about money, were you?' The question hung, unanswered.

Barzini watched and kept his counsel as the discussion intensified around the table. Twice the crystal decanter was refilled from the sideboard as the evening wore on. At its end he had his fee for the job in Agardo, which paled into insignificance when compared to the fee for the next assignment, which in turn depended totally on the deliberations of one hundred and fifteen elderly cardinals across the other side of the darkened city. Close to midnight the meeting broke up, possibly for the first time in many hundreds of years utterly dependent on decisions out of their control.

* * *

The blonde, still at her desk in the lobby, looked up bleary-eyed as the hum of the lift announced its decent. However, the lobby doors did not open, and the hum died away. Frowning she returned to her magazine. The side of the hotel in deep shadows concealed an ancient roller shutter door. From the outside it looked as if it had not moved for years. A large industrial waste container, overflowing with junk, sat in front. Smoothly and silently the entire door rose upwards, complete with waste container. It had barely stopped moving when a beige-coloured Fiat 3700 van drove out and into the street. Silently the door slid down to earth, leaving the street quiet and undisturbed except for the howls of the cats and the van's engine fading into the darkness.

* * *

Two days later, as the city held its breath, the ballot papers of the one hundred and fifteen cardinals were put into a brazier beneath a chimney in the Sistine Chapel. Using dry straw this time, the ballot papers produced a white smoke which under the watchful eyes of the world's press, announced that one third of the world's population had a new Pontiff. The next day, under the dome of St Paul's, Albioni Luciani solemnly accepted his position and to the Cardinal President's questions, 'Do you accept, and what name will you take?' broke into one of his famous smiles, as with radiance and confidence he answered 'I accept and take the name John Paul the First.'

It was the 26 August 1978. From the ranks of richly dressed cardinals, Paul Casimir Marcinkus dabbed his perspiring face delicately with his silk handkerchief. Across the city on that sweltering day, on the fifth floor of the four-storey Ambrose Hotel the flickering television image played to a silent group of three men: Roberto Calvi, head of the Banco Ambrosiano, known as the Priests' Bank in Milan and principal investor in the Institute of Religious Works, otherwise known as the Vatican Bank; Vincent Carone, the tough New York police officer who represented the Sovereign Knights of Malta and with connections to New York mafia's Genovese crime family; and Umberto Ortolani, known as the 'Vatican fixer' for his wide range of contacts within all factions of the Church, and again a member of the Sovereign Knights of Malta.

CHAPTER 61

Some days before, and 600 miles to the west and ever so slightly to the north in the Massif du Canigou, hidden by the Forest of Rialsesse, with only the tips of it turreted roofs showing amid the waving treetops, a magnificent castle lay all but hidden from the outside world. Only a few had ever set eyes upon it; the nearby village of Rennes-le-Château, absorbing the conspiracy-theory-driven tourist interest. On the upper level, a study contained rows of damask leather bound ledgers covering an entire wall. Those same walls flickered to the lunchtime news from CNN showing images of the dome of St Peter's caused the room's single occupant to pause momentarily her munching of the delicate Roquefort cheese and flavoursome French onions. Taking an appreciative sniff, she savoured the bouquet of her glass of 1954 Mouton Rothschild while the CNN coverage followed the newly crowned Pontiff into St Peter's to the tumult of the assembled crowd.

After setting down her wine glass, she picked up the telephone and asked to be connected to the Hotel Ambrose in Rome. Moments later, the single white telephone next to the three observers in Rome rang. Ortolani glanced at the other two, his eyes wide. On the third ring he picked it up, held it to his ear, but said nothing. Moments after that, he merely said 'Je comprends' and replaced the instrument. Somewhat paler, he rejoined his companions.

* * *

Some four weeks' later, in an office in Milan, Roberto Calvi had occasion to lose some of his expensively acquired tan. The long overseas call from the President of Ambrosiano SA, the Panamanian offshoot of Banco Ambrosiano, had somehow foreshadowed the next call. The heavily accented president was informing Calvi of the probable default on a $10,000,000 loan to an industrial conglomerate in Guatemala. The president had asked Calvi's advice on handling the issue, because it had been Calvi himself who had set up the deal prior to El Presidente's appointment. Naturally the president felt the need to confer with higher authority.

Calvi had replaced the receiver slowly. The perspiration on his brow was caused not so much because the Guatemalan conglomerate had defaulted, but that it was not his money he had invested. Neither was it Banco Ambrosiano's. Probably, the Institute for Religious Works did not know precisely how they achieved the rate of return on their funds through Banco Ambrosiano; but Vincent Carone's friends in New York and Sicily did. The thought of telling them of the failed investment caused more perspiration to gather on his tanned brow. The telephone stirred again and, irritated he picked it up.

'Casimir Marcinkus, sir,' came the soft Milanese voice.

'Put him through,' snapped Calvi. 'No, no, Your Eminence, he's here and he needs to see you sir.' Seconds later the heavy teak door to Calvi's top-floor office overlooking Milan resounded to the knock of his secretary.

'Mr Marcinkus, sir,' she began, but she got no further as the burly Archbishop blundered into Calvi's office. 'Roberto! It's Albioni . . .'

Calvi quickly held a finger to his lips. 'Thank you, Maria, that will be all.'

Maria, rolling her eyes between the two, shut the door softly.

'Albioni's *assessore* rang me this afternoon. He wants a meeting on Friday, in two days!'

Roberto countered smoothly, 'My dear Marcinkus, our new Pontiff has been scuttling round Rome this past month pressing flesh and getting to know his Curia. Sooner or later, he will want to know how it is financed.'

Marcinkus flapped his hands, sweating profusely. 'His *assessore* says he wants to talk about the miners of Agardo.'

Calvi stopped and exhaled slowly. 'I see, I see.' he said, returning to his large desk. A long silence followed. 'Two days, you say?'

'Yes, yes.'

'That will be the twenty-ninth, then.'

Marcinkus merely nodded. Exhaling deeply, Calvi sat in his large leather chair. He took a slim pocketbook out of his Armani jacket and flicked it open with one hand. Dialling on the old-fashioned dial took a moment and Calvi pressed the receiver to his ear. Looking Marcinkus in the eye, he uttered one word into the mouthpiece, 'Silvio?'

* * *

Sister Vincenza sighed as the chimes of her old mother's clock rang through the tiny apartment. The clock had been with her now for over thirty years in every sort of dwelling, from the tiny cell of her first calling, through to the richly furnished flat she had now as housekeeper to Albioni Luciani, or Pope John Paul I now – as she proudly reminded herself. Shuffling into the tiny kitchen she put on the milk for Albioni's coffee and filled a small brandy glass with his favourite cognac. Ready at last, as she had been every night for the last twelve years, she let herself out of her apartment in the papal palace and padded softly and slowly up the carpeted stairs. In the gloom, she failed to see the hooded figure until he stepped out in front of her. The edge of the tray caught the monk square in his midriff and with an explosive sigh he folded double and sat down, gasping. Sister Vincenza's eyesight was poor, so she never saw both his hands grasp the flask and the cognac glass and let the tray fall to the floor.

Sitting down hard Barzini looked up at the astonished nun. 'Pardon me, Sister, I am so clumsy.'

'No, no,' she fussed 'are you alright?'

'Yes, I think so,' he said eyeing both hands, which held the flask and the glass. 'Now, there's a bit of divine intervention for you! Not a drop spilt for some lucky devil. I wish I had that for supper.'

'Shush!' admonished Sister Vincenza 'it's the Holy Father's'.

'Oh Lord,' mumbled Barzini. Blushing, he got to his knees and looked for the tray. It had fallen behind Sister's legs and by the time she had picked it up, the glass of cognac held no trace of the tiny brown pill. Barzini pulled his hood up and mumbling goodnight padded softly down the stairs.

* * *

On Friday, 29 September 1978, Vatican Radio announced to an astonished world that John Paul I, pope for thirty-three days, had passed away unexpectedly in his sleep. Accordingly, a new conclave would now decide the next Holy Father.

Unnoticed in the media frenzy descending on Rome, Sister Vicenza's funeral was held the day before her beloved Albioni's on 2 October. Widely assumed to have died of a broken heart the day after the Pontiff's death, the simple ceremony was held in the Magdalena Chapel within the Vatican walls. It was attended by no less than eighteen cardinals, still in a state of shock at the premature death of John Paul I. At the rear of the tiny chapel three hooded members of the Order of the Sons of Sion stood silently: witnesses to Sister Vicenza's confessional taken just prior to her death by one of their members: Father Barzini.

Soon afterward the conclave in the Sistine Chapel elected the 264th successor to St Peter. As he took his solemn vows under the dome of St Peter, Karol Wojtyla raised his eyes, pausing only briefly at the dark clad figures in the congregation.

CHAPTER 62

Thomas raised the flat of his hand to shield his aching eyes from the glare of the sun. Beating down from the mountain peaks of Kordestan in northern Iran it concentrated its fierce power in the valley bottom along which they were making slow progress. There was silence on the cart on which Sebastian and Thomas were enduring the torment of the heat and flies. For the tenth time that day he leant wearily forward so the swaying back of the seat on the ox cart rubbed less against his tender back. In an effort to distract himself, he took to minutely surveying the faded chequered pattern of the old bus seat, so lovingly installed on the front the cart: the irony of the pattern on its faded fabric was not lost on Thomas.

The bus depot of the Falls Road was never far from his mind, where its fresh green and yellow buses were all fitted out with seats covered in a hard-wearing cloth that looked much the same. God knows how this seat had made it to the dusty mountains of Iran.

This run called for all his reserves of patience and stamina and once again he had to swivel round and check the rear of the covered wagon and, seeing that the corner of the wooden crate was visible once more, he had to heave more of the stinking fish boxes that filled the cart bed over its precious cargo.

This would have driven a lesser man to insanity he decided; but then he was not a 'lesser man'. In fact, he was actually a dead man who had been given a third chance to stay alive. Almost eight months before he had said goodbye to his last glimpse of blue sky as that foul stinking hood was pushed over his head.

In spite of his predicament, he had in that moment thanked God he had not suffered the fate of the rapist before him, whom Thomas had watched being hauled skyward with neither hood nor bonds. The entire square had erupted with applause as he tore his neck to shreds in an effort to relieve the excruciating pressure exerted by the thin steel cable. His grotesque fight for life ended as his bowels emptied down his lifeless legs sending their contents to land softly where he had stood moments before.

Oddly, Thomas had watched the proceedings with a strange detachment. Only the rough fitting of the hood provided his much-needed rush of adrenalin as he hyperventilated in the stifling darkness. He felt rough hands slip a noose over his head and pull the slipknot tight behind his ear. To his right an unintelligible shout in Farsi caused him to start praying: something he had not done since he left Burtonport when he was sixteen. 'Holy Mary Mother of God, pray for us sinners now, Holy Mary' and that had been the moment when his mind had distantly registered urgent blasts of car horns and slamming doors. Shots rang out, but before he could return to his prayer a mighty force pulled him skyward. Bound though they were, his legs kicked the air as the noose tightened. His windpipe was constricted as he fought for air. A red mist began to cloud the edges of his vision. Then blackness – for how long, he had no way of knowing. But as he slowly felt the hard ground of the square beneath him he was doused in a flood of stinking water which went straight up his nose. Gasping and retching he rolled over, streaming water and mucus into the sandy ground. A further bolt of water was enough to bring his head up to survey a forest of booted legs around him. Strong hands picked him up and he found himself supported by two soldiers as they dragged his inert form to the police station in the corner. There, Thomas was flung into a cell and deposited on the only cot in the room before he faded into unconsciousness.

He awoke sometime later as his cell door was opened. He moved to sit up on the iron cot and tried to swallow, but the pain from his throat made him retch. There was a table in the cell on which stood a glass of water. His hand stretched toward this magical elixir, but as his fingers encircled the glass his wrist was gripped by an iron hand. Once again, he cried in pain.

'Not so fast my friend,' said a voice, followed by a deep chuckle. 'In fact, not so fast Thomas O'Neil of the Irish Republican Army, previously based in the Belfast and the Northern Ireland bus company depot off the Falls Road in that city.'

Thomas stayed shock still for a moment, then slumped in relaxation, but still the hand remained. 'You'll forgive me for not getting up to greet you then,' he countered, thinking wildly. 'Only my hand seems to be stuck'. Again, he swallowed and winced in pain.

'Of course, how unthoughtful of me. Perhaps I should leave you with some throat lozenges and resume our discussion in a day or so? After all, I'm in no rush and for you every day is a bonus is it not?'

The cell door had shut quietly, and Thomas had leant back against the bed. For three days they left him, the only interruptions being the opening of the door for his two meals a day and the foul walk down the dingy corridor with his bucket of urine and faeces. By the third day his nightmare in the square had almost faded, but when the details seemed hazy feeling around his neck brought it all flooding back.

For his next visit, two of them came into his cell, as the sergeant dragged in a couple of small chairs for the 'guests'. When he left, a packet of red, white and gold landed on the desk: Marlboros, part of his cargo all those weeks ago.

Lieutenant Al Zubair sat back and expelled the rich smoke in Thomas' face. Inspector Shalid, who sat next to him, would never know how much he enjoyed that. Thomas' fingers twitched as he moved to the packet. His hand closed round the cigarette and this time, unbelievably, no dark-skinned hand gripped his wrist and denied him his prize. Al Zubair's slim Dunhill lighter did the rest.

'So, Thomas "me boy", what shall we do with you now?' Lieutenant Al Zabir's Iranian accent attempting mimicry of the harsh Belfast tones of years ago.

Leaning back nonchalantly, Thomas expelled a stream of smoke and, feeling unaccountably confident he looked the lieutenant in the eye. 'You tell me. It was you who stopped the party, not me'.

Al Zubair's eyes creased at the corners. 'You are an expert at your trade Mr Thomas,' he began. 'It took us many, many months to track the import of cigarettes and alcohol into the naval base'. Thomas acknowledged this truth with merely with a nod of his head.

'As I said,' replied Thomas, 'You stopped the party, not me'. He felt a growing sense of patience; this after all was the Middle Eastern way, to obfuscate endlessly until a point could be made. Lieutenant Al Zubair hesitated, his thoughts masked behind his dark eyes. His uncle, who had also arrived at the police station, had seemed more interested in the monk that was to accompany Thomas' body home.

'If you're so damned good at smuggling contraband in, perhaps could you smuggle some out?'

Thomas scratched his throat to conceal his surprise. 'Well, it's possible. But after Trump backed out of the nuclear treaty in 2018, you are the most watched nation on earth,' and he pointed his finger to the sky.

'True. True', flushed Al Zubair, surprised at Thomas' perception, 'But they watch for oil and military movements, they do not concern themselves with the little people of the mountains.'

Thomas leant back and chuckle. 'You mean where's the best place to hide a body? A graveyard of course,'

'Quite, quite', beamed Al Zubair. 'But I did not mean only one border to cross, you may have several, and even a sea journey.'

'You have something on your mind?' grunted Thomas.

'Northern Ireland firstly. Then others will take it to the UK,' came the direct reply.

Silence for a moment, then Thomas laughed harshly. He pushed back his chair and stood up. 'Your generosity overwhelms me kind sir,' he said with a mock bow. 'Stay and I hang: smuggle something into Northern Ireland and I'll be dead in a week,' he said bitterly.

'Perhaps, perhaps not. Your quarrel with the Irish Republicans is not of our doing, but if you handed over to them the means of ending their struggle with the British once and for all, don't you think that your Irish cousins would welcome you?'

Thomas snorted in derision, his eyes wildly dancing between the two urbane Iranians. 'I betrayed an entire unit all those years ago. The Paras shot them all: I saw it with my own eyes. Unless they believe me dead, do you know the punishment for traitors on the Falls Road?'

'Worse than a dusty square in a foreign land?' shot back Al Zubair.

Slowly Thomas sat down, a certain weariness overcoming him. 'What exactly would I be smuggling?'

Al Zubair masked the triumph in his eyes. 'Soon, soon.' Then he paused and changed the subject, 'Father Sebastian, you asked for him?'

'His order has a monastery back in my hometown. I used to have an uncle there. I thought perhaps they could get word to my folks.'

Al Zubair shifted in his seat. 'Are you aware of the Sons of Sion support for the IRA?'

For the second time Thomas laughed. 'You know little of Northern Ireland politics, Lieutenant. Every God-fearing Catholic supports the RAH deep down. There isn't a parish priest who will condemn an active soldier who dies in the line of duty against the Brits.'

'I'm not talking about passive support, Thomas O'Neil,' Al Zubair interrupted icily. 'We understand the order is still, shall we say, active in providing facilities and funds for a wide range of active service units.'

'Well, there you have the edge on me,' said Thomas sarcastically, sensing the interview drifting away.

Al Zubair shrugged his shoulders and got to his feet, 'Ah well, perhaps you should think of the possibilities over the next day or so: we're in no rush'.

So, saying, the door opened and the two left the cell without another word.

* * *

Days later the door opened again, and Thomas was beckoned out of the tiny cell. To his surprise, a short walk down the dilapidated corridor saw him in a small, enclosed yard with a square of the bluest sky above he had not seen for a long time. He savoured the air and the heat on his upturned face.

'Welcome back to the land of the living,' said the surprise voice behind him before he and Father Sebastian were embracing in genuine delight. The pair then commenced a slow circuit of the yard talking animatedly although, after a while, Father Sebastian merely listened and looked occasionally at Thomas: with his arms folded in his voluminous sleeves, his face betrayed little of his thoughts. At the end of the allotted exercise time, Father Sebastian left with a firm handshake, to depart as he had come on a bus to the distant Turkish frontier.

CHAPTER 63

At the border, which Sebastian crossed by foot, he noted the one-way nature of the traffic. Outside the small Kurdish border town of Cukurca, UN officials waited to greet the trickle of refugees allowed to leave Iran. Next to the UN Toyotas stood sharp-eyed Americans in local garb watching the vehicles inching towards the border. Approximately one in four were turned off to a side compound where their contents were minutely examined for breach of UN resolutions and sanctions.

Sebastian grimaced wryly: the real sanction busting went on every night along the tortuous border pathways and secluded tracks. From a friendly imam at the local mosque, he retrieved his ancient Honda motorcycle and, habit streaming behind, drove off towards the mountains of Kurdistan and the outpost of Hakkari, home to an ancient fortress of the Order of Sion. It was late afternoon when Sebastian finally drove up the dusty track from the valley to the darkening fortress: actually, more of an outpost left over from the third Crusade. Built in 1141, it had been almost continuously occupied by the order throughout the Ottoman empire and the upheavals of many wars from the Middle Ages to the Second World War. Only a dozen brothers lived in its gloomy portals, being changed seemingly on a whim by instructions from Rome. (Father Sebastian's own last posting had been at Burtonport some eight years previously.) Pushing his motorcycle into what used to be the stables, he went directly to the small chapel on the western side of the building. The last of the day's sun shone through the exquisite west window, making up for its small size by its dazzling array of colours that filled the tiny chapel with warm hues. He knelt at the small altar to give thanks for a safe journey. With his head bowed, he felt rather than heard another kneel next to him.

For long moments both men knelt side by side, as men in this place had done for centuries. Eventually Sebastian bade the abbot good evening. Abbot Dovarich was an ex-military policeman from the Turkish armed forces, who coolly waited for Sebastian to begin. Their conversation lasted long enough for them both to shift uncomfortably on their knees before they stood up with some difficulty and left the tiny chapel.

The next day Abbot Dovarich drove out of the small courtyard in his battered Moskovich saloon and took the main road to the local capital, nestling in the Armenian Highlands. He parked his car carefully in the main street of the bustling town and sauntered towards the railway station. Abbot Dovarich knew that all of life can be found around a railway station: fresh new arrivals; old lags waiting to take advantage; confusion; noise; and above all, a highly mobile population departing and arriving from all parts of Turkey, Syria, Iran and Northern Iraq. A railway station is also the finest source of stolen mobile phones for miles.

In his last five years at Hakkari he had had to do this on two occasions. Muffled from the early chill in the air with his fur-lined jacket and with his woollen cap pulled well down, he went into the little bar behind the goods yard. The noise and hubbub died briefly as he entered but resumed once everyone there had eyed the latest entrant as 'one of them', rather than the vicious civilian police. Dovarich sought a wiry, miserable looking man at the bar. Recognising Dovarich, the man slid an empty glass towards him. As the barman busied himself the two remained silent, until another customer called for his attention.

Draining half his glass, the wiry man spoke. 'Don't tell me. Let me guess,' and stained, uneven teeth flashed a smile at Dovarich. 'GSM-enabled, charged, not yet reported stolen?'

Dovarich merely nodded. After his first visit, Wasim had known immediately the 'client's' requirements. Although Wasim's name was the only thing Dovarich knew about him and that discovery had been a slip of the tongue. So, he was not surprised when, a slim silver Nokia miraculously appeared in Wasim's walnut coloured hand. Without appearing to look, he thumbed rapidly across its screen and lifted the handset to his face. Nobody watching from more than half a metre away would even know he had a phone. Wasim whispered for several seconds, then the phone disappeared, as did the remaining contents of his glass.

For the next half-hour the two men engaged the sullen barman in desultory conversation. After Wasim's fourth refill, the bar door opened and a pale youth in his late teens slipped into the smoky atmosphere, brushing against Wasim as he made his way to the rear of the premises. Contact had been made. Dovarich merely felt his left-hand pocket jostled slightly and then Wasim was gone. Slipping his hand inside the pocket the smooth tablet-like form of a mobile phone had taken the place of the bulky envelope stuffed with cash.

On the road back to Hakkari, a lay-by beckoned where the international lorry drivers would sometimes sleep over on their way to Russia. At present it was empty and Dovarich drove to the end of the carpark overlooking the swollen River Zab on its way to the Iranians further south.

Sitting on a large, rounded boulder, the roar of the river drowned everything around him – the distant road now inaudible over the rushing torrent – the phone lit up in his hands as he dialled a number. She answered from her room in the castle. The one lined with the damask leather bound volumes.

Their conversation lasted no more than ten minutes and moments later the silver tablet was broken down into its component parts and was being swirled down the river. Meanwhile the elderly Moskovich saloon had driven away out of the car park.

* * *

One week after Father Sebastian had left Iran he walked back towards the dusty control building, to present his papers to the guard in reflecting sunglasses. This produced a flurry of activity in the scruffy office, where Sebastian stood patiently, his face a mask, as phones rang and papers were shuffled.

In due course Sebastian saw a cloud of dust approaching, which metamorphosed into a dusty, silver coloured Mercedes 'S'-Class saloon, its windows an impenetrable black. The eyes of the border guard darted between the monk in front of him and the sinister saloon, which he gestured to halt. When it stopped, Sebastian walked towards the car rear window which lowered, and a smiling Lieutenant Al Zubair offered him a lift. Compromised, Father Sebastian settled into the soft leather as the vehicle whisked him south.

During Sebastian's absence, Thomas had been treated with complete indifference by his jailers. There was no attempt to talk to him or interrogate him; rather they just ignored the charge in their midst. Thomas used the time to reflect, however. The abrasions on his neck had virtually gone but on one occasion when he found a sliver of broken mirror in the exercise yard he could detect an angry weal under the skin on the left of his neck. Fingering the weal always provoked the same thoughts. Why? Why had the execution of a small-time smuggler of cigarettes and alcohol been halted? And halted in such a fashion. Thomas had discerned the relationship between Zubair and his uncle.

The one thing he knew was that the reason for his salvation lay primarily in his smuggling skills: his ability to slip across borders at will, assume local identities and above all do all this without any discernible help. So, why the questions about Father Sebastian?

Thomas turned this over and over in his mind when he had told Father the content of his 'interview' leaving nothing out; and the look of interest on Sebastian's face had not been lost on him. In any case where the hell was he? It was the uncertainty that gnawed at him. Was all this some game in which he would be marched back to the square? The memory of those Mercedes saloons in the square came flooding back. Somehow, he doubted it.

* * *

Lieutenant Al Zubair lowered the rear window and observed the robed monk just outside the city of Khorramshahr, 'It suits me to drop you here my friend: that way we are both protected'.

Father Sebastian nodded, perspiring quickly in the sudden temperature change from the rear of the Mercedes to the side of the highway in southern Iran. 'I understand. Destroy those numbers when you have credited the account. Half now, half on delivery'.

Al Zubair nodded formally, and the black glass slid back into position. The car glided away leaving the dark figure taking his first steps along the highway. 'The monk should be back in with our prisoner in a couple of days,' Al Zubair reflected. His hand opened to reveal the slip of paper passed to him: a series of numbers denoting international bank sort codes, identification codes and account numbers. Banco Ambrosiano, Milan. Al Zubair had never heard of it, but he shrugged, putting the scrap of paper carefully in his top pocket as he reached for the vehicle's cell phone.

General Bagheri answered at once with a single grunt. Al Zubair detailed the previous conversations in the rear of the car to the silent general. On one occasion, Al Zubair had checked he was on the line; 'Uncle, are you listening?' Only a grunt ascertained that he was.

Al Zubair had kept the question of money to the end. 'Anyway, uncle they want two million dollars: half immediately and half when the cargo arrives in ...'

'Shh, shh,' came the admonishment.

A pause followed as the vehicle swished along.

'Well,' chuckled the general finally, 'it's a lot cheaper than funding the Al Samud missile programme and they can't fly that far, or for that matter hit anything'.

Al Zubair's teeth flashed white in the darkness as the two men roared with laughter.

* * *

Thomas didn't bother to stand up when the cell door bolts were drawn. He could tell by the strips of sunlight on the cell floor that it was roughly his mealtime and as such provoked no mouth-watering anticipation. But when Father Sebastian stooped as he entered the cell, Thomas let out a sigh of relief as he caught sight of the tall figure in his dusty habit.

CHAPTER 64

Across the Great Salt Desert a sandstorm whirled, and the wind howled. Ninety metres underground however, it was a different tale. The huge facility hummed and whirred with quiet activity. Tannoy announcements sent technicians scurrying from one item of plant to another in response to commands from the central control console behind which stood the spectacled Dr Schlatter. In spite of the sixty-eight-degree air conditioning provided by his employees, Dr Schlatter was perspiring heavily as he wheeled his chair along the banks of switches and dials making minute adjustments.

The project had far exceeded his expectations. After his somewhat tense introduction to his targets and requirements by the oily Abbasi and the sinister Izadi, he had resigned himself to his task. Judi had been brought along and, in the rear of the large cavern a set of apartments had been fashioned that would have not looked out of place in fashionable Geneva.

Although he had witnessed the grinding poverty on his journey here, in part due to the heavy sanctions imposed by the international community on the Iranian regime, no expense had been spared in the accommodation he and Judi were now enjoying; apart from windows the couple lacked nothing.

In another part of the cavern identical living quarters had been created for Mohsen Fakrizadeh, the senior Iranian scientist at the plant. Dr Schlatter had formed a reasonable relationship with him and had commiserated with him on being held underground for so long. Mohsen had agreed but said the threat from Mossad was such that he could only visit his wife in Tehran infrequently.

So pleased was Izadi with the increase in production, he had taken Judi shopping to Tehran at a government-only-supplied store: although they had travelled in separate vehicles in accordance with the strict protocols monitored by the morality police. Judi had come back breathless and wide-eyed at what she described as a private shopping mall that contained every western luxury, which had been created behind the walls of one of the government buildings. She had been even more impressed to find there were no tills of any description, and that she was limited in what she could shop for only by the size of the Mercedes' boot.

Mohsen's and Judy's trip the second time was different. As the large lift doors had opened opposite the control panel where Dr Schlatter worked, the car erupted at speed and flew across the cavern floor. The rear door had been flung open and a terrified Judi had flown into the control room and launched herself at an astonished Dr Schlatter. Tears coursed down her swollen cheek as she held him tight, her body racked with sobs. Izadi had entered the control room after her, breathing hard with his eyes flushed with anger. He too slumped into a chair and apologised coldly to Dr Schlatter for the emotional condition of his wife. His account of what had happened sounded like a scene from a Hollywood action movie.

He explained that the two Mercedes saloons had left Tehran and headed south. Judi was in one Mercedes with Izadi and a driver, whilst Mohsen Fakhrizadeh was in another. Fakhrizadeh's car had slowed to overtake a pickup that had been left on the side of the road with the bonnet raised. As his car drew level, the rattle of heavy machine gun fire reached the occupants of Judy's car. Reacting instantly, the driver stamped on the accelerator and swerved past the scientist's blazing Mercedes. Judi, glancing from the window saw immediately that it was riddled with bullet holes. She also saw that Fakhrizadeh's eyes were staring sightlessly at her through the shattered window. The rear of the pickup, which had previously been shrouded by a tarpaulin, showed that it was fitted with twin mounted machineguns that were spitting bullets at the car. However, as they raced away to safety, Judi could see that both machineguns and pickup were unmanned: there was no one behind the guns and the pickup was empty.

The convoy did not stop but drove at speed into the entrance of the Fordo facility.

By the time the vehicle had negotiated the lift, Izadi had calmed somewhat, but it was with a smouldering angry stare that he observed Dr Schlatter comfort his sobbing wife whilst he reported on the assassination of yet another key scientist.

Chapter 65

After Thomas's initial joy at having Father Sebastian back, his life had settled once again into monotonous uncertainty. The days passed and he was no wiser as to his fate. Of the lieutenant there was no sign, and Father Sebastian was strangely relaxed about staying around Thomas. Walking around the exercise yard one afternoon Sebastian said casually 'We're leaving in three weeks apparently'.

'We', muttered a startled Thomas.

'Yes, my abbot wants me to spend a while with our brothers in Ireland and we can journey there together'.

'I don't take passengers or partners on my trips' muttered Thomas darkly. 'Whatever these buggers are up to, a trip is a trip. Take the goods; get them in and get out'.

Father Sebastian lips smiled but his eyes did not. 'Thomas, I am your passport out, without me ...', he glanced at Thomas' neck meaningfully.

Thomas stared back and asked waveringly, 'What's going on Father? What are you doing with a death row smuggler heading towards Ireland?'

'God works in mysterious ways, Thomas.'

Thomas laughed harshly, 'Listen Father. I called because I haven't been to a Mass since I was fourteen and I was hours away from a necktie party. How am I supposed to take a package – and a monk for Christ's sake – 3,000 miles across the Middle East and Europe without attracting attention?'

'I think you'll find we're capable', shot back Father Sebastian.

'"We"? You keep saying "we"; "we", as in who? You, me, the Iranians, and who else?'

Father Sebastian merely nodded and left Thomas alone in the small yard. 'Well, me boy', mused Thomas, alone again, 'you've two choices', as he fingered the scar on his neck.

* * *

Thomas had been taken from his cell some weeks after Sebastian's second visit. He had experienced a momentary panic when they had escorted him out of the station and down the street towards the main square. In the corner sat a horribly familiar crane, its engine ticking over quietly. He must have paused momentarily because Lieutenant Al Zubair had touched his elbow somewhat reassuringly. A Mercedes 500D long-nosed flat-bed lorry was parked in front of the crane with what appeared to be a cargo of cut date palms lashed to its rear body. The cab was finished in multi-coloured panels with Farsi script decorating much of it.

Thomas was puzzled and watched as an Iranian soldier in fatigues clambered up the uneven load and with a whirling motion of his hand, summoned the hook downwards from the crane. The hook on the end of the steel cable disappeared into the topmost fronds and immediately the soldier leapt off the load, circling his hands to the crane driver as he did so. When entire load of swaying palms cleared the deck of the lorry, it left in place a beautifully constructed timber box approximately one metre long by half a metre wide.

Thomas and Al Zubair walked towards it and Thomas examined the dummy palm fronds swaying gently some fifteen feet above them, inside which was the cunningly created frame that had left room for the box underneath.

A small ladder was placed at the truck's side members and Al Zubair motioned Thomas upwards, following behind carrying a small pry bar. Thomas watched as the slim officer bent to the top panel of the box. Working swiftly around its perimeter the lid was gently eased off and, with a final screech of nails, came away to reveal another inner case, made largely of polystyrene but lined with a dull metal about five millimetres thick. Thomas ran his finger along the edge of the crate, curious to understand the purpose behind this elaborate ruse.

Al Zubair paid no attention, but applying gentler movements this time prised the top layer of the lead-protected polystyrene free. A force gripped Thomas' chest. He fought for words, but none came. Four times his eyes, wild and disbelieving, swept from the shiny cylinder nestling in its protective wrapping, to Al Zubair's dark eyes. When he did find his voice, he asked blankly, 'Is that what I think it is?', already knowing the answer as the circular arrangement of three triangles on the shiny casing winked up at him.

'That depends on what you think,' replied the smiling Al Zubair.

'Why the fuck are you showing me? What do I know about them?'

'You know nothing my friend,' agreed Al Zubair.

Another deeper voice chimed in, coming round the cab of the truck, 'But you do know how to get it to Ireland, don't you, Mr O'Neil?'.

Thomas whirled and stared at an impassive General Bagheri standing with two other officers. 'You're fucking mad the lot of you. Just hang me and get on with it'.

Al Zubair flashed an alarmed glance at the general who made a calming motion to his nephew and the three men watched as Thomas stalked off into the square, his shoulders set, occasionally stopping and turned around to reveal his face flushed with anger.

General Bagheri put an arm around his nephew's dejected shoulders. 'We should take coffee,' and he gently steered his young relation out of the square.

'But ...'

'But nothing, Lieutenant', the general said firmly. 'It's the Irish way'. Forty minutes later they returned to find that Thomas had procured a pad of paper and was carefully drawing and measuring the large crate on the back of the lorry. Presently he stood back and gave the general two pieces of the pad covered on both sides with neat script.

For several long minutes not a word was said. Then the general looked up, 'Anything else?'

'Yes. Three things my friend. Who knows about this?'

General Bagheri replied, 'Myself, Commander Hossein Salami, Commander Saeed Izadi, Sebastian and yourself'.

Thomas nodded, 'OK. Keep it that way. Next, the boat. It's lying at the Ayia Napa boatyard in Cyprus: it needs bringing to Latakia. No variations. No excuses.' The general nodded. 'And I'll need a million pounds sterling'.

Thomas immediately realised he should have asked for more, as without a pause the general nodded. But then he added, 'You'll have to collect it in person from our embassy in Dublin'.

Thomas stuck his hand out with a grin to the startled general, not missing the look that Al Zubair gave his uncle.

CHAPTER 66

In a disused warehouse on the edge of Khorramshahr, Thomas' requests arrived in very short order. Sebastian, now clad only in a grubby dish dash, wandered around the pile of old lorry wheels, axles, chassis and welding gear. Across the floor, the bending figure of Thomas was silhouetted against a shower of welding sparks as the odd contraption took shape.

After several days, surrounded by discarded scrap, a frame of sorts stood ready in the workshop. Comprised of two lightweight alloy chassis sections, it stood completely twisted on four old truck wheels of differing sizes. Sebastian frowned, with this they had to reach the Mediterranean over 1,000 miles away, across deserts teaming with aggressive soldiers, under skies patrolled by all-seeing drones and satellites? Walking round the contraption he pushed it gently with one hand. To his utter amazement it rolled quietly and smoothly across the workshop floor to rest with a light bump against one wall. Perplexed, he followed it and pulled it backwards. It felt no heavier than a golf cart he had had occasion to use one year on a visit to Rome. Frowning, he examined the frame closely as the sound of a heavy diesel engine came from the unit's entrance. It was the fitting of the axles that gave the contraption its ungainly look. In fact, whilst the frame which was to take a load bed looked as if it would fall apart at any moment, Sebastian saw the portal axles had been beautifully crafted and fitted specifically to take wheels of different sizes. The unit's doors opened wide, and Thomas got up to guide in the rear of a large lorry. Before long, its contents lay on the floor and Thomas continued his work.

Forty-eight hours later, with just his hand resting on a rear corner, Thomas pushed the cart out of the workshop. Its ironwork was lost now under a layer of shabby, coarse timber and with each wheel sporting a different, dirty colour.

'Taxi to Latakia, my friend?' he asked Sebastian with a broad grin. He was still chuckling at Sebastian's face when a large lorry pulled up sharply and, under Thomas' guidance reversed to the rear of the cart and stopped.

Al Zubair jumped out caught a whiff of the appalling stench rapidly filling the warehouse and promptly emptied the contents of his stomach over the lorry's wheel. Holding his hand to his mouth, he stumbled away.

Then it hit Sebastian. The contents of his stomach took on properties of their own as they rose quickly up his throat and exited his mouth in a spray.

The stink was unbelievable: a cloying heavy smell that could be traced to the mound of leaking boxes now covering the cart's bed. The new wooden crate that had been disclosed in the square those weeks ago, now disappeared under boxes of indeterminate age stamped with the name of a fish merchant in Abadan.

Thomas stood next to Sebastian, his arms folded and a look of complete satisfaction spreading across his face. 'As I said, my friend, Latakia or bust.'

'Latakia' spluttered Sebastian, not trusting his stomach to disgorge any further contents. 'Yes, Latakia by-the-sea,' came the amused response. 'Where the good ship *Lollipop* awaits us on the Syrian coast.' Sebastian looked at him in complete bewilderment.

One last act remained. The two dun-coloured oxen procured by General Bagheri arrived sporting large doleful eyes. A foul stream of decaying fish oil was seeping from one corner of the cart where Thomas had placed a bucket under the dripping putrefaction. When it was half-full, he took an old rag and smeared it liberally across the gleaming beasts. The two observed Thomas with their soulful eyes, as their tails swished at the large cloud of flies that now hovered over them. Thomas declared departure to be the next day and after browbeating Al Zubair to bring several bottles of whisky to his cell, retired for the evening.

* * *

Sebastian stood uncertainly the following grey morning: of Thomas there was no sign. Impatiently he leant against the cart, where its smell was slightly more bearable in the chill of the dawn. He felt the frame move slightly behind him and as he turned the stooped figure of an Iranian peasant had taken the reins of the bullocks.

Sebastian was about to remonstrate with the man when he was struck dumb: the scruffy local turned to the monk, and with a heavy Irish accent greeted him, 'Top o'the morning to you sir! Talib's the name, smuggling's the game'.

Laughing uproariously as he clambered up to sit on the cart, he gave the oxen a gentle nudge and set them on their way. Sebastian had grabbed his bag and swung himself up next to a wizened, bent, distinctly dirty Thomas who was wearing the same kind of tatty garment as he was. Strangely enough, seeing this he found himself feeling a little more confident about what the two of them were embarking on.

* * *

Thousands and thousands of years ago the Karun and Diyala rivers had carved vast flood plains through modern-day Iran and had provided the fertility and fabulous wealth of Persia of old. Alongside the now turgid rivers, ancient routes had been worn, marked by trees or large boulders since time immemorial. Like much of the rest of the world, modern Iran now relied on fast motorways to traverse its vast terrain, leaving the old routes to decay. The Iran Thomas and Sebastian witnessed in the long weeks across the arid landscape and into the mountains bore little relation to the society of today. Courtesy and politeness abounded and what little curiosity arose about the cart's contents proved Thomas' hunch right. With the need for all faithful Muslims to wash prior to prayer five times a day, curious onlookers were soon discouraged from getting too close, including the most curious policeman when the sun was high and flies buzzed around the cart. For his part, Sebastian marvelled at Thomas' cunning that had discovered that rotting fish was a staple fertiliser and its trading blended perfectly into the life of rural Iran.

On occasions of course, the main carriageway had reasons to cross the mighty Karum. Huge berms thrown up to convey the highway towards the river itself caused Thomas and Sebastian to make detours from the ancient track. Approaching one such crossing, the track itself disappeared forcing the pair to take the highway for a mile or so before rejoining the track on the northern side of the berm. Thomas urged his oxen on and drove steadily up the soft verge of the tarmac, all the while dripping putrefaction from the corners of the cart. Presently the speeding traffic slowed and halted allowing the filthy, tattered cart slowly to overtake the twentieth century's finest machines as they queued patiently in the shimmering heat. A checkpoint.

Thomas and Sebastian also waited patiently behind a couple of vehicles that had stopped in front of the group of heavily armed men in the uniform of the IRGC. Thomas bowed his head, listening. He caught a snatch of conversation. They were looking for Zionist infiltrators who had assassinated an senior Iranian scientist; he could not catch the name.

Keeping his eyes lowered and clasping his hands together Thomas slid off the cart and stumbled towards the officers. One started to approach but backed off when the ghastly smell from the cart reached him. Thomas paused just in front of his oxen and with head bowed concentrated on the officer's feet.

'You filthy peasant and son of a whore! Get this stinking specimen away!' the officer screeched, his face turning puce behind his clasped handkerchief.

Thomas remained calm and made to lead his oxen into an impossible gap between two huge lorries. One of the drivers, with great amusement – more at the officer than the hapless Thomas – shifted his truck into reverse with a grinding of gears. Inching backwards, he halted to a chorus of cries as the next lorry sounded its horn. Still the gap remained impossibly small. Thomas paused then led his charges slightly towards the steep drop to the flood plain.

By now the officer was incandescent with rage and frustration. Screaming at Talib he pointed to the checkpoint barrier, all the while holding the handkerchief to his nose. But as Thomas nudged his charges forward the barrier opened and he drove slowly through the check point with no more than a respectful raised hand and 'May Allah bless your children'. A short distance on, he turned off the highway once again onto the ancient cart way. Nobody even looked at him.

Their days blended into weeks as they crossed with little difficulty the porous northern border of Iran and Iraq and thence into Syria. Throughout the long journey, they kept up their alibi through the sale of rotten fish from the rear of the cart, the contents of which would be replaced by half a dozen boxes or so at the beginning of every week by a drab, nondescript lorry that appeared out of nowhere.

Their long trek afforded them both plenty of time to reflect on the bizarre nature of their undertaking. For his part, Sebastian realised that Saeed Azadi's choice of 'mule' was masterful. Thomas kept his payment side of the bargain to himself whilst he mulled over the look that Al Zubair had shot his uncle over the subject. For the moment, though, he was content that the arrival of the bomb would restore his standing with the Derry Brigade's commanders.

* * *

Casting glances towards the Nahr al Kabhur River, Thomas found a track leading to a deep pool invisible from the road.

'Time for a change, me boy,' he chuckled as he urged his faithful oxen down the narrow lane. Out of sight from the road, he drove the cart into a shallow pool until the wheels were submerged in the clear water. Taking his shovel, he proceeded to empty the cart of the weeks of accumulated fish scale and filth. The same shovel used broadside on, washed wave after wave of water over the cart and the basking oxen.

Cleaner and decidedly more fragrant, the cart rejoined the sandy road alongside the highway, but not for long. In the distance stood a shimmering pile of metal resembling a grotesque pyramid, each block represented by a cube of crushed steel. On the outskirts of Abu Kamal the Anfal Metal Company of Syria proudly boasted that it crushed as many scrap vehicles a day as were imported new to the country.

Getting closer, Sebastian could see a wall of steel cubes fencing in acre after acre of vehicles piled high on each other. A dozen crane jibs poked brazenly above the walls lowering huge dish-like magnets to God knows where behind the steel walls, only to reappear with a hapless motor vehicle, its wheel spinning like the legs of a trapped metallic insect until it was dropped with a crash into the jaw of a giant crusher.

It was into this metal hell that Thomas slowly drove his cart until he pulled up outside a huge, corrugated shed. There, Thomas leapt lightly down and embraced a burly Syrian welder who, with his goggles pushed high on his glistening forehead, grasped Thomas in delight before the pair wandered off down wide aisles of scrap vehicles.

Some little time elapsed before the two re-appeared and, after a firm handshake, the welder disappeared back into his corrugated shed while Thomas eyed Sebastian and told him, 'Well, we'll stop the night. Room service is non-existent, but we do get breakfast!'

Sebastian grimaced and clambered down. On his left, a mountain of crushed vehicles revealed a small office door through which he entered an air-conditioned office complete with a bed and a table, all concealed in a steel shipping container buried within the scrap mountain.

'I'll be across the road in the shed, if you want me,' Thomas explained. 'Otherwise, I'll see you in the morning.'

* * *

Shortly after dawn, Sebastian awoke in the narrow camp bed as a blue-overalled young boy brought a tray with sweet Arab tea and local naan bread, figs and olives. Standing in the doorway under an archway of scrap vehicles, he savoured the sweet tea and crispness of another glorious day. Of Thomas there was no sign as he glanced up and down the scrap yard.

As if to answer his thoughts, the huge, corrugated doors opposite screeched open to reveal the nose of a Toyota Hi-Lux pick-up: probably the most common vehicle on the roads of the entire region. Behind its dusty windscreen, a grinning Thomas gunned the engine and the pick-up lurched forward, pulling behind it their transport of the last 600 miles. Gone were the oxen and, now fitted with a steel drawbar its ungainly twisted chassis had been cleverly corrected so it ran straight and true. On what now passed for a well-used flatbed, there stood a vintage Churchill milling machine resplendent in a new coat of glistening blue paint.

Thomas leapt from the cab. 'Top of the morning, sir!' he cried in mock tones, bowing to an astonished Sebastian. 'Talib Al-Majid at your disposal!'

Closing the Toyota door with a flourish he pointed proudly at the emblazoned door panel: 'Al-Majid Machinery Removals' the legend ran. Sebastian wandered over to the waiting pick up looking at it in amazement. From every bearing and thread protruded thick grease. Likewise, the machine bed of the machine glistened under a coat of oil.

Thomas wandered up, 'Pile of scrap, of course, but its smart enough to pass muster to the locals, and it'll be enough to get us to Latakia.

Two days later in the utter luxury of the noisy non-air-conditioned cab of the Toyota, they dropped finally down the Al-Ansariyyah mountains to the small port of Latakia framed with the glistening Mediterranean as its backdrop. Again, in what was obviously a well-rehearsed routine, Thomas sought a large scrap yard based in an old quarry. As the unit drove through the large iron gates, Sebastian raised his eyebrows slightly at the legend over the entrance: Anfal Metal Co of Syria. The trailer was reversed under an overhead crane as Sebastian undid the large webbing straps. In no time, the trailer rose slightly on its springs as the dusty blue monster it had been carrying was swung away and deposited on a pallet further down the yard. The hook returned, gliding softly towards Thomas on the bed of the trailer. With a large pry bar he removed the fish-oil-stained plywood sheets from the floor and, grasping the hook, guided it under the small straps around the dusty box in the well of the trailer.

After the crane had lifted the crate clear, Thomas slid back the heavy plywood base off the trailer. Then the hook descended a final time to slow movements of Thomas' wrist. Once again the trailer settled under its load – a new one this time – and Sebastian again found himself a bemused observer as he watched Talib bend over the wooden crate. He was holding a small container in one hand and a stencil in the other. After the container was shaken vigorously Sebastian watched as the words 'Volvo Marine' followed by 'Penta 245' appeared in fresh letters on the rough timber. A dozen partly worn commercial vehicle tyres in the bed of the pickup completed the mundane cargo of the little combination. Then they departed and without further ceremony, blended perfectly into the late afternoon traffic entering the bustling port of Latakia.

* * *

Thomas smelt it first. Breathing deeply through his nostrils he filled his lungs with pleasure. Sebastian's quizzical look was returned by a guffaw of triumph. 'It's the sea, Sebastian, the sea! Can't you smell it, man.'

Warmer and dustier it may have been, but Thomas' childhood still flashed in front of him: huge green Atlantic rollers crashing on shore, which, ironically would now be his eventual destination.

As dusk settled, the Toyota made its way into the nearly deserted commercial section of the port. Harsh arc lights created pools of brilliance, contrasting with stygian shadows around silent iron shapes in the harbour, where Thomas confidently piloted the pickup along the deserted quays until, towards the rear of the harbour, he stopped and honked the horn twice. Then the two sat in silence, waiting.

Sebastian heard a slight movement, a creaking and whirring as if a mechanical monster was stirring in its sleep. Then the huge riveted, latticed ironwork not two yards from his window slid forwards and the huge overhead crane rumbled to a stop above them. Thomas got out and clambered up the access ladder to the crane's controls. In the softly illuminated glass cabin, Sebastian could see the two men discussing and pointing. Thomas' hand appeared with a wad of notes and with much pointing and gesticulating, hands were shaken and Thomas finally descended the ladder.

CHAPTER 67

Thirty years ago, she would have graced the pages of 'quality broadsheet' papers: fast and elegant, the epitome of seagoing luxury for a wealthy client. Probably her gleaming white hull would have been photographed against the blue of the Mediterranean or Caribbean, sporting nubile, scantily clad girls relaxing on the foredeck as she carved a creamy wake through the sea's, smooth glittering surface. But time and money move on. The motor cruiser before them rocked gently at her moorings under the sliding spot lamps of the crane. Her immaculate teak decks were faded and scuffed now, the white cabin work, which was once gleaming now offered just the flat and weary drabness of idle neglect.

Sebastian watched from the quay above as Talib worked in the open centre section of the cruiser. In due course a void opened, to reveal a large stainless-steel tank. At Thomas' silent bidding the crane plucked it out of the motor cruiser's bowels and placed it smoothly on the deck next to where Sebastian was standing. The hook then moved balletically to the trailer, where it collected the stencilled box and placed it in the well under the tank. The tank was then reinserted, and Thomas clambered up the steel ladder.

Sebastian watched as the Toyota and trailer were disconnected and parked independently of each other in a melée of various vehicles, most of which were scrap, at the rear of the crane. Moving from wheel to wheel, Thomas deflated all the tyres, letting each wheel settle on its rim. He then jacked up the pick-up and trailer in turn to remove a wheel from each, so that both vehicles listed over despondently. Finally, he took three aerosol cans of common spray lubricant and liberally coated the pickup and trailer. 'Twenty-four hours of this,' he said, raising his palms in the hot dusty air 'and they'll look as if they've been there for years'.

Sebastian gazed thoughtfully at his departing back as Thomas negotiated the vertical iron ladders at the dockside with alacrity. Sebastian, though, took a little longer, uncertain of his footing in his long, travel-stained habit.

There was a little deck between the cruiser's forward and aft cabins, where Sebastian joined Thomas and took in the sight that made feel even more dismayed. Peeling paint, cracked windows and a swirl of windblown rubbish in the corners completed the boat's derelict appearance. It required a bit of fumbling around a sturdy teak door before Thomas managed to unlock it at four separate points. Pushing it open, he descended a few steps into the main saloon. He turned on a switch illuminating dim lights which indicated that the battery's last gasp was barely sufficient only to lighten the gloom and no more. Sebastian followed as Thomas moved to the cockpit and watched Thomas' dirty white robes in front of the large console where rows of lights winked on. Next, his hand moved to a large red button which he depressed for a few silent seconds. Incongruously in the scruffy surroundings, a diesel coughed under the decking and caught, running smoothly with barely a murmur. The second diesel caught immediately and likewise settled to a rich purr. The lights in the cabin burst into a bright, ambient glow and Thomas swung around with a satisfied look on his face. 'Give her twenty minutes and we'll shower and freshen up. Meanwhile I think we'll drink to the first half of the mission'.

Sebastian was slowly turning, gaping at the sight that met his eyes. The interior of this part of the boat looked as if it had left the shipyard that morning. Deep-buttoned leather couches lined the bulkheads and rich varnished teak boards trembled under his feet. Thomas opened a cabinet revealing a well-stocked selection of drinks and poured two fingers of amber fluid into a pair of beautiful crystal tumblers. The two men sat down gratefully and chinked glasses. 'Never judge a book by its cover,' winked Thomas as he raised his glass.

Minutes later, he had proudly taken Sebastian aft, through the scruffy mid-ships to an equally contrasting aft cabin split into two well-appointed bedrooms with full en-suite facilities. To Sebastian's growing amazement, he then pulled a concealed brass ring and lifted a large hatch into the engine space, from where the heavy insulated hatch let out the muted roar from the two gleaming powerful marine engines pulsing gently side by side.

'This'll take us to Ireland, then?' Sebastian said looking at Thomas, who merely nodded.

'Even the Atlantic after the Straits of Gibraltar?' pressed Sebastian.

'Gibraltar? Even further, me boy.'

Half an hour later Sebastian followed an expensive smelling Thomas up the rusty deck ladder. The dirty white dish dash and rope sandals of Talib had been replaced by faded, but immaculate, Versace jeans, a polo top and scuffed deck shoes of soft brown leather. A Rolex Oyster of some forty years' vintage completed Thomas' new appearance: that of a wealthy Mediterranean 'cruiser' of expensive but unobtrusive taste. Sebastian likewise sported faded, but well-fitting Gucci jeans and a casual jacket, all of which strangely fitted him perfectly.

The two sauntered into the brighter area of the port towards the bars and clubs coming alive for the evening. While Thomas sauntered across the street and entered a brightly lit bistro, Sebastian excused himself and nipped into a phone booth where fed in the requisite coins, lifted the received and punched in a telephone number that began: 0039.

The meal was superb after the long weeks of travel and stench, and the two men comfortably let a few hours, and a couple of bottles, slip away. When the evening drew to a close, Thomas threw a sheaf of banknotes on the table and muttered nonchalantly, 'Do the honours, Sebastian. I'll just have to see about our deck ornaments'.

Sebastian frowned as Thomas approached a couple of tanned, leggy beauties at the bar, who had been making eyes at them all evening. He watched even more bemused as Thomas whispered something in the darker-haired girl's ears and the three roared with laughter as Thomas' arms encircled their slim waists conspiratorially.

CHAPTER 68

'Did it change?' she mused. The dark greens of various hues seeming to stretch to the horizon, her viewpoint clear from the crenelated tower soaring from the forest floor. A keener eye, or maybe a younger eye she wryly thought, would see a ring of cliffs hiding the huge natural bowl, or sink hole, her home had resided in for 700 years. The cliffs made of the same creamy limestone as the castle itself had long ago given up their buttery golden glow to the amorous attention of creepers and lianas. Only occasional gaps where disease or animals had gnawed the thick tendrils revealed the cliff's warmth of tone and in those gaps, just visible, was the evidence of a bygone age: gaps but square ones; regular lines of mortar; empty windows missing only a friendly figure waving to the fields below. There was too the occasional glimpse of smaller stump holes set at angles up or down it mattered not, where once children pattered up and downstairs, precariously clinging to the rock face. Before her time, and that of her many ancestors, the castle had stood in a bowl of fertility where its fields yielded their bounty to its secret community keeping its own existence secret: a dark and dangerous thing. This was where precious few down the centuries had been entrusted with 'the word'. Labourers and clerks born and died, not knowing of another world.

Eleanor Plantard St Claire sighed as she had done increasingly of late as she absent-mindedly pushed away a wisp of her once luxuriant russet curls and tightened the shawl around her. The pictures in the long gallery had since her earliest memory given her an uncanny sense of destiny, leaving her with the curious feeling that her childhood had begun in the spring of 1312 when the proud Knights of Jerusalem had been burnt at the stake on that clear Paris morning.

The picture had, of course, darkened over the years, as many of the portraits in the gallery had, but still the unknown artist had captured the agony of the roasting knights, their white surcoats bravely contrasting with bright crimson of the flames. Only De Molay, his head bare and his mouth open in his last moments was roaring, 'Within a year'. That was the caption of the painting. And so it had proved. His Holiness, Clement V, and King Philippe of France had indeed passed away within twelve months of that treacherous spring morning.

Clement V's last papal bull had been to bequeath 'the word' to the care of her ancestors: Henri and her namesake Eleanor. In hindsight it seemed so simple, so elegant, as her other favourite picture told in glowing colours. The rock basin, a product of the limestone sub-strata, created in glacial runoffs millions of years ago, had provided a perfect hideaway. Shielded from the prying world as it had been, by the impenetrable interlocking valleys of the Razès and, in the Middle Ages, supporting colonies of lepers.

Up to the late 1400s the castle remained hidden, content to rest as the secret depository of its masters in the papal palaces of Avignon. Much of the worldwide Inquisition had been funded from here via the non-too-delicate care of the Dominican Order. Given their instructions by Gregory IX, its members carried out their bidding to be the 'sword of the Lord' with considerable enthusiasm. It was, she supposed, during this period, when heretics' property became the Church's, that successors to the Knights of Jerusalem in the guise of the Order of Sion, had laid down the path that led to her standing there.

Eleanor had hoped, as countless Grand Nautoniers of the Order had before, to carry the fight to the final victory over the Infidel. She had known when her thin hands had found the hardening lump in her stomach that she may not have time. As she passed the picture of de Molay, daily his words 'Within a year', seemed to strike her with sonorous resonance. Her term of office since inheriting the mantle from her father at when she was still only twenty-eight had spanned over forty years. Forty years in which the world had changed, seemingly ignorant and immune from the guidance and leadership of the last 700 years.

The Order had started the second half of the twentieth century with its fighting reserves bursting its doors. Eleanor's father and predecessor had succeeded in having a very good war indeed. Gold and valuables had literally flowed across Europe in the darkness and confusion, but even then the seeds of the next thirty years of impotence had been sown. A curtain had fallen from the Baltic in the North to the Adriatic in the South. A curtain smothering the freedoms and beliefs of a quarter of the world's Catholics. The book of 'daily orders' – a series of heavily bound damask leather volumes recording all of the Order's activities from its founders to the current day – had detailed Eleanor's struggle throughout her time of office. Her masters, hidden within the Curia and hierarchy of the tiny distant state, communicated only sporadically the same way they had done for hundreds of years. Over the centuries the family had controlled their destiny ruthlessly without the slightest compunction, Urban's words echoing down the years.

Eleanor's great grandfather had been the Grand Nautonier who ended the community around the castle. Arriving back from Paris late in the nineteenth century, he had the foresight to see the fledgling developments spawned earlier by the Montgolfier brothers. Flimsy hot air balloons and flying machines, although presenting a negligible risk in his lifetime had threatened their future existence.

Members of the brotherhood who had knowledge of the 'special place' under the castle, had been put on wooden boats in the dark, fast flowing waters of the cavern. Ostensibly to explore further down the subterranean river, all had been dashed to their deaths in the rapids and falls that only the Grand Nautonier knew of. For months the region had been alive with strange rumours of bruised and battered bodies and splintered boat remains in the various river systems as the subterranean flow erupted in different locations.

It was then, at the dawn of the twentieth century that the mighty forest was laid down, and now more than nine decades later their mature topmost branches completely filled the natural basin and crept up the castle walls, so that just the topmost turrets betrayed the castle to casual observers. From the ground, a tortuous private drive leading down the steep cliffs dissuaded visitors from venturing further; in any case the curious and inquisitive had by now centred on the village of Rennes-le-Château. The otherwise non-descript village had soared to prominence in the late nineteenth century with the arrival of a new priest, one Bérenger Saunière. After some initial difficulties with the Church authorities, which entailed the newly installed priest being suspended for a year, he had managed to strike a relationship with Eleanor's great grandmother the Countess of Chambord who was at that time married to the current Grand Nautonier. The records of the order showed an advance of some 30,000 francs, an astonishing amount, roughly equivalent to four times the priest's salary, to effect repairs to the derelict medieval church of St Mary Magdalene.

Eleanor smiled to herself at the memory. The volumes relating to that period recorded in dry and dusty tones the amount of the loan and its purpose. But she had her great grandmother's ribbon-tied letters from the young Bérenger and they told of a different side to the stiff, formal countess. The letters written in a flowing hand detailed the lust and passion between the unlikely pair. Descriptions of bed chambers and secret places within the castle where their trysts took place had given a then-young Eleanor her first insight into the grown-up world. A world she only knew from formal dinners and occasions from the secret life of the Order of Sion within her closeted walls.

In common with her ancestors and generations to come the countess had sought to dominate this young and vibrant priest: in short to 'own' him as her mannequin. She showered him with gifts and wealth, using with abandon the reserves of the Order. In spite of the fire within the countess' loins for her young lover, she had with considerable foresight managed to shift the change in fortunes for the priest entirely to his parish.

With the connivance of the priest's housekeeper, Marie Denarnaud, seemingly secret documents had been 'discovered' in a hollow pillar within the crumbling church. Saunière had duly reported the 'find' to an incredulous countess, who had in turn directed him – as she had been instructed – to his bishop. The bishop, following full instructions from Vatican sources, had duly referred the young priest and his ancient documents to an Abbé Bieil at Saint-Sulpice in Paris. Bieil subsequently interpreted that the documents referred to the ancient and long-removed treasures of the Visigoths and, prior to them, the contents of the looted temples of Jerusalem.

Saunière had returned to the poor village in the south of France and overnight became rich beyond his wildest dreams. The countess had watched inscrutably from afar as he constructed a magnificent villa and created a superb library of rare manuscripts and art. With the 'samples' she had secreted in the church, the world's attention became focussed on the sleepy village and not the half-hidden and secretive castle some twenty miles distant in the Razès and the forest of Rialsesse.

When shortly before Saunière's death in 1915 a tombstone was unearthed with the words 'This treasure belongs to Dagebert II and Sion King and he is here dead', the feeding frenzy of would-be treasure hunters was only eclipsed by the cataclysmic events of 1914. The countess, tiring of the affair, had sought to finally distance the castle from Saunière and had used the Order to arrange his death, seemingly of a stroke. Years later as the mystery of Rennes-le-Château rumbled on, the discovery that Saunière's coffin had been ordered six months prior to his death had further deepened the enigma.

That had all been two world wars and a lifetime or more ago, but its repercussions were still felt as strongly as they had ever been. Their memory sent a shiver through Eleanor, who pulled the shawl round her tightly: the night air under the turret's roof was cool and the forest's deepening blackness contrasted with the indigo of the sky. A commotion from below led her grey form to the crenelations. As she peered down into the softly lit courtyard she pressed her lips together. Her daughter and namesake – so many Eleanors had come and gone – threw back her head and laughed seductively with her male companion.

Eleanor's watery blue eyes crinkled at the edges as she fondly remembered her lengthy initiation to her birthright of Grand Nautonier. Long hot summers of fun, laughter and passion: suitor after suitor, tryst after tryst. Then, and only then, the moment that would define her life and calling. Her final decision; resented, fought over, but in the end accepted as the price of her life's work. Similarly, in turn, her late husband Jacques – God, how she missed him – and her decision over their two offspring. Who would carry Urban's message onwards?

Initially, she privately admitted it was Hugh who caught her eye. Tall, well-built, decisive and quick: on the face of it a natural choice. And yet, deep down she knew he needed more. The Order demanded a special kind of ruthlessness and determination: a leader capable of taking decisions that affected not only individuals, but the destiny of countries and the path of governments. From the moment of the twins' birth, Hugh had acquiesced to his sister's leadership. Jest and fool they did, but a flash of her cool blue eyes brought him tumbling swiftly to heel.

* * *

If Eleanor and Jacques noticed, they did not care to admit that Eleanor was subjugating her intuition to that of her husband's desire to see a male heir. It was only when she was approaching her fifteenth birthday that the young

Eleanor's ability to deal important events in her life with icy detachment was becoming apparent. And her mother knew precisely when that defining moment had been reached.

After much persuasion, brother and sister had acquired a pair of pedigree Chartreux cats and the race was on to see whose could have a litter first. But after a particularly damp winter in the castle, the onset of mild asthma had been diagnosed in Eleanor and she, with characteristic firmness of mind, had decided to rid the castle of her children's cats. Summoned to her study, her daughter had received the blow coolly with only a fractional dilating of her disconcerting blue eyes. By contrast her brother had fled to his room, not to re-appear for two days. Later Eleanor had found her daughter in the barn where the two cats had delivered their litters a day or so apart. She recalled the scene as vividly as if it were yesterday. As Eleanor had stood in the doorway framed by the late sun, her daughter had glanced up at the darkening of the door. She sat cross-legged on a bale of hay, softly stroking the purring feline, all the while whispering entreaties to her. The mother cat stretched luxuriously allowing her to stroke the soft fur of her chin. As Eleanor watched this scene, she saw her daughter's hand steal behind her back: seeking each suckling kitten she found unerringly each tiny neck and with an audible snap lay the inert form against its mother's swollen nipples. Six tiny forms lay dead behind her back as she slipped her hand round the purring mother's neck. The slightly louder crack accompanied her smile to her mother as she acknowledged her presence. Her eyes had never blinked.

* * *

Hidden from view against a darkening sky, Eleanor watched below with pride as her offspring flirted and flattered her young beau. They were all the same, these young men drawn to the younger Eleanor's beauty and vivacity. Mavericks from other orders, usually the Dominicans or Franciscans, and of late, the upstart Opus Dei and the Sovereign Knights of Malta, all unknowingly playing the game, all innocent of the courtship rituals in which Eleanor Plantard St Claire toyed with them. For the secret she guarded, one that had been handed down over hundreds of years, was one never to be divulged until the marriage bed.

The courting before knew no bounds, had no rules. As with the elderly Eleanor, only the strongest, most ruthless ambassadors would be the victors. A chink of weakness would be utterly exploited and the hapless suitor would at best be sent to some outlying monastery for life, or at worst would forfeit his life entirely, often in the bizarre pursuit of pleasure of the keepers of the secret order.

Whilst the world watched and acquiesced to the subservience of women in a religious organisation that venerated one woman above all, the backbone of part of the Order's strength owed some, if not all, of its characteristics to the allure and power of sexually avaricious, predatory females down the ages who had sought and captured the very toughest and hardest males for the role ahead.

Eleanor Plantard St Claire watched the setting sun cast its orange glow across the underbellies of the high fluffy clouds; the richest of blues, pinks and yellows overlaying the dark forest. Her jaw clamped firmly: the last time it had been the same, her decision and hers alone.

It was almost a medieval decision it its enormity. Late August 1978, a decision that reverberated around the world: a decision that she had come to regard as the defining decision of her calling. The seemingly untimely ending of one Holy Father's life had heralded in the next: a successor to the line of popes stretching back to St Peter, who almost single-handedly had been responsible for the breaking down of the Iron Curtain and the collapse of the brutal regime that had created it – none of which could have been achieved without a little unsung help, of course.

Eleanor stepped inside from the chill evening air and made her way to the 'Long Room' below the castle roof. Venerated over the years, it had been used as the official boardroom of the Sons of Sion for over seven centuries. Certain members of the hierarchy of the Roman Catholic Church on this earth had at one time or another met her to discuss matters too delicate for the all-hearing officials and staff in the various papal residences. Decisions that had affected entire nations had been made here under a shadow of the original Van Eyck painting depicting Urban directing his first Crusade. The picture had recently been skilfully lit from hidden corners in the room emphasising the brilliance of Urban's message and his directions, whilst leaving the fleeing infidel hordes barely visible in the penumbral darkness around the painting. It was this scene that drew Eleanor and whether it was back in 1978, or more recently in the summer of 1982 when it had become necessary to 'suicide' a senior member of the Banco Ambrosiano in London, it was the picture's guiding message that enabled her to decide. She gazed at the painting, the room in virtual darkness with only the colours of the Van Eyck shining with translucent brightness down the ages.

The artist had depicted Urban, eyes blazing at the Infidel below, as he directed his blood red cross-adorned knights at them. Beneath the painting on a simple oak lectern lay a large damask red leather-bound book. Faded and worn, it lay open as Eleanor's gnarled finger traced the words of her ancestor Henri de Montfort's as he was expelled from Acre 700 before:

Let us not in this hour of defeat harbour a single thought that this is the end. Rather say that this is the beginning of the end for the Infidel across the world. Urban II's call from Clermont will be honoured, if it takes until the end of time.

Eleanor reflected that it may well be her destiny and hers alone to finish this journey. She had sanctioned the bomb's movement out of Iran. Now she had resolved, she would wait. Latest reports put Father Sebastian and the Irishman at the western end of the Mediterranean having just left Malta.

CHAPTER 69

As Eleanor gazed at the painting, barely 280 miles away the bow of a motor cruiser was nudging itself through the muddy outflow of the Rhône as Thomas threaded a way through the outer breakwater of the first port at the mouth of the huge river. Seeking anonymity, he moored alongside three rusty river dredgers.

Thomas glanced at his companions. Layla at once caught his eye from her reclining position on top of the aft cabin and arched seductively, her eyes twinkling as her gaze slid away. Thomas' jaw clamped together. The journey across the Mediterranean had been uneventful and trouble free. From leaving Latakia the vessel had made its way to its first 'Western' port of Larnaca. There within a remarkably short space of time the shabby down at heel cruiser had responded amazingly to Thomas' energetic cleaning and polishing. Within two days, its classic lines, gleaming mahogany top deck and glistening white paint earned its share of envious glances as she rode comfortably with other expensive sea-going cruisers. Her age lending a certain 'chic' amid the acres of gleaming stainless steel and polished white fibreglass. As a personal reward for his labours, he had crooked his finger at Layla, the taller of the two 'passengers' who, by unspoken agreement, was 'his': her price for maritime hitchhiking her way around the Mediterranean.

Eyeing her scantily clad figure Thomas had pulled out a wad of warm dollars and with a pat on her sweetly oscillating backside had sent her and Sofia into Larnaca. A good couple of hours later a battered taxi had pulled up on the warm stone blocks of the quay above them, to squeals of feminine laughter.

Boxes and expensive looking carrier bags had been deposited with great enthusiasm by the excited girls. Not long after, to a wave of expensive perfume, the cruiser sported four immaculate members of the 'Med set': gleaming new Gucci loafers; obligatory white slacks; and expensive Henry Lloyd tops completed the image. Anonymously and now with perfect camouflage, the cruiser had slipped up the Mediterranean heading westward. Meandering along day after day through blue glittering waters, calling at leisure at the many whitewashed ports, the cruiser shipped its happy cargo onwards. Thomas decided the pleasure so far was all his; Sofia, the shorter of the two girls, had taken to sunbathing nude on the aft cabin roof. Surreptitiously Thomas had adjusted the rear-view mirror as the two men guided the vessel on. From the two girls huddled figures and their glances towards the forward cabin, it was obvious which was the happier bunny, he decided.

Sebastian never discussed the subject, but it was apparent that only a platonic friendship was being forged in the small aft cabin. Whilst in the master cabin under the fo'c'sle, nightly new boundaries of pleasure were discovered. Even so, as the little cruiser crept into the medieval Maltese port of Valetta by the second week Thomas was beginning to flag.

Since his days in Belfast, Thomas paid little attention to world events. He had observed that things were fractionally easier in Syria following the departure of President Assad and noted too the increased presence of American naval units in the course of their passage. Israel appeared to be fighting on all fronts following the 7 October Hamas incursion, and now Iran was entering the fray.

Sebastian, on the other hand, remained glued to the BBC World Service almost hourly. The two men were in the outer harbour of Valetta when the radio was turned on and they heard the announcement, 'This is the BBC from London, on Friday the thirteenth of June. The Israeli Defence Ministry has announced the deaths of General Bagheri, Commander Hossein Salami and Commander Saeed Izadi in targeted attacks on the Iranian military'.

Sebastian stared at the radio and at Thomas, 'The three we met!'

A loud horn sounded, the little boat had drifted into the path of a rusty cargo vessel and Thomas rapidly corrected his course. His attention was diverted by the alacrity in which Sebastian nimbly leapt to the stone quay as soon as the vessel berthed.

He strode purposefully away, looking neither right nor left, leaving Thomas bemused and Sophia even more disappointed. Pouting, she turned over on the deck towel as a passing cruise ship's crew lined the rails to enjoy the view.

Sebastian returned later and ducked into the forward cabin. He took a small item from his pocket and slipped it beside the binoculars in their teak bracket close to the wheel. Thomas looked up from the chart table where he was plotting their next course.

'One incoming call only, Thomas. If I'm not around, get me. It's important.'

Thomas grimaced and nodded. An hour later as the sun set over the ancient port the device bleeped twice. Sebastian picked it up and looked at the illuminated display. 'Yes' was all he said as he moved beside Thomas who was still at work. He stepped to one side so that Sebastian's elegant fingers could trace the line from the tiny island of Malta westwards across the Mediterranean towards the Straits of Gibraltar. Raising his eyes quizzically he asked Thomas, 'A week and a half to Gibraltar. And another week, or two, depending on the weather in the Bay of Biscay. Yes? Yes. Four weeks at most.'

A pause and a stillness, and distant look stole over Sebastian, 'I understand.' Then he thumbed the off button on the phone, slid open the elegant mahogany-framed cabin window and tossed the phone out into the inky waters, before raising the heavy signet ring to his lips and kissing it.

Whatever conversation had precipitated that exchange back in Malta had been left undiscussed until now as the they put into Port St Louis on the mouth of the Rhône. Sebastian had kept glancing at the chart as they headed ever northwards. It was when the glistening blue sea had started to turn muddy brown with the Rhône's discharge, that finally Sebastian had turned to Thomas to comment, 'Odd way to Gibraltar?'

Thomas, still staring ahead, replied, 'Who said I was going to Gibraltar?'

'Well, I asked if it was a week and a half to go!' exploded Sebastian in frustration.

'So, you did. So, you did. And it was,' Thomas said laying on the Irish accent. 'But we just weren't going that way! You'd just better pray that this baby's dimensions are right.'

Sebastian frowned but said nothing. This was Thomas' responsibility, not his. And it would be Thomas who would suffer cruelly if things did not go according to plan.

For his part, Thomas' relationship with Layla grew ever closer in direct contrast to Sofia's attempts with Sebastian. By the time the foursome sauntered down the dock leading to the port of St Louis, Thomas' hand had slipped down the rear of Layla's firm warm bottom whilst they meandered along, flanked on either side by the two 'friends'. 'Pity really, that all good things come to an end,' Thomas thought as Layla's warm oscillations filled his palm.

In the small square, the foursome agreed to go their separate ways for the afternoon, meeting in four hours' time at the Bar du Midi overlooking the harbour. The girls wandered off with a wad of cash each, heading for the boutiques of the small port.

With one final lingering look at Layla's departing rear, Thomas told Sebastian, 'Right, me boy. Plan B'. Then he handed over a pre-written list of requirements, went through each item carefully and then said to the bemused monk, 'See you back at the boat in forty minutes.'

Sebastian's task was no mean feat, and he had to resort to a battered taxi to get him and the mountain of provisions back to the dock. Even so, as the scruffy Peugeot 305 rattled along the warm quay he could see Thomas' figure already at work with forward mooring rope and down at the aft a faint cloud of blue smoke indicated that the engines were ticking over.

Without saying a word Sebastian paid off the cabby and loaded the boxes and bags into the centre well deck. But when he caught the driver's stare as he turned the vehicle round next to the bollard that Thomas was bent over, Sebastian followed his gaze. The Henri Lloyd top, Gucci loafers and faded white slacks had gone. Thomas now picked up the loose end of the forward line and minced slowly down the quay swinging the rope in a seductive fashion. His tight leather trousers, open burgundy silk top and vivid necktie were as nothing to his heavily mascaraed face and pouting rouge lips. Having seen enough, the cabby spat derisively on the quay and roared away.

Tapping an astonished Sebastian on the shoulder with a limp-wristed movement, Thomas winked lasciviously, 'Don't you just love cruising, sailor!' So saying, he ducked down below and immediately the boat moved away from the jetty leaving behind a small pile of boxes and assorted feminine garments on the departing quay as Thomas opened the throttle and swept the boat in an arc to the harbour entrance. He resisted all attempts by Sebastian to discuss their northward passage up the deep and powerful Rhône, but by the next day the boat had merged with the general river traffic and passed the ancient papal seat of Avignon.

CHAPTER 70

Eleanor had sat in the darkened room gazing at the picture. For three days she had been oblivious to the entreaties of her daughter to eat and rest. On the third day she descended from the heights of the hidden castle at last, called her daughter and had the old Mercedes brought to the courtyard. Marcel, her driver for twenty years, was surprised to be instructed to hand the keys to the young Eleanor, who eased her long legs behind the thin-rimmed steering wheel. Her mother had called at her small 'office' on the way to the car and now clutched a brand-new mobile phone, its screen still obscured slightly by sticky cellophane. The elderly Mercedes 450 SEL had made its way smoothly up the steep drive cut into the sandstone cliff. At the top, an ancient gate blocked the way. Pointing a small remote through the windscreen commenced an ever-widening crack to appear in the centre of the rusty ivy-clad gates. They moved slowly inwards complete with piles of leaves and fallen branches cleverly attached to the bottom frame. The car swept through onto a sandy single track and with a deepening roar sped away. Behind it the gates had already closed and a crooked *Propriété Privée* sign discouraged further interest. Apart from the swish of the tyres the silence in the car was absolute.

Eleanor's gnarled fingers ran over the phone's smooth casing as she stared at the passing forest. Her daughter too maintained the silence, flicking her eyes from the road and watching her mother's face in the rear.

'And how was young Petre last night, dear?' The fractional emphasis on 'young' causing a flush of darkness to Eleanor's neck.

'Why do you ask, Mother? Is it the same? Are you still waiting?' she snapped back, guiltily aware that her days of fun were drawing to a close.

The gnarled fingers stroked their owner's stomach reflectively. 'You know, as you always have, that you have to carry on when I am gone. I'd had you at your age.'

The car surged forward as her daughter stamped angrily on the accelerator. 'Why do I have to chose before I become Grand Nautonier? Why?'

A sigh came from the back, then a long silence. 'You must be the strength behind the Order, my dear. You and you alone must select the hardest and most ruthless of your children to carry on.'

Leaning forward, she rested one bony hand on her daughter's shoulder. 'As Clement knew all those centuries ago, it is we who have the survival instinct.'

Her daughter's smooth hand crept up to rest on hers. 'I know, I know,' she said huskily.

Her mother kept her hand there a moment then with a steely look leant back in the soft leather seat. 'This year's selection of novices to work in Rome must contain your choice, my dear. In three weeks, young priests from all over the world will begin their postings at the Vatican. Go there and choose,' she concluded, with words that were as final as they were firm.

* * *

The car had slipped unobtrusively onto the N19 running along the River Dordogne mingling with farm traffic and laden holiday cars as it slowed.

Sometime later, Eleanor peered at the small screen and said, 'We've no signal. Can we climb a little?'

An affirmative grunt from the front preceded the car swinging off the D4 towards the hilltop village of Domme where, in due course, the car crunched slowly to a halt in the main square. Early in the day the only people around had been the ice-cream sellers setting up stalls and bicycle hirers adjusting chains ready for the tourist onslaught. But now it was quiet.

Eleanor parked beneath a plane tree stepped out, and opened the rear door for her mother. As if she had aged in the last three days, she leant heavily on the young woman's arm. Mother and daughter moved slowly to the low rampart beyond which the entire Dordogne valley lay spread. Pigeons waddled expectantly in front of them as they approached the low wall. Eleanor's gnarled fingers, more nimble than their arthritic condition belied, thumbed the smooth buttons on the slim handset as she keyed in: 0039.

Leaning against the railing, her lips moved in silent conversation, which lasted for the best part of half an hour. Finally, she stood stiffly erect, flicked the small phone from her wrist and watched its descent to strike the first ledge where it flew into a dozen pieces that continued their cascade downwards. 'It's done, and we can go', she said simply.

Her daughter did not ask, but she knew a defining moment in her life had been reached. That night she was summoned to her mother's bedchamber. In the few hours since they had arrived back at the castle, the older woman seemed to have aged and shrivelled. Beads of sweat dotted her forehead, as she lay propped by five or six pillows. Her claw-like hands clasped her stomach and sitting silently by her bed, Eleanor wept as she held her mother's frail wrist as a further spasm of pain caused her to moan and the deep lines at the corners of her eyes deepened further.

In sympathy she leant forward to speak, 'Mother,' she began.

But Eleanor Plantard St Claire opened her eyes, blue piercing eyes, to look at her daughter and say, 'Go now, my child. Go to Rome. Seek Cosimir Marcinkus and Cardinal Ratzinger. Make your choice from this year's intake. It is time, my child: your time. You must finish what I have begun. Soon you will need all your strength.' Without elaborating, the eyes closed and her shallow breathing resumed.

Slowly Eleanor rose and left the dimly lit bedchamber and her mother's frail figure dwarfed by the huge bed. Firmly she closed the door.

CHAPTER 71

Brigade Commander Maher was a cautious man. To the rest of the world the Troubles were over, signed away by a British prime minister intent on leaving his legacy, and aided by Maher's own commanders eyeing a comfortable retirement in politics. But not in Maher's mind. The memory of his dad beaten half to death in the shipyard was still raw. And then again by the vicious British soldiers intent on 'keeping the peace.'

Sure, since the Good Friday Agreement he had used his unique talents for anyone and anybody with the wherewithal to pay. The crime gangs of Dublin had been particularly lucrative, even though he had given a good percentage to the Order of Sion in the monastery for the use of their facilities. But now? A possibility of hitting the British State so hard it would be his own personal legacy.

If he thought about the choice of target he had said little. All he knew of the place was its famous Gold Cup and that came courtesy of his passion for horses. The meeting in the boardroom at the monastery had been no different than any other over the years, but it was her icy blue eyes that worried him. Just who was this Chevalier Hegarty? Or did the dowdy, fussy secretary wield more power than she let on.

Maher did not dwell too long on these concerns. Always a meticulous planner, he possessed not only the ruthless ability of many of his compatriots but also, rarely among them, a cool head. Whilst the use of the monastery was known only to himself, this team would have to be brought in with no knowledge at all of their whereabouts. Success would bring down the full wrath of British intelligence and the establishment. The trail had to go cold many, many miles away.

Maher had slipped unnoticed into West Belfast just past one o'clock in the morning. O'Dare's Dairies was ablaze with light as tankers delivered the products of countless Irish cattle, whilst electric milk floats stood patiently, connected umbilically to their charging machines. Pulling his cap low and turning up his collar, he had slipped into the cashier's office. Presently a younger man left the depot with a wide grin on his face to return to his wife's bed. A surprise day off, with pay too!

Maher piloted the moaning electric float around the still darkened streets of the Ardoyne. At five addresses, he had walked up the short paths with his chinking bottles, leaving one of those bottles at each house marked with the sign of a cross scratched on the foil lid with his nail. Later, after leaving the dairy, he had driven to the Royal Belfast golf course and waited.

One by one, five nondescript saloons made their way into the car park. Presently six men set off around the course. The cool north-easterly had kept most of the members away that morning and as the club's pro sat drinking his coffee he watched with a small shake of his head as the group tee'd off. Resuming his perusal of the morning paper, he dismissed the six from his mind. At the eighth hole, furthest from the club house and almost close enough to the sea to touch its glittering surface, the six gratefully sank into a bunker and out of the keen wind blowing in from the sea.

Maher took up position at the rear of the bunker and eyed the five. 'Sorry for the precautions, boys,' Dylan nodded, his face serious, it was his Uncle Michael who had gone to the bus depot all those years ago to sort out a traitor. Michael had never come home; thanks to the Paras, neither had seven other members of the Belfast Brigade. The girl Clodagh, daughter of Kieran, Thomas O'Neil, the young depot 'gofer', others faded in his memory. Seven bodies the army press release had said: a total active service unit But Dylan knew there had been only six coffins ordered. The question was: Who wasn't it? Shutting his mind, though, he concentrated on what Maher was telling him. Only three times had they been summoned like this and always for the 'big ones': kept in reserve, deadly sleepers waiting only for the call.

They listened quietly for twenty minutes. Maher's unusual eloquence silencing their objections; only at his last statement did they look at each other, wide-eyed.

Later, in the car park, Maher had driven straight out, deliberately leaving the five together. As he knew they would, the group bunched together, 'Well do we trust him that much?' said Cian, the youngest of the group.

Sean and Connor nodded sagely. Dylan interrupted strongly. 'If what he says is true; this could be the end of the struggle,'

They stood silently in the wind for a moment, privately going over they had been told. And then nodded at each other in agreement. 'See you on Friday, then'. Dylan said with a wolfish grin and strode away.

Maher had watched the impromptu gathering from the road above the village of Craigavad. Satisfied by what he had seen, he lowered his binoculars, restarted the car and drove slowly back to Belfast.

* * *

Friday morning arrived preceded by the moaning progress of the milk float driven down Dylan's street. On cue, as he stepped out of his darkened door, a battered transit van bearing the legend O'Dare's Dairies had followed the milk delivery. Dylan climbed in, taking care not to catch his Berreta strapped to his calf. In the light of one small twelve-volt bulb he flashed his grin to the band of five sitting on and around large boxes. When the door was shut and the van moving, Maher's voice cut from the front of the cab, 'OK boys, on with them', his tone brooking no opposition.

An hour so later the swaying band of men in the rear of the van, made even more uncomfortable by an as yet unnamed member puking over the angular boxes, sensed the vehicle halt. Mayer was tired, the lanes and byways over the Sperrin and Glendowan mountains had served a purpose but he needed to keep the secret a while longer. As the garage walls slid smoothly upwards, he growled a reassurance to the comically masked group slumped in the rear.

* * *

At the time the van had been leaving Belfast, Pat O'Connor had been adjusting his uniform and opening the main door of his Garda office in Burtonport. As the lights flickered on and his hands mechanically prepared the first of many steaming mugs of coffee, his eyes fell on his open daybook. 'Oh, be Jesus!' he exclaimed, eyeing the neat entry in his own handwriting. He screwed his face up. Two weeks before, Father Hegarty from the monastery up the road had informed him of today's arrival of two brothers by sea from a brother community in Portrush, Northern Ireland. Technically they would be crossing the border and Father Hegarty, as was his meticulous way, informed the Garda so customs formalities could be observed. And now Pat had forgotten. Thanks to his sister's wedding last week, more time than usual had been spent in Maggie's Bar.

He lifted the phone to call his counterpart in Customs House, Ballyshannon, further down the coast. Thinking further, he replaced the handset firmly. 'Sod it,' he thought. 'Two monks arriving on the next tide, so what?'

CHAPTER 72

At that moment the motor cruiser's salt-stained bows were nudging across Gweebarra Bay. Thomas looked through wind-worn eyes at the tiny village he had left so long ago, while Sebastian scanned the coast for the towers and outline of his long-awaited destination.

In these dank northern waters, their camp journey up the Rhône seemed so long ago. Thomas' heavy make-up, flamboyant clothes and outrageous behaviour to all passing traffic ensuring no French authorities questioned the steady progress of the motor cruiser. Sebastian's perplexity had eased as their craft had nudged from the Rhône, via the Saône and Yonne rivers into the Canal De Bourgogne and onwards to the Seine. Taking the quiet backwaters past Armançon and Migennes, Thomas's insistence of the crucial boat dimensions became clear. Limited by French VNF regulations, navigation was restricted to vessels of one-point-eight-metre draught below the waterline and three-point-five metres air draught above it. By lowering the small mast with nothing more than her navigation lights, the cruiser glided through the locks with centimetres to spare. Joining the English Channel at Le Havre the vessel had successfully sanitised its Mediterranean past and merged beautifully with the local traffic.

From there, they hugged the French coast as far as Ushant preferring the casual French naval security to the eagle-eyed Royal Navy, Sebastian had set a course northwards up the west coast of Ireland. Not until they called at Ballybunnian, on the mouth of the Shannon, did Thomas permit Sebastian to use a telephone kiosk. Yet again, despite passage of time since his last known call, the conversation was so brief it could not have comprised more than half-a-dozen words.

* * *

Pat had ridden his ancient black bicycle down to the small jetty as he spotted the motor cruiser nudging its way round the headland. Thomas and Sebastian adopted a suitably languorous expression as they waited in the salt-encrusted boat. Pat leant his bicycle against the jetty wall and welcomed the brothers welcomed.

At Sebastian's prior suggestion, Thomas fumbled under his garments for his passport all the while chatting amiably to Pat on the stone quay. When Pat heard the faint twang of his local accent he flapped embarrassingly with his hands. 'No. No, Father. Don't you be worrying yourself with paperwork. Father Hegarty telephoned me to warn me in advance.'

Mumbling their thanks, the two brothers clambered up to the quay.

'Oh, by the way,' Thomas said to the Garda officer. 'Finnigan's will be collecting the boat later if you could keep the quay road clear, you know the size of his truck! The boat'll be going up to the monastery. One of the engines needs some work and, fortunately for our limited funds, one of our brothers is a qualified engineer'. A wave of acknowledgement sent them on their way.

Sebastian knocked once on the oak door on the upper floor of the monastery and without waiting strode in.

Colm Hegarty met him half across the room. 'Sebastian! Good to see you at last!' as the two embraced. Thomas stood uncertainly in the doorway: delivery of any item was the most deadly time, and he was on his guard.

Even so, he stepped into the room and was astonished at the opulence he saw all around him. Some kind of medieval knight stood at the far end of the room, its antique armour looking as if it would be more at home in a wealthy millionaire's study. As the other two continued their bonhomie, Thomas crossed to the window and caught sight of the Finnigan's huge low-loader slowly entering the monastery's grounds.

'All the way from Khorramshahr to Burtonport, Gentlemen! I think I'd call that "Job Done", don't you?'

'Yes indeed,' chuckled Hegarty. 'I think it calls for a little celebration!'

As whiskey began to warm his stomach Thomas started to feel himself relax; perhaps after all it would be a good day. He would be collecting his bounty in Dublin in two days, but in the meantime, he was going to make use of the luxurious facilities the brothers seemed to enjoy. As he soaked the journey away in the huge jacuzzi, for the first time he allowed his mind to dream: a million pounds – that would buy a new, no not a new, and excellent second-hand anonymous cruiser, leaving over half in his account in Zurich with plenty in reserve to trade with; in two days, then he would be off. No more cigarette runs up the Euphrates for him. The warmth from the spirit caressed his thoughts, perhaps he could find Layla again, and he let his mind drift down that delightful avenue.

Eighty feet below Thomas' warm, dreamy world, five men sat on upturned milk crates around a large sandpit. Spread out in the sand in front of them lay the model of part of their target town: complete with roads, traffic lights, all manner of housing and a small railway track. Using snapshots and an enlarged British Ordnance Survey map, the town had been painstakingly recreated using scale versions of the buildings to create a living map. Central to the model was huge doughnut-shaped building surrounded by vast car parks. The group had been studying and discussing this model for four days now, with Maher all the while speaking quietly but firmly as he pointed out the various routes and issue with an old billiard. The team interjected at times as ideas and plans formed, were modified and refined.

Now the time was approaching and above them, two heads listened carefully. Elizabeth and Colm sat opposite each other at the long table following the coarse Belfast accents which came clearly to them over the sound system. Colm raised his head, with a satisfied look in his eyes. Patiently, he waited until those blue eyes sought his.

Elizabeth looked at him. 'They're good, they're very good,' she said softly 'They could do this.'

Colm nodded sagely. 'Maher's only used this team together on two previous occasions, they won't be missed by either the brigade or army intelligence.'

Elizabeth raised a small hand silencing him immediately. The voices came over clearly. 'They're planning on leaving in forty-eight hours.'

'The return ticket is what matters.'

Elizabeth nodded, 'See to it.'

Colm remained where he was. As his Grand Nautonier had done before, many miles away, he sat along with his thoughts. The shadows lengthened and the soft lighting came on in the room; opening a small bureau he poured himself two fingers of his favourite single malt. The Talisker seared his tongue as he swirled it round. Turning, he observed for the thousandth time the armoured figure behind his chair. Courage came with his second tumbler as he awaited Thomas' inevitable presence on the eve of his bounty collection.

The same raw spirit seared Thomas' throat as he watched a mellow Colm Hegarty and his mind wandered. He felt uneasy – no not uneasy: uncomfortable. Hegarty was going to ask something else, he knew it. Surreptitiously as Hegarty dreamily eyed the armoured figure at the end of the room, Thomas let the remains of the whisky run into the deep pile carpet. His mind was clear.

With an imperceptible click, the door opened behind Thomas and Elizabeth entered. Hegarty seemed to steel himself before picking up the telephone in front of him. 'Michael? Our guests in the cellar will have those sandwiches now.'

Under Hegarty's and at Elizabeth's bidding, Thomas descended an interminable series of stone stairs. Passing at one stage a small, barred grill in the circular stairwell through which Thomas spied rows of empty pews facing a darkened altar.

The bottom of the stairs led into a broad, low-ceilinged passageway floored with ancient uneven slabs. From a door to their left, silently and without preamble, a cowled figure had glided in front of them holding aloft a tray of hors d'oeuvres and gently steaming dishes. The smell made Thomas' mouth water, and he increased his pace after Father Michael towards the open oak door from which coarse laughter could be heard.

Father Michael entered followed by Thomas. The room erupted into loud cries of appreciation while he swiftly made his way to a long table at the far end of the room. As one, the five men rose and clustered round the monk.

'Whoa, boy!' Maher shouted, 'Where's your manners. Let him serve it for God's sake!'

Impatiently he strode up to the five sheepish men. Father Michael had rapidly laid the small plates and dishes out on a low table at the end of the room and just as quickly left. For a brief moment the six men turned their backs on the room and bent to the succulent feast laid before them.

That was when Thomas felt a grip to his elbow and turned round to face a pair of ice-cold eyes. But it was not the eyes that made his mouth go dry: in Elizabeth's hand the Russian AN94 seemed ridiculously large. Another in Colm Hegarty's meaty hands looked like a child's toy.

Curiously, Thomas did not feel fear; the hand that gripped him had firmly pushed him to one side. The noise in the confines of the low cellar was deafening. With an ability to fire at 1,800 rounds per minute and pierce body armour at 100 metres, the bullets chewed the course sandstone blocks at the end of the cellar. Of the six men clustered there, five dissolved in a red mist of disintegrating body parts. It was over in seconds. The silence as profound as the preceding noise

It was Elizabeth who walked to the end of the room where Maher lay, still breathing shallowly. Thomas watched horror-struck as she lowered the weapon and said, 'Dieu le veut' and then pulled the trigger a second time.

As the last bullet fired and the hammer clicked on an empty chamber, Hegarty move next to him. 'Now then, Thomas,' he asked smoothly. 'How would you like to fulfil a pope's command?'

CHAPTER 73

The damp bulk of Mount Errigal somehow seemed to finish a chapter for Ben. Was it really only so short a time since his Land Rover had crested the mountain in that driving rain and he had spied Burtonport for the first time? Ben had dragged the elderly machine out of the presbytery garage before dawn that morning, leaving the hood down for the long journey open to the elements. The drive gave him time to reflect and brought to mind his first night trip to the monastery. Unanswered questions crowded in and he frowned in concentration.

Shaking his head in frustration, he stamped on the accelerator and chuckled to himself: a deepened engine note, and an increase in vibration and noise was all his right foot action produced, the needle remained obstinately quivering at around fifty miles per hour. Flat out across the Glendowan Mountains, Ben relished with perverse delight at his obstinate choice of transport. He would make the most of his next few days' leave, glad he had used the Land Rover as an excuse not to fly to Rome immediately.

The approach after turning off the A480 had lifted Ben's spirits; in the distance down the village road he could see the early morning sun glint off the guardhouse windows and the ubiquitous red and white striped pole against the dark green hedge. A lightly armed corporal stood rooted in the centre of the road and Ben's lips compressed as he pressed the accelerator. The deepening engine rate from the approaching hoodless, camouflaged Land Rover caused the corporal to slip the strap of his Heckler & Koch off his shoulder. Grinning with delight, Ben stamped on his brakes and squealed to a halt. He tugged his Berghaus open as he stood behind the flattened windscreen and shouted at the bemused corporal, 'Stand to attention you slovenly oaf and salute your senior officer!'

Chas paused, unslinging his weapon and made to salute, 'Ben, you bastard! The dog collar confused me!'

Ben leapt from the idling Land Rover and embraced his friend from the Guatemalan jungle. 'Still not got a proper job then?' he said as he dug Chas in the ribs. Chas gasped, eyeing the dog collar, not sure whether to clip his old troop leader or laugh.

Ben relaxed, 'Good to see you Chas. How're the boys?'

'All well, Ben, I mean Father.' Chas blushed, a rare thing in an SAS trooper. 'How's the boss?'

'Same as ever, you know, tells you what you need to know.'

'Is he on camp?'

'Mm, yes,' nodded Chas, 'usual office.'

Ben's knock on the heavy door brought a gruff 'Enter' and the waft of stale pipe tobacco as he entered. Instantly he was two years younger and bidding goodbye to this gruff commander whom he would have followed to the ends of the earth. Colonel Parker stood as he crossed the polished floor and saluted formally. 'Ben, good to see you!'

In due course an orderly brought tea and scones and the shadows lengthened as the two chatted. 'Still got the ops in Guatemala then?' Ben pressed.

'Never ending, Ben. Never ending. As soon as we finish one drug baron, his brother or cousin springs up again. But, you know, battles move on and now I've been given the latest intelligence to follow, which makes that lot in South America seem like conker fights.'

Ben waited patiently. His old boss sighed and picked his cup up, then caught sight of the clock on his desk, put it down firmly and, pointing at his wall safe, asked, 'Shall we?'

Without waiting for an answer, he poured two stiff measures from the decanter conveniently housed with his confidential papers.

'Anything come of those two security enquiries I told you about?'

'No, no, nothing really,' said Ben noncommittally: Raffy's face in the study that dark night flashed momentarily in front of his. 'You haven't had any contact with a group called the Sons of Sion have you?'

'Sons of Sion?' echoed Parker. 'Sounds like some religious order. Can't say I have. Why?'

'Oh, it's probably nothing, but they have a monastery overlooking Gweebarra Bay where I was stationed and, well ...' but there he stopped. 'Oh, it's nothing. Don't worry. But let me know if my records are accessed again will you, sir?'

'Of course,' muttered Colonel Parker, who took a sip before saying, 'You know you're still under the Official Secrets don't you?' Ben's back stiffened as he nodded. 'We've pulled back seventy-five percent of our units to Hereford and asked those who've recently left, if they would like another three years. You met Chas?'

Ben raised his eyebrows. Normally the regiment would be spread thinly around the world, their fearsome capability and reputation achieving the work of dozens of 'conventional' troops or law enforcement officers. To pull back this number meant a huge commitment.

Colonel Parker got up stiffly and perched on the corner of his desk. 'You know our maxim Ben: once is chance, twice is coincidence, more than three, well it's war.' He looked at Ben under his shaggy eyebrows. 'You're a lucky man, Ben. You're out of it now.' He paused: no rancour in his voice. 'We've had, over the last eighteen months, several items of intelligence pass across my desk and those of others. On their own they mean little. But, together, well ...

'Two years ago the Paras helped to "neutralise" an IRA active service unit in Belfast. They'd been operating from the local bus depot, and we'd got a deep mole in, a female who in turn recruited a young lad in the depot itself. Anyway, the local IRA rumble him and arrange a necktie party. Fortunately, the Paras get wind and raid the garage, as our mole and her informer are due to play at being puppets. Instead of surrendering, the unit fights and no-one gets up. The commanding officer reports he's shot seven IRA men, but we hear only six coffins were needed. We think our mole's man got away. Then a whisper comes via our own B Squadron operating round Qum Qasr in Iraq with the UN Weapons Inspectors, that some local guy who'd been smuggling cigarettes and booze into Iraq had also been playing the other side and had been caught smuggling American cigarettes into an Iranian naval base across the waterway. So, he's due for the long drop after Friday prayers.

'No big deal,' Colonel Parker shrugged, 'Local matter. But apparently then he's rescued by the arresting officer, as the rope is tightening round his neck, with the assistance of his uncle, who just happens to be none other than one General Bagheri, Head of the IRGC, himself.

'We also hear he's maybe not local, but a dead IRA man from Belfast.' He paused and let Ben absorb all this while he refilled the two glasses. And Ben did indeed remain silent.

'So, we've got two pieces of intelligence from either side of the world,' the colonel continued. 'On their own they mean nothing. But next we find out from pathologists in Zurich that when they've examined the wreck of a top nuclear scientist's car that happened to collide with a laden petroleum tanker, neither of the before bodies is that of the owner of the car.'

Ben raised his eyebrows, 'So what you're saying, it's an insurance scam perhaps?'

'Except that the owner of the Mercedes sports car is, or was, the leading light in the Central European Atomic Research Facility, CERN for short, and he is nowhere to be seen, along with his beautiful wife of eight months.

'On top of that, Ben,' George said, spreading his palms upwards, 'if there is a God, then Mossad are next to him, as they reveal that a contact in Tehran's top hotel, The Espinas Palace , says a top scientist and his wife are ensconced in the most expensive suite guarded night and day by an elite unit of Basij, the fanatical volunteer wing of the IRGC – as you probably know.'

Colonel Parker went to the darkened window and pulled the curtains, before continuing. 'As you can see, we have a presumed dead, ex-IRA smuggler saved from the gallows, a disappearing nuclear physicist, and Iran. But do you know what really, really worries me?' Ben waited. 'Someone looking remarkably like Dr Schlatter flew into Shannon airport last week, hired a SUV and disappeared. Now, do you follow?

'Our American cousins can only come up with the fact that they're "fairly sure" Iran had 450 kgs of enriched uranium which President Trump is convinced he's obliterated with the attack on Fordo with the B-2s and their bunker buster payloads. But what if they're wrong, Ben?'

Ben felt at last the need to respond. 'You always said follow your instincts, sir.'

'I told you Ben, it was to use yours!' he growled.

Ben gasped slightly, 'I'm a man of the cloth now. The info's fascinating but why tell me?'

'Thought you might keep your nose to the ground, that's all. No harm done, is there? Just keep an eye open for our Swiss doctor on your travels round your parish,' and with that he passed a passport-sized picture across the desk.

'Sorry, sir. I don't think you understand. My first posting was Ireland, but my second is the Vatican and I somehow don't think I'll find him there!'

The colonel opened his mouth and rocked back in his chair. 'Dear God, I do apologise. That's an old fool grasping at straws for you. I told you you're out of it now and I meant it,' and he reached across the desk for the passport photograph.

'No,' said Ben softly, his hand suddenly closing over the slip of cardboard, 'I'll keep it just the same. I may be going back.' Raffy's face passed fleetingly, disturbingly, across his mind.

* * *

Ben noted with childish pleasure the fitment of the new electric gates to Mountford Hall. Shame really to relegate his and his brother James' actions all those years ago to the dustbin of history. He watched and marvelled at the smooth action of the huge wrought iron gates. How many times had his father peremptorily called out from the front of the Bentley: 'Ben!' or 'James!', seemingly at random but, in reality indicating who was in favour or not. More often, it seemed, it was Ben. The number of times he had been sent scampering from the warmth of the Connolly seats to pit his puny frame against those monstrous iron gates and then the final ignominy, his father would let his window glide downwards as he passed Ben and say 'Close them tight, there's a good lad,' as he sped up the long gravel drive, his brother James' head immobile in the rear window.

Now as he drove up the long drive, deliberately scattering gravel over the immaculate lawns, he grimaced sardonically. Dorothy, his mother, let out a squeal of delight as he walked unannounced into the sun-dappled morning room his parents habitually used. Sir Roderick, more formally, carefully folded his copy of *The Times* before rising to greet his eldest son.

Ben had deliberately said nothing before of his posting: a habit from his Hereford days. But his mother clapped her hands in delight, 'Why you'll only be a few hours from James: he's in Florence.'

'It's 150 miles, Mother,' Ben patiently explained.

'Well, he is your brother. You should make the effort,' she rejoined.

'James was in Rome some years ago,' added his father, his unseen agenda being that Ben was yet again behind his sibling in his chosen path.

'Mm,' observed Ben dryly, 'it took me longer to fight a few battles in Guatemala than I thought.'

Sir Roderick dipped his head as if to look at Ben over non-existent glasses, 'All the same, I'm sure you'll want to look him up, he's near the Duomo studying with the Neocatechumenals.'

Ben looked sharply up. 'Who did you say? The Neocatechumenals?'

'I believe that's their name,' rejoined Sir Roderick.

Ben paused, it was Raffy who had alerted him to their existence during one of their frequent discussions. Ben had no knowledge of the sect, except that Raffy had dismissed it as another variation on the Opus Dei. How strange, he thought, that his studious, scholarly brother was working with a group widely vilified for their fundamental view of Catholic life.

Probing gently, he watched his father's and mother's eyes avert their gaze as he discussed the objectives of the various sects. As cradle-Catholics, his parents obviously had some kind of reservation about James' decision, but as Ben had always given them the bigger challenge in raising two sons, James' studious path had gone unremarked.

* * *

Later that day, Ben decided that the time had come to swap his military kitbag for a suitcase that more befitted his posting, and he was tidily packing the clothes neatly laid out on his bed with Sandhurst-like precision when Sir Roderick knocked softly and entered the room. He was carrying a small, faded box.

'Ben', he began without preamble, 'This is yours now,' and he opened the box to reveal an old-fashioned signet ring with a double-headed eagle upon a black background. 'You couldn't have it whilst serving, clearly. But you may find it useful in Rome. It's been in our family for over 700 years – and it's not the only one,' he added, without elaborating. Then he nodded formally to Ben and left. His son gazed at the ring, slipping it over his finger. As he did so, he felt the hand of history on his shoulder.

* * *

Father Ryan had been his usual exuberant self when he answered the telephone; his delight at Ben's posting to the Vatican was undisguised. Plainly that information would not remain quiet in the diocese, Ben thought wryly. A pupil of Father Ryan in Rome in so short a time!

Father Ryan enquired solicitously if he had enjoyed his first posting, after some mirth when Ben told him of his dreams when first told of Father Raffique Alhambra. Fruity Merseyside accents chuckled at his imagination.

'Well, it will be warm where you're off to now Ben.'

Ben murmured his agreement.

'No, Ben, I mean it could be hot,' came the serious response along the line.

'Don't worry Father, I can take care of myself and if the worst should happen, I've always got your number!'

'You've served in the jungle, Benjamin. Watch where you tread,' and the telephone clicked off at the other end of the line. Father Ryan studied the silent instrument for a long time, lost in thought then, with an equally thoughtful genuflect at the silent instrument, he left the study.

CHAPTER 74

Ben was amused to see the Carabinieri officers at the customs and passport control. The large, bustling Fiumicino Airport was a seething mass of humanity. Lines of travellers snaked across the gleaming concourse, papers were brandished, bags opened, and voices raised. In contrast, to the left of the huge arrivals board, a line of black-clad figures moved smoothly past the checkpoint. Only an elderly officer, his paunch resting on the desk in front, giving a cursory glance to the various documents brandished briefly in front of him. After collecting his luggage from the melée on the carousel, Ben was ejected into the warm afternoon sun in less than ten minutes.

As the black-clad 'Presbyters' as they were known trickled out of the gleaming concourse they were pounced upon by Rome's finest cabbies, all competing for a lucrative twenty-mile fare paid for by the Vatican. His destination seemed to be well known by the cabbie and after a hair-raising forty-five-minute journey through traffic where the national speed limit appeared to be just the minimum requirement, Ben was deposited at the Centro Peregrinatio ad Petri which temporarily acted as the Vatican clearing house for accommodation for priests on secondment. Ben shuffled forward, one of a long line of cassock-clad figures to a series of incongruously modern desks set on the marble floor under a soaring medieval roof. As he took his turn at one desk, waiting patiently for the starched coif of the nun sitting behind it to acknowledge him, he looked carefully around.

'Name?'

'Sorry, Father Benjamin Mountford.'

'I see,' and a well-manicured finger ran down the list of typewritten names. Ben was briefly aware of another figure that materialised at his side.

'Ah! Good afternoon, Father Mountford. Allow me to introduce myself,' a firm hand found its way into Ben's palm. 'Sister Aloife of the Order of Sion. That'll be fine now, Sister Megan,' she said firmly. 'I'll handle Father Mountford's accommodation.

'There appears to have been a delay from your diocese in confirming your details, so we've put you in a little hotel near the station. It's on the Metro, so you'll be fine for your work here'.

She flipped expertly through a loose-leafed file in the crook of her arm. 'Here it is, Hotel Ambrose, Via Principe Amedeo just off the Via Giovanni Giolitti. I see they've treated you to a top-floor room. Aren't you the lucky one!'. Her mouth smiled at Ben, but her eyes remained cool as she handed a photocopied map of the city and a letter confirming the booking.

Slightly perplexed not to be with his peers lodged at the Domus Internationalis Paulus VI Ben again settled into the rear of a taxi. He gave the cabbie the address only to hear a snort of derision, 'What! Your first day and they put you up off the Via Giovanni Giolitti? Your bishop must have told them you're a bad boy!' he roared, laughing at his own joke. The idea of a priest, however humble, being put up in the rundown area around the Stazione Termini tickled him no end and he was still chuckling as he dropped Ben at the end of a small scruffy cul-de-sac behind the Basilica of Santa Maria Maggiore.

* * *

Ben shrugged and walked up the worn steps. The smell of tobacco gone stale and overuse of bleach assailed him as he walked across the scrubbed wooden floor to the bowed head of the bleached receptionist, who looked up briefly, continued chewing gum and pushed the register across to Ben.

She watched him rapidly fill out his details, leaning back and thrusting her breasts towards him before she unhooked a solitary key from the empty top row. She let her gaze linger over his broad back as he headed for the lift and then picked up the telephone receiver. Her call was taken immediately and tersely answered before being cut off. Upstairs, two flickering monitors burst into life just as Ben pushed open the door to his room.

* * *

Even though she had baulked at her mother's ultimatum, Eleanor had resignedly grown to anticipate such a moment in her life. On her coming of age some eleven years previously, she had disappeared into the 'bowl' as she called it, her private personal childhood playground surrounding the castle.

There she had howled at the injustice of her fate to the silent trees and rocks where tumbled-down ruins of buildings from the thirteenth century mocked her self-pity.

Her mother had explained her destiny to her directly and without preamble. She would marry and carry the Order forward; it was written and in her blood: destiny was not a personal choice for a Plantard St Claire. But later, as she had reflected on the hand that fate had dealt her, she decided to play the game. She would select a mate as her mother instructed, and he would be the fittest and the meanest – but, by God, she reserved the right to choose.

And so it had been for the last decade. An apparent life of chastity amongst men whose decision to marry God would lead to a life of denial, temptation and frustration. Eleanor had learnt well to exploit their fantasies in such a way that she literally held the power of life or death over her chosen beaux. Her favoured hunting grounds among new priests seconded to the Vatican and the younger members of various orders, particularly Opus Dei and the Sovereign Knights of Malta, had laid bare a fascinating mix of zealotry and passion. She exploited to the full her hapless victims' expressions of fulfilment, afterwards watching their angst as their downfall consumed them.

In this, Eleanor discovered a delicious control, having her latest flame called away by his bishop to a far-flung outpost: just as she had brought him to the edge of madness, she then discovered the ecstasy of his agony. The burden of her calling could not, would never be, revealed until her marriage night. As the years slipped by, her biological clock ever ticking to the constant reminding of her mother, she became ever more determined in her pursuit of her ultimate mate.

Three years previously she had an assignation in one of the Vatican museums, the Room of the Chiaroscuri. Beginning a desultory conversation with the elderly curator as they admired the coffered ceiling designed by Raphael and the personal weapons of Pope Leo X Medici, the curator intimated that further weapons and instruments of the Inquisition were housed beneath the museum out of the gaze of the public. Not something the Vatican was keen to display these days, the curator had said, shaking his head sadly. 'The past is all forgotten now, Miss: people forget our power, now we are curiosities only,' he mused.

Murmuring her agreement she casually probed about the hidden collection. Old Giulio Penni had looked after the collections in the various museums for the best part of his fifty-eight years. Suddenly he seemed to lose years, and he became animated, his eyes twinkling with enthusiasm. 'Oh! I'm not sure a lady would want to see those.' he smirked. 'The old IOR took all its pleasure before executing sentence on the poor blighters.'

'Go on,' murmured Eleanor politely.

'They say a man at the point of death is at his most powerful, if you get my meaning,' said Giulio suddenly overcome. Eleanor kept her face neutral, shaking her head slightly. 'You know, Miss, down there.' Giulio hissed, jabbing his hands below his belt.

CHAPTER 75

After his initial disappointment at the location of his lodgings, Ben had thrown himself into the intricacies of Vatican life. Unlike any other posting, the small city state was quite literally a country within a country. Allowed a week by the College of Curia to organise his affairs, almost as a 'fresher' week at university, Ben threw himself into the life of the Vatican's administrators. He was introduced to the Vatican's own bank: it was a condition of his calling to the Curia that all his worldly affairs be administered from the Vatican. Accordingly, he completed account transfer forms from his local Bank of Ireland in Burtonport and pushed the paperwork across the desk to the frock-coated official. After examining it cursorily, the man nodded and informed Ben it would take a few days to complete the international transfers, but if he needed cash he could withdraw immediately from the bank itself. Ben nodded briefly and left the ornate banking hall.

While he made his way out through the huge glass doors, the serious faced official ran his index finger once more down Ben's account application. Tapping his finger against his surname, he pursed his lips. muttered a brief apology to the next earnest looking applicant, left his position and walked briskly to the rear of the building clutching Ben's account application.

Once before in his mundane existence he had an occasion to alert a certain authority within the bank and to his utter surprise he had been handsomely rewarded in his next pay packet. The name on the form in his hand matched that on an 'aware' list circulated only last week. The official had little interest as to why the name was on the list, but he did know what to do about it.

He made his way along carpeted corridors, quiet, except for purposeful conversations half overheard through open doors, he came eventually to a large open floor, divided into waist-high working areas. Each little square held a glowing screen and the bowed head of an operator. Seated at a raised dais at the end of the room the official could see his manager, who took Ben's form, glanced at it and then dismissed his colleague with a grateful, 'Bene'.

Soon after, a leather-clad dispatch rider appeared at the manager's desk, listened briefly to the instructions he was given and strode purposefully from the room. Only a matter of minutes later, he was weaving in and out of the chaotic traffic through which he hurried to the Hotel Ambrose, arriving there in less than a quarter of an hour. The envelope he delivered remained in the postbox of the hotel reception until it was collected by a figure clad in a dark robe, who took it to the lift in the corner of the lobby.

* * *

Eleanor had left the Château Val Dieu driving the elderly Mercedes 450SEL through a veil of tears. The ivy-clad gates had swung silently behind her, bringing yet more floods of tears which made her blink and spurred her to drive furiously down the single sandy track. She would not see her mother again; of that she was sure. Forced out of the old woman's bedroom by those icy eyes, she had meekly obeyed, as she always had. Her mother, pale and wasted, a shadow of herself, from that day they had driven to Domme and that lengthy telephone call she had made there. From then, it had seemed, the malignant growth had entered into a race with Eleanor: the two locked into a battle in which there was only one outcome. To tearful entreaties, Eleanor had been forced to swear that she would go to Rome.

Her mother, who was becoming weaker by the day, had alternately pleaded and berated her daughter, desperate to ensure the Order's succession. Only once in the 700 years of its existence had one Grand Nautonier failed to pass her mantle to a living relative. But Eleanor's dalliance in choosing a mate had brought her mother despair. Not only did she desire to see her daughter succeed, but her mother needed to confide the contents of the telephone call some four weeks previously, realising belatedly that her chance of concluding the greatest success in her order's long history was remote.

* * *

The road along the Mediterranean coast was heavily used and with minimal border surveillance. Flying was quicker and trains sometimes more comfortable, but both entailed paperwork, payment and identification at some stage. Eleanor travelled as she habitually did, in nondescript everyday clothes, the superb maintenance and special tuning of the Mercedes largely hidden under its metallic brown dusty and dented paintwork.

Eventually the salty tears stopped, and she found herself leaving the road from Quillan onto the one that would take her round the Golfe du Lion to

Orange. The irony that the route went past the old papal palace at Avignon never failed for her. Seven hundred years had passed since the issuing of the papal bull, ostensibly ending in brutal fashion the reign of the Templars. Seven hundred years in which its secret successor had aided and abetted its persecutor with blind and total loyalty.

After Suffering the thundering A9 for several more miles, Eleanor took the exit at Orange and climbed away from the bustling centre on the road leading eventually to her favourite halt at Digne, where she stopped at the restaurant, to sit on the terrace overlooking the rolling hills of Provence stretching to the sea in a lavender haze.

Once a Nautonier selected a mate, it would only be in extreme and unprecedented circumstances that could she return to Rome. From then on, she did not exist. Banished as her ancestors had been to the mountains and plains of Canigou she would only be required to serve as steward for the organisation until such times as she was summoned by secret decree.

Although she had undertaken this journey before, each time with the same aim, on this occasion it was different; as if her mother's illness had acted as some kind of wake-up call. She observed in a detached manner her life before, musing that she was already using the term 'before' as if, by default, there was to be an 'after'.

In truth, her mother had prepared her well for her role. It was not a role of choice, but one of birth. Eleanor did not feel the need to discuss the rights and wrongs of her calling. Her life had a purpose. It was true that she had rebelled mightily in the past and her mother had indulged her mutinous periods with calm patience, observing her wild liaisons with fond memories of her own. She had known this day would arrive for her daughter, as it had for herself.

Skilfully over the years, Eleanor had let her children into the minutiae of the Order's activities. From an early age, she had allowed her daughter to be party to the secrets of the vast cavern beneath her home. Careful to guard its secrets, young Eleanor had accepted from an early age the need to choose her friends carefully. Her mother had wisely not kept her children locked away during their teenage years but rather encouraged a freedom that would have been frowned upon in a traditional upbringing. However, only suitors of a certain calling were ever permitted to be around the young Eleanor.

Under her mother's careful tutelage, she encouraged and mercilessly discarded those who could not match her expectations or ambitions. Whilst she had known that one day she would succeed, Eleanor had only carefully redacted dealings with the day-to-day activities of the Sons Of Sion: the unspoken, deniable, syndicate of the Order of St Anthony. One day – and with a shiver as she realised it was fast approaching – she would be privy to the secrets of 'the book': the leather-bound volume that lay at the end of the long line of similar volumes in her mother's 'thinking room' under the sloping roof of the chateau.

In those volumes were detailed decision after decision that each successive Grand Nautonier had made over the centuries. Decisions that had affected the lives of men, the survival of governments and the future of nations. Decisions that had sent the Sons of Sion to change history. Only on her succession to Grand Nautonier would she know it all. Only on the death of the present Grand Nautonier would that knowledge be passed on.

* * *

Continuing her reflective mood, Eleanor took her time down the Route Napoléon through the fragrantly perfumed capital of Grasse. It was late afternoon as the dusty vehicle drew up outside the Hôtel Hermitage. At the prices charged per night, discretion was assured and Eleanor found herself in her usual suite with its the fabulous view overlooking Monaco harbour. She had a great fondness for her regular suite here: it had been the scene of many a wild liaison.

She arose early the next morning to start the second leg of her leisurely drive to Rome. Almost on autopilot, as she meandered along the Golfo di Genova, her thoughts turned to what might have been only twelve months earlier. An Englishman from London, from Ealing Abbey no less, had been sent to Florence by the bishop. Of the many sects that flourished on the right wing of the Church, the Neocatechumenals were perhaps one of the most secret: barely did their name make public reading. Cunningly referring to themselves as 'The Church' had, in one stroke, circumvented the objections of many a conservative parish. Further, in order to distance themselves from the rest of the Church they eschewed the political boiling pot of Rome for the cooler suburbs of Florence. They were based ostensibly around the medieval Duomo in the centre of the city, although the order maintained a training and recruitment centre behind the Santa Maria Maggiore church off Via de' Cerretani.

Of all her previous beaux, Father James Mountford was the one she found most difficult to erase from her memory, partly she suspected in a wry moment because he and he alone had been chastely immune to her feminine charms. Something about the Englishman stirred her and she studied his features minutely as he completed the formalities, she had placed a small pencil cross against his name on her list and passed it to her tame manager at the Vaticana Bank. The next day, as part of their general introduction to the Vatican and Rome itself the new arrivals were each assigned a sister well versed in the history and operations of the Vatican City. Duly, with much laughter and comment in the large hall, each was introduced to his guide for the following week. Eleanor had observed these ceremonies over a number of years and had honed her predatory instincts to a fine point. Resignedly, each new arrival queued patiently, a look of polite interest being cast at the line of generally older, sallow-faced nuns.

With practice, and keeping her starched coif well over her face, Eleanor would manage to get close to her intended choice without her 'victim' having a glance at her. Only as the two met in front of the introducing *asessore* would she reveal her face. Eleanor was a classic south European beauty of faintly dusky clear skin and wide firm lips. Her eyes were of a dazzling blue, passed down over the generations, and the reaction of the novice at first glimpsing her face usually gave an indication of how long it would take her to bed them.

Father James had been one such intended choice. With a well-practised flick of her hood she had introduced herself as Sister Eleanor of the Order of Sion. Father James' strong aristocratic features registered quickly the diminutive beauty in front of him, uncomfortably aware of her frank appraisal through those piercing China blue eyes. She had taken him on a whirlwind tour, through seemingly endless rooms and corridors all filled with hurrying, busy people administering the minutiae of the headquarters of the faith of a third of the planet. Of particular interest to the scholarly Father James were the Vatican archives.

For Eleanor, the game was about the chase and delicious choice of timing. She likened herself to a chess grand master, carefully orchestrating events and movements. In James, she quickly detected a formidable intellect who had spent his life preparing to join the Church. (For James Mountford, unknown to Eleanor, the journey had started hundreds of years before, his bloodlines almost mimicking the rise and fall of Roman Catholicism in England.)

She had similarly acquired the habit of skirting over various topics in a seemingly random manner, as all the while her sharply analytical eyes watched for the faintest flicker of interest. By experience she had this to a fine art, observing not only the man's eyes but also the muscles around his eyes and the extreme corners of his mouth. James gave little away except for his passion for mountain climbing and skiing. Eleanor treated these with a certain scepticism as, given the Pontiff's own widely publicised enthusiasm, all aspiring members of the Curia professed similar pastimes.

But two or three days into their Vatican introduction, she had raised the issue of the Vatican archives. At once James' pupils had fractionally dilated and the corners of his mouth puckered in interest. Sensing a situation she could exploit, she duly obtained the necessary passes from her cardinal and arrived at the desk of Alfonso the archive keeper.

Sister Eleanor St Claire and Father James Mountford were duly entered laboriously into the visitors' book. After a brief enquiry James had set off down the dusty, shelf-lined corridors and stopped at the earliest recordings. Watching curiously, Eleanor saw him leaf through the records and histories of various early Crusader families, in which he became so engrossed that he was oblivious to her growing impatience and discomfort in the musty passages.

In the end she moved close behind him to peer over his shoulder to see that he was reading the wording of the papal bull issued by Clement V that had ended the Crusader movement. James was motionless, with just a finger moving slowly across the page as he tortuously translated the early Latin. Slowly Eleanor pushed against his back, her breasts rising and falling – nothing. She pushed harder and his finger stopped moving. A deep crimson began to suffuse his neck. Eleanor quickly slid past him and covered the movement by selecting another small leather-bound volume from the shelf.

The moment passed as Eleanor engaged James' eyes frankly. 'Why the interest in this section?'

James chuckled, covering his faint discomfiture. 'My family go back a long way,' he began, 'and it was always a rumour that an ancestor of ours was amongst the last Crusaders with de Molay when they were executed for heresy.' Eleanor raised her eyebrows.

James sighed, 'I'd love to spend some study time here, but I'm only in the Vatican for the week.'

Before she could stop herself, Eleanor interjected, 'I'll get some research done for you, if you like.' James smiled, a faint blush colouring his cheeks.

* * *

Eleanor herself was no stranger to these musty vaults since she had spent many an hour in her younger days following the history of her mother's order. The archives are only revealed to the public fifty years after the death of the pontiff in question, unless the College of Cardinals decides that even the passage of fifty years would not spare the embarrassment of the current Church hierarchy. Such items and manuscripts would be held in a permanent archive, secretly located in sealed away from prying eyes. Given her elevated status, even Eleanor had only been allowed in there once and then the decrepit librarian, Alfonso, did not afford her much time to delve into the dusty boxes and files.

Dumb and going deaf, Alfonso had worked in the archives since leaving school at the age of fourteen. His father before him had held the same position and it was widely acknowledged that the knowledge he had garnered over the years would be priceless in the wrong hands: not that the Curia lost any sleep over it. Alfonso lived over the shop in a grace and favour apartment and his entire working life, and some said more, was spent underground documenting and filing in the long dusty corridors between the packed shelves of documents. His face was the colour of putty from his long life out of the sun's rays, yet he would receive a constant trickle of visitors who, having been screened for suitability by their local bishop, would then have to appeal in writing and in person before a special panel of senior members of the Curia who would determine the applicant's suitability for access to the archives. Even so, having gained this rich prize to the world's most consistent and preserved records of the last 2,000 years, Alfonso would remain with his guest, constantly watching and fussing over the slightest disturbance of anything from his, or more correctly, the Vatican's archives.

* * *

When the archives closed, he spent all his spare time in the secret archives behind massively locked doors. Here, sometimes for the entire night, he would remain closeted away, working under half a dozen ancient electric lamps, as he painstakingly put together the documents, discussions and decisions of the Roman Catholic Church that must never see the light of day. Fond though he was of 'his' library, he did reluctantly admit that 'other' people could, but seldom did, gain access. They were the serving Pontiff and any member of the College of Cardinals with their respective secretaries, the Grand Master of the Sovereign Knights of Malta and finally the Grand Nautonier of the Knights of St Anthony and the Sons of Sion, or her immediate successor.

Eleanor stood before the pasty-faced little man, having handed him a small parchment card her mother had given her before her departure. 'It's been a long time, a long time indeed, Madam Plantard St Claire.' He bowed stiffly as Eleanor registered his voice with surprise. 'But I thought . . .'

'Everybody does my lady.'

Chatting amiably, the two had locked the archive doors and descended the worn stone stairs as if they had known each other all their lives.

'Your mother's not well?' he observed directly.

Eleanor shot him a sharp glance. Buried he may be in these dark dungeons and cut off from the outside world, but he missed nothing.

'She came first some forty years ago,' he mused. 'Since then, only two or three times, but she did spend a lot of time here in the summer of '78. My father used to say the archives are our strength from the past. Without knowing the reasons, the decisions, our forebears took, how can we have the courage to take our own?'

Eleanor nodded, in agreement.

Alfonso carried on, 'The records you have in the chateau, my lady, you know,' he paused, selecting his words deliberately, 'the thick, hand-tooled, damask, Moroccan leather ledgers in the long room at the top of the tower.'

Eleanor eyed the diminutive, little man as he fumbled with a large bunch of ancient keys. 'What of them?' she asked sharply. The chateau's archives were, next to the secrets of the bowl, etched as inviolate in her soul. Just what did this man know?

Alfonso drew himself up as Eleanor stooped and entered the dungeon. 'They only tell you half a tale,' he said and shut the door firmly behind them.

Eleanor pressed her lips together and gazed around the little room. It was hewn out of huge blocks of stone, cemented together with ancient mortar. The floor was an expanse of worn flagstones leading to an empty water trough and rough iron cot in the corner. Huge rusting iron bars remained high up the wall near to the curved stone ceiling. Any light they may once have let into this gloomy cell was now extinguished by rough twentieth-century breeze blocks and crude mortar. Apart from the yellow glow coming from the rusting bulkhead light on the wall, the room was bare. Completing her inspection in silence, she turned to Alfonso. So engrossed had she been studying the small cell, his shuffling steps to the water trough had gone unnoticed. Now, holding Eleanor's gaze in his eyes he twisted the ancient tap above the trough. A stream of clear water issued forth and splashed into the empty trough, its tinkling, gushing noise amplified in the small cell. Patiently Eleanor watched the trough as it started to fill. Presently, shifting her feet impatiently, she caught Alfonso's eye. Nodding as if understanding her, he held his hand up placatingly. Gradually the trough's level approached the rounded edge and as it did so Alfonso turned the tap slowly until the trough was brimming full and starting to leak from a small copper overflow pipe onto the floor.

He beckoned to a bemused Eleanor, stepped up onto the edge of the trough, motioning her to do the same. The pair stood awkwardly holding onto each other's shoulders, legs slightly apart over the deep brimming trough. Alfonso reached down with his hand and finding the tap, twisted it slowly into the wall. Eleanor's bewilderment increased and, about to frame a tart question, opened her mouth. As she did so, beneath her feet the surface of the still water trembled and a rumbling, grating noise emanated through the soles of her feet. With a slight movement of the surface of the water, slopping some over her toes, she sensed a sideways movement. The noise increased and in front of her the rusting bulkhead light slid slowly to the right of her vision. Gripping Alfonso's bony shoulders, she twisted her head. The entire wall of the cell, complete with iron cot and the couple clinging together over the trough, was rotating to a grumbling grating noise. Slowly and smoothly the wall twisted round until the remaining light from the cell diminished to virtually nothing. Alfonso's right hand let go Eleanor's shoulder for a moment and brushed against a passing wall. Light flooded the room as the couple slid into it. Barely taking in her surroundings Eleanor was brought to a halt by a small jolt, and she stepped gratefully off the trough.

The chamber in which they stood had been out of the volcanic pumice-like tofa and stretched into the distance towards which oak frames supported shelf after shelf of boxes: boxes of all shapes and sizes and in a vast array of materials. On one row of shelves, they were all of a uniform leather, bound with a looped chain and sealed with a wax seal on the side. The next row contained wooden chests, their iron bindings red with age, locked with a padlock bigger than a man's hand. Moving past the rows of shelves Eleanor ran her finger over the smooth adzed finish, a frown creeping over her face. There was something about the oak frames that seemed familiar and yet ... yet she had never been allowed access to this room. She knew now, wryly, that her previous access had been a ruse. Her mother had known she was not ready for this and had kept her to the public archives.

* * *

Her thoughts drifted as she realised with a start she had cruised down the length of the Riviera di Levante with her mind on autopilot. It was the signs for the approach to Pisa that had brought her subconscious to a halt; she shook her head to clear it. Father James, her one failure. She paused at the side of the busy road: ahead lay the left fork for Florence, straight on lay Rome. Her research in the secret archive had revealed much and, to her utter amazement, most of which she could never reveal; but there was enough to tempt James with. Her mouth curled in anticipation: she had the bait, but could she use it on blood relations? With a wicked grin she swerved left for Florence.

To her utter chagrin and later cold anger, Father James had received her with a distant aloofness. Even her morsel of research produced no more than a polite interest. Even Father James' invitation to dinner had turned out to be a formal affair in the rectory with nine other members of the Neocatechumenals earnestly discussing the day's lectures. As she moved to kiss him on his left cheek, the Italian way, she felt his eyes rebuff her with a cold haughtiness.

'You should try your research on my younger brother,' he said coolly. His nuance was not missed by her.

'Brother?' Eleanor said neutrally.

'He's taken holy orders late in life after a spell in the army; he would enjoy the challenge.' James' eyes narrowed as he watched Eleanor's expression.

Eleanor kept her gaze steady and uninterested, 'Where's his parish?'

'Oh, yours – for twelve months. He's in tomorrow's intake. I'll be down to see him this week.'

Eleanor had driven away thoughtfully. One thing for sure, she knew who would be introducing who to the Vatican. Vaguely excited, she piloted the large car south, feeling curiously fulfilled.

The next day, after the investiture ceremony in the College of Cardinals, Eleanor had gone to see the ever-reliable manager at the Vatican Bank who, with a polite, stiff bow had proffered the next typewritten list of sixty-seven additions to the Curia. Eleanor's elegantly manicured finger had skimmed down the list, finding at last the name she sought: Father Benjamin Cadogan Mountford. She tapped the surname thoughtfully. What, if? What if he was? But she sniffed, peremptorily dismissing her idle dream. Marking his name instead with a small, neat cross, she nodded briefly to the manager and left.

As the new arrivals were being processed on their first morning, Eleanor had slipped unobtrusively into the gathering of white-coifed figures, keeping her head down. Nominally a sister of the Franciscan Order, she used its cover only to her advantage when absolutely necessary. With impeccable timing she arrived at the desk of the elderly sister as Ben stood schoolboy-like in front of her.

'Father Benjamin Mountford,' he proffered to the bowed head. Her gnarled finger ran down her list.

'Welcome Father,' and without turning her head she raised her hand beckoning from behind her. Eleanor glided forward, pursued by the frown of the sister she had deftly slipped in front of.

'Sister Eleanor, Father. Pleased to have you in Rome,' A phrase she had practised over the years. Her small slim hand held briefly onto Ben's as she raised her head and looked him directly in the eyes. Instantly she saw James in him ... but more. The firm, almost hard handshake belonged to a rangy six-foot tall, tanned man of almost athletic proportions. His figure, beaten by weather and climes far from Europe, displayed an openness that lifted her heart. At the same time, she saw firmness in his jaw and a glint in his eye. Perhaps she imagined that? Perhaps she willed herself to imagine that?

Ben clasped her hand and looked back intently. Eyes? Not again, surely? Eyes of the coolest blue, but not in a face from northern lands? Fixing him with her gaze was a southern Mediterranean beauty who caused a tightness in his chest.

Eleanor released his hand, pushing it fractionally away from herself. Businesslike at once, she led Father Ben away from the throng to the doorway of the enormous hall. As they were lost from sight, the bank manager, watching from high up, picked up a telephone and dialled a number off the Via Principe Amadeo. The conversation was entirely one-sided and lasted no more than thirty seconds.

CHAPTER 76

The four men sat with an easy camaraderie established over a long period of time: thirty or so years for some. It was not often they sat together; only in extreme circumstances would the four ever risk being associated with each other. They had arrived over the last three days, all converging slowly, invisibly, on the small hotel off the Via Principe Amadeo.

Carone had arrived first, two days ago, maintaining his secrecy till the last by taking a room on the third floor, dressed as a migrant worker employed on a refurbishment job nearby. With his New York Police experience, he had known just how to ghost past the receptionist who would have only the faintest recollection of a middle-aged man in worn working men's clothes. The clientele of the Hotel Ambrose, like the owners, kept themselves to themselves. It was a dormitory hotel: no food was served, so no guests mingled in the dining room. The only opportunity for contact would be the brief daily visit to the reception in the disinfectant scrubbed lobby.

Marcinkus had arrived next. Decidedly uncomfortable and slightly queasy from his journey across Rome in one of the hotel's anonymous beige Fiat vans, he had nearly vomited over himself as the van had driven swiftly round the descending spiral roadway under the hotel. Juddering to a halt the portly Archbishop had been flung against the van's bulkhead as it stopped in the silent cellars. Marcinkus had glared at the innocent-faced driver, had grabbed his luggage and walked unsteadily down the dimly lit cellar to the lift at the end.

As the lift whirred, another engine noise was heard from the descending roadway. This time a powerful purr preceded the Mercedes' arrival. Entirely black, including the windows, the limousine glided to a halt next to the van that had so recently discharged its puffing occupant. The driver's door sprang open and a man in sunglasses, dressed in black as if he too were part of the car, moved smartly to the rear door. After scanning the dimly lit cellar, including the hapless driver of the van, he opened the door. There was a pause while a rapid conversation was ended abruptly on a mobile telephone, then the car's occupant alighted elegantly. His gaze fell on the van driver who for no reason shivered and turned his eyes away. In silence Lucio Gallé strode to the lift.

Umberto Ortolani was the last to appear. For a lunchtime summons, he had left it until late morning due to some local business difficulties. The taxi driver had raised his eyebrows at the request for the Hotel Ambrose but choked off his comment as he felt Umberto's small black eyes boring into him. The driver had taken his fare in silence and with a shrug watched the expensively dressed man nimbly skip up the worn steps to the seedy hotel. Likewise, the blonde receptionist caught a whiff of his expensive cologne. She took in his immaculate manicure and half hidden Patek Philippe watch. Involuntarily, she stretched her neck and pushed her breasts forward. Umberto, if he noticed, merely nodded, palmed the small brass key and headed for the lift.

Membership had been good for the four, who sat relaxed and at home in the luxurious surroundings, where a waft of rich cigar smoke curled up from Marcinkus. The banter was one of rich men, enjoying life. But amongst them all harboured the question: why? Why now? And why did the Grand Nautonier need to come in person. Even in that hot August of 1978 it had merely taken a telephone call to send Barzini on his way.

Of the four, Gallé felt least perturbed. Brought in following the 'suicide' of Roberto Calvi to rescue the millions of missing Vatican dollars, he was confident in his ability to acquit himself of his responsibilities. Gallé lent back in his comfortable chair: he alone in the room had never met the Grand Nautonier. Previous meetings, and there were few enough of them, had kept the large chair at the head of the table symbolically empty.

* * *

In the sun-drenched Piazza St Pietro, Eleanor began describing the vast space. 'It was originally Bernini's design to link the two arms with a vast triumphal arch to pass underneath as the pilgrims sought access to the Piazza. But, in fact, the arms of the colonnades remained open, seen by later generations as the welcoming arms of the Catholic faith, once entered to be clasped to the bosom of St Peter.'

Ben let the diminutive sister continue, only half listening to the history of St Peter's Basilica. In truth, he was overawed by the size and presence of the square. In times of crisis in his life he had, for one reason or another, come back to his birth religion. Now, he had the honour of serving here for the next twelve months, in what he wryly supposed, was the the clerical equivalent of duty at Buckingham Palace. Walking slowly up the centre of the vast piazza, the double colonnades encircled him and the dome of St Peter's beckoned.

An acquired habit of Ben's from his Hereford days enabled him to keep a deadpan face no matter what his mind registered. Seeing no reaction, Sister Eleanor moved on as the pair entered the mighty double doors. 'On the right you now see Michelangelo's "Pietà" completed when he was twenty-four, now protected from the public following a vandal attack some years ago.'

Ben's eyes followed her and he cast his own over the sensitive and evocative piece of the limp torso of Jesus held in Mary's arms. She was not to know his thoughts were with the museums and their archives. Directly his eyes caught hers and a modest lowering of her eyelids.

The pair moved slowly onwards beneath the mighty dome supported by its four enormous pillars. They paused under the relief of St Veronica's handkerchief; used to wipe the face of Christ as he hung dying on the cross. Ben gazed upwards at the relief, his mind inexplicably crowded with images of Raffy.

Eleanor paused, watching Bens features. 'What troubles you, Father?' she gently enquired.

'Nothing. It's nothing,' he insisted, surprised at his own emotion. 'I've neglected a friend in need,' letting his voice trail uncertainly.

'Can I help?' Eleanor murmured. She felt a curious affinity with the tall priest, that was not altogether unpleasant.

* * *

The two continued their walk up the nave of the mighty edifice. Somehow Eleanor sensed the moment, uncertain as to its significance. They drifted on, their voices low against the perpetual hum of conversation in Catholicism's holiest shrine. Ben could not help his rising frustration at the lack of silence, his mind slipped back to operations in the Guatemalan jungle: those precious moments before dawn when it seemed life stood still as if in awe of the daily birth of the sun. Here above all should it not be a place of awe? And yet, and yet … Loud American tourists and chattering Japanese intermingled. Respect. He wryly decided, there was none. The site was a curiosity, yet another 'must visit' on the itinerary of world-weary culture tourists.

Suddenly he felt as if he knew this place's creator. He saw Michelangelo with his vision for the world's most holy shrine, a place of silent prayer and reflection, perhaps a soprano's rendering soaring to its impossible ceiling. Yet here he stood amid the bustle and he could not help but think of Jesus in the temple as he cast out the moneylenders.

Again, Raffy's face floated before him and the voice of Father Ryan warning him, 'Beware of the jungle, Benjamin. Beware of the jungle'.

Feeling strangely uneasy, he asked Sister Eleanor with a confidant open smile to ask, 'And you Sister? What is it that brings you here?'

'Well,' she answered softly, taken aback, 'I'm here to escort new arrivals like you, as are my fellow sisters.'

'No. No,' muttered Ben, 'I was thinking personally, sister.'

Eleanor modestly cast her eyes downwards, 'Oh, you could say I've been on this journey all my life, as my forebears have.

'But you're here to learn about this place, you don't need me to ...'

But the tall black-clad figure had stepped in front of her to ask the white coiffed figure, 'So, what does a sister do when not on duty?' meeting her startled upturned blue eyes with equanimity.

Just in time, Eleanor managed to raise her hand to cover a non-existent blush, as she bowed her head to hide her quick smile of triumph.

* * *

Later in the shower, she gratefully sluiced away the effects of Rome's stifling heat. Running her hands over her taut body she permitted herself another smile. At once she stamped her foot. Slowly, she reminded herself, slowly.

Sheer silk underwear, her favourite Janet Reger from London, and a three-seasons' out-of-date Versace summer dress completed her outfit. With a delicious touch of irony, Eleanor had elected to meet Ben in the snack bar by the Vatican Museums adjoining the Sistine Chapel. An early evening suited Eleanor on two counts: it would avoid the subliminal invitation as evening drew to a close, and tomorrow she had the meeting with the respective Grand Masters to contend with. She would treat the evening lightly. With possibilities.

* * *

'A soldier then,' she said reflectively, looking at Ben later as the two shared a chilled Frascati. 'Where did you say you served?' she asked, watching him over her frosted glass.

'I didn't, but here and there.' Ben replied easily, feeling relaxed in this woman's company. 'Royal Green Jackets, my father's regiment; pen pusher really, but I got to travel a bit,' he shrugged non-committally.

'And what did theological college have to say to a serving soldier?' she murmured.

'Oh, well, you see I was at college before.' his voice trailed.

'Go on.'

'Well, it's a long story, but I met a girl in Liverpool. It was only the once you understand, but old Father Ryan used to send us out, I think with the aim of meeting and resisting sins of the flesh. Anyway, I didn't. Couldn't.' He shrugged his shoulders expressively.

She raised her eyebrows fractionally, leaning back against the smooth aluminium chair.

He exhaled sharply. 'After the first night she disappeared.'

'Go on,' she pressed.

He shook his head as if to eject the thoughts. 'It's history now. A long time ago.'

They both took reflective draughts of the wine.

Hoping that the subject had changed, Ben smiled: a warm engaging smile, 'OK, OK!' he said in mock surrender. 'Tell me why I'm enjoying a drink with a nun in the Vatican for God's sake!'

The two chuckled and with a smooth, practised movement Eleanor had another bottle of Frascati brought over. Ben chinked glasses with her in a mock toast to themselves and deep wells of mirth bubbled from the pair. It was a warm evening; the city was relaxing around them, life felt good. Ben felt his shoulders relax too as the light refreshing wine took hold.

'So,' continued Eleanor softly, pausing with the glass halfway to her slightly parted lips, 'what happens to relationships,' she fractionally raised her glass, 'when you marry the Church, Father?'

Ben acknowledged with a half-smile. 'My CO told me when I left the regiment that all I was doing was swapping one fight with another – and I don't think he was wrong.'

Eleanor's eyes fractionally dilated. The wine emboldened him to a degree he had not felt for some time. 'I think our Church has given up fighting as it were. What I mean is, I come from a long line of Catholics, some of whom have laid down their lives in pretty awful circumstances for the Church. Nowadays we all like to think that that part of our history is all behind us, but we forget the world is still a dangerous place and we must never forget to fight for what is right.'

Eleanor interjected light-heartedly, 'I only wanted to know ...'

Ben held his hand up sternly, 'I know. I know,' he said, 'but our faith is under threat as never before from within and from outside. Internally we have pressures to accept practices and dogmas unthinkable fifty years ago. And no one, from the theological colleges upwards appears to give a damn.

'Sometimes,' he said, 'it takes an outsider to see threats that cradle-Catholics miss. My old colleague Father Raffique, who was a convert from Islam, spent hours and hours researching the early church and the development of various sects, only to warn me against them as if they represented the threat. But he got it wrong, I suspect. The threat is from within the main body. In accepting the importation of other religions, we have weakened or even dismissed the huge role that the Church played in western, and by implication, worldwide civilisation. We have become apologists for all we achieved. For political reasons we now accept into the West a religion that has atrophied for a thousand years. The time when Islam gave the world an early civilisation has passed and been turned backwards by an increasingly extreme and vicious clergy. But for the discovery of hydrocarbons, it would have withered and failed. We need to become soldiers again, and to do that we need fresh, strong blood. Man was not born to be alone. We learnt in the regiment that teams are better than individuals.'

Eleanor had sat silent, listening carefully without interruption. When she next engaged Ben's eyes her lids were lowered and her gaze direct. For no apparent reason Ben felt a shiver go down his back.

'Would you say the threat was greater from outside or within?' she lightly questioned, draining the last of the bottle equally into the two glasses.

'Mm,' said Ben, pausing a moment. 'Within. Within ourselves and within soft-left, consensus politics.' A silence settled over them.

'We ... That is, I, don't think you're wrong,' she said softly, correcting herself and lifting her delicate chin. 'But get the map out. Look at the spread of Islam since the fourteenth century compared to our efforts, even in our missionary heyday: they've spread like cancer. They are the threat Ben, why I could ...'

But Ben interrupted her, leaning forward to emphasise, 'Some would say that Islam is one of the great religions, Sister.

'Because we let it become that', she spat, her eyes flashing. 'It's a jungle out there.'

Ben leant back, studying her features anew, his face a mask and Father Ryan's words burning his soul. 'I agree' he said presently 'and the strong and the bold survive.'

Eleanor tilted her head graciously at the riposte and smiled openly. 'I can see your tutors at the seminary had a challenge with you,' she said, warmly smiling with her eyes.

Then she cast her eyes to her unadorned wristwatch. 'My, look at the time. I'm afraid you'll have to excuse me.'

Ben stood, momentarily flustered. Eleanor thumbed a few notes out from an elegant clip and left them on the table.

Ben opened his mouth.

'My treat,' she said smoothly. 'I am meant to be showing you around, remember. And no doubt we can continue our discussion. But it will have to be the day after tomorrow: I'm busy, I'm afraid?'

Quaintly she extended her hand, fingertips down, to which Ben felt his lips inexplicably drawn. She turned and it seemed a cab drew up behind her without bidding.

As she opened its rear door, Ben recovered sufficiently to call out, 'How shall I contact you?'

'You won't. I will. I promise.'

But which Order?'

'Didn't I say? Oh, Sons of Sion.'

And with that the cab door slammed, and the vehicle moved swiftly into the thinning evening traffic.

Colm Hegarty's words came to Ben as he watched the cab disappear, its driver anonymous in some kind of dark hood, 'We are members of an order, not a democracy'.

He decided to walk back across the city, his mind a maelstrom. Out across the Viale Vaticano he strode purposefully, heading for his hotel. Colonel Parker's words came to him again, 'Once is chance, twice is coincidence, three times is war'. Spying a public telephone booth, he slipped in and dialled the code for England: the colonel would not be in bed yet.

* * *

'Sir, Mountford here, not too late?' Ben quickly slipped into his clipped military speech.

'Ben!' came the booming voice, 'By God, that was quick. Only telephoned your bishop this afternoon.'

'Sir?' Ben replied, puzzled.

'We've had another attempt at your records Ben, and I was trying to get in touch via your diocese.'

Ben swiftly explained the apparent coincidence. 'Who from sir, do we know?'

'You bet,' chuckled the colonel. 'Got a return contact number and all. Our WAAF was really onto the case when your name flashed up.'

Ben waited expectantly.

'Ben,' came the voice solemnly, 'look at your watch. In ten minutes, hang up, walk away and find another telephone box. Then ring me with its number and I'll ring you back. Understood?'

'Affirmative, sir,' acknowledged Ben, his heart rate rising.

'The call came through two days ago, Ben, from the Irish Embassy,' the voice paused.

'Ireland, sir?'

'No, the Irish Embassy, I said.'

'Sir?' Ben frowned in the airless booth.

'The Vatican Office of the Embassy of the Republic of Ireland,' Parker paused again. 'Now, call me old-fashioned but: you, Ireland and my disappearing, supposedly dead nuclear physicist keep bouncing round my head. Have you anything to add?'

'This scientist, sir. You say you lost track of him out of Shannon airport, if I remember.'

Colonel Parker interrupted, 'Yes. Yes, I did. But we picked him up again travelling up the west coast.' Ben listened intently.

'Pure luck really, but he must have had some altercation or other with one of the locals in Sligo. Anyway, the Garda who attended the RTA used his name, and his registration number to do a PNC check over their short-wave radios. Then, as God was really smiling that day, the Yanks were training our 5th Para Brigade intelligence boys in the use of a UAV and were flying it over Lough Erne in Fermanagh. Anyway, they pick up the registration number on the waveband frequency scanners and bingo were following the good doctor live via sat-cam up the coast of Ireland.'

'You said you lost him, sir, a second time?'

'Mm yes, he drives through a little town named Burtonport and turns up into the Erigol Mountains.'

Ben's grip on the receiver tightened.

'Ten minutes, Ben.' The telephone clicked.

Gritting his teeth, he put the receiver down and exited the stifling booth. Looking in both directions, he could not see the telltale yellow of a telephone booth within eyesight and headed on towards the station.

Eighty metres behind him and on the opposite side of the road the taxi edged forward, its 'for hire' sign extinguished.

By the time Ben had found another telephone booth, he was outside Rome's main railway station. Of the row of a dozen booths, eight were occupied, one had the contents of an Italian reveller's stomach left over its cradle, and three were empty. Selecting the one with occupied booths either side Ben rapidly dialled up Parker's number. Speaking briefly, he pressed the disconnect button with his finger, all the while keeping the receiver to his ear. He turned round, idly scanning the busy concourse, waiting for the instrument to ring. As he did so a cab glided to a halt not ten yards away. His eyes moved to the crowds exiting the station, but as he did so the cab's driver turned momentarily towards him. As soon as the cabbie saw Ben looking in his direction, he turned back again. Of his face Ben could see nothing, but the man did appear to be wearing some kind of hood, which was strange in Rome's evening warmth, but even stranger as this was the second hooded cabbie Ben had seen that night. Then the telephone rang once, 'Mountford,' uttered Ben, his eyes on the cab.

'As I was saying,' cautioned Colonel Parker's unruffled voice, 'he turned up towards the mountains, but then took a small track through some trees. Unfortunately, the UAV was on a video-tracking-only training flight and had not had its ground-searching radar or heat detectors activated. Anyway, the track exited the trees following the fall line along the mountain. From digital enhancement, a small bungalow could be seen through the foliage. By this time, we've got the local Garda onto it.'

Ben's lips compressed in a mirthless smile as he struggled to define Officer Pat's idea of 'on to it'.

'Anyway, the UAV doesn't leave the area until the Garda turn up. But the cottage is empty, as is the garage. No Land-Cruiser, no Dr Schlatter.'

'Sir, the track up from Burtonport. Were there any other buildings in the area?'

'Apart from the small cottage no – unless you count the monastery about a quarter of a mile away.'

Ben listened, his mind racing, and his eyes fixed on the cabbie who was now talking into a small hand-held device. Monastery; the pub in Burtonport; Seamus's, 'I tell you something's not right,' as he muttered into his dark beer.

'Mountford, you there? Hello!'

'Yes, yes sir, sorry I was watching . . .' and then the taxi pulled away into the traffic. Shaking his head, he dismissed the cab and leant back in the warm booth. 'That monastery, sir. I don't think I told you this when I was in Hereford. Well, one night I took it upon myself to do a recce.'

'On a monastery? Are you mad?'

Ben persisted, leaving nothing out. As he got to the part about the infrared beam, its appearance even now crystal clear in his mind, Parker interjected, 'Ten minutes,' and the instrument hummed impotently at him.

It took three more random telephone booths to finish his story and by the time he had criss-crossed the area looking for different booths it was growing dark as he entered the dim, disinfectant smelling lobby of his hotel. The blonde receptionist slipped reluctantly out of the night office, smoothing down her short skirt. Beyond her Ben could see the outstretched legs of a well-built male with a can of lager balanced on one knee.

She handed him his key diffidently and turned to go back into the small office. 'Oh! Pardon, Padre. I forgot. A small parcel arrived earlier. And she reached underneath the counter, making no effort to hide the view as she leant down. Ben met her eyes as she handed over a small, heavy box: it was postmarked Northern Ireland. Nodding his head briefly in thanks, he headed for the lift.

The parcel was well wrapped with a double layer of old-fashioned heavy brown paper around a further layer of bubble wrap film. The whole, heavily covered in a kind of cargo tape. Ben sat at the small cheap desk, consumed by his task. At last, the final layer surrendered revealing a small oak casket approximately five inches square. The wrapping had contained a letter, addressed to him at his hotel. He noted that the letter's Dublin postmark was dated the day before he had arrived in Rome. A small brass plaque was set on the top of the box, such as one would have engraved for a school sports trophy.

Ben sat and stared at the neat engraving. For several minutes he sat immobile until at last, his hand drifted to the buff envelope. Fumbling with its sealed flap, he could not take his eyes from the glowing brass plaque – Father Raffique Alhambra 1959–2025.

Slowly Ben's fingers opened the buff envelope. There were two sheets of old-fashioned, heavy quality manila and the top sheet bore the legend Linsell Phelan & Co and was signed by a David Greenhalgh. Ben remembered the little man doffing his hat in front of the presbytery as Maria disappeared through the front gate.

Dear Father Mountford,

It is with sincere regret we have to inform you of the sudden death of Father Alhambra.

He was released into the care of the diocese during the unfortunate police investigations. I, myself, delivered Father Alhambra to the care of the brothers and he appeared in good health, albeit concerned about the police allegations.

Unfortunately, following a short illness that night, he passed away in the monastery.

As you know he was a refugee and a convert from Islam, and accordingly we have no records of relatives to whom we can return his ashes. Bishop Casey and I are of the opinion you would like to scatter his remains at what was for Father Alhambra his first refuge after fleeing Iraq.

With my sincere condolences,

David Greenhalgh, Linsell Phelan & Co.'

The second letter, headed using the same typeface Ben noted, was from the diocesan office of Bishop Casey expressing his condolences at Father Alhambra's passing.

Long moments passed for Ben as he sat in his austere room staring at the casket. Absently he removed the lid and stared at the fine grey ashes within. Suddenly he saw Raffy in the study that night, the look of pure terror on his face and the theatrical locking of the door.

Ben's mind drifted. His breath, warm in the cool night air on that Irish hillside, the fine red pencil of light bisecting it. Suddenly he blinked, his lethargy fell from him like a cloak and he felt the course of adrenalin surge through his veins.

The envelope. Maria's removal of it from the presbytery table, what had prompted him to hide the original? If she had taken it, would he now be alive?

Or in Rome for that matter? From behind a slightly loose leather covered cardboard back panel in his case, he retrieved Raffy's letter that he had retrieved, seemingly an age ago, from the tabernacle in Burtonport.

He read Raffy's letter in the anonymous security of the communal bathroom, inside one of the WC cubicles, with the hot taps running full bore filling the bathroom with steam and a stool jammed under the door handle to prevent anyone from entering. When he had finished, he was on the point of putting it back in his pocket when he had a better idea and tucked under the linoleum out of sight behind the lavatory bowl.

Back in his room, Ben dismissed his churning thoughts and knelt at his bed in prayer. After twenty minutes he got into bed and slept soundly for two hours. When he awoke, refreshed and determined, dawn was just lightening the sky.

He had a plan. Accordingly. he left the hotel, bidding the ever-present receptionist a cheery good morning. He walked briskly but was soon virtually jogging until he made a sharp turn down a small street where he stopped, counted to ten and returned to the main street retracing his steps slowly. He repeated this twice, each time he scanning the traffic for a ducking figure or a hurriedly turned face. Nothing.

Relaxing now, he made his way leisurely across the wakening city. Eventually he came to the east bank of the Tiber, just south of the Ponte Cavour. Walking slowly along the Lungotevere Marzio he spied his destination, the pale bulk of Castel St Angelo beckoning in the early light. This was where, he was convinced, Raffy's writings had led him. Looking at his watch, he cast his eyes up and down the commercial quarter overlooking the river. Finding a small stationer's and copy business, he settled down just along the street to await its opening.

CHAPTER 77

A lfonso visibly started as he looked up. Ben's rubber-soled combat boots had been put to good effect and he had managed to approach the bowed elderly head at the reception desk without alerting him. Ben beamed at Alfonso and produced his creased authority from Bishop Casey to view the archives. Alfonso, warming to the genial stranger, omitted his usual scrutiny and pushed the visitors' book to Ben without prompting.

While Alfonso busied himself at the table behind the reception desk, Ben's fingers lightly skimmed the previous entries and stopped when he found what was looking for: Sister Eleanor Plantard St Claire, Sons of Sion. The entry below that caused his eyes to widen fractionally. Unknown to Ben, Alfonso was also taking interest in what he had found: the mirror he was looking at was old, but it faithfully reflected the one above Ben's head and the view it afforded of the open visitors' book. Having seen what he needed to see, the old man cleared his throat as Ben was reaching for the pen to add his own entry.

Next came the typewritten postcard containing the question to which section of the archive the visitor required access. Ben hesitated a moment, then boldly wrote: 'Sons of Sion' and pushed it back to the curator.

Ben noted Alfonso's attempt to disguise his startled reaction. Recovering himself, the curator nodded briefly, although Ben saw his eyes flicking sideways towards a small door inset under the huge spiral ramp that led up into the centre of the building. Instead though, Alfonso shuffled off up the ramp leading to the main level. Ben followed the elderly man's gait, wondering about that glance to the small door and what lay beyond it.

As they proceeded upwards, the gentle curves on the beautiful, frescoed ceiling proclaimed Paul III's personal motto: *Festina Lente* at which Ben grimaced as he made the translation: 'Make haste slowly'. He was admiring the beautiful carvings and mildly erotic frescoes, images of a different era he surmised with faint amusement, when his mind was suddenly arrested with a blast of ice-cold clarity. Raffy, he knew, would not have risked his life or exhibited the level of terror Ben had witnessed, only to introduce Ben to what amounted to a glorified library to which he had just gained access to using the flimsiest of forgeries. Alfonso's involuntary glance was the key he decided.

Ben's fingers found a small coin, a coin of such insignificant weight it barely registered in his fingers. Rolling it gently off his fingertips it fell on the smooth stone of the gently sloping ramp, slightly behind the puffing Alfonso. Immediately Ben detected a faint movement of his silver head. So! A few yards further on, Ben flicked another coin, well to the left of Alfonso. Again, the slight, imperceptible movement. Ben's mind was made up. To the back of Alfonso's silver head he called softly, 'This isn't where Sister Plantard St Claire and Father James came is it?' No reaction from the shuffling figure.

Ben caught up with him easily and firmly spun him around in the crook of his arm. The pair sat on the low curving balustrade, the chamber silent, its ornate mosaic floor some eighty feet beneath them. Ben glanced casually round to make sure they were alone. Then he deftly hooked his boots around the carved stone pillars supporting the balustrade, leant backwards gently over the void, gripping the elderly man's shoulders as he toppled backwards. Alfonso threw his arms out and he cried in terror.

'So, we do have a voice, then,' Ben gently observed, all the while his arm keeping the squirming man firmly over the void. After a moment Ben let the wriggling man come back to balance on the stone balustrade. Keeping his arm firmly round him, Ben let his heaving breaths subside a moment.

'What is it that a sister of the Sons of Sion and Father James Mountford came to see, my friend? Is it further up here,' he indicated with his hand towards the remainder of the ramp, 'or were we closer downstairs?'.

No reply, just Alfonso's wildly gyrating eyes as he began to struggle again. Ben hooked both his feet firmly behind the pillars and leant swiftly back once more. Alfonso's wail of terror echoed around the marble mausoleum, 'No! No! I promise. Let me back, please. I beg!'

Swiftly, Ben pulled himself back, his stomach muscles gratefully relaxing: further out of condition than I thought, he grimaced. They retraced their steps and back at the bottom of the ramp Alfonso took a huge well-worn key from his belt and unlocked the door leading to stone stairs descending into the gloom. With a tug, Ben yanked the key from its chain and standing at the top of the stairs in the crude light of bulbs from the curved ceiling, carefully locked the door behind them. Then the pair descended into the darkness.

* * *

Across the mosaic floor, now dappled with sunlight, Barzini's cowl-clad figure thoughtfully put down the tourist leaflet he had been so assiduously studying. Hearing the old man's cry, Barzini had sought refuge behind the huge Doric columns and had overheard it all. He paused at the sturdy wooden door beneath the curving ramp listening intently but heard nothing. When the door refused to budge, he produced a small bunch of fine steel skeleton keys and began to work them in the lock.

* * *

Ben followed the shuffling figure of Alfonso, his eyes narrowed. He had scared the old man all right, but somehow, he sensed, he would not get all that he wanted out of him. Not yet at any rate. At the foot of the first flight of stairs Alfonso's gnarled hand reached to the wall and another ancient brass switch clicked satisfyingly as they went through a stone archway. The old man paused momentarily, his head moving fractionally to the left, then he resolutely turned right and set off down a long stone corridor, faster this time. Ben sensed his decision and in the same instant knew immediately Alfonso was leading him away from his goal.

342

As he followed the shuffling figure, his mind sprang into a sharpness that he had not experienced since leaving Hereford. His breath, silvery in that red pencil beam on that Irish hillside, Colm Hegarty in that boardroom with the armoured knight behind him, his cool grey eyes unfathomable as he told Ben they were 'part of an order not members of a democracy'. Eyes, blue eyes, the mysterious Elizabeth who was she? Maria turning up out of the blue followed immediately by the oily solicitor David Greenhalgh. And then, and then Raffy's unexplained death at the monastery, his ashes delivered to him to mourn. Or as a warning?

Ben's hand strayed to his pocket; he felt the large iron key he had ripped from Alfonso's belt. At least he was safe down here, he thought. Colonel Parker's face came to mind: trust your instincts all the time he used to say. And that recollection did it. Instinctively Ben knew he was not safe: in fact, he sensed mortal danger.

Barzini halted, frozen in mid-step as he descended the worn steps. Hearing returning footfalls he glanced around. No cover and no other option. So, he quickly unscrewed the light bulb above him, biting his lip as it seared his fingertips and then shrinking against the wall as he saw the elderly curator being frogmarched past the bottom of the stairs by his companion.

After negotiating two more flights of worn steps Ben's spirits were rising with confidence. They stopped at an ancient wooden door, its surface gnarled and worm-eaten with large square-headed bolts embedded across its surface. Alfonso produced a key, larger by half than the one Ben had relieved him of and rusty with age and lack of use. His eyes were downcast in defeat he turned to the door and inserted the key. Once again Barzini halted, this time slipping a small black shape from under his armpit. Ben reached past Alfonso and keeping eye contact, twisted the old key, in the same movement pushing the door inwards. Through it he found a small cell, which he illuminated after finding the old light switch to reveal that the cell was empty: devoid of any furniture, although there was a water trough, with a tap above on one wall.

Barzini paused further back along the passage from where he could see the open cell and the light spilling out across the floor and where, incongruously, he heard the sound of running water. Holding his Beretta at shoulder height, he softly approached the open door when suddenly the gushing sound stopped, and he froze. Moments later a deep grating noise emanated through the open door, coupled with a gentle movement in the floor that he sensed through the soles of his boots. He felt his way cautiously round the edge of the stone door jamb and risked a quick glance just in time to see a section of the solid stone wall at the end of the cell glide back into place.

The rotation stopped on the other side of the wall and the water in the trough slopped slightly over Ben's feet. The room they were now in was of an identical construction to the one they had just left, lined with the same finely dressed stone; but this one stretched away into the darkness and was made all the more confining by the shelves and racks that filled the small space. Alfonso was the first to move, stepping down from the trough, his stooped back straightened as he stood proudly in what Ben realised with undoubtedly his domain.

'Not so fast my friend; not so fast,' he said, grabbing the elderly curator by the shoulder as he made to set off into the darkness. 'Is this where Sister St Claire came?' He paused absorbing the scene. 'Why?' he went on without waiting for a reply.

Alfonso merely looked at him, a sadness in his eyes. Ben paused, waiting for a reply but none came. He pushed Alfonso against the wooden shelves. Angry, he saw Raffy's look that night, the box of ashes, Hegarty's stare. He needed answers, and he needed them now. His right hand moved to the elderly man's chin. Seeking and finding the nerve behind his jaw, Ben began to squeeze, the coldness in his eyes terrifying Alfonso more than the sense of creeping paralysis from his neck down.

'You need both of us to get out,' Ben hissed as the old man's eyes closed to the waves of nausea overwhelming him. Ben's mind clicked and he stepped back. After a moment Alfonso was strong enough to stand unaided, and he rubbed his jaw reflectively. 'This way,' he muttered sullenly, and stumbled off in between the dusty shelves.

By Ben's calculations they walked a good forty yards back into the archives. Lit intermittently by yellowing bulbs in bulkhead fittings, it was faintly musty and smelt of the centuries; but as he followed, he saw in Alfonso's careful walk that he was completely at home here. His fingers trailed lovingly over faded crimson, leather, hand-tooled ledgers that lay stacked in between chests of indeterminate age constructed of wood and sometimes leather, most sporting large iron bindings and ancient locks.

It did not take many minutes for Ben to pick up the dates on the shelves. In spidery handwriting on neat rectangles of faded cardboard, they recorded chronologically the records of the Roman Catholic Church from the first millennium. He had barely time to ponder the significance of this, before the elderly man stopped. Running a single gnarled finger along dry faded leather book spines he had halted at a particularly thick volume. In faded, chipped gold leaf at the top of the spine Ben saw 1314 as Alfonso's hand carefully pulled the volume from the shelf.

Without bidding from Ben, the old curator carefully laid the large volume down on a small table nearby. His fingers flicked carefully through the stiff parchment pages until he stopped and straightened. Then he looked at Ben when he said, 'This is what Sister St Claire was interested in. What did you say your surname was, Father?'

'Father Mountford,' Ben replied, uncertainly.

'Then you need to read this, Father.' he replied gravely, turning the volume to Ben. 'You have Latin I presume?'

Ben nodded briefly, running his finger along the neat manuscript. Translating as he read, the text read:

> In the year of our Lord anno domini 1314 under the bull of
> His Holiness Clement V Vicar of Christ on Earth the
> following souls are condemned to death for the crime of
> heresy, may their souls rest in peace: Jacque de Molay, Grand
> Master, Knights of Jerusalem; Ambrose le Vaal, Grand
> Chancellor of the Knights of Jerusalem; Godfroi of Ghent,
> Knight of the Order of Jerusalem.

Ben's finger stopped as he read the next passage. Alfonso watched the young, bowed head, his finger immobile on the yellowing parchment. For long moments the silence in the underground archive was absolute, the only movement both men's rising and falling chests. Ben was the first to move, taking in a swift breath he visibly squared his shoulders and continued with his finger, painstakingly translating the words, his lips moving soundlessly. Eventually, Alfonso could stand no longer on his old legs and he quietly slid to the floor, resting his back gratefully against leather volumes as Ben continued turning the pages one by one.

Eventually Ben stood up stiffly and returned the huge volume to its rightful place. He said nothing but helped the elderly librarian to his feet and in silence the two took their place over the water-filled trough and clasped each other as the wall slowly revolved.

The sudden grating caught Barzini unawares. He had had little choice but to wait in the bare cell not knowing whether his quarry would return by this route or not. As it was, he made his exit from the cell a trifle too late, and he had barely slipped out of the room when the two figures appeared waltz-like on the rotating trough.

Barzini fled noiselessly up the passageway heading for the first flight of stairs. Pausing, he could hear the pair making rapid progress towards him. At the foot of the first staircase, he made his decision. As he mounted the first step, he instantly regretted it: he only had the use of his skeleton keys, and

Father Mountford and the elderly archive curator would be upon him as he fumbled with them.

Leaping nimbly up the stairs, he saw the first missing bulb and his jaw clenched. At the top he reached up and seared his fingers for the second time as he unscrewed the glowing bulb there.

Ben and Alfonso mounted the staircase and climbed uncertainly to the inky blackness to the top. Alfonso was leading, his hand on the worn guide rail, and he never knew what hit him. With his target silhouetted against the passageway below, Barzini's foot caught the elderly man under the chin and his head snapped back with an audible crack as he somersaulted backwards. Ben never stood a chance; Alfonso's frame tumbled backwards out of the gloom without a sound and swept him down the stairs. Instantly, subconsciously, Ben relaxed and rolled with the flailing body and the two hit the bottom of the stairs in a tangle of arms and legs. Bruised and aching, Ben still managed to roll to one side and lie still: however, a glance at the angle of Alfonso's neck and his staring eyes told him all he needed to know.

From above he heard footsteps at the top of the stairs. Slowly and carefully, someone was descending the stone steps. The only part of Ben's body visible was his right boot. Quickly he unlaced it and wriggled his foot out, grimacing as he stood and looked around. Barzini paused three steps from the bottom. The crumpled figure of Alfonso told its own tale. Father Ben's leg disappeared behind the stone wall and did not move. Barzini's shoulders relaxed and he started down, the pistol extended in his hand. That was his second mistake.

The oak shelf had probably aged a couple of hundred years and hardened with age, its edge whistling out of the darkness caught Barzini squarely on the bridge of his nose. His reflexes had just sufficient time to pull the trigger sending a round ricocheting down the corridor as his head exploded in stars. Pausing only to re-tie his boot and pick up Barzini's weapon, Ben glanced at his garb with a grimace and mounted the stairs two at a time.

Presently, breathing hard, he stepped into the mosaic floored hallway and closed the door behind him. Turning the key in the lock and leaving it there he strode out into the sunshine and disappeared into the crowds.

CHAPTER 78

After some hesitation Eleanor had turned into the small cul-de-sac off the Via Principe Amadeo. There it was, just as her mother had described: the Hotel Ambrose, nestling anonymously in the corner of the nondescript street, the epitome of a down at heel working men's lodging. As if for reassurance, she fumbled for the small brass cruciform key in her purse, passed to her by her mother's gnarled and twisted hands. She reflected fleetingly that it was probably the last time she would touch her mother alive. So, pressing the key to her lips, she strode towards the hotel.

* * *

The four men sat at the polished table, three of them had arranged the fresh white surcoats around their chairs. Their faces were impassive while they waited, as the Council had waited for hundreds of years for the arrival of their Grand Nautonier. Only Ortolani, sombre in black from head to toe, displayed any kind of animation. Impatiently chewing, he glanced at his watch and the slim folder in front of him. Where the hell was Barzini, he pondered? Unlike him to be late. The possibility of failure never occurred to Ortolani and he shook his head as if to rid himself of this nagging worry.

The hum of the lift sent the three men to their feet and Ortolani to the double doors. As he opened them, Eleanor swept into the room, her face ignoring his look of surprise. Silently she took her place at the head of the table and for a moment she stood observing each man. None returned her stare. She wore a medieval surcoat clasped at her throat with a gold encrusted ruby the size of a pigeon's egg.

* * *

Earlier that day in an anonymous office housed at the rear of the Institute for Religious Works, Hugh Claire had received a short, shocking phone call. An international call, it caused his normally ebullient features to slide into solemnity and his shoulders sagged as he placed the instrument back on its cradle and sat immobile for a while, staring into space.

In a sense, he had awaited this moment for much of his adult life. Plantard St Claire carried neither rancour nor jealousy at his sister's succession over him; in fact he had carved out a successful position for himself and the Order within the Vatican Bank. As senior aide to the Vice President of the Institute for

347

Religious Works, he was placed high enough to affect clandestine transfers of funds and associated activities, but yet remain anonymous on the world stage.

He picked up the telephone and told his secretary to allow no more incoming calls. With any disturbance now taken care of, he crossed the room and deftly swirled the dial of a small wall safe, opened the door and extracted two items. A small cylinder wrapped in brown paper he placed on the corner of the desk, but the square wooden casket some five inches square he placed reverently on his blotter.

Back in his chair, he opened the smooth wooden lid and gazed at the gold encrusted ruby brooch, the size of a small egg that lay inside. Regarded by the ancients as a symbol of freedom, charity, dignity and above all divine power, it had been cut from the throat of a Moslem pilgrim to Mecca in 1185, by Raynald of Châtillon. Unfortunately, the pilgrim in question happened to be the fourth cousin of Salah al Din Yusuf Ibn Ayyub, better known as Saladin. In swift and bloody retribution, Saladin invaded Jerusalem in July 1187 and annihilated the Crusader army at the Battle of Hattin. Reynaud was executed excruciatingly by Saladin personally, but the ruby made its way to the Order to be passed from Grand Nautonier to Grand Nautonier on each other's death and was worn to address meetings of the Inner Council.

He picked up the telephone again and dialled directly the personal *assessore* to the Holy See and Pontiff in person. Within one hour, Hugh was gently ushered into a sparsely furnished room on the top floor of the Vatican apartments. He placed the two items on the desk as he heard the door close gently behind him. In silence the seated figure raised his head slightly to study them. With considerable difficulty the frail figure raised his head further and their eyes met: pale rheumy eyes meeting a cold blue stare. Hugh Plantard St Claire sat down slowly.

* * *

A few hours later, in an altogether more sumptuous apartment overlooking the Cortile del Belvedere, he stood in front of his sister and clasped the brooch to her creamy white surcoat. Then he swiftly knelt in front of her as she held the paper cylinder in her right hand. She gazed down at her brother and her eyes slid to her right hand. More important than the bauble at her throat, she carried confirmation of Clement V's ambition: an ambition that was nearer fulfilment now than at any time in the preceding 700 years.

* * *

The surcoat was made the finest linen and from its folds as it hung from her slight frame its rich crimson silk lining could be seen. Eleanor's delicate hands appeared from behind those folds bearing a small wrapped cylindrical parcel. Turning to Ortolani, she nodded briefly. He crossed in silence to the panelled wall behind her and gently removed the heavy framed Van Eyck and, laying it on the table in front of the men, deftly worked on its back with a small tool. In moments he had removed the painting from its frame and placed it out on the polished surface. Glancing at Eleanor, he picked up the cylinder and with sure movements removed its heavy wrapping paper and unrolled the ancient canvass onto the table next to the painting. Its edges folded back on themselves obstinately, as if they were not ready for the light. Muttering, Ortolani crossed the room for a second time to a small cabinet and returned with four heavy grit-like balls, which he placed on the rebellious corners. The five in the room stared silently at the painting, each alone with his thoughts.

Eleanor began, 'His Holiness Clement V gave that painting to my ancestors over 700 years ago following the execution of de Molay and the top twelve commanders of the Sovereign Knights of Jerusalem. It was handed to us to keep the eternal flame burning for a secret organisation, the likes of which the world had not seen before.'

Then she paused to look at the armoured figure at the end of the room. The men behind her stared, transfixed by the ancient cross carefully stitched onto the brilliant white linen. It was faded and ragged, held only by a fine, barely discernible white mesh, but the original blood red cross, faded by down the centuries, still held their eyes. 'The cross you see on my back before you,' continued Eleanor, 'was taken from de Molay's cell the night before his execution by the King of France. Handed down by Grand Nautonier, it has become the symbol of our fight and support for the Holy Roman Church.'

She stopped and turned slowly, her long linen surcoat rustling on the floor around her. 'When the two halves of the painting come together, then Urban's prophecy will come true.' Her voice rose, sternly and with a depth she never knew she had. 'Death to the enemies of Christ, death to the infidel unbeliever!' Raising her arm from her surcoat's rich folds her eyes bored into each of the men, 'Dieu le veut!' she cried.

As one they rose their right arms, and repeated, 'Dieu le veut! Dieu le veut!' Then Eleanor sought Ortolani's eyes and he removed her cloak, before a further nod indicated that the five should sit.

Various historians had pointed out over the centuries the apparent imbalance of the Van Eyck work. The magnificent portrayal of Urban II on his throne in front of the Cathedral of Clermont, massed thunderclouds above, and yet a ray of the brightest sun falling on him and his court. Biblical in its portrayal, Urban's outstretched mitre followed by adoring soldiers resplendent in shining armour, splashed with the blood red cross patée. Now in front of

349

the silent men, they understood the message brought by the diminutive woman at the head of the table. The rent in the canvass, its edge as sharp as if it was cut yesterday, nestled up to its famous brother.

Over the centuries the original Van Eyck had been seen as a largely symbolic work; its apparent message clearly showing a few terrified mujaheddin of Saladin, their traditional white dish dash and turbans in bloody disarray as they fled the armoured cavalry of Urban II. The addition of the missing half instantly completed the image the artist had intended to convey. The few fleeing infidel had turned into a full-scale rout. Soldiers, women, children and animals were shown in panic-stricken flight across the sands of Arabia. From the right-hand side of the now balanced picture, the richness and culture of Europe was depicted in its fine buildings and fabrics from where the artist led the eye across to the deserted wastes of Arabia. Nestling in those blood-soaked sands, as the Crusaders ran amok in the seething, fleeing humanity, rose a structure familiar to millions who made the once in a lifetime pilgrimage to the home of the Prophet. Under Van Eyck's brush, the black square of the Kaaba was shown rent by cracks and falling masonry, corpses lay littered around its darkened walls, horribly mutilated or showing signs of a pox-ridden death. Across the canvas stared Urban II, his face impassive, surrounded by rich golden light and his massed armies.

Eleanor broke the silence, 'Enough of history. Now, to the future,' she said firmly. Rapidly the two paintings were cleared away and from under the table Ortolani produced two large rolls of paper. The first, spread out using the same heavy grit balls, revealed a large-scale map of the Arabian Peninsula, with the borders of Saudi Arabia clearly marked in red. The second roll was more of an engineering drawing that, to untutored eyes, made no sense at all. Eleanor moved softly round the table, a long narrow pointer in her delicate fingers as she talked. If the men registered any shock at her words, none showed it.

* * *

It was almost an hour before Eleanor concluded her soft discourse. 'You've addressed the warning from Burtonport?' she asked Ortalini, her eyebrows raised. However, if Ortolani was surprised that she knew he had received information that morning, he kept it well hidden.

'Barzini's attending to it as we speak, ma'am.' She picked up the uncertainty in his voice and raised her eyebrow fractionally. As she did, a telephone bleeped from his jacket, the relief evident on his face as he answered it. 'Si?'. Unintelligible noises came from the handset into the room. Ortolani frowned, his face changed to a deathly pallor, 'Si, si, I understand, I'm on my way now. Don't worry he won't talk.' He thumbed the handset and slipped it back into his jacket. His worried eyes sought Eleanor's. She was already appraising him coolly.

'Barzini followed the man Burtonport warned me about.' Eleanor nodded softly. 'He went to the Archives and somehow got Alfonso to take him our archives.' He paused.

'And?' softly uttered Eleanor.

'That was my local contact in the Carabinieri over on the Lungotevere. When the staff locked up this afternoon, they couldn't find the curator. Someone noticed the key in the door of the cellars and went down. There they found Barzini semiconscious with his face a mess and old Alfonso, the curator, dead at the foot of the stairs. Barzini's in custody and that's where I'm going. Don't worry.'

'I'm not the one worrying.' Her eyes caught his and he shivered. 'Let me know of the outcome. Meanwhile I have a date for tonight. By the way, you haven't got a picture of who Barzini was following have you? You never know – someone less talented may spot him?'

Ortolani fumbled in the folder on the table and handed Eleanor several typewritten sheets with a photograph stapled to the top corner. Suddenly it was her turn to match his pallor.

Chapter 79

This is the BBC from London, on Tuesday 17 July at 12.00 GMT.

The British Seismological Society this morning announced news of an earth tremor from the Saudi Arabian peninsula measuring more than 7.4 on the Richter Scale. Confirmation is difficult owing to the exclusion of non-Muslims from the epicentre located around the Holy City of Mecca. As further details are released, we will bring you the information later in the bulletin.

Further News: In a surprise announcement this morning, Vatican Radio announced the private visit of the Saudi Grand Mufti for an audience with Pope Leo XIV. The Vatican has kept the visit low-profile, following the previous pope's unsuccessful visit to the Greek Orthodox Church some years ago. It is hoped that the Grand Mufti, who is widely regarded as a moderate Sunni cleric, will help the Vatican to bring conciliation to the current turmoil in the Middle East. His visit is not without criticism from within his own ranks, and particularly the Wahhab Sunnis of Saudi Arabia. Sources in Iran speak of the betrayal of Islam to the West. There will be considerable interest in the Grand Mufti's visit from the large number of senior Muslim clerics gathered for a special Haj in the holy city of Mecca.

Ben sat on the edge of his bed in his sparsely furnished room. He had retrieved Raffy's carefully penned pages, and they lay scattered at his feet on the worn linoleum; he held the final sheet for a long time without really looking at it.

A shrill ring from the cheap bedside telephone startled him. When it rang a second time he lunged across the bed to pick it up.

The receptionist was bored, indifferent, 'Sister Eleanor says she will send a car in half an hour.'

He mumbled his agreement and slowly replaced the instrument. Was she part of this? Was he seeing ghosts? His mind rationalised. Rubbing his shoulders ruefully, he realised his bruises were no ghosts: somebody, somehow wanted him very much quiet about his access to the hidden archives.

A glance at the angle of Alfonso's neck had told him he would not be volunteering any more information. That left the mysterious figure he had laid low; the one who knew his business and had been waiting in the shadows at the top of the stairs. Shaking his head he collected up Raffy's manuscripts and put them hurriedly back under a loose corner of the bathroom linoleum.

He was washed and changed and making small talk with the peroxide receptionist when a car horn sounded outside. To his surprise it was a long, black Mercedes with darkened windows and Vatican number plates. He opened the rear door wide and warily to check the interior before entering. Frowning at himself, he sank back into the soft upholstery.

The driver was taciturn, merely grunting at Ben's attempt at conversation as he wove the big vehicle through the heavy traffic. Ben soon gave up and leant back, to look out of the windows as they cruised through the city. His knowledge of Rome's geography was scant, but it was with slightly rising consternation he realised the Mercedes was making its way towards the Ponte Sant'Angelo, the very bridge he had crossed that morning.

His hunch was probably right: no one would have discovered the elderly archivist by now unless the monk he had rendered unconscious had managed to raise the alarm. So, he kept his face impassive to the rear-view mirror as the driver pulled up just short of the famous bridge in front of a modern glass and stainless-steel restaurant frontage.

The driver remained silent as he held open the rear door. Ben got out, noted that pavements were surprisingly uncrowded and was about to comment on that when he was rewarded by a thump of the door closing and the vision of the car merging smoothly into the evening traffic. Setting his shoulders he pushed open the restaurant's glass door.

She was sitting on the mezzanine overlooking the busy restaurant. The little area held only four tables and three of them sported a sign reading *riservato* on their pristine tablecloths. Perfect, she had decided.

She saw the maître'd intercept the tall man at the door and watched as, with his head bowed, he listened to Ben. With a nod and a gesture, he threaded his way through the busy diners to the spiral staircase leading to the mezzanine floor. He was devilishly good looking she mused as she rose to greet him, offering a small, outstretched hand to his lips.

She had carefully chosen her dress for the evening: nothing too expensive; sophisticated yet simple enough for a sister to wear. Set against her slightly olive complexion, the cream linen dress fell three-quarter length to just above her elegant calves; edged with the finest of fine blue brocade it matched perfectly her clear blue eyes. She wore no jewellery except for a golden crucifix on a light chain that hung tantalisingly above the cut of her dress.

Her choice of restaurant, the latest most fashionable in the Trastevere district with its decor of pale wood, stainless steel and soft lighting, was stunning.

Ben was mesmerised. Was this the sister he had been introduced to only yesterday? He was aware of his interest quickening as they engaged in small talk over the menu. When the maitre'd's feet could be heard on the stairway, Eleanor let Ben order in halting Italian: crostini potatoes with goat's cheese and rocket to start, followed by the classic veal dish Ossobuco.

Eleanor studied the wine list, however, before asking, 'Do you have a preference, Ben?'

'No. No, you choose.'

'Very well: Châteauneuf-du-Pape, the Beaucastel, please,' she said firmly, handing back the wine list. 'It was the preferred wine of the Papacy in the fourteenth century when we, I mean the Pope, was exiled in Avignon during the Schism'.

Ben raised his eyebrows. Changing subject, she continued, 'Did you enjoy your visit to the archives?'

Ben returned her quizzical look 'Yes. Fortunately, I had authorisation from my bishop in Ireland to access the private archives, for which I was deeply grateful. Our family have been Catholics for over 700 years; I was keen to do some research but alas, I ran out of time. And the archivist had another visitor, a monk I believe. Perhaps I'll get the chance to go back tomorrow'.

Ben continued smoothly, 'How long did you say you were in Rome for?'

'My duties mean I visit rarely, Ben. So, not long, I'm afraid.'

'Yes, I saw your name in the visitors' book.' He did not elaborate and let the conversation lapse awkwardly.

Eleanor let the small silence develop as the first course arrived. 'I took a Father Mountford there once ... a relation?'

Ben nodded effusively. 'My brother. He's with some order in Florence, Neocatechumenals I think.' Eleanor nodded, her eyes cool. 'Part of the Opus Dei, aren't they?' Ben pressed.

'Perhaps. Perhaps not. We tend to keep ourselves to ourselves.'

'We? You mean, your Sons of Sion?'

Eleanor swallowed the last piece of goat's cheese elegantly and dabbed her lips with her napkin. 'Some orders are just rhetorical discussion groups, but some carry swords beneath our pious exteriors,' she continued softly so Ben had to lean forward to catch her words. 'We sent Escriva 'out' in 1928 and his organisation has been hugely successful in arresting the decline of our values and influence.'

Ben raised his hand slightly, 'You say, Escriva. He's the founder of Opus Dei? Came out? Out of what, if he was the founder?'

Eleanor sipped her wine carefully and said little as the large white plates of steaming veal arrived. She looked at Ben after the waiter had gone; the restaurant's distant hubbub weaving a cocoon of privacy. She felt her mother's hand on hers, knowing that the mantle of Grant Nautonier had passed. This was her decision and hers alone. She felt empowered.

Lifting her chin fractionally, her blue eyes regarded Ben softly when told him, 'You're a soldier, Ben. Battles are not the end of a war: the struggle is unceasing.'

Ben's thoughts flashed briefly to Colonel Parker's last words, while Eleanor continued, 'Opus Dei was conceived as a response to the worldwide surge in Communism in the early part of the last century. We needed a backbone to counter the greatest threat to our Church since the Reformation. It took us fifty years, but we stood firm, and history records the result.'

Ben smiled. 'You're not surely claiming credit for the fall of Communism?'

'In no small measure, Ben: in no small measure. It was no coincidence that Communism wasn't defeated in military terms. After all, wasn't it Stalin who dismissed our threat? But that it imploded, starting with John Paul's homeland.' Ben had to agree and nodded sagely.

'Ben, the twentieth century has been an unwelcome diversion for the true soldiers of Christ.' She paused, watching him carefully. 'Did you win the war in Guatemala, Ben?' she asked softly, her knife elegantly slicing into the pale meat. He kept his face impassive, but his Adam's apple bobbed up and down. Eleanor watched and waited as the silence developed.

Ben nodded slowly, the instant question forming but resolutely pushed to the back of his mind. 'Some wars are never ending,' he began.

'Exactly!' she interjected.

He ignored the interruption and carried on, 'As my last CO observed. Life is a constant fight of good versus evil is it not?'

Triumphantly her eyes sparkled. 'Archbishop Marcinkus himself has said many times "You can't run a church on Hail Mary's alone."' Ben nodded; he was aware of the archbishop she mentioned: he oversaw the Vatican Bank.

She continued vivaciously, lightness in her tone: a new confidence. 'Think of us as one army, Ben. Some preach. Some administer. Some attend to finances. And some fight for our future.'

'You mean like a specialist unit?' interjected Ben innocently, raising his eyes. She nodded emphatically. Ben continued, 'You mean the Swiss Guards in the Vatican?' his face open.

Eleanor answered with a disdainful sniff, but acknowledging the riposte with a gracious bow of her head. She smiled, 'The veal's excellent, is it not?' Ben concurred watching her eyes: blue eyes. Eleanor continued, 'We recruit right at the start Ben, at theological colleges all over the world. Only a dozen or so a year, selected usually for some degree of military discipline or ancestry. They become our sleepers, sometimes dormant for years.'

'Sounds like blackmail to me,' Ben said slowly.

'Sometimes yes: young priests are extremely susceptible to certain forms of flattery.'

The eyes: blue eyes. Maria forcing his back over the hall table in that distant presbytery; Elizabeth coolly appraising him from her ancient typewriter back in Liverpool.

'Some, of course, we lose as they leave the priesthood. And some,' she paused, looking into his eyes, 'return.'

Ben felt the velvet glove closing round him. He ignored her last words. 'So, who do you fight today, Sister, now that Communism is dead?' he smiled openly.

Eleanor said nothing for a minute or two as they savoured their meal and sipped the superb wine: a favourite of past popes, indeed. Ben glanced round the restaurant. This too was a favourite with the Vatican hierarchy, judging from the amount of black smock shirts and liturgical purple. Even so, it was no different to any smart restaurant anywhere in the world: good food, great wine, conversation and interesting company. Eleanor's soft tones drew his attention back to the table.

'We fight an enemy almost as old as ourselves,' she continued. 'One that many credit with civilising influences that gave us the Renaissance; an enemy whose written word has not changed for 1,300 years and whose influence in the last one hundred has been nothing short of disastrous for Western Christianity.' There was steely look in her eyes when she told him, 'We fight an enemy with no regard for his own life either now, or when we started in the first Crusade.'

Ben blinked at the historical span of her argument. 'Surely great religions try to live peacefully together?'

Her eyes blazed fractionally and for a moment Ben felt a shiver go up his spine. 'Evangelism is just a public policy,' she spat. Ben leant back thinking that this the moment when the otherwise perfect evening would start to turn ugly. But he was spared when the dark look in her eyes was replaced by a sparkle and the smile that started to form on her lips. He laughed in relief, and she joined in, chuckling with happy mirth.

He might have puzzled at this sudden change in mood, but her eyes were flirting with him now as she asked archly, 'And will you remain married to the Church, Father?'

'I was taught a long time ago that a team is more important than the individual,' he fenced. She pursed her lips as if making her mind up. She made as if to speak but he continued softly, 'You analyse the struggle correctly, but a little extremely?

'The views of the silent majority do not tend to get heard; in a sense we're governed by what the media and elected leaders think; which, in fact, should be the reverse. The media and politicians should react to our thoughts.

'All over the world, the old order – or perhaps the order that has dominated the last fifty years – is in retreat.'

She observed him with rapt attention, her food forgotten. 'Just maybe,' she thought, 'Just maybe, please God, he is the one.' She shifted on her chair in response to a different sensation and slipped her bare foot over Ben's.

He feigned no interest, taking a long sip of wine and continuing 'My family, God knows, has seen its share of fighting over the years: either for God or Country, or sometimes both,' and he let the sentence hang.

'Your ancestors fought for Rome before,' Eleanor stated flat and deadpan.

'Yes, I saw in the archives today. It's odd, really. I mean, we've had a picture of a Henri de Mountford in the library at home with a castle in the background. Now I know it to be the Temple Mount in Jerusalem.'

'Was he wearing the cross patée?' she asked softly.

'Pardon?' 'The cross patée: the crimson cross of the one true Church?' her eyes sparkling.

'Well yes, he has the surcoat over his armour. But the Templar leaders were executed in the 1400's, surely?'

'It was a public betrayal and execution of the Knights of Jerusalem,' she continued, her voice lower and with a throaty timbre about it that stirred Ben. 'You saw your ancestor, yes?' Ben nodded, only hours before his finger had softly glided down the ancient parchment, his surname leaping out at him over the centuries.

Eleanor leant back studying Ben and for a moment he felt as if his inner self-being was carefully taken apart. What was it with him and women with blue eyes like hers? He shifted in his seat, becoming uncomfortable under her gaze.

'But a de Mountford did not die with De Molay,' she continued, aware that she was starting to weaken the armour of his resolve. 'As our records show, there was an amazing deception by Clement V,' she said in admiration.

Ben raised his glass, 'If I recall, fourteen Knights of the Temple of Jerusalem were executed in Paris by burning at the stake.'

Eleanor leant forward again, her heavy gold crucifix dangling temptingly above the valley of her breasts. Ben was intrigued by this woman. His brain felt the same forced arousal as his by now, almost painful, erection. She watched his eyes as her own began to smoulder with victory. 'You asked me who we fight? Let me ask you in return; as a military man, what was wrong with the attacks on and before 11 September 2001?'

Ben sniffed in surprise, his ardour cooling somewhat. 'Well,' he began, 'total surprise, but the response far outweighed their effectiveness. They twitched the tail of the tiger without a thought to the consequence. And in a similar vein the attacks on 7 October resulted the same. Whipping up religious fervour and little else, they left their heartlands undefended and turned the majority against them. At least initially.'

Eleanor nodded, 'Some say that their biggest mistake was leaving a trail direct to their homelands.'

Ben was intrigued at her line of thought. 'Difficult to fly a passenger aircraft into buildings in the heart of New York and not leave a trail, I would have thought.' Eleanor merely inclined her head with another of her little smiles. Her foot sought his and a small warm toe wriggled in the hairs of his lower leg.

CHAPTER 80

Payment for the meal, dismissed by Eleanor with a firm shake of her head, appeared to consist of a scribbled signature on the bill proffered by the maitre'd. They had barely stepped out of the restaurant when the long low Mercedes 500 SEL pulled silently to the kerb. At the driver's invitation, they ducked into the softly lit interior and sat back as the car soundlessly glided away.

Eleanor had carelessly draped her cashmere shawl over the armrest between them, and while she kept up a rapid-fire of conversation with the burly, cowled driver, her fingers were busy under the shawl describing slow, lazy circles of every increasing diameter on Ben's inner thigh. Ben was on the point of losing control when the vehicle halted at the huge wrought iron gates of the Giardini Vatican and, much to his disappointment Eleanor withdrew her hand and lowered her window. Immediately one of the uniformed Swiss Guards stooped to her, sixteenth-century halberd grinding on the floor.

No sooner had the electric window slid to a halt and the rugged features of the Guard appear, than with a flash of a card in her slim hand, he stood quickly to attention. The car barely slowed as he bellowed his order and to Ben's amusement a detail of his guard appeared from nowhere to push open the huge gates. Slipping through, they entered the largely secret and private gardens of the Vatican.

Eleanor left the window down but replaced her hand and continued as she had done, letting the heavy scents of the gardens at dusk steadily pervade the car. Once more Ben felt himself being equally steadily aroused to the point of ecstasy and he leant back in the seat savouring this tsunami of delightful sensations.

When the car glided to a halt a second time, it was beside a small door set in the main building. From his brief perusal of his guide to the Vatican, Ben picked out skyline of the Vatican Museum, amongst other things, home to the Cappella Sistina. The couple got out in silence and, as the car glided away, Eleanor produced a key with which she opened the small oak door and turned on a light switch.

To Ben's astonishment, he found himself in the entrance to the famous chapel where, every day, thousands of tourists queued to catch a glimpse of the celebrated paintings and frescoes within.

'All the world hastened to behold this marvel and was overwhelmed, speechless with astonishment,' Eleanor said in hushed tones, leading Ben by the hand. He nodded in acknowledgement of Vasari's familiar litany, his neck craning to see the marvels around him. 'Botticelli, Pinturicchio and Ghirlandaio on the walls,' she pointed out with her outstretched arm, 'and the granddaddy of all on the ceiling, Michelangelo himself,' she paused, guiding his arm around her slim waist. 'However, some say the ceiling of the Gesu by I'l Baciccia is better.' She let the provocation lie pregnant in the atmosphere.

'And where would I see that?' he responded lightly.

'Why, I have a copy in my apartment upstairs,' she responded with a warm open smile. 'Shall we?'

Keeping his arm firmly round her waist, they headed for a small flight of stairs signposted to the Vatican Lapidary Gallery. As they mounted them, windows overlooking the Cortile del Belvedere gave a glimpse into a darkened private world, within the lights ablaze in greater Rome.

At the top of the stairs, frowned upon by the various renditions of past popes adorning the walls, the couple paused. Eleanor's lips puckered in amusement as she caught Ben watching her chest rise and fall beneath the thin material of her dress. In front of them in gold letters on a varnished nameplate lay the legend Borgia Apartments and an ornate arrow leading left.

At once it was obvious from the wealth and the decor of the passage that they were now in the part of the Vatican not frequented by tourists: the Apostolic Palace. The carpet sank beneath their feet, laid on a floor of the palest polished oak. At intervals along the long corridor, waist-high marble plinths sported busts and figurines of past popes of a quality and luminosity not seen downstairs. From the ceiling, at slightly larger intervals, gold and crystal chandeliers cascaded a beautiful soft golden light over the entire corridor. Large, polished doors led off the corridor, furnished with beautifully cast and polished door handles and locks. Letting his arm slip from her waist, Eleanor softly and silently led Ben along this magnificent corridor. At the very end she turned, a brass key in her hand, as though that was the cue he had been waiting for,

In a fluid move, Ben slipped his hands round her waist and pushed her against the huge door, her eyes, her blue eyes, gazed up at him dilating with every second. She snaked her bare forearm around his neck and brought his lips to hers. She held back fractionally refusing his bid to part her lips, then she raked her nails through the thin material of his shirt down one side of his spine. Involuntarily Ben's buttocks clenched and he thrust forward. Slowly his tongue found hers. Freeing herself breathlessly she put the key in the lock and pushed open the door.

If Ben had been astounded at the passageway to her apartment, it was nothing compared to the sight that now met his eyes. Every wall was covered in the most ornate frescoes from artists represented throughout the Vatican. The room was a complete temple to the Baroque, but as Ben looked around in awe, he saw that voluptuous figures of women and men were engaged in far more lascivious behaviour than those on public display below.

Eleanor's feet clicked loudly on the mosaic floor as she led him across the magnificent room. The next set of doors were no less ornate than the first, but the rich clicking of the door catch had barely faded when the next, smaller room revealed itself. Shocking in its simplicity, it was floored in the palest of ash, and the walls were completely plain save for a detailed plaster fresco around the top.

Light from invisible sources softly filled the room, in the centre of which stood a small altar. This too was stunning in the simplicity of its white marble and matching altar cloth overhanging its edges. Against it leant a magnificent medieval sword and at its rear stood a simple wooden cross. In front of the altar, two plain kneelers lay in front of a simple oak rail. While a perfect cone of white light fell on a glistening object centred on the altar. Legend held that Joseph of Arimathea had drunk from this chalice for forty-two years during his imprisonment. It stood bronzed and mature, tall and slim. Thin stemmed, it flared sensuously into a beautiful bowl flanked by two handles of perfect proportion. The Chalice of the Eucharist, drank from by Jesus at the Last Supper, known throughout the ages as the Holy Grail, stood in the cone of light.

Eleanor let go of Ben and knelt at the small altar; he followed suit. For long moments the pair knelt, silent in that private sanctuary. Ben's hands were clasped together but he could not take his eyes off the gleaming vessel.

Eleanor softly cleared her throat, 'Those that drink from the Chalice have the strength to vanquish the enemies of the one true Church, Ben. And the sword was used by Charles Martel at the Battle of Tours in AD732 when the Muslims were routed.

Here was the understanding he had been searching for. Was this the end of his lifelong quest?

As if seeking assurance, he turned his head from the altar to stare at the beautiful woman at his side. A sense of resolve and inner peace suffused him; the sense grew until he knew with absolute certainty where his destiny lay. He thought of himself leaning against the giant aircraft's wheel in the heat of Guatemala, the small buff envelope in his hand. He had reached another crossroads in his life.

Nodding, his mouth incapable of speech, he rose and took her hand. The only other door in the room led to a master bedroom. With its door closed behind them, as if to protect the previous room's contents she uttered just three words, 'Dieu le veut', and threw herself eagerly at him.

Eleanor had spent so long arousing him that he felt he was going to explode from the top of his head. Like two teenagers, they tore and ripped at clothing and then paused breathless and naked to eye each other briefly. Not only was Eleanor insatiable, but he also found to his mild surprise a youthful vigour he had not experienced since his encounter at the seminary in Liverpool.

* * *

The first storm passed, and she lay on her back in the large bed. The breeze from the open windows teased her nipples, red, raw and erect, her crucifix lay in a small pool of perspiration in between her breasts. Propping himself up on his elbow, he watched her chest rise and fall. He brushed her lips gently, sensuously, with his and she arched her neck, cat-like forcing him to kiss her throat. He kept his eyes open and watched her as his tongue flicked lightly across her body. This prompted her to grasp his head and guide him, softly moaning with abandon. This time she kept her eyes closed and as he rose above her, he watched her face contort in exquisite agony. Even so, he felt strangely detached. As he gently rotated his hips he saw a passport on the bedside table.

The storm subsided a second time and, as the two lovers lay entwined, Ben reached for the dark brown document. Flicking idly through with one hand, whilst one eye was buried on her damp chest, he watched the international entry and exit stamps march across the pages. As the last page fluttered quietly down, he caught the passport number: 003. He knew there were only 400 such passports issued in the Vatican and the sudden realisation left him completely out of his depth. For the first time in his life, he felt uncertain. Twice more that night she awoke him with her soft demands, rousing him to heights he never knew possible. Eventually they slept, foetal-like as dawn broke the sky.

But when he woke, his mind was instantly alive. He rolled up and sat on the bed. She slept; her hair plastered across her cheek and an arm out flung. He eyed his surroundings and silently shook his head. Another door opposite the one they came in opened to a beautiful marble shower room, where doused himself in a bracing cascade of cold water. Strangely Father Michael's words came to him as the needle jets stung his bare skin. As he stepped out of the shower and wrapped a large fresh towel around him, his eyes fell on his kitbag. Yes, his kitbag from his hotel room. Opening it he saw every item had been washed and pressed.

A small noise made him look up. 'I had your things brought over, Ben, forgive me, but I thought it easier that way.' He could only nod mutely as she advanced across the marble. 'You don't want me to send them back, do you?' she murmured as her arm encircled his neck.

'Oh, my God,' he thought. 'Raffy's letter!' as his hand drifted to the warm cleft that seemed so naturally to fit his palm.

CHAPTER 81

Al Bahah, Hijaz Mountains, Saudi Arabia: Eight months earlier.

Michael Lindeman leant back in his large leather chair: for the second time in as many minutes he glanced at his Patek Philipe watch that nestled insignificantly in the blonde hairs on his thick wrists. He looked longingly at the top drawer of his filing cabinet. No, he decided, it was not worth it. When His Highness Hussein Al-Saud, Minister of the Interior of the Kingdom of Saudi Arabia was due to pay a visit to his site it would be better protocol if no alcohol was in view. Especially as, worryingly, the phone call had indicated that the Grand Mufti would be accompanying his Royal Highness.

Wearily he glanced at his watch again. Despite the reassuring hum of the air conditioning his portacabin felt the buffeting of an early evening sandstorm. He glanced outside; already the gangers were exhorting the crew to lash the sand covers over the plant and machines. The uniform pale grey of all the Amadeus Corp SA's equipment was being covered quickly by the dull-coloured tarpaulins. He watched as the huge red letters AC, familiar round the world on oilrigs, container ships and road haulage vehicles disappeared.

Two days, he fumed: for two days the crew would drink themselves stupid in the illicit shebeens of Jeddah, while hundreds and thousands of dollars' worth of pipe-laying equipment lay muffled and inactive against the raging sandstorm. An inactive plant and a high-level visit from the minister and, for God's sake, the Grand Mufti. A sense of foreboding crept over him.

His Highness Hussein Al-Saud beamed at him in open friendship from beneath his red and white ghutra. 'Mikel! My friend. As-Salamu alaykum! How are you? You are well?' Michael shook his hand, mildly surprised at the warmth of his greeting. He caught the look in his eyes and involuntarily cast his own to the darker figure accompanying His Royal Highness. Black taqiyah, black thobe and full white beard, he made no effort to greet Michael but merely bowed stiffly in greeting.

The three men took their seats in the little office, sipped tea and discussed pleasantries relating to Michael's personal life and the opening season of the hunt in the vast Rub-Al-Khali desert to the south of them. Presently, His Royal Highness clapped his hands together, indicating that the real business was about to begin. 'Mikel my friend,' he began. He went on to thank the Amadeus Corporation for their scheduled completion on time and ahead of budget for the vast de-salination plant on the coast at Jeddah. He described in glowing, almost effusive terms for the benefit of his companion, the production of clean drinking water from the salt of the Red Sea. It had been every Minister of the Interior's dream to bring clean sweet water to Mecca, the holiest city in Islam nestling beyond the Hijaz Mountains. 'Mikel, tell our learned friend how fast you make progress for us'.

Michael rose from his desk, picked up a small laser pointer and moved to a detailed map on his office wall. With a small bow to the expressionless Mufti, he showed out the route of the pipeline from Jeddah, past Al Bahah into the mountains: illustrating his method of cut and cover, he showed the process of laying the one-and-a-half-metre pipeline under the desert.

Progress, he said, had so far been a creditable 200 metres per day; with a roll of his eyes to the gathering noise of the wind outside, he confirmed that the project was still on schedule to turn the taps on in Mecca by July the following year. The most difficult part of the project was yet to come, however, in that the pipeline had to climb over Hijaz mountains. This would necessitate a large pumping station to be built at the site of the meeting.

His Royal Highness' face took on a lugubrious expression, 'Mikel, my friend. My learned colleague has come to help us with a small matter.'

'Here it comes,' thought Michael.

When the Grand Mufti spoke, it was in flawless Harvard English, 'The benefits of this pipeline are immeasurable to us, as you know. For many years the existence and continued growth of our most Holy City has been hampered by the levels of water available in the mountain water table. As you also know, these levels had been steadily falling over the last decade requiring us to use some 10,000 water tankers for the Haj'.

Mike nodded, silently thinking, 'Come on, get to the point!' But he smiled effusively at his guests.

'Your pipeline will solve all our problems and further enhance the Prophet's Birthplace.' He paused and placed his fingertips together thoughtfully. 'However, our law forbids any infidel to set eyes on the Kaaba.'

Michael grunted explosively. 'Indeed, indeed, and that is why, with the consultation of the Interior Minister, we shall halt the pipeline some two miles from the Kaaba in order that our eyes shall not fall upon it'.

The Mufti nodded slowly, 'But that is my point, effendi.' He used the familiar greeting silkily. 'It is written that the Hijaz Mountains to the East and the boundless desert in the West are the boundaries beyond which no infidel may cast his eyes'.

Michael paused: it was not the Arab way to raise direct objections to a point, he must agree with the protagonist. 'Of course, you are right,' he conceded. 'Perhaps we shall have to end the pipeline here. After all your tankers will still have a much smaller journey than driving all the way to the coast.' The Grand Mufti nodded, satisfied his legal ruling had been accepted by a foreigner.

His Royal Highness cleared his throat softly, 'If I may be so bold as to make a suggestion?' the cleric inclined his head. 'What if Amadeus Corporation could take the pipeline to the Holy City without setting eyes on our most Holy Kaaba?'

The cleric paused a moment, lost in thought. 'That would indeed be acceptable to the Senior Council of the Ulama. However, I would be intrigued as to how you would effect this?' His dark eyes sought Michael.

Michael opened his mouth to respond but his Royal Highness continued smoothly, 'Then that is settled. We shall tunnel under the Hijaz mountains direct to the heart of the City.'

Michael threw his hands up in the air and looked in bewilderment at the two urbane men in front of him. 'You can't just tear up an entire civil engineering project like that! Why, the whole project is set up for cut and cover operation only. There's no tunnelling equipment here; no personnel. Need I go on?' his shoulders slumped, 'And that's before we renegotiate all the contract, Your Royal Highness.'

Both their eyes met. 'By how much would your costs increase Mikel, as an estimate?'

'You want me to conjure up a cost for a major civil engineering project on the back of a cigarette packet?' Michael's disdain was clear.

Not long after, he watched as the government Mercedes left his compound. As His Royal Highness had so reasonably pointed out, the howling sandstorm had stopped operations for two days, so that should be sufficient time to re-calculate the costs. Michael beamed and waved at the departing car, shutting his office door he picked up the heavy crystal paperweight from his desk and revolving like a discus thrower, hurled it at the blueprint of the pipeline on the wall. Then he picked up the phone.

CHAPTER 82

Franz Lindeman rested his fingertips on the rim of the mahogany and stainless-steel steering wheel. It was the only pressure it needed. Behind him the Riva's twin-Chrysler V8s roared discreetly, and the beautiful teak boat carved a white furrow in the bay of Bahia Blanca. Glancing behind him, absently wiping a strand of his silver hair misplaced by the air steam, he smiled fondly. At the end of a thirty-meter line Eva, his young wife was effortlessly mono skiing out of the boat's creamy wake. Her tanned, lithe figure attracted not only his gaze. But his reverie was broken by the telephone. Frowning at the disturbance, he picked it up from its cream leather cradle in front of the shimmering dials of the dashboard. 'Ja,' was all he said. His eyes creased as he spoke to his son calling from the other side of the world. 'Two days you say, Michael? That's fine. Very fine. Don't worry, I'll call the board together.'

* * *

Six months after the end of the Second World War a battered Argentine freighter operating under the flag of a neutral country had dropped anchor in the Bay of Bahia Blanca. The three lean, travel-worn Germans had gratefully disembarked from the down at heel vessel and watched with trepidation as the Skoda lorry, now rusty from its long journey on deck, was swung out over the quay.

Bearing a letter embossed with the Vatican seal, they had sought out the Banco Ambrosiano in the city. In a short space of time, they had a further letter of introduction to a port official at the harbour.

Franz Lindeman had sat patiently watching the balding little man read it. Then, in a trice, the man had risen from the desk, pulled the shutter down on his office window and escorted Franz to a dilapidated three-storey building overlooking the dock, which had been empty for several years. Once busy with seamen awaiting the next berth to Europe, it now echoed to their footsteps across its floors, disturbed only by the cooing of the pigeons that had adopted the roof space. Franz, who had a smattering of Spanish, had been selected from the trio to be the go-between. The port official had left him with the keys and had disappeared, and Franz was about to leave the building himself when its door darkened, and a habit-clad figure approached him. 'Father Paolo,' he introduced himself, 'and you are Mr Kuchler?'

'No, no, Lindeman: Franz Lindeman.' As the two shook hands, Lindeman wondered how this man of God, far away in the sanctuary of South America, knew his partner's name.

Later that evening the three Germans sat in their hotel looking at each other. Van de Goltz broke the astonished silence. 'He gave you the building. Deeds, title, keys and everything?'

Lindeman nodded, sipping his beer. 'He knew how much Hudal let us keep. He knew how much we'd used as bribes to get here. And he knew the bank account details and how much we'd left in the secret tank under the lorry.'

Kuchler's eyes narrowed, 'He wants what in return?'

Lindeman continued smoothly, 'A condition of their investment is ...'

Kuchler broke in gutturally 'Their investment, you say! Why, Hudal took three-quarters off us at the Wawel Palace!'

But Lindeman held his hand up placatingly. Opening his folded leather-flying jacket he extracted half a dozen sheafs of paper. Kuchler picked them up and scanned them quickly, his face a deepening crimson. The bank statement of the newly formed Amadeus Corporation SA showed a balance increase of some twenty-five percent since they had opened it less than two weeks previously. He raised his eyes to Lindeman, mute with his questions.

'We've to attend Mass every four months, at the Catedral de Nuestra Señora de La Merced in the town where we are to make a donation to the Sons of Sion in cash, decided by us and the brothers in the preceding meeting. From time to time, they will relay certain instructions to us, which he did not specify. Apart from that we are free to run and build our own future'.

* * *

Years later, the origins of the Amadeus Corp were never very far from Franz Lindeman's thoughts as he brought the gleaming Riva back to its berth under the offices they had started in decades ago. Using their discipline and industriousness the three had managed to acquire their twentieth vehicle by the time Germany was defeated in 1945. With the world's attention on the chaos of post-war world, the trio quietly got on with the job of building their business empire.

With no overheads to speak of and initially living on the top floor of the converted mission they aggressively bought contracts and vehicles from indigenous Argentine companies. Initially taking neither dividend nor salary, they very soon ran most of the road transport of southern Argentina. It was a busy time filled mainly with beef exports from the Pampas to a hungry Europe and it was not long before the first war-surplus liberty ship sporting the pale grey livery of the fledgling corporation sat in the harbour.

From running the farms, to transporting the beef; from owning the abattoirs and canning factories and transport to Europe – the three dapper Germans controlled it all. It was not too long before the merchant fleet expanded into whaling off South Georgia. A construction division was added, although it only had one customer introduced from the brothers at the monastery. Whilst in the air, the fledging economies of emerging South American countries discovered the speed and convenience of Amadeus Corporation's fleet of redundant Dakota DC10s and Junkers 52s.

From their original thrice-yearly visits to Abadia Nuestra had grown an increasingly large torrent of cash flowing into the monastery's coffers. Once, Lindeman's bookkeeper, ignorant of the destination of large amounts of money, suggested using the new automated credit system. Transferring funds in between institutions was surely easier than cash? But, Brother Paolo had turned the request down flat. 'Cash, Franz, is all we need for our fight. We need no paper trail for others to follow.' And that was that. A small price to pay, Franz reflected, for his and his colleagues' increasingly opulent lifestyle.

Lindeman was atheist to the core, but he could not help noticing an increasingly vocal and well-organised opposition movement building. He was first aware of this in Argentina, but watched as it spread over the entire continent, fanned by insurgent Communist elements. Whilst seemingly ineffective, much of the opposition was to be found supported by the Catholic Church in the form of the monks belonging to the Order of Sion, based at the monastery and other locations.

He moored the Riva fastidiously as he always did. Its sleek form bobbing up and down under the curved stone arches of Amadeus Corp Headquarters. Eva had stepped lithely from the boat, and he watched her departing backside with a wry smile. Life was good for Franz Lindeman. No, it was bloody marvellous, he reflected. Despite losing his first wife some three years ago, Eva had given him a brand-new spring in his step. He skipped up the worn stone steps alive and alert for his ninety-five years ready for the long meeting that awaited him.

The three silver-haired gentlemen sat at their respective mahogany, leather-topped desks, facing each other at the points of a triangle across the polished stinkwood floor. His son's phone call took up most of the long discussion. The two cowled brothers of the Sons of Sion ensured that all details were properly covered before they allowed the meeting to break up.

CHAPTER 83

It was fine. By God, it was going to be fine. Michael took the laser measurements again from his small handheld Psion and translated them laboriously to the long engineering drawing on his office wall. The deadline his father had set was immovable, so much so that his father had travelled from his base in Argentina to impart it to his son.

Michael had been astonished at the flurry of activity his phone call had provoked. True to his word, he had sought an audience with His Royal Highness Hussein al-Saud. Instead of being shown into the magnificent marble and silk-lined office of the minister, he had been collected by a fleet of custom-built, open-topped Range Rovers and taken on a two-day shooting and hawking party in the desert. There, in the fastness of the Najd Desert, Michael and His Royal Highness had re-negotiated the increase in contract terms, closely linked to a substantial increase in the cash payment from Amadeus Corp to the Minister's private account in Geneva.

Now, months later, Michael paced the tiny cabin, a damp extinct cigar clamped between his lips. For week now he had made regular trips down the escarpment to Jeddah to the huge engineering shops based on the outskirts of the port. He had put the TBM machine jaws into the back of his pickup and hawked them from machine shop to machine shop. Carefully, reluctantly he had shown the worn, blunt teeth of the tunnel boring machine to tutting, head-shaking engineers. The Hijaz Mountains, far from consisting of the golden sandstone and chalks of Arabia, had comprised of tough igneous rocks which were so hard that his TBM, one of the best available in the world and purchased from London's Elizabeth Line's underground contractors, had singularly failed to keep up the progress required. Instead of the forecast thirty metres per day, the two-metre tunnel was grinding its way forward at less than a third of that rate.

Michael's lips clamped firmly together as he eyed the calendar on the wall. To make matters worse, his site accountant had been replaced, under his father's instructions, by a surly overweight local accountant, Saleem Al Jahib, who had claimed full knowledge of construction accountancy procedures. In fact, he had single-handedly reduced the Amadeus Corp debt credit rating in the Gulf to one of junk status. The problem had been the insistence of the Ministry of Finance to pay the project in stage payments linked to the forward progress of the TBMs as they bored steadily westward. Even the much-trumpeted arrival of South African mining engineers had not produced the increase in tempo.

The project was in deep trouble. Men and equipment stood idle in the searing heat, geared to removing 300 square meters of spoil per day and were not moving more than a third of that. On top of all that, this was the day when Saleem had omitted to pay the wages of the truck drivers. Worse still, the delivery of the new sections of the blue polypropylene water pipe had been halted because the last month's invoice had not been paid.

Michael glanced again at the calendar. Only two days before the contract deadline. The TBM had in fact broken through a week ago and was within 150 metres of the boundaries of the Holy City, but his appointment with the bank in the morning was no option. The project was going bust. Without further funding from Amadeus Corp Group or the Interior Ministry; the TBM would be switched off tomorrow. Just as his father had instructed.

Chapter 84

Ireland: Two months before

The day after the demise of the IRA team, Thomas had sat in the back of the Mercedes while Colm Hegarty, dressed in olive fatigues and a non-descript hacking jacket, had piloted the vehicle along a corridor, deep within the bowels of the monastery. Entering a lift of sorts, Thomas had been astonished to find himself driving out of a garage attached to a small bungalow in dense woodland. The journey to Dublin had taken all day utilising tiny back roads.

Hegarty, who had given little away from his first offer to double Thomas' contract, was ostensibly taking him to Dublin to collect his 'fee'. Thomas had little idea what to do with his money, but at Colm's suggestion he transferred the bulk of it to the Banco Ambrosiano.

As they stood outside Colm's bank in the warm sunshine on O'Leary Street, Thomas gripped Colm's arm, 'Time to explain, Hegarty? Not that I'm interested, you understand.' The explanation came in a corner booth of the Liffy Arms, where the two sat in semi-darkness while the thump of the jukebox drowned all conversation as they put their heads together.

Later, back at the monastery, Thomas regarded Sebastian with a newfound respect as the plans for the voyage unfolded. The salt-encrusted motor cruiser had duly appeared in the monastery yard. In short order, a scaffold had been erected around her and with squealing protest from pulley blocks, the cargo so carefully inserted in Latakia was hoisted clear. Moments later, to Thomas' quiet amazement, a box identical in every way rumbled across the courtyard on a small dolly: even down to the stencilled markings it was its twin. From the noise of the protesting blocks, it weighed the same too as it was lowered into the centre of the boat.

Later that evening, it had taken a single movement of the derrick on the trawler, *Mulligan's Mother*, to hoist the plain wooden crate from the flatbed truck on the quayside at Burtonport into the hold. Thomas had been dropped off by Colm Hegarty at the top of the main street to check on the location of the local Garda's car. True to form, it was parked outside Maggie's bar. Thomas quickly placed his hand on the bonnet; it was still warm. Pat would be inside for several hours. The pickup crept passed and parked on the harbour wall.

Before the sun rose on the next day *Mulligan's Mother* had slipped her moorings and headed west across a darkened Atlantic: by sunrise Ireland had long disappeared below the horizon.

Colm, Sebastian and the woman conversed earnestly in the small wheelhouse. Colm addressed the woman as Elizabeth and obviously deferred to her in some way: the passage from Latakia had clearly stood him in good stead.

Thomas relaxed a little and made his way aft to the small pallets, shrouded in lashed tarpaulins as he had requested. Now *Mulligan's Mother* was lost in the Atlantic amongst tens of other fishing vessels; a few Irish and British, but the majority being Spanish boats out of Bilbao, pillaging British and Irish fish stocks. Thomas watched as the Irish crews spat overboard as the huge Spanish factory ships steamed relentlessly back and forth. It would have taken a keen observer to spot that *Mulligan's Mother* ploughed a steady course westward with little attention to her fishing gear.

By the evening of the second day, they had left the multitudinous fishing fleets behind and except for the occasional slab-sided container ship, were alone. Colm brought the little boat onto a heading for the Straits of Gibraltar, trusting that the change of course here would disguise their actual point of departure.

Darkness saw the ship transformed into a hive of activity. Setting the engines at slow ahead and after engaging the autopilot to maintain their course, the four struggled into the olive overalls from the monastery and under Thomas' firm instruction set to work with the contents of the small pallets. Elizabeth was given the task of painting the wheelhouse a dazzling shade of white; while the black, rust-streaked hull, with the three men sitting on suspended planks, slowly changed colour to a glistening royal blue. Many hours later, Thomas left a paint-splattered Colm and Sebastian to attend to matters on deck.

When dawn rose on the fifth day, land-based birds whirled around them as the dark hunk of the Rock of Gibraltar came into view. The *Sally Ann*, registered in Padstow according to the plate on her stern, touted for business as she headed for the North Mole in Gibraltar's outer harbour. Along her flanks she carried the notice 'Dive ship for hire', whilst her small deck sported a rack of yellow air tanks, above which dive suits of every size, shape and colour hung in the breeze.

As they idled up to the fuelling bowser on the quay, a group of American tourists watched through expensive binoculars. Leaving the others below deck under strict instruction, Thomas chatted with the Port Fuelling Manager as he counted out payment in American dollars. Two thousand gallons later, Thomas sauntered back to the *Sally Ann*, alongside which the group of Americans, they could only be Americans Thomas decided, had congregated.

'Say, Fellah!' boomed the tallest man, as he stuck his thumbs in his waistband. 'How much per day for the five of us?'

Thomas grimaced, 'I'm booked, I'm afraid, for a week. But I'll come back in seven days. Any good?

'Depends on how much,' drawled another thickset man.

'Five thousand dollars a day,' Thomas said softly as he bent to the mooring rope; the group turned and sauntered off, muttering. 'Suit you,' said Thomas, as he leapt down to the deck.

The *Sally Ann* followed her course eastwards: the full length of the Mediterranean. They made a brief visit to Valletta, where Thomas decided to remain on board to clear a sticky injector on the elderly marine diesel. He watched as Colm and Sebastian disappeared along the harbour wall, but Elizabeth had remained on board and was watching him at work on the engine. She unsettled him, he decided. She did not say much, but when she did, Colm and Sebastian listened very carefully. It was her eyes he decided: pale blue and icy cold. One to watch as he set to on his injector pump.

Later, as the now smooth-running *Sally Ann* burbled out of the darkening harbour, Thomas watched Colm, Sebastian and Elizabeth on the fantail of the boat. Colm had his head inclined and was talking. Presently he took a small silver cell phone from between his shoulder and passed it to Elizabeth. She spoke animatedly for several minutes on occasion looking at Colm and Sebastian. Then she turned and sought out Thomas behind the glass in the wheelhouse. He could hear nothing, but she took the small phone from her ear and flicked it into the inky sea. Then she spoke briefly to Colm and disappeared down the companionway.

Colm stepped lightly into the wheelhouse. 'A hundred and eight degrees about, Thomas. We need to drop Elizabeth back at Valletta.'

Thomas grimaced 'What's up? She forgot confessional?'

Colm smiled but his eyes remained cool. 'Elizabeth goes to prepare for the next phase. Cancer is rarely cured in one operation.'

Half-an-hour later the *Sally Ann* once again nudged up to the darkened pier. Elizabeth stepped out of the cabin and, carefully judging the movement on the gentle swell, stepped onto the stone steps leading upwards. As she disappeared Thomas could not make out her outline: she appeared to have lost a lot of weight, and her hair had changed shape. When she reached the top of the steps in the gloom, Thomas could not be sure, but she appeared to be a lot younger. Lights from the harbour reflected off her glasses as she raised an arm in farewell – or was it a salute?

Never mind that, however. Thomas spun the wheel and the *Sally Ann* glided gently away from the harbour wall and towards the open sea once again. Casting a glance into the oily waters of Valletta harbour, Thomas pondered on the significance of the second cell phone to be tossed unceremoniously into the water.

On the second day out, a large freighter followed them steadily from the west. Of some thirty thousand tons, she passed them 200 yards to port. Colm waved briefly at a figure on the open bridge as the freighter pulled ahead. She was painted in a uniform pale grey with the letters AC on her single funnel and the name on her stern read *City of Bahia Blanca* Buenos Aires. The figure on the departing freighter continued to watch from behind his glasses as the two vessels drew apart.

On the fourth day the *Sally Ann* entered Port Said and Thomas went briefly ashore to book a sailing on the next lock movement for the Suez Canal. It was important to travel with the correct mix of vessels within the locks as the larger vessels, unable to manoeuvre in the close confines ran the risk of swamping smaller boats making the passage. The three made good use of the leisurely passage and in the dark nights the letters adorning the boat were carefully obliterated. Soon the *Sally Ann* sported no more than her deep blue hull and glistening superstructure. On the second night whilst at anchor in the Great Bitter Lake the *Sally Ann* became, at Colm Hegarty's behest, *The Wind of Change*, port of registry: Marseille. The newly named *Wind of Change* entered the glittering Gulf of Suez with the arid fastness of the Sinai on the port side. A new determination and lightness came over Colm and Sebastian and they laughed and joked with Thomas. As the tip of the Sinai fell away behind them and the Red Sea opened up the grey form of the *City of Bahia Blanca* could be seen ahead. By nightfall they had caught up with her and at Colm's instruction pulled alongside. It did not go unnoticed to Thomas that although the vessel appeared brightly light, all the lamps were heavily shielded: in the gloom, someone would have to be on top of them to observe the swift deployment of a large crane from the deck of the freighter.

After the simple deal crate disappeared skywards to be loaded onto the freighter, Colm snapped, 'Right! Abandon Ship!'

Thomas grabbed his few possessions and, with his nerves on fire, scrambled up the lowered ladder. As he reached the deck some thirty feet above, he turned and watched Sebastian in the trawler's wheelhouse. He saw Sebastian fix the wheel in a set position, watched him adjust the engine controls and then nimbly skip across the deck and leap the widening gulf to the ladder. The *Wind of Change* began to describe a lazy circle in front of the freighter. Leaning on the rail Thomas felt the deck tremble as her engines increased in tempo. Water boiled at her stern, and she went full ahead. Thomas frowned: the abandoned *Wind of Change* was heading right across their swiftly moving bows. His warning shout was cut short as the *City of Bahia Blanca* struck the little trawler amidships. The deep flare of the freighter's bow pushed her sideways and underneath the foaming black sea. In seconds she had rolled over and with a shuddering, tearing screech passed under the freighter's hull. Thomas felt a secondary thud moments later as the trawler struck the underside of the freighter for the last time. But when he glanced at the bridge, Colm and Sebastian were enjoying a glass of beer. In salute they raised their glasses to him.

With a finality borne of his previous experience, Thomas suddenly realised his own usefulness was expiring. There was a wariness about him, then, when he mounted the steps to the bridge, where Colm and Sebastian greeted him with smiles and a glass of beer.

'If I were you, Thomas O'Neil,' said Sebastian, clapping him on the back, 'I'd be thinking now my job's over and I'm waiting for the bullet.' Colm nodded, suddenly subservient under Sebastian's lead.

Thomas merely raised his eyebrows, 'The thought had occurred, yes. General Bagheri gave me a termination contract, it's true. But he thought he'd sent his missile to the Little Satan's eyes and ears.'

Sebastian indicated the dry, dun-coloured foothills of the Hijaz Mountains. Thomas looked at the two other men. He had figured out roughly where the bomb was going. Colm interjected, a new spirit stealing across his face. Thomas had seen him speak once before in the long, sun-dappled office at the monastery. His voice took on a dreamy quality. He gripped the rail and stared at the mountains. 'We are no terrorists, Thomas. We do not use cowards or weaklings with explosives strapped to their bodies. We do not fly aeroplanes into skyscrapers nor drive trucks up to embassy gates. These are the actions of a corrupt and evil society that has no coherence to fight as one. We will not attack in pinpricks that goad and frustrate our enemy. Neither do we insist our foot soldiers achieve martyrdom in heaven. For 800 years, Thomas, we have lived to fight another day and that day is fast approaching. In all our Crusades we singularly failed to cut the cancer emanating from the sands of Persia.

'Now', Colm paused and looked over Thomas' shoulder to the mountains on the horizon. 'Now we return for our final Crusade. Thousands of our forebears felt the infidel steel at the Battle of Hattin. Ironic isn't it that descendants of Saladin should hand us the means to finish our struggle. But fear not, Thomas, the masterstroke will behead the main body, but there will always be offspring that need cauterising.'

Thomas' mind was racing – relieved, but racing at the same time. 'You think you'll get away with detonating that?' he jerked his thumb amidships.

'Not think, Thomas. Not think. The only people who know about the bomb and its whereabouts are dead, courtesy of Mossad and the Americans. General Bagheri and Hussein Salami were assassinated by drone. And Saeed Izadi died in a bombing raid. The bomb's signature emission will be identified by the Americans and Mossad as Iranian.'

Sebastian cut in, 'And the world will look in the opposite direction.'

Colm cleared his throat and his eyes grew hard. 'Not everyone will, Thomas. Have you met the good Dr Schlatter yet?'

The trio made their way aft. On the rear deck sat a large forty-foot container unit, a bank of air-conditioning fans roaring away from on top. Colm opened the steel access door and the three entered the cool interior. Dr Schlatter looked up from his workbench, his thick glasses magnifying his large eyes as he blinked rapidly into focus. Recognising Colm and Sebastian, he broke into a satisfied grin. 'I'm ready. It's perfect. All I need is the access code and mobile phone number for detonation.' Colm nodded sagely.

The deal crate that Thomas had last seen open in that dusky square an age ago sat in the centre of the makeshift workshop. Wonderingly, he walked over it and peered inside. There was the dull silver cylinder, nestled just as he remembered in its polystyrene nest, only now a veritable forest of wires led from the small rectangular access hatch to a small knee-level workstation next to it. Dr Schlatter was holding a box containing a foam cradle in which sat a Nokia phone. As the three of them looked on, he held aloft a similar model to demonstrate detonation. At his thumbed command, a bleep of the autodial could be heard. The last bleep fell silent. All eyes switched to the panel on top of the open bomb. At the first ring a red light illuminated, and Dr Schlatter looked round in triumph.

Reaching behind him, he pulled a coil of fine copper cable. 'You'll need this of course: the cell phone frequency doesn't reach underground, so the device will have to have access to open air within 200 metres or so.'

Colm nodded. 'When I know the digit sequence from our remote operation, then the device is live?' Dr Schlatter nodded effusively.

'There's nothing to prevent detonation?' pressed Sebastian.

'No. No. Absolutely nothing.' Then he paused, as if he was unsure how to phrase what was coming next. 'Then my job is over,' he asked, looking at the grave faces, with his own betraying a naïve misunderstanding of his final words. 'Then Judi and I will be free? As you promised?'

Sebastian nodded gravely. 'General Bagheri gave you his word. As soon as the BBC World Service confirm detonation of a device, Judi will be escorted to the nearest border and released.' Dr Schlatter almost wept with relief as the three men left his workshop. Colm exhaled outside in the warm, damp Gulf air.

CHAPTER 85

Michael Lindeman's sweat cooled rapidly in the chill air conditioning of the local branch of Bank Hapoalim SA. As usual in the Gulf in the early days of July, streets sweltered under a forty-five-degree heat and the transition from air-conditioned vehicle to street and into the bank caused rivulets of sweat under his collar.

His visitor's uncomfortable movement was not lost on Riduan Boasyir, the branch manager. Coolly elegant in his immaculate dish dash he leant forward. 'Mikel, my friend, I urge you, call in funds from your father; the bank cannot and will not extend its credit any further. I do not understand why your parent company and father, whom we have had many dealings with, appear to be letting you go bankrupt.'

Michael had a pained look across his face. 'Riduan, I told you, its group policy to let local contracts stand or fall. My father is a hard man,' he lifted his shoulders expressively.

'Please, effendi,' the manager pleaded, 'make the call now'. He indicated the telephone on the desk.

Michael made as if to pick it up and then held back. 'Riduan, I don't understand. You're pulling the plug when we've less than two weeks to go: I can't take the pipeline with me!'

Riduan watched impassively, leant back and softly repeated, 'Make the call Michael.'

Michael threw his hands up but pulled the instrument to him. Seconds passed as the call winged its way round the globe. In the offices overlooking the harbour Franz Lindeman scooped up the phone, his old pale eyes hard when he answered, 'Ja'.

'Father. It's Michael. I'm with our local bank manager. We're going to be closed in twenty-four hours unless the group stand behind the debt. Under the circumstances, father, it's only two week's work.' The phone crackled explosively, and Michael held it away from his ear. 'Yes, but ...' Again, the phone barked. 'I understand, sir, perfectly.' Michael had turned a shade paler and replaced the dead handset.

Riduan rose formally and said, 'I'll send the foreclosure team in tomorrow, first thing. So sorry it had to end this way, Mikel.' He offered his hand, but Michael was already on his way out of the office. Outside on the baking pavement, he hailed his driver from across the street.

Sinking gratefully into the soft leather and feeling the rush of cool air on his face, he smiled through the darkened windows. Perfect, just perfect. As the car ground slowly through the Jeddah traffic, not 400 yards behind it sat a flatbed Mercedes in a dull olive green. Its cab contained three men, all in the local white dish dash although their hands and faces had been carefully stained with walnut juice. The plain deal crate sat lashed behind the cab.

Presently, the traffic thinned and the single-track road up to the foothills of the Hijaz Mountains contained only two vehicles. Michael drew up to the site entrance and waited whilst his driver opened the chain link gate. Half-a-dozen of the labourers who had not been paid that week hung around as the car sped past and rocks bounced off its dusty bodywork as Michael's stony face stared ahead. The Mercedes truck followed bumper to bumper as the chain link gate was closed to the angry group.

When darkness fell the small crowd at the gates melted away and Michael dismissed the driver for the night. The tunnel entrance yawned dark and cool in the base of a craggy sandstone cliff some distance from the silent offices. Colm, Sebastian, Michael and Thomas shook hands in front of the Mercedes truck. Thomas watched as Colm and Sebastian's dish dashes were removed. A moment later, over their olive-green fatigues a white, knee length surcoat reflected eerily in the moonlight. On the front and on the back was stitched a bold blood-red cross patée.

'From Hugh de Payens to Jacques de Molay,' said Colm in a voice deep with passion. 'For all our knights lost in battle and for Pope Urban II, who started this battle, and under our new Pope we will finish. We commit our actions to the most Holy Roman Church and to God. In nomine Patri ...'

Thomas watched the blond-haired site manager who was spellbound by the two monks. Surreal in the moonlit arid landscape, their surcoats flapped in the light breeze. Behind them sat the crate that had come so far. Colm raised his voice from the Latin, and proclaimed, 'Dieu le veut!' and raised his clenched fist to the darkened cliffs.

Michael quickly slid the rough deal crate onto a small inspection trolley, and once it was loaded they pushed it effortlessly into the tunnel mouth. Michael reached down to a small panel and it glided soundlessly forward into the darkness. Sebastian went to the Mercedes and came back lugging a great coil of fine wire. This he placed in the load tray of a rugged quad bike.

'The inspection hatch is further up the valley, below a jagged outcrop of rock,' said Michael. 'You can't miss it: the drill derrick's still there. Open the hatch and the tunnel is twenty metres below you, so you'll have plenty of cable. The trolley is programmed to stop under the hatch. Connect the two jack plugs into the top of the bomb and press the green button, and then it'll keep going until the tunnel face. Leave the mini satellite dish on the derrick framework and get back before dawn.' Sebastian ran through his instructions and departed leaving a low plume of dust from the quad.

Michael's last task was to start one of the giant bulldozers and ram the tunnel-boring machine into the tunnel. He drove it in at an angle so there could be no possibility of it being removed.

Back in the portacabin, the three men chinked glasses. 'To Pope Urban II,' Colm uttered. Thomas frowned but raised his glass all the same.

'Dieu le veut!' echoed Sebastian, a peculiar smile stealing across his face. The silence in the small office was absolute and prolonged. Colm cleared his voice, briskly. 'Now, if you'll excuse me, I have an appointment with a Grand Mufti.'

CHAPTER 86

Ben held her against the marble shower wall. Her legs encircled his waist and her arms forced his mouth onto hers. Oblivious to the hissing nozzles, the two rutted under their warm streams. Slowly their breathing returned to normal, and her legs slipped weakly to the floor.

Eleanor pushed wet strands of hair from her face and held him against the wall. 'What if you had the chance to change history, Ben, for the next 1,000 years; to right the last 700 years? What if you could finish our Crusade? Final victory for God's one true Church. Would you? Would you take that chance?'

Her breathing now was imperceptible, and rivulets of water ran down her body. Her eyes bore into Ben's very being. Ice blue eyes that he felt dissecting his innermost soul. More. He had once faced a female leopard in the mountains of Armenia. Her eyes had been the same. Now, as then, his life hung in the balance. She waited for his reply. The hand of her mother and of her mother's ancestors over the centuries was upon her. Ben stepped out of the shower and began towelling himself roughly.

'Go on,' he began. She lifted her chin fractionally, a gleam in her eyes. He continued cautiously, 'I would not be the first of our family to further the cause.'

Breakfast was served on her little balcony opening out onto the Cortile del Belvedere. Coldly, methodically Eleanor spoke. Ben listened, as she outlined her argument against the world's second largest religion. Dismissively describing the rise of fundamentalism in the divided Islamic world as the rantings of a few mad clerics, coupled with availability of unlimited money.

Ben found himself drawn deeper with this woman than he had ever known. Eleanor gave him almost everything, but not quite. She was not that ready, but she had committed herself further with this man than anybody before. Coldly, she knew if he was not the right one, she had given him a death sentence.

* * *

Ben knew that Raffy's letter was a fatal threat to him. He felt reasonably sure she did not have it, so after the breakfast was cleared away, he made his excuses, citing lectures. He kissed her fully, lingeringly, on her lips and took his leave. He avoided the queues for the Sistine Chapel at the northern end of the Cortile del Belvedere and made his way reflectively through the ornamental gardens of the Cortile della Pigna, leaving the complex by the shop, thinly patronised at that time in the morning, and past the Pio Clementino Museum.

Ben found a phone booth in a quiet side street and made the call. 'Sir? Mountford, in Rome,' his mind on overdrive, he slipped into military brusqueness.

'Ben!' boomed the voice at the other end of the line. 'Thank God you rang. Didn't have a clue where you were. They said you'd vacated your lodgings'.

Bens lips compressed in the heat of the phone booth. 'Vacated or re-located?' he wondered. He pressed on firmly, 'sir. That scientist. The one the ops guys lost near the monastery.'

The line spluttered and he held the receiver from his ear, 'But that's precisely what I want to talk to you about,' barked Colonel Parker.

'Go on, sir.'

'I gave the task of following the doctor's trail to our old unit. So, Chas and the boys start at an abandoned cottage that was the nearest building to his last known point. They find nothing inside the cottage, and it probably hasn't been used for some time. But when they open the garage, somehow, they trip a switch because the whole garage floor sinks down like some giant lift. At this stage the entire unit are carried downwards too fast to extricate themselves.'

The colonel paused and sniffed down the line. Ben knew he was cursing the unit for committing all its members with no back-up. He grimaced, imagining the carpeting Chas would have received over that one. 'Anyway, the lift stops, and the team find themselves in some kind of cellar. It's a garage of sorts with various motor vehicles parked against the walls. One of the vehicles is the good Doctor Schlatter's four-wheel drive. The engine's cold and the place is empty. Further along the cellar, Pete enters a small cell cautiously, but the place is abandoned. It contains a model, Ben, on the floor, a model with a street layout, intersections, the lot.'

Ben listened grimly and his hand tightened on the receiver.

Colonel Parker began again. 'The end of the cellar has a stone wall with the evidence of automatic fire embedded in it, the surface is chewed to buggery and in the debris small fragments of tissue and evidence of blood: lots of it. Someone's had a firing squad down there.' He paused, catching Ben's thought unawares. 'Ten minutes, Ben, phone me back.'

Ben left the fetid heat of the phone box and cast his glance up the Via Vittoria and set off at a determined pace. Behind him, on the opposite side of the road, a dark saloon glided forward.

Colonel Parker answered at once and continued, 'Anyway, the unit secure the cellar and report in. I give the go-ahead for further investigation, and they climb out of this cellar complex into the monastery that I told you about.' Ben's mind switched to his and Raffy's reception by the brotherhood.

Parker continued, 'The place is semi-abandoned and all they find is eighteen or nineteen monks at evening vespers.'

'How old were they, sir?' Ben interjected.

'Old? Oh, God knows. But well over sixty or seventy,' came the puzzled reply.

'Not when I was there, George. They were all late-twenties, or early-thirties. In fact, very like our age profile in the service, sir.'

'Mmm,' replied his old CO, resignation creeping into his voice. 'Ben, something isn't right here. I've got a mysteriously resurrected nuclear scientist; disappearing monks; and, from the forensic DNA analysis, the blood in the cellar belongs to at least two or three members of an IRA cell that we know for a fact they only use on their big ops.'

Parker continued, sharing his confidences with Ben, 1,300 miles away. 'What if the Continuity, or the Real IRA have somehow got hold of a device?'

'A device, sir?' Ben countered,

'Well, we do have a missing nuclear scientist here and what's more... Sorry, Ben: ten minutes.' The phone clicked.

Ben shook his head in exasperation and flung open the booth door unnecessarily hard. He glanced up and down the street, belligerent but unseeing. The figure in the dark saloon sank further behind the steering wheel.

Something bothered Ben as he walked rapidly up the hot street. He could not help feeling that Colonel Parker's problem was somehow connected to him. But try as he might, he could not unravel the thread.

His only factual connection was that he happened to have spent the night with a sister from the same order as the Irish monastery. Sister? Was that all she was? Expensive means? Cars collecting her? And that fabulous apartment. Passport number: three? Just who was she? His mind was full of questions but few answers.

He found the next glass booth in a little shopping mall off the Via Vittoria. Slipping adroitly into its warm confines, he turned his back on the angry gesticulations of a swarthy Italian woman who had just been about to enter it. Barzini drove past the entrance to the mall in time to see her start beating the glass. He watched Ben's turned back and picked up the cell phone.

Colonel Parker continued gruffly down the new connection. 'Ben, without going through the proper channels just yet, there is a chance we may recall you.'

Ben raised his eyebrows, 'sir, about that monastery. You know what I told you in Hereford.'

'Yes. Yes,' cut in Parker testily, 'I was coming to that. In the courtyard of the monastery, of all things we find an old motor cruiser. I say old, because she'd obviously been at sea for a while from the look of her. But while we had a forensics team there, someone decided to take a closer look. Something's been hauled in or out because there's a scaffolding frame and lifting blocks over her. One of the lads, Sean Daly, has recently transferred from the SBS; so, out of curiosity, he peeks at the engine. You there?' boomed Parker. '

'Sir,' Ben nodded, unsure why he was getting all this information.

'You know our Q-boats? You know the thing: average, scruffy, nondescript appearance, but top-notch running gear tuned and maintained to the nth degree? Well, this boat was, it certainly was', he muttered down the line.

Then the colonel paused, and Ben sensed an uncertainty. Ben was not strictly a serving officer, but all the same he had signed the Official Secrets Act. 'Go on, sir' he said softly.

The colonel continued, his voice grave over the miles. 'One of our forensic boys has a flash of inspiration and inspects the centre bilge bay under the rigged scaffold. Under a false floor, he finds a new machine crate with "Volvo Penta 245" stamped on it.'

Ben frowned in irritation at the stifling heat inside as the woman's voice rose to a shriek outside.

'Bear with me, Ben,' Colonel Parker chuckled intuitively 'Anyway, so what? A spare engine in a boat that's obviously been at sea some while, except, Ben, the crate's warm.'

'Warm, sir?'

'Note my choice of words, Ben, the crate, not the brand-new engine', he paused, and Ben deliberately bit his lip.

'Next, they decide to run a check on the boat with, amongst other things, a Geiger counter', Ben's mind snapped back into focus. 'Ben, it goes off the scale, something in that boat is radioactive in a big way. We organise a full nuclear decontamination unit, seal the monastery and fly in a full nuclear weapons' programme team and mobile laboratory. But after two days, the team declare the boat free of nuclear material.'

'Free, sir? But I don't follow, you just said the Geiger counter . . .'

'Yes. Yes. I did. I said the boat was free of radioactive material itself, but it had recently carried a highly nuclear cargo.

'How much do you know about radioactive decay, Ben?'

'Bugger all, sir,' replied Ben, totally focussed now on the handset in his hand.

'Thought so. Ten minutes, Ben. Ten minutes.' Click.

Pushing open the booth and dodging the flailing handbag of the enraged woman, Ben ran lightly out of the shopping mall and back on to the Via

Vittoria with his mind in turmoil. Nuclear device? What was described as 'the final solution'? Eleanor's soft voice saying, 'What if you cut off the head of the serpent, Ben? What if you have the final solution?'

None of it made sense as he stood in the stifling morning sunshine. He had a call to make, though and set off again towards the railway station where he could be sure of finding an empty phonebooth.

* * *

Barzini muttered into his phone as he kept pace with the hurrying figure on the opposite pavement.

'He's changing phones every ten minutes,' breathed Carone to the icy blue eyes at the head of the table. 'It's classic subversion tactics. No one has a chance of an intercept and if they did, they'd only hear part of the conversation. This man's a pro.' Eleanor looked at him appraisingly.

* * *

Once again outside the station Ben found an empty booth as he had hopped. Colonel Parker continued as if nothing had happened to interrupt him. 'Refining uranium into weapons-grade material produces what the scientists call its 'half-life' of radioactive decay. Some products, dependent on the level of refining, have a half-life comparatively short, say eighty or ninety years, others such as weapons-grade fissile material can be radioactive for hundreds of years.' Ben nodded frowning.

'Therefore, that's why in the event of a nuclear attack, everything the enemy has would remain radioactive and inoperable. You follow?' Without waiting for a reply, he carried on. 'Well, these rates of decay can be measured just as if measuring the heat loss on a pan of water and the rate of cooling gives a figure that our lads can work with in conjunction with BNFL and others to identify the missing material. But it gets better than that, Ben; the temperature fall, and rate of decay, identifies the origin of the nuclear material and source of uranium ore. Each uranium mine's products have a different "signature". Just as a diamond can be identified whether it is South African or Russian, Ben. The rate of decay from the heat signature in the hold of that cruiser has been identified as the uranium ore yellowcake from the mines of Niger, West Africa.'

Ben's mind spun, 'Niger? What's that to do with your theory?'

Colonel Parker continued ominously. 'Because that's where the Iranian Nuclear Programme acquired the ore from to refine at Natanz and Fordo.' Parker continued, 'The IAEA said that they had enough to build nine bombs, and we are of the opinion that it's all destroyed. But what if we're wrong Ben?'

Ben interrupted, watching his wristwatch, 'And are you saying, sir, that there is a possibility that the device, if it exists, is from an Iranian weapons' programme?'

'Remember Gaddafi supported the IRA for years with the backing of Iran, Ben. What if the IRGC has found a way to give the IRA a weapon? And if it has, where is it now? None of our intelligence is revealing any activity at all from all three terrorist groups. It's as if nobody has missed the team from the monastery.'

'If it's a deep team, sir, there will be only one or two people aware of their mission anyway.' Parker grunted in agreement. 'And apart from the conclusion that there has been a weapon in the cruiser, what else?'

'I was saving that,' grunted Parker. 'There's a model in the cellar, Ben.' He paused, as if tired. 'It's Cheltenham, Ben: GCHQ. They aim to blind us. They've learnt, Ben. These Irish bastards. Manchester was a large bomb, 1,000 pounds in a truck. But ten years on, it's given Manchester one of the best urban redevelopments seen in England for a long time. If they do this, we would be electronically blind and deaf for twenty years given the likely contamination.'

'Sir, you haven't a bomb yet,'

'Anything and anybody that can carry a Geiger counter is out Ben. It's just a question of time, and now we know the target.'

Ben interrupted, 'sir, what if that's what you're supposed to think?'

'I've respected you for a long time, Ben,' came the soft reply, 'But this wasn't a trail laid out for us. Remember our chat before your posting? Information gleaned from widely disparate intelligence sources coupled with a slice of luck. We, Ben, have evidence of a weapon on Irish soil. A fight or struggle over the weapon and a model of the intended target.'

Ben agreed, glancing at his watch. 'You remember what I told you about that monastery? Well, on my last ops I had occasion to chase an assassin into another Sons of Sion monastery.' Briefly he outlined the facts of the assassination of Bishop Condera.

The colonel interrupted, 'Ben, you've gone soft in Rome. Are you telling me a bunch of monks may have an interest in a nuclear device?' and he chuckled.

Ben compressed his lips, 'Only in as much as Islamic clerics in London have expressed support for 11 September, sir'. He placed the receiver on the cradle and exhaled slowly. This was spiralling out of control, he thought. First, he needed to recover Raffy's letter: if that had remained undisturbed, he felt safe. Someone had tried to access his military records, but Parker seemed satisfied that only a standard background had been uncovered. The phone calls were untraceable, and he was sure that there had been no attempt to follow him. Sister Eleanor intrigued his mind and body, but was a fanatical determination to follow fundamental Catholic tenets proof of terrorist activity? Perhaps not.

After their last call had ended, Colonel Parker looked unseeing for a long time at the silent phone. He trusted Ben implicitly; he had always thought outside the box and his decision to enter the Church was completely in character. Something was bothering Ben, and if it bothered Ben, it bothered Parker.

He went to the large cabinet in his austere office and then sat under the reading lamp above his desk in silence. Colonel George Parker was old-school, but he knew asymmetric warfare was developing at pace, led by audacious raids by the Ukrainians on an enemy ten times their size, and inspired by the Israeli Mossad agents infiltrating Iranian proxy groups and destroying them with explosive pagers and mobile devices. The utter precision of the American raids on those nuclear facilities in Iran had been possible only because of the incredible level of communications and technology the West possessed. It did not take a genius to realise that the power of electronic eavesdropping and surveillance.

Parker picked up the phone. Ben was wrong, just plain wrong. 'Get me the Chief of Defence Staff: Whitehall,' he barked.

CHAPTER 87

Ben skipped up the freshly scrubbed and bleached steps of the Hotel Ambrose and told the blonde receptionist that he had checked out the day before and had left some paperwork in his room.

'I'd be surprised if it's still there', she muttered, tautening her chest as she reached behind her for the key. 'The brothers were very thorough when they came for your luggage'. 'Brothers?' Ben asked, raising his eyebrows. 'Yes, you know, from the Sons of Sion: they always come in cases like this.' She didn't elaborate.

The lift halted at the top floor and Ben quickly walked down the linoleum corridor. His room yawned emptily at him as he went to the loose linoleum behind the lavatory. His heart leapt as his searching fingers touched the folded sheets of Raffy's letter. He stood for a moment, his mind racing.

Certain now that he was all right, he started to analyse his concerns he had briefly discussed with his old CO. His mind ticked off his contacts and observations since that evening in Guatemala. He paused on the way to the door and looked up. A scrape of a chair and footfall led his eyes tracking across the ceiling. He was on the top floor, he knew. He entered the lift and pressed the ground floor button. The receptionist came out of the little back office to the hiss of the doors closing in the small vestibule and was taken aback that Ben had left the building so quickly.

She returned to her magazine, but in the lift shaft Ben crouched amid the oily cables, his heart pumping. Staring up the dimly lit shaft, he counted five sets of doors. His hunch was right. The top floor was not the top at all. He had just two choices, to climb the lift shaft and hope no one used it or wait until someone needed the fifth floor. His decision was taken from him. By his side the greasy cables tautened and whirred, and he felt himself drawn upwards. One, two, three, it was not slowing down. Ben anxiously eyed the approaching shaft head. He crouched on all fours around the greasy cables, but still the lift rose smoothly. Tensing himself, he flattened his torso against the ventilated ceiling panel of the lift and waited for the impact. Ever so gently the steelwork pressed into this back and stopped.

He was prostrate in the seven or eight inches at the top of the shaft, his eyes pressed close to the slatted top of the lift. Ben held his breath. The doors sighed open and three people shuffled into the narrow space. His nostrils flared, it could not be! Surely not. But Eleanor's warm perfume drifted upwards, and her voice stirred Ben as she spoke authoritatively to the two men.

Ben's only movement was his eyeballs as they swivelled across the slatted vent. The smaller of the two men cut a sinister figure, dressed in black from head to toe. His silver hair was cut expensively, and his tanned, swarthy complexion remained icy as he listened to the other man speak. Ben had no way of proving it, but from the vivid scars and purple bruising of Barzini's face, he knew who it was he had laid out in the Vatican archives.

Eleanor was brandishing some sheets of paper, 'You let me deal with this, you understand?' Without deigning to wait for an answer she carried on. 'Tomorrow, wait until the news breaks out on the BBC or CNN. It will be vague to begin with, but we must not act before. You must make sure the rumours of the Iranian Shia involvement reach the Sunni population before the Americans and Mossad confirm it. It's timed to coincide with the Grand Mufti entering St Peters to receive father's Holy blessing. Have you got the . . .' But the lift had come to a halt and the doors opened. The three moved into the small lobby and Ben lost the conversation over the receding footfalls.

He remained immobile for an age on the top of the lift, debating whether to return to the fifth floor, but was unsure if it was empty or not. Somehow, he had to reach Colonel Parker again. Something was planned in Rome which would be momentous enough to be on the BBC or CNN. Maybe he was wrong about the bomb. He could not see how it fitted into his current predicament, but as he lay there, he could not help but think back on Eleanor's words.

He waited a full ten minutes before slipping back the roof panel and landing silently on the balls of his feet inside the lift. Pausing with his ear to the door he pressed the button on the panel. As soon as the doors were wide enough apart, he slipped through the gap and strode quickly down the lobby, waving at a surprised receptionist as he rapidly left the building. Gazing at his departing figure the blonde young woman frowned and looked back at the closed lift doors.

* * *

The phone had rung interminably. In the end, Ben had tried two other kiosks on the Via Giovanni, but to no avail. Unsure now, he wandered along. To the riverside of the Spanish Steps a small area of specialist electronic goods shops had sprung up. He found himself in front of a television shop window watching the mute pictures on the other side of the glass. At the top corner of animated screens, a satellite transmission from the BBC World Service was showing the world familiar outlines of Big Ben and the ornate gates of No 10. The reporter was clutching his microphone and speaking directly to the camera, but it was not the reporter that Ben was watching. Behind him huge concrete berms were being lowered into place around the Palace of Westminster. Likewise, the entrance to Downing Street now resembled the entrance to a nuclear bunker. Discrete distance shots of hooded men on top of various public buildings told Ben exactly why Colonel Parker was not answering his phone. He had dismissed Ben's concerns and had concentrated his troops around key objectives. As if to underline Parker's dismissal of Ben's opinions, the camera cut to an aerial view of the doughnut-shaped building that was GCHQ at Cheltenham. Scorpion light tanks could be seen clearly manoeuvring on roundabouts and junctions. Military helicopters circled. Ben nodded to himself. So be it: Colonel Parker had made his decision.

CHAPTER 88

The strains of 'Laudate Dominum', her favourite Mozart work, softly filled the apartment. Reclining on the huge double bed, she swirled the ruby red wine around the glass, taking a deep draught she sniffed appreciatively at its rich aroma. One of a new generation of winemakers from Rossi de Toscana, Paulo Massi's Vintage Sangiovese was simply superb. Satisfying as it was, though, it did nothing to assuage Eleanor's mind.

She took a second reflective sip as she studied the photocopied sheets. She read it twice. The research was good, very good, although much of what Father Alhambra Raffique had written was in the public domain, it disturbed her to find so much committed to paper about her secret organisation and aims written by someone she had never met. Too late, of course, even though the author was no longer.

What worried Eleanor now was the second man to have read what she held in her hand. A second man who she very much hoped would rise to her challenge and his destiny after tomorrow. Especially after tomorrow. She glanced at the bedside table holding the innocuous syringe filled with dark fluid. Her glance roved the empty side of the bed. Now she understood her mother's words. Only she could decide. Only she could make or destroy 700 years of destiny.

A faint click from the apartment's outer door made up her mind. She rolled off the bed and with a quick movement placed the photocopied sheets and syringe under the mattress. Coolly, she ensured the syringe was within finger reach of the edge of the bed: she may need it in a hurry. But not until tomorrow. Glass in hand and totally naked, she went to greet Ben. Not until tomorrow.

* * *

The specially chartered 747 lifted off from Jeddah International and banked steeply to the east. Climbing hard over the Hajiz Mountains it basked in the late evening sun as the dun-coloured mountains below revealed their rugged topography under the lengthening shadows. The huge aircraft levelled briefly before climbing on a gentler angle over the featureless Rub-al-Khali desert. Even at 7,000 feet the human sprawl around the city of Mecca could be discerned. Columns of people, ant-like in the late sun, crept towards the central mosque. Even at this height the faint black square of the Kabba was discernible. Swift shadows darted across the desert landscape, and scanning the indigo sky he saw them close in on the port wing. Shark-like, the Saudi F-15s slowed to the lumbering speed of the 747 and tucked themselves behind and just under the wing. He knew two more would be on the starboard side, accompanied by the flight leader above and behind them, watching carefully.

Very carefully, the elderly Grand Mufti settled in his seat. He did not fly often, and the sensation discomfited him. Leaning back, he closed his eyes, he would need his rest for tomorrow. Almost unreported, he was flying to Rome, to the Vatican no less, for a private audience with the Vatican Council and Pope Leo XIV. He was no fool, but he had decided in his own way to sacrifice himself in the cause of Islam by seeking discourse with Western leaders, via the one man in the whole world respected by both parties.

His nephew had been murdered in Najaf not many months previously, and before the death of Mohammad Baqir al-Hakim, leading Shiite cleric Abdul Majid had also lost his life at the Imam Ali mosque.

He was convinced that he would have an influence on the Holy Father, who in turn would speak to Washington. The fools who lead Hamas and their suicidal attack on Israel cared little for the result of attacking the most powerful military in the Middle East. For all their rhetoric, Israel and its allies were annihilating them and their proxies in Hezbollah and the Houtis.

He knew he was running enormous risks, not only from the Wahhabi Sunnis in Saudi who viewed his trip as nothing more than treachery, but also from extreme elements of the Badr Brigade, the military wing of SCIRI. His age and revered status had persuaded the Islamic Revolutionary Council to quietly back his journey. Hotheads such as Bin Laden and the young cleric Muqtader al-Sadr had over the years merely angered the Coalition forces into ever more draconian measures. He knew with weary resignation that it was the activities of the fundamentalists that flashed across Western television screens on a nightly basis, with the pictures of young men beating themselves in the street and women clad from head to toe in black burkas. It was little wonder the West viewed Islam with deep, dark suspicion. He sighed heavily.

He also knew that he was the oldest member of SCIRI they could send. He was expendable. His failure or demise would play directly into the hands of the militants. He hoped that the entire ruling body of SCIRI that he had left behind at Mecca for the Haj would support his efforts in his absence. The presence of some three million pilgrims clustered around the Kabba would ensure a coup could not succeed.

He twitched his toes in his open sandals. At least when he returned, the results of his meeting with the Argentinan contractors would be bearing fruit and the perennial water shortage of the Holy shrine would be at last resolved. The huge new de-salination plant on the coast would at last assuage the thirst of millions of pilgrims. Thanks be to Allah! His Highness Hussein Al Saud, Minister for the Interior of the Kingdom of Saudi Arabia had in yesterday's audience informed him as to the progress of the long-awaited pipeline from the vast new installation. In spite of the failure of the previous construction company and the appointment of the liquidators, new contractors had been found who were willing to complete the massive project. Al Bukum had informed the Minister they were available to commence immediately and work twenty-four hours a day to complete the pipeline. What a pity the Shia pilgrims coming to the Kaaba for July would not enjoy the benefits of fresh, clean, piped water, he wryly thought.

Chapter 89

Ben awoke in the gentle moonlight that softly invaded his eyes, and gradually the room, in shades of blues and greys.

He had dreamt, or had he thought? The two processes merged so he knew not what conscious thought or sublime dreaming was. He saw Colonel Parker and his troop, their features etched sharply on his mind chasing hither and thither across a stylised map of England. They were hunting. Above the busy landscape, Eleanor's face swam softly into focus looking at Ben – with pity? Or fondness? He hoped the latter.

He stirred and rolled over. His groin ached and his midriff felt the bruises where she had gripped him in between her thighs. His mouth smiled at the memory, and he nuzzled the pillow. It smelt of her. It smelt of her hair and her perfume. But it was cold.

His eyes snapped open. The moonlight cast dark and uneven shadows over the rumpled and disorganised sheets. She had gone. Ben rolled catlike to the edge of the bed and sat up; his feet cool on the marble floor. The silence was palpable; his nerves were on fire. She had given him everything, last night, with every fibre of her body. Eventually the two lay entwined in the damp sheets. She had looked at him, in that deep possessive feminine way, as she wrapped her limbs around him.

'Are you the one, Ben?' she had muttered huskily. He had started to compose an answer, but her eyelids had drooped, and she had sighed and fallen asleep in his arms.

He rose and padded softly to the tall windows. Beneath the apartment the darkness of the Cortile del Belvedere stretched emptily away under the silver moonlight. He could hear a faint, baritone murmur; he turned and walked barefoot towards it. The small door in the corner of the private chapel adjoining her apartment was open and a soft, indistinct light emanated from its aperture. He drew closer.

Through the open door he could see the beginnings of pale blue walls, so softly lit that first it was night within. He could hear deep steady voices recanting Latin. Cautiously, he edged to the door and stole a glance into the room. What he glimpsed was sufficient to have him gasping for breath. He stood with his back to the wall while his breathing subsided.

The plain white altar was illuminated from a single dazzling source above. The same that had so poignantly spotlighted the bronzed chalice two nights previously. The voices continued now louder and clearer: 'In nomine Patri ...' Ben slowly put his eye around the door again.

Colm Hegarty in the cardinal red of high office had stooped to the figure kneeling at the altar. Placing the host on the communicant's parted lips he softly intoned the words of the Mass. Turning to the altar, he lifted the chalice and proffered it to Eleanor's lips. The bright light above the altar cascaded down on the little scene and highlighted the tints of her hair. It was as though she wore a halo of golden fire. But it was not even for this powerful scene that drew Ben's breath. She wore a simple cotton shift, clinched at her slim waist with an ornate leather belt. At her hip trailed the medieval sword he had seen the previous evening. Her chest was ablaze with the crimson red of the cross patée of an early Crusader.

A movement to the left of the altar arrested his thoughts. Concealed from Ben behind the white marble a third, much older, figure lifted his hand in blessing. He remained seated, his frail head bowed under his cream silk zucchetto, his voice wavering. Slowly, with trembling voice he blessed Eleanor as she sipped from the ancient chalice.

She remained kneeling for some minutes, her head bowed. Then she rose and stood silently in front of the altar. Colm placed the chalice reverently in the centre of the altar. He slowly walked round Eleanor, standing next to her in front of the two leather kneelers. The two gazed at the glowing chalice until with one voice they raised their right hands and 'Dieu le veut!' rang out. The seated figure, his head further bowed, nodded in affirmation.

Behind the little group, Ben could see a door softly open. In the penumbral shadows at the far end of the room he could see two *asessores* of the Papal Office advance. Gently, reverently, they escorted the figure out of the chapel. As the far door clicked softly home, Ben turned and glided silently back to the bed.

He had just regularised his breathing as he felt her warm naked figure slip in beside him. He stirred, feigning disturbance and grunted sleepily. Eleanor watched his chest rise and fall slowly. With a single elegantly manicured nail she raked softly down his ribs; he stirred slowly. Ben knew in an instant his fate was being decided. Presently she slipped an arm around him and dozed off.

* * *

For the second time that night he awoke to a cold bed. This time the early sun streamed in through the open windows: mid-July in Rome was a time of high summer and cloudless skies. He could hear Eleanor around the apartment singing to the early morning request show from the local radio station. Drying himself off from the shower and entering the small breakfast room he slipped his hand around her waist and nuzzled her neck. She dropped her wooden spoon and turned to Ben. He had rarely seen a woman so radiantly, confidentially happy. She looked absolutely on top of the world, her skin glowed, her lips were full and her eyes danced with him. They kissed fully, Ben pushing her against the stove until she squealed in protest and broke away laughing. He looked at her, unsure as to the reason for her mood. She was as he would imagine a bride on her wedding day.

Breakfast was a light-hearted affair; her infectious, joyous mood pervaded the apartment and Ben's mind. With a ridiculous sense of well-being and confidence, he felt giddy and excited in the presence of this woman. Seated opposite each other as the golden light streamed into the elegant apartment, Ben felt completely at one with himself and Eleanor. She slid her small, bare foot along his leg playfully, 'I couldn't tell you before but . . .'. She paused and in the instant Ben's mind flashed over the last few years of his life. Right from his experience in Liverpool, to Guatemala, to Burtonport, and the fate of Raffy. Colonel Parker's humorous condemnation of his concerns bit deeply as he waited breathlessly for her to continue. His mouthful of delicious, scrambled egg turned to dust as he watched her.

If Eleanor noticed his abrupt look, she didn't react, but continued, her eyes dancing in fun. 'We have a visit today from the Grand Mufti of Saudi Arabia to the Holy Father. News has only just broken, as the Kingdom did not want to create interest in his visit from the wrong quarter.'

Her lips compressed and she looked at Ben. 'The Holy Father is to conduct Mass and a service of reconciliation in private before their talks.'

Ben interrupted catching her enthusiasm. 'The Grand Mufti? Here in Rome?'

'And I shall be there, Ben, to witness the whole event'.

She glanced away and her lips smiled as she rose from the table. Suddenly Ben knew whatever his premonition was, it was going to happen today. A Grand Mufti coming in peace to the camp of the infidels no less, and the Sons of Sion, at least in the shape of Eleanor, on hand to witness the talks. If the talks succeeded in defusing the public perception of Christianity versus Islam, East versus West, then the ramifications for world peace would be incalculable. If, on the other hand, a tragedy befell the Grand Mufti, 9/11 would be as a pinprick compared to the forces unleashed against the West.

Ben's mind whirred and he barely registered the light kiss on his cheek as Eleanor left the apartment. With crushing clarity, he saw Colonel Parker's face; he knew now he was wrong, Parker was right. The Sons of Sion had no interest in a nuclear device, or Northern Irish politics, nor had they need to. A Grand Mufti was being delivered to them. Like a lamb to the slaughter. And somehow Eleanor held the key. He knew the reason for her mood. Last night's secret Mass made sense now, as well as her peculiar garb.

He changed quickly, slipping into the dark clothes and soft soled boots he had worn all that time ago to investigate the monastery. Donning his bulky vestments of office over this attire, he left the apartment.

The first rule of any mission was sharing your intention and intelligence. Glancing at his watch, he saw that he had little over an hour before the arrival of the Grand Mufti and, in a phone booth outside the Pia Clementino Museum, he dialled Colonel Parker's number.

Ring, ring. Ring, ring. He glanced frustratedly up and down the street. No answer. He hung up and tried again, no luck. Again, he glanced up the street. The black Mercedes arrested his vision; he frowned and turned away, holding the phone in the crook of his neck.

He disconnected and dialled again: the same national code, but a different telephone number.

The phone at Mountford Hall rang once before it cut to the answering machine. Ben's mouth opened in frustration, but he changed his mind and spoke rapidly and at length. In the fly-blown mirror he could see the black limousine creep along the kerb towards him. As he finished speaking, he saw the door open and Barzini's bruised features slip out. He exited the cubicle and ran nimbly up the museum steps.

Barzini followed, the slim hypodermic concealed in his thick hand. At the rear of the museum atrium the exit to the Cortille della Pigna was guarded by a uniformed member of the Swiss Guard. Ben composed himself and with a reverent nod eased past into the area accessible only to the College of Cardinals. Barzini glared at the six-foot guard. The glare was returned with equanimity. Barzini ground his nails into his palms in frustration as he turned and walked away.

* * *

Out of respect of the Islamic custom of quiet contemplative prayer, the Vatican authorities had declared St Peter's Basilica closed for the day. This acceding to the traditions and diktats of the Islamic faith had not gone unremarked in the corridors and offices of the Vatican. Dominated by the right wing and increasingly orthodox Opus Dei, the basilica organist had secretly been instructed to pay Elgar's 'Lux Eterna' as the small procession of imams glided softly up the nave towards the baldachin canopy under which awaited the head of the worldwide Catholic Church. Ben slipped unobtrusively to the left of the Gloria della Cattedra, leaving him a clear view over the huge altar resting on the tomb of St Peter. From the portico where he had been received, the Grand Mufti slowly passed the ancient marble columns, originally from the Basilica Constantine. In between them stood a single silent line of members of the order of Sons of Sion.

If he understood the message, the Grand Mufti gave no sign, as he walked with measured pace and considerable dignity towards the diminutive figure. On either side of the Pontiff stood a crimson-clad cardinal. Ben recognised with a start the craggy features of Colm Heggarty whose eyes, Ben felt sure, had picked him out through the shadows and swirls of incense – but perhaps it was his imagination.

The piped tones of the 'Lux Eterna' faded away to the corners of the great basilica as the small procession came to a halt in front of the ornate canopy of the baldachin. Under its domed portico the frail white figure made to rise, assisted by the two scarlet cardinals. At the same time the cone of light illuminating the Pontiff slowly increased its intensity. The effect was subtly to darken the rest of the huge edifice. Ben's eyes slid away from the unfolding ceremony down the ranks of darkened figures. Amid a rising tide of consternation he could not immediately see her diminutive figure. She held the clue, he was certain, but beyond that ... Again, his eyes scanned the black figures – nothing. His spirits sank, he felt uncertain: foolish, even.

It was her movement that gave Eleanor away; she glided silently down the east aisle behind the huge pillars. He started forward down the opposite aisle, pausing theatrically at each column and waiting until her dark figure had cleared the opposite one. She was headed for the entrance to the Piazza St Pietro where a brilliant shaft of sunlight entered the basilica. As she reached

Michelangelo's Pieta he glanced back, uncertain. His mind fleetingly remembered another time and place. The night-shrouded garage in Guatemala City; the nun looking at her outstretched hand glistening redly in the gloom. Then the cough of the starter motor. His head swivelled back and forth as he passed the last column.

As if perfectly choreographed, Ben and Eleanor walked into the shaft of sunlight in unison. Her eyes sparkled as she acknowledged him. Then she produced a small mobile phone which she held to her ear. The rest of the basilica was in gloom, in direct contrast to the cone of brilliant white light that fell on the figures beneath the baldachin. Ben tore his eyes from the nave as the frail figure placed his hand upon the Grand Mufti. Suddenly he knew he was utterly safe. As his eyes slid away, he saw Colm Hegarty's jaw lift the beginnings of a smile, evident even at that distance.

The moment his brain registered Hegarty's expression, his eyes had slid towards the first of the nuns next to the craggy cardinal. With a start that seared his soul, he saw Maria smiling at him from beneath her coif.

Maria! The woman of a thousand dreams who had so enchanted him at the seminary and then miraculously appeared in Ireland as Raffy had been arrested. The woman who seemed so inextricably linked with the dowdy, mysterious Elizabeth. Suddenly, within the space of a few blinding seconds in this holy place he had the answer to the jigsaw puzzle his life and faith had become: 'We are members of an order, not a democracy.'

Colm's determined features stared at him. Eleanor kneeling in that private sanctuary receiving the Holy Father's blessing; and his ancestor's name in those secret archives. Time seemed to pause, suspending itself. And in this moment of almost divine lucidity Ben's brain experienced a calmness and clarity of thought he had never had before. He saw Eleanor, this beautiful, feisty enigma of a woman who had come into his life; but also, he saw the mission her order shared. A mission seven centuries in the execution. To finish what Urban II had begun at Clermont in 1095. A purity and conviction of purpose seemingly so far limited to the Islamic forces against them. But no longer.

Ben saw a future – no, his own future – swept clear of the concessions and vacillations of the last 700 years. Onward Christian soldiers, marching with the one true Church. A waking of the power they had enjoyed for centuries and the final Crusader victory.

When Eleanor removed the phone from her ear, her eyes blazed in triumph as she looked directly at him. The invitation was plain, and he darted forward. She flicked the small silver phone high into the air, glinting in the sunlight before Ben deftly caught it and looked at the illuminated screen: 'Connected' was its only message.

Two thousand miles away, the sands beneath the tented city housing three million pilgrims returned in an instant to their silicon components. The entire Najd desert was lit by a searing flash with the intensity of many times that of the midday sun. Its golden, purple, violet and grey hues lit the Hijaz Mountains with a clarity that defied description. Some thirty seconds after the initial vaporization and flash of light came an air blast flattening everything within a thirty-mile radius. After that followed the strong, sustained, awesome roar that heralded doomsday, as though the Creator himself had said 'Let there be light'.

* * *

The *City of Bahia Blanca* was barely making steerage way off the Yemen coast heading towards the Gulf of Aden. A thin ethereal sea mist blanketed all sound. Dr Schlatter was leaning against the fantail with Father Sebastian when suddenly, in the north, a light of incredible intensity pierced the gloom. Dr Schlatter stood up, uncertain, and shielded his gaze. One and a half minutes later came a shattering roar. His eyes wildly sought Sebastian's, but they had barely time to take in the small, snub-barrelled pistol in his huge hand as the good doctor's skull exploded in a flash of light. He was dead before his body splashed into the warm sea.

* * *

Ben caught up with her across the huge piazza among the throng of pilgrims. She had removed her coif with a sweep of her hand, and her hair was blowing carefree in the breeze. Eleanor looked round and saw him approaching, and her eyes met his with a look of unconfined happiness. Then she turned away, an enigmatic smile playing on her lips, increasing her pace ever so slightly as she extended her fingers back to him and waited for the feel of his hand in hers. With all his doubts now banished, Ben darted forward.

* * *

This is the BBC. We interrupt this programme to bring a special news bulletin. The American Institute of Seismology in conjunction with the Pentagon and intelligence sources in the government of Israel have just issued the following statement:

Following detailed analysis of the alpha and beta shock waves from the earthquake in Saudi Arabia reported this afternoon, and with further evidence from J-STARS surveillance, it is almost certain that the shock waves emanated from a nuclear device detonated just below ground level. Early indications from shockwave analysis indicated the atomic particles to be part of the Iranian stockpile at Fordo, which had been presumed destroyed. American forces in the region have been placed at DEFCON 2.

CHAPTER 90

The simmering heat of summer had long since passed in the bowl and the trees planted by her grandfather all those years ago had assumed their autumn hues beneath a somewhat pale, crisp, blue sky.

High up in the turret room, she wrote as countless Grand Nautoniers had before in the smooth parchment pages of the damask leather volumes, the faint scratching of her pen in harmony with the crackle of the first log fire of winter. Her eyes moistened as she recorded the passing of the previous Grand Nautonier: now the latest entry on an exceedingly long list.

But they quickly dried and hardened as the events of the summer unfolded in measured prose on the pale pages. When it was done, she permitted herself a satisfied smile as she slid the closed volume into its place on the shelf and looked again at the painting. Did she imagine it? Or was Urban II smiling at her as well?

Outside, on the open balcony, she leant against the crenelations overlooking her domain with a sense of deep fulfilment. The sound of his footfall disturbed her reverie and Ben's forearm snaked around her waist as he nuzzled her neck.

Content and replete, she intertwined her fingers with his. Feeling for a moment the buttery softness of his signet ring, she ran the top of her finger over its ancient surface, seeing in her mind the double-headed eagle on a black shield with the engraved gold band.

'You've written the ledger?' It was a statement, more than a question.

'Mm,' she replied, nuzzling him back. 'The first of our many entries Father Mountford.'

Her eyes were sparkling in the way he now understood so well as she pressed his hand down below her belly in blissful confirmation.